Praise for the novels of *New York Times* bestselling author

DEBBIE MACOMBER

"Macomber is known for her honest portrayals of ordinary women in small-town America, and this tale cements her position as an icon of the genre."
—*Publishers Weekly* on *16 Lighthouse Road*

"Debbie Macomber is one of the most reliable, versatile romance authors around."
—*Milwaukee Journal Sentinel*

"Debbie Macomber shows why she is one of the most powerful, highly regarded authors on the stage today."
—*Midwest Book Review*

"Macomber has a gift for evoking the emotions that are at the heart of the genre's popularity."
—*Publishers Weekly*

"Macomber is no stranger to the *New York Times* bestseller list. She knows how to please her audience."
—*Oregon Statesman Journal*

"Macomber's storytelling sometimes yields a tear, at other times a smile."
—*Newport Newss, VA, Daily Press*

"Overflowing with small-town atmosphere, a warm sense of family, and engaging secondary characters, this story will resonate with many American fans."
—*Library Journal,* on *Return to Promise*

Dear Reader,

I can't tell you how delighted I am that these books are being reissued in two special volumes—*Navy Brides* (available in April) and *Navy Grooms* (July). I've often been asked when my Navy books will be published again—and here they are, with the addition of my brand-new front-list title for Silhouette Special Edition, *Navy Husband,* which appears in *Navy Grooms*.

As you may know, I live in a navy town, across Sinclair Inlet from the navy shipyard in Bremerton. Aircraft carriers, submarines and destroyers are all part of the view. I know I'll never forget the first time I saw an aircraft carrier. As the *Nimitz* sailed into port, I saw the wives, girlfriends, parents and kids of the sailors onboard. (Husbands, too!) I felt that I was part of a significant and moving experience.

I wrote the first five Navy books in the 1980s, and of course many of the things we take for granted now—especially methods of communication, like cell phones and e-mail—didn't exist then. (Not surprisingly, you'll see lots of e-mail use in *Navy Husband*!) But I think the situations in these stories are universal. They have to do with the men and women who balance love for each other with love for their country. That can become difficult, for them and their families, especially during times of military deployment. It's something we've all been very aware of the past few years.

I hope you enjoy these books, whether you've read them before or this is your first encounter with them. I love hearing from my readers. You can reach me at P.O. Box 1458, Port Orchard WA 98366, or visit my Web site at www.debbiemacomber.com.

Debbie Macomber

DEBBIE MACOMBER

Navy Brides

If you purchased this book without a cover you should be aware that this book is stolen property. It was reported as "unsold and destroyed" to the publisher, and neither the author nor the publisher has received any payment for this "stripped book."

ISBN 0-7783-2248-3

NAVY BRIDES

Copyright © 2005 by MIRA Books.

NAVY WIFE
Copyright © 1988 by Debbie Macomber.

NAVY BLUES
Copyright © 1989 by Debbie Macomber.

NAVY BRAT
Copyright © 1991 by Debbie Macomber.

All rights reserved. Except for use in any review, the reproduction or utilization of this work in whole or in part in any form by any electronic, mechanical or other means, now known or hereafter invented, including xerography, photocopying and recording, or in any information storage or retrieval system, is forbidden without the written permission of the publisher, MIRA Books, 225 Duncan Mill Road, Don Mills, Ontario, Canada M3B 3K9.

All characters in this book have no existence outside the imagination of the author and have no relation whatsoever to anyone bearing the same name or names. They are not even distantly inspired by any individual known or unknown to the author, and all incidents are pure invention.

MIRA and the Star Colophon are trademarks used under license and registered in Australia, New Zealand, Philippines, United States Patent and Trademark Office and in other countries.

www.MIRABooks.com

Printed in U.S.A.

CONTENTS

NAVY WIFE

Dedicated to
the women behind the men
who "go down to the sea in ships."
The backbone of the navy—the navy wife.

Special thanks to

Sandy Campanelli,
wife of Command Master Chief John Campanelli,
USS *Nimitz*

Lee Knichel,
wife of Lieutenant Commander Ray Knichel,
USS *Nimitz*

Debbie Korrell,
wife of Chief Steven Korrell, USS *Alaska*

Rose Marie Harris,
wife of MMCM Ralph Harris, retired, U.S. Navy

Chapter One

After walking over to the window in her brother's empty apartment, Lindy Kyle paused and let her tired gaze rest on the view of downtown Seattle. Dusk was settling over the steel jungle, and giant shadows from the skyscrapers fell into the maze of concrete across the picturesque waterfront. In another mood Lindy would have been struck by the intricate beauty of what lay before her, but not now.

Seattle, as Steve had claimed, really was a lovely city. When she'd arrived, she'd been so preoccupied with trying to find the address of the apartment and the appropriate parking space for her Volkswagen Rabbit in the lot behind the building that she hadn't taken the time to notice anything around her.

Now she sighed at the panorama that lay before her. "I'm actually here," she said, mainly to hear herself speak. She'd come to expect a lot from one western city. She felt as an immigrant might have years ago, sailing into New York Harbor, seeking a new way of life and freedom from the shackles of the past. Lindy had been bound, too, in the chains of grief and unhappiness.

Dramatically she posed, pretending to be the Statue of Liberty, her right hand held high as if gripping a lighted torch, her left firmly clasping imaginary stone tablets. "Okay, Seattle, give me your tired, your poor, your huddled masses yearning to breathe free." Lindy sucked in a shaky breath and battled back tears. "Seattle, calm my fears. Clear my head." She dropped her arms and swallowed at the growing knot in her throat. "Heal my heart," she added in a broken whisper. "Please, heal my heart...."

Exhaling raggedly, she dropped her arm and admitted it was too much to expect–even from a place that had once been honored as the most livable city in the United States. Far too much to ask.

Suddenly exhausted, Lindy picked up her suitcase and headed down the narrow hallway toward the two bedrooms. She opened the first door and stood in the doorway examining the room. The closet, which was partly open, displayed an organized row of civilian clothes hanging inside, crisp and neat. A framed picture or two rested on the dresser, but Lindy didn't pay attention to those. This had to be the bedroom of Rush Callaghan, her brother's roommate. Currently both men were at sea serving six-month tours of duty. Steve was an officer aboard the submarine *Atlantis*, somewhere in the Pacific upholding God, country and the American flag. Lindy had no idea where Rush was and didn't particularly care. Men weren't exactly her favorite subject at the moment.

She closed the bedroom door and moved on to the next room. A dresser drawer hung open, mismatched socks draped over its edge. Bulky-knit sweaters were carelessly tossed on the ledge above the closet and shoes were heaped in a pile on the floor.

"Home, sweet home," Lindy said with a soft smile. She really was fond of her brother, and although he was nearly ten years older, her childhood had been marked with memories of his wit and warmth. She laid her suitcase across the unmade bed, opened it and reached for Steve's letter. "Come to Seattle," he'd written in his lazy, uneven scrawl. "Forget the past and make a new life for yourself." Steve had had first-hand experience with pain, Lindy knew, and she respected his judgment. He'd survived the emotional trauma of divorce and seemed to have come out of it with a new maturity.

"You'll know which bedroom is mine," Steve's letter continued. "I can't remember the last time I changed the sheets so you might want to do that before you crash."

Crashing certainly sounded inviting, Lindy mused, sinking with a sigh onto the edge of the unmade bed.

Although she'd nearly memorized Steve's words, Lindy read completely through the letter once more. Clean sheets were in the hall closet, he explained, and she decided to tackle making the bed as soon as she'd unpacked her things. The washer and dryer were in a small laundry room off the kitchen, the letter went on to say.

When she finished reading, Lindy placed Steve's instructions on top of the dresser. She stripped off the sheets, carried the bedding into the laundry room and started the washing machine.

When the phone rang it caught her off guard, and she widened her eyes and placed her hand over her heart as shock waves washed over her.

It rang one more time before she decided to answer it.

"Hello?"

"Lindy, it's your mother."

"Oh, hi, Mom." Lindy smiled at her parents' habit of identifying themselves. She'd been able to recognize her own family's voices since she was a child.

"I take it you've arrived safely. Honey, you should have phoned–your father and I've been worried."

Lindy sighed. "Mom, I just walked in the door not more than ten minutes ago. I was planning to phone after I fixed myself something to eat."

"Did your car give you any problems?"

"None."

"Good." Her mother sounded relieved.

"Everything's fine–just the way I said it would be," Lindy added.

"What about money?"

"Mom, I'm doing great." A slight exaggeration, but Lindy wasn't desperate–at least she wouldn't be if she found a job reasonably soon. The unemployment problem was one she hoped to correct first thing in the morning.

"I talked to your Uncle Henry in Kansas City and he said you should think about applying at Boeing…that airplane company. He claims they're always looking for someone with a degree in computer science."

"I'll do that right away," Lindy answered in an effort to appease her mother.

"You'll let us know when you've found something?"

"Yes, Mom. I promise."

"And don't be shy about asking for money. Your father and I–"

"Mom, please don't worry about me. I'm going to be just great."

Her mother expelled her breath in a long, anxious sigh. "I do worry about you, sweetie. You've been so terribly unhappy. I can't tell you how disappointed your father and I are in that young man of yours."

"Paul isn't mine anymore." Lindy's voice trembled a little, but she needed to say it out loud every now and then just to remind herself of the fact. For four years she'd linked all thoughts of her future with Paul; being without him felt as though a large part of herself was missing.

"I saw his mother the other day, and I'll have you know I took a great deal of pleasure in looking the other way," Grace Kyle continued, with more than a hint of righteous indignation.

"What happened between Paul and me isn't Mrs. Abram's fault."

"No. But she obviously didn't raise her son right–not if

he could do something this underhanded and despicable to you."

"Mom, do you mind if we don't talk about Paul anymore? Ever?" Even the mention of his name brought with it a sharp pain, yet part of her was still hungering for news of him. Someday, Lindy vowed, she'd look back on these awful months and smile at the memory. Someday, maybe. But not now.

"Lindy, of course I won't talk about Paul if you don't want me to. I was being insensitive–forgive me, sweetie."

"It's all right, Mom."

A short, throbbing silence followed. "You'll keep in touch, won't you?"

"Yes," Lindy answered and nodded. "I promise."

After a few more minutes of filling her parents in on the news of her trip, Lindy replaced the receiver. The washing machine went into the spin cycle behind her, and she tossed a glance over her shoulder. That was the way her world felt lately, as if she were being put through a churning wash. The only question that remained to be answered was if she'd come out of this drip-dry and wrinkle free.

Rush Callaghan stood on the bridge of the USS *Mitchell*, a pair of binoculars gripped tightly in his hands. He paused to suck in a deep breath of tangy salt air and sighed his appreciation for the clear, clean scent of it. Being on the open seas stirred his blood back to life after three long months of shore duty. He relaxed, home at last, as the huge 1,092-foot-long aircraft carrier cut a wide path out of Puget Sound and into the dark green waters of the north Pacific. Rush was more than glad. He had recognized from the time he was a boy that his destiny lay on the swirling waters of the world's oceans. He'd been born on the sea and he'd known ever since that this was where he belonged, where he felt truly alive.

Rush had dedicated his life to the sea, and in turn she had become his mistress. She was often demanding and unreasonable, but Rush wouldn't have had it any other way. A gentle breeze carried with it a cool, soothing mist. The spray came at him like the gentle, caressing fingers of a woman riffling through his hair and pressing her body against his own. Rush grinned at the picturesque image, knowing his lover well. She was gently welcoming him back into her arms, but Rush wasn't easily fooled. His mistress was fickle. Another time, possibly soon, she would lash out at him and harshly slap his face with cold, biting wind and rain. Her icy fingers would sting him with outrage. It was little wonder, Rush thought, that he'd come to think of the sea as his lover, since she often played the role.

When the *Mitchell* had pulled out of the Bremerton shipyard eighteen hours earlier, Rush had left nothing to tie him to the shore. No wife, no sweetheart, nothing except a Seattle apartment where he stored his worldly goods. He wasn't looking to build any bridges that would link him to the mainland. He'd learned early in his career that a wife and family weren't meant for him. If the waters of the world were his mistress, then the navy would be his wife. There'd been a time when he'd hoped to divide his life, but no more.

A quick exchange of angry words followed by an outburst of disgust from his fellow officer, Jeff Dwyer, caught Rush's attention and he lowered his binoculars.

"Problems?" he asked when Jeff joined him on the bridge.

Jeff's mouth tightened and he nodded. "The captain's just ordered us back."

"What the hell?" Rush felt a hot surge of anger pulse through him. "Why?"

"There's something wrong with the catapults. Apparently maintenance doesn't have the necessary parts to repair the problem."

Rush swore under his breath. The catapults were used to

launch the Hawkeyes, Intruders, Tomcats and other aircraft from the carrier runway. They were vital equipment for any assignment at sea.

Fortunately the squadrons flying in from two navy airfields on the West Coast–a hundred planes were scheduled to rendezvous with the *Mitchell*–had yet to arrive. As chief navigator it was Rush's job to guide the carrier through the waters; now it was up to him to head the *Mitchell* back to the shipyard.

"I've already sent out word to the airfields," Jeff informed him. "They've turned the planes back."

Frustration built up in Rush like a tidal wave. After three months shore duty and a mere eighteen hours at sea they had to bring the *Mitchell* home to port with her tail between her legs.

"How long?" Rush asked between clenched teeth.

"Maintenance doesn't have a figure yet, but if it's as bad as it looks, we could be sitting on our butts for at least a week."

Rush spat a four-letter word.

"My sentiments exactly," Jeff answered.

Rush let himself into the dark apartment and set his seabag just inside the door. The way things were working out he could be here awhile. The realization angered him every time he thought about it. He moved into the kitchen and set the six-pack of cold beer on the counter. He rarely indulged himself this way, but tonight he was in the mood to get good and drunk.

Not bothering to turn on any of the lights, Rush took one chilled aluminum can and carried it with him into the living room, pulling off the tab as he went. Standing in front of the wide picture window, he offered a silent toast to the glittering lights of the waterfront several blocks below. He took a large swig of beer. Tonight something cold and alcoholic suited his temperament.

He took another long drink, sat on the sofa and propped his feet on the coffee table. What he needed was a woman. One sexy as hell, with big breasts and wide hips to bury himself in–one who would relieve his angry frustration. Rush frowned. The crude thought wasn't like him. He rarely allowed his mind to indulge in such primitive fantasies. But tonight, after watching weeks of planning and months of hard work go down the drain, Rush wasn't in the mood for niceties.

Against his will, Rush remembered the look in his friend Jeff's eyes when he'd stepped off the gangplank. Jeff had been hurrying to get home to his wife, Susan. Rush didn't need much of an imagination to know what Jeff was doing about now–and it wasn't drinking cold beer in a dark living room. He allowed himself to grin. Jeff and Susan. Now that was one marriage Rush wouldn't have bet good money on. But Susan Dwyer had pleasantly surprised him. When Jeff had left Bremerton earlier in the week, there'd been no tears in her eyes, only smiles. She'd been a good wife to Jeff from the first. Susan wasn't a clinger or a complainer; the only bonds she'd wrapped around her husband had been in his heart.

Rush had seen subtle changes in his friend since his marriage. He'd been looking for major ones. Over the years Rush had witnessed the power a woman could wield over a sailor's life often enough to recognize the symptoms. But Susan Dwyer hadn't been like some of the others, and Rush had silently admired her–and envied Jeff. His friend had gotten damn lucky to find a woman like Susan. Luckier than Rush.... But then Rush had given up trying.

The sound of someone moving behind him jerked Rush into action and he vaulted off the sofa. The bathroom door closed and he heard the rush of running water. What the hell! Someone was in the apartment. It had to be Steve. He moved down the hallway, looked inside his roomate's bedroom and cocked his eyebrows in astonishment. A silk robe was draped across the end of the bed and the room was littered with female paraphernalia.

Rush released a slow, exasperated breath. He'd been afraid something like this might happen. Steve was still working his way through the pain of his divorce and it had left him vulnerable. Rush was all too familiar with the seductive wiles a woman could use to cloud a man's better judgment. And now it appeared that some schemer was taking advantage of his friend's generous nature, planting herself in their apartment. Apparently Steve was still susceptible to being tricked and used. Well, Rush wouldn't stand for it. A surge of anger at the thought of someone taking advantage of his friend's kind heart made him clench his fists.

He'd gladly handle this situation, he decided. He'd get rid of her, and if Steve asked for an explanation later, Rush had the perfect excuse. After all they had an agreement about this place and it didn't include inviting women to move in. His mouth tightened into a narrow line. From what little he could see, this one had made herself right at home. Well, no more.

With beer in hand, he leaned against the wall, crossed his legs and waited. Within a couple of minutes the bathroom door opened and the woman stepped out. Her dark eyes rounded before she let out a soft gasp.

Obviously startled half out of her wits, the woman's hand flew to her heart, gripping the lacy edge of her pajamas. "Who are you?"

Dear God, wouldn't you know it, Rush groaned inwardly. This wasn't just any woman, but one as sexy as the one he'd been fantasizing about, with nice, round breasts and long, inviting legs. One look and Rush could understand why his friend had set her up in this cozy arrangement. Lord knew she was tempting enough. Her sheer baby-doll pajamas revealed peekaboo nipples, firm hips and shapely legs. It took him a full second to realize her hair was dark and nothing like that of the blondes that usually appealed to his friend.

She continued to stare at him, eyes as round as golf balls, her hands pressed flat against the wall behind her. She opened her mouth and stammered, "Wh-what are you doing here?"

Other than the small gasp, Rush noted, she revealed no real fear. "Isn't that supposed to be my question?" he taunted, and his mouth twisted into a cool, appraising smile. She didn't make an effort to cover herself, but perhaps she wasn't aware of how the muted moonlight played over her pajamas, giving him tantalizing glimpses of her full breasts. Then again, maybe she was.

"You must be Rush."

"So Steve mentioned me?" That surprised him.

"Yes…of course." The woman worked her way past him and retrieved her robe from the foot of the bed, quickly donning it. She made an effort to disguise her uneasiness, but Rush noted that she was trembling. Even from where he was standing he could see that her heart was pounding like a jackhammer. She glanced his way once, silently appealing to him with those huge brown eyes of hers, but Rush was unmoved. If she thought to practice her charms on him, then she could think again. Steve Kyle was his friend and he wasn't about to let his buddy be used by this woman or anyone else.

As nonchalantly as possible Rush followed her into the bedroom, ignoring the soft scent of jasmine. "How long have you been here?" Her clothes hung in the closet and her things were lined atop the dresser. He lifted the sleeve of a blouse and let the smooth feel of silk run through his fingers. From the look of things, she'd settled right in as though she owned the place. Perhaps she assumed she did; but she'd learn soon enough.

The woman didn't answer him right away. Instead, she moved out of the bedroom and into the kitchen and turned on the lights. "Only a couple of days."

"You didn't waste any time, did you?"

She looked at him as though she hadn't understood his question. "No."

He snickered. "I thought not."

Her gaze left his and rested on the partially empty six-pack of beer. The sight of that seemed to make her all the more nervous and she rubbed the palms of her hands together as though to ward off an unexpected chill. "You've been drinking." Her words sounded like an accusation. The woman's judgmental attitude only served to amuse Rush. He had to give her credit, though; under like circumstances he didn't know if he could have exercised such an impudent spirit.

In response to her statement he reached for another beer. His mouth twisted into a sardonic smile. "Care to join me?" he asked, gesturing toward the four remaining cans.

"No thanks." She tightened the cinch on her robe and squared her shoulders.

"Somehow I didn't think you would." Rush tossed his empty can into the garbage and reached for another. More to irritate her than anything, he took a long, slow drink, letting the cold liquid slide down his throat.

She watched him and braced her hands against the back of the counter. "How long will you be… staying?"

She had one hell of a nerve. "I think I should be the one asking questions, don't you?"

"I–I suppose."

She continued to stare at him with those wide, appealing eyes, and Rush struggled to ignore the false innocence of her silent entreaty.

"I take it Steve didn't let you know I was coming."

"No, he forgot to mention you." It was apparent to Rush that his roommate probably had no intention of letting him know. It would have been easy enough to let the matter slide since Steve would be returning from sea duty before Rush was due back into port.

"I'm Lindy."

He didn't acknowledge her greeting.

As though to cover her embarrassment, she opened the refrigerator and took out a carton of milk.

Rush watched her actions carefully and noted that the inside of the fridge was well stocked. The observation only served to irritate him more. Knowing how generous Steve was, Rush didn't doubt that he'd given her the money to get set up in the apartment.

Lindy poured herself a glass and replaced the milk. "This does make things a bit awkward, doesn't it?"

Again Rush ignored her. Instead of answering her question he pulled out the chair opposite her and sat down, nursing his beer. As hard as he tried, he couldn't take his eyes off her. She was more than just pretty. Delicate, he decided, with a soft injured look about her. Damn, he fathomed better than he would have liked what must have led Steve to invite this woman to move in. In addition to the fragile beauty, she was soft and feminine–the kind of woman a lonely sailor imagines sleeping in his bed, waiting for him. Rush understood all too well, but he didn't like the idea of some woman using his friend. Not when Steve was ripe for pain.

She took a quick swallow of the cold milk, her soft, dark eyes hardly leaving his. Rush was growing more uncomfortable by the minute. He didn't want her here, didn't want her anywhere near this apartment. As far as he was concerned she was trouble with a capital *T*. She must have sensed this because he noticed her fingers tighten around the glass. Obviously she didn't plan to make this easy.

"It would help if we could reach some kind of agreement to share the place–at least until you leave again," she said, looking both embarrassed and uneasy.

His slow answering smile was as cool as Rush could manage. He wasn't about to let a woman sway him out of doing what he must, unpleasant as the task seemed. "Listen, honey," he said brusquely, "the only one of us who's going to be leaving is you. And the sooner the better. So pack your bags; I want you gone before morning."

Chapter Two

So Rush Callaghan was kicking her out of the apartment, Lindy mused. Terrific. What else could go wrong? The answer to that was something she didn't want to find out. Oh Lord. She'd known Steve's invitation was too good to be true. Nothing was ever going to be right for her again–she'd been sabotaged by fate while still in her prime….

A quick calculation of her limited funds suggested that she could possibly last two weeks if she rented a cheap hotel room and ate sparingly. Two weeks and she'd be forced to return to Minneapolis a failure. The thought wasn't a comforting one. Her parents would gladly take her in, but their excessive concern right now was more suffocating than she could bear.

With deliberate calm Lindy drank the last of her milk, carried the glass to the sink and rinsed it out. All the while her thoughts were a churning mass of wary doubts.

She would leave, she decided, because Rush Callaghan had decreed that she must. But she could see no reason to hurry. Simply because he was an officer used to giving orders and having them followed didn't mean she had to jump at his every command.

"Did you hear me?" Rush asked, his narrowed gaze following her deliberate movements.

"I'll be out before morning," was the only answer she

would give him, and she forced those words to come out as stiffly as starched sheets.

It gave Lindy fleeting satisfaction to witness the surprise in Rush's eyes. He stared at her almost as if he'd been looking forward to an argument, to sharpening his wits on hers. Apparently he'd thought she would stand up and issue some kind of challenge. Well, Lindy just wasn't in the mood to put up much of a fight. If he wanted her out, then fine, she'd pack her bags and leave.

Wordlessly she opened the dishwasher and set the glass inside. His eyes followed her suspiciously, apparently disliking her cool compliance. For the first time he looked unsettled, as though it was on the tip of his tongue to suggest that she could stay until morning. But if the thought crossed his mind, that was as far as it went. He said nothing. Lindy supposed he was right. She could see no reason to prolong the inevitable. But damn it all, she'd never felt so helpless and lost in her life. A condemned man walking to the hangman's noose had as many options as she seemed to have at the moment.

Lindy turned and left the kitchen. She tried to walk away proudly, but her shoulders sagged with abject defeat. She heard the kitchen chair scrape against the floor as Rush stood and followed her.

Standing in the doorway to her bedroom, Rush glanced at his watch. Lindy pulled out her suitcase from under the bed and looked in the direction of her clock radio, noting the late hour.

As though it went against his better judgment, Rush stuck his hand in his uniform pocket and murmured, "Listen, tomorrow morning is soon enough."

"Not for me, it isn't."

"What do you mean?"

"Never mind," Lindy said with a righteous sigh.

"Lord, how like a woman," Rush murmured to the ceiling, the words tight and controlled. "She tosses a dart at me and then refuses to acknowledge it. What she really wants me to know is that she couldn't bear to be in the same room with me. Well, honeybunch, the feeling is mutual!"

Some of Lindy's control slipped at his taunt, and she angrily jerked a blouse off a hanger. "I don't suppose you stopped to think that I didn't move in here without an invitation. Steve invited me. I have his letter right here to prove it if you'd take the time to read–"

"Unfortunately Steve didn't clear this cozy little arrangement with me," he interrupted, "and I have no intention of sharing this place with you or any other female."

"You men think you're really something, don't you?" Lindy cried, jerking yet another blouse from a hanger. "You like being in control, dictating whatever you wish on nothing more than a whim."

He looked surprised that she'd revealed any emotion. Good heavens, just what did he expect from her? Lindy didn't know, and at this point she simply didn't care. When she'd finished emptying her closet, she whirled around to face him.

"All along Steve's been telling me what a great friend you are, a terrific guy. You should meet him, Lindy. I know you'd like him," she said sarcastically, mimicking her brother's praise. She cast Rush a disparaging look. "Some roommate you turned out to be. I'll tell you one thing, mister…"

"Spare me, would you?"

"No." Lindy slammed the lid of her suitcase closed. "You're all alike. Every last one of you is just like Paul."

"Paul?"

Her index finger flew at his chest and she heaved back in indignation. "Don't you dare mention his name to me. Ever!"

"Lady, you brought him up, I didn't!"

"That was a mistake. But then I seem to be making a lot of those lately."

"Your biggest one was moving in here."

"Tell me about it," she returned with a sneer. "Well, you needn't worry. I'll be out of your way in a few minutes." She yanked the suitcase off the bed and reached for her coat, preparing to leave. Boldly she paused and raised her eyes to meet his. With her lips curved upward, she regarded him with open disdain. "Steve is really going to be upset about this."

"I'll deal with him later." The look he was giving her said that if anyone had a right to be angry, it was him. As though Steve had been the one to let *him* down.

With a carefully manufactured calm, Lindy stopped at the front door, set down her suitcase and slipped the key to the apartment off her chain.

Rush held out his hand and she pressed it into his waiting palm. Once again he looked as if he wanted to say that she could stay until morning. She didn't know what stopped him–probably his pride. Men had to have their pride. No doubt he was aware that she'd take delight in throwing the invitation back in his face.

Lindy watched as Rush's dark eyes narrowed, then she sadly shook her head. For years she'd been hearing Rush's name exalted. According to Steve, Rush Callaghan was both an officer and a gentleman. In the space of fifteen minutes, Lindy had quickly discovered he was neither.

"Bad judgment must run in the family," she said, more for her own ears than his. "If Steve thinks you're so wonderful, then my mistake about Paul seems like a minor miscalculation of character." With that she picked up her lone suitcase and pulled open the front door.

Rush's hand reached out and gripped her shoulder, stopping her. "Family? What exactly do you mean by that?"

"Steve Kyle, my brother. You know, the man who pays half the rent for this place? The one who wrote and claimed I was welcome to live here until I found a job?"

His fingers closed painfully over her shoulder and his eyes simmered with impatient anger. "Why the hell didn't you say you were Steve's sister?" He reached for her suitcase, stripped it from her hands and jerked her back inside the apartment. Rush slammed the door shut after her and studied her as though seeing her for the first time.

"Don't tell me you didn't know!" she shouted back. "Just who the hell did you think I was?" The answer to that was all too obvious and a heated flash of bright color invaded her neck and cheeks. "Oh, honestly, that's…disgusting."

Rush raked his fingers through his hair in an agitated movement and walked a few steps past her before turning around to confront her once more. "Listen, I didn't know. Honest."

"Does this mean I'm welcome to spend the night in my own brother's apartment?"

He let that taunt pass. "Yes, of course."

"How generous of you."

Rush picked up the suitcase and carried it back into Steve's bedroom, his jerky movements revealing both his chagrin and his anger. Lindy followed him, no longer sure what to make of this man. She knew Steve's invitation had been a spur of the moment thing. The two men easily could have gotten their wires crossed. From experience Lindy knew how letters could get held up in the military, and it was likely that Rush hadn't known she was planning on moving in. Still that didn't excuse his arrogant attitude toward her.

Lindy was two steps behind the man who Steve claimed was his best friend. Rush set the suitcase back on top of the mattress and hesitated before turning around to face her once more.

"I apologize. Okay?"

She answered him with an abrupt nod. His apology was followed by a short, uneasy silence. Lindy didn't know what to say. After a tense moment, she murmured, "I think the entire incident is best forgotten."

"Good." Rush buried his hands in his pockets, looking as uncomfortable as Lindy felt. "Of course you're welcome to stay in the apartment as long as you like. I'm hoping to be out of here by the end of the week."

"I thought you'd already left. I mean…"

Apparently he knew what she meant. "I had, but there were some mechanical difficulties and the *Mitchell* is back in the shipyard for repairs."

"For a week?" After nearly drowning in love and concern from her parents, Lindy had been looking forward to living alone. Well, so much for that–at least for now.

"Possibly longer, but don't worry about it. You're welcome to stay," Rush murmured, still looking uncomfortable.

Lindy guessed that he didn't often make apologies. "Thanks, but I have no intention of burdening you any longer than necessary. As soon as I've found a job, I'll be on my way."

"'Night," Rush said abruptly, taking a step in retreat.

"Good night," Lindy returned with a weak, dispirited smile.

Rush walked out of the room and Lindy closed it in his wake and leaned against the frame. Her mind was whirling. She knew even before she climbed between the sheets that she wasn't likely to sleep any time soon. Rest, like contentment, had been a fleeting commodity these past few weeks.

Rush smelled fresh coffee when he woke the next morning. With some reluctance, he climbed out of bed and dressed. He'd made a heel of himself and he wasn't eager to face Steve's sister with his head throbbing and his mouth tasting like something floating in a skid-row gutter. After he'd left Lindy the night before, he'd tried to sleep, given up an hour later and gone back to drink the rest of the six-pack of beer and watch television. Now he was suffering the consequences of his folly.

He sat for a moment on the edge of his bed, his head in his hands. For years he'd heard stories about his friend's younger sister. How intelligent she was, how clever, how pretty. Steve was more than fond of his sister. He adored her and now Rush had gone and insulted her, and in the process maligned his best friend. He should have realized that Steve wasn't fool enough to set a woman up in their apartment. Hell, Steve was still so much in love with his ex-wife that he couldn't see straight.

Damn it all, Rush mused, irritated with himself. He shouldn't have downed those first two beers. If his head had been clearer, he might have recognized her name.

Rush frowned. He vaguely recalled Steve telling him about some fancy job with a large insurance company that was supposed to be waiting for Lindy once she graduated from college. Come to think of it, he thought Steve had said she was engaged to be married this summer, as well. He wondered what she was doing in Seattle, but after their poor beginning he wasn't about to drill her about her job or problems with her fiancé.

Lindy sat at the kitchen table with the morning newspaper spread out in front of her. She chose to ignore Rush. As far as she was concerned the man had all the sensitivity of a woman-hating Neanderthal. Okay, so they were going to be sharing the apartment for a while. A week, he'd said. She could last that long if he could.

Rush walked over to the coffeepot, poured himself a cup, then muttered something that sounded faintly like a growl. Lindy supposed that was his own prehistoric version of "good morning." She responded in kind.

"What was that?" he demanded.

"What?"

"That disgusting little noise you just made."

"I was just wishing you a good morning."

"I'll bet," he muttered, lifting the steaming mug to his lips. He took a sip, then grimaced as if he'd scalded his tongue. He paused to glare at Lindy as though to blame her for his troubles.

Swallowing a chuckle, Lindy stood, deposited her coffee cup in the kitchen sink and left the table, taking the morning paper with her. It wasn't until she was in her bedroom that she realized she was smiling–something she hadn't felt like doing in a long while. Maybe having a man around to thwart and frustrate wasn't such a bad idea. With few exceptions, she'd recently come to view the opposite sex as both demanding and unreasonable. Rush Callaghan certainly fit the mold.

Gathering her clothes and a few personal items, Lindy headed for the bathroom. She'd discarded her robe and had just leaned over the tub to start her bathwater, when Rush strolled in.

"Are you planning to–" He stopped abruptly, his jaw slack.

Reluctantly Lindy straightened, gripping the front of her gaping pajama top with one hand. Color mounted in her cheeks like a red flag rising as she realized that her bent position over the tub had probably granted Rush a bird's-eye view of her rounded derriere. The flimsy baby-doll top no doubt gave him an equally revealing study of her breasts through the thin material. Incensed with herself as much as at Rush, she jerked a towel off the rack and wrapped it around her middle.

"Sorry," he muttered and quickly moved out of the room. He stood just across the threshold, watching her as though he couldn't jerk his gaze away. He swallowed hard once before stiffly stepping away.

Lindy walked over and purposefully closed the door. To be on the safe side she locked it.

"Just how long are you planning to be in there?" Rush

shouted, apparently not feeling the necessity to disguise his bad mood.

Lindy reached for her Timex. She looked at the watch and gave herself fifteen minutes. "I'll be out before eight." She expected an argument, but if Rush had any objection he didn't voice it.

Once Lindy was soaking in the hot bathwater, she found herself grinning once more. It was obvious that Rush Callaghan wasn't accustomed to having a woman around. The thought pleased her, but it didn't surprise her. The man was a grouch and dictatorial to boot, acting as though it were a woman's duty to humbly submit to his every command. There weren't many females who would be willing to put up with that kind of chauvinistic attitude. Lindy certainly wouldn't.

Nor had she been oblivious to his admiring appraisal. Just the memory of his slow, hungry look was enough to lift her mood considerably. After Paul, it did her ego a world of good to realize another man found her appealing. Plenty of doubts had surfaced over the past few weeks regarding her feminine charms, and it gave Lindy a cozy feeling deep down to realize she possessed enough allure to tempt a man.

Now that she had time to think about it, Lindy admitted that Rush wasn't so bad-looking himself in a fundamental sort of way. Until a woman recognized his condescending ways, Rush would undoubtedly fascinate her. He was well over six feet tall, with a muscled, whipcord leanness that spoke of discipline and control. His broad shoulders tapered to narrow hips and long legs. Without much effort, Lindy could picture him standing at attention in full-dress uniform, surveying all that was before him with an arrogant tilt of his square jaw. Lindy was surprised at the sudden strong charge of pleasure the thought gave her. Her mind conjured him standing tall and immovably proud, shoulders squared, gaze focused straight ahead. With the thought, some of the pique she'd been feeling toward him vanished.

But what intrigued her most about Rush Callaghan, she decided, were his eyes. Although he hadn't said more than a handful of words to her this morning, his dark blue gaze was highly expressive and more than able to telegraph his sour mood. She'd gained a good deal of pleasure in provoking him and then watching his brows crowd his eyes, narrowing them into slits of cool, assessing color. Later when he'd confronted her in the bathroom, those same clear blue eyes had revealed much more.

As her mind continued to play with the thoughts, Lindy scooted down into the hot water, raised a washcloth and idly drizzled the water over her smooth, flat stomach.

In the hallway outside the bathroom door, Rush paced like a stalking, caged tiger. He'd checked his watch every damn minute for the past five. Just how long did it take a woman to bathe, for God's sake? Too damn long, for his tastes.

Finally accepting the fact that pacing wasn't going to hurry her any, he retreated into his bedroom and sat on the edge of the mattress. In an effort to be honest with himself Rush admitted that it wasn't the fact that Lindy was hogging the one facility in the apartment that irritated him so much. It was the tantalizing figure she'd presented to him when he'd inadvertently walked in on her.

Her firm young body had all but taken his breath away, and when he checked his hands he found he was still trembling with the effects of the brief encounter. He hadn't a clue as to why she would wear that silly piece of lace. The silky see-through fabric didn't hide a damn thing.

Like an innocent, he'd moved into the bathroom only to be confronted by the sweet curve of her buttocks and the milky white skin of her long, shapely legs. Rush could swear the woman's legs went all the way up to her neck.

If that sight hadn't been enough to hammer the breath from his lungs, having her turn around and confront him had. Her full pink breasts had darkened at the tips as she struggled to hold the front of her pajamas together. Not that her efforts had done much good. Her nipples had hardened and pointed straight at him as though begging to be kissed. Even now the image had the power to tighten his groin and make his breath come in harsh, uneven gulps.

A week. Oh Lord. He wondered if he could last that long. He inhaled deeply and closed his eyes. He hoped the *Mitchell* would be ready to sail by then because he didn't know how much longer he could contain himself around Lindy. He knew he had to avoid a relationship with her at all costs. In addition to being his best friend's sister, Lindy was hurting, Rush realized. Something had happened–he didn't know what, didn't need to know–but he'd recognized the heavy shadow of pain and grief that hung over her head like a dark thundercloud. Something had knocked her world off kilter. And Rush wasn't in a position to right it. He wasn't anyone's savior. In the meantime, the best thing that could happen was for him to keep his eyes and ears to himself and pray the *Mitchell* left ahead of schedule.

Lindy found Rush was in the kitchen when she returned from job hunting late that afternoon. Her day had gone amazingly well and she felt greatly encouraged. After filling out dozens of forms and passing a series of tests, she was scheduled for an interview at the Boeing Renton plant for the following Monday. The salary was more than she'd hoped for and the benefits substantial. She held high hopes for the interview. Perhaps the worm had finally turned and her luck was going to change. She certainly hoped so. But in the meantime she felt obligated to keep job hunting in case something else turned up between now and then. Besides she didn't relish lingering around the apartment, bumping into Rush everytime she turned around.

"Hi," Lindy greeted Rush cheerfully, draping the strap of

her purse over the back of the kitchen chair. She was in the mood to be generous with her reluctant roommate. After her fruitful day of job hunting, she was actually beginning to feel a little like her old self.

It was obvious, however, from the vicious way Rush was scrubbing away at the dishes that his earlier dark mood hadn't improved.

He grumbled a reply, but didn't turn around. "Listen, I've got a schedule posted outside the bathroom so there won't be a recurrence of what happened this morning."

A schedule for the bathroom? He had to be joking! "Okay," she answered, having difficulty disguising her amusement. She opened the refrigerator and took out a cold can of soda, closed the door and momentarily leaned against it. It struck her then that she was hungry. She'd eaten lunch hours before, but with her limited funds she couldn't afford a fancy restaurant meal and had opted, instead, for a fast-food chicken salad. She had started to search through the cupboards when Rush turned around and nearly collided with her

"Excuse me," he said stiffly.

"No problem." She pressed herself against the counter as he moved past.

From the way he skirted around her, one would think she was a carrier of bubonic plague.

Without another word, Rush wiped his hands dry, rehung the dish towel and moved into the living room to turn on the television.

Since he didn't appear to be the least bit communicative, she wasn't about to ask him if he'd eaten or if he was hungry. Far be it from her to appear anxious to share a meal with Rush when he obviously wanted to ignore her. They weren't on a Sunday-school picnic here, they were merely polite strangers whose presence had been forced on each other.

Sorting through the cupboards, Lindy brought out spaghetti noodles and a bottle of spicy Italian sauce. After weeks of a skimpy appetite, it felt good to think about cooking something substantial.

The sausage was frying up nicely and the faint scent of fennel and sage wafted through the kitchen. Lindy brought out an onion and had begun dicing it to add to the meat when the knife slipped and neatly sliced into her index finger.

The sight of blood squirting over the cutting board shocked more than hurt her. She cried out in a moment of panic and rushed to the sink, holding her hand.

"Lindy, are you all right?"

She ignored the question. The cut hurt now. Badly. Closing her eyes, she held her finger under the running water.

"What happened?" Rush demanded, joining her at the sink.

"Nothing." Already the stainless steel was splashed with blotches of blood.

"You cut yourself!"

He sounded angry, as though she'd purposely injured herself in a futile attempt to gain his sympathy. "Are you always this brilliant or is this show of intelligence for my benefit?" she asked through clenched teeth. He looked stunned for a minute as though he didn't understand a word of what she was saying. "Any idiot could see I've cut myself," she cried, her voice raised and laced with a healthy dose of fright.

"Let me take a look at it."

She shook her head forcefully, wishing he'd go away so she could assess the damage herself. The terrible stinging had been replaced by an aching throb. She couldn't keep herself from bouncing, as if the action would lessen the pain.

"Give me your hand," he demanded, reaching for it.

"Stop shouting at me," she yelled, and jerked away from him. "As far as I'm concerned this is all your fault."

"My fault?" His expressive blue eyes widened.

"Any fool knows better than to keep sharp knives around." Lindy knew she wasn't making sense, but she couldn't seem to help herself.

"For God's sake, stop hopping around and let me get a good look at it."

Using his upper body, he trapped her against the counter. She really didn't have any choice but to let him examine the cut. Biting unmercifully into her bottom lip, she unfolded her fist, while gripping her wrist tightly with her free hand.

His touch was surprisingly gentle and she watched as his brow folded together in a tight frown of concern.

"It doesn't look like you're going to need stitches."

Lindy expelled a sigh of relief. With no health insurance, a simple call to the hospital emergency room would quickly deplete her limited funds. And although her parents were willing, Lindy didn't want to ask them for money.

"Here." With a tenderness she hadn't expected from Rush, he reached for a clean towel and carefully wrapped it around her hand. "It looks like the bleeding has stopped. Wait here and I'll get a bandage."

It was all Lindy could do to nod. She felt incredibly silly now, placing the blame on him for having a sharp knife. He left her and returned a couple of minutes later with some gauze and tape.

"I didn't mean what I said about this being your fault," she told him, raising her eyes to meet his.

His eyes widened momentarily, and then a smile flickered in their blue depths. "I know," was all he said.

Although she was willing to credit her loss of blood with the stunning effect of his smile, there was no discounting the way her heart and head reacted. The simple action left Lindy warmed in its afterglow long after her finger was bandaged.

Three days passed and Rush and Lindy became a little more comfortable with each other. There were still a few awkward moments, but Lindy discovered that they could at least sit across the table from each other and carry on a decent conversation without risking an argument.

Rush tended to stay out of her way–and she, his–but there were certain times of the day when meeting was inevitable. In the mornings when they were both hurrying to get ready to leave the apartment, for instance. Twice Rush had gone out in the evening, leaving abruptly without a word. Lindy hadn't asked where he went and he didn't volunteer the information, but Lindy had the impression that he was simply avoiding being at close quarters with her.

Since it seemed silly for them to cook separate meals, they'd reached an agreement that Lindy would prepare the meals and Rush would do the dishes.

Rush was sitting in the living room when Lindy let herself into the apartment on Friday afternoon. She tossed her purse aside and slumped down on the opposite end of the sofa away from him.

"Any luck?" he asked in a conversational way, watching her.

Lindy noted that he looked tired and frustrated. "No, but I'm hoping everything will come together at the interview on Monday."

He stood, rammed his hands into his pockets and looked away from her, staring out the window. "I'm not exactly filled with good news myself."

"Oh?" She studied him closely, wondering at his strange mood.

"Without going into a lot of detail," he said, his voice tight, "the problem holding up the *Mitchell* isn't going to be easily fixed."

Lindy nodded and drew in a ragged breath, not sure what was coming next.

"It's going to take as long as a month to have the parts flown in," he continued.

"I see." She straightened and brushed aside a crease in her blue skirt, her fingers lingering over the material. "I suppose this means you want me to leave then, doesn't it?"

Chapter Three

"Leave?" Rush echoed, looking both surprised and angry.

Lindy bounded to her feet, her hands clenched at her sides in tight fists. "It's a perfectly logical question, so don't snap at me."

"I'm not snapping."

"A turtle couldn't do it better."

"Are you always this prickly or is it something about me?" He was glaring at her, demanding a response, the look in his eyes hot enough to boil water.

Although his voice was deliberately expressionless and quiet, Lindy knew by the tight set of his jaw that he was getting madder by the minute. Not that she cared. The man drove her absolutely loony. She'd never known anyone who could control his emotions the way Rush did. Oh sure, he laughed, he smiled, he talked, he argued, but in the entire four days that she'd been living in the apartment with him, he'd revealed as much sentiment as a wooden Indian. Even when she'd cut her finger and hopped around the kitchen like a crazed kangaroo, he'd been as calm and collected as though he handled hurting, frightened women every day of his life. Nothing seemed to faze Rush. Nothing.

"Well, you needn't worry. I'll go," she announced with a proud tilt of her chin. "It won't be necessary for you to ask twice." She bent down and reached for the strap of her purse, her heart pounding like a charging locomotive. Moving was something she should have done the minute she realized she wasn't going to have the apartment to herself.

"Damn it, Lindy. I didn't say you had to leave."

She blinked. "You didn't?"

"No. You jumped to conclusions."

"Oh." Now she felt like a bloody idiot. It was on the tip of her tongue to apologize. She'd had a rough day; the heel had broken off her shoe and the job she'd gone to apply for wasn't the least bit as it had been advertised. Although they'd offered it to her, she'd decided against it. Good grief. She wouldn't have been anything more than a glorified desk clerk. Maybe she shouldn't be so particular, but after four years of college she wanted so much more than to file papers and answer a telephone.

Maybe she was feeling a little guilty because she'd told Rush she hadn't had any luck when she'd actually gotten a job offer. And refused it.

They stood not more than five feet apart and his piercing gaze locked with hers, burning straight through her proud resolve.

When Lindy spoke her voice was husky with emotion, and her heart began a heavy muted pounding against her rib cage. "I lied."

Rush's eyes clouded, then hardened, and Lindy felt the dread crowd its way into her throat. Rush wasn't the type of man who would take something like this lightly.

"What did you lie about?"

"I got offered a job today. I turned it down." With her long tapered nails biting into the flesh of her palms, she explained the circumstances. "I thought you should know because... well, because I plan to rent my own place as soon as I can after I find something. But it looks like I could be around awhile."

A smile flickered over his lips and he appeared to relax a little. "I can stand it if you can."

"That's debatable."

They were both grinning then, and Lindy felt the uneasy tension seep from her limbs. Now that she'd explained things to Rush she felt much better. In fact, possibly for the first time, she was completely at ease with him. It wasn't that he intimidated her so much as he challenged her. She felt as if she had to be constantly on her guard with him. Watch her step, keep the peace–that sort of thing.

"You must be hungry." she said, turning toward the kitchen. "I'll get dinner going."

"Lindy."

She twisted around, her eyes questioning.

"Since it's Friday and we've both had a trying week, how about going out for a pizza?"

The minute Rush issued the invitation, he was convinced he'd done the wrong thing. His biggest concern was that he was giving Lindy the wrong impression. When the repairs on the *Mitchell* were finished he'd be leaving, and he didn't want to give his best friend's sister the idea that there could ever be anything romantic between them. The circumstances in which they were living were tempting enough, and here he was adding to the tension by deepening the relationship to something beyond their polite but strained friendship.

Hell, he wasn't even sure why he'd suggested they go out. The last couple of nights he'd purposely left the apartment and sat in a bar on the waterfront, nursing a drink or two. The best way to deal with this awkward situation, he'd decided, was to stay away from Lindy as much as possible. Remove himself from temptation, so to speak. Because, damn it all, Lindy Kyle was one hell of a tempting morsel. Her young, firm body was ripe and it had been too long since he'd had a woman. Every time he was in the same room with her, he felt the charge of electricity arc between them. Until today, he'd been able to deal with it, and now he was purposely exposing them to God only knew what.

He wanted to be angry with her–needed it to dilute the effect she had on him. When she'd admitted she'd lied, he'd felt a reassuring irritation surging up inside him, rough and heated. As far as he was concerned, women weren't exactly known for their integrity. Although disappointed in her, he'd made a conscious effort to control his ire, knowing it wouldn't do any good to blow up at her.

And then she'd told him about turning down the job, her clear brown eyes soft and filled with contrition for having misled him. Her eager, young face had been as readable as a first-grade primer. She'd stood before him, so forthright and honest, and he'd felt something deep and fundamental move inside him. Before he'd even known what was happening, he'd offered to take her to dinner.

It was more than that, too. Steve's letter had finally caught up with him, explaining what had happened to Lindy. The poor kid had been through a lot. Apparently she'd been deeply in love with this Paul Abrams, and she'd been crushed when he'd broken the engagement. Rush had been crippled by emotional pain once himself. He knew from personal experience how devastating letting go of a loved one could be.

After reading his friend's long letter, Rush's opinion of Lindy had altered. Not that he'd made any dyed-in-the-wool assumptions about her before the letter's arrival. The fact was, he chose to think of her as little as possible. But after reading what Steve had written, he'd discovered that he admired Lindy for picking up the pieces of her life and forging ahead despite rejection and defeat.

Something else Steve had mentioned had strongly affected Rush. Throughout everything, Lindy hadn't shed a tear. Her entire family continued to worry about her because she was taking everything far too calmly, holding up much too well. It wasn't natural, Steve had claimed, sounding very much like the concerned older brother he was. Almost grudgingly, Rush found himself appreciating Lindy's courage and unsinkable pride. Not so long ago he'd been left to deal with the trauma of a lost love. He could still remember the pitying looks sent his way after Cheryl. The effort and control it had demanded on his part to pretend nothing was wrong, that losing Cheryl didn't really matter, had drained him. When all the while, every breath he drew had been a reminder that he'd been a fool to ever have trusted the woman. And worse, to have loved her.

Rush could identify with Lindy's attitude all too well. He would have walked over hot coals before he'd show his pain to anyone, friend or foe. Apparently she felt the same way. Maybe that was the reason he found himself wanting to spend more time with her, looking for a way to be her friend.

A Michael Jackson song blared loudly from the pizza parlor's jukebox and, much to her surprise, Lindy found herself tapping her foot to the music and wanting to snap her fingers. Rush sat across the booth from her, looking more relaxed and at ease than she could ever remember seeing him. A tall, frosty pitcher of beer rested in the middle of the table.

Lindy had already downed two thick mugs of ale and was feeling the dizzying, warm effects of the alcohol. Rarely had she tasted better pizza, and she'd pigged down three enormous slices, astonishing them both. Now she felt content and happy, two states of mind that had been sadly lacking in her life recently.

"If there was a big enough floor space, I'd want to dance," she told Rush, who instantly looked relieved–no doubt because he'd chosen a restaurant without one. Lindy giggled.

"What's so funny?"

"You!"

"I'm glad you find me so amusing."

"Don't take it personally. It's just that it feels so good to sit back and relax like this."

"That amuses you?"

"Yes, because you look like you've just been granted a pardon from the governor because you don't have to dance. And something else."

His dark brows shot up. "There's more?"

"Oh yes. For the first time since we met, I don't feel I have to keep my wits sharpened around you." She said it with a smile, hoping her good mood would cut any sting from her words. "In case you didn't know it, Rush Callaghan, you can be one hell of an arrogant jerk. Imagine posting a schedule to use the bathroom!"

His eyes narrowed, his jaw clenched in mock consternation, and still he looked every inch the sturdy, capable naval officer she knew him to be.

"There are a few truths about yourself I could enlighten you with as well, Lindy Kyle."

"Perhaps," she conceded.

He was teasing her and Lindy found herself warming to him. When he chose to, Rush could freeze out an Eskimo with one piercing glare. She hated to think of the men on the *Mitchell* facing his wrath because, although she hadn't seen it in full force, she'd witnessed enough to know his anger would be formidable. Discovering this gentler, fun-loving side of his nature had been an unexpected surprise.

Still smiling, Rush stood and threw a couple of dollars onto the table. "Come on, let's get out of here before someone pushes aside a few tables and starts up a band."

Lindy laughed and reached for her sweater and purse. Rush's hand lightly touched the small of her back as he guided her out of the restaurant. "So you really aren't going to take me dancing?" she asked, once they were outside in the cool June air.

"Not on your life."

Lindy released a slow, expressive sigh and glanced up into the dark warmth of his gaze. A small taste of excitement filled her, and some of the heavy feeling that had weighted her heart for so many interminable weeks lifted.

"Would the lady consider a walk instead?" Rush said, his voice oddly tender, indulgent. He lifted his hand and rested it against her shoulder, his touch amazingly light.

Lindy had the impression that he'd rather not have his hand where it was, but that he couldn't help himself, and she waded through a surge of elation. It was marvelous to feel like a woman again, and she was highly aware of her power, however fleeting.

They strolled toward the busy Seattle waterfront, weaving in and out of the crowds that lingered on the sidewalk. The air was clean and fresh, smelling of tangy salt and seaweed, and although the sun had set, the gentle breeze carried with it a pleasing warmth.

Rush bought them coffee from a seafood bar and they silently walked along the pier, staring at the lights from the ferryboat as it glided across the murky green waters of Puget Sound.

"Can I see the *Mitchell* from here?" Lindy asked.

"No. It's in the shipyard in Bremerton, which is all the way across the Sound."

"You really love the sea, don't you?"

Rush's fingers momentarily tightened their grip on her shoulder. "Yes, I do. Did Steve ever tell you I was born on a ferryboat?"

"No."

"I think my destiny was cast then. My mother named me Rush because they were hurrying to get her to the hospital in time. Unfortunately, or fortunately, depending on how one chooses to look at it, I was born on the water."

"And have been at home there ever since," she added in a soft whisper.

He nodded and their eyes met in a brief exchange of rare understanding. Rush continued talking, telling her a little of his youth and his early days at Annapolis. He made a striking figure, leaning against the edge of the pier, Lindy noted. He paused and smiled down at her. His eyes narrowed briefly with appreciation and it was as if they had become two different people for this one special night.

Rush looked younger, Lindy mused, more open. For the first time since she'd arrived in Seattle, she felt that she was beginning to appreciate this complex man. Maybe because he was really talking to her, sharing a small part of himself with her. There was no pretense between them tonight. Somehow Lindy realized how rare it was for Rush to expose this amiable, sensitive part of himself, to let down his guard and throw caution to the wind. She felt as though she'd been granted a rare gift, one that she would look back on years from now and treasure.

They left the pier a few minutes later, discarded their Styrofoam cups and continued strolling down the busy sidewalk until they reached Waterfront Park. Lindy braced her foot against the bottom stair, which led to an observation deck and a museum on the second level.

"It's a beautiful night," Rush commented, staring into the sky.

Lindy had the feeling he was about to suggest they head back to the apartment. She didn't want the evening to end. Everything was too perfect for them to leave so soon.

"Come on. I'll race you up the stairs," she called, letting the breeze carry her challenge. Not waiting to see if he was going to follow her, she grabbed for the railing and hurled herself up the concrete steps, taking two at a time.

The wind, which had recently picked up, whipped her hair from her face as she made a mad dash up the stairway, doing her best to swallow her laughter.

"Lindy."

Rush's exasperated voice was directly behind her, and not wishing to be outdistanced, she lurched forward.

He beat her easily and was waiting for her, blocking her way when she breathlessly reached the top.

"You little fool."

Still panting and laughing, she tried to leap around him but almost lost her balance. A look of horror crowded his face as he reached out to grab her, but Lindy quickly darted in the opposite direction. Rush tried to block her there, as well, and she shrieked with the sheer joy of the moment and scooted sideways from him.

"Lindy, stop."

She dodged to her left and when he followed her, she darted to her right, then triumphantly stumbled past him, running to the railing, her eyes wild with joy.

"I won," she declared triumphantly, swinging around to face him.

Rush collapsed on the park bench, barely winded. "You cheated."

"Oh, honestly. Can't you admit it when a woman outsmarts you?"

"I'd admit it if it was true."

"My foot, you would." Lindy slumped down on the bench beside him, her breath coming in uneven, shallow gasps. Good Lord, she was out of shape. She let her head fall back so her hair rushed away from her face, granting her a feeling of complete freedom.

Lindy exhaled, dragging the oxygen through her lungs. "Oh, Paul, I can't remember a night when I've had more fun." The instant the name slipped through her lips, Lindy tensed. "I meant…Rush."

The excitement that had galloped through her blood just seconds before felt like a deadweight pressing against her chest. For one crazy moment she was paralyzed. She had trouble breathing, trouble moving, trouble thinking. Scalding tears burned in her eyes, and the huge lump in her throat felt as if it were monumental.

Moisture rolled down the side of her face, burning her skin like acid, and she sucked in a trembling sob.

"Lindy, are you all right?"

Rush brushed away a tear and his finger felt incredibly warm against her icy cold cheek.

"Something must have gotten into my eye," she lied, turning away so he wouldn't be able to see the extent of her emotion.

"Here."

He pressed a white handkerchief into her numb fingers, and she made a quick job of wiping her face dry. "I think we should be heading back. Don't you?"

"Anything you say."

He sounded so concerned when it was the last thing she wanted. Suddenly Rush was the last person in the world she yearned to be with. Escape seemed of paramount importance. Somehow she found her way to her feet, although the cement seemed to buckle beneath her shoes. With some effort she managed to keep her balance and rush away from the bench.

It would have been too much to hope that Rush would let her go. But oddly enough he seemed to appreciate her mood, remaining silent as he matched his quick steps to hers. Side by side they started up the hill toward First Avenue.

The climb was steep and Lindy was winded by the time they'd gone only a few blocks.

"I'll get a taxi," Rush said.

"No. Don't, please." She wanted to walk–needed to wear herself out physically so she could collapse in her bed exhausted. It was the only way she could guarantee she would sleep. The simple act of putting one foot in front of the other, climbing up one street and then the next one, seemed to help her contain her emotions.

By the time they reached the apartment building, Lindy's lungs ached and her calf muscles violently protested the strenuous exercise. She waited impatiently while Rush unlocked the front door.

He held it open for her, and in that moment she detested him for the small display of manners. Paul had impeccable manners and look what he'd done to her. Look what he'd reduced her to.

Without even glancing in Rush's direction she paused just inside the living room and said, her voice weak and faltering, "Thank you for dinner."

He didn't answer her for what seemed an eternity, and she had the impression he was willing her to turn around and face him. But she knew she couldn't without dissolving into wretched emotion.

"Anytime, Lindy." His words were low and as smooth as velvet.

"Good night." The sooner she got away from Rush the better.

"'Night." Again his voice was so gentle, so tender.

She made it all the way to the bathroom door before her gaze blurred so badly with tears that she had to stop and wipe the moisture from her eyes. Drawing in several steadying breaths between clenched teeth gave her some relief. She'd be damned before she'd cry over Paul Abrams.

Damned. Damned. Damned.

Without being aware of how it happened, Lindy found that she had stopped and braced a shoulder against the wall, using it to keep her upright, needing its support. She pinched her nose with her thumb and index fingers, willing back the release of torrential tears.

"Lindy, you need to cry."

The words seemed to come from a far distance, echoing around her in a canyon of despair. She dropped her hand and looked up to find Rush standing beside her.

"No," she said forcefully. "I won't."

"Don't let him do this to you."

She tried to push Rush away, but her effort was puny and weak. "You don't know anything," she cried. "How could you?"

"I know what it is to hurt."

"Not like this." No one could ever hurt this much. No one.

"Listen to me," he said, and his hands gripped her shoulders. But even his fingers were gentle when she wanted them to be hard and punishing. "Cry. Let it out before the grief strangles you."

"No." Still she resisted, wildly shaking her head. "No. I hate him. I hate him."

"I know, honey. I know."

The dam broke then, and the tears that had been pent up inside her soul, shoved down and ignored for so long, bled from her eyes. A low, mewing sound slid from the back of her throat, nearly choking her. Sobs overtook her, huge, oxygen-robbing sobs that shook her shoulders and made her breast heave.

Rush didn't try to hold her and she was grateful because she couldn't have borne being restrained. Unable to remain upright, she braced her back against the wall and slumped to the floor. She gently rocked back and forth, weeping bitterly for the innocence she had lost, and wailing for the love she had given so freely to a man who didn't deserve it. She cried until there was nothing left inside her.

Lindy started to retch when her tears were spent, and she knew she was about to lose her dinner. Rush's hand under her elbow helped her to an upright position and into the bathroom. He stood behind her as she leaned over the toilet. She thought she felt his hand on her back, but she couldn't be sure.

When she was finished he handed her a damp washcloth. She held it to her face, letting the coolness soak away some of the terrible red heat. Her eyes burned like fire, her throat felt gritty and coarse, and her hands shook.

"Here." Rush handed her a glass of water.

She felt an abundance of shame at having allowed him to see her like this, and worse, that he should be the one to take care of her. She sank to the edge of the tub, afraid her shaky legs could no longer support her.

"You're going to be all right now," Rush told her confidently. "It's over."

She couldn't look at him but nodded because it seemed the right thing to do. Rush had no way of knowing what Paul had done to her. No way of knowing that the man she'd loved and planned to share her life with had married another woman while Lindy proudly wore his engagement ring. Rush Callaghan didn't know a damn whit about shattered dreams or the pain of a broken heart. He would never allow himself to be hurt this way.

"Come on," he said. "I'll take you into your room."

She stood with his help, and he tucked his arm around her waist as he led her into her darkened bedroom. Gently he brushed the wet strands of hair from her face and lowered her onto the mattress in a sitting position.

"I trust you don't need anyone to undress you."

"No, I'm fine."

"It's a damn good thing," he said, and there was more than a trace of a smile in his words.

He started to walk away from her but paused just before he reached the door, turning back to her. "You're a beautiful woman, Lindy Kyle, and someday there'll be a man who will love you the way you deserve to be loved."

Her mother had said almost those identical words to her. At the time, Lindy hadn't been ready to accept them; she wasn't sure she could now. All through college there'd only been Paul. Every thought of the future had been linked with him. Every dream. Every ambition. She felt as if fate had sent her tumbling into oblivion, uncaring what ill fortune befell her.

But it wasn't in her to argue with Rush. Instead she brought her feet up onto the bed and pressed her head against the feather pillow. Her eyes ached unmercifully and she closed them.

"Did you hear me?" Rush demanded softly.

She wanted to shake her head that she hadn't, but there wasn't enough spirit left in her to challenge him. "I'm too selfish to pine away for Paul Abrams," she said, her soft voice trembling. "I'm not willing to be miserable any more."

Her words seemed to please him. "You're one hell of a woman, Lindy, and don't you forget it."

"Right." She couldn't contain the sarcasm. Although she kept her eyes closed, Lindy knew it was a long time before Rush left the doorway. His presence all but filled the room. Only when he'd slipped away did she feel comfortable enough to relax and sleep.

Lindy woke around two, her throat dry and scratchy. Her temples throbbed, and her eyes were red and swollen. She didn't turn on any lights as she made her way into the kitchen, preferring the shield of darkness.

The drapes were open and the city lights flickered in the distance. Taking the cold glass of water and the aspirin with her, Lindy stood at the window and expelled her breath in a long sigh. She'd made such an idiot of herself in front of Rush. The thought of facing him in the morning was almost more than she could bear.

Fresh tears dampened her face at the memory of the humiliating way she'd sobbed and moaned and rocked with grief. She exhaled a quivering breath and brushed her cheeks free of moisture.

"It's over, Lindy, there's no need to cry anymore."

She whirled around to discover Rush sitting in the darkened room, watching her.

"I'll cry if I damn well please," she hissed.

"There's no need to now."

Lord, she hated it when men thought they were so wonderfully logical. Everything seemed to be so cut-and-dried for them.

"Who made you king of the universe?"

He chuckled at that.

"I don't find that the least bit amusing. I honestly want to know what makes you think you know so damn much about human nature that you can decree when enough tears have been shed?"

"I know."

Lindy slapped her hand against her side in an action meant to reveal her disgust. "So the big lieutenant commander has spoken." She whirled around and placed the water glass down with such force that the liquid sloshed over the sides.

"How could you possibly know about loving someone and then losing them? You can't imagine what it's like to have your heart ripped from your chest and be left with a gaping wound that refuses to heal." She was yelling at him now, but not because she was angry. The memory of the way she'd broken down in front of him was more than embarrassing. Heated words were her only defense.

Rush was out of the chair so fast that it shocked her. He loomed at her side like a dragon, his jaw as tight and contorted as she'd ever seen it.

"I know more than I ever cared to." Each word dripped with ice, his message clear.

They stood, their gazes locked in the moonlight, glaring at each other, refusing to look away. She saw his pain then, as raw and jagged as her own. His guard was down. He'd lowered it for her tonight when she'd spilled out her heart, leaving himself exposed and trapped in pain-filled memories.

"Rush," she whispered, "I'm sorry. I didn't know." Slowly,

she lifted her hand and touched his shoulder, wanting to offer him comfort the way he had helped her. “I didn’t know.”

He reached for her then, crushing her in his arms, burying his face in the curve of her neck. He didn’t fill in the details. He didn’t need to.

Chapter Four

Lindy slept on the davenport across from Rush, but the sweet luxury of oblivion escaped him. Even now, hours later, he couldn't forget the unselfconscious way she'd wrapped her arms around him and held him, her tears soaking through his shirt. Rush wasn't sure who she was crying for anymore: him or her. It didn't matter.

Her body felt unbelievably good against his own, and her warmth had chased away the arctic chill that had seemed to cut all the way through to the marrow of his bones. He didn't like to think about Cheryl and rarely did these days. But somehow being a witness to Lindy's anguish had brought the memory of his own bobbing uncontrollably to the surface of his mind. Like a cork, the remembrance of his love and foolishness had refused to sink, and he'd been left to deal with the pain that had suddenly seemed as fresh and real as it had been eight years ago.

The memory of Cheryl had weighed on him like a steel cloak, tormenting his heart and mind. He'd loved her with a love that was pure and innocent. A love so rare that he never hoped to feel such deep, heart-wrenching emotion again. Leaving her to go to sea had been the most difficult thing he'd ever done. Every day of the tour he'd written to her, spilling out his heart. On payday he'd sent her every penny he could, living on a bare minimum himself because it was important to him that she have the things she needed.

When he'd reached home port, he couldn't get off the aircraft carrier fast enough. After six months at sea, he was dying to hold her again, dying to love her. But she hadn't been at the dock. Bitterly disappointed, the only thing Rush could reason was that she was ill. Well, he'd been partially right. Only her sickness was of the nine-month variety. From what he'd learned later, sweet innocent Cheryl had shacked up with another sailor a week after he'd left San Diego. She'd apparently hoped to pass the baby off as Rush's. Rush, however, hadn't needed a degree in math to calculate the dates.

It might have made things easier for him if they'd fought. He might have been able to release some of the bitter anguish he'd experienced over her infidelity. But instead he'd simply told her goodbye and walked away, the diamond engagement ring he'd intended to give her seeming to sear a hole through his palm.

In the weeks and months that followed, his mind played crazy tricks on him. He tried to convince himself the baby was his, although God knows it was impossible. He heard from a friend that Cheryl married some poor schmuck fresh out of officer training within a month after Rush had left her.

A couple of years later he'd run into her in a bar. Her big blue eyes had clouded with tears as she'd told him they'd let something good slip away. With a wedding band on her finger, she'd placed her hand high on his thigh and suggested they get together for old times' sake. Rush had thought he was going to vomit, she repulsed him so completely.

He never saw her again, never wanted to. Cheryl had taught him valuable lessons, ones destined to last a lifetime. She'd destroyed a part of him that could never be resurrected.

The first faint light of dawn seeped into the sky, extinguishing the stars one by one, and still Rush couldn't sleep. But the even meter of Lindy's breathing as she lay sleeping on the sofa was a soothing balm and gradually he felt the rigid tension leave his limbs.

They'd sat for hours, his arm around her, her head nestled over his heart. Neither had spoken—or wanted to. It was a time to remember. A time to forget. When she'd fallen into an exhausted sleep, he'd gently slipped free of her hold and lowered her head onto the sofa.

She was going to be all right now.

So was he.

Lindy squinted as the sun flooded the living room and seemed to rest, full force, on her face, disturbing her deep sleep. Her neck ached, and it was then that she realized that her only pillow had been the small flat decorative one from the couch. She felt disoriented until the memory of what had happened between her and Rush gushed through her mind like melting snow rushing down a mountainside during a spring thaw. She groaned and covered her face with her hands, embarrassed anew.

Slowly, almost against her will, she sat up and opened her eyes. She felt empty inside, depleted. Shaky.

A quick survey of the room told her Rush wasn't anywhere in the immediate vicinity, and she sighed with relief.

Coming to her feet, she brushed the mussed dark hair away from her face and stumbled into the kitchen. The coffee was made and a note propped against the base of the machine. Lindy reached for the slip of paper and blinked several times in an effort to clear her vision. Rush had duty and wouldn't be home until late afternoon.

Thank God.

She wasn't up to confronting him. Not now, anyway. What could she possibly say to him after she'd stripped herself emotionally naked and exposed her soul? Lord, she didn't know, but she'd figure it out later. Right now she wanted a hot bath and some breakfast, in that order.

By five that afternoon, she'd washed windows, baked a fresh apple pie and scrubbed the shower. Occupying herself with a dozen domestic tasks until she was forced into the inevitable confrontation with Rush.

She was frying pork chops for dinner when she heard the front door open, and she tensed, instantly filled with dread.

An awkward silence ensued when he stepped into the kitchen. Since she wasn't sure how to begin, she glanced around nervously and offered him a falsely cheerful smile.

Rush was frowning and she watched as his gaze bounced around the apartment, growing darker and more irritated with each passing moment.

Despite her best efforts, Lindy felt completely unstrung, and still Rush just stood there, looking straight through her with those impassive blue eyes of his.

"I baked a pie." It was an absurd thing to say, but Lindy was quickly losing a grip on her determination to be cheerful and pleasant.

"That's not what I smell."

Lindy saw him wrinkle up his nose a couple of times, sniffing. "What are you?" she asked, forcing a light laugh. "A bloodhound?"

Obstinately Rush refused to respond to her attempt at good humor. If anything, his face grew more marred by dark shadows and anger kindled in his eyes. "It smells like pine needles in here."

"Oh." Why, oh why, couldn't he play her game? He had to know how difficult all this was for her. "I scrubbed down the cupboards. I think I was supposed to dilute the cleaner more than I did."

Her back was braced against the counter, her fingers gripping the edge. She could feel a pulse come alive in her temple. She'd had all day to make up her mind what she was going to say to Rush, how she was going to act, but her conclusions had been vague and fearful. That was when she'd decided she wouldn't utter a word about what had happened, praying he wouldn't, either. She should have realized Rush wouldn't let her forget it.

"You've been busy."

She nodded eagerly. "Yeah, I decided to spruce up the place a bit."

Her efforts didn't appear to please him. Damn, but she wished he'd say or do something to help her. He had to know what she was going through.

"You said something about pork chops being your favorite dinner," she offered next, almost desperate. All the while, her eyes pleaded with him. She'd just found her footing with this man, and now she was floundering again, her feet slipping out from under her every which way she turned.

"That was thoughtful." Still he frowned, his brow crowding his eyes, darkening them all the more.

Lindy rushed to the stove and used a cooking fork to turn the sizzling meat. She dared not look at him, and when she spoke the words strangled her. "I wanted to thank you, I guess."

"For what?"

Obviously Rush wasn't going to exert the least bit of energy to help her. The stoic look of the wooden Indian was properly in place once more and she wanted to hate him for his ability to disguise his emotions so effortlessly.

"Lindy."

She ignored him, flipping the frying meat when it was totally unnecessary.

"Lindy, turn around and look at me."

She shook her head.

"Those pork chops are going to turn into rubber if you cook them much longer."

Forcefully she turned off the burner and slapped the cooking fork on the stove top. "I could hate you for this," she muttered between clenched teeth.

"Well don't, because it isn't any easier for me."

Her chest was heaving with indignation when she slowly turned so that they faced each other once more. Nothing about him said he was the least bit uncomfortable. They could have been discussing the weather for all the reaction Rush revealed.

"Well?" she demanded, not having a single clue as to what he was thinking. He wore the hard mask of disciplined self-control, and she longed to slap it from his face.

"I'm embarrassed, too," he admitted finally.

"You? Whatever for? I was the one who made a complete idiot of myself. I was the one who was wailing like a banshee." She whipped the hair from her face. "What could you possibly have to be embarrassed about?"

He looked as if he were going to answer her, but Lindy wasn't about to let him. An entire day of worry and frustration was banked against her fragile control.

"Why couldn't you have let it drop?" she continued. "Trust me, I was willing to forget the entire incident. But, oh no, Mister Know-It-All has to rub my nose in it."

The muscle in his clenched jaw leaped so hard his temple quivered, and a strange light flared in his eyes. "I didn't want any pretense between us."

Defiance and pride filled Lindy's breast and her long nails threatened to snap as she continued to grip the countertop behind her. "I don't, either," she whispered after a moment, willing now to release her resentment and accept the wisdom of his words.

"I'd like us to be friends."

She nodded, dropping her gaze to the freshly waxed kitchen floor. "Lord knows, I could use one."

He smiled at that, and when she glanced up she noted that his eyes had softened perceptibly.

"How did you know apple pie is my favorite?"

Relaxing, Lindy returned his smile. "A fine naval officer like you should know the answer to that. Apple pie has to rank right up there with hot dogs and the American flag."

They both laughed aloud then, but not because she'd been especially clever. The matter had been settled between them and they were on an even keel once more. They could be friends.

"Well, how do I look?" Lindy asked Rush Monday morning. She stood beside the kitchen table, where he sat reading the paper and drinking coffee. Her interview wasn't scheduled until noon, but she'd been dressed and ready since eight, pacing the living room. Lord, he swore she'd straightened the same stack of magazines ten times.

"You're going to do great."

"You didn't even look at me," she accused, her hands clenched together in front of her. She was a picture of efficiency in her dark blue business suit, white blouse and navy pumps. If it were up to him, he would hire her on the spot.

"You look wonderful," he said, meaning it. Too damn good for his own peace of mind, if the truth be known.

She checked her wristwatch and nibbled nervously on the corner of her bottom lip. "I think I'll leave now."

"Good idea." To be truthful, he'd be glad to have her out of the apartment. But not because she was making a nuisance of herself. Oh sure, her pacing was beginning to get on his nerves, but far more profound than that–Lindy was beginning to get to him. Bad.

She reached for her purse. "I'll see you later."

"Break a leg, kid."

"Thanks."

Her quick smile ate like a sweet-tasting acid all the way through him. He'd been a fool to think their nonrelationship would fall neatly back into place after Friday night. He'd been a first-class idiot to believe they could just be friends. Oh, they were that all right, but God knew he hungered for more. Much more.

Rush's breath escaped on a long, disgusted sigh as he pushed his coffee cup aside. Every time he looked at Lindy his body started to throb. It wasn't even funny. In fact it was downright embarrassing.

He leaned back in the chair and folded his arms over his chest, trying to reason matters out. Lindy was years younger than he. Ten, at least. And she'd been hurt, the pain much too fresh for her to trust her feelings. To further complicate the situation, she was Steve Kyle's little sister. Rush might be able to overlook the first stickler, but not the second or the third. Lindy was too vulnerable now, too susceptible. And Steve Kyle was much too good a friend to lose because Rush couldn't maintain his self-control.

Lord, he wished she'd get that damn job and move out of the apartment. And out of his life. Once she'd cleared out, maybe things would go back to normal and he could concentrate on matters that were important to him.

That wasn't true, Rush admitted even as he thought it. He liked having Lindy around, liked her being there when he came in after a frustrating day aboard the *Mitchell*. Liked talking to her in the evenings. That was the problem in a nutshell. He liked every damn thing there was about Lindy Kyle.

Rush was mature enough, disciplined enough, to ignore the physical attraction, although God knows it was difficult. A thousand times he'd cursed the memory of that morning when he had found her in the bathroom, and seen her all soft and feminine. His mental picture of the way her breasts had peeped out at him, firm and round and proud, had the power, even now, to eat a hole straight through his mind. For his own sense of well-being he couldn't allow his thoughts to dwell on how good she'd felt in his arms, or how she'd fallen asleep with her head resting securely over his heart. Nor did he choose to think about how he'd sat and stroked her hair, drinking in her softness, marveling in her gentleness.

Lindy's allure, however, was much more profound than the physical. In the space of one week she'd managed to reach into his heart, dragging the emotion out of him like hidden scarves from the sleeves of a clown. Each one more colorful than the last. Each one a surprise. Lindy made him feel vulnerable, threatening him in ways he'd never expected to experience again.

He wanted to stay away from her, avoid her as he had in the beginning. But Lindy was like a magnetic field that drew everything to itself. He couldn't be anywhere near her and not want her. Physically. Emotionally. Every damn way there was to want a woman.

He stood then, determined not to think about her anymore. A cold shower was what he needed to wake him up to a few fundamental facts. He wasn't an inexperienced youth, unable to control himself. Rush had been around the block more times than he cared to count.

With a fresh set of clothes, he stepped into the bathroom and shut the door. He hesitated, closed his eyes and slumped against the side of the sink. Inhaling the faint flower scent of Lindy's perfume, he released a groan that came from deep within his chest. The fragrance wove its way around him like an early morning mist, tempting him, enticing him, reminding him of everything he swore he was going to forget.

With his jaw knotted so tight his teeth hurt, Rush reached for the shower dial and turned it on full force. Grimly he wondered how much cold water it would take to distract him from the ache in his groin.

"Rush." Lindy threw open the front door of the apartment. "I got the job." Filled with joyous excitement, she tossed her purse aside and whirled around the living room like a ballerina, her arms clenched tightly over her breasts.

She was so dizzy she nearly stumbled, but she didn't care. Breathless and laughing, she stopped and braced her hand along the back of the sofa. "Oh, come on, Rush, you've got to be home!"

A quick check of the rooms told her he wasn't. The minute she'd been free, Lindy had hurried out of the Boeing offices, dying to tell Rush that the job was hers. The money was great. More than great. Wonderful. Health insurance, paid vacations, sick leave. And ten days off at Christmas. The whole nine yards–or was that ten? She didn't know. What she did know was that this wonderful, fabulous job was hers.

She couldn't have asked for a better position. The woman who would be her supervisor had taken Lindy around to meet her co-workers and everyone had been so nice, so friendly. Lindy had known almost immediately that she was going to fit right in.

"Rush," she called out again, in case she'd missed him somehow.

His name fell emptily into the silence. Oh well, he'd hear her good news soon enough. She went into her bedroom and changed into jeans and a soft pink ten-button Henley shirt, pushing the three-quarter length sleeves up past her elbows. She reached for her purse and as an afterthought scribbled Rush a note that said she was going out to buy thick T-bones, and when she got back they would celebrate.

By the time Lindy returned from the Pike Place Market, Rush was on the lanai and the barbecue was smoking.

"Hi," she called out, and set the grocery bag on the counter. "I got the job."

"I didn't doubt for a minute that you would."

Rush looked wonderfully relaxed in casual slacks and a light blue sweater that set off the color of his eyes to a clear cornflower blue. The sun glinted through his dark hair, and when he turned to smile at her, his face fairly danced with happy mischief, as if he'd known all along she'd do well and was as pleased as she that she had gotten the job. And exceedingly proud.

"Well, you might have shared some of that confidence with me," Lindy told him with mock disgust. "In case you didn't notice, I was a wreck this morning. Imagine leaving two hours before an interview." She could chide herself about it now, but she'd felt as if an army of red ants had decided to use her stomach as a place to dig their farm.

"I was confident enough to buy a bottle of champagne to celebrate," he informed her, moving into the kitchen and opening the fridge. He brought out the bottle and set it on the counter with all the ceremony and flair of a wine steward.

"Oh Rush, we can't drink this," she whispered, reverently examining the bottle. This wasn't the normal cheap champagne Lindy was used to drinking at Christmastime, but an expensive French variety, decorated with a gold seal and a fancy blue ribbon.

"Why not?" His brows shot up.

"It's too good.... I mean, I can't even pronounce the name of it." She tried, her tongue stumbling over the French vowels. In high school she'd taken a couple of years of the language, but she could never be considered fluent.

"You can't say champagne?" His voice dipped with sarcasm while tiny pinpricks of light shimmered in the depths of his eyes.

"Oh stop. You're being deliberately obtuse."

Already he'd peeled away the decorative top foil. "If anyone has reason to celebrate, it's you."

Lindy sighed and nodded, utterly content. "I can't tell you how pleased I am."

"You don't need to," he teased. "Anyone within a five-block radius could feel your happiness." His gaze held hers briefly before he dragged it away and started working to remove the cork.

Lindy felt strangely breathless and dizzy with joy. She was truly happy, when only a few weeks before she'd doubted that she'd ever experience elation or excitement again. Now she felt as though destiny had finally caught up with her again, and she was riding the crest of a wave, surging ahead, grabbing at every good thing that came her way. And lately, since she'd met Rush, there seemed to be so much to feel good about.

The sound of the cork popping and the bubbly liquid spraying into the sink caused Lindy to gasp, then giggle.

"Here, here," she cried, handing Rush one of the tall narrow glasses he'd set out. She didn't want any of this precious liquid to be wasted. God only knew how much Rush had paid for the bottle.

"A toast," Rush said, handing her a glass and taking his own. Tiny golden bubbles popped to the surface as if to add their own congratulations. "To Lindy Kyle, computer expert," Rush murmured, completely serious.

"I'm not really an expert."

"Are you always this argumentative, woman?"

"All right, all right," she laughed and licked the moisture from her fingertips. "IBM owes everything to me. Mr. Wang himself calls me his friend." Her eyes were laughing, her joy and enthusiasm exuding with every breath, because it was impossible to contain them.

"Mr. Wang?" Rush asked her. "What about Mr. Callaghan? Is he your friend?"

"Oh most assuredly. The very best kind there is."

"Good."

Lindy thought his voice sounded slightly husky, pleased, but before she had time to analyze it or study him further, Rush poised his glass next to hers. Gently they tapped the delicate rims together and Lindy tasted a sample. The smooth liquid was wonderfully light and mellow and so delicious that she closed her eyes to properly savor it.

"This is marvelous stuff," she said, taking another sip.

"I thought you'd like it."

"I bought us steaks," she said, suddenly remembering the sack. "And enough vegetables to open our own fifty-item salad bar."

Rush chuckled. "You get the salad together and I'll manage the steaks."

"That sounds like a workable plan."

"Good grief," he chided, unwrapping the thick T-bones from the white butcher paper. "You're already using office lingo."

Lindy resisted the urge to swat his backside as he returned to the lanai, and turned her attention to the variety of fresh vegetables for the salad.

She finished before Rush did, and taking her champagne glass with her, joined him outside. It had rained for part of the week, but the sun was out this afternoon and the breeze was fresh and clean.

"The coals aren't quite hot enough yet," he told her, leaning against the wrought-iron railing, looking at ease with himself and his world.

Perhaps it was the champagne or the fact she'd stood too long in the sun. Lindy wasn't sure which to blame. But standing beside Rush she suddenly felt the overwhelming need to have him kiss her, the overpowering desire to glide her moist lips back and forth over his and taste the champagne on his tongue.

"Lindy?" He was frowning at her, and for a moment she was sure he'd read her thoughts. "What is it?"

"Nothing." She shook her head for emphasis, pushing down the impulse. It was insane, stupid, wrong. And yet something kept driving her. Something primitive and completely unmanageable. Before she could change her mind, she took both their wineglasses and set them aside, her hands shaking.

Rush watched her like a man in a trance.

She leaned forward and planted her hands on his shoulders, her intense gaze holding his.

At her touch, she felt a quiver work its way through his lean, hard body. He stiffened, his shoulders at attention as though a visiting admiral were passing by for inspection. But still he didn't try to stop her, didn't gently push her away as she thought he might. His hands bunched into tight fists at his sides.

Filled with purpose, and more determined than she had been about anything in a long time, Lindy stood on tiptoe and briefly touched her lips to his.

It was better than she'd thought, better than she'd dreamed. She cocked her head so their noses wouldn't present a barrier and kissed him again. Lightly. Tentatively. Shyly.

Rush stood stiff and motionless, but a low moan slipped from deep within his throat. His dark eyebrows cramped his piercing blue eyes, and he glared at her. If he hoped to intimidate her with a look, he failed. Lindy felt incredibly brave, ready to take on a fully armed armada if need be. Surely managing one weary sailor wouldn't be so difficult.

Rush closed his eyes then opened them, searching her face, his look tormented. He seemed to be telling Lindy to stop. Begging her to move away from him because he hadn't the will to move himself. But Lindy had no intention of following his silent demand. None. Instead she smiled boldly up at him, her heart in her eyes.

Rush claimed her lips then, and groaned anew as if holding her were the last thing in the world he wanted to do. His mouth clung to hers, warm and demanding as his tongue plundered the dark, sweet secret of her mouth, taking all that she offered.

His hands pulled her tight against him and he continued to kiss her again and again until she was flushed and trembling and her blood felt as if it could boil.

"Oh God, Lindy. No. No. This isn't right." His voice was tortured and barely audible. But still he didn't release her.

Chapter Five

Rush's face was hard. Harder than at any time Lindy could remember. His eyebrows were pulled down over his eyes, which were busily searching her face, seeking answers she couldn't give him.

Gently, his hands at her waist, he broke her hold on him and turned away, but not too far, because she was able to view his profile in the afternoon sunlight. He sucked in a giant breath and savagely jerked his fingers through his hair, his face dark and ravaged with what looked like guilt and regret.

"Rush," she whispered. "Listen...."

"No, you listen...."

The same mindless force that had driven her to kiss him led her now, and she moved behind him, wrapping her arms around his torso and fiercely hugging his back. She could feel the coiled resistance in him, but refused to release him.

"Lindy, damn it, you're not making this easy." His hands moved to break her hold and release himself from the trap of her arms.

At least Lindy thought that was his intent. But instead his fingers closed over her knuckles, squeezing her hands together with such force she nearly gasped with pain. But when his hand touched hers something seemed to snap inside him and he relaxed, causing her to melt all the more intimately against him.

She was shocked by how good Rush's body felt. He was tall and lean and hard and he stirred some inherent need in her.

An eternity passed before either moved. They hardly seemed to breathe. Lindy would have held onto Rush until the Second Coming if he hadn't broken free of her clasp and moved away from her. His breath was choppy then, as though it had cost him a great deal to leave her arms. His intense blue eyes stubbornly avoided hers.

"I think it would be best if we forget that ever happened," he said gruffly, and seemed to be engrossed in placing the steaks on the barbecue.

"I'm not going to forget it." Lindy didn't know why she felt she had to argue with him, but she did. "I thought you were the one who was so keen on us being honest with each other."

"This is different." He shook enough salt over the meat to preserve it into the next generation. Pepper and garlic powder followed, so thick they practically obliterated the juicy T-bones.

"You said it was important there be no pretense between us," she pressed. "And you're right."

"Damn it, Lindy. Just what the hell do you want from me?" He remained hunched over the barbecue, refusing to meet her eyes. "Do you want me to tell you I find you attractive? Fine. You turn me on. I hope to hell you're satisfied now."

She couldn't have stopped the spontaneous smile that joyously sprang over her face had their lives depended on it. Just knowing Rush was attracted to her gave Lindy a giddy sense of power.

"I find you appealing, too," she admitted, having trouble keeping the elation out of her voice. Actually that was a gross understatement. She was drawn to Rush the way a thirsty flower is to rain.

"Well, you shouldn't, because..." he paused and forcefully exhaled a breath, looking both angry and confused.

Lindy's heart thudded expectantly. "Why not? Is it so wrong?"

Rush rose slowly to his feet then, faced her and placed his hands on her shoulders in a brotherly fashion, his eyes clear. Determined.

"Lindy, listen to me. You've been badly hurt recently. Devastated by a man you loved and trusted, and now everything seems to have turned around. You've got a reason to be happy, to celebrate. But my being here is much too convenient. It's only natural that you feel attracted to me, living at close quarters the way we do. You're a young, passionate woman, filled with the love of life and...you're excited now. I don't blame you, especially after everything you've been through. Your pride suffered a major setback not so long ago, and here I am like a savior, the means of salvaging it all."

"Rush...no."

"But Lindy," he continued, unwilling to let her cut him off, "you're too vulnerable right now. The attraction you feel toward me is only natural under the circumstances. But you've got to understand something important here. Given the same situation, you'd experience these identical emotions toward any healthy, red-blooded male. It's not really me who appeals to you, it's the thought of another close relationship."

"You can't honestly believe that. Why, that's ridiculous, Rush Callaghan."

"No, it isn't. Think about it, Lindy. Think hard. You want a man tonight." His voice was rough with intensity. "I can understand your feelings, sympathize with what's happened to you, but making love wouldn't be right. I'm not the one for this, and I refuse to take advantage of you. Find someone else to build your ego."

"I find that insulting," she told him earnestly, but without anger. She had thought he might try to avoid her by starting an argument, and she refused to swallow the bait, no matter how much he irritated her.

"I'm not saying this to offend you. You're the one who insisted upon honesty. You got it." He returned to the steaks, as calmly as if they'd been discussing something as mundane as stock prices or the outcome of a baseball game.

"You're making this difficult," she said next.

"I plan to make it impossible."

"Honestly, Rush. Would you stop handling me with kid gloves? I'm a woman."

"Honey, that's one thing you won't find me arguing about." His words were followed by a harsh chuckle. "Now, come on. Be a good little girl and eat your steak."

The dishwasher was whirling softly in the background when Lindy reached for the telephone a couple of hours later. As soon as their meal had been completed, Rush had left her without so much as a word to tell her where he was going or when he intended to come back. The bloody coward!

"Hi, Mom," Lindy said when her mother picked up the receiver on the third ring.

"Lindy, sweetheart, is everything all right?"

"It's wonderful. I got a job with Boeing and start first thing in the morning."

"That's terrific."

Lindy could hear the relief in her mother's voice, and smiled, remembering again how great she'd felt when the personnel director had offered her the job.

"Sweetheart, I couldn't be more pleased. I knew everything would work out, given time."

"I have more good news."

"More?" her mother said, and laughed softly.

"I've met someone."

"You have?" The question was followed by a brief, strained silence. "Isn't this rather sudden?"

Lindy could all but hear the excitement drain out of Grace Kyle's voice to be replaced by weary doubt. "Now, before you say anything, let me tell you something about him. He's wonderful, Mom, really wonderful. He's helped me so much, I can't even begin to tell you everything he's done for me. He's a good, kind person. Honorable."

"Oh, Lindy," her mother said with a sigh, "do be careful."

"I will, Mom. I promise." The comedy of the situation struck her then, and she started to giggle.

"What's so funny?" Her mother obviously hadn't stopped to think things through.

"Mom, I'm twenty-two years old and when I told you that I'd met someone, you said I should be careful, like I was seven years old again and about to cross a busy street alone for the first time."

"But, Lindy, you're hardly over–" Grace paused and exhaled a disgusted, uneven breath. "I refuse to even mention his name."

"Paul." Lindy said it for her. "He can't hurt me anymore. I refuse to let him."

"That's nice, sweetheart. Now tell me–where did you meet this young man you think so highly of?"

Lindy gnawed on her lower lip. Explaining her living arrangements to her mother would surely be cause for concern, but Lindy wasn't in the habit of lying. "I met him a few days after I arrived in Seattle."

"Oh. And what's his family like?"

"Mom, we've only known each other a little while. I haven't met his family."

"But I think you should find out about them, don't you?"

"I suppose. In time. Listen, Mom, I just wanted to call and let you know that everything is going terrific. I've got a good job and I couldn't be happier. Really."

"I'm so pleased for you."

"I know. I feel good about everything, and I don't want you to worry about me anymore because nothing's going to hold me down again."

"I knew you'd find your footing, given time."

"I have, Mom."

"Goodbye, sweetheart."

"'Bye, Mom. Give my love to Dad."

"I will."

Lindy thought she heard a trace of tears in her mother's soft voice when she replaced the receiver. She was surprised to note there was a hint in her own.

With Rush gone, the apartment felt like an empty tomb and the evening dragged by. Lindy watched television for a while, worked a crossword puzzle and added an extra coat of pink polish to her nails. By eleven she was tired and ready to give up her vigil. Rush had been determined to get away from her, to leave her alone to recognize the foolishness of her actions. She knew what he was thinking as clearly as if he'd announced his intentions. Only it hadn't worked. If anything, Lindy was more determined than ever to get him to face the truth of what was happening between them.

Discouraged, she undressed and climbed between the cool sheets. But sleep wouldn't come. Instead all she could think about was how good it had felt to be in Rush's arms. How good and how remarkably right.

She recognized there was some validity to what he'd claimed. But he was wrong to think she was using him. The feelings she had for Rush had absolutely nothing to do with what had happened with Paul. The attraction she felt for Rush was because of who he was. She'd meant every word she'd said to her mother. Rush Callaghan was an honorable man, and there seemed to be few enough of them left.

Rush had given her a priceless gift. Her freedom. His patience and tenderness had released her from the shackles of pain and remorse. He'd held her hand and shown her the way out of the dark shadows. He'd led her gently into the warm healing glow of a summer sun.

If he were with her now, discussing matters the way he should be, Lindy knew exactly what he'd say to her. He'd tell her she was grateful. She was, but it was far more than gratitude she felt toward Rush. He'd taken her wounded heart and breathed new life into it. He'd let her feel again when her every nerve ending had been numb, and her very existence had seemed pointless.

She couldn't stop thinking about how perfect she'd felt in his arms, her breasts flattened against his broad chest, her nipples hard and erect. Just the memory was enough to stir her senses back to life. That brief time with Rush had produced an incredible range of new awarenesses. His kiss had been warm and tender, his lips lingering over hers as though this moment and place were out of time and meant for them alone.

His tender touch had brought with it the sweetest, most terrible yearning to be loved by him. Completely. Totally. Lindy didn't need anyone to tell her that when Rush Callaghan gave his heart to a woman, she would be the most incredibly fortunate female alive.

Lindy had just begun to scratch the surface of his multifaceted personality. Over the years, Rush had built several thick protective layers around himself, and Lindy had only managed to peel away the top few, to gain a peek inside. But she believed with all her heart that underneath he was sensitive and strong, daring and bold, and yet in some ways almost shy.

In time, Rush would realize she knew her own mind—and her own heart. In no way was she rebounding from Paul. Her former fiancé had actually done her a big favor, although it had been difficult to recognize it at the time. Paul was weak. Blinded by her love, she hadn't seen it before. Paul didn't possess the principles Rush did, either. Rush, on the other hand, was noble, reliable and completely trustworthy. Lindy would stake her life on it. Her judgment had been poor once, but she'd learned something from Paul, and although the lesson had been bitterly painful, she'd been an apt student. She knew an honorable man when she saw one. And Rush Callaghan fit her definition to a T.

Still awake at midnight, Lindy bunched her pillow in half and rolled onto her stomach. She might as well climb out of bed and wait for him as toss and turn all night. She'd no sooner made the decision to get up when she heard the front door open.

Relieved, Lindy smiled and eagerly threw aside the blankets. She slipped her arms into the sleeves of her robe and headed out her bedroom door, impatient to talk to him.

Rush was just coming down the hallway.

"You're home," she greeted, not even trying to disguise her pleasure. It wasn't one of her most brilliant statements, but she didn't care.

He grumbled something that she couldn't make sense of.

"You didn't need to leave, you know."

"Yes, I did." He kept as far away from her as space would allow.

"Rush, we need to talk."

"Not now."

"Yes, now," she insisted.

"You have to go to work in the morning. Remember?" he argued, and rubbed his hand wearily over the back of his neck. "And for that matter so do I."

Lindy took a step toward him, and stopped. The cloying scents of cheap perfume and cigarette smoke clung to him like the stench of an infection. Shocked, Lindy tensed and braced herself against the wall to avoid getting any closer to him than necessary. She felt as though he'd driven a stake through her heart, so violent was the rush of pain. Rush had left her arms, scoffed at her timid efforts at lovemaking and gone to another. Someone with far more experience than she.

She glared at him through wide, angry eyes. "You're disgusting." She spat the words vengefully with all the vehemence her heart could muster. Then she whirled around and returned to her room, slamming the door with such force that the picture of her family on the dresser tumbled to the carpet.

Rush didn't bother to follow her and Lindy was glad.

She was trembling uncontrollably when she sank onto the edge of her mattress. The honorable man she'd been so willing to place on a pedestal possessed clay feet. Clay feet and a clay heart.

Lindy may have slept at some time during the long night that followed, but she doubted it. She was so furious she couldn't allow herself to relax enough to sleep. She had no hold on Rush, she realized. There was no commitment between them. A few kisses were all they'd ever shared, and yet she wanted to throttle him.

Apparently she wasn't as apt a student as she'd thought, and she didn't know which had disappointed her more–Rush's behavior or her own inability to judge men.

Rush heard Lindy tossing and turning in her room long after he'd retired to his own room. He knew what she believed and had purposely let her go on thinking it, hoping she'd forget this silly notion about letting a romance develop between them. That had been his original intention. But when he'd seen the flash of pain in her eyes, he knew he couldn't go through with it. Unfortunately Lindy wasn't in any mood to carry on a levelheaded conversation, he'd decided. He'd explain things in the morning.

Rush had gotten out of the apartment as soon as he could following dinner, afraid of what might happen if he stayed. The truth of the matter was that it had taken every damn bit of restraint he'd possessed to walk away from Lindy. The cold beer he had nursed in a sleazy waterfront bar was small compensation for his considerable sacrifice.

His biggest problem was that he believed every word he'd said to Lindy. She was vulnerable right now. Vulnerable and trusting. A lethal combination as far as Rush was concerned. If he loved her the way she wanted, she'd wake in the morning filled with regrets. Rush couldn't do that to her. Hell, if he was honest, he couldn't do it to himself. He wasn't so much a fool not to recognize that loving Lindy once would never be enough. A sample would only create the need for more. Much more.

The simple act of kissing and holding her had nearly defeated him. When she'd leaned up and brushed her lips over his, his body had fired to life with a heat that had threatened to consume him. It had demanded every part of his considerable self-control not to lift her into his arms and carry her into his bedroom.

The sweet little witch must have known it, too. She'd pressed her softness against him, fully conscious of what the intimacy was doing to him. And then she'd paused and looked up at him, her eyes wide and trusting and filled with such delectable love that it was more than a mere man could resist. He'd kissed her until he'd felt her weak and trembling in his arms. He had no idea what had stopped him then, but whatever it was, he was grateful.

Escape had been his only alternative, and he'd left the apartment when he could. He didn't want to be in the bar, but after a brisk walk there hadn't been anyplace else he knew to go. A woman who often loitered there had strolled up to his table, sat down without an invitation and tried to start a conversation. Rush had glared at her and told her wasn't in the mood for company. Apparently she'd taken his words as a challenge and before he could stop her, her arms were all over him.

Rush didn't realize the scent of her sickeningly sweet perfume had stayed with him until he saw Lindy's look of complete disgust.

He was going to settle that matter first thing in the morning.

It was with a sense of righteousness that Lindy snapped a rock-music tape into her cassette player and turned it up full blast. Tapping her foot to the loud music, she wove the hot curling iron through her hair and waited. Within a couple of minutes, Rush staggered into the bathroom, apparently having just awakened, looking as if he intended to hurl her portable stereo out the living room window.

"Is that really necessary?" he shouted.

With deliberately slow movements Lindy turned down the volume. She regarded him with wide, innocent eyes. "What did you say?"

"Is that god-awful music necessary?"

It gave her a good deal of pleasure to smile sweetly back at him and ask, "Did I wake you? I'm so sorry, Rush."

"I'll bet," he grumbled and turned to stumble back to his room.

Lindy loved it.

Her sense of timing couldn't have been more perfect some time later when they met again in the kitchen. He grumbled something that sounded faintly like a plea for coffee. He had just gotten down a mug and started to pour himself a cup when she switched on the blender full blast. Hot coffee splattered over the counter and Rush jumped back, cursing savagely.

He whirled around to face her and once more Lindy gave him her brightest smile. She finished her task and asked, "Would you like some orange juice?"

"No," he grumbled.

She swallowed a laugh and with a good deal of ceremony, poured herself a glass.

Rush was studying her with a tight frown. "Now I know

what they mean when they say 'hell hath no fury like a woman scorned.'"

Lindy gave him a vague look. "I'm sure I don't know what you mean."

"Like hell," he exploded. "Exactly how long is it going to take you to properly mete out justice?"

"Rush, I think you got out of the wrong side of bed this morning. You seem to be imagining all sorts of things. What could I possibly be angry about?" Already she was feeling better. Okay, so maybe her revenge was a tad childish, but Rush deserved everything he got–in triplicate.

"Damn it, Lindy. You've got the wrong idea here."

"Wrong idea about what?" She batted her thick lashes a couple of times for effect and had the satisfaction of seeing him clench his jaw. From experience Lindy knew mornings had never been Rush's favorite time of day. He looked disoriented, out of sorts and more than a little lost in knowing how to deal with her. As far as Lindy was concerned, Rush's confusion was poetic justice.

"While I'm still alive and breathing," he managed, "I think you'd better know there's been a minor misunderstanding here."

"I haven't the slightest idea what you're talking about," she returned, her look as earnest as she could make it and still hold back her amusement.

His hand slammed against the counter. "And I'm sure you know exactly what I'm talking about," he countered, unable to restrain his fury. "You've tried and convicted me without knowing the details."

The particulars were the last thing Lindy wanted to hear. "Spare me, please," she told him, the amusement of her game vanishing. "You can sleep with a harem for all I care." It astonished her how easily the lie slipped from her lips. Rarely had she been more bitterly disappointed in anyone than she had been in Rush.

"Lindy…"

She cut him off with a quick shake of her head. "I wish I had more time to sort this out," she lied again, but not as smoothly this time. "But in case you've forgotten, I've got a job to go to."

She walked away from him and was already in the living room when she paused to add, "You were right about one thing, though. I'm not ready for another relationship." She turned to face him then. "You don't need to worry about trying to clear the air. I understand, Rush, far better than you know."

His eyes held hers and a strong current of energy passed between them. As always she could read little in his impassive expression. But he must have agreed with her because he said nothing, and she hurriedly walked away, eager to escape.

It was while she was brushing her teeth that a sheen of tears brightened her eyes. After everything that had happened to her, it was a surprise. She'd assumed she had more control of her emotions than this; she blamed the tears on lack of sleep.

With her purse in her hand she headed for the front door. She'd learned several lessons in the past few months, but they didn't seem to be getting any easier.

Walking down the hallway, she was forced to pass Rush, who was sitting on the sofa in the living room. She forced a smile and squared her shoulders, prepared to move past him with her head high.

Just as she reached him, Rush's arm reached out, grabbed her hand and stopped her cold. His eyes held her more tightly than any vise.

"I won't have you face your first day on the job with doubts. There was no one last night, Lindy. No one but you."

She blinked back the surprise and uncertainty, not sure what to believe. The evidence had reeked from him.

Rush tugged at her arm, bringing her closer. When she was within easy reach, he wrapped his arm around her waist and brought her down onto his lap. She landed there with a plop. His hands found their way to her face and he turned her head so her unwilling gaze was forced to meet his.

"I can't let you go on thinking I could've touched another woman after kissing you." His eyes filled with an emotion so powerful that Lindy couldn't speak. Gone was the mask–lowered or destroyed, she didn't know which–and what she saw in his wonderful eyes gave flight to her heart. His look was innocent, youthful almost. Seeking. He needed her to believe him, was pleading with her in a way she knew was foreign to this proud man.

Tears pooled in her eyes, and she nodded, silently telling him that she trusted his word.

The pad of his thumb wiped the moisture from the high arch of her cheek.

"Damn it, Lindy. We're in one fine mess here," he said, his voice gruff with emotion. "I want you like hell. What are we going to do?" His warm mouth, only inches from hers, brushed lightly over her parted lips.

Lindy just managed to stifle a groan and kissed him back softly, her mouth lingering over his own, needing his warmth.

By this time he'd wrapped her in his embrace. As though they had all the time in the world, Rush brought her lips down to his own with an agonizing slowness. The kiss was filled with such aching tenderness, such sweet torment that the fresh tears rolled unheeded down the side of her face.

"I should have trusted you," she told him brokenly. "I should have known."

"Lindy…don't cry, please. It's all right. It doesn't matter." He pulled her more completely into his embrace and held her tightly.

The memory of his look when he'd stumbled into the bathroom caused her to laugh and cry at the same time.

"Honey…please. I can't bear the thought that I've made you cry. You are crying, aren't you?"

Lindy laughed aloud, then sobbed. She reached for his hand to kiss his knuckles. "Did you burn yourself when you spilled the coffee?"

He looked at her as though they should give serious consideration to having her committed to a mental facility. "No," he said tightly.

"I'm so sorry," she told him, spreading kisses over the edge of his jaw. "Oh, Rush, I thought horrible things of you. I thought–"

"I can guess," he muttered, cutting her off.

"But you're good and honorable and I was so wrong."

He chuckled and shook his head. "If you had a hint of what I was thinking of doing right now, you'd amend the honorable portion."

It was difficult to read his expression, but what she saw there caused her to wrap her arms around his neck and kiss him with a hunger that left them both shaking.

"Shall I tell you what I'm thinking, Rush Callaghan?"

Chapter Six

"Rush, guess what?" Breathless with excitement, Lindy let herself into the apartment and stopped abruptly, swallowing the remainder of her good news. Another man was standing next to Rush, and it looked as though the two had been arguing, or at least heatedly discussing something.

For the first time in recent memory, Rush didn't look pleased to see her. Apparently she'd arrived at the worst possible time. Her dark eyes met his and she offered a silent apology. His brief smile both reassured and warmed her.

After an awkward moment, Rush stepped forward. "Lindy, this is Jeff Dwyer. Jeff, this is Lindy Kyle, Steve Kyle's little sister."

Jeff resembled a fat cat who had just been presented with a pitcher of rich cream. The corners of his mouth twitched with the effort to suppress a smile, and his eyes fairly danced with mischief and delight. "I can't tell you how pleased I am to meet you, Lindy."

"Thank you." Her gaze moved from Rush to Jeff and then back to Rush, who gave her a fleeting smile that revealed his chagrin. He wasn't overly pleased about something, but he wasn't angry, either.

"Since Rush didn't bother to explain, I will," Jeff went on to say. "We're both officers aboard the *Mitchell.* Rush and I've worked together for the past four years." He hesitated and rubbed the side of his jaw. "Until recently I thought I knew everything there was about my fellow officer, but I guess I was wrong."

Rush placed his hands in his pants pockets, ignoring the comment. "Jeff and his wife Susan are visiting downtown Seattle this afternoon."

Jeff couldn't have looked more pleased. Lindy didn't know what was happening between the two men, but she'd apparently loused things up for Rush.

"Sue's having the twins' pictures taken at one of those fancy studios," Jeff continued. "She didn't seem to need me, so I thought I'd stop off and see my good buddy Rush."

Lindy nodded, not knowing how else to respond.

"How long have you–ah, been living here?" Jeff asked.

Unsure, Lindy's gaze sought Rush's.

"It's not what you're implying, Jeff." Rush's frown was fierce as he glared at his friend. "In case you didn't hear me the first time, I'll say it once more. Lindy is Steve Kyle's little sister."

Again the edges of the other man's mouth moved spastically. Jeff looked to be exerting a good deal of effort to hold back his amusement. The more pleased the other man's look became, the darker Rush's frown grew.

"I heard you," Jeff said.

"Isn't it about time for you to pick up Susan and the kids?" Rush asked in an emotionless tone that was devoid of humor.

Jeff made a show of looking at his wristwatch. "I suppose," he admitted reluctantly. His gaze drifted to Lindy. "It was a pleasure to meet you. A real pleasure. Next time, I'll bring Sue along."

"I'd like that."

Rush was already standing next to the front door when Jeff left her. Lindy could vaguely hear the two exchange farewells followed by a couple of heated whispers.

"What was that all about?" she asked, once Rush had returned.

"Nothing."

"Don't give me that, Rush Callaghan. I know better."

He lapsed into silence for a moment. "Jeff came over to investigate a suspicion."

"Oh?"

"How did your day go?"

His effort to change the subject wasn't subtle, but Lindy could tell pressuring him to explain what had been going on between him and Jeff Dwyer wouldn't do her any good.

"Oh," she said, her eyes rounding with excitement. "I nearly forgot." Her hands eagerly started digging through her purse, tossing aside her compact and eel-skin wallet in her rush. Triumphantly she held up two tickets. "I got box seats for the Mariners' game tonight." When Rush just stood there staring at her, she blinked back her disappointment. She'd hoped he'd be as enthusiastic about attending the game as she was. "You do like baseball, don't you?"

His nod was decidedly absent. "Box seats?"

"On the one-hundred level. A girl I work with got them through the office. She can't go tonight, and asked if I could use them." Lindy had been so eager she could hardly make it back to the apartment fast enough, convinced Rush would want to see the Mariners play as much as she did. But looking at him now, she wasn't sure what to think. "Why are you looking at me like that?" she demanded, a little piqued.

"Like what?"

"Like that.... Just now."

He shrugged. "I was just thinking about something Jeff said. I'm sorry. Did you say something I missed?"

Slowly Lindy shook her head. He hadn't told her any part of his conversation with his friend, and Lindy knew it would be useless to even try to get him to discuss the details with her.

"Do you want to go to the game or would you rather skip the whole thing?" She tried to sound nonchalant, but she was really hoping Rush would want to attend the game.

"The game, of course. Don't you think you'd better change clothes? Starting time is in another forty-five minutes."

"Right." Still confused, Lindy moved down the hallway to her bedroom. She didn't know what to make of Rush today. They'd been getting along so well lately, spending as much time together as possible, cramming all they could into the days and nights before the *Mitchell* left.

In three days they'd done something together every night. Tuesday he'd taken her to the Woodland Park Zoo, and they'd fed peanuts to the elephants and been splashed while watching the playful antics of the seals. Wednesday they'd gone on a picnic on the shores of Lake Washington, where Rush had lain on the sweet-scented lawn, resting his head on her thigh while he nibbled on a long blade of grass. Thursday they'd eaten fish and chips on the waterfront and strolled hand in hand in and out of the tourist shops that dotted the wharf. Each night they'd laughed and joked and talked freely. And each night Rush had kissed her. Once. And only once. As though anything more would be too much temptation for him to handle. Rush treated her with kid gloves, touching her as if he were handling live ammunition. His kiss was always gentle, always controlled–too controlled to suit Lindy. If she hadn't felt the soul-wrenching reluctance and regret in every part of him when he gently left her arms, she would have been deeply discouraged.

Lindy knew that Rush was having problems dealing with the emotions she aroused in him. He didn't trust their attraction. Didn't trust her, believing she couldn't possibly know her own heart so soon after Paul. And perhaps, Lindy realized, Rush didn't trust himself. He'd certainly gone out of his way to behave like an endearing older brother–except when he lowered his guard just a little each night to kiss her. He wanted her. He'd told her as much, and she wanted him. But the time for them wasn't right.

As fast as she could Lindy changed out of her work clothes and rejoined Rush in the kitchen, prepared to hurry to the baseball game. He took one look at her and burst out laughing.

"What's so funny?"

"You. I thought you said we were going to watch the game. You look like you plan to participate in it."

She'd chosen faded jeans, a Mariner T-shirt and Steve's old baseball cap. "Have you got a problem with this, fellow?" she asked him, her eyes sparkling with fun and laughter.

Still grinning, Rush shook his head. "Come on, Babe Ruth, we've got a game to see."

They were settled in their box seats with foot-long hot dogs, a bag of peanuts and cold drinks by the time the first pitch was tossed. Rush had never been much into baseball. Football was his game, but he couldn't have refused Lindy anything. Her energy and enthusiasm for life were like a breath of fresh tangy air after a storm at sea. Being with her stirred his senses to vibrant life and made him glad for who and what he was. There were odd moments, now and then, when he resisted the magnetic pull he felt toward her and recounted the arguments—that she was too young, too vulnerable and his best friend's sister. But each day the echoes from his conscience came back weaker and his arguments sounded flatter. He was losing the battle, convinced he was being swept away in the whirlpool with little control over what was happening to either of them. For the most part Rush had given up the struggle and was living one day at a time, spending time with Lindy, savoring the moments they were together. But he couldn't, wouldn't allow the fickle Fates to carry him where they would, knowing full well they'd place him with Lindy, warm and willing, in his bed.

Jeff Dwyer knew him well enough to have guessed something had changed Rush's life. The day before, Jeff had confronted Rush and suggested that he revealed all the symptoms of a man in love. Rush had denied that, probably a lot more forcefully than he should have, because Jeff had gone on to enumerate the changes he'd seen in Rush since the *Mitchell*'s arrival back in Bremerton.

Not willing to drop the matter, Jeff had shown up at the apartment. He seemed to take delight in informing Rush that he'd been watching him closely of late. Jeff had noticed how quickly Rush left work the minute his shift was over, as if he couldn't wait to get back to his apartment. It used to be that Rush hung around awhile to shoot the bull with the other guys. No more. Rush was out of the shipyard like greased lightning. And furthermore, Jeff had claimed, Rush walked around with a cocky half smile, as though he found something highly amusing. As far as Jeff was concerned, these telltale symptoms added up to one thing: a woman.

Rush hadn't argued with his friend. He'd simply refused to discuss the subject. A lot of good it had done him. Just when he'd thought he was making headway and Jeff was about to drop the entire matter, Lindy had come bursting in the front door. Her eyes had glowed and sparkled as they sought him, confirming everything Jeff had been saying ten times over.

At his side, Lindy roared to her feet cheering. Lost in his thoughts, Rush hadn't been watching the game and now he saw that the Mariners had just scored. He joined Lindy and shouted once for effect.

Lindy laughed gleefully, turned to him and hugged his waist, her eyes alive with joy. With hardly a pause, she sat back down and reached for the bag of peanuts. Rush took his seat as well, but his mind was whirling. He wanted to kiss Lindy at that moment, and the need was so strong in him that it demanded all his restraint not to haul her into his arms right then and there. He reached for the peanuts himself and noted grimly that his hands were trembling with the need to touch her.

The game must have gotten good, because several times during the next few innings Lindy scooted to the edge of her seat and shouted advice to both player and umpire. As far as Rush could tell; he'd responded appropriately throughout the game. He'd cheered and hissed a couple of times, applauded and booed when Lindy did, but he hadn't a clue what was going on in the field. Dealing with what was happening to his own emotions was all he could handle for now. He was plowing through mine-infested waters with Lindy, and he was gradually losing his grip on his control with each minute he spent in her company.

Following the baseball game they walked from the Kingdome back to the apartment, a healthy two miles. Personally he would have preferred a taxi, but Lindy was in a mood to walk. She chatted as they strolled along, hand in hand. She was pleased that the home team had won and soon Rush felt himself caught up in her good mood.

Lindy didn't know what was wrong with Rush, but he hadn't been himself all evening. He'd hardly spoken during the entire game, and although he seemed to be paying attention, she could have sworn he hadn't noticed a blasted thing.

For her part, Lindy felt great. More than great. She felt wonderful! And so much of this newly discovered inner peace was due to loving Rush. She even knew the precise minute she'd recognized the truth about her feelings for her brother's friend. It had been the morning of her first day at Boeing, when he'd told her he couldn't let her think he'd touched another woman after kissing her. Even now, the memory of his words had the power to bring tears to her eyes. For days she'd yearned to tell him how her life had changed since she'd met him. But her words would only embarrass him, so she'd kept them locked inside her heart until she was convinced she'd choke on them.

When they reached the apartment, Rush held open the door for her to precede him inside. Lindy stepped into the living room, but didn't turn on any lights. The view of the Seattle skyline from the window drew Lindy there.

"Isn't it lovely?" she said, looking out over the glimmering lights of the waterfront. All seventy-five floors of the Columbia Center were lit, as was the Smith Tower.

Rush stood behind her, but said nothing.

Lindy turned and slipped her arms around his middle, pressing her ear to his broad chest, hugging him, savoring the peace of the moment, knowing he wouldn't allow it to last long.

His lips brushed the top of her head and she smiled. From experience Lindy knew that he tensed before he kissed her, as though gathering together his reserve of self-control. True to form, he stiffened and she smiled because she was beginning to know him so well. Eager now, she raised her head and tilted it to one side to receive his kiss. As it had been on previous nights, his mouth was warm and moist as it glided smoothly over hers. In welcome she parted her lips and slipped her arms up his chest to lazily loop them around his neck.

His kiss was light. Petal soft. Controlled.

Already his hands were braced on her shoulders, cupping them as he prepared to ease himself out of her arms. Lindy felt as though she were starving and a delectable feast was within easy reach, and yet Rush wouldn't allow her more than a sample.

"No," she objected in a tight whisper. She raised her hands to touch his face, her fingertips gliding over his features, hoping to memorize each one, burn it into her heart so that when he left her she could bear the parting.

"Lindy, don't," he groaned, and squeezed his eyes closed. He gripped her wrists and brought her fingers to his lips, kissing the tips.

"Hold me for just a little while longer." She thought for a moment that he was going to argue with her, but he didn't. With her arms draped around his neck, she pressed her cheek over his and felt him relax ever so slightly. But it wasn't nearly enough to satisfy her, and unable to resist, she turned her head and nuzzled his ear with her nose. Her mouth grazed his clenched jaw. Her lips worked their way across his brow, over his eyes and down the side of his nose to nibble on his lower lip. She hesitated, then ran the moist tip of her tongue over the seam of his lips.

Rush's arms tightened around her and he whispered her name on the tail end of a plea for her to stop.

He wanted her. She could feel the evidence boldly pressing against her thigh, and the knowledge of his desire gave her a heady sense of power. Led by instinct, she edged as close as possible to him and rotated her hips once, biting back a cry at the pleasure the action gave her even as it created a need for more. So much more.

"Oh God," he moaned through clenched teeth. "Lindy, don't do that."

"All I want you to do is hold me for a few minutes more. Is that so much to ask?"

"Yes," he returned, and his breath came in hot, quick gasps.

If he had planned on arguing with her, he didn't follow through–apparently having decided it was a losing battle. His hands, which until that moment had been on either side of her waist, moved slowly upward as though drawn there by a force stronger than his will.

Lindy's breasts strained against the fabric of her T-shirt with the need to experience his touch. Slowly his palms encircled her breasts, cupping them, weighing her ripe fullness.

Her soft moans echoed his.

"Lindy, no," he breathed, and the words seemed to stagger from his lips, low and reluctant. "Tell me to stop. Remind me what a good friend your brother is." His thumbs rotated around her nipples, which beaded into hard pebbles and stood proudly at attention. Rush groaned once more.

He kissed her then, hard, thrusting his tongue deep into her mouth as if to punish her for making him want her so desperately. She used her hands to hold his head as her eager tongue met his and they dueled and stroked against each other.

He broke away from her and sucked in deep, uneven breaths. "This has got to stop," he whispered fervently into her hair. "Now."

Lindy found she could say nothing. She searched his handsome face for some sign, anything that would explain why it was so urgent for them to stop kissing when she felt so right in his arms. Her heart was pounding in a hard, fast rhythm that made her feel breathless and weak.

Yet at the same time she was filled with an awesome sense of power. Standing on tiptoe, she slanted her mouth over his and used her tongue to torment him, probing his mouth with swift, gentle thrusts.

"Oh God, Lindy." He kissed her then, firmly, leaving her in no doubt that he was the one in control, not she.

Without Lindy being sure how he'd managed it, Rush had her T-shirt off and her bra unfastened and discarded. The next thing Lindy knew, they were both on the sofa, she in a reclining position, Rush above her. He kissed her face, her forehead, her eyes and lips, again and again, until she lost count. Then his mouth worked its way down the delicate line of her jaw to her neck. She sucked in a wobbly breath when his moist, hot lips found one of her nipples and drew it into his mouth for his tongue to torment. When he'd finished with it he moved to the other nipple, licking it until it ached and throbbed, taut and firm.

He kissed her lips repeatedly, and waves of erotic sensation lapped over her like water pounding relentlessly against the shore.

Lindy was throbbing everywhere. Her mouth, her tongue, her breasts, her belly and the area between her thighs. Her fingers wove their way through his hair.

"Rush." She whispered his name in a tormented whisper. "I love you so much."

He stilled, and after a torturous moment he raised his head. Poised as he was above her, his eyes feasted on her, studying her for what seemed an eternity. Then he shook himself as though coming out of a mindless fog. "You don't mean that. You don't know what you're saying."

"I know exactly what I'm saying." She held his head with her hands and said it again. "I love you." She punctuated each word with a swift kiss on his lips.

Rush's brow folded into a dark, brooding frown. "You can't possibly mean that. Lindy, for God's sake, you barely know me!"

"I know everything I need to." She smiled up at him, not willing to listen to any more of his arguments.

As though he wasn't sure how to respond, Rush slowly disentangled their limbs one by one, the whole time looking as if he didn't have a clue how they'd ended up that way. When he'd finished, he sat on the edge of the sofa and wiped a hand back and forth over his face.

"Lindy, listen."

"No. I'm not going to because you're going to argue with me, and I won't let you." She sat upright, their thighs so close they touched.

"It's only natural…."

Lindy slid off the sofa and pressed one knee to the floor so she could look him in the eye, but his gaze stubbornly refused to meet hers.

"I know exactly what you're going to say."

His face was tight with what looked like embarrassment as he reached for her T-shirt and handed it to her. Lindy smiled and slipped it over her head.

"I love you," she repeated, feeling more sure of herself every time she said it.

"Lindy…."

"I'm not too young to know my own mind." When his gaze shot to her, she knew she'd stumbled over one of his objections. "I'm twenty-two years old, for heaven's sake. I'm not a child."

He opened his mouth to argue with her, but she pressed her finger over his lips to silence him. "Now this is the biggie. You're worried about what happened with Paul and you think all this emotion I feel for you has to do with him. I can understand your concern, and in the beginning you might have been right. But not now. I was mulling this over the other night. Thinking about how low I was when I moved to Seattle and how I was convinced nothing good would ever happen to me again. Then I met you, and, Rush…" she stopped, biting into her bottom lip as the emotion filled her eyes.

"There's no need…."

"Yes, there is." Her hands cupped his face, her gaze delving into his, showing him all the love that came shining through from her heart. "When I think about everything that led me to move to Seattle I haven't a single regret. Not one. All the pain, all the disillusionment was worth it. In fact, I'll always be grateful to Paul because it was through him that I found you."

"Lindy, stop. Don't say any more."

"But I have to. Don't you see?"

Rush closed his eyes and pressed his cheek next to her tear-stained one. His breathing was as labored as her own, but otherwise he didn't move.

"It took what happened with Paul for me to find you, appreciate you, understand you. I love you so much.... I can't keep it inside anymore."

"Oh, Lord, don't say that."

Once more, she pressed her finger over his lips. "I don't want anything from you. Nothing. You didn't ask for this, and I've probably embarrassed the hell out of you by blurting it out. I apologize, but Rush–my noble, honorable Rush–I do love you."

She stood then, her legs a little shaky. "Having gotten that off my chest, I'm going to leave you."

"Lindy?" His gruff voice stopped her.

"Yes?"

He had the look of a man who'd been pulled apart on a torture rack. He rubbed a hand down over his face and then shook his head. "Nothing."

The following morning Lindy woke to hear Rush rummaging around the kitchen, albeit quietly, no doubt hoping to escape without having to confront her. She climbed out of bed and greeted him with a warm smile.

"'Morning."

He grumbled something in return.

"Did you sleep well?"

He gave her a look that told her he hadn't. "I've got watch today."

"Yes, I know."

"It's Saturday. How come you aren't sleeping in?"

She dropped her eyes. "I wanted to be sure of something."

"What?"

"That you believe what I told you last night."

His gaze found hers and Lindy could tell he was struggling within himself. The stern look he wore so often in the morning softened somewhat, but when he spoke his voice remained gruff. "Listen, I'm not much of a conversationalist at this time of day, and now probably isn't the best place to discuss this." He paused as though to compose his thoughts, sighed and then continued. "I want you to know, I'm truly flattered that you think you love me."

"But–"

"But," he cut in, "you can't trust what you're feeling right now. So let's leave it at that. Okay?"

"Leave it?" she flared. "Rush, no…."

"I'll be your friend, Lindy, but that's all I ever intend to be."

"My friend?"

"And that's it, so don't argue." He downed the last of his coffee and set the cup in the sink with as much force as if he intended to shove it down the drain. "I'll see you later."

"Okay. If that's the way you want it."

"I do."

"Then I'd be honored to have you for a friend, Rush Callaghan."

He paused, his back to her. "No more kissing, Lindy. I mean that."

"No kissing," she echoed.

"We're going to live as brother and sister from here on out."

"Brother and sister." Lindy knew that would last until about lunchtime tomorrow, if that long.

"And if it proves too difficult for us, then I'll make arrangements to live aboard the *Mitchell*."

"If you think it's for the best," she agreed, doing her best to swallow her amusement. Rush's reaction was exactly as she'd guessed it would be. "If that's what you honestly want."

His hand slammed against the counter. "You know it isn't," he said, and whirled around to face her. "Damn it all to hell. Have you the slightest notion of how close we came to making love last night?"

She nodded.

"I've never known a woman who could tie me into knots

the way you do. I promised myself I wasn't going to touch you again, and here it is seven-thirty in the morning and I want you so damn much I hurt."

Silently she stepped to his side and looked up at him, her eyes wide and innocent.

"Damn it, Lindy," he groaned. "Why do you have to be so beautiful?" He slipped his arms around her waist and exhaled sharply. "Now kiss me before I go. I'll be back as soon as I can."

Obediently she twined her arms around his neck and raised her lips to his. "Anything you say, big brother."

Chapter Seven

Freshly ground hamburger squished between Lindy's long fingers as she meshed the meat and spices together to form patties for the barbecue grill. It was a lovely summer afternoon in a week that had begun with such marvelous promise.

The front door opened and Rush let himself in to the apartment.

"Hi," Lindy called out, pleased to see him. He was fifteen minutes later than usual, and she'd hoped he hadn't missed the ferry, which ran hourly. "How do barbecued hamburgers sound for dinner?"

"Fine."

The word was clipped and impatient, as though what she served for their evening meal was the least of his concerns. Surprised at his gruff tone, Lindy turned around to find him standing in the doorway, his brow furrowed in a frown so tight it darkened his face.

"Did you have a bad day?"

"No."

Something was obviously troubling him, but from the hard set of his mouth, she knew it wouldn't do her any good to ask. In an effort to ignore his surly mood, she hurried to tell him her good news. "I got word from Steve. The *Atlantis* is due in as early as next week."

Rush acknowledged the information with a curt nod.

"There's cold pop in the fridge if that interests you."

Apparently it didn't because Rush left her and moved into the living room to turn on the television. Lindy finished her task, washed the hamburger goop from her fingers and joined him there, sitting on the arm of the sofa. She rested her elbow gently on Rush's shoulder while Susan Hutchinson from Channel 7 relayed the latest news-making incident from the Persian Gulf.

When Rush pulled out of Bremerton, Lindy knew the *Mitchell* would be headed for those same trouble-infested waters. Her heart thudded heavily in her chest as she battled to control her anxiety. She hated to think of Rush in any danger and wished the *Mitchell* was headed for the South Pacific or somewhere equally pleasant.

Rush must have sensed her fears because he wrapped his arm around her and gently squeezed her waist. Her hand slid over his shoulder and she kissed the top of his head, loving him more each minute of every day.

"Lindy?"

"Hmm?"

The tension in his shoulders was so severe, she wondered how he could hold himself stiff for so long and still breathe.

"When I leave, I don't want you clinging to me."

She blinked, not sure she understood what he was saying. He seemed to be implying she would make a scene on the dock, weeping and gnashing her teeth because the man she loved was heading out to sea. That he would even imagine such a thing was an insult. The other implication was even more offensive.

"Are you suggesting that once you leave I should start dating other men?"

A week seemed to pass before he answered. "Yes. I think that would be a good idea."

Lindy was slow to react to what he was suggesting. Her

emotions went from surprise to mild irritation, then quickly broadened to out-and-out fury. She jerked her arm off his shoulder and leaped to her feet. "Well, thank you very much."

"For what?"

If it hadn't been so tragic, so painfully sad, Lindy might have laughed. She'd never felt as close to any man as she had to Rush these past two weeks. When she'd declared her love, she hadn't been looking for white lace and promises. The words had been seared against her tender heart and she hadn't been able to hold them inside a minute longer. She hadn't asked anything of him, but she certainly hadn't expected this intolerable pat on the hand, telling her she was too young, too immature or too stupid to know her own mind.

"For God's sake, think about it, will you?"

"What?" she returned in like voice. "That I'm still a baby and certainly incapable of sound judgment? How about the fact that I'm looking to prove myself after Paul? What I feel for you is obviously some rebounding thing to soothe my injured ego. Right? Is that what you want me to think about, Rush? Unfortunately I can't come up with a single reason I should, since you've already shoved those things in my face at every opportunity."

His jaw was clenched so hard that his temple went white. "You're fresh out of college…."

"And still tied to Mama's apron strings. Is that what you mean to imply?"

"No."

Oh, the gall of the man. Rather than continue arguing, Lindy returned to the kitchen. She was so furious that she clenched her hands into hard fists and exhaled several times to gain control of her simmering rage. She gritted her teeth as she went about fixing their meal. If Rush was so keen for her to start dating someone, then Lindy could see no reason why she should wait until the *Mitchell* left Puget Sound. A small sense of satisfaction lifted the corner of her mouth in a soft sneer as she thought about having men come to the apartment to pick her up and the pleasure she'd derive from introducing them to Rush. Oh, he'd really love that. She might even stay the night with a friend from work and let Rush stew, thinking she was with another man. Then she'd see exactly how eager he was to have her meet someone else.

Lindy braced her hands against the counter and hung her head in abject defeat. Behaving that way was childish and immature and impossibly stupid. Sure, she'd make Rush suffer, but *she* would end up being the one with a broken heart and myriad regrets.

Rush seemed to be telling her something more. Yes, he hungered for her physically. The circumstances in which they were living were rife with sexual tension. Each day it became more difficult to ignore the fire between them, and more than once they'd gotten close enough to the flames to singe their self-control.

The realization hit Lindy then, the impact as strong as if Rush had slugged his fist into her stomach. In some ways it would have been easier if he had. Rush didn't love her. He pitied her after what had happened with Paul. All his tenderness, all his concern, everything he'd done had been born of pity. She'd mistaken his touch, his soul-wrenching kisses for passion when, from the beginning, all he'd really felt was compassion for her.

"Where's my book?"

Rush's question came at her as if from outer space. She turned to discover he stood not more than five feet away, looking irritated and impatient. She hadn't a clue what he was talking about.

"My book?" he repeated. "The one that was in the living room last night. What did you do with it?"

Still numb, she raised her hand and pointed toward his bedroom. "I set it on your dresser."

Since there was so little time in the morning, Lindy had gotten into the habit of straightening up the apartment before she went to bed. The night before Rush had been at a meeting, and she'd retired early, tired from a long day, before he'd gotten home.

"I'd appreciate it if you left my things alone," Rush said in a low growl. "Move whatever you want of yours, but kindly keep your hands off mine."

Answering him with anything more than a shake of her head would have been impossible. Lindy didn't know what had gone wrong, but in the space of fifteen minutes her world had been badly shaken. First Rush had told her he wanted her to start seeing other men and then he'd jumped all over her for putting his book away. Nothing seemed to make sense anymore.

The insight came to her then—it seemed to be the night for them—Rush wanted her out of the apartment. When she'd gotten the job with Boeing, it had been understood she'd need to wait for a couple of paychecks before she could afford to rent her own place. They hadn't actually discussed it, and at the time Lindy had let the subject drop because she'd wanted to spend as much time as she could with Rush. He hadn't asked her about it, and she'd assumed that he wanted her with him just as much. Once more, she'd been wrong.

Quickly calculating her limited funds, she realized that with what remained of her savings and her first check, which was due on Friday, she could possibly afford a studio apartment. If she asked around at the office, there might even be someone there who was looking for a roommate.

The muscles in her throat constricted as she fought down the regret. She'd been such a fool.

Rush noted that Lindy left the apartment as soon as she'd finished preparing their dinner, not bothering to eat anything herself. For that matter he didn't have much of an appetite either, but he sat down at the table, propped his book open in front of him and pretended an interest in both the book and the dinner.

It had been on the tip of his tongue to ask Lindy where she was going, but he'd swallowed the question, realizing how stupid it would sound after the way he'd laid into her earlier. He hadn't meant to start a fight, hadn't even been looking for one. It had just happened, and he was as shocked by his insensitive demands as Lindy had been. He hadn't meant a thing he'd said. The hurt in her expressive dark eyes returned to haunt him now. When he'd asked her about the book, she'd stood looking at him in confusion, the violet smudges that appeared beneath her eyes a silent testimony to the trauma his words had inflicted.

As for the suggestion she see other men, that was downright idiotic. Talk about inflicting self-torture! He wanted to see Lindy with another man about as much as he desired a bladder infection.

The problem, Rush knew, was that he loved Lindy Kyle. She was stubborn, headstrong, proud… warm and vibrant. She might as well have branded his heart, because he belonged to her.

Rush pushed his plate aside and wearily wiped a palm across his eyes. Hell, this was the last thing he'd planned would happen. He was thirty-two years old, for God's sake. Mature enough to recognize when he was headed for trouble. He'd known what was going to happen with Lindy from the first night he'd seen her standing, all soft and feminine, in the hallway outside Steve's bedroom. He'd known the morning she'd blasted the rock music loud enough to hurl him out of bed because she was hurt and angry. He'd known when she'd held his head between her hands and stared into his soul and whispered so sweetly that she loved him.

Rush stood and walked out onto the lanai, hands buried

in his pants pockets. The dark green waters of Puget Sound were visible and Rush snickered softly. So much for not seeking a bridge to tie him to the mainland. He was trapped on shore now and he dreaded leaving. He used to think of the navy as the only wife he'd ever need. But recently, when he crawled into bed at night, it was Lindy he longed to wrap his arms around. Lindy he longed to love. He wanted her to be a permanent part of his life. She was laughter and sunshine. She'd made him feel again, laugh again, love again. He couldn't bear to think of what the future would be like without her. Two weeks. He'd only been with Lindy for two weeks. Before that she'd been a name, the sister of a good friend. He couldn't ask her to share his life based on a two-week acquaintance. It was crazy. No, he'd be patient with her, force himself to wait. The six-month separation would do them both good. Time would test the strength of their love. Time would reveal the truth.

It was only a little after eight-thirty when Lindy returned to the apartment. She would have preferred to stay away much longer, but after reading through the evening newspaper for apartment rentals and wasting money on a horrible movie she didn't know where else to go or what else to do. Eventually she'd need to return anyway, and knowing Rush, he'd probably left the apartment, as well.

He wasn't in the living room or kitchen, and she didn't bother to check any of the other rooms, not wanting a recurrence of their earlier argument. It was obvious he wasn't in the mood for company.

Sitting at the table, Lindy spread out the classified section and read the apartment-for-rent advertisements once more.

Quite by accident she found a section she hadn't thought to look at before: roommates wanted. She read a couple of those and decided to phone the one that looked the most promising.

"Hello," she said brightly when the woman answered. "I'm calling about your ad in the paper."

Rush walked into the kitchen, hesitated when he saw her and opened the refrigerator to take out a cold can of pop. Lindy strove to ignore him as much as possible. Her fingers gripped the pen unnecessarily hard as she doodled while the woman on the other end of the line explained a few of the details regarding her ad.

"It says here that you're looking for a nonsmoker. I…I don't smoke and I've recently moved into the area and need a place to live. I…have a job."

"Lindy."

Rush called her name, but she pretended she hadn't heard him. Besides she was already involved in one conversation and if he chose to be rude that was his problem.

Undeterred, Rush waved his hand in front of her face. "Get off the phone."

"Excuse me a minute please." Lindy spoke to the woman, enunciating each word as she held her temper by a fragile thread. She pressed the receiver to her shoulder blade and glared up at Rush. "Just what do you think you're doing?" she hissed between clenched teeth.

"There's no need for you to find an apartment," he told her, returning her heated stare.

"I beg your pardon, Rush Callaghan, but this is my life, and if I choose to leave this apartment, I'll do so with or without your permission."

Rush cursed beneath his breath and walked away from her.

"I'm sorry to keep you waiting," Lindy said sweetly into the telephone receiver. "Perhaps it would be best if we met?"

"Damn it, Lindy," Rush shouted, twisting around to face her once more. "Will you kindly get off the phone so we can talk?"

He might as well have been speaking to a stone wall for

all the attention Lindy paid him. "Yes, Tuesday afternoon would be fine."

Rush's returning glare was hot enough to peel thirty-year-old wallpaper off a wall, but still Lindy ignored him.

"You won't be meeting whoever that is," he told her sternly, looming over her. "You're only wasting time."

"Kindly excuse me again, would you?" Lindy asked softly, deliberately calm. She turned to Rush then and half rose from her chair. "Would you shut up? I can't hear a word she's saying."

"Good."

He was making Lindy more furious by the minute, and she tried to tell him as much and still keep control of her temper. "I'm sorry to keep interrupting our conversation," she said to the woman on the phone.

Rush walked around the table a couple of times, looking like a man trapped in a small space–or a shark circling its kill. Finally he stopped, standing directly across from her. He closed his eyes and rubbed a hand along the back of his neck as though to relieve an ache there, then paused and looked at her. "Lindy, I'm leaving."

The words were nearly shouted. She hesitated and prayed for patience, and when that didn't work, she counted to ten. Flippantly she raised her hand and waved goodbye. Still, he didn't move.

"I'm twenty-two," Lindy answered the woman's question. "No...no you needn't worry about that sort of thing. There isn't anyone important in my life at the moment." She swallowed tightly at the lie.

She exchanged a look with Rush and feared he was going to explode. "I thought you were leaving," she whispered heatedly, cupping her hand over the mouthpiece. "Don't let me stop you."

"Not the apartment," he raged, staring at her as though she were completely dense. "The *Mitchell* is sailing out."

"I know.... In two weeks."

"The catapults are being tested tomorrow and possibly Wednesday. If everything works out we'll be gone by the beginning of next week."

"The beginning of next week," she echoed, hanging up the phone. She kept her hand on the receiver feeling numb with shock, numb with fear. "But you said it would be at least a month."

"As I recall, I told you it could be as long as a month. As it happens, it's only two, possibly three weeks."

"Oh, Rush." She turned to him, her eyes wide with a hundred emotions she didn't know how to define. She'd accepted long ago that their time together was limited. But she'd counted on every minute of these remaining weeks. Needed them. Needed Rush.

"It shouldn't come as any great surprise," he told her, and pulled out a chair to sit across from her.

"It isn't.... It's just that... I don't know." Her stomach twisted into hard knots and for a painful moment she couldn't breathe. She was stunned, and she felt Rush's eyes slowly search her face. With everything in her, she met his gaze, determined to appear cool and composed. Her heart might be quivering with apprehension, but she'd die smiling before she'd allow him to know it. He'd already told her once that he didn't want her clinging to him when he left. And she wouldn't. She'd stand on the dock with a smile on her lips and a tear in her eye, and wave until her arm dropped off, but she'd never let him know it was killing her.

"About tonight," he started again. "I didn't mean any of what I said."

He dropped his gaze, but not before Lindy saw a strange mixture of regret, desire and remorse. In the two weeks they'd been together, Lindy had thought she'd witnessed all Rush's moods. She'd seen him at his cynical best, when he'd been purposely aloof and brash. She'd experienced his comfort, his tenderness as he held her in his arms while she sobbed against his chest. And she'd heard the music of his laughter, stood transfixed by his sometimes warm-heated, playful moods. Oh Lord, she was going to miss him. Miss everything about him.

"Lindy, I'm sorry for what I said."

His hand reached for hers, rubbing warmth back into her chilled fingers. She shook her head, hoping that would suffice as acceptance of his apology.

They were silent for a moment, caught in the surging tide of their individual thoughts.

"I don't have any right to ask you to wait six months for me."

"I'll wait," she offered quietly. Lindy had no other choice.

"If you meet someone else…"

"Is that what you want?"

"No." Anger flared briefly in his eyes. Then his expression changed to that cool, watchful look he wore so often. "No," he repeated softly.

"That isn't what you said earlier." She tried to laugh, but the sound of her pain was carried in the mirth.

"I didn't mean it. Not a word."

"You don't believe that I love you, do you?"

He waited a long time before he answered. "I don't know. I think it's too soon after Paul for you to know what you're feeling."

Lindy closed her eyes in an effort to control the urge to argue with him. She did love him, and never more than now. She'd just learned he'd be sailing out of her life for half a year, and her only thought was how she would manage without him.

She watched as a small pulse started in his temple. "I don't want to leave you, Lindy."

Her gaze shot to his, and her eyes widened with astonishment. Rush loved the sea. The navy was more than his career. It was his life, the very reason he got out of bed every morning. She'd listened for hours while he described for her the warm sensations that went through him when he was on the open seas. She'd felt his pride and exhilaration when he spoke of standing alone against the force of a fierce storm. He loved everything about navy life. It was his dream, just as the oceans of the world were his destiny.

And he didn't want to leave her. What he felt for her was stronger than the lure of the sea.

Tears shimmered in her eyes and she bit hard on her lower lip to hold them at bay. Rush wouldn't tell her he loved her–not with words. It would have been more than she could expect. But by admitting that he didn't want to leave her, he said everything.

When Lindy had composed herself enough to look up at Rush again, she felt the tension in every line of his lovingly familiar face.

"I want you to stay at the apartment," he said, and his hand continued to rub hers, holding her fingers in a grip that was almost painfully tight. "Steve will be back soon, but he'll only be here a few weeks, if that long."

Lindy nodded.

"Then the place will be empty for months."

Again she acknowledged his words with an abrupt movement of her head.

"It would be better if there was someone living here. As it is now, an empty apartment is an invitation to burglars. You'd actually be doing Steve and me a favor if you agree to say."

"I'll…I'll want to start contributing toward the rent."

"Fine. Whatever you want. When Steve arrives the two of you can work it out."

"What about when Steve is here?" Lindy asked. "Where will I sleep?"

"He can have my room."

"But what about when you're both here?"

Rush frowned, and then a strange, almost humorous light entered his eyes and a soft smile crowded his face. "Let's cross that bridge when we get to it. Okay?"

"Okay."

"Anything else?" he asked.

She dropped her gaze to his hand, which was holding hers. "I love you, Rush, and I'm going to miss you like hell."

He raised her hand to his lips, closed his eyes and kissed it gently.

The coffee was ready by the time Rush met Lindy in the kitchen the following morning. Although she'd been physically and mentally exhausted, she'd hardly slept, managing three, maybe four hours of rest at the most. Now her eyes burned and she felt on the verge of tears.

Rush joined her at the table. He wordlessly reached for the morning newspaper and buried his face in it, not speaking to her–apparently pretending she wasn't there. Lindy stood it as long as she could.

"Would you like some breakfast?" she asked.

He shook his head. The stupid newspaper still presented a thin barrier between them.

Whereas Lindy had felt loved and reassured after their talk the night before, this morning she felt lonely and bereft. Rush hadn't sailed away yet, but he might as well have for all the companionship he offered.

"I think I'll get dressed now," she whispered, hoping that would gain his attention.

"Fine."

"Stop it, Rush."

That worked, and he lowered the paper, peering at her over the top of the page, his face clean of expression. "Stop what?"

"That!" She pointed an accusing finger at the newspaper. "I hate it when you do this."

"What hideous crime am I guilty of now?"

"You haven't left yet…. I'd think you'd want to spend every minute you could with me…. Instead you're hiding behind the *Post-Intelligencer* so you won't have to look at me."

"You're being ridiculous."

"I'm not. It's almost as if you can hardly wait to get away from me."

With deliberately slow movements he folded the newspaper and set it aside. "Is it because I didn't want any breakfast? Is that what's upset you so much? You know I seldom eat this early."

"No…of course that's not it."

"What is it then?"

"I…don't know." Lindy felt like such a fool. She didn't know why she was acting like this, but she couldn't stand it when Rush treated her this way. She could deal with his anger far more easily than this intolerable patience.

"What exactly do you want from me, Lindy?"

"I want some emotion," she cried.

"What?" he barked, clearly not understanding her.

"Not tears. I want you to…oh, never mind. Go back to reading your precious paper with that same stoic expression you always wear in the morning. I humbly apologize for having interrupted your reading time."

Lindy couldn't get to her bedroom fast enough. She took small pleasure in slamming her door. Her intention had been to dress as quickly as she could and leave the apartment. Instead she found herself sitting on the edge of her bed, trembling and teary eyed, confused and suddenly feeling utterly, desperately alone.

When her bedroom door flew open, Lindy gasped. Rush's gaze pinned her to the bed as he silently stalked across the room.

"Damn it, Lindy." The words were ground out through his teeth before he sank onto the bed beside her. His arms tightened around her trembling body, pressing her down against the mattress. His hands found and cupped her breasts as he buried his face in her hair, spreading a wildfire of kisses along her cheeks and face, but avoiding her lips.

All Rush had to do was touch her and the desire curled in her belly like an anchor rope ready to plunge her into dark, inviting depths of passion.

His fingers tightened on her shoulders as he raised his head and stared down at her. He looked as though he were trying to stop himself but couldn't. Then his mouth closed hungrily over hers, rubbing back and forth, his tongue probing hers.

Lindy's arms found his back and she arched her spine, grinding her hips against him, needing him so desperately she could barely breathe. The longer Rush kissed her, the deeper she sank into the turbulent waters of desire. She felt like she was drowning, oblivious to everything except the primitive need to be loved by Rush.

"Oh, Lindy...." The words came out softly as he lifted his head from hers. He paused and dragged in a heavy breath, held it a moment then expelled it. "Well," he whispered, "is that enough emotion for you?"

Chapter Eight

Lindy liked Susan Dwyer the minute the two met. Susan's reddish-brown hair was naturally curly, and although it was styled fashionably short, it managed to fall in an unruly array surrounding her pert face. She possessed the largest, liveliest brown eyes that Lindy could ever remember seeing on anyone. They sparkled with intelligence and vitality, glinting with warmth and curiosity as they studied Lindy.

"Jeff has talked of little else since he met you the other day," Susan confessed.

"It was certainly nice of you to invite Rush and me over for dinner," Lindy returned. Twin boys, about eighteen months of age with reddish caps of curly hair like their mother's stood at the edge of their playpen, silently regarding the two women through large, doleful brown eyes. They'd recently awakened from a late-afternoon nap and looked mournfully toward Susan in the hope that she'd abandon her dinner guests and play with them.

"A meal is a small price to pay to meet you."

Lindy smiled at that. "I take it Rush hasn't said much about me?"

"Are you kidding? He's been so tight-mouthed one would think you were top-secret information."

"That sounds like Rush." Lindy's gaze sought him out and

found him and Jeff on the back patio, lighting up the barbecue grill. Just watching him gave her a solid, warm feeling deep inside her breast. She'd found him attractive before, but now, set against this low-key social background, dressed casually in jeans and a striped shirt, looking relaxed and at ease, she found she loved him all the more.

"Rush and Jeff have been friends a lot of years," Susan went on to say. She opened the refrigerator, brought out a large bowl of potato salad and set it on the kitchen counter. "Jeff knew the first day after the *Mitchell* returned that something had happened to Rush. He mentioned it to me right away, but it wasn't until last week that he knew that Rush had found a special woman."

"Rush is the one who's special." Lindy continued to study him, trying to put the knowledge that he'd be leaving out of her mind long enough to enjoy this one evening with his friends.

Susan turned around and her gaze followed Lindy's. "He's happier now than I can ever remember seeing him. More serene. You've been good for him, Lindy–really good. I didn't used to like Rush.... Actually I was only reciprocating what he felt toward me. I think I may have reminded him of someone he knew a long time ago. Although Jeff's never told me this, I believe Rush may have tried to talk him out of marrying me."

"I've never known a man who can frown the way he does," Lindy said with a soft sigh. "I swear one of those famous looks of his could curdle milk a block away."

Susan hooted. "I know exactly the look you mean."

"How long have you and Jeff been married?" From everything Rush had told Lindy about Susan, and he'd spoken of little else on the hour-long ferry ride to Bremerton, Rush held his friend's wife in the highest regard. She was surprised to hear he'd once felt differently.

"We've been married about two and a half years now."

Jeff said something that caused Rush to chuckle. The low, modulated laugh seemed to shoot into the sky. Then they both laughed.

Surprised, Lindy and Susan turned around.

"I don't think I've ever really heard Rush laugh quite like that.... So free," Susan murmured, as she gazed at the two men. "He's always been so cynical, so stoic. I never really knew what he was thinking. When we first met he terrified me."

"I know what you felt," Lindy said slowly. "The first couple of days after I met Rush, I found myself wanting to thwart him. He can be such an arrogant bastard."

"And at the same time there's something so appealing about him," Susan answered thoughtfully. "And I'm not talking about how good-looking he is, either, although God knows he's handsome enough. But even when he openly disapproved of me, I couldn't help admiring and respecting him. It took time to earn his trust, and despite everything I was glad he was Jeff's friend. There's something inherently strong about Rush. Strong and intensely loyal. I've always known Rush would look out for Jeff no matter what the circumstances. It helped when Jeff had to leave.... Knowing he would be with Rush."

"He's the Rock of Gibraltar, I know," Lindy answered softly, loving him so much her heart ached. "Loyal and constant." She tried not to think about the huge aircraft carrier sailing out of Bremerton, taking Rush thousands of miles away from her. She attempted to push away all thoughts of how empty her life would be after the *Mitchell* left.

"What's it like?" Lindy whispered, hardly aware the words had slipped from her mouth.

Intuitively, it seemed, Susan knew what she was asking. "I don't sleep for the first week. No matter how many times Jeff leaves, it's always the same. For seven days I lie in bed and stare at the ceiling, my stomach in knots. As much as I try I can't seem to stop fretting and worrying. Finally I'm so exhausted my body takes over, and I'm able to sleep."

"Rush told me you are one of the strongest women he knows…. The best kind of navy wife."

Susan's countenance softened and her cheeks flushed to a fetching shade of rose pink. She dipped her head a little and murmured, "How sweet of him to say so."

"What does Jeff say about your sleeping problems?" Lindy asked.

Susan shrugged. "He doesn't know."

"But…"

"He has enough worries and responsibilities aboard the *Mitchell* without me burdening him with more. As much as possible I send him off with a smile and handle anything that arises as best I can while he's gone."

"I'm afraid," Lindy admitted reluctantly. "Not because Rush is leaving. I…I can accept that. But I worry about them sailing in the Persian Gulf." Every night, it seemed, the news was filled with reports of violence in the troubled waters of the Middle East. Before they'd left the apartment she'd heard reports about gunboats that had attempted to attack the U.S. Naval forces that very afternoon. Lindy hadn't mentioned to Rush what she was feeling, knowing he'd brush off her concern. She wanted to be strong, wanted to be brave for both their sakes.

Susan's dark eyes clouded and her chin trembled just a little. "After what happened to the *Stark*, we're all concerned. You aren't alone. But if any of us wives were to dwell on the danger, we'd soon be basket cases. I try to put it out of my mind as much as I can. I believe in Jeff, too. He's damn good at what he does and he's part of the most advanced naval fleet in the world. My security rests in the fact that he can take care of himself and his men. Rush can, too."

"I haven't told Rush how afraid I am."

"Good." Susan's gentle smile was encouraging.

"I…love Rush." The words came out hoarse and broken. She didn't have the security Susan and the other navy wives had. Rush had done nothing more than ask her to wait for him. At most, she could be considered his girlfriend, his sweetheart. "I don't want to lose him." She dropped her gaze and rubbed her open hands down the front of her jeans, more fearful than ever over what the future could hold. "I've only known him two weeks…. I can't believe I feel this strongly."

"It was like that with Jeff and me. We married within a month after we met, and he left for six months in the South Pacific almost immediately afterward. Talk about worry!"

"But I thought that area was relatively peaceful."

Susan cast an affectionate look toward her husband. "It wasn't that. I…I was more concerned about how attractive Jeff would find those lovely Polynesian girls."

"Oh." Lindy hadn't thought of that.

Susan blushed a little. "I was pregnant at the time, feeling completely miserable and about as sexy as a tuna casserole. Naturally we didn't know it was twins and I was desperately sick every morning. The highlight of each day was when the mail was delivered. I'd wait all morning and pray there'd be a letter from Jeff. When one finally did arrive, Jeff wrote in detail, telling me about this erotic show he and Rush had managed to see while on shore leave on a small island whose name I can't even pronounce. Topless dancers and the whole bit. I was so upset I cried for days, convinced he didn't love me anymore, and if he did that he'd never want to make love to me again." She pressed her hands over her small breasts. "In case you haven't noticed, I'm not exactly richly endowed in that area."

"I'm not exactly Dolly Parton myself."

They laughed together in an easy camaraderie, as if they'd known each other for a long time instead of just a few short hours.

"Anyway, I didn't write back. Every time I thought about him gawking at those other women and their gorgeous boobs, I got all the more furious. Here I was, heaving my guts out every morning and my loyal, true-blue husband was living it up on shore leave on some exotic island and writing home about how randy he was."

"I don't blame you for not writing back. I'm not sure I would have, either."

"Oh, Lindy," Susan said, pressing her hand on Lindy's forearm, her eyes wide and serious. "It was a terrible thing to do. Jeff about went crazy. He didn't know what had happened to me, and I think it nearly broke him mentally. I got the most soul-wrenching, tormented letter from him, begging me to let him know what had happened. His mind had worked everything into such a terrible state that he was convinced I'd lost the baby–we didn't know it was *babies* then–or even that I might have left him for another man. When I finally wrote and told him how unhappy I was that he'd gone to a stupid topless show he made me promise never, ever to do anything like that to him again."

"Was Jeff here when Timmy and Tommy were born?"

Hearing their names mentioned, the twins cooed and stamped their feet, wanting out of their playpen prison. Susan was busy putting the finishing touches on the relish plate, so Lindy lifted first one and then the other, balancing them on her hips. The two were an armful, but Lindy managed, briefly wondering how Susan coped with them twenty-four hours a day.

"It worked out that Jeff was home for the birth, but we were lucky because he was scheduled for sea trials on my due date. The boys obliged us by arriving ten days early."

Timmy wound his fingers through Lindy's hair while Tommy took pleasure in playing with the spaghetti strap of her summer top.

"Rush is the boys' godfather," Susan explained. "The only

times I've ever seen him let down his guard were with them—and then tonight with you. He'd make a wonderful father someday."

"I think he would, too," Lindy said, kissing the chubby cheek of each twin. The boys laughed and Timmy tried to lean over and grab a pickle from his mother's hands.

"Just a minute, son," Susan told him. "Dinner's almost ready."

To keep the pair entertained until their mother dished up their dinner plates, Lindy bounced them up and down on her hips in a jaunty, trotting step around the kitchen. She was laughing, her face flushed and happy, when she looked up to discover Rush standing on the other side of the sliding glass door, watching her.

His deep blue eyes were so intense that her breath caught in her throat. Lindy thought for a moment that she might have done something to anger him. His gaze had narrowed, but there was a light shining from it that didn't speak of anger, but of something else, something far stronger that she couldn't define. A muscle worked in his cheek, and he seemed to be taking in every detail of her as she bounced the chubby cherubs on her hips.

Jeff must have called him because Rush turned abruptly and left without saying a word.

"Here, I'll take one of the boys," Susan offered, lifting Tommy from Lindy's hip. She carried the squirming child outside where two high chairs were positioned side by side next to the round picnic table.

Lindy followed her onto the patio and slipped Timmy into his seat.

"I learned a long time ago that it's best to feed the boys before Jeff and I even try to eat."

Lindy noted Susan had dished up foods her young sons could eat with their hands: chicken legs, finger-Jell-O, pickles and potato chips made up the twins' meal.

"They're getting so independent. They make a terrible fuss if I try to spoon-feed them anymore."

"Can they feed themselves?"

"For the most part." Susan was busy strapping in each toddler. "Believe me, it's a test of patience because more food lands on the floor and wall than ever makes it into their mouths. Afterward it's easier to squirt them down than to try to wash their hands and faces."

Lindy laughed at the visual image of Susan holding the boys while Jeff brought around the garden hose.

Rush's friend strolled to his wife's side and slipped his arm around her slim waist. Susan was a full head shorter than her husband and fit neatly into his embrace. "Are you ready for me to put the steaks on the grill?"

Susan nodded and leaned her supple form against her husband. She went up on tiptoe and brushed a kiss over his cheek. She paused then and smiled up at him. "Anytime you want."

Lindy watched, fascinated by the tender exchange between husband and wife. From what little Susan had told her she knew the couple had gotten off to a rocky start. They'd worked hard to find happiness together and it showed. Jeff and Susan didn't require words to communicate. A shared look, a soft sigh would often be all that was required. How Lindy envied them. How she wished everything was settled between her and Rush. But it wasn't. And he'd be leaving her in just a few, intolerably short days.

They caught the nine o'clock ferry back to Seattle. Jeff dropped them off at the terminal and after Susan and Lindy had shared hugs and Lindy had kissed the boys goodbye, Lindy and Rush walked onto the waiting boat.

Although he shouldn't have been, Rush was astonished at the way Lindy and Susan had become such fast friends. The two had talked and laughed as if they'd known each other since childhood. Now that he thought about it, the two women were quite a bit alike. Both were intelligent, sensitive and personable. And both were in love with navy men. It took a special breed of woman to fit into the military lifestyle, to accept the long separations, brief reunions and the fact that family must always come second in their husbands' lives.

Both Lindy and he had come away from the evening refreshed. Jeff had given definition to the unknown emotions Rush had been dealing with the past two days. Rush had asked his friend how he managed to leave Susan and the twins and not look back–and had witnessed the instant flash of regret that shot into his friend's eyes. Jeff had explained that the last days before he sailed were always the worst. He didn't want to leave Susan, didn't want to think of not being able to love her for months on end. Nor did he like to think about all that he was missing in his children's lives. He'd been at sea when their first teeth had come in, and on sea trials when they'd taken their first steps. Now he'd be leaving them again, and his mind was crowded with everything he wasn't going to be there to experience.

Then Jeff had asked Rush if he'd had a fight with Lindy recently. Rush's astonishment must have shown because Jeff had laughed and said the same thing happened to him and Susan every time he found out when he'd be sailing. Like clockwork. His fault, usually. But he and Susan had made a promise to each other long ago. No matter what they fought about, they never left anything unsettled between them.

"I'm going to stand outside," Lindy said, cutting into Rush's thoughts. The ferry had been underway for about twenty minutes. She stood and buttoned her sweater before heading for the weather deck.

"Sure. Go ahead," Rush answered. He didn't mind the long ride to and from the shipyard each day. Most of the navy personnel lived in Kitsap County, across Puget Sound from Seattle. But Rush preferred the cultural advantages of living in a big city.

Rush watched as Lindy moved outside the passenger area and stood against the stern, her hands on the rail. The wind whipped the hair from her face and plastered her thin sweater against her soft curves.

Just watching Lindy, Rush felt his heart constrict. When she'd been holding Timmy and Tommy, laughing with them, bouncing the twins on her hips, Rush hadn't been able to tear his gaze away from her. The earth could have opened up and swallowed him whole and he swore he wouldn't have been aware of it.

Seeing her with those two babies had been the most powerful, most emotional moment of his life. The sudden overwhelming physical desire for her was like a knife slicing into his skin and scraping against a bone–it had gone that deep. Not once, not even with Cheryl had he thought about children. He enjoyed Jeff's sons. They were cute little rascals, but seeing Lindy with those babies had created a need so strong in him he doubted that his life would ever be the same again. He wanted a child. Son or daughter, he didn't care. What did matter was that Lindy be their mother.

Even now, hours later, his eyes couldn't get enough of her as she stood, braced against the wind. He thought about her belly swollen with his seed, her breasts full and heavy, and the desire that stabbed through him was like hot needles. The sensation curled into a tight ball in the center of his abdomen. He'd longed for her physically before now. The thought of making love to her had dominated his thoughts from the first morning he'd stumbled upon her in the bathroom wearing those sexy see-through baby-doll pajamas.

But the physical desire he was experiencing now far exceeded anything he'd previously known. And it was different in ways he couldn't even begin to explain.

Unable to stay parted from her a minute longer, Rush left his seat and stepped outside, joining her at the railing.

Wordlessly he slipped his arm over her shoulder. Lindy looked up at him, and her eyes were unusually dark and solemn. The effort it cost her to smile was revealed in the feeble movement of her mouth.

"Lindy?"

She pressed her index finger across his lips the way she did when she didn't want there to be questions between them. Although she strove valiantly to prevent them, tears filled her sweet, adoring gaze. Inhaling a wobbly breath, she pressed her forehead against his chest in a vain attempt to compose herself.

Rush wrapped his arms around her, needing to comfort her, feeling strangely lost as to what to say or do, and not completely understanding what was wrong. Her lithe frame molded against him and he reveled in the feel of her softness pressed to him. "Honey, what is it?"

She shook her head. "Susan said…"

"She offend you?" Rush couldn't imagine it, and yet the anger rose in him instantly.

Lindy swiftly jerked her head from side to side. "No…no, of course not." Her arms were around his middle now, her eyes as dry as she could make them. But her chin quivered with the effort.

She lifted a hand and touched the side of his face, her eyes full of such tenderness that it was all Rush could do to meet her gaze.

"Do you remember the night we met?"

He grinned. "I'm not likely to forget it. I nearly tossed you into the street."

"You were perfectly horrible. So uncompromising…so unreadable."

"So arrogant," he added, regretting every harsh word he'd ever said to her.

The corner of her mouth quirked with a swift smile. "A good dose of healthy arrogance to put me in my place as I recall."

He brushed the hair from her face and nodded, resisting kissing her, although it was difficult.

"I disliked you so much.... I actually looked forward to thwarting you. I could hardly wait for you to leave. And now...now I dread it. I wish I could be more like Susan. She's so brave."

"She's had far more experience at this than you." Rush searched her face, and under his scrutiny the normally cool, composed features began to quiver with unspoken anguish. He understood then. She was afraid, almost desperately so, and bravely holding it all inside. Pierced to the quick by his own thoughtlessness, he tightened his grip on her and breathed in the sweet flowery fragrance of her silky dark hair.

"Honey, nothing's going to happen to me."

"But...the gunboats...the missiles."

"I'm coming back to you, Lindy."

She brushed her hands down her cheeks to wipe away the sheen of tears. "You think I'm being silly and emotional, don't you? This isn't wartime, and nothing is likely to happen, but I can't help thinking..."

He took her by the shoulders then, gripping her tightly. "No," he said sternly, his heart filling with a mixture of concern, tenderness and understanding. His mind groped for the words to comfort her. "You're not overreacting. It is going to be dangerous. I'm not trying to whitewash our assignment. But, Lindy, my sweet Lindy, I've never had anything more to live for than I do right this minute."

"You'd better come back to me, Rush Callaghan." She said it as though it were a fierce threat and the consequences would be dire if he didn't.

Death was the only thing that would keep him from Lindy. Unless... The thought was as crippling to him as the fear of him dying was to Lindy. "Then you'd better be waiting for me."

Her sturdy gaze held his and his hands slid from their grip on her shoulder to stroke her slim, swanlike neck.

"You still don't trust my love, do you?" she asked, looking sad and disappointed.

"Yes," he answered, nodding his head for emphasis. "I believe you." He wasn't sure he should–she was so young, so susceptible–but God help him, he needed everything Lindy was so generously offering him.

He took her hand and brushed his lips over her palm and then, because he couldn't resist and didn't give a tinker's damn who was watching, he kissed her mouth.

It was ten by the time the *Yakima* docked in Seattle. The hike to the apartment was a steep climb, but the night was so gorgeous that Lindy didn't want to hurry home. Every minute left was precious and wasting even a single one would be a crime.

"Let's go to the park," she suggested.

Rush looked bewildered for a moment, and asked, "What park?"

"The one here on the waterfront."

"Whatever for?"

Lindy laughed and slapped her hand noisily against her side. "So much for romance."

"Romance?"

"Come on, Rush. I'm finished crying. When you sail off into the sunset, I'll be there wearing a smile. All I ask is for you to humor me a little before you go. If that means taking a short detour to look at the stars from Waterfront Park, I think you should at least be willing."

"Lindy–" he said her name on the tail end of a sigh "–you've got to get up and go to work in the morning."

She thought for a moment he might refuse her, but he

didn't. He slipped his arm around her waist and guided her in the direction of the park.

They climbed the stairs to the second level and stood at the railing, overlooking the quiet green water. The lights from Harbor Island and West Seattle flickered like moonbeams dancing in the distance.

Lindy folded her hands over the cold steel rail, Rush behind her, his chin resting on the crown of her head. "Remember the last time we were here?" Lindy asked, thinking of their wild race up the stairs and the joy she'd experienced in having bested him.

"Yes." Rush's low voice carried a frown.

Lindy twisted around and gazed up at him. "Why do you say it like that?"

"You called me Paul. Remember?"

It took her a second to recall that and all that had happened afterward. "Was that really such a short time ago?" It felt like years instead of just a few weeks.

"Yes." His brow pleated with a grim look.

"No wonder you think I can't possibly know my own heart," she whispered, a little desperately. "No wonder you've never told me how you feel."

His brows lowered even more, shadowing his face as though he'd realized he'd never said it. "I love you, Lindy."

She closed her eyes and let the words rain down over her heart like velvety smooth flower petals, relishing each one, holding them close so she would have them later when she needed them. "I know," she whispered, the tears back in her voice. "I just wanted to hear you say it one time before you left."

Chapter Nine

"Lindy?" Rush dropped his hands from her shoulders. His mind was buzzing, as active as any hive. He felt weak from her touch, weak from the effect of her tears, weak with a desperate need to hold her and make her his own. He'd loved unwisely before, and had given up the dream of ever finding happiness again. And then Lindy, his sweet beautiful Lindy, had slammed into his life, and Rush knew he would never be the same again. His heart felt as if it would burst as he pulled her closer, breathing in the perfumed scent that was hers alone.

"Yes?"

Rush couldn't believe the thoughts that were bouncing around in his mind like Mexican jumping beans. Nothing seemed to keep them still. He loved Lindy. He desired her in a way that went miles beyond the physical. Her courage, her honesty, her spirit–each had shattered every defense he'd managed to erect over the years. From the moment they'd met, she'd played havoc with his heart.

"Rush?" She was staring up at him with wide, inquiring eyes.

"I think we should get married." There. It was out. He watched as the surprise worked its way over her features, touching her eyes first, narrowing them as though she wasn't sure she'd heard him right. Then the excitement and happiness broke out and glowed from every part of her, followed almost immediately by swift tears that brimmed in her clear, brown eyes. When her teeth bit into her lower lip, Rush wasn't sure what to think. She tossed her arms around him, and Rush felt the shiver work through her despite the warmth of the June evening.

"Yes, I'll marry you." Her answer was issued in a small voice that pitched and faltered like a boat bobbing in a storm at sea. "When?"

"We'll buy the ring tomorrow."

She nodded, her eyes bright and eager. "I'll arrange to take off early enough so we can get to the courthouse before it closes."

"The courthouse?"

"For the license." She cast him a stern look that convinced him she would make a wonderful mother.

Once he understood the implication, Rush frowned, unsure how to proceed. "But I don't want to get married *now*."

The happiness that had been shining from her face faded, then vanished completely to be replaced by a stunned, hurt look.

"I see," she whispered, and took a step back, away from him. "You want us to wait six months until you return from this tour?"

It made a hell of a lot of sense to Rush, and when he spoke his voice was soft yet inexorable. "Of course."

"I see."

"Would you quit saying that like I'd just suggested we live in sin?"

Rush could tell that she was struggling to compose her thoughts. Confusion and another emotion he couldn't define tightened her brow, and she looked to be on the verge of breaking into tears—but these weren't tears of sudden happiness.

"I need to think," she announced, stiffly turning away from him and hurrying down the concrete stairs.

Rush, watching her run away from him like a frightened doe, held up his hands in a gesture of utter bewilderment. They couldn't get married so soon. For God's sake, they'd known each other less than three weeks.

Lindy walked as fast as her legs would carry her, and her heart was pounding so hard she could feel it all the way to her toes. She was a little embarrassed, because she'd assumed that Rush meant for them to marry right away, and she was troubled, too. She didn't want to wait, and she couldn't think of a way of explaining to Rush all the strong and conflicting emotions that were churning inside her.

Within a matter of seconds, Rush's quick-paced steps joined hers.

"For God's sake will you tell me what you find so damn insulting?" he demanded.

Lindy stopped and looked up at him, loving him so much her heart threatened to burst. His eyes seemed unusually dark and, as always, unreadable as he buried his thoughts and his pain deep within himself.

"Insulting? Oh Rush," she whispered contritely, "never that."

"Then why did you take off like a bat out of hell?"

She dropped her gaze to the sidewalk. "I don't want to wait.... When you leave Saturday I want to be..."

"Lindy, that's crazy."

"...your wife," she finished.

Rush's jaw clamped shut, and Lindy saw the muscles in his lean cheek jerk as a hodgepodge of doubts clouded his mind. She didn't blame him, but if he was willing to make a commitment to her now, it seemed fruitless to wait six months.

"I've been through one long engagement," she whispered fiercely. "I have no desire for another. I'll marry you, Rush, and consider myself the luckiest woman alive. But when you place a ring on my finger there will be two, not one."

"Do you realize how ridiculous you sound?"

She watched him intently, her eyes riveted to his. "Yes, I suppose I do, from your point of view."

"In other words, it's all or nothing?"

"No," she answered softly. "I'd marry you tonight if I could, or six months from now if that's what you choose. But if you love me enough to want me as your wife then why should we wait? That's what I don't understand."

His eyes hardened. "But you might regret…"

"No," she cut in, shaking her head so hard her hair whipped across her face. "I swear to you I'm not going to regret it."

Rush inhaled and cast an imploring look to the dark sky as though seeking guidance, and if not that, then divine intervention.

"I don't even want to discuss it."

"Fine," Lindy said with a sigh.

The remainder of the walk was completed in silence. When Rush unlocked the apartment door, Lindy stepped inside, intent on going to her bedroom to give them both space and time to think matters through.

Rush's hand reached for hers, stopping her before she'd gone more than a few steps.

Surprised, she glanced up at him, the light so dim she could barely make out his features.

"It's not right to hurry this when we've only begun to know each other," he said in a tone that was low, husky and deliberately expressionless.

Gently Lindy brushed her fingertips across the taut line of his jaw. "I'm not going to repent at leisure, if that's what you're worrying about. You seem to find it so important that we wait, so we will. But I love you enough right now. I don't have a single doubt that our marrying is the right thing, and nothing is going to change my mind."

"Lindy, it's crazy."

"Marry me now, Rush."

He shook his head. "Six months is soon enough. You need..."

"Me? You're the one who seems to be having all the doubts."

"I'll marry you in six months, Lindy," he said sternly.

Maybe, her mind tossed back. Maybe he would.

Rush studied her for a full minute. "I want you to wear my engagement ring."

The ring finger on her left hand remained dented from the year in which she'd worn Paul's diamond. Unconsciously she rubbed her thumb back and forth over the groove now, reliving anew the desolation that engagement had brought her. The emotion rippled in her chest, each wave growing broader in its scope. She didn't want to be Rush's fiancée–she'd been Paul's for so long. She'd lost Paul and she could lose Rush, too, in a hundred different ways.

"Will you?" he asked, his voice as unemotional as if he were requesting the time.

Once more Lindy would be forced to face the truth. Rush loved her enough to want a commitment from her but not enough to make her his wife. She would be a fiancée. Again. But not a wife.

A strange light flared in his eyes that she faintly saw in the darkness. "It's important to me."

She sucked in a deep breath and felt all the resistance inside her collapse. Gone was her pride; gone was her conviction; gone was her stubbornness. He wanted to wait. She would. He wanted her to wear his ring. She would do that, too.

"Yes," she whispered brokenly. He needed that assurance. It was Lindy who required more.

Hours later something woke Lindy. Unsure what had stirred her from slumber, she rolled onto her side and rubbed the sleep from her eyes. Across the room a shadow moved and she noted Rush's profile outlined in the doorway of her bedroom. He was leaning against the frame of her door, his head dropped as if he were caught in the throes of some terrible quandary. Something about him, about the way his shoulders slouched and his head drooped, told her this was the last place in the world he wanted to be…or the first.

"Rush, what is it?" She raised herself up on one elbow.

Her words seemed to catch him unawares, and he jerked his head up and straightened. Moving to her side, he sank to the edge of the mattress. Tenderly he brushed the unruly hair from her forehead, his face so intense it seemed knotted. He didn't speak, and Lindy had no way of knowing his thoughts. He groaned then, and his mouth claimed hers in a fiery kiss that threatened to turn her blood to steam. He lifted his mouth from hers and tucked her head beneath his chin, rubbing his jaw back and forth over her crown as if to soak in her softness.

Lindy dragged in a shuddering breath, her senses fired to life by his touch. She'd assumed when she first woke that he wanted to make love to her, but that wasn't his intention. No lover would hold a look of such torment. His eyes were fierce, savage and yet unimaginably tender.

He studied her, and his warm hands stroked her face as though to memorize each loving feature. The smile that touched the edge of his mouth was fleeting. And still he didn't speak. His thumb lightly brushed over her lips, and he closed his eyes briefly as if to compose his troubled thoughts.

"I love you, Lindy," he whispered, in a voice that was at once gruff and soft. "I love you so much it scares the hell out of me."

His arms went around her, holding her as close as he could with the blankets bunched between them. Inhaling a deep breath, he buried his face in her neck.

Lindy's fingers riffled through his dark hair and she lowered her lashes, cherishing this moment, although she wasn't sure she understood it.

"Tomorrow," he told her. "I want you to take off early. We have an appointment at the courthouse."

The longest–and shortest–days of Lindy's life were the three they were required to wait before their wedding. Rush made the arrangements with a navy chaplain, and Jeff and Susan Dwyer stood up for them. The ceremony itself lasted only a few short minutes. Rush stood close at Lindy's side, and she couldn't ever remember him looking more handsome than in full-dress uniform. When he repeated his vows, his voice was strong and confident. Lindy's own was much softer, but equally fervent.

Afterward they went to an expensive restaurant for dinner and were met by several other couples, all navy people, all friends of Rush's. Names and faces flew past Lindy, and after a while she gave up trying to keep track of who was who. She managed to smile at each one and made the effort to thank them for coming to share this day with her and Rush.

Once they were seated, Lindy placed the bouquet of baby's breath and pink rosebuds in her lap. Susan sat on her left and Rush on her right. Rush was talking to Jeff who sat on the opposite side from him. Rush's fingers closed around Lindy's and communicated his frustration at being trapped with all these people when he wanted to be alone with her. Lindy felt the same way. Rush was her husband and she was dying with the need to be his wife in every way. They had such little time left together. Three days and two nights to last them half a year.

"Do you think we're both crazy?" Lindy leaned over and whispered to Susan. There'd been so little time to talk before the ceremony.

"I think it's the most wildly romantic thing I've seen in years." Her new friend's eyes sparkled with shared joy. "A blind man could see how much Rush loves you."

"I honestly didn't think he'd do it," Lindy confessed.

"What? Marry you?"

"Yes, before he left anyway. He wanted to wait until he returned in December, and…then he didn't. I hardly had time to think once he made up his mind. The past three days have zoomed by. I feel as if I've been on a spaceship–everything's a blur. We've been up every night past midnight discussing the arrangements."

"Didn't you have to work?"

Lindy nodded and suppressed a yawn. "I didn't dare ask for any days off since I've been working such a short time. I regret that now, because I think my supervisor would have understood. But Rush didn't want me to jeopardize my job."

"You'll need it once he's gone," Susan said with a wisdom that must have come from her years as a navy wife. "It's important for you to keep busy. Rush knows that. Having a job to go to every day will help the time he's gone pass all the more quickly. The transition from being together almost constantly to being alone will be smoother, too."

"What about you?" Lindy knew that Susan didn't work outside the home. Her friend couldn't with Timmy and Tommy still so young.

"I manage to do some volunteer work with some of the other navy wives," Susan explained. "We help each other. Once everything settles down, I'll introduce you around."

Lindy smiled, more than willing to meet the others and make new friends. She wanted to do everything that was right to be a good wife to Rush. There was so much to learn, so much to remember. Susan was already a valuable friend, and now she was willing to show Lindy the ropes.

When they left the restaurant, several couples stood outside waiting, and Lindy and Rush were bombarded with flying rice.

Rush had chosen a hotel close to the restaurant for their wedding night. He'd checked in before the ceremony and had their luggage delivered to the suite.

"I didn't think I was ever going to get you alone, Mrs. Callaghan," he whispered to her in the elevator, wrapping his arms around her waist and looking very much as though he wanted to kiss her.

"And exactly what are you planning to do once you have me all to yourself?"

"Oh Lord, Lindy." He breathed in a giant whoosh of oxygen. "You have no idea how hard it's been to keep my hands off you these past few days."

"Yes, I do," she answered softly, blushing just a little. "Because it's been equally difficult for me."

The elevator came to a smooth halt and the door glided cheerfully open. With Rush's hand at her waist guiding her, they walked down the long narrow hallway to the honeymoon suite.

When they reached the room, Rush gently scooped her up and into his arms, managing to hold onto her, juggle the keys and unlock the door.

Rush carried her into the room, slammed the door closed with his foot and gently laid Lindy upon the huge king-size mattress.

Lindy's arms curled and locked around his neck and, unable to wait a minute longer, she smiled up at him, raised her head and kissed him. Rush groaned and pressed her deeper into the pillows, covering her upper body with his own. Her breasts felt the urgent pressure of his chest, her nipples already tingling with the need to experience his touch. The hammering rhythm of his heart echoed hers and seemed to thunder in her ears. Lindy had waited so long for this night.

Poised above her as he was, Rush's mouth dipped to capture hers.

"I can't believe we're finally here," he whispered, his mouth scant inches above hers.

"I can't believe we're actually married."

"Believe it, Lindy." The moist tip of his tongue outlined her bottom lip.

"I'm going to be a good wife to you," she whispered fervently, planting her hands on either side of his face and guiding his mouth to hers, taking his tongue in her mouth. "You won't regret marrying me…. I promise."

"I have no regrets. Dear God, Lindy, how could I?" Again and again his mouth claimed her until she lost count.

"Lindy, Lindy," he whispered against her neck. "I don't think I can wait much longer…. I wanted to do this slow and easy, but already I feel like I'm going to explode, I want you so much."

They kissed again tempestuously, their mouths grinding hard, their tongues meeting. The kissing sparked the coals of their desire with an urgency that left Lindy trembling in its wake.

Reluctantly, his breath coming in uneven gasps, Rush moved away from her enough to start unbuttoning his jacket. Lindy noted that his movements were abrupt, impatient.

With trembling, uncooperative fingers, she reached for the zipper at the back of her gown, letting the satin and lace knee-length dress fall to the floor.

She was about to slip the pale pink camisole over her head when Rush stopped her.

"Let me," he murmured, his eyes consuming her with a need he couldn't disguise.

She nodded and let her hands fall slack at her sides.

He stood before her–so tall, so solemn, so intent. Lindy could feel the spiraling desire wrap itself around them both, binding them to each other as effectively as any cord. His hands reached for the garment's hem and she raised her arms to better aid him. The silky material whispered against her skin as he drew it over her torso, and Lindy heard Rush's soft gasp as her breasts sprang free.

To her surprise, his hands came up to caress her neck and not her breasts. His touch was unbelievably light, as though he feared the slender thread of his control would snap. His hands gently stroked the sloping curve of her neck and then traveled down to her shoulders, his fingertips grazing her soft, smooth skin. Lindy's eyes grew heavy under the magic he wove around her and her body felt warm and restless. The fresh, clean scent of him filled her and her head rolled to one side. She was caught so completely in the spell he was weaving around her that she feared she might faint with her need for him.

With the softest of touches his hands found her breasts, fitting to their underswell, lifting them, weighing them as though on a delicate balance. The thumb on each hand grazed an already erect nipple. Lindy must have moaned or emitted some kind of sound, because he whispered, "I know, honey, I know."

Something like a flame began to warm the pit of her stomach–Lindy could think of no other way to describe it. The sensation grew more heated and more intense with every passing flick of his thumbs, until her nipples became throbbing velvet pebbles beneath his fingertips. When Lindy was convinced she could endure no more of this sweet torture, Rush lowered his mouth to hers. Gently, moistly, he kissed her lower lip, tugging at it with his teeth. Then he repeated the process and feasted feverishly on the upper.

Rush broke away from her long enough to finish undressing, then lowered himself to the mattress, propped beside her and slightly over her. The hand he slipped beneath her back felt cool and smooth against her heated flesh. He used it to arch her toward him, and she gasped when his hot mouth closed over a breast, feasting on one and then the other in turn.

The fire that had started in her stomach spread its flickering flames through her until Lindy felt she was about to be consumed by the heat Rush had generated.

If he didn't take her soon, she was convinced she'd melt with her need. Everything in her seemed to be pulsating. Her breasts throbbed and the apex of her womanhood beat its own pagan rhythm until Lindy tossed her head back and forth, trapped in a delirium of sexual tension.

Rush kissed and caressed her endlessly, his mouth exploring her breasts, her soft belly, her long legs until Lindy thought she'd go mad. Every nerve in her body was shouting with need. Once he had reduced her to quivering helplessness, Rush changed positions so that he was poised directly above her.

His knee parted her thighs and she willingly opened to him. Rush guided himself into position so that the tip of his engorged manhood was pressed against her moist opening.

"Lindy," he whispered hoarsely, "I…love… you." With each word his pulsating warmth plunged deeper and deeper into her, until he was so far inside her, so firmly locked within her, she was sure he had reached her soul.

Slowly, gradually he began to move, and his swollen heat created the most delicious, most pleasing friction against the most intimate of her surfaces.

Lindy's hands clutched at his broad back, wanting him closer, needing him. She was filled with a tautness, an indescribable demand that became more intolerable with every heart-stopping stroke until she was sure she would scream.

As she struggled to catch her breath, Rush's hands caressed her once more, finding her tingling breasts and then the flat of her stomach.

"Rush…oh Rush…." She tossed her head from side to side, completely lost in the pleasure.

"Kiss me," he pleaded. "Give me your tongue." He put a hand under her head, lifting her mouth to his. Gingerly she explored the hollow of his mouth, running her tongue over his smooth, even teeth. His lower lip was full and when she nipped at it the effect on him was electric. He drove into her again and again, gaining momentum with each thrust until there was only the insistent friction and the sweet, sweet pangs of an all-consuming pleasure. When he climaxed, Lindy felt him throbbing in the innermost recesses of her body and smiled, depleted and utterly content.

Panting, Rush rolled over and pulled her on top of him. He was as breathless as if he'd run for miles, and Lindy's own breathing was as labored as his. Exhausted, she closed her eyes and pressed her flushed face to his heaving chest, allowed herself to be transported, floating in the warm aftermath of his love.

Lindy slept in his arms and Rush watched her, astonished at the woman who was now his wife. Even though he would do nothing to change the deed, he knew deep in his heart that they should have waited before marrying. But he'd wanted her so desperately, and the thought of losing her had been more than he could bear. So he had sealed their future. It was what Lindy wanted–it was what he wanted.

These past weeks with Lindy had begun to fill the emptiness in his soul. His heart had found a home with her. She had wiped away years of cynicism with her smile, erased the bitterness from his memory with her tenderness, healed him and given him a reason to live.

A thin ribbon of sunlight peeked through the crack in the drapes but Rush dared not raise his wrist to check the time for fear of disturbing Lindy's sleep. Lord, what a woman he'd found. Twice more during the night they had made love, and each time she had opened herself to him, holding back nothing. As their bodies had come together, their souls had merged as well. Their lovemaking was as Rush had always known it would be. He could hardly bear the thought of waiting six months to love her again. And they only had one night more.

"Rush." She tossed his name over her shoulder. "I've got to push your things aside if I'm going to get all my stuff into your closet."

"Then do it," he said, delivering another armful of dresses and blouses to her.

They'd decided to transport her personal things into Rush's bedroom; she could sleep in his room when he was away, which only made sense.

"I can't believe you hauled all this to Seattle in that dinky Rabbit you drive."

"I did."

She was so intent on her task that she didn't notice that Rush had moved behind her. He slipped his arms around her waist and hugged her, resting his chin on her shoulder, kissing her neck. Lindy finished pushing the hangers to one side before twisting around and shyly kissing him back.

"Is that everything?" she questioned, looping her arms around his neck.

"Just about. You know, there are better ways to spend a honeymoon."

Her lashes fluttered down. "Yes, I know, but…but I thought you'd be exhausted by now. I mean…well, you know."

Rush started unfastening the buttons of her blouse. "I find that you bring out the animal side of my nature."

Already Lindy could feel her body starting to respond. "You seem to be doing the same thing to me."

"We've got a million and one things to do," he muttered, but his fingers were intent on only one task.

"I know," Lindy returned, pulling his shirt free from his waistband.

He stripped the blouse from her shoulders and removed her bra. Her breasts stood out firm and round. He fondled each one, then kissed them in turn. "Did I ever tell you about the morning I walked in on you in the bathroom?"

"Yes," she whispered hoarsely.

"I thought at the time your nipples were begging to be kissed."

"They are now, too."

Rush groaned. "Oh God, Lindy, I'm never going to get enough of you before I leave."

"But not for any lack of trying," she whispered back, threading her fingers through his hair. Tossing back her head, she whimpered softly as he sucked her breast with the hunger of a starving man. Already his hands were at the snap of her jeans, working that open and then tugging at the zipper. Lindy's fingers were equally busy.

They could hardly make it to the bed fast enough. Wordlessly Rush spread her legs and lowered his body into hers. At his first thrust, Lindy felt an electric charge shoot through her and she cried out.

Their lovemaking was a hungry, wild mating that was both tender and fierce and left them so exhausted they fell into a deep, drained sleep.

A sharp sound broke into Lindy's consciousness, but she resisted waking, not wanting to tear herself away from the warm, lethargic feeling of being held in Rush's arms.

"What the hell?"

Lindy's eyes shot open to discover her brother standing in the doorway of Rush's bedroom. Before she could move or speak, Steve had tossed his seabag on the floor and stormed into the room. With one sweeping motion, he hauled Rush out of bed and slammed him against the wall.

"Just what the hell are you doing in bed with my sister?" he demanded, his fist poised in front of Rush's face.

Chapter Ten

"Steve!" Lindy screamed. "We're married." She bolted upright and clenched the blankets to her naked breasts with her right hand while holding out her left in proof.

"Married!" Steve exclaimed on a long, slow breath. Gradually he released his grip on Rush's neck. "What the hell! But you hardly know each other. You can't possibly…. You wouldn't."

"It happens that way sometimes," Rush explained, and reached for his pants.

"I don't believe this." Steve shook his head as though the action would dissolve the image before him, then turned and stalked out of the room. He paused at the doorway and looked back. "We need to talk."

Lindy wasn't sure which of them Steve wanted to speak with. What was clear was that Lindy hardly recognized her own brother. His solid, sturdy good looks hadn't changed in the time since she'd last seen him. He was still lean and handsome, the way she'd always remembered him, but his eyes had been so hard, so cruel, as though he would have relished an excuse to fight, even if it was with his best friend.

Rush sat on the edge of the mattress and Lindy moved behind him, looping her arms around his neck. "Are you all right?"

"It's not exactly the way I cherish being woken."

"Me, either." Her teeth nibbled his earlobe, and she rubbed her bare breasts against his back, loving the tingly feeling the action provoked. She grinned with satisfaction as she felt Rush's shoulders tighten and knew he'd experienced the same kind of delicious pleasure.

"Lindy, for God's sake, stop. I've got to go out there and talk to your brother."

The regret in his voice was enough to raise her blood pressure and she sighed, wishing her brother had chosen another time and day to make his appearance.

"I'm coming with you," Lindy said when Rush had finished buttoning his shirt.

"Honey, listen," Rush said, his voice low and thoughtful. "I think it might be better if Steve and I had a few minutes alone first."

"Why?"

"I want to tell Steve how things went between us," Rush explained. "If he's going to be angry, then I'd rather he was upset with me."

"Hey, Rush, come on. We're in this together." She reached for her clothes and was dressing as quickly as her fingers would allow. "It isn't as if you seduced me, you know. In fact it was more the other way around. You've been a perfect gentleman from the minute we met.... Well, other than that first night–but that's understandable when you think about it.... I think we should both talk to Steve. He is my brother and..."

Rush moved around to her side of the bed and stood in front of her.

Lindy was prepared to argue with her husband if he was determined to be obstinate, but when she glanced up his eyes were filled with such love and tenderness that all her determination to stand at his side and face her brother evaporated.

"Ten minutes," he said, taking her by the shoulders. "That's all I ask."

Denying Rush anything in that moment would have been impossible, and she nodded.

Her husband-of-a-day rewarded her with a quick but infinitely thorough kiss, his tongue darting into her mouth and shooting ripples of pleasure down the full length of her body. When he released her Lindy sank back onto the corner of the bed, her legs too weak to support her.

Rush left the bedroom and closed the door. Lindy stared at it helplessly, unable to move. Almost immediately the raised, angry voice of her brother followed as he demanded to know what the hell Rush thought he was doing marrying his little sister. Lindy didn't hear her husband's reply, but whatever he said apparently didn't appease Steve, because shortly afterward Steve started in again. Lindy grimaced at some of the language, impatient to speak to her brother herself. She was an adult and certainly capable of choosing her own husband.

She gave Rush the ten minutes she'd promised, but it was difficult. As the endless seconds ticked past, Lindy tried to remember the last time she'd seen Steve. Before he'd divorced Carol, Lindy realized. That was what?–one and a half years ago now. Steve had been happy then, excited, full of life. Could it really have been only eighteen months ago? She hardly recognized Steve as the same man. He looked so much older than his thirty-three years, and she wondered if the divorce was responsible for the changes in him. From what her parents had told her, Steve and Carol had broken up shortly after their visit to Minneapolis, and the divorce had been final for over a year. No one knew any of the details. Steve hadn't explained a thing, and Lindy hadn't asked. What went on between her brother and Carol was their business, not hers.

When Lindy couldn't stand it any longer, she stood and walked out of the bedroom. Both men stopped and turned around to face her. Anger flashed from their eyes, and it looked as if they were about to resort to physical violence. Lindy knew she'd timed her entrance perfectly.

"It's good to see you again, Steve," she said with a soft smile, walking to her husband's side and slipping her arm around his waist.

Her brother grumbled something in reply.

"Aren't you going to congratulate Rush and me?"

Steve's eyes hardened as they clashed with Rush's. "I'm not sure."

"Why not?" Lindy feigned a calmness she was far from feeling and smiled up at Rush, letting her warm gaze speak for her.

"Lindy, just what in the hell do you think you're doing?" Steve demanded, looking more upset by the minute. "You've been in Seattle how long? Three, four weeks?"

"Are you saying Rush will make me a terrible husband and that I've made a dreadful mistake? Obviously you know something about him that I don't."

"That's not what I mean and you know it," Steve shouted. He paused long enough to rake his fingers through his hair, mussing the well-groomed effect. "What about Paul Abrams?"

Lindy met her brother's gaze without emotion. "What about him?"

"You loved him…or so you said. Hell, the last time I heard from you, your heart was broken and you didn't know if you wanted to go on living. Remember?"

"Of course I remember."

"And that's all changed?" His voice carried a harsh sound of reprimand. "It didn't take you very long to forget him, did it? So much for undying love and devotion. Well, little sister, did you ever stop to think what could follow next? If your affections can change overnight, what's going to happen when Rush has sea duty? Are you going to divorce him once he's out of sight because you find yourself attracted to another man?"

Lindy felt her husband tense at her side. She wasn't pleased with Steve's insinuation, either, but she was willing to let it pass. "As you recall, Paul was the one who conveniently forgot about me. Thank God he did, otherwise I would never have met Rush."

"You're saying that now. God, what a mess." Steve abruptly turned away and marched to the other side of the room. Just as sharply, he turned back to face them. "Of all the people in the world, I thought you were the one I could trust the most."

His comment was directed at Rush.

"She's just a kid." The look Steve tossed his friend suggested Rush had resorted to robbing a day-care center.

"I'm twenty-two," Lindy cried, piqued.

"Damn it, Lindy. You don't know a thing about marriage."

"She knows enough about being a wife to satisfy me," Rush answered calmly.

"She's too young for you," Steve shouted, and started in again with hardly a breath. "Any fool could see she married you on the rebound. I thought you were smarter than this, Callaghan. You took advantage of her."

"If he'd taken advantage of me," Lindy cut in, growing more impatient with her sibling by the moment, "he wouldn't have married me."

"Of course he married you. He knew I'd beat the hell out of him if he didn't."

From the tight expression her brother wore, Lindy could see that he'd relish the opportunity to fight with Rush.

"Steve, stop it," she pleaded, holding out her hands. "I'm married, and although you seem to think it's some great tragedy, I don't. I plan on being a good wife to Rush. This isn't an overnight fling. We're committed to each other."

"I don't give this so-called marriage three months."

Rush's hands knotted into tight fists, but when he went

to step forward, Lindy stopped him. Her husband had done an admirable job of keeping his cool, but Steve's accusations were beginning to wear on them both, and Lindy could tell Rush wouldn't put up with much more.

"Have you told Mom and Dad?"

"Of course. I'm not ashamed of what we've done." But she'd waited until after the ceremony to announce she was married for fear her mother would try to talk her out of it. When she did phone her parents, Grace Kyle hadn't been able to disguise her shock and had started to weep. When her father had come on the line, he'd been equally stunned, almost embarrassed, stumbling over his words, clearly not knowing what to say. It wasn't until Rush had talked to both her parents that Lindy's family had made an effort to offer their congratulations.

Steve's eyes narrowed. "I should kick your teeth down your throat for this, Callaghan."

Rush's mouth quirked into a half smile. "I'd like to see you try."

"Stop it, both of you!" Lindy cried, shocked at both men. "I don't know what's the matter with you, Steve, but this is my honeymoon. I have only one night left to spend with my husband, and I don't intend to waste it arguing with you."

"The *Mitchell* is leaving in the morning?"

Once more Steve's question was directed to Rush as he chose to ignore Lindy.

Rush nodded.

The two men stood not more than ten feet apart and glared heatedly at each other, issuing silent challenges. Steve broke away first, picked up his seabag and headed toward the door.

"I'll leave you two alone."

"It would be appreciated," Rush answered.

Steve turned back to face his friend and Lindy couldn't remember when his dark eyes had been more intense. "You hurt her, Callaghan, and you'll answer to me personally."

The tension in the room was so electric it was a miracle lightning didn't flash from the ceiling. It seemed to arc and flow between the two men, ready to ignite at any moment.

"I thought you knew me better than that," Rush answered through clenched teeth.

"I don't trust anyone. Not anymore. Just remember what I said. If Lindy's ever unhappy, I'm going to hold you responsible."

A throbbing, wounded silence filled the room after the front door slammed. Lindy sat on the davenport and forcefully expelled her breath. "What is his problem?"

"When was the last time you saw your brother?" Rush wanted to know, taking the seat beside her and reaching for her hand.

"About a year and a half ago. Steve and Carol drove to Minneapolis when Steve was on shore leave. They were so much in love and so happy, we were all stunned when a few months later we got a letter that said he'd filed for divorce. We never knew why. I think he would have told me had I asked, but I never did. What happened between him and Carol is their business."

"The divorce changed him," Rush explained softly.

"You're telling me. But his letters were never like this. He was always so encouraging, so upbeat. When he heard what happened with Paul, his letter helped me so much. He understood so well what I was going through, but now I feel like I hardly know him."

"He's upset," Rush answered after a moment. "He'll come around once he has time to think things through. He knows us both, probably better than anyone else."

Lindy nodded. "I'm not fickle and my brother knows that. I didn't marry you on the rebound. I swear that, Rush. I love you."

Rush's face broke into a slow, relaxed grin and he draped his arm over her shoulders. "And I love you, wife."

Lindy tucked her head beneath his chin and snuggled into his warm embrace, cherishing the closeness they shared. She didn't expect anyone else to understand something she couldn't explain herself. Finding Rush was like stumbling upon her other half. With him she was whole.

"What went wrong with Steve and Carol?" Lindy asked quietly as her thoughts drifted back to her brother. She was concerned about the changes she saw in him.

Rush was silent for a long moment. "I'm not sure. Like you, I felt it was his and Carol's business, but I'm almost certain she was unfaithful."

"No way." If Lindy knew anything about her ex-sister-in-law it was that gentle, sweet Carol would never cheat on Steve. "She just isn't the type."

"Then I haven't any idea what went wrong."

"How sad," Lindy murmured. It was obvious to her that Steve had changed drastically since his divorce. Although she couldn't believe Carol had been unfaithful to her brother, that would explain Steve's statement about not trusting anyone anymore.

"I think we could both learn a valuable lesson from what happened with your brother's marriage," Rush said, his voice tightening.

"What?" Lindy asked, and raised her head to study her husband's face. His eyes had darkened slightly and she wasn't able to read his thoughts, but she had a good idea what he was thinking. And she didn't like it. Not one damn bit. "Are you going to start lecturing me, Rush Callaghan?"

"Lecturing you?"

"Yes. I have a fair idea of what you're going to say."

The muscles of his face relaxed into a half smile as he leaned against the back of the davenport and crossed his arms. His knowing eyes came alive with mischief. "Oh, you do, do you?"

"You were about to give me some dopey line about what

we're experiencing now being some kind of euphoric stage all lovers go through."

"I was?"

"Yes, you were. You were going to say we're experiencing a time when everything and everyone is perfect. There's no one else on the planet but us and nothing else but our newly discovered love."

Rush's brows arched, but if he was portraying anything other than amusement, Lindy couldn't tell.

"And…"

"There's more?" he asked, and laughed, his rich baritone sounding relaxed and amused.

"Oh, I'm just getting to the good part." She stood and rubbed the palms of her hands together, sorting through her thoughts.

"Well?" he pressed, having trouble disguising his amusement.

"You're about to tell me that the tension is gone. We've stepped over the line, entered the bedroom and now that territory has been charted."

"Not as much as I'd like, but we'll make up for lost time later." Rush's words were more promise than comment.

"Don't interrupt me."

"Sorry." He didn't look the least bit repentant.

"You're going to tell me we're about to step off cloud nine and should expect to be hit with a healthy dose of reality. We could be headed for trouble now. If we aren't careful, what happened to Steve and Carol could happen to us."

All traces of amusement faded from Rush's eyes and his face tightened. Lindy knew she was right. "By this time tomorrow, you'll be gone." She forced herself to offer him a brave smile. "And I'm going to be alone."

Rush stood. His eyebrows were pulled down into a heavy ledge of concern. "That's right, Lindy. Up until this point everything's gone smoothly for us. Our whole world has been telescoped into a two-part universe. After tomorrow everything will change, and I doubt that it'll ever be exactly the same again. In two weeks you could be wondering how you ever imagined yourself in love with me."

"That will never happen." She shook her head hard for emphasis.

"In two months, you'll have forgotten what I look like."

From his narrowed, tight expression, Lindy knew he wouldn't listen to any denials. She hadn't started this conversation to argue with him. The last thing she wanted was for them to spend their remaining hours fighting.

"You're married to a man you hardly know who's going to be leaving you for half a year. The next time I see you, it'll be close to Christmas."

She crossed her arms and cleared her throat loudly. "Have you finished?"

"Finished what?"

"Your lecture."

"Lindy, I'm serious. I–"

"You're not saying anything I haven't already thought about a hundred times. I love you, Rush, and I've never been more sure of anything in my life. My feelings aren't going to change in ten days or ten years."

Tenderly he wrapped her in his arms then, and held her close. If there was anything more he wanted to tell her, he left it unsaid.

Hours later Rush lay on his back in bed with Lindy nestled, sleeping, in his arms. He hadn't been able to sleep, dreading the thought of leaving her. Getting married the way they had was possibly the most irresponsible thing he'd done in his life. But he didn't care. Given the same set of circumstances he'd marry Lindy again. Gladly.

She astonished him. She was so sure, so absolutely confident they'd done the right thing. Her unwavering trust had been contagious. God knew, he'd wanted her badly enough. Steve seemed to think he'd taken advantage of her, and perhaps he had, but that couldn't be changed now. Lindy was his wife, and by all that he considered holy, he planned to be a good husband to her.

He closed his eyes and inhaled the fresh scent of jasmine and perfume that was Lindy's alone, knowing full well that within a few hours he would be walking away from her.

Rush thought his heart would burst with the love he felt for his wife. He softly kissed the crown of her head, cradled in the crook between his neck and shoulder.

Lindy Callaghan was some kind of woman. They'd made love together, their bodies moving in perfect synchronization, as though they'd been married for years. All afternoon and evening, they'd teased and played lovers' games, pretending they had forever. But it wasn't enough. Not nearly enough. Rush wanted her again. Now. But he had the feeling making love to her a thousand times wouldn't be enough to satisfy him.

Lindy woke from a sound sleep when Rush pushed the thin fabric of her nightgown aside, his fingers light and quick. She hardly felt his movements until his mouth closed greedily over her nipple. She sucked on her bottom lip to keep from whimpering as the hot stab of pleasure pierced her. Her head ground into the pillow with every moist stroke of his tongue. And when his teeth gently tugged at the raised peaks of her breasts, it felt as if he were pulling at a thread that was linked to the heart and heat of her womanhood. She moaned anew at a pleasure so intense it was akin to pain, and still Rush sucked at the pebbled hardness. Again and again, like a butterfly flitting from flower to flower, he sampled the sweetness of the nectar from her breasts until he was pleasurably sated.

When she was sure she was about to melt with liquifying,

pulsating need, Rush lifted his head. He lay on his side and slid his hand down the smooth length of her stomach until his caressing fingers tangled in the nest of wispy hair. He paused.

Lindy stopped breathing as his fingers slowly delved deeper, charting fresh territory as they sought the opening to the moist warmth. With his probing finger inside her, Lindy lifted her bottom and rotated her hips, saying without words what she wanted. Rush's mouth returned to her nipple and the hot cord of pleasure joining her breasts and the core of her womanhood was drawn even tighter as he connected the two ends.

When he had nearly driven her to the limits of sanity, Rush moved his body over hers. In one unbroken action, he entered her.

They both gasped at the strength of the undiluted pleasure.

Their eyes met and locked in the darkness. He was buried as deeply inside her as he could go, and still he didn't move. Lindy felt his limbs tremble as he struggled to gain control of his raging desire. She moaned in protest and squirmed beneath him, grinding her hips against him until he cried out her name in an agonized plea.

"Honey…please…don't do that."

"I can't help it." Once more she raised her bottom enough to experience the intimate friction she craved so desperately.

"Lindy." He hissed her name again through clenched teeth. "For pity's sake, don't…. Every time you do that…oh, Lindy…."

She gazed up at his tortured face and lifted her head to kiss him. He responded by thrusting his tongue in her mouth while all ten fingers tunneled through her hair.

He started to move then in a long, slow stroke that plunged him deep within her. She whimpered when he withdrew, but he quickly sank into her again and again and again, bringing them to a shared climax several moments later. Together they cried out, their hearts sailed and they soared into a new shining universe as their voices shouted in joyous celebration.

Still sheathed inside her, Rush whispered urgently, "You're mine, Lindy. Mine."

"Yours," she whispered in return. "Only yours."

Lindy had never seen so many people gathered in one place in her life. It seemed the entire navy had come to watch the tugboats tow the *Mitchell* out of Sinclair Inlet.

Susan Dwyer stood at Lindy's side on the long pier, looking at the huge aircraft carrier as it sliced through the dark green waters. Helicopters from the local television stations hovered overhead and small planes zoomed past to get pictures of the carrier as it was tugged away from the Bremerton shipyard.

"How do you feel?" Susan asked, shouting above the noise of the cheering crowd.

"I don't know." Lindy shook her head, feeling a little numb. A lump rose in her throat. When she'd kissed Rush goodbye, she'd felt the reluctance and tension in him, but no shrinking. As much as he wanted to stay with her, as much as he longed for them to be together, he longed for the sea more. He was going to leave her because it was his duty, his destiny. He belonged to the navy, and she had only been granted second rights.

"I'm not going to cry." That much Lindy knew.

"Good girl." Susan was dry-eyed herself. "You're going to do just fine. We both are. These six months will fly by. Just you wait and see, and before we know it they'll both be back, randy as hell and–" She stopped abruptly and heaved in a deep breath. "Who am I trying to kid? It's going to be the pits." Her gaze clouded and she bit into her trembling bottom lip. "I think I'm pregnant again."

Lindy didn't know what to say. "Does Jeff know?"

"Nope. I went off the Pill last month when they left the first time. There didn't seem to be any reason to keep taking them when Jeff was going away for all those months. I forgot to take the stupid things half the time anyway. Then Jeff was home and I didn't even think about it until yesterday morning."

"Why then?"

"I threw up."

"Oh, Susan. Are you going to be all right?"

"If I said yes, would you believe me?"

"Probably."

Her friend sighed. "Well, don't. I have miserable pregnancies. And I don't think Jeff's going to be pleased, either. We'd agreed to wait at least another couple of years."

Lindy found a tissue in her purse and handed it to her friend, who quickly wiped the moisture from her pale cheeks.

"Tears are another sure sign with me."

"I'd better keep track of these symptoms," Lindy muttered absently.

Susan paused, blew her nose and turned to face Lindy. "What do you mean?"

"Rush and I weren't using any birth control, either.... It wasn't the right time of the month for me to start the Pill, and well, to be honest, we didn't discuss it."

"Oh, Lindy, how do we let these things happen?"

Lindy didn't have an answer to that. Not once during the last two nights had she given any thought to the fact that she could become pregnant. It certainly wouldn't be any great tragedy, but she would have preferred to wait a year or two before they started a family. Rush hadn't said a word, either. It seemed improbable that he hadn't thought of the possibility.

"You want to come back to the house with me and share a hot fudge sundae and a jar of pickles?" Susan asked seriously.

Lindy shook her head. "My brother arrived yesterday. We haven't had much of a chance to talk."

"Keep in touch."

"I will," Lindy promised.

Steve was watching the newscast that showed the *Mitchell* pulling out of Puget Sound when Lindy entered the apartment. He didn't so much as look away from the television screen when she entered the living room, and Lindy paused, anticipating the worst.

"If you're going to yell at me, do it now and get it over with," she said, standing just inside the room. After saying farewell to Rush she didn't need anything more to dampen her already low spirits.

Her brother leaned forward and pressed the remote control, turning off the television set.

"Dear God, Lindy, what have you done?"

"I just said goodbye to my husband," she answered him, in a steady, controlled voice.

"Why'd you marry him?"

"For the usual reasons, I assure you."

Steve wiped a hand down his face. "I wish to hell I could say how happy I am for you, but I can't. I know you too well, Lindy. This marriage just isn't going to work. You're not the type of woman who's going to accept the life-style the navy demands. How can you possibly expect to know a man well enough to marry him in three weeks?"

"I know everything I need to."

"I suppose he told you about Cheryl?"

She squared her shoulders and stiffened her spine in a defiant gesture. She knew there'd been someone else, but Rush hadn't filled in the details. She hadn't told him everything about Paul, either.

"Did he?" Steve pressed.

"No," she flared.

"You're married to a man and you know nothing about his past."

"I love Rush and he loves me. That's all I need." Lindy was painfully conscious of her brother's adverse feelings toward her and Rush, but she was at a loss to understand his hostility. Unless his divorce had completely tainted his views on marriage.

Steve shook his head, his face pinched in a deep frown. "I'm afraid you've made the biggest mistake of your life, Lindy Kyle."

She stepped into the room and sat on the sofa arm. "The name's Lindy Callaghan, now."

Chapter Eleven

Susan Dwyer met Lindy at the front door. "Welcome," she said, bringing her inside the house. A group of women sat in the living room and smiled enthusiastically when Lindy entered the room. She recognized several of the faces from the restaurant where she and Rush had eaten their wedding dinner, but remembering all their names would have been impossible.

"Hello," Lindy said, cordially nodding her head toward the others. She took the only available chair and crossed her long legs, hoping she gave the appearance of being at ease. Susan had invited her over for a late lunch the week before, but her friend hadn't mentioned that anyone else would be present.

"I thought it was time you got to know some of the other wives," Susan said as a means of explanation.

"And if no one else is going to say it, I will," an attractive blonde with wide blue eyes piped up. "We're all anxious to get to know you better."

"We've all been crazy about Rush for years. I'm Mary, by the way."

"I'm Paula," the blonde who'd spoken first added.

"Hello, Mary and Paula." Lindy raised her hand.

Four of the others quickly introduced themselves. Sissy, Elly, Sandy and Joanna.

"Did you get the wives' packet?" Joanna wanted to know scooting to the edge of her seat.

Lindy's eyes shot to Susan. "I don't think so." The *Mitchell* had been gone almost a month now and because Lindy had been so busy with her job and worrying about her brother, she hadn't been able to get together with Susan as soon as she'd wanted.

"I'll take care of that right now." Joanna opened a briefcase and brought out a thick packet. She stood and delivered it to Lindy. "This is a little something the navy hands out to new wives so they aren't completely in the dark about what they've gotten themselves into having married a man in the military."

"A sort of finding-your-sea-legs-while-still-on-land idea," Susan explained.

Lindy opened the packet to find several brochures and booklets. There was one on the social customs and traditions of the navy–guidelines for the wives of commanding officers and executive officers, another on overseamanship, and several others, including one that gave the history of the U.S. Navy.

"An issue of *Wifeline* should be in there, too."

"Joanna's one of the ombudsmen for the *Mitchell*," Susan explained.

Lindy wasn't sure what that meant. "Oh," she said weakly, hoping she didn't sound completely stupid.

Joanna must have read the confusion in her eyes, because she added. "I act as a liaison between the command and the families. If you have a problem with something, come to me."

"Wonder Woman here will take care of it for you," Sissy commented and smiled at Joanna. "I know she's helped me often enough."

"I'm not completely sure I understand," Lindy admitted, with some reluctance. Although Steve had been in the service fifteen years, as long as Rush, Lindy had little technical understanding of the way the military worked.

"Let me give you an example," Joanna said and tapped her index finger against her lips while she thought. "Let's say you get sick and need to go to the hospital when Rush is on a cruise, and there's some kind of screwup there and they won't take you."

"Call Joanna." Seven voices chimed in unison.

"I see."

Joanna playfully cocked her head and slanted her mouth in a silly grin, which caused the others to laugh. "Mainly my job is to be sure that no one feels they need to face a problem alone. When you married Rush, you married his career, too. You belong to the navy now just as much as Rush does. If you've got a problem there will always be someone here to help."

"That's good to know." Lindy hadn't thought about it before, but what Joanna said made sense. The knowledge that someone was there to lend a helping hand gave her a comforting sense of belonging. Although she knew Susan was her friend, Jeff's wife had been her only contact with Rush's life.

"When the guys are around there aren't that many problems, but once they're deployed we have to stick together and help each other," Sissy added, and a couple of the others nodded their agreement.

"What do you mean there aren't that many problems with the guys around?" Mary, a slim redhead, cried. "I don't suppose anyone happened to mention to Lindy the hassles of shifting responsibilities and…"

"Hey, the poor girl just got married. Let's not hit her over the head with everything just yet."

"No," Lindy interrupted. "I want to know."

"It's just that we–meaning we wives–are left to handle the domestic situations when the men are at sea. It's not as if we have a whole lot of choice in the matter. Someone's got to do it. But then once our husbands sail home we're supposed to return to the docile role of wife and mother and automatically let the men take over. Sometimes it doesn't work that well."

"I don't imagine it would," Lindy said thoughtfully, and sighed inwardly. Briefly she wondered what problems the years held in store for her and Rush. She'd never thought about the shifting roles they'd need to play in their family life. It was a little intimidating, but she'd only been a bride for a month and didn't want to anticipate trouble.

"Every time Chuck's due back home, I get sick," Mary confessed, looking disgusted with herself. "It's all part of the syndrome."

"The homecoming is wonderful, but Wade and I tiptoe around each other for days for fear of saying or doing something that will ruin our reunion," another wife explained.

"We choose to ignore the obvious problems and pass over strife until it's time for him to be deployed again."

"That's when it really hits the fan," Susan inserted.

"What do you mean?" Lindy was curious to know. She could understand what the others were saying, although she hadn't been married long enough to experience with Rush a lot of what the women were warning her about. But the time would come when she was bound to, and she was eager to recognize the signs.

"It seems we're all susceptible to arguing before our husbands' leave," Joanna explained.

Lindy remembered how Rush had purposely picked a fight with her the afternoon he'd learned the repairs to the *Mitchell* had been completed.

"Rush jumped all over me for putting his book away," Lindy told the others. "I didn't understand it at the time. It was so ridiculous, so unreasonable and not like him at all."

The others nodded knowingly.

"I imagine it was about that time that Rush realized he loved you," Susan added smoothly. "Jeff pulled the same thing. He always does. The day he comes home and suggests it's time I go on a diet, I know what's coming. He's just learned when he'll be deployed. Jeff loves what he does, but he loves me and the kids, too. It's a crazy kind of tug-of-war that goes on inside him. He dreads leaving, hates the thought of all those months apart, and at the same time he's eager to sail. He can hardly wait to get out on the open seas."

"Try to make sense out of that if you can," Mary grumbled. "But this is all part of being a navy wife."

"And then there's the constant knowledge that we can be transferred at any time."

"Say, did anyone else hear the rumor that the *Mitchell* could be reassigned to Norfolk?"

"It's just gossip, Sissy," Joanna answered. "There's no need to worry about it now."

"See what I mean," Susan told Lindy with a soft laugh.

"You mean the *Mitchell* might transfer its home port to Norfolk?" Already Lindy was thinking about what would happen with her job if Rush was to be stationed in another state. She'd have to go with him and leave Seattle. Of course she could always find another job, but she didn't relish the thought. A growing knot of concern started to form in her stomach.

"The *Nimitz* was transferred from Norfolk to Bremerton," Sissy reminded the group.

"Two joys of navy life," Mary muttered disparagingly. "Deployment separation and cross-country moves."

"If worse comes to worst, we'll survive."

It was apparent to Lindy that Joanna was the cool voice of reason in this friendly group. Lindy still had trouble keeping track of who was who, but felt that she was going to fit in nicely. It was as though she were being welcomed into a sorority. The other navy wives' acceptance of her was automatic, their reception warm.

"We always survive," Susan added softly. "Now, as I said earlier, we're not going to knock poor Lindy over the head with everything in one afternoon."

"Yeah, we plan to give it to you in small doses."

"Has anyone else stopped to figure out how much time married couples are separated if the husband is in the navy?" Mary asked, holding a calculator in her hand. Her fingers were punching in a long list of numbers that she called out at regular intervals. "According to my figures, during a twenty-year enlistment–" her fingers flew over the keys "–the husband and wife will spend six years apart."

"Six years?" Lindy repeated while the numbers whirled around her head.

"It's not so bad," Susan said, and patted Lindy's hand to tell her she understood her friend's distress. "In small doses."

"While I've got everyone here," Joanna added, snapping her briefcase shut and setting it aside. "Remember you need to have your letters mailed by the fifteenth of each month."

The other women nodded, apparently already aware of the deadline. Susan had explained to Lindy earlier that because the *Mitchell* was deployed in unfriendly waters, the mail would be flown in with supplies only once a month.

"When are we going to eat?" Sissy asked, craning her neck to peek into the kitchen.

"Every time Bill's gone, Sissy gains ten pounds."

"I work it off once he's home, so quit teasing me."

"I could make a comment here, but I won't," Sandy muttered, and the others laughed.

"Well, if a certain someone doesn't feed me soon, I'm going to fade away before your very eyes." Dramatically Sissy placed the back of her hand against her forehead and released a long, expressive sigh.

"Okay, okay," Susan said with a laugh. "Lunch is served."

Everyone stood at once and moved into the kitchen. The table was arranged with a variety of salads, buffet style. Plates and napkins were arranged at one end and the forks fanned out attractively.

"I brought the recipe for the Cobb salad, in case anyone's interested," Paula commented.

"I wish you had said something," Lindy complained under her breath to Susan. "I could easily have brought something."

"You're our guest of honor."

"We're all dying to know how you met Rush," Sissy said and Joanna moved Lindy to the front of the line and handed her a plate.

"I think he's sexy as hell, and Doug told me he could hardly believe Rush would marry someone he only knew two weeks."

"Well, actually," Lindy murmured as an embarrassed flash of color entered her cheeks, "it was closer to three weeks."

The women laughed.

Sissy pressed her hand over her heart and sighed. "That's the most romantic thing I've heard in years and years."

Elly's shoulders moved up and down as well in an elongated sigh. "I always knew when the big man tumbled, he'd fall hard."

"He's so handsome," Mary interjected.

"So dedicated," Paula added.

"Until the night of your wedding dinner, he was always so…detached and distant. We all noticed the change in him."

"Thank you," Lindy answered softly.

"I bet he's a good lover."

"Sissy!"

Lindy laughed because although the others had been quick to chastise their friend they eagerly looked in her direction for a response. Not willing to disappoint them, she wiggled her eyebrows a few times and nodded.

"I knew it. I just knew it," Sissy cried.

"Are we going to eat, or are we going to talk about Lindy's love life all afternoon?" Joanna asked.

The women looked at each other, came to some sort of tacit agreement and set their plates aside.

* * *

"Are you all right?" Jeff asked Rush as he moved past his friend to the engine-order telegraph.

"Fine." The word was as sharp as a new razor. Rush wasn't willing to discuss his problems with anyone, not even Jeff.

"There's got to be some logical explanation why Lindy hasn't written."

"Right," Rush answered, but he avoided looking at his friend, doing his best to look busy. He didn't want to be rude, but he wasn't going to discuss his troubles either.

"Susan's letter says the wives' association had Lindy over for lunch recently."

"Is that supposed to reassure me?"

"I think it should." Jeff unfolded Susan's thick letter and scanned its contents. "Lindy's kept in close contact with Susan and the others."

"That doesn't mean a damn thing."

"Apparently they had a wedding shower for her."

That made him feel a whole lot better, Rush mused sarcastically. Lindy seemed to have forgotten she had a husband, but she was busy accepting wedding gifts.

Jeff paused and cleared his throat. "It seems the wives went together and got Lindy a long silk nightie."

Rush didn't respond. His jaw was clenched so tightly that he was convinced his back molars would crack. He'd been four interminable weeks without a single word from Lindy. A whole damn month. The knot in his stomach was tight enough to double him over. His nerves were shot. He found himself snapping at his men, behaving irrationally, becoming angry and taking it out on everyone else. And worse, he wasn't sleeping. For two nights now he hadn't been able to so much as close his eyes. Every time he did, the images that filled his mind were of Lindy with another man, presumably Paul. The hot surges of anger and adrenaline that shot through him were so strong that any chance of falling asleep was a lost cause. Lindy might as well have taken a knife and cut open a vein as not written.

Unwillingly Rush's mind leaped to a memory of how it had been with Cheryl. At first there'd been a flood of letters, filled with all the right phrases, everything a man longs to hear when he's separated from the woman he loves. Then Cheryl's letters had petered out to a handful in a month, and then just a sporadic few before his return.

But damn it all to hell, Lindy was his wife. He'd slipped a diamond ring on her finger and committed his life to her. He'd expected more of her than this. But apparently she took her vows lightly because she'd sure as hell forgotten him the minute he was out of sight.

It was a mistake to have married her. But he'd been so much in love with her that he'd refused to listen to the calm voice of reason. He'd lost one woman and feared losing another. He should have known standing before a preacher wasn't going to make any difference, but he would never have believed Lindy could do this. All her reassurances about knowing her own heart had fooled him. She'd been so positive they were doing the right thing. None of that confidence was worth a damn now. They'd both made a mistake. A bad one. At the rate things were progressing, this marriage could be the single worst disaster of his life.

"I'm going below," Rush announced, walking away from the gyrocompass repeater, which indicated the *Mitchell*'s course. The sight of Jeff holding a letter from home was more than Rush could take. He needed to escape before he said or did something he'd regret.

Jeff nodded, but his brow was creased with tight bands of concern.

Once in his compartment, Rush lay on his back with his hands cupped behind his head. Steve was right. Rush had known it the minute his friend had said as much. Lindy had married him on the rebound, and now that he was gone she'd realized what a terrible error in judgment she'd committed and wanted out.

They'd been living in a fairy tale, forced to share the apartment the way they were, and like a fool Rush had gotten sucked into the fantasy. Lindy had been wounded by love and Rush had been a convenient source of comfort to her damaged ego.

Now that he was gone, Lindy realized their mistake. The muscles of his stomach knotted when he realized how helpless he was in this situation. Lindy didn't love him.

Now all he had to worry about was if she was pregnant. Not using any protection had been a conscious decision on his part. They hadn't even talked about it the way couples should–hadn't discussed the possibility of starting a family so soon. It wasn't that Rush had been so eager for Lindy to get pregnant, he realized with a flash of insight. But he hadn't wanted a repeat of what had happened with Cheryl. If Lindy's stomach was swollen with a baby when he returned, he didn't want any question in his mind about who was the father.

Rush refused to believe he'd actually done anything so stupid as to play that sort of silly mind game. Lindy wasn't going to cheat on him–he refused to even consider the possibility. But then he'd honestly assumed she loved him, too–the same way he loved her. It hadn't even taken her a month to forget him.

Lindy let herself into the apartment and stopped when she found her brother sitting in front of the television, watching a late afternoon talk show. Steve's behavior was really beginning to concern her. He'd been assigned shore duty, and when he wasn't working he sat around the apartment with a lost, tormented look that reminded her of how she'd felt when she'd first arrived in Seattle. His behavior wasn't the only thing that was getting on her nerves. He'd become so cynical and so sarcastic about life. His thinking seemed so negative that she didn't like to talk to him anymore. There'd been a time when she'd admired him for the way he'd handled the emotional trauma of the divorce, but his letters had been a convenient front. It became clearer every day that the healing process hadn't even started in Steve. He still loved Carol, and he needed to either patch things up between them or accept the divorce as final. Otherwise it was going to ruin his life.

"Hi," she said, and walked into the kitchen, setting down the grocery bag on the counter. "What's Oprah got to say today?"

"Who?"

"The woman whose program you're watching."

"Hell, I don't know. Something about nursing mothers."

"And that interests you?"

"It's better than staring at some stupid game show."

"It's a beautiful day. You should be outside."

"Doing what?"

Lindy sighed. "I don't know. Something. Anything."

Steve stood and came into the kitchen. "Do you want me to do something for dinner? Peel potatoes, that sort of thing?"

She thanked him for his offer with a smile. "I've got everything under control." Opening the refrigerator, she set the milk inside and decided now was as good a time as any to wade into shark-infested waters. "Is Carol still living in Seattle?" Lindy asked the question and then turned to face her brother.

"Carol who?"

His words may have been flippant, but he couldn't disguise the instant flash of pain in his eyes.

"Carol Kyle, your wife."

"Ex-wife," he corrected bitterly. "As far as I know she is."

"I think I'll give her a call."

A year seemed to pass before Steve answered. "Before you start meddling in someone else's troubles, you'd better take care of your own, little sister."

Lindy's heart flew upward and lodged in her throat. "What do you mean by that?"

Steve pointed toward the mail that was stacked on the kitchen table. "You must have put the wrong address on that long letter you've been writing all month to Rush, because it's been returned."

"Oh, no." A sickening feeling invaded her limbs and her eyes widened with dread. "Returned? But why?" She reached for the thick manila envelope and checked the address. "Oh, Steve, what will Rush think if he doesn't get any mail from me?"

"The only thing he can assume under these circumstances. That you married him on the rebound and regret it."

She raised her hands in a gesture of abject defeat. "But I don't feel that way, not at all."

"Lindy, sit down. You look like you're about to faint." Her brother pulled out a chair and carefully lowered her into it. He walked a couple of times around her, as though gathering his thoughts on how to handle the situation.

Tears of frustration were hovering just beneath the surface. She'd faithfully written Rush each night, pouring out her heart to her husband, reassuring him each day how much she loved him and how proud she was to be his wife. She'd written about meeting the other wives and told him about the social get-together they were planning to celebrate the halfway mark of the six-month cruise. She'd drawn a picture of the lacy silk nightie the girls had given her as a wedding gift and told him how eager she was to model it for him.

There were weeks when she'd scribbled long epistles as many as six and seven times. Since the mail was only going to reach him once a month, Lindy had written it in journal form, marking the days.

To her surprise, this long separation wasn't anything like he'd suggested it would be. Rush had warned her that two weeks after he was gone she'd start to wonder how she ever imagined herself in love with him. Two weeks from the day he left, Lindy had made a giant card to tell him exactly the opposite had happened. If anything she loved him more than ever.

Over and over she had read the thick letter she'd received from him, until she had set each precious line in her memory. Rush's letters had been her lifeline to sanity.

The realization that he had received only a short one from her early after he sailed out of Bremerton, if that, was almost more than she could bear thinking about.

"What are you doing?" Steve asked, when Lindy reached for the phone.

"Calling Susan."

"What good is that going to do?"

"I…I don't know." But Lindy had to talk to someone before she went loony. Susan would know what to do.

"Hello?" Susan answered on the third ring, and Lindy could hear the twins crying in the background.

"Susan, it's Lindy. Something terrible has happened, and I don't know what to do." She was speaking as fast as she could, her voice raised and shaky.

"Lindy? Slow down. I can't understand a word you're saying."

"My letter to Rush came back," Lindy explained, doing her best to keep her voice as even as possible, although it wobbled like a toy top winding down after a long spin.

"Did you have the right address?"

Lindy reached for the envelope and read off Joanna's street numbers.

"Lindy," Susan muttered, interrupting her. "That's not the mailing address for the *Mitchell*."

"I know…. It's Joanna's. She said we were supposed to get all the mail to her by the fifteenth. Remember?"

"You weren't supposed to mail it to *her*," Susan cried. "It was supposed to be mailed, period."

"But I thought she was in charge of that."

"No, Lindy, Joanna doesn't have anything to do with the mail."

"Oh God, Susan, what will Rush think?"

Susan hesitated, then sighed. "It isn't that bad. I wouldn't worry about it, since it's only the one letter. He'll receive the others."

Lindy felt like weeping all the more. "But there was only the one letter. A long, long one…. Oh Susan, Rush must believe…I hate to even think about it. He'll assume I don't love him."

The line was silent. "The important thing is not to panic."

"I think it's too late for that."

"Now calm down," Susan muttered, and Lindy could picture her friend chewing on her lower lip, trying to come up with something. "Jeff will tell him."

"Tell him what?"

"Everything. How you've gotten involved in the wives' association and that we're seeing each other regularly. Rush is a smart man, Lindy. Give him credit for some intelligence."

"Right," Lindy said, nodding her head once. "He'll figure it out…. He knows I love him." Lindy gnawed on her lip, remembering how the women's group had told her if she had any problems, she should contact Joanna.

A long silence stretched over the wire before Susan spoke. "Should I call Joanna or do you want to?"

The phone rang just after midnight. Lindy rolled onto her stomach and checked the time. She hadn't been sleeping well and had only turned off the light fifteen minutes before. The call was probably some prankster and she wasn't eager to answer it, figuring Steve would. By the third ring, Lindy gave up on her brother and reached for the telephone receiver.

"Hello." She tried to make her voice sound as gruff and unfriendly as possible.

"This is a ham-radio operator in Anchorage, Alaska," the male voice explained. "A call is about to be transmitted to you from aboard the USS *Mitchell.* Talk as you would normally, but each time you're finished speaking you must say *over*. Do you understand?"

"Yes…."

"Okay. Go ahead and hang up and I'll connect you in about fifteen minutes."

Lindy's hand was shaking so badly she could barely replace the receiver. Rush. Somehow, someway, Rush had found a means of contacting her. She scooted off the bed and paced barefoot across the carpet, waiting. Fifteen minutes had never seemed to drag by more slowly.

When the phone rang, she nearly tore it off the nightstand.

"Lindy? Over."

The line sounded as if it were coming from the moon. Static filled the air. Popping and hissing.

"Yes, this is Lindy. Over."

"I only want to know one thing. Are you pregnant? Over."

Chapter Twelve

"You want to know what? Over," Lindy asked incredulously.

"Are you pregnant or not? Over." Rush demanded a second time. The long distance wire popped and hissed, making it almost impossible to hear him clearly.

"Not. Stop yelling at me and let me explain."

Silence followed.

A third voice interrupted. "Over?"

"Over," Lindy repeated.

"I'm listening. Over." Some of the bitter anger was gone from Rush's voice, but his frustration and anxiety were evident even through the poor quality of the connection.

"There was a screwup with the letters. I'll explain it later. Over."

"Explain it now. Over."

"I mailed the letter to Joanna instead of the address you gave me. Over."

"Joanna who? Over."

"Joanna Boston. She's an ombudsman for the *Mitchell.* I thought she was handling all the correspondence. I didn't realize it would go through the normal channels. Over."

"In an entire month you only wrote me one letter? Over." The words were shouted into her ear.

"It was sixty-two pages long. Over." Lindy returned at equal volume.

Silence crackled like a morning breakfast cereal, and when Rush spoke again, his voice was more subdued, but still tense. "Do you regret the fact that we're married? Over."

"No. Do you? Over."

Rush seemed to take his own sweet time answering, and when he did his voice was almost a whisper. "Not now. Over."

"I love you," Lindy whispered, "I…I told you before you left that I know my own heart, and I do. Over."

"When I didn't get any mail, I thought you'd decided to… hell, I don't know what I thought. Over."

"I'll write every day, I promise. I'm not going to make the same mistake twice with the mail business. Over."

"Damn good thing. I nearly went berserk. Over."

"I'm really sorry, Rush. I felt terrible when the letter was returned. Over."

"I understand. Over."

They were married and hadn't seen each other in two months and there didn't seem to be anything more they had to say.

"I have to go. Over," Rush said, after an awkward moment.

"I know. Goodbye, Rush. Don't worry about anything at this end. I'm doing okay. Your letters help…. I'm really sorry about what happened with yours. It won't happen again. Over."

"Goodbye, Lindy. I need you. Over."

The line went dead then and she was left holding the receiver in her hand. A tingling, burning feeling worked its way from her fingers down her arm and through her torso to settle in her stomach. Rush had been so angry with her. She couldn't blame him for being upset, but once that matter had been cleared up their conversation had remained awkward and stilted. They didn't have a lot to say to each other. His life was so far removed from hers now that there was nothing to share. He was a naval officer; she worked for an airline manufacturer. Their lives had briefly crossed paths for a three-week span and, when it came time to separate, they'd resisted and held on to each other. For the first time since Rush had been deployed, Lindy wondered if she had done the right thing in marrying him. At that moment it didn't feel right. Not for her, and from the way it sounded, not for Rush, either.

Lindy leaned back against the headboard and released a slow, agonized sigh. The shaking started then, and she gripped her hands together in a futile effort to control the trembling. She had married a man she barely knew, on an impulse. Doubts whizzed through her mind like buzzards circling a crippled animal, waiting for it to die. The picture was all too graphic in Lindy's troubled mind. She was stumbling and her family, particularly her brother, were all waiting for her to fall so they could tell her what a fool she'd been.

Lindy shook her head to dissolve the nightmarish image. She was being ridiculous. She loved Rush, and he loved her. He'd just ended their conversation by telling her of his need for her. A man like Rush Callaghan didn't say those words lightly. The circumstances they were trapped in had led to this negative thinking. These doubts would be gone by morning and she'd feel as strongly as ever about her commitment to Rush.

Swallowing at the hard lump in the back of her throat, Lindy turned off the bedside lamp and lay back down, resting her head on the pillow that had once been her husband's. Everything was going to work out fine. She'd done the right thing by marrying Rush. They were deeply in love with each other and if there were a few rocky roads ahead, that was to be expected. They'd weather those just fine.

But Lindy didn't sleep that night.

* * *

The tall waiter handed Lindy the oblong menu with the gold tassel. "This is a pleasant surprise," she said, looking across the linen-covered table at her older brother. Her relationship with Steve had gone much better this past month. He rarely mentioned Rush, and she stayed away from the subject of Carol. It wasn't exactly solid ground they stood on, but stable enough for the two of them to coexist without too many personality problems. The gesture of dinner was a delightful one, and Lindy wasn't about to refuse. They both needed a break from the humdrum of daily life.

These last couple of days Steve had been almost like his old self–teasing, joking and laughing. If she hadn't known him better, Lindy might have been fooled. She toyed with the idea of talking to Steve about the doubts that had been haunting her since the ship-to-shore call from Rush. She was terribly frightened that she'd done the wrong thing in marrying him, and she was unsure what, if anything, she could do about it.

"I figure I owe you at least one evening out before I leave," Steve said as a means of explanation for the unexpected invitation.

"You didn't need to pick the most expensive restaurant in town."

Steve glanced over the top of his menu and shrugged. "What else have I got to do with my money?"

"You could start dating again." She offered the suggestion flippantly, not really meaning it. Like Rush, Lindy had recognized almost immediately that her brother was still in love with his ex-wife.

"I could," Steve answered thoughtfully. "But I won't."

"I know," Lindy said, understanding perfectly.

"What do you know?"

It was almost as if they were children again, Lindy mused–the way his eyes sparkled with mischief and his mouth quirked with a teasing half smile.

"Well?" he pressed.

"I know you won't date again."

Slowly Steve set the menu aside, his fingers lingering over the gold tassel. The humor drained out of his eyes. "The lobster sounds good, doesn't it?"

Lindy didn't want to introduce a subject that would embarrass or intimidate her older brother. Any mention of Carol was taboo and they both knew it. Sadly she recognized that talking over her fears about her marriage wasn't going to work, either. She didn't know what she'd tell Steve anyway. She was scared to death she'd married the wrong man, terrified that everything her brother had accused her of was true.

Her biggest concern was that she'd accepted Rush's proposal on the rebound and her marriage was based on emotional insecurity. Two weeks wasn't sufficient time to know a man well enough to commit her life to him. Even the regrets Rush had prophesied were beginning to come true. There were days when she had to struggle to remember what her husband looked like. A thousand unknowns haunted her. His phone call had only served to remind her how arrogant he could be, and the letters from him that had followed were filled with his angry frustration at not hearing from her.

Although Steve seemed more open than he had been, Lindy didn't feel she could discuss her doubts. Her brother was struggling with his own problems.

"Then lobster it is," she said, forcing her voice to sound airy and bright.

Steve picked up his butter knife and slowly ran the blade down his long fingers. "I wanted to take you to dinner for another reason, too."

"I'm a rotten cook and another night of my special enchiladas with homemade salsa was more than your stomach could tolerate?"

"Close," Steve answered, and chuckled. But his eyes quickly sobered and he lowered his gaze. "Actually I owe you an apology, sis."

"Oh?" This was a major surprise.

"I was wrong to come down on you and Rush the way I did." He lay the butter knife down and reached for the salad fork, absently stroking the tines. Every mannerism revealed his regret at the way he'd chastised her earlier. "If I'd gone out and handpicked a husband for you, I couldn't have found a better man than Rush Callaghan."

Lindy's gaze rested on the delicate floral design of the place setting.

"You saw what you wanted," Steve continued, "and went after it. It takes a special kind of woman to do that, Lindy, and although I'll admit I had my fears, you've managed to calm every one of them."

"He is wonderful."

"You both are."

Lindy's nod was decidedly noncommittal. She could feel the emotion gathering in the back of her eyes. How could Steve sound so certain about her and Rush when she was struggling to believe in her own marriage? He made her happiness sound like a foregone conclusion when she was dog-paddling in a mire of self-doubts, struggling to stay afloat. A week before he would have taken her in his arms and comforted her. Tonight he made her sound like Joan of Arc for being so brave and true. There was no justice left in the world. None.

"Attribute my foul mood to the fact that I was shocked by your news. That and a strong brotherly instinct to protect my baby sister. I think the two of you are going to do exceptionally well together."

With trembling hands Lindy smoothed the pink linen napkin in her lap, hardly able to breathe normally, let alone find words to answer her brother. His original disdain for her and Rush's marriage had a lot more to do with his own unpleasant experience with nuptial bliss than anything else. Lindy's greatest fear was that she'd made the same mistake her brother had.

After an awkward moment, Lindy murmured, "I appreciate the apology, Steve, but it wasn't necessary."

Her brother shook his head, dismissing her words. "Rush will be good to you, and you're exactly the right kind of woman for him. I expect you'll both be very happy."

"We're going to try." The words were squeezed out of Lindy's throat. If he didn't stop soon, she was going to embarrass them both by bursting into tears.

"Give this marriage everything you've got, Lindy." He set down the fork and reached for the water glass. "Hold on to the happiness with both hands. Don't ever let anything stand between you."

His eyes were so full of pain that Lindy had to look away. She felt certain he must have read all the fear in her eyes. How sad it was that the two of them, who had once been so close, could sit across from each other and ignore what was on their hearts.

Reaching for the menu once more, Steve released his breath in a long sigh. "What do you say we start off dinner with a Caesar salad?"

"Sure," Lindy answered, forcing herself to smile.

My dearest Lindy,

I feel like a first-class idiot, shouting at you the way I did on the phone the other night. I jumped to conclusions, thinking the worst when I didn't get any mail from you. Lindy, I can't even begin to explain what was going on inside me. Jeff tried to tell me there was some logical explanation why you hadn't written, but I wouldn't listen. It was as though my greatest fears were hitting me in the face. I couldn't sleep; I couldn't eat. In my mind, I was absolutely certain Paul had come back and told you he'd made a mistake and you'd left with him. I know it sounds crazy now, but at the time, it made perfect sense.

From the day when the mail was handed out and I didn't get any, I've been acting like a real ass. Jeff must have gone to the chaplain because the next thing I knew I got called in to talk to him. He was the one who arranged the ship-to-shore call. Thank God he did.

After we talked, I was ready to free-fly. There's no way to explain how much better I felt. Has anyone ever told you what a sweet, sexy voice you have? And when you told me you still loved me, I nearly broke down and wept. I was so relieved. God, Lindy, I don't even know how to explain how good it felt to know everything's all right.

After the things I said to you in my last letter, I wouldn't blame you if you wanted to bag this whole marriage, but I'm hoping to God you don't. All I can say is, I'm sorry.

Honey, it's been less than three months and I'm already keeping track of how many days until I see you again. Try to arrange some additional time off in December, if you can, will you? I'm going to take you to bed and I swear it'll be a full week before we venture out of the bedroom. I guess that tells you how I'm feeling right now.

Before I met you I was this sane, ordinary man who was content with his life and sure of his goals. Two weeks after I meet you, and I'm a completely different person. There's a wedding band on my finger and I'm thinking about how nice it would be to become a father. I've even been toying with the idea of buying a house. What do you think? You can bet I do a lot of thinking about making love to my wife. Mostly I'm wondering what the hell I'm doing on the other side of the world.

I saw something yesterday that drove that point straight through my gut. We got orders to lend assistance to a Saudi oil tanker that had been hit by a Harpoon-type missile. One of our frigates pulled up alongside to help control the fire, and we sent a couple of Sea Kings with fire-fighting equipment and took their injured aboard. It really hit home that there could be trouble here, and this part of the world isn't sitting around enjoying crumpets and tea. I'm not telling you this to worry you, Lindy. I needed to see that burning tanker to take care of some business matters I should have done a long time before now. If anything happens to me, I want you to know you'll be well taken care of financially.

I've got to close this letter for now, but I'll write more later. Lots more. I love you, Lindy. It frightens me how much.

Dearest Rush,

Reading your latest letter was the best thing that's happened to me since our wedding. I've been feeling so confused and blue lately. After your letter, I felt like singing and dancing. I love you, husband. I don't have a single lingering doubt.

Did you hear the shouts of glee all across America this morning? No, we haven't landed on the moon or captured a Caribbean island. School started and those cries were the happy voices of mothers all over the land. At least, that's what Sandy and Mary and several of the other navy wives told me today. I've gotten to be good friends with several of them. Did you know that Sissy Crawford's real name isn't Sissy? It's something completely different, like Angela or Georgia. The other wives started calling her that because she hates it so much when Bill's at sea, and she's so sure everything's going to go wrong that the women started calling her Sissy in a friendly, teasing way. The name stuck. I don't know if I should tell you what they've been calling me. Actually it's kind of embarrassing, but by the same token it's true. Randy. Don't worry. Susan made them stop. Good grief, we could all call each other that.

As for taking time off in December, you've got it, fellow!

It's been over three months since you sailed…were deployed. Are you impressed with the navy lingo I'm picking up? Three months since we kissed; three months since we made love; three months since I've slept in your arms.

And another three to go.

I've got good news. I got a raise, which was a pleasant surprise. I'm working out well with Boeing and they seem to appreciate my obvious talents. I decided to put the extra money in a savings account so we'll have a little something to fall back on when it's time for me to give up working to stay home with the children. It's difficult for me to imagine myself a mother when being a wife is still so new. I don't think we need to rush into this parenting business—do you? I wish we'd talked about these matters before you left. I have no idea how you feel about starting a family. When you asked if I was pregnant, it didn't exactly sound as if you'd have been pleased with the prospect if I had been.

Anyway, we're halfway through the tour and we've both managed to survive thus far. Susan and I and a bunch of other navy wives are celebrating Halfway Night this weekend. I don't know if I'm supposed to tell you this, so keep it under your hat because the other husbands are going to get insanely jealous. You, on the other hand, are sure to be coolheaded, mature and reasonable about this sort of thing, and I'm confident it isn't going to bother you.

The nine of us are carpooling it to a Seattle nightclub to see some male strippers. Doesn't that sound like fun? Susan and I have been looking forward to this night for weeks. In fact we've had the reservations since the first week in August. As you've probably guessed, this is a popular club.

Believe me, Rush, you're not going to say anything that will frighten me anymore than I already am about what's happening in the Middle East. Reports are on the news every night. All I ask is that you take care of yourself.

Steve left Monday for a week of sea trials, so it's really been lonely around here. It's the first time I've been in the apartment completely alone since I arrived in Seattle. It gives me lots of time to write to you so I don't mind.

I suppose you know by now that Susan is pregnant. She's feeling surprisingly good, especially after the doctor confirmed that there's only one baby. Susan's hoping for a girl this time.

I'm going to mail this off since I don't want a repeat of what happened last month. Remember, I love you. Please don't take any crazy risks.

Lindy,
What the hell do you mean, you're going to see a male strip show! You're damn right I didn't tell the others. Good God, they'd stage a mutiny. As for me being mature and coolheaded, you couldn't be more wrong. I don't like it. Not one damn bit.

My dearest, darling Rush,
The male strippers were sexy as hell. What gorgeous bodies! What cute buns. What attractive…never mind.

We had a fantastic time, but, quite honestly, it was too much for us men-starved navy wives. We talked it over and agreed this kind of entertainment would be better served later in the tour when we could count on our husbands being home soon. We decided to go back for a Final Fling the week before the Mitchell is scheduled to arrive home.

I love you, Rush Callaghan. Take care of yourself.

Love,

Lindy

P.S. Would you ever consider wearing spurs and a cute little cowboy hat to bed?

"Line 314," Lindy murmured absently, answering the phone at her desk.

"Lindy, it's Steve."

Something in the pitch of her brother's low-modulated voice, something in the way he said her name instantly alerted Lindy. Goose bumps shot up and down her spine. Not once in all the weeks that Lindy had worked for Boeing had her brother telephoned the office. She didn't even know where he'd gotten her work number.

"What's wrong?"

Steve hesitated. "I just heard a news bulletin over the radio. There's been a report of an accident aboard the *Mitchell*."

"Oh, God." The words were wrenched from her heart. "Rush.... Did they say anything about Rush?"

"No, but it's much too soon. Don't panic, Lindy. There are nearly four thousand men aboard the carrier. The chance of Rush being a fatality is minute."

Lindy closed her eyes and cupped her hand over her mouth as terror gripped her. Her heart roared in her chest so loudly that it nearly drowned out her brother's words.

"I think it would be a good idea if you left work and met me at the apartment."

She nodded, unable to find her voice.

"Lindy?"

"I'm on my way." Already she was clearing her computer terminal, doing only what was absolutely necessary so she could leave.

"Lindy, can you drive? Do you want me to come get you?"

"No…. I'm fine. When did it happen? How?"

"They're not exactly sure, but the preliminary reports are mentioning a plane crash."

"How many are dead?"

"Sweetie, listen. The only reason I phoned was so you wouldn't hear the news yourself or from someone at the office and panic. I'm telling you everything I know. I called the base and they're setting up an information center for wives and family. Once you're home I'll take you there."

"I'll meet you as soon as I can." Worry had already clogged Lindy's throat by the time she replaced the receiver. Her supervisor was just walking into her office when Lindy scooted her chair back from the desk.

"You heard? Someone just told me there was something about the *Mitchell* on the radio. Take whatever time you need."

"Thanks." Lindy grabbed her purse, her legs so weak she could hardly walk.

The drive from Renton to the apartment normally took fifteen to twenty minutes. Lindy made it in ten and had little memory of the ride. She dared not turn on the radio for fear of what she'd learn. The entire time she was driving, she prayed, mumbling the same desperate plea over and over again. An aircraft carrier was a huge ship, a city unto itself, able to house as many as six thousand men. The possibility of Rush being a fatality was infinitesimal. He was the chief navigator. The bridge was possibly the safest place of all. He would be free from harm. At least that was what Lindy kept telling herself.

Steve was waiting for her when she burst in the front door. "Did you learn anything more?"

He looked terribly pale, and nodded. "Lindy, sit down."

"No!" she screamed, knotting her fists. "Tell me! Is he dead? Is he?"

Steve raked his hands through his hair. "I don't know. Apparently an Intruder was landing and a wing caught on the arresting gear. It cartwheeled on the flight deck, spewing wreckage," he hesitated. "They haven't released any names yet. Five are known dead."

"Dear God."

Her brother placed his hands on her shoulders and his eyes revealed his own personal torment. She knew in that minute that he would have given his soul not to be the one to tell her this.

"What is it?" she asked, in a voice that was as calm and as accepting as she could make it.

"The latest information reports that part of the plane careened into the bridge."

Lindy shut her eyes and it was the last thing she should have done. Instantly she felt her legs give out as her mind conjured up the worst possible scene of bodies being hurled through space and men screaming in agony. Fire seemed to have erupted everywhere. Lindy gasped and her hands shot out.

Steve managed to catch her, pressing her head against his shoulder. "Rush is going to be all right," he murmured, while his hand smoothed her hair.

"No," she said, in a whisperlike sound. "He isn't." If there was any action or any trouble, Rush would be there right in the middle of it.

Steve escorted Lindy to the naval base, where an information center had been set up. The first person Lindy saw was Susan. The two women looked at each other and started sobbing. Timmy and Tommy, not knowing what to make of everything, were soon crying, too. Lindy took Tommy and attempted to comfort him, but the youngster wanted his mother and squirmed in Lindy's arms.

"Jeff?" Lindy finally managed to ask.

"I don't know. What about Rush?"

Lindy heaved in a calming breath. "I haven't heard."

It seemed hours passed before any additional information was released, and then the names of the injured were read. Neither Jeff nor Rush were listed. Lindy didn't know whether to be happy or terrified. The only choices that remained were that both men had somehow magically escaped the explosion or were among those listed as dead.

Steve was at Lindy's side as much as possible, doing what he could. One look at her brother told Lindy he suspected the worst. As much as she could, Lindy tried to be positive. If Rush had died in the explosion, she reasoned, she would have felt it. Deep within her heart, she would have felt a part of herself die. She wouldn't be this calm, this accepting.

People milled around everywhere. Wives, children, parents. Rather than sit and worry, Lindy mingled with the others, talking, praying and crying–sometimes all three at once.

It was when she turned to find Steve at her side that she knew word had finally come through. She looked up to the brother she had always loved, the brother who had shielded her from whatever pain he could, and Lindy smiled. She realized at the time how odd that was.

Her brother slipped his arm around her shoulder and his jaw jutted out in a gesture of grief and pain.

"Rush is listed as missing."

Chapter Thirteen

"What do you mean missing?" Lindy asked. "Rush couldn't have just disappeared." It astonished her how calm she felt, how controlled, as though they were discussing something as mundane as the tide tables or what to fix for dinner.

"Lindy, I think you should prepare yourself for the worst."

"That would be silly," she said, turning back to the little boy she'd been talking to and purposely ignoring her brother. "Rush is fine. I know he is. There's been some screwup and he's going to be furious when he learns the way the navy has everyone so worried about him."

"Lindy…." Steve hesitated, and his brow creased in thick folds of concern and regret. "I hope to God you're right."

"Of course I am."

Steve left her then and Lindy sank into an empty chair. Her hands shook so badly that she clenched them together in her lap, her long nails cutting crescents of pain into her palms. Soon her arms were shaking, then her legs, until her whole body felt as if it were consumed by uncontrollable spasms.

Susan took the chair beside Lindy and wrapped her own sweater around Lindy's shoulders. Susan held it there until some of the intense cold she was experiencing seeped away and a steady warmth invaded her limbs.

Lindy tried to smile, failed, and whispered one word. "Jeff?"

"He's fine."

Lindy nodded once. "Good."

"They'll find him, Lindy," Susan said, her voice thick with conviction, although she was struggling with her own fears. "I know they will. Jeff won't let anyone rest until they do."

"I know." Lindy remembered how Susan had once told her that she didn't worry so much about Jeff at sea because she always knew Rush would be there to watch out for her husband. The truth of what Susan was telling her now was the only slender thread Lindy had to hang on to. Jeff would turn hell upside down until he learned what had happened to Rush.

Soon the other wives joined Lindy, scooting their chairs and forming a protective circle around her. No one did much talking. No one tried to build her up with false hopes. No one suggested she try to eat or get some sleep. Or leave.

That night cots were brought into the information center for those who wished to stay. Lindy insisted the other wives go back to their families, but each one in turn refused. They were special sisters, bonded together in ways that were thicker than blood.

"No one's leaving until we find out what happened to Rush," Susan said, speaking for them all.

The others managed to sleep that night in the cots provided. Lindy tried, but couldn't. Every time she closed her eyes that same terrible scene flashed through her mind, and she was convinced she could hear Rush cry out in torment. As the hours slowly, methodically ticked away, Lindy sat and stared into space. In the darkest part of the night, surrounded by silence, she tried to prepare herself to accept Rush's death, but every time she entertained the notion, such piercing pain stabbed through her that she shoved the thought from her mind. This interminable waiting was the worst nightmare of her life.

Food was brought in the following morning and the others ate, but Lindy knew it would be impossible for her to hold anything down.

Susan handed her a glass of orange juice. "You didn't eat anything yesterday. Try this," she said softly, insistently. "You're going to need your strength."

Lindy wanted to argue with her friend but hadn't the fortitude. "Okay."

Another eternity passed, a lifetime–hours that felt like years, minutes that dragged like weeks, seconds that could have been days. And still they waited.

"He's dead," Lindy sobbed to the others late that afternoon, although just saying the words aloud nearly crippled her. "I know it. I can feel it in my heart. He's gone."

"You don't know it," Susan argued, and her own eyes shone brightly with unshed tears. Her hands trembled and she laced her fingers together as though offering a silent prayer.

"Don't even say it," Sissy cried, her face streaked with moisture.

Joanna gripped Lindy's fingers with her own and knelt in front of her, her gaze holding Lindy's. "He's alive until we know otherwise. Hold tight to that, Lindy. It's all we've got."

Lindy nodded, her eyes so blurred with tears that when she looked up to find her brother standing over her, she couldn't read his expression. A powerful magnetic force drove her to her feet.

"Tell me," she whispered urgently. "Tell me."

"He's alive."

Lindy didn't hear anything more than that before she broke down and started to weep, covering her face with her hands, her shoulders heaving with the depth of her relief. But these tears were ones of joy. A sheer release from the endless unknown. She tossed her arms around her brother's neck and he gripped her waist and swung her around. Susan and the others were jumping up and down, hugging each other, laughing and crying as well.

When everyone had settled back down, Steve gave them the rest of the information. "They found Rush buried under a pile of rubble; he's lost a lot of blood and in addition to internal injuries, his arm has been severely cut. He's being flown to Tripler Army Hospital in Hawaii for microsurgery. Apparently the nerves in his left arm were severed. He's unconscious, but alive."

"I'm going to him," Lindy said with raw determination, as though she expected an argument. Nothing would stop her. She wouldn't believe Rush was going to live until she saw him herself. Touched him. Kissed him. Loved him.

Steve nodded. "I already made arrangements for you to fly out today."

A pumpkin and a picture of a witch decorating the wall across the room from him were the first things Rush noticed when he opened his eyes. His mouth was as dry as Arizona in August and his head throbbed unmercifully. A hospital, he determined, but he hadn't any idea where.

Carefully and with a great deal of effort, he rolled his head to one side and stared at the raised rail of the bed. He blinked, sure he was imagining the vision that was before him.

"Lindy?"

The apparition didn't move. Her fingers were gripping the steel railing and her forehead was pressed against the back of her hands. She looked as though she were sleeping.

Rush tried to reach out and touch her, gently wake her, but he couldn't lift his arm. Even the effort sent a sharp shooting pain through his shoulder. He must have groaned because Lindy jerked her head up, her eyes wide with concern. When she saw he was awake, she sighed and grinned. Rush swore he'd never seen a more beautiful smile in his life. The pain that stabbed through him with every breath was gone. The ache in his head vanished as the look in his wife's eyes immersed him in an unspeakable joy that transcended everything else.

"You're real," he murmured. He refused to believe that she was a figment of his imagination. His head remained fuzzy and his vision blurred, but Lindy was real. He'd stake his life on that.

She nodded and her hand brushed lightly over his face, lovingly caressing his jaw. "And you're alive. Oh, Rush, I nearly lost you."

She bit into her bottom lip and Rush knew she was struggling not to cry. He wished he could have spared her all worry and doubt.

"Where am I…? How long?"

"You're in a hospital in Hawaii. Two days now."

He frowned. "That long?" Now that his eyesight was clearing, he could see the dark smudges under Lindy's eyes. She was as pale as death, as though recovering from a bad bout of flu. And much thinner than he remembered. Too thin. "You look terrible."

She laughed, and the sweet, lilting sound wrapped itself around his heart, squeezing emotion from him. Dear God, he loved Lindy. So much of the accident remained clouded in his mind. All he could remember was hearing a horrendous noise and seeing a ball of fire come hurling toward him. Everything had happened so fast that there had barely been time to do anything more than react. All he knew was that he didn't want to die. He wanted to go home to Lindy. His Lindy. His love.

The next thing he remembered was pain. Terrible pain. More acute than anything he'd ever experienced. He knew he was close to dying, knew he might not make it, and still all he could think about was Lindy. Dying would have stopped the agony; slipping into the dark swirling void of death would have been welcome if only it would end the torment, but Rush chose the pain because he knew it would lead him back to Lindy.

"Have you looked in a mirror lately?" she asked, her lips twitching with a teasing smile. "You're not exactly ready to be cast as Prince Charming yourself."

"You've been sick?" he pressed, his tongue faltering over the words. It was a struggle to keep awake, the pull back to unconsciousness greater with each second.

"No, just worried. It took them nearly forty hours to find you after the accident and until then you were listed as missing."

"Oh God, Lindy, I'm…sorry."

"I'm fine now that I know you're going to be all right." Again her fingers touched his face, smoothing the hair from his brow, lingering as though she needed the reassurance that he was real.

"How many…dead?"

"Seven. Three on the flight deck and four on the bridge."

Rush's jaw tightened. "Who?"

Lindy recited the names and each one fell upon his chest like a boulder dropped from the ceiling. "…good men," he said after a moment, and was shocked at how fragile his voice sounded.

"More than twenty suffered serious injuries."

Rush felt himself drifting off; he resisted, but the pull of the tide was too powerful for him to fight. "How bad…"

"The burn victims are the worst."

He nodded and that was the last he remembered.

When he woke again the room was pitch-dark. He felt a straw at his mouth and he sucked greedily. "What time is it?"

"Two a.m."

"Lindy, is that you?"

"Do you need something for the pain?"

He shook his head. "No." Her fingers curled around his own and he held on to her, savoring her touch. He slept again.

Lindy sat in a chair at her husband's side. She'd tried to sleep countless times, but the rest her body craved continued to elude her. Just as she'd start to drift off, the horror of those two days of not knowing if Rush was dead or alive returned and snapped her awake. She'd come so close to losing him. Seven men had died. Honorable men. And Rush had come a hairsbreadth from making the count eight. The men who had died were husbands, fathers, lovers–and now they were gone.

Standing, she walked over to the window. Palm trees swayed in the late afternoon breeze. The sun shone and the ocean lapped relentlessly against the white, sandy beach. The flawless beauty of the scene should have soothed her troubled spirit, but it didn't. Instead she felt a cold hard feeling settle in her lungs. It spread out, making her breathing labored and causing her throat to ache. Those men had died, and for what? Lindy had no answers, and every time she closed her eyes the questions started to pound at her, demanding answers when she had none.

"Lindy?"

She took a minute to compose herself, pasted a smile on her face and turned around. "So Sleeping Ugly is finally awake. How are you feeling?"

"You don't want to know."

Concern moved her to his bedside. "Should I get the nurse? She said if you needed something for pain, I could…"

"I'm doing okay." His brows folded into a tight frown as he looked up at her. "You're still looking like death warmed over."

She forced a cheery laugh and decided to put her makeup on with a heavier hand before her next visit. "That's a fine thing to say to me!"

"When was the last time you had a decent meal?"

She opened her mouth to tell him, but paused when she realized she didn't know herself. "I'm fine, Rush. You're the patient here, not me."

He looked for a minute as if he were going to argue with her, but he didn't. "If you're not hungry, I am."

"I'll see what I can scrounge up."

She returned a few minutes later, carrying a tray. But it was soon apparent that Rush had no appetite and had used the excuse of hunger as a ploy to get her to sample something.

Three days passed. Rush grew stronger with each one, and Lindy grew paler and thinner. She still couldn't sleep–not more than an hour at a stretch.

A week after Rush arrived in Hawaii, Lindy strolled into his hospital room to discover her husband sitting up for the first time. His left arm was in a cast and hung in a sling over his chest. The swelling in his face had gone down considerably, and he looked almost like his old handsome self once more. Lindy paused and smiled, perhaps her first genuine one since she'd arrived in this tropical paradise.

"You're looking fit."

"Come here, wife," he said holding out his one good arm to her. "I'm tired of those skimpy pecks on the cheek you've been giving me. I'm starved for you."

Lindy walked across the room like a woman who'd been wandering in the desert and been offered a glass of water. Once Rush had his arm around her, his mouth claiming hers, she felt whole again. He smelled incredibly good and tasted of peppermint.

The fears and doubts that had been hounding her all week dissolved in the warmth of his hold. When he lifted his head and smiled, Lindy felt weak and breathless in his embrace.

"Lindy, dear God, I've nearly died, I've wanted to hold you so much."

Angry, selfish thoughts flooded her mind, and she clamped her mouth shut. He'd nearly died, yes, but it was from a terrible plane crash and explosion that didn't have anything to do with her. But when Rush directed her mouth to his, she was engulfed in his kiss, lost and drowning. Nothing else mattered. As his lips closed over hers, demanding and hungry, he reclaimed everything that had once been his: her heart, her body, her soul. There was nothing left inside her to protest. He owned her so completely, so unquestionably, that she hadn't the will to say or do anything. All she could do was submit.

She wrapped her arms around his neck and leaned into him, giving him her tongue when he sought it, taking his when it was offered. Their need for each other was urgent. Fierce. Savage, yet tender. Nothing else in the world made sense except this. Only the driving need Lindy felt to be a part of Rush.

Moisture appeared in the corners of her eyes and Rush sipped away her tears. He kissed her eyes, her forehead, her cheeks, her lips, and nuzzled tenderly at her neck while his fingers tunneled through her dark hair.

"Lindy," he breathed. "My love, my own sweet love." His long fingers brushed the wisps of bangs from her face and wiped away the last trace of tears, as though she was the most precious thing he had ever touched.

"I talked to the doctor this morning," he whispered. "I'm going to be released at the end of the week."

Lindy's tender heart swelled with unrestrained joy.

"We have one night, love, just one night before I fly back to the *Mitchell*."

For one frenzied moment, Lindy was sure she'd heard him incorrectly. Going back? He couldn't possibly be returning to the Persian Gulf after what had happened.

"No." She freed herself from his grip and took a step back. "You can't go back!"

"Honey, I have to. It's my job."

"But…"

"What did you expect me to do?"

Lindy wasn't sure what she'd assumed would happen. Anything but having him return to the same nightmare.

"Honey, listen. We've only got six weeks of the cruise left. Hell, for all I know we could even be headed back sooner than that, depending on the amount of damage we sustained. Six weeks isn't such a long time. I'll be home before you know it."

Somehow Lindy managed to nod. They had precious time left, and the thought of spending these last days together arguing was intolerable. After all, there wasn't much she could say. She'd thought–or at least hoped–he'd be coming home with her now. She needed him sleeping at her side to chase away the demons and dissolve the horror from her mind.

Rush may want to make love to her, Lindy realized, but he wanted to get back to his ship more. She'd noted that when he started talking about the *Mitchell* his eyes had seemed to spark with new life. He didn't like lying around the hospital; she would have been surprised if he had. Rush longed to go back to his ship, back to his men. He wanted to leave her behind, safely tucked away in a Seattle apartment while he was gallivanting all over the world, risking his life. Risking her peace of mind. Risking their happiness.

"I hope that hotel room of yours has a double bed," Rush said, smiling up at her.

"It does," she assured him, averting her gaze to the scene outside the window.

Something was wrong with Lindy. Rush knew it, felt it every time she walked in the room. She looked a little better–at least he knew she was eating regularly. Some color had returned to her pale cheeks when they'd walked in the sunshine.

Rush tried to draw her out, tried to get her to tell him what was troubling her, but she held it all inside and he didn't press her. He would be leaving the hospital early that afternoon and leaving Lindy first thing in the morning. She'd been through a great deal and so had he. If what was bothering her was important, she'd say something to him.

The petite blond nurse who had been assigned his room strolled in, holding a small white cup and a glass of water. She was young and pretty, the kind of woman who might have attracted his attention before he met Lindy. Now he only had eyes for his wife and barely gave the woman more than a second glance.

"Pill time," she announced cheerfully.

Rush grumbled and held out his hand. The blue-eyed nurse waited while he took the two capsules and swallowed down a glass of water.

"Where's your wife this afternoon?"

"She'll be by later," Rush explained. He was surprised Lindy wasn't there already. Lindy was as keen as he was to get out of this sterile environment, but he was far more eager to get his wife into bed. One damn night was all they had. He wished to hell it could be more. It seemed their entire married life had been crammed into three all-too-short nights.

"I hear you're leaving us."

He nodded. He didn't like the antiseptic smell here, and he swore the food must taste better in prison. It had been torture to be this close to the ocean, to smell the clean tangy scent of it and be prohibited from doing anything more than gaze at the blue waters. He was anxious to get back to the *Mitchell.* He felt a lot like someone who had fallen off a horse and needed to climb right back on again. He'd been mentally shaken by the accident, his courage tested. He needed to set foot on the bridge, look down on that flight deck and know he was in control once more.

"I don't know when I've seen a woman more in love with her husband. Or more worried," the pretty blond nurse went on to say. "When your wife first arrived, I thought we were going to have to admit her. I swear she was as pale as bleached flour. I suppose you know she wouldn't leave your side. For three days, she didn't move. The doctors tried repeatedly to assure her you were going to be all right, but she wouldn't believe it. Not until you woke, and even then she refused to go."

Rush rested his head against the thin pillow and held in a sigh until his chest ached with the effort. He'd known that every time he woke Lindy had been with him, but he hadn't realized she'd spent every minute at his side.

"I hope you appreciate that woman," the nurse continued.

"I do," Rush countered. Tonight he'd show Lindy just how much.

Lindy was determined that this one night with Rush would be as perfect as she could make it. She planned to blot out all her doubts and grab hold of what happiness she could before Rush returned to the Persian Gulf. She yearned to encapsulate these last hours together and hold them in her memory until he returned safely to her in December.

"How are you feeling?" she asked, once they were inside her hotel room.

"A little weak," Rush admitted reluctantly. "But I'm getting stronger every day."

She helped him into a chair. It was on the tip of her tongue to suggest he wait a few more days before flying across the world and rejoining his ship, but she knew it would be useless. She knew Rush. She'd seen that hard look of determination he wore more than once. He wouldn't listen to her.

"I thought we'd order dinner from room service," she said, standing awkwardly in the middle of the floor.

He nodded. "Good idea." He hesitated and gave her a look that was almost shy. "I have another good idea, too. Come to me, Lindy. I need you."

She couldn't have refused him had her life depended on it. He stood, reached for her hand and walked her to the bed. He kissed her once, hard, his tongue delving into her mouth, stroking hers. His right hand was fumbling with the buttons of her blouse, but the left one was incapable of giving much assistance. With their mouths still linked, Lindy brushed his hand aside and helped him. When she was finished with her own, she freed his uniform shirt from his waistband and unbuttoned it for him.

"Thanks," Rush breathed hoarsely, when she'd finished the task. Lindy paused, biting her lip as she ran her hand over the dark-furred chest. The muscles of his abdomen felt hard and sleek, the curling hairs wispy against the tips of her fingers.

"I want you like hell," he groaned.

Lindy let her eyes fall and released a short, delicate chuckle. "I can tell." His free hand cupped her breast and her nipple blossomed and grew incredibly hard. "I want you, too."

He flicked his thumb over the rose tip of her breast and she moaned.

"I can tell," he repeated thickly.

They finished undressing each other with trembling hands. Lindy helped Rush with the parts he couldn't manage, and he helped her the best he could. Soon they were lying on the mattress, their bodies on fire for each other.

When he moved on top of her, Lindy smiled up at him, craving the fiery release his body would give her. Still trembling, she closed her eyes and gave herself over to this experience. She allowed herself to be swallowed up in his tenderness, and when he entered her, her body answered in perfect counterpoint to his. Rush's touch, his lovemaking, was a balm, a healing potion for all they had suffered. Tears wet her face and his lips found them. Intuitively he knew she needed assurances and he gave them to her with the ebb and flow of his body into her own. No matter what the future held, he seemed to be telling her, no matter what happened in the next six weeks, they would have this night to hold on to and to remember.

They made love again after dinner, and he held and kissed her long after midnight. While Rush soundly slept, Lindy climbed out of bed and cuddled up in the chair across from him.

She'd tried so hard to put the fear behind her, but she couldn't. A hundred times in the past week, she'd hungered to tell him how she'd nearly gone crazy with worry, and she hadn't said a word. She wanted to explain how every time she closed her eyes the same freakish nightmare haunted her sleep. But again and again she'd held her tongue, gliding over what was important for fear of shattering the peace of these past days together.

In a few hours Rush would return to his ship and she would go back to Seattle. She'd been wrong not to tell Rush what she was feeling, wrong to allow him to assume she could go on playing this charade. Steve was right. He had been all along–she wouldn't make a good navy wife. It wasn't in her to bid her husband farewell time after time and handle whatever crisis befell them with calm acceptance.

Twice now Lindy had found herself deeply in love, convinced she knew her own heart each time. Confident enough to wear the rings each man had given her. Both times she'd been wrong. She wasn't the type of woman Rush needed. She wasn't strong enough to endure months of loneliness and deal with the knowledge that she would always take second place in her husband's life.

Hot tears scalded her eyes and when she could restrain them no longer, she let them flow freely down her face, no longer willing to hold them back.

Rush raised his head from the pillow, looking disoriented and groggy. He turned and stared at his sobbing wife.

"Lindy," he breathed her name into the night. "What's wrong?"

"Do you love me, Rush?"

"Of course I do." He threw back the sheet and sat on the edge of the bed. "You know I do."

"If you love me...if you really love me, you'll understand...." She paused.

Rush moved off the bed, knelt down in front of her and took her two hands in his one. "Understand what, honey?"

"I want you to get out of the navy."

He tossed his head back as if she'd slapped him. "Lindy, you don't know what you're asking."

"I do know. I know you love it. I know you've always loved being on the sea. But there are other jobs, other ways.... I can't bear this, Rush, not knowing from one day to the next if you're going to be dead or alive. Let some other man put his life on the line. Someone without a wife. Anyone but you."

"Lindy–oh love." He pressed his forehead on her bent knee and seemed to be pulling his thoughts together. When he raised his head, his eyes were hard. "The navy is my life. It's where I belong. I can't walk away from a fifteen-year commitment because you're afraid I'm going to be injured again."

Lindy felt as though her heart were crumbling, the emotional agony was so intense. She pulled her hands free of his grasp and stiffened. "Then you leave me no choice."

Chapter Fourteen

"I don't leave you any choice? What do mean by that?" Rush demanded.

Lindy didn't know. All she did know was that everything the other wives had warned her about was happening. Rush and she had such little time together and, not wanting to say or do anything to disrupt these precious few days, Lindy had skimmed the surface of their relationship, ignoring the deep waters of unhappiness and strife. They'd avoided any chance of conflict in their marriage until everything was ready to burst inside her.

"Well?" he repeated.

"I don't know," she admitted reluctantly. "I want you to do something else with your life. Something outside of the navy that isn't dangerous. You've got me to think about now…and children later. Maybe you think I'm being selfish, but I want you to be a husband and father before anything else. The navy is first with you now and I'll always be a poor second. I hate it."

Rush rammed his fingers through his hair. "Honey, you can't change a man from what he already is. You don't have any idea what you're asking me to do–it'd be impossible."

"You don't seem to understand what you want of *me*," she countered sharply. "You claim you love me. You claim you want our marriage to work. But I'll always play second fiddle in your life, and I can't. I just can't deal with that. If playing hero is so important to you, then fine."

Rush's lips tightened and he stood and walked away from her.

"I love you, Rush." Her voice was taut, strangled. "All I'm asking is for you to love me as much as I do you."

"I do love you," he shouted.

"No." She shook her head with such force that her hair went swirling around her face. "You love the navy more."

"It's been my life for fifteen years."

"I want to be your life now."

"God, Lindy, you want me to give up everything that's ever been important to me." He threw back his head as a man in agony would, closed his eyes and then glared at the dark ceiling.

Lindy bounced her index finger against her chest. "I want to be the most important person in your life."

"You are!"

"No," she murmured sadly. "I'm not. Look at you. You nearly died on that stupid aircraft carrier and you can hardly wait to get back. I can feel the restlessness in you. It's like you've got to prove something."

Rush whirled around to face her then, his eyes wide, his body taut. "You knew what I was when we got married. You were perfectly aware how I felt about the navy then. You were willing to accept it as my career. What happened to that unshakable confidence you had that we were doing the right thing to rush into marriage? Lord, I can't believe this."

"I was confident I loved you. I'm sure of it now."

"The navy is part of me, Lindy. A big part of who and what I am. Don't you see that?"

"No." Her voice cracked, and she sobbed once.

The sight of her tears seemed to tear at him and Rush knelt beside her and pulled her into one arm, holding her tightly, as though he felt her pain and was desperate to do anything he could to alleviate it. Lindy wept against his shoulder, her arms moving up and clinging to his neck. His mouth sought and found hers and he kissed her into submission while his hand worked its magic on her body, destroying her will to argue.

Before Lindy knew what was happening, Rush had her back in bed and his mouth was sucking on her breast; he was tormenting her nipples with his tongue, and she was being devoured by the licking flames of desire.

"No…no," she sobbed, and pushed him away. She jumped out of bed, her shoulders heaving with the effort it had cost her to leave his arms. "You aren't going to use me this way!"

Rush rolled on his back and closed his eyes in angry frustration. "Use you! Now it's a sin to make love to you, too?"

"It is when you use lovemaking to bury an issue."

"Can you blame me?" he shouted, his patience obviously on a short fuse. "I'm flying out of here shortly. I won't see you until the middle of December–if then, from the way you're talking. I'd prefer that we spend our last hours making love, not fighting. If that's such a terrible crime, then I'm guilty."

The alarm rang, and the tinny sound echoed around the room, startling them both. Lindy glared accusingly at the clock radio. Already it was time for Rush to leave her, and she hadn't said even half of what was in her heart.

Without a word her husband climbed out of bed and started dressing in his uniform. He had some difficulty, with his left arm in a cast, but he didn't seek her help, and she didn't offer.

Numb with pain and disbelief, Lindy watched him. Nothing she'd said had mattered to him. Not one word had seemed to reach him. He was so intent on getting back to the *Mitchell* that nothing, not her love, not her demands or her pleas, was important enough to delay him.

Once he finished buttoning his shirt, Rush picked up his things that littered the room, preparing to leave.

Lindy hated the way he ignored her so completely. For all the notice he gave her, she might as well have been an empty beer can. Savored for the moment of pleasure it brought, discarded once used.

She was kneeling in the middle of their bed, and the tears streaked her face. "It's either the navy or me," she said, and her voice wobbled as she struggled not to beg him.

Rush paused at the door, his hand on the knob, but he didn't turn around to look at her. "I love you, Lindy, but I can't change what I am because of your fears. I could leave the navy, but it wouldn't be the right decision for either of us. If you're going to force me to decide, then I have to go with what I am."

Lindy felt as though he'd struck her. She closed her eyes and covered her face with both hands. The door of the hotel room opened, and desperate now, she scooted off the bed. "Rush."

He paused.

"When the *Mitchell* returns, I won't be on that dock waiting for you!" She shouted the words at him, in a voice that was threatening as a shark's jaw. "I mean it. I won't be there."

His shoulders were stiff, his head held high and proud. "Then I won't expect you," he said, and walked away from her without looking back.

Steve was waiting for Lindy when she stepped out of the jetway that led into the interior of Sea-Tac Airport. He brushed a quick kiss over her cheek and took the carry-on bag from her hand. When he lifted his head and looked at her, he paused and frowned.

"How was the flight?"

Lindy shrugged, praying she didn't look as bad as she felt. "Fine."

"How's Rush?"

"He couldn't be better," she answered, unable to keep her voice from dipping with heavy sarcasm. "He's all navy–you know him. God, country, apple pie–the whole patriotic bit. He nearly lost his arm. He nearly bled to death, but he couldn't enjoy a few days in paradise because it was more important for him to get back to the *Mitchell.* He's got a job to do, you know. He alone is going to uphold world peace. You didn't tell me what a hero I married, Steve."

Looking stunned, her brother stopped and glared at her, his eyes wide and filled with surprise. "Exactly what is your problem?"

"Nothing," she flared. "Everything," she amended.

"What happened?"

She didn't want Steve to be gentle and concerned. Not when she was being forced to admit her blunder. "You were right from the first. I made a mistake.... A bad one. I'm not the kind of woman who will ever make a good navy wife.... You knew that from the beginning."

Steve's frown deepened. "I've come to think differently in the past few weeks. Lindy, when we got the news there'd been an accident aboard the *Mitchell*, you were as solid as a rock. It was me who fell apart at the seams. Don't you remember how I kept telling you you should prepare yourself for the worst? Everything I said and did was wrong. You were like an anchor during that whole time. I was the one leaning on you for strength."

Lindy's smile was weak and gentle as she placed her hand on her brother's forearm. "You were wonderful. I thank God you were there."

"But you love Rush. Dear God, Lindy, you were so strong and brave when we learned he was missing, and yet I was afraid it would have killed you if the damage control party hadn't found Rush in time."

"Yes, I love him. But I'm not willing to take second place

in his life. With Rush–" she paused and looked up at him, her gaze narrowing "–and with *you*, the navy will always come first."

"Did you tell Rush this?"

She nodded, and her eyes filled with an unspeakable sadness. "He knows exactly how I feel."

"What are you going to do now?"

"I…I don't know."

Steve placed his free arm around her shoulder and squeezed gently. "Don't decide anything yet. You're hurting and miserable. You've got several weeks to think matters through and then, once Rush is safely back in Seattle, you two can sort things out."

"I told Rush I wouldn't be there to meet him when the *Mitchell* sails home. I meant it, Steve. He put the navy first. He was the one who chose his career over me."

Steve's mouth and eyes thinned with frustration. "You sent Rush back to the *Mitchell* with that piece of good news? Come on, Lindy. It's time to grow up here. So you were worried about him. That's only natural. But don't try to suffocate him now because eventually it'll kill your marriage. Rush isn't the kind of man who's going to let someone else dictate his life. You knew that when you agreed to be his wife."

Lindy pulled herself free from her brother's hold. "I didn't expect you to understand."

"For God's sake, Lindy, you want to castrate a man because he's got a job to do and feels honor-bound to do it? What kind of logic is that?"

"I'm not going to talk about it anymore." Quick-paced, determined steps carried her down the concourse and away from her brother. She should have known better than to even try to talk to him. Steve Kyle was as much into patriot games as Rush.

"Lindy," her brother called, catching up with her. "I can't

let you ruin your life like this–and Rush's in the process. Any idiot can see how much you two love each other."

"I don't want to hear this. It's none of your business, so keep your opinions to yourself."

"I can't!"

"Get your own house in order, big brother, and then you can start cleaning mine. Until then, stay out of my affairs." Lindy regretted the harsh words the minute they tumbled over her tongue. Steve looked at her as though she'd stabbed a knife into his chest. A muscle in his jaw leaped to life and she saw her brother mentally withdrawing from her, as if a mechanical door were slowly lowering, blocking her out.

His eyes narrowed and hardened as his angry gaze briefly met hers. "If that's the way you want it."

It wasn't, but she didn't know how to retract those cruel words. He didn't bother to wait for an answer and marched away from her. Lindy caught up with him in the baggage claim area and they rode into the city in a stilted, uneasy silence.

"I didn't mean what I said earlier," Lindy told him, once they were inside the apartment.

Her brother didn't look at her. "Yes, you did," he said after a moment, and walked away from her.

"I seem to be batting a thousand lately," Lindy confided to Susan. She'd been back from Hawaii almost three weeks now, but this was the first opportunity she'd had to visit her friend. "In one short week, I managed to alienate both my husband and my brother."

"Have you heard from Rush?" Susan asked, replenishing the coffee in both their cups.

"No. But then I didn't expect to."

"Have you written him?"

Lindy reached for her coffee cup, cradling it with both hands, letting the warmth burn her palms. "No."

Susan pulled out a chair and slumped down. She was nearly five months pregnant and just starting to wear maternity tops. She looked soft and fragile, but underneath she was as tough as leather. Lindy would have given everything she owned to possess the same grit and fortitude as her friend.

"From what I can tell, you've put yourself in a no-win situation," Susan said softly, sadly.

"My God, Rush was nearly killed. It was so close. The doctors said–" Lindy paused and bit into her bottom lip to control the emotion that rocked her every time she thought about the accident.

"He could have gotten hurt in a car accident driving to an office just as easily. Would you suggest he never sit in a car again?"

"No. Of course not." Her hands shook as she raised the mug to her lips and took a sip. "The accident taught me something more. Whatever it takes to be a good navy wife, I don't have it. I couldn't stand on that pier and smile the next time Rush gleefully sails off into the sunset. I can't take these long months of separation. I always thought married people were one, a unit, two people sculpting a life together. It's not that way with Rush. It won't ever be that way–not as long as he's in the navy. I can't be like you, Susan. I wish I could, but it's just not in me."

"You'd rather be separated for a lifetime?" Susan questioned, frowning.

"Yes. It would be easier than dying by inches. No. Oh God, Susan, I don't know what I want anymore."

Her friend didn't say anything for a long time, and when she did, her voice was gentle, understanding. "I stopped counting the times I've said goodbye to Jeff a long time ago. Every time I stand out on that pier and watch that huge carrier pull away, I think I'll never be able to do it again. Letting Jeff go, and doing it with a smile, takes everything there is inside me. You've got it wrong, Lindy. You think I'm so brave and good, but I'm not."

"But you are."

"No. I'm just a woman who loves her man."

"I love Rush, too," Lindy returned defiantly.

"I know, and he loves you." The tip of Susan's finger circled the rim of her coffee cup as she averted her gaze, her look thoughtful. "I don't think I'll ever forget the night I first met you. We were in the kitchen chatting, and Rush and Jeff were fiddling around on the patio with the barbecue. Remember?"

Lindy nodded.

"You were holding one of the boys and I saw Rush look at you. Lindy, there's no way I can describe the longing that came into his eyes. Just watching him stare at you with such tenderness made me want to weep. It was as if you were the Madonna holding the baby Jesus. In that moment, I knew how much your love had changed Rush, and how important you had become to him in those short weeks.

"You might succeed in getting him to leave the navy, but in time you'll regret it. I know Rush will. Eventually it would cripple him, and in the process, you. If ever there was a man who was meant to lead others, meant to serve his country, it's Rush."

"Why is it always the woman who has to change?" Lindy cried. "It's not fair."

"You're right," Susan agreed, with a sad smile. "It isn't fair. All I can say is, if you try to change Rush and succeed, he won't be the same man you fell in love with, or the same man you married."

Lindy bowed her head, more confused than ever.

"Rush took your words to heart," Susan added, looking both disheartened and disappointed.

Lindy jerked her gaze up. "How do you know that?"

"He doesn't expect you to be waiting for him when the

Mitchell docks next month. Jeff wrote that Rush has volunteered for the first watch."

"What does that mean?"

"It means he's going to remain on board as officer of the day the first twelve hours after the crew is dismissed. He told Jeff he didn't have any reason to hurry home since you weren't going to be there."

"But, I didn't mean I wouldn't be at the apartment!"

Susan shrugged. "How was Rush supposed to know that?"

The phone rang twice and Lindy glanced at her watch, calculating if she had enough time to answer it before meeting Susan and the other navy wives. She had no intention of being late for this last fling before the *Mitchell* docked. Taking a chance, she hurried into the kitchen.

"All right, all right," she grumbled, and reached for the receiver. "Hello?"

Her greeting was followed by a short silence, and then a soft female voice asked, "Is Steve Kyle available, please?"

"Carol? Is that you?" Lindy's heart started to pound with excitement. She'd been wanting to talk to her former sister-in-law for weeks.

"Who's this?"

Carol's voice was far from fragile and she could almost picture the petite, gentle blonde squaring her shoulders and bringing up her chin.

"It's Lindy."

"Lindy! I didn't know you were in Seattle."

"Six months now."

"You should have called. I'd love to see you again."

"I wanted to contact you," Lindy said, her spirits lifting as a Christmas song came over the radio, "but Steve wasn't in favor of the idea. How are you?"

"Good. Real good. Well, tell me–are you Mrs. Paul Abrams

yet?" The question was followed by a light, infectious laugh. "The last time I saw you, Paul had just given you a diamond ring and you were floating on cloud nine."

It was difficult for Lindy to remember those days. She may have been fooled into thinking she was happy, but that contentment had been short-lived. She would never have been the right woman for Paul. Once again she thanked God he'd had enough foresight to have recognized as much.

"I married Rush Callaghan," Lindy told her.

A short, shocked silence followed. "You did? Why that's wonderful–congratulations. I've always had a soft spot in my heart for Rush."

The last person Lindy wanted to discuss was her husband, especially the way matters were between them now. "Steve isn't here at the moment, but he'll be back soon. I'll tell him you called." Lindy hesitated and then decided she couldn't hold her tongue any longer. "I don't know what happened between you two–Steve never told me–but whatever it is, I hope you can patch it up. He misses you dreadfully." Lindy knew her brother would have her hide if he knew she'd told Carol that.

Carol laughed, but the mirth couldn't disguise her pain. "He's gotten along fine without me, and I've learned to manage without him, too. Leave a message for him, will you?"

"Of course."

"But tell him–" Carol added quickly, "–tell him it isn't overly important."

"Sure. I'll be happy to."

"It was nice talking to you again, Lindy. Really nice. I'm pleased for you and Rush. Be happy, you hear?"

Lindy nodded, although she knew Carol couldn't see the action. "I will," she mumbled. "I will."

Rush stood at the bridge ready to be relieved of duty. The sky was a deep shade of pearl gray and he expected it to start raining any minute. The foul weather suited his mood. The *Mitchell* was home, and his friends had hurried off the carrier and down the gangway to a happy reunion with their wives and families, eager to spend the holidays with their loved ones.

Rush had stood on the bridge, hungrily scanning the crowds through his binoculars, hoping with everything in him that he'd find Lindy there. He would have given his retirement pay to have found her among the well-wishers, waiting for him.

But Lindy hadn't been there, and a small part of Rush had died with the knowledge. Cheryl hadn't been there for him, either. Rush shouldn't have been surprised. Lindy had told him in Hawaii she had no intention of standing on the gangway, and she'd meant it. He was a fool to even have expected her.

His watchful gaze scanned the outline of the city of Bremerton and the Christmas decorations that hung from the streetlights. For the past six weeks of the cruise, he'd closed himself off from thoughts of Lindy, mentally chastising himself for exposing his heart a second time. Over and over again, he'd told himself women were too fickle to be trusted. But now that he was in port everything had changed and he knew he would eventually have to face her.

Marrying Lindy had been a gamble–he'd known it the day he slipped the wedding band on her finger. Her brother had had every reason to come down on him so hard. His friend was right. Rush had taken advantage of Lindy. He'd cashed in on her pain and insecurities, used her infatuation with him for his own purposes. It wasn't any wonder Lindy was confused and miserably unhappy now. Everything that had happened between them was his fault and he accepted full responsibility. Lindy wasn't ready to be a wife and she wanted out.

Rush didn't blame her.

His relief arrived and, after making the necessary notations in the log, Rush picked up his seabag and headed down the steep gangway. A stiff, cold breeze hit him and he paused to raise the collar of his thick wool jacket. There was no reason to hurry, and his steps were heavy.

His left arm was free of the cast now, but he still hadn't regained full use of it. His shoulder ached almost unbearably at times, but Rush had welcomed the pain. The physical throbbing somehow helped overshadow the mental agony of what had happened between him and Lindy.

Halfway down the gangway, something made him glance up. He stopped, his heart thundering against his rib cage, unable to believe his own eyes. There, alone at the end of the pier stood Lindy. The strong wind plastered her long coat to her torso and beat her thick dark hair roughly about her face. Her hands were buried in her coat pockets and she'd raised her chin, her loving eyes following his movements, patiently waiting.

Years of discipline, weeks of control, snapped within Rush as he dropped his seabag and started walking toward her. His chest felt as though he was on fire, he was fighting so hard to bury the emotion that pounded through him. His pulse started to beat in his temple. She'd come. His Lindy had come.

Rush quickened his pace and Lindy started running toward him, her arms outstretched. He caught her and pulled her into his embrace, burying his face in her soft hair, breathing in her delicate scent.

He tried to speak and found he couldn't. His tongue might as well have been attached to the roof of his mouth, and after a half second, he gave up trying to voice his thoughts. It came to him then how unnecessary words really were.

He sighed and reveled in the warm glow of Lindy's love at full strength. It worked on him like a healing potion, a relentless tide surging against him at full crest. It was as though they had exchanged their wedding vows there, at that moment on that pier, so strong was the love that flowed between them.

"Rush," she cried, tears in her voice. "I'm sorry, so sorry."

She held him so tightly that Rush could barely breathe. He closed his eyes, letting his heart and mind soak up her words. Each one tenderly removed the barbs of doubt that had tormented him, each one healed the pain and deep sense of loss these past weeks of separation had brought him. Each word confirmed what he'd always known but had been afraid to admit, fearing it would cripple him for life. He loved Lindy, loved her beyond anything else there could ever be in his world. He loved her more than the thrill of navigating the oceans, more than serving his country and commanding men. From the minute she'd given him her heart, Rush had only one mistress, only one wife, and that was Lindy.

"I love you," she said fiercely. "I've been such a fool." Lindy felt home at last in Rush's arms. This was where she belonged, where she planned to stay. It had taken these long weeks apart for her to realize what a fool she'd been to risk losing this wonderful man. Everything Susan had said was true, and Lindy had finally recognized the truth in her friend's words.

"You?" His voice was strained and husky with emotion. "If anyone was a fool, it was me. I should never have walked away from you in Hawaii."

The muscles in his lean jaw bunched and she kissed him, not able to wait a moment longer. Her hands lovingly stroked the sides of his face, relishing touching him so freely. Her mind groped for the words to explain.

"I was wrong, Rush, so wrong to try to force you to choose between me and the navy."

"Lindy, stop." He held a hand to her mouth to cut off her words. "Listen to me, my love. The reenlistment papers are in my pocket. I haven't signed them, and I won't."

She broke away, her face tight with disbelief. "You most certainly will sign those papers, Rush Callaghan."

From the look he gave her, Lindy knew she couldn't have shocked him more had she announced she was six months pregnant. His gaze narrowed as he studied her.

"The last time we talked, you were dead set against the navy. You wanted to be first in my life. I'm telling you I'm willing to give you what you want."

"You came so close to dying," she reminded him softly, and her voice trembled slightly with remembered pain. "I don't know if you're even aware of how badly you were injured."

He shook his head.

Rush had changed in so many ways since Hawaii. His shoulders were broader and his eyes less clouded, letting her look into his heart and know his thoughts.

"I couldn't bear the thought of losing you, Rush. It terrified me. I decided that if I was going to be forced to give you up, I'd rather get it over with quickly instead of letting go of you a little at a time. That was why I asked you to give up the navy. That was why I told you I wouldn't be here when you returned. Believe me, I know how crazy that sounds now. But at the time I felt I was doing the right thing."

"That's the most twisted piece of reasoning I've ever heard."

"I know," she whispered, dropping her gaze.

"Lindy, I meant what I said about those reenlistment papers. If you want a civilian for a husband, I'll do my damnedest to adjust."

She met his intense gaze and smiled through her tears. "Sign the papers, Rush. I've done a lot of maturing these past six weeks. You wanted a navy wife and by God, you've got one."

He stared at her and a strange, unidentifiable light flared in his gaze, darkening and then lightening their cornflower blue.

"You mean it, don't you?"

She nodded vigorously. "You bet I do. I may make mistakes along the way, but I'm willing to learn. I love you, Rush."

"I love you, wife."

"Navy wife," she amended.

Rush laughed and folded her in his arms, holding on to her as though he never planned to let her go. When they broke apart, Rush retrieved his seabag, and with their arms wrapped around each other's waists, they stepped forward toward tomorrow–a naval officer and his first mate.

NAVY BLUES

Dedicated to
Mary Magdalena Lanz,
July 2, 1909, to May 1, 1988
Beloved Aunt

Special thanks to
Rose Marie Harris, wife of MMCM Ralph Harris,
retired, U.S. Navy; Debbie Korrell,
wife of Chief Steven Korrell, USS *Alaska;*
Jane McMahon, RN

Chapter One

Seducing her ex-husband wasn't going to be easy, Carol Kyle decided, but she was determined. More than determined—resolute! Her mind was set, and no one knew better than Steve Kyle how stubborn she could be when she wanted something.

And Carol wanted a baby.

Naturally she had no intention of letting him in on her plans. What he didn't know wouldn't hurt him. Their marriage had lasted five good years, and six bad months. To Carol's way of thinking, which she admitted was a bit twisted at the moment, Steve owed her at least one pregnancy.

Turning thirty had convinced Carol that drastic measures were necessary. Her hormones were jumping up and down, screaming for a chance at motherhood. Her biological clock was ticking away, and Carol swore she could hear every beat of that blasted timepiece. Everywhere she turned, it seemed she was confronted with pregnant women, who served to remind her that her time was running out. If she picked up a magazine, there would be an article on some aspect of parenting. Even her favorite characters on television sitcoms were pregnant. When she found herself wandering through the infant section of her favorite department store, Carol realized drastic measures needed to be taken.

Making the initial contact with Steve hadn't been easy, but she recognized that the first move had to come from her. Getting in touch with her ex-husband after more than a year of complete silence had required two weeks of nerve building. But she'd managed to swallow her considerable pride and do it. Having a woman answer his phone had thrown her for a loop, and Carol had visualized her plans swirling down the drain until she realized the woman was Steve's sister, Lindy.

Her former sister-in-law had sounded pleased to hear from her, and then Lindy had said something that had sent Carol's spirits soaring to the ceiling: Lindy had claimed that Steve missed her dreadfully. Lordy, she hoped that was true. If so, it probably meant he wasn't dating yet. There could be complications if Steve was involved with another woman. On the other hand, there could also be problems if he wasn't involved.

Carol only needed him for one tempestuous night, and then, if everything went according to schedule, Steve Kyle could fade out of her life once more. If she failed to get pregnant...well, she'd leap that hurdle when she came to it.

Carol had left a message for Steve a week earlier, and he hadn't returned her call. She wasn't overly concerned. She knew her ex-husband well; he would mull it over carefully before he'd get back to her. He would want her to stew a while first. She'd carefully figured the time element into her schedule of events.

Her dinner was boiling on the stove, and Carol turned down the burner after checking the sweet potatoes with a cooking fork. Glaring at the orange-colored root, she heaved a huge sigh and squelched her growing dislike for the vegetable. After she became pregnant, she swore she would never eat another sweet potato for as long as she lived. A recent news report stated that the starchy vegetable helped increase the level of estrogen in a woman's body. Armed with that information, Carol had been eating sweet potatoes every day for the last two weeks. There had to be enough of the hormone floating around in her body by now to produce triplets.

Noting the potatoes were soft, she drained the water and dumped the steaming roots into her blender. A smile crowded the edges of her mouth. Eating sweet potatoes was a small price to pay for a beautiful baby…for Steve's baby.

"Have you called Carol back yet?" Lindy Callaghan demanded of her brother as she walked into the small kitchen of the two-bedroom apartment she shared with her husband and Steve.

Steve Kyle ignored her until she pulled out the chair and plopped down across the table from him. "No," he admitted flatly. He could see no reason to hurry. He already knew what Carol was going to tell him. He'd known it from the minute they'd walked out of the King County Courthouse, the divorce papers clenched in her hot little hands. She was remarrying. Well, more power to her, but he wasn't going to sit back and blithely let her rub his nose in the fact.

"Steve," Lindy insisted, her face tight with impatience. "It could be something important."

"You told me it wasn't."

"Sure, that's what Carol said, but…oh, I don't know, I have the feeling that it really must be. It isn't going to do any harm to call her back."

Methodically Steve turned the page of the evening newspaper and carefully creased the edge before folding it in half and setting it aside. Lindy and Rush, her husband, couldn't be expected to understand his reluctance to phone his ex-wife. He hadn't told either of them the details that had led to his and Carol's divorce. He preferred to keep all thoughts of the disastrous relationship out of his mind. There were plenty of things he could have forgiven, but not what Carol had done–not infidelity.

As a Lieutenant Commander aboard the submarine USS *Atlantis*, Steve was at sea for as long as six months out of a year. From the first Carol hadn't seemed to mind sending him off on a three-to-four month cruise. She even used to joke about it, telling him all the projects she planned to complete when he was at sea, and how pleased she was that he would be out of her hair for a while. When he'd returned she'd always seemed happy that he was home, but not exuberant. If anything had gone wrong in his absence–a broken water pipe, car repairs, anything–she'd seen to it herself with barely more than a casual mention.

Steve had been so much in love with her that the little things hadn't added up until later–much later. He'd deceived himself by overlooking the obvious. The physical craving they had for each other had diluted his doubts. Making love with Carol had been so hot it was like a nuclear meltdown. Toward the end she'd been eager for him, but not quite as enthusiastic as in the past. He'd been trusting, blind and incredibly stupid when it came to his ex-wife.

Then by accident he'd learned why she'd become so blasé about his comings and goings. When he left their bed, his loveless, faithless wife had a built-in replacement–her employer, Todd Larson.

It was just short of amazing that Steve hadn't figured it out earlier, and yet when he thought about it, he could almost calculate to the day when she'd started her little affair.

"Steve?"

Lindy's voice cut into his musings, and he lifted his gaze to meet hers. Her eyes were round and dark with concern. Steve experienced a small twinge of guilt for the way he'd reacted to his sister and Rush's marriage. When he'd learned his best friend had married his only sister after a dating period of a mere two weeks, Steve had been furious. He'd made no bones about telling them both the way he felt about their hurry-up wedding. Now he realized his own bitter experience had tainted his reasoning, and he'd long since apologized. It was obvious they were crazy about each other, and Steve had allowed his own misery to bleed into his reaction to their news.

"Okay, okay. I'll return Carol's call," he answered in an effort to appease his younger sibling. He understood all too well how much Lindy wanted him to settle matters with Carol. Lindy was happy, truly happy, and it dismayed her that his life should be at such loose ends.

"When?"

"Soon," Steve promised.

The front door opened, and Rush let himself into the apartment; his arms were loaded with Christmas packages. He paused just inside the kitchen and exchanged a sensual look with his wife. Steve watched the heated gaze and it was like throwing burning acid on his half-healed wounds. He waited a moment for the pain to lessen.

"How'd the shopping go?" Lindy asked, her silky smooth voice eager and filled with pleasure at the sight of her husband.

"Good," Rush answered and faked a yawn, "but I'm afraid it wore me out."

Steve playfully rolled his eyes toward the ceiling and stood, preparing to leave the apartment. "Don't tell me you two are going to take another nap!"

Lindy's cheeks filled with crimson color and she looked away. In the past few days the two of them had taken more naps than a newborn babe. Even Rush looked a bit chagrined.

"All right, you two," Steve said good-naturedly, reaching for his leather jacket. "I'll give you some privacy."

One glance from Lindy told him she was grateful. Rush stopped Steve on his way out the door and his eyes revealed his appreciation. "We've decided to look for a place of our own right away, but it doesn't look like we'll be able to move until after the first of the year." He paused and lowered his gaze, looking almost embarrassed. "I know this is an inconvenience for you to keep leaving, but..."

"Don't worry about it," Steve countered with a light chuckle. He patted his friend on the back. "I was a newlywed once myself."

Steve tried to sound casual about the whole matter, but doubted if he'd succeeded. Being constantly exposed to the strong current of love flowing between his friend and his sister was damn difficult, because he understood their need for each other all too well. There'd been a time when a mere look was all that was required to spark flames between him and Carol. Their desire seemed to catch fire and leap to brilliance with a single touch, and they couldn't get to bed fast enough. Steve had been crazy in love with her. Carol had appealed to all his senses and he'd ached with the desire to possess her completely. The only time he felt he'd accomplished that was when he was making love to her. Then and only then was Carol utterly his. And those times were all too brief.

Outside the apartment, the sky was dark with thick gray clouds. Steve walked across the street and headed toward the department stores. He didn't have much Christmas shopping to do, but now appeared to be as good a time for the task as any.

He hesitated in front of a pay phone and released a long, slow breath. He might as well call Carol and be done with it. She wanted to gloat, and he would let her. After all, it was the season to be charitable.

The phone rang just as Carol was coming in the front door. She stopped, set her purse on the kitchen counter and glared at the telephone. Her heart rammed against her rib cage with such force that she had to stop and gather her thoughts. It was Steve. The phone might as well have been spelling out his name in Morse code, she was that sure.

"Hello?" she answered brightly, on the third ring.

"Lindy said you phoned." His words were low, flat and emotionless.

"Yes, I did," she murmured, her nerves clamoring.

"Do you want to tell me why, or are you going to make me guess? Trust me, Carol, I'm in no mood to play twenty questions with you."

Oh Lord, this wasn't going to be easy. Steve sounded so cold and uncaring. She'd anticipated it, but it didn't lessen the effect his tone had on her. "I…I thought we could talk."

A short, heavy silence followed.

"I'm listening."

"I'd rather we didn't do it over the phone, Steve," she said softly, but not because she'd planned to make her voice silky and smooth. Her vocal chords had tightened and it just came out sounding that way. Her nerves were stretched to their limit, and her heart was pounding in her ear like a charging locomotive.

"Okay," he answered, reluctance evident in every syllable.

"When?" Her gaze scanned the calendar–the timing of this entire venture was of primary importance.

"Tomorrow?" he suggested.

Carol's eyes drifted shut as the relief worked its way through her stiff limbs. Her biggest concern was that he would suggest after the Christmas holidays, and then it would be too late and she would have to reschedule everything for January.

"That would be fine," Carol managed. "Would you mind coming to the house?" The two bedroom brick rambler had been awarded to her as part of the divorce settlement.

Again she could feel his hesitation. "As a matter of fact, I would."

"All right," she answered, quickly gathering her wits. His

not wanting to come to the house shouldn't have surprised her. "How about coffee at Denny's tomorrow evening?"

"Seven?"

Carol swallowed before answering. "Fine. I'll see you then."

Her hand was still trembling a moment later when she replaced the telephone receiver in its cradle. All along she'd accepted that Steve wasn't going to fall into her bed without some subtle prompting, but from the brusque, impatient sound of his voice, the whole escapade could well be impossible…this month. That bothered her. The one pivotal point in her plan was that everything come together quickly. One blazing night of passion could easily be dismissed and forgotten. But if she were to continue to invite him back one night a month, several months running, then he just might catch on to what she was doing.

Still, when it had come to interpreting her actions in the past, Steve had shown a shocking lack of insight. Thankfully their troubles had never intruded in the bedroom. Their marriage relationship had been a jumbled mess of doubts and misunderstandings, accusations and regrets, but their love life had always been vigorous and lusty right up until the divorce, astonishing as it seemed now.

At precisely seven the following evening, Carol walked into Denny's Restaurant on Seattle's Capitol Hill. The first year she and Steve had been married, they'd had dinner there once a month. Money had been tight because they'd been saving for a down payment on the house, and an evening out, even if it was only Saturday night at Denny's, had been a real treat.

Two steps into the restaurant Carol spotted her former husband sitting in a booth by the window. She paused and experienced such a wealth of emotion that advancing even one step more would have been impossible. Steve had no right to look this good—far better than she remembered. In the thirteen months since she'd last seen him, he'd changed considerably. Matured. His features were sharper, clearer, more intense. His lean good looks were all the more prominent, his handsome masculine features vigorous and tanned even in December. A few strands of gray hair streaked his temple, adding a distinguished air.

His gaze caught hers and Carol sucked in a deep, calming breath, her steps nearly faltering as she advanced toward him. His eyes had changed the most, she decided. Where once they had been warm and caressing, now they were cool and calculating. They narrowed on her, his mistrust shining through as bright as any beacon.

Carol experienced a moment of panic as his gaze seemed to strip away the last shreds of her pride. It took all her willpower to force a smile to her lips.

"Thank you for coming," she said, and slipped into the red upholstered seat across from him.

The waitress came with a glass coffeepot, and Carol turned over her cup, which the woman promptly filled after placing menus on the table.

"It feels cold enough to snow," Carol said as a means of starting conversation. It was eerie that she could have been married to Steve all those years and feel as if he were little more than a stranger. He gave her that impression now. This hard, impassive man was one she didn't know nearly as well as the one who had once been her lover, her friend and her husband.

"You're looking fit," Steve said after a moment, a spark of admiration glinting in his gaze.

"Thank you." A weak smile hovered over her lips. "You, too. How's the Navy treating you?"

"Good."

"Are you still on the *Atlantis*?"

He nodded shortly.

Silence.

Carol groped for something more to say. "It was a surprise to discover that Lindy's living in Seattle."

"Did she tell you she married Rush?"

Carol noted the way his brows drew together and darkened his face momentarily when he mentioned the fact. "I didn't realize Lindy even knew Rush," Carol said, and took a sip of the coffee.

"They were married two weeks after they met. Lord, I can't believe it yet."

"Two weeks? That doesn't sound anything like Rush. I remember him as being so methodical about everything."

Steve's frown relaxed, but only a little. "Apparently they fell in love."

Carol knew Steve well enough to recognize the hint of sarcasm in his voice, as if he were telling her what a mockery that emotion was. In their instance it had certainly been wasted. Sadly wasted.

"Are they happy?" That was the important thing as far as Carol was concerned.

"They went through a rough period a while back, but since the *Mitchell* docked they seem to have mended their fences."

Carol dropped her gaze to her cup as reality cut sharply into her heart. "That's more than we did."

"As you recall," he said harshly, under his breath, "there wasn't any fence left to repair. The night you started sleeping with Todd Larson, you destroyed our marriage."

Carol didn't rise to the challenge, although Steve had all but slapped her face with it. There was nothing she could say to exonerate herself, and she'd given up explaining the facts to him more than a year ago. Steve chose to believe what he wanted. She'd tried, God knew, to set the record straight. Todd had been her employer and her friend, but never anything more. Carol had pleaded with Steve until she was blue with exasperation, but it hadn't done her any good. Rehashing the same argument now wasn't going to help either of them.

Silence stretched between them and was broken by the waitress who had returned to their booth, pad and pen in hand. "Have you decided?"

Carol hadn't even glanced at the menu. "Do you have sweet-potato pie?"

"No, but pecan is the special this month."

Carol shook her head, ignoring the strange look Steve was giving her. "Just coffee then."

"Same here," Steve added.

The woman replenished both their cups and left.

"So how is good ol' Todd?"

His question lacked any real interest, and Carol had already decided her former boss was a subject they'd best avoid. "Fine," she lied. She had no idea how Todd was doing, since she hadn't worked for Larson Sporting Goods for over a year. She'd been offered a better job with Boeing and had been employed at the airplane company since before the divorce was final.

"I'm glad to hear it," Steve said with a soft snicker. "I suppose you called this little meeting to tell me the two of you are finally going to be married."

"No. Steve, please, I didn't call to talk about Todd."

He arched his brows in mock consternation. "I'm surprised. What's the matter, is wife number one still giving him problems? You mean to tell me their divorce hasn't gone through?"

A shattering feeling of hopelessness nearly choked Carol, and she struggled to meet his gaze without flinching. Steve was still so bitter, so intent on making her suffer.

"I really would prefer it if we didn't discuss Todd or Joyce."

"Fine. What do you want to talk about?" He checked his watch as if to announce he had plenty of other things he could be doing and didn't want to waste precious time with her.

Carol had carefully planned everything she was going to say. Each sentence had been rehearsed several times over in her mind, and now it seemed so trite and ridiculous, she couldn't manage a single word.

"Well?" he demanded. "Since you don't want to rub my nose in the fact that you're marrying Todd, what could you possibly have to tell me?"

Carol gestured with her hand, her fingers trembling. "It's Christmastime," she murmured.

"Congratulations, you've glanced at a calendar lately." He looked straight through her with eyes as hard as diamond bits.

"I thought…well, you know, that we could put our differences aside for a little while and at least be civil to each other."

His eyes narrowed. "What possible reason could there be for us to have anything to do with each other? You mean nothing to me, and I'm sure the feeling is mutual."

"You were my husband for five years."

"So?"

She rearranged the silverware several times, choosing not to look at Steve. He wore his anger like a tight pair of shoes and sitting across from him was almost too painful to bear.

"We loved each other once," she said after a drawn-out, strained moment.

"I loved my dog once, too," he came back. One corner of his mouth was pulled down, and his eyes had thinned to narrow slits. "What does having cared about each other have to do with anything now?"

Carol couldn't answer his question. She knew the divorce had made him bitter, but she'd counted on this long time apart to have healed some of his animosity.

"What did you do for the holidays last year?" she asked, refusing to argue with him. She wasn't going to allow him to rile her into losing her temper. He'd played that trick once too often, and she was wise to his game.

"What the hell difference does it make to you how I spent Christmas?"

This wasn't going well, Carol decided–not the least bit as she'd planned. Steve seemed to think she wanted him to admit he'd been miserable without her.

"I…I spent the day alone," she told him softly, reluctantly. Their divorce had been final three weeks before the holiday and Carol's emotions had been so raw she'd hardly been able to deal with the usual festivities connected with the holiday.

"I wasn't alone," Steve answered with a cocky half smile that suggested that whoever he was with had been pleasant company, and he hadn't missed her in the least.

Carol didn't know how anyone could look so damned insolent and sensuous at the same moment. It required effort to keep her chin up and meet his gaze, but she managed.

"So *you* were alone," he added. The news appeared to delight him. "That's what happens when you mess around with a married man, my dear. In case you haven't figured it out yet, Todd's wife and family will always come first. That's the other woman's sad lot in life."

Carol went still all over. She felt as though her entire body had turned to stone. She didn't breathe, didn't move, didn't so much as blink. The pain spread out in waves, circling first her throat and then her chest, working its way down to her abdomen, cinching her stomach so tightly that she thought she might be sick. The whole room seemed to fade away and the only thing she was sure about was that she had to get out of the restaurant. Fast.

Her fingers fumbled with the snap of her purse as she opened her wallet. Her hands weren't any more steady as she placed several coins by the coffee cup and scooted out of her seat.

Mutely Steve watched Carol walk out of the restaurant and called himself every foul name that he could come up with from his extensive Navy vocabulary. He hadn't meant to say those things. Hadn't intended to lash out at her. But he hadn't been able to stop himself.

He'd lied, too, in an effort to salvage his pride. Lied rather than give her the satisfaction of knowing he'd spent last Christmas Day miserable and alone. It had been the worst holiday of his life. The pain of the divorce had still ached like a lanced boil, while everyone around him had been celebrating and exchanging gifts, their happiness like a ball and chain shackling his heart. This year didn't hold much prospect for happiness, either. Lindy and Rush would prefer to spend the day alone, although they'd gone out of their way to convince him otherwise. But Steve wasn't stupid and had already made other plans. He'd volunteered for watch Christmas Day so that a fellow officer could spend time with his family.

Gathering his thoughts about Carol, Steve experienced a healthy dose of regret about the way he'd behaved toward his ex-wife.

She'd looked good, he admitted reluctantly–better than he'd wanted her to look for his own peace of mind. From the moment they'd met, he'd felt the vibrant energy that radiated from her. Thirteen months apart hadn't diminished that. He'd known the minute she walked into Denny's; he'd felt her presence the instant the door opened. She wore her thick blond hair shorter than he remembered so that it fell forward and hugged the sides of her face, the ends curling under slightly, giving her a Dutch-boy look. As always, her metallic blue eyes were magnetic, irrevocably drawing his gaze. She looked small and fragile, and the desire to protect and love her had come at him with all the force of a wrecking ball slamming against his chest. He knew differently, but it hadn't seemed to change the way he felt–Carol needed him about as much as the Navy needed more salt water.

Sliding out of the booth, Steve laid a bill on the table and left. Outside, the north wind sent a chill racing up his arms and he buried his hands into his pants pockets as he headed toward the parking lot.

Surprise halted his progress when he spied Carol leaning against the fender of her car. Her shoulders were slumped, her head hanging as though she were burdened by a terrible weight.

Once more Steve was swamped with regret. He had never learned the reason she'd phoned. He started walking toward her, not knowing what he intended to say or do.

She didn't glance up when he joined her.

"You never said why you phoned," he said in a wounded voice after a moment of silence.

"It isn't important…I told Lindy that."

"If it wasn't to let me know you're remarrying, then it's because you want something."

She looked up and tried to smile, and the feeble effort cut straight through Steve's resolve to forget he'd ever known or loved her. It was useless to try.

"I don't think it'll work," Carol said sadly.

"What?"

She shook her head.

"If you need something, just ask!" he shouted, using his anger as a defense mechanism. Carol had seldom wanted anything from him. It must be important for her to contact him now, especially after their divorce.

"Christmas Day," she whispered brokenly. "I don't want to spend it alone."

Chapter Two

Until Carol spoke, she hadn't known how much she wanted Steve to spend Christmas Day with her—and not for the reasons she'd been plotting. She sincerely missed Steve. He'd been both lover and friend, and now he was neither; the sense of loss was nearly overwhelming.

He continued to stare at her, and regret worked its way across his features. The success of her plan hinged on his response and she waited, almost afraid to breathe, for his answer.

"Carol, listen..." He paused and ran his hand along the back of his neck, his brow puckered with a condensed frown.

Carol knew him well enough to realize he was carefully composing his thoughts. She was also aware that he was going to refuse her! She knew it as clearly as if he'd spoken the words aloud. She swallowed the hurt, although she couldn't keep her eyes from widening with pain. When Steve had presented her with the divorce papers, Carol had promised herself she would never give him the power to hurt her again. Yet here she was, handing him the knife and exposing her soul.

She could feel her heart thumping wildly in her chest and fought to control the emotions that swamped her. "Is it so much to ask?" she whispered, and the words fell broken from her lips.

"I've got the watch."

"On Christmas…" She hadn't expected that, hadn't figured it into the scheme of things. In other words, the excuse of Christmas wasn't going to work. Ultimately her strategy would fail, and she would end up spending the holiday alone.

"I'd do it if I could," Steve told her in a straightforward manner that convinced her he was telling the truth. She felt somewhat less disappointed.

"Thank you for that," she said, and reached out to touch his hand, in a small gesture of appreciation. Amazingly he didn't draw away from her, which gave her renewed hope.

A reluctant silence stretched between them. There'd been a time when they couldn't say enough to each other, and now there was nothing.

"I suppose I'd better get back." Steve spoke first.

"Me, too," she answered brightly, perhaps a little too brightly. "It was good to see you again…you're looking well."

"You, too." He took a couple of steps backward, but still hadn't turned away. Swallowing down her disappointment, Carol retrieved the car keys from the bottom of her purse and turned to climb into her Honda. It dawned on her then, hit her square between the eyes. If not Christmas Day then…

"Steve," she whirled back around, her eyes flashing.

"Carol." He called her name at the same moment.

They laughed and the sound fell rusty and awkward between them.

"You first," he said, and gestured toward her. The corner of his mouth was curved upward in a half smile.

"What about Christmas Eve?"

He nodded. "I was just thinking the same thing."

Carol felt the excitement bubble up inside her like fizz in

a club soda. A grin broke out across her face as she realized nothing had been lost and everything was yet to be gained. Somewhere in the distance, Carol was sure she could hear the soft, lilting strains of a Brahms lullaby. "Could you come early enough for dinner?"

Again, he nodded. "Six?"

"Perfect. I'll look forward to it."

"I will, too."

He turned and walked away from her then, and it was all Carol could do to keep from doing a war dance, jumping up and down around the car. Instead she rubbed her bare hands together as though the friction would ease some of the excitement she was feeling. Steve hadn't a clue how memorable this one night would be. Not a clue!

"Your mood has certainly improved lately," Lindy commented as Steve walked into the kitchen whistling a lively Christmas carol.

His sister's words stopped him. "My mood has?"

"You've been downright chipper all week."

He shrugged his shoulders, hoping the action would discount his cheerful attitude. "'Tis the season."

"I don't suppose your meeting with Carol has anything to do with it?"

His sister eyed him skeptically, seeking his confidence, but Steve wasn't going to give it. This dinner with his ex-wife was simply the meeting of two lonely people struggling to make it through the holidays. Nothing less and certainly nothing more. Although he'd been looking for Carol to deny that she was involved with Todd, she hadn't. Steve considered her refusal to talk about the other man as good as an admission of guilt. That bastard had left her alone for Christmas two years running.

If Lindy was right and his mood had improved, Steve decided, it was simply because he was going to be out of his sister and Rush's hair for the evening; the newlyweds could spend their first Christmas Eve together without a third party butting in.

Steve reached for his coat, and Lindy turned around, her dark eyes wide with surprise. "You're leaving."

Steve nodded, buttoning the thick wool jacket.

"But…it's Christmas Eve."

"I know." He tucked the box of candy under his arm and lifted the bright red poinsettia he'd purchased on impulse earlier in the day.

"Where are you going?"

Steve would have liked to say a friend's house, but that wouldn't be true. He didn't know how to classify his relationship with Carol. Not a friend. Not a lover. More than an acquaintance, less than a wife.

"You're going to Carol's, aren't you?" Lindy prompted.

The last thing Steve wanted was his sister to get the wrong impression about this evening with Carol, because that's all there was going to be. "It's not what you think."

Lindy raised her hands in mock consternation. "I'm not thinking a single thing, except that it's good to see you smile again."

Steve's frown was heavy with purpose. "Well, don't read more into it than there is."

"Are the two of you going to talk?" Lindy asked, and her dark eyes fairly danced with deviltry.

"We're going to eat, not talk," Steve explained with limited patience. "We don't have anything in common anymore. I'll probably be home before ten."

"Whatever you say," Lindy answered, but her lips twitched with the effort to suppress a knowing smile. "Have a good time."

Steve chose not to answer that comment and left the apartment, but as soon as he was outside, he discovered he was whistling again and stopped abruptly.

* * *

Carol slipped the compact disk into the player and set the volume knob so that the soft Christmas music swirled festively through the house. A small turkey was roasting in the oven, stuffed with Steve's favorite sage dressing. Two pies were cooling on the kitchen counter–pumpkin for Steve, mincemeat for her. To be on the safe side a sweet-potato-pecan pie was in the fridge.

Carol chose a red silk dress that whispered enticingly against her soft skin. Her makeup and perfume had been applied with a subtle hand. Everything was ready.

Well, almost everything.

She and Steve were two different people now, and there was no getting around the fact. Regretting the past was an exercise in futility, and yet Carol had been overwhelmed these past few days with the realization that the divorce had been wrong. Very wrong. All the emotion she'd managed to bury this past year had seeped to the surface since her meeting with Steve and she couldn't remember a time when she'd been more confused.

She wanted a child, and she was using her ex-husband. More than once in the past week, she'd been forced to deal with twinges of guilt. But there was no going back. It would be impossible to recapture what had been between them before the divorce. There could be no reconciliation. Even more difficult than the past, Carol had trouble dealing with the present. They couldn't come in contact with each other without the sparks igniting. It made everything more difficult. They were both too stubborn, too temperamental, too obstinate.

And it was ruining their lives.

Carol felt they couldn't go back and yet they couldn't step forward, either. The idea of seducing Steve and getting pregnant had, in the beginning, been entirely selfish. She wanted a baby and she considered Steve the best candidate…the only candidate. After their one short meeting at the restaurant, Carol knew her choice of the baby's father went far beyond the practical. A part of her continued to love Steve, and probably always would. She wanted his child because it was the only part of him she would ever be able to have.

Everything hinged on the outcome of this dinner. Carol pressed her hands over her flat stomach and issued a fervent prayer that she was fertile. Twice in the past hour she'd taken her temperature, praying her body would do its part in this master plan. Her temperature was slightly elevated, but that could be caused by the hot sensation that went through her at the thought of sharing a bed with Steve again. Or it could be sheer nerves.

All day she'd been feeling anxious and restless with anticipation. She was convinced Steve would take one look at her and instantly know she intended for him to spend the night. The crux of her scheme was for Steve to think their making love was *his* idea. Again and again, her plans for the evening circled her mind, slowly, like the churning blades of a windmill stirring the air.

The doorbell chimed, and inhaling a calming breath, Carol forced a smile, walked across the room and opened the door for her ex-husband. "Merry Christmas," she said softly.

Steve handed her the poinsettia as though he couldn't get rid of the flower fast enough. His gaze didn't quite meet hers. In fact, he seemed to be avoiding looking at her, which pleased Carol because it told her that the red dress was having exactly the effect she'd hoped for.

"Thank you for the flower," she said and set it in the middle of the coffee table. "You didn't need to do that."

"I remembered how you used to buy three and four of those silly things each year and figured one more couldn't hurt."

"It was thoughtful of you, and I appreciate it." She held out her hand to take his coat.

Steve placed a small package under the tree and gave her

a shy look. "Frangos," he explained awkwardly. "I suppose they're still your favorite candy."

"Yes. I have a little something for you, too."

Steve peeled off his heavy jacket and handed it to her. "I'm not looking for any gifts from you. I brought the flowers and candy because I wanted to contribute something toward dinner."

"My gift isn't much, Steve."

"Save it for someone else. Okay?"

Her temper nearly slipped then, but Carol managed to keep it intact. Her smile was just a little more forced when she turned from hanging his jacket in the hall closet, but she hoped he hadn't noticed.

"Would you like a hot-buttered rum before we eat?" she offered.

"That sounds good."

He followed her into the kitchen and brought the bottle of rum down from the top cupboard while she put water on to boil.

"When did you cut your hair?" he asked unexpectedly.

Absently Carol's fingers touched the straight, thick strands that crowded the side of her head. "Several months ago now."

"I liked it better when you wore it longer."

Gritting her teeth, she managed to bite back the words to inform him that she styled her hair to suit herself these days, not him.

Steve saw the flash of irritation in his ex-wife's eyes and felt a little better. The comment about her hair wasn't what she'd wanted to hear; she'd been waiting for him to tell her how beautiful she looked. The problem was, he hadn't been able to take his eyes off her from the moment he entered the house. The wisecrack was a result of one flirtatious curl of blond hair that swayed when she moved. He hadn't been able to look past that single golden lock. Neither could he stop staring at the shape of her lips nor the curve of her chin, nor the appealing color of her china blue eyes. When he'd met her at Denny's the other night he'd been on the defensive, waiting for her to drop her bombshell. All his protective walls were lowered now. He would have liked to blame it on the Christmas holidays, but he realized it was more than that, and what he saw gave him cause to tremble. Carol was as sensuous and appealing to him as she'd always been. Perhaps more so.

Already he knew what was going to happen. They would spend half the evening verbally circling each other in an anxious search for common ground. But there wasn't one for them...not anymore. Tonight was an evening out of sequence, and when it had passed they would return to their respective lives.

When Carol finished mixing their drinks, they wandered into the living room and talked. The alcohol seemed to alleviate some of the tension. Steve filled the silence with details of what had been happening in Lindy's life and in his career.

"You've done well for yourself," Carol admitted, and there was a spark of pride in her eyes that warmed him.

Steve didn't inquire about her career because it would involve asking about Todd, and the man was a subject he'd sworn he would avoid at all costs. Carol didn't volunteer any information, either. She knew the unwritten ground rules.

A half hour later, Steve helped her carry their meal to the table.

"You must have been cooking all day."

She grinned and nodded. "It gave me something to do."

The table was loaded with sliced turkey, creamy potatoes, giblet gravy, stuffing, fresh broccoli, sweet potatoes and fruit salad.

Carol asked him to light the candles and when Steve had, they sat down to eat. Sitting directly across the table from her,

Steve found he was mesmerized by her mouth as she ate. With all his might he tried to remember the reasons he'd divorced Carol. Good God, she was captivating–too damn good to look at for his own peace of mind. Her hands moved gracefully, raising the fork from her plate to her mouth in motions as elegant as those of a symphony director. He shouldn't be enjoying watching her this much, and he realized he would pay the price later when he returned to the apartment and the loneliness overtook him once more.

When he'd finished the meal, he leaned against the shield-back dining-room chair and placed his hands over his stomach. "I can't remember when I've had a better dinner."

"There's pie…"

"Not now," he countered quickly and shook his head. "I'm too full to down another bite. Maybe later."

"Coffee?"

"Please."

Carol carried their dishes to the sink, stuck the leftovers in the refrigerator, and returned with the glass coffeepot. She filled both their cups, returned it to the kitchen and then took her seat opposite him. She rested her elbows on the table, and smiled.

Despite his best intentions through a good portion of the meal, Steve hadn't been able to keep his eyes away from her. The way she was sitting–leaning forward, her elbows on the tabletop–caused her breasts to push together and more than amply fill the bodice of her dress. His breath faltered someplace between his lungs and his throat at the alluring sight she made. He could have sworn she wasn't wearing a bra. Carol had fantastic breasts and Steve watched, captivated, as their tips beaded against the shiny material. They seemed to be pointing directly at him, issuing a silent invitation that asked him to fondle and taste them. Against his will, his groin began to swell until he was throbbing with painful need. Disconcerted, he dropped his gaze to the steaming cup of coffee. With his hands shaking, he took a sip of his coffee and nearly scalded the tender skin inside his mouth.

"That was an excellent dinner," he repeated, after a moment of silence.

"You're not sorry you came, are you?" she asked unexpectedly, studying him. The intent look that crowded her face demanded all Steve's attention. Her skin was pale and creamy in the muted light, her eyes wide and inquiring, as though the answer to her question was of the utmost importance.

"No," he admitted reluctantly. "I'm glad I'm here."

His answer pleased her and she smiled, looking tender and trusting, and Steve wondered how he could ever have doubted her. He knew what she'd done–knew that she'd purposely destroyed their marriage–and in that moment, it didn't matter. He wanted her again. He wanted to hold her warm and willing body in his arms. He wanted to bury himself so deep inside her that she would never desire another man for as long as they both lived.

"I'll help you with the dishes," he said, and rose so abruptly that he nearly knocked over the chair.

"I'll do them later." She got to her feet as well. "But if you want to do something, I'd appreciate a little help with the tree."

"The tree?" The words sounded as foreign as an obscure language.

"Yes, it's only half decorated. I couldn't reach the tallest limbs. Will you help?"

He shrugged. "Sure." He could have sworn that Carol was relieved, and he couldn't imagine why. The Christmas tree looked fine to him. There were a few bare spots, but nothing too noticeable.

Carol dragged a dining-room chair into the living room and pulled a box of ornaments out from underneath the end table.

"You're knitting?" Steve asked, hiding a smile as his gaze fell on the strands of worsted yarn. Carol had to be the worst knitter in the world, yet she tackled one project after another, seeming oblivious of any lack of talent. There had been a time when he could tease her about it, but he wasn't sure his insight would be appreciated now.

She glanced away as though she feared his comment.

"Don't worry, I'm not going to tease you," he told her, remembering the time she'd proudly presented him with a sweater she'd made herself–the left sleeve had been five inches longer than the right. He'd tried it on and she'd taken one look at him and burst into tears. It was one of the few times he could ever remember Carol crying.

Carol dragged the chair next to the tree and raised her leg to stand on it.

Steve stopped her. "I thought you wanted me to do that?"

"No, I need you to hand me the ornaments and then stand back and tell me how they look."

"Carol…if I placed the ornaments on the tree, you wouldn't need the chair."

She looked at him and sighed. "I'd rather do it. You don't mind, do you?"

He didn't know why she was so determined to hang the decorations herself, but it didn't make much difference to him. "No, if you want to risk your fool neck, feel free."

She grinned and raised herself so that she was standing on the padded cushion of the chair. "Okay, hand me one," she said, tossing him a look over her shoulder.

Steve gave her a shiny glass bulb, and he noted how good she smelled. Roses and some other scent he couldn't define wrapped gently around him. Carol stretched out her arms and reached for the tallest branch. Her dress rose a solid five inches and exposed the back of her creamy smooth thighs and a fleeting glimpse of the sweet curve of her buttocks. Steve knotted his hands into fists at his sides to keep from touching her. It would be entirely plausible for him to grip her waist and claim he was frightened she would tumble from her perch. But if he allowed that to happen, his hands would slip and soon he would be cupping that cute rounded bottom. Once he touched her, Steve knew he would never be able to stop. He clenched his teeth and inhaled deeply through his nose. Having Carol standing there, exposing herself in this unconscious way, was more than a mere man could resist. At this point, he was willing to use any excuse to be close to her once more.

Carol lowered her arms, her dress fell back into place and Steve breathed normally again. He thought he was safe from further temptation until she twisted around. Her ripe, full breasts filled the front of her dress, their shape clearly defined against the thin fabric. If he'd been guessing about the bra before, he was now certain. She wasn't wearing one.

"I'm ready for another ornament," she said softly.

Like a blind man, Steve turned and fumbled for a second glass bulb. He handed it to her and did everything within his power to keep his gaze away from her breasts.

"How does that one look?" Carol asked.

"Fine," Steve answered gruffly.

"Steve?"

"Don't you think that's enough decorations, for God's sake?"

His harsh tone was as much a surprise to him as it obviously was to Carol.

"Yes, of course."

She sounded disappointed, but that couldn't be helped. Steve moved to her side once more and offered her his hand to help her down. His foot must have hit against one leg of the chair because it jerked forward. Perhaps it was something she did, Steve wasn't sure, but whatever happened caused the chair to teeter on the thick carpet.

With a small cry of alarm, Carol threw out her arms.

With reflexes born of years of military training, Steve's hands shot out like bullets to catch her. The chair fell sideways onto the floor, but Steve's grip on Carol's waist anchored her firmly against his torso. Their breathing was labored, and Steve sighed with relief that she hadn't fallen. It was on the tip of his tongue to berate her, call her a silly goose for not letting him place the glass bulbs on the tree, chastise her for being such a fool. She shouldn't put herself at risk over something as nonsensical as a Christmas tree. But none of the words made it to his lips.

Their gazes were even, her haunting eyes stared into his and said his name as clearly as if it were spoken. Carol's feet remained several inches off the floor, and still Steve held on to her, unable to release her. His heart was pounding frantically with wonder as he raised a finger and touched her soft throat. His gaze continued to delve into hers. He wanted to set her back on the carpet, to free them both from this invisible grip before it maimed them, but he couldn't seem to find the strength to let her go.

Slowly she slid down his front, between his braced feet, crimping the skirt of her dress between them. Once she was secure, he noted that her lower abdomen was tucked snugly in the joint between his thighs. The throbbing in his groin began again, and he held in a groan that threatened to emanate from deep within his chest.

He longed to kiss her more than he'd ever wanted anything in his life, and only the greatest strength of will kept him from claiming her sweet mouth with his own.

She'd betrayed him once, crippled him with her deceit. Steve had sworn he would never allow her to use him again, yet his arguments burned away like dry timber in a forest fire.

His thumb found her moist lips and brushed back and forth as though the action would be enough to satisfy either of them. It didn't. If anything, it created an agony even more powerful. His heart leaped into a hard, fast rhythm that made him feel breathless and weak. Before he could stop himself, his finger lifted her chin and his mouth glided over hers. Softly. Moistly. Satin against satin.

Carol sighed.

Steve groaned.

She weakened in his arms and closed her eyes. Steve kissed her a second time and thrust his tongue deep into her mouth, his need so strong it threatened to consume him. His hand was drawn to her breast, as if caught by a vise and carried there against his will. He cupped the rounded flesh, and his finger teased the nipple until it beaded and swelled against his palm. Carol whimpered.

He had to touch her breasts again. Had to know for himself their velvet smoothness. Releasing a ragged sigh, he reached behind her and peeled down her zipper. She was as eager as he when he lowered the top of her dress and exposed her naked front.

Her hands were around his neck, and she slanted her mouth over his, rising to her tiptoes as she leaned her weight into his. Steve's mouth quickly abandoned hers to explore the curve of her neck and then lower to the rosy tips of her firm, proud breasts. His moist tongue traced circles around the pebbled nipples until Carol shuddered and plowed her fingers through his hair.

"Steve…oh, I've missed you so much." She repeated the sentence over and over again, but the words didn't register in his clouded mind. When they did, he went cold. She may have missed him, may have hungered for his touch, but she hadn't been faithful. The thought crippled him, and he went utterly still.

Carol must have sensed his withdrawal, because she dropped her arms. Her shoulders were heaving as though she'd been running in a heated race. His own breathing wasn't any more regular.

Abruptly Steve released her and stumbled two paces back.

"That shouldn't have happened," he announced in a hoarse whisper.

Carol regarded him with a wounded look but said nothing.

"I've got to get out of here," he said, expelling the words on the tail end of a sigh.

Carol's gaze widened and she shook her head.

"Carol, we aren't married anymore. This shouldn't be happening."

"I know." She lowered her gaze to the carpet.

Steve walked to the hall closet and reached for his jacket. His actions felt as if they were in slow motion–as if every gravitational force in the universe was pulling at him.

He paused, his hand clenching the doorknob. "Thank you for dinner."

Carol nodded, and when he turned back, he saw that her eyes had filled with tears and she was biting her bottom lip to hold them back. One hand held the front of her dress across her bare breasts.

"Carol…"

She looked at him with soft, appealing eyes and held out her hand. "Don't go," she begged softly. "Please don't leave me. I need you so much."

Chapter Three

Carol could see the battle raging in Steve's tight features. She swallowed down the tears and refused to release his gaze, which remained locked with her own.

"We're not married anymore," he said in a voice that shook with indecision.

"I…don't care." Swallowing her pride, she took one small step toward him. If he wouldn't come to her, then she was going to him. Her knees felt incredibly weak, as though she were walking after being bedridden for a long while.

"Carol…"

She didn't stop until she was standing directly in front of him. Then slowly, with infinite care, she released her hold on the front of her dress and allowed it to fall free, baring her breasts. Steve rewarded her immediately with a swift intake of breath, and then it seemed as if he stopped breathing completely. Carol slipped her flattened hands up his chest and leaned her body into his. When she felt his rock-hard arousal pressing against her thigh, she closed her eyes to disguise the triumph that zoomed through her blood like a shot of adrenaline.

Steve held himself stiffly against her, refusing to yield to her softness; his arms hung motionless at his sides. He didn't push her away, but he didn't welcome her into his embrace, either.

Five years of marriage had taught Carol a good deal about her husband's body. She knew what pleasured him most, knew what would drive him to the edge of madness, knew how to make him want her until there was nothing else in their world.

Standing on the tips of her toes, she locked her arms tightly around his neck and raised her soft lips to gently brush her mouth over his. Her kiss was as moist and light as dew on a summer rose. Steve's lashes dropped and she could feel the torment of the battle that raged in his troubled mind.

Slightly elevating one foot, she allowed her shoe to slip off her toes. It fell almost silently to the floor. Carol nearly laughed aloud at the expression that came over Steve's contorted features. He knew what was coming, and against his will, Carol could see that he welcomed it. In a leisurely exercise, she raised her nylon-covered foot and slid it down the backside of his leg. Again and again her thigh and calf glided over his, each caressing stroke moved higher and higher on his leg, bringing her closer to her objective.

When Steve's hand closed, almost painfully, over her thigh, Carol knew she'd won. He held her there for a timeless moment, neither moving nor breathing.

"Kiss me," he ordered, and the words seemed to be ground out from between clenched teeth.

Although Carol had fully intended to comply with his demand, she apparently didn't do it fast enough to suit her ex-husband. He groaned and his free hand locked around the back of her head, compelling her mouth to his. Driven by urgency, his kiss was forceful and demanding, almost grinding, as if he sought to punish her for making him want her so much. Carol allowed him to ravage her mouth, giving him everything he wanted, everything he asked for, until finally she gasped for breath and broke away briefly. Steve brought her mouth back to his, and gradually his kisses softened until Carol thought she was sure her whole body would burst into flames. Sensing this, Steve moved his hand from the back of her head and began to massage her breast in a leisurely circular motion, his palm centering on her nipple. Her whole torso started to pulsate under his gentle touch.

Carol arched her spine to grant him easier access, and tossed back her head as his fingers worked their magic. Then his hand left her breast, and she wanted to protest until she felt his fingers slip around her other thigh and lift her completely off the carpet, raising her so that their mouths were level, their breath mingling, moist and excited.

They paused and gazed into each other's eyes. Steve's were filled with surprise and wonder. Carol met that look and smiled with a rediscovered joy that burst from deep within her. An inner happiness that had vanished from her life the moment Steve had walked away from her, returned. She leaned forward and very gently rubbed her mouth across his, creating a moist, delicious friction. Gently her tongue played over the seam of his lips, sliding back and forth, teasing him, testing him in a love game that had once been familiar between them.

Carol gently caught his lower lip between her teeth and sucked on it, playing with it while darting the tip of her tongue in and out of his mouth.

The effect on Steve was electric. His mouth claimed hers in an urgent kiss that drove the oxygen from her lungs. Then, with a strength that astonished her, he lifted her even higher until his mouth closed over her left breast, rolling his tongue over her nipple, then sucking at it greedily, taking in more and more of her breast.

Carol thought she was going to go crazy with the tidal wave of sensation that flooded her being. She locked her legs around his waist and braced her hands against his shoulders. His mouth and tongue alternated from one breast to the other until she was convinced that if he didn't take her soon, she was going to faint in his arms.

Braced against the closet door, Steve used what leverage he could to inch his hand up the inside of her thigh. His exploring fingers reached higher and higher, then paused when he encountered a nylon barrier. He groaned his frustration.

Carol was so weak with longing that if he didn't carry her voluntarily into the bedroom soon, she was going to demand that he make love to her right there on the entryway floor.

"You weren't wearing a bra," he chastised her in a husky thwarted voice. "I was hoping…"

He didn't need to finish for Carol to know what he was talking about. When they were married, she'd often worn a garter belt with her nylons instead of panty hose so their lovemaking wouldn't be impeded.

"I want you," she whispered, her hands framing his face. "But if you think it would be best to leave…go now. The choice is yours."

His gaze locked with hers, Steve marched wordlessly across the living room and down the long hallway to the bedroom that had once been theirs.

"Not here," she told him. "I sleep there now," she explained, pointing to the room across the hall.

Steve switched directions and marched into the smaller bedroom, not stopping until he reached the queen-size bed. For one crazy second, Carol thought he meant to drop her on top of the mattress and storm right out of the house. Instead he continued to hold her, the look in his eyes wild and uncertain.

Carol's eyes met his. She was nearly choking on the sadness that threatened to overwhelm her. Tentatively she raised one hand and pressed it to the side of his face, her eyes wide, her heart pounding so hard she was sure the sound of it would soon bring down the walls.

To her surprise, Steve tenderly placed her on the bed, braced one knee against the edge of the mattress and leaned over her.

"We aren't married…. Not a damn thing has been settled between us," he announced, as though this should be shocking news.

Carol said nothing, but she casually slipped her hand around the side of his neck, urging his mouth down to hers. She met with no resistance.

"Make love to me," she murmured.

Steve groaned, twisted around and dropped to sit on the side of the bed, granting her a full view of his solid back. The thread of disappointment that wrapped itself around Carol's heart was followed by a slow, lazy smile that spread over her mouth as she recognized his frantic movements.

Steve was undressing.

Feeling deliciously warm and content, Carol woke two hours later to the sound of Steve rummaging in the kitchen. No doubt he was looking for something to eat. Smiling, she jerked her arms high above her head and stretched. She yawned and arched her back, slightly elevating her hips with the action. She felt marvelous. Stupendous. Happy.

Her heart bursting with newfound joy, she reached for Steve's shirt and purposely buttoned it just enough to be provocative while looking as if she'd made some effort to cover herself.

Semiclothed, she moved toward the noise emanating from her kitchen. Barefoot, dressed only in his slacks, Steve was bent over, investigating the contents of her refrigerator.

Carol paused in the doorway. "Making love always did make you hungry," she said from behind him.

"There's hardly a damn thing in here except sweet potatoes. Good grief, woman, what are you doing with all these leftover yams?"

Carol felt sudden heat rise in her cheeks as hurried excuses crowded her mind. "They were on sale this week because of Christmas."

"They must have been at rock-bottom price. I counted six containers full of them. It looks like you've been eating them at every meal for an entire week."

"There's some pie if that'll interest you," she said, a little too quickly. "And plenty of turkey for a sandwich, if you want."

He straightened, closed the refrigerator and turned to face her. But whatever he'd intended to say apparently left him when he caught sight of her seductive pose. She was leaning against the doorjamb, hands behind her back and one foot braced against the wall, smiling at him, certain he could read her thoughts.

"There's pumpkin, and the whipped topping is fresh."

"Pumpkin?" he repeated.

"The pie."

He blinked, and nodded. "That sounds good."

"Would you like me to make you a sandwich while I'm at it?"

"Sure." But he didn't sound sure of anything at the moment.

Moving with ease around her kitchen, Carol brought out the necessary ingredients and quickly put together a snack for both of them. When she'd finished, she carried their plates to the small table across from the stove.

"Would you like something to drink?" she asked, setting their plates down.

"I'll get it," Steve said, apparently eager to help. "What would you like?"

"Milk," she responded automatically. She'd never been overly fond of the beverage but had recently made a habit of drinking a glass or two each day in preparation for her pregnancy.

"I thought you didn't like milk."

"I...I've acquired new tastes in the past year."

Steve grinned. "There are certain things about you that haven't changed, and then there's something more, something completely unexpected. Good God, woman, you've turned into a little she-devil, haven't you?"

Carol lowered her gaze and felt the heated blush work its way up her neck and spill into her cheeks. It wasn't any wonder Steve was teasing her. She'd been as hot as a stick of dynamite. By the time he'd undressed, she'd behaved like a tigress, clawing at him, driven by mindless passion.

Chuckling, Steve delivered two glasses of milk to the table. "You surprised me," he said. "You used to be a tad more timid."

Doing her best to ignore him, Carol brought her feet up to the edge of the chair and pulled the shirt down over her legs. With feigned dignity, she reached for half of her sandwich. "An officer and a gentleman wouldn't remind me of my wicked ways."

Still grinning, Steve lounged against the back of the chair. "You used to be far more subtle."

"Steve," she cried, "stop talking about it. Can't you see you're embarrassing me?"

"I remember one time when we were on our way to an admiral's dinner party and you casually announced you'd been in such a rush that you'd forgotten to put on any underwear."

Carol closed her eyes and looked away, remembering the time as clearly as if it had been last week instead of several years ago. She remembered, too, how good the lovemaking had been later that same evening.

"There wasn't time for us to go back to the house, so all night while you strolled around, sipping champagne, chatting and looking sedately prim, only I knew differently. Every time you looked at me, I about went crazy."

"I wanted you to know how much I longed to make love. If you'll recall, you'd just returned from a three-month tour."

"Carol, if *you'll* recall, we'd spent the entire day in bed."

She took a sip of her milk, then slowly raised her gaze to meet his. "It wasn't enough."

Steve closed his eyes and shook his head before grudgingly admitting, "It wasn't enough for me, either."

As soon as it had been socially acceptable to do so, Steve had made their excuses to the admiral that night and they'd hurriedly left the party. The entire way home, he'd been furious with Carol, telling her he was certain someone must have known what little trick she was playing. Just as heatedly, Carol had told Steve she didn't care who knew. If some huffy admiral wanted to throw a dinner party he shouldn't do it so soon after his men return from deployment.

They'd ended up making love twice that evening.

"Steve," Carol whispered with ragged emotion.

"Yes?"

"Once wasn't enough tonight, either." She dared not look at him, dared not let him see the way her pulse was clamoring.

Abruptly he stopped eating, and when he swallowed, it looked as if he'd downed the sandwich whole. A full minute passed before he spoke.

"Not for me, either."

Their lovemaking was different this time. Unique. Unrepeatable. Earlier, it'd been like spontaneous combustion. This time was slow, easy, relaxed. Steve led her into the bedroom, unfastened the buttons of the shirt that she was wearing and let it drop unheeded to the floor.

Carol stood before him tall and proud, her taut nipples seeming to beg for his lips. Steve looked at her naked body as if seeing her for the first time. Tenderly he raised his hand to her face and brushed back a wisp of blond hair, his touch light, gentle. Then he lowered his hands and cupped the undersides of her breasts, as though weighing them in a delicate measure. The velvet stroke of his thumbs worked across her nipples until they pebbled to a throbbing hardness. From there he slid the tips of his fingers down her rib cage, grazing her heated flesh wherever he touched her.

All the while, his dark, mesmerizing gaze never left hers, as though he half expected her to protest or to stop him.

Carol felt as if her hands were being manipulated like a puppet's as she reached for his belt buckle. All she knew was that she wanted him to make love to her. Her fingers fumbled at first, unfamiliar with the workings of his belt, then managed to release the clasp.

Soon Steve was nude.

She studied him, awed by his strength and beauty. She wanted to tell him all that she was feeling, all the good things she sensed in him, but the words withered on her tongue as he reached out and touched her once more.

His hand continued downward from her rib cage, momentarily pausing over her flat, smooth stomach, then moving lower until it encountered her pelvis. Slowly, methodically, he braced the heel of his hand against the apex of her womanhood and started a circling, gyrating motion while his fingers explored between her parted thighs.

Hardly able to breathe, Carol opened herself more to him, and once she had, he delicately parted her and slipped one finger inside. Her eyes widened at the stab of pleasure that instantly sliced through her and she bit into her lower lip to keep from panting.

She must have made some kind of sound because Steve paused and asked, "Did I hurt you?"

Carol was incapable of any verbal response. Frantically she shook her head, and his finger continued its deft movements, quickly bringing her to an exploding release. Wave upon wave of seething spasms, each one stronger, each one more intense, overtook every part of her. Whimpering noises escaped from deep within her throat as she climaxed, and the sound propelled Steve into action.

He wrapped his arms around her and carried her to the

bed, laying her on top of the rumpled sheets. Not allowing her time to alter her position or rearrange the sheets, Steve moved over her, parted her thighs and quickly impaled her.

His breathing was ragged, barely under control.

Carol's wasn't any more even.

He didn't move, torturing her with an intense longing she had never experienced. Her body was still tingling in the aftermath of one fulfillment and reaching, striving toward another. Her whole person seemed to be filled with anxious expectancy…waiting for something she couldn't define.

Taking her hands, Steve lifted them above her head and held them prisoner there. He leaned over her, bracing himself on his arms on either side of her head. The action thrust him deeper inside Carol. She moaned and thrashed her head against the mattress, then lifted her hips, jerking them a couple of times, seeking more.

"Not yet, love," he whispered and placed a hand under her head, lifting her mouth to his. Their kiss was wild and passionate, as though their mouths couldn't give or take enough to satisfy their throbbing need.

Steve shifted his position and completely withdrew his body from hers.

Carol felt as if she'd suddenly gone blind; the whole world seemed black and lifeless. She started to protest, started to cry out, but before the sound escaped her throat, Steve sank his manhood back inside her. A shaft of pure light filled her senses once more and she sighed audibly, relieved. She was whole again, free.

"Now," Steve told her. "Now." He moved eagerly then, in deep, calculated strokes, plunging into her again and again, gifting her with the sun, revealing the heavens, exploring the universe. Soon all Carol knew was this insistent warm friction and the sweet, indescribable pangs of pleasure. Her body trembled as ripple after ripple of deep, pure sensation pulsed over her, driving her crazy as she remembered what had nightly been hers.

Breathless, Steve moved to lie beside her, bringing her into the circle of his arms. An hour passed, it seemed, before he spoke. “Was it always this good?”

The whispered question was so low Carol had to strain to hear him. “Yes,” she answered after a long, timeless moment. “Always.”

He pressed his forehead against the top of her head and moaned. “I was afraid of that.”

The next thing Carol was aware of was a muffled curse and the unsettling sound of something heavy crashing to the floor.

“Steve?” she sat up in bed and reached for a sheet to cover her nakedness. The room was dark and still. Dread filled her–it couldn’t be morning. Not yet, not so soon.

“I’m sorry. I didn’t mean to wake you.”

“You’re leaving?” She sent her hand searching for the lamp on the nightstand. It clicked and a muted light filled the room.

“I’ve got the watch today,” he reminded her.

“What time is it?”

“Carol, listen,” he said gruffly, “I didn’t mean for any of this to happen.” All the while he was speaking, Steve’s fingers were working the buttons of his shirt and having little success in getting it to fasten properly. “Call what happened last night what you will–the holiday spirit, a momentary slip in my better judgment…whatever. I’m sure you feel the same way.” He paused and turned to study her.

She leaned forward, resting her chin on her raised knees. Her heart was in her throat, and she felt shaken and miserable. “Yes, of course.”

His mouth thinned and he turned his back to her once more. “I thought as much. The best thing we can do is put the entire episode out of our minds.”

"Right," she answered, forcing some enthusiasm into her voice. It was working out exactly as she'd planned it: they would both wake up in the morning, feel chagrined, make their apologies and go their separate ways once more.

Only it didn't feel the way she'd anticipated. It felt wrong. Very wrong.

Steve was in the living room before she moved from the bed. Grabbing a thin robe from her closet, she slipped into it as she rushed after him.

He seemed to be waiting for her, pacing the entryway. He combed his fingers through his hair a couple of times before turning to look at her.

"So you want to forget last night?" he asked.

"I…if you do," she answered.

"I do."

Carol's world toppled for a moment, then quickly righted itself. She understood–it was better this way. "Thank you for the poinsettia and candy." It seemed inappropriate to mention the terrific lovemaking.

"Right." His answer was clipped, as though he was eager to be on his way. "Thanks for the dinner…and everything else."

"No problem." Stepping around him, Carol opened the door. "It was good to see you again, Steve."

"Yeah, you, too."

He walked out of the house and down the steps, and watching him go did crazy things to Carol's equilibrium. Suddenly she had to lean against the doorjamb just to remain upright. Something inside her, something strong and more powerful than her own will demanded that she stop him.

"Steve," she cried frantically. She stood on tiptoe. "Steve."

He turned around abruptly.

They stared at each other, each battle scarred and weary, each hurting. Each proud.

"Merry Christmas," she said softly.

"Merry Christmas."

* * *

Three days after Christmas, Carol was convinced her plan had worked perfectly. Thursday morning she woke feeling sluggish and sick to her stomach. A book she'd been reading on pregnancy and childbirth stated that the best way to relieve those early bouts of morning sickness was to nibble on soda crackers first thing–even before getting out of bed.

A burning sense of triumph led her into the bathroom, where she stared at herself in the mirror as though her reflection would proudly announce she was about to become a mother.

It had been so easy. Simple really. One tempestuous night of passion and the feat was accomplished. Her hand rested over her abdomen, and she patted it gently, feeling both proud and awed. A new life was being nurtured there.

A baby. Steve's child.

The wonder of it produced a ready flow of emotion and tears dampened her eyes.

Another symptom!

The book had explained that her emotions could be affected by the pregnancy–that she might be more susceptible to tears.

Wiping the moisture from the corners of her eyes, Carol strolled into the kitchen and searched the cupboard for saltines. She found a stale package and forced herself to eat two, but she didn't feel any better than she had earlier.

Not bothering to dress, she turned on the television and made herself a bed on the sofa. Boeing workers were given the week between Christmas and New Year's off as part of their employment package. Carol had planned to spend the free time painting the third bedroom–the one she planned to use for the baby. Unfortunately she didn't have any energy. In fact, she felt downright sick, as though she were coming down with a case of the flu.

A lazy smile turned up the edges of her mouth. She wasn't

about to complain. Nine months from now, she would be holding a precious bundle in her arms.

Steve's and her child.

Chapter Four

With his hands cupped behind his head, Steve lay in bed and stared blindly at the dark ceiling. He couldn't sleep. For the past hour he hadn't even bothered to close his eyes. It wouldn't do any good; every time he did, the memory of Christmas Eve with Carol filled his mind.

Releasing a slow breath, he rubbed his hand down his face, hoping the action would dispel her image from his thoughts. It didn't work. Nothing did.

He had never intended to make love to her, and even now, ten days later, he wasn't sure how the hell it had happened. He continued to suffer from a low-grade form of shock. His thoughts had been in utter chaos since that night, and he wasn't sure how to respond to her or where their relationship was headed now.

What really distressed him, Steve realized, was that after everything that had happened between them, he could still want her so much. More than a week later and the memory of her leaning against the doorjamb in the kitchen, wearing his shirt–and nothing else–had the power to tighten his loins. Tighten his loins! He nearly laughed out loud; that had to be the understatement of the year.

When Carol had stood and held out her arms to him, he'd acted like a starving child offered candy, so eager he hadn't stopped to think about anything except the love she would give him. Any protest he'd made had been token. She'd volunteered, he'd accepted, and that should be the end of it.

But it wasn't.

Okay, so he wasn't a man of steel. Carol had always been his Achilles' heel, and he knew it. She knew it. In thinking over the events of that night, it was almost as though his ex-wife had planned everything. Her red dress with no bra, and that bit about placing decorations on the tree. She'd insisted on standing on the chair, stretching and exposing her thigh to him…his thoughts came to a skidding halt.

No.

He wasn't going to fall into that familiar trap of thinking Carol was using him, deceiving him. It did no good to wade into the muddy mire of anger, bitterness, regret and doubt.

He longed to repress the memory of Carol's warm and willing body in his arms. If only he could get on with his life. If only he could sleep.

He couldn't.

His sister, Lindy, had coffee brewed by the time Steve came out of his bedroom. She sat at the table, cradling a cup in one hand while holding a folded section of the *Post-Intelligencer* in the other.

"Morning." She glanced up and greeted him with a bright smile. Lately it seemed his sister was always smiling.

Steve mumbled something unintelligible as a means of reply. Her cheerfulness grated against him. He wasn't in the mood for good humor this morning. He wasn't in the mood for anything…with the possible exception of making love to Carol again, and that bit of insight didn't suit him in the least.

"It doesn't look like you had a good night's sleep, brother dearest."

Steve's frown deepened, and he gave his sister another noncommittal answer.

"I don't suppose this has anything to do with Carol?" She waited, and when he didn't answer, added, "Or the fact that you didn't come home Christmas Eve?"

"I came home."

"Sure, sometime the following morning."

Steve took down a mug from the cupboard and slapped it against the counter with unnecessary force. "Drop it, Lindy. I don't want to discuss Carol."

A weighted silence followed his comment.

"Rush and I've got almost everything ready to move into the new apartment," she offered finally, and the light tone of her voice suggested she was looking for a way to put their conversation back on an even keel. "We'll be out of here by Friday."

Hell, here he was snapping at Lindy. His sister didn't deserve to be the brunt of his foul mood. She hadn't done anything but mention the obvious. "Speaking of Rush, where is he?" Steve asked, forcing a lighter tone into his own voice.

"He had to catch an early ferry this morning," she said, and hesitated momentarily. "I'm happy, Steve, really happy. I was so afraid for a time that I'd made a dreadful mistake, but I know now that marrying Rush was the right thing to do."

Steve took a sip of coffee to avoid looking at his sister. What Lindy was actually saying was that she wanted him to find the same contentment she had. That wasn't possible for him now, and wouldn't be until he got Carol out of his blood.

And making love to her Christmas Eve hadn't helped.

"Well, I suppose I should think about getting dressed," Lindy said with a heavy dose of feigned enthusiasm. "I'm going to get some boxes so Rush and I can finish up the last of the packing."

"Where's your new apartment?" Steve had been so preoccupied with his own troubles that he hadn't thought to inquire until now.

As Lindy rattled off the address Steve's forehead furrowed into a brooding frown. His sister and Rush were moving less than a mile away from Carol's place. Great! That was the last thing he needed to hear.

Steve's day wasn't much better than his sleepless night had been. By noon he'd decided he could no longer avoid the inevitable. He didn't like it, but it was necessary.

He had to talk to Carol.

He was thankful the apartment was empty when he arrived home shortly after six. Not willing to test his good fortune, and half expecting Lindy or Rush to appear at any minute, he walked directly to the phone and punched out Carol's number as though punishing the telephone would help relieve some of his nervousness.

"Hello?" Carol's soft, lilting voice clawed at his abdomen.

"It's Steve."

A pregnant pause was followed by a slightly breathless "Hi."

"I was thinking we should talk."

"All right." She sounded surprised, pleased, uncertain. "When?"

Steve rotated his wrist and looked at the time. "What are you doing right now?"

She hesitated. "I…nothing."

Although slightly awkward, their conversation to this point had felt right to Steve. But the way she paused, as though searching for a delaying tactic, troubled him. Fiery arrows of doubt hit their mark and he said, "Listen, Carol, if you're 'entertaining' Todd, I'd prefer to stop by later."

The ensuing silence was more deafening than jungle drums pounding out a war chant.

It took her several seconds to answer him, and when she did, the soft voice that had greeted him was racked with pain. "You can come now."

Steve tightened his hold on the phone receiver in a punishing grip. He hated it when he talked to her like that. He didn't know who he was punishing: Carol or himself. "I'll be there in fifteen minutes."

Carol replaced the telephone in its cradle and battled down an attack of pain and tears. How dare Steve suggest Todd was there. Suddenly she was so furious with him that she could no longer stand in one place. She started pacing the living room floor like a raw recruit, taking five or six steps and then doing an abrupt about-face. And yet she was excited–even elated.

Steve had taken the initiative to contact her, and it proved that he hadn't been able to stop thinking about her, either.

Nothing had been right for her since Christmas Eve. Oh, she'd reached her objective–exceeded it. Everything had gone according to plan. Only Carol hadn't counted on the doubts and bewilderment that had followed their night of loving. Their short hours together brought back the memory of how good their lives had once been, how much they'd loved each other and how happy those first years were.

Since Christmas Eve, Carol had been crippled with "if onlys" and "what ifs," tossing around those weak phrases as though she expected them to alter reality. Each day it became more difficult to remember that Steve had divorced her, that he believed her capable of the worst kind of deception. One night in his arms and she was fool enough to be willing to forget all the pain of the past thirteen months.

Almost willing, she amended.

It took vindictive, destructive comments like the one he'd just made to remind her that they had a rocky road to travel if they hoped to salvage their relationship.

Before Steve arrived, Carol had time to freshen her makeup and run a brush through her thick blond hair. She paused to study her reflection in the mirror and wondered if he would ever guess her secret. She doubted it. If he couldn't read the truth in her eyes about Todd, then he wasn't likely to recognize her joy, or guess the cause.

Thinking about the baby helped lighten the weight of Steve's bitterness. Briefly she closed her eyes and imagined holding that precious bundle in her arms. A little girl, she decided, with dark brown eyes like Steve's and soft blond curls.

The mental picture of her child made everything seem worthwhile.

When the doorbell chimed, Carol was ready. She held the door open for Steve and even managed to greet him with a smile.

"I made coffee."

"Good." His answer was gruff, as though he were speaking to one of his enlisted men.

He followed her into the kitchen and stood silently as she poured them each a cup of coffee. When she turned around, she saw Steve standing with his hands in his pockets, looking unsettled and ill at ease.

"If you're searching for traces of Todd, let me tell you right now, you won't find any."

He had the good grace to look mildly chagrined. "I suppose I should apologize for that remark."

"I suppose I should accept." She pulled out a chair and sat.

Steve claimed the one directly across from her.

Neither spoke, and it seemed to Carol that an eternity passed. "You wanted to talk to me," she said, after what felt like two lifetimes.

"I'm not exactly sure what I want to say."

She smiled a little at that, understanding. "I'm not sure what I want to hear, either."

A hint of a grin bounced from his dark eyes. "Forgiving you for what happened with Todd…"

Carol bolted to her feet with such force that her chair nearly fell backward. "Forgiving me!" she demanded, shaking with outrage.

"Carol, please, I didn't come here to fight."

"Then don't start one. Don't come into my home and hurl insults at me. The one person in this room who should be seeking forgiveness is *you*!"

"Carol…"

"I should have known this wouldn't work, but like a lovesick fool I thought…I hoped you…" She paused, jerked her head around and rubbed the heels of her hands down her cheeks, erasing the telltale tears.

"Okay, I apologize. I won't mention Todd again."

She inhaled a wobbly breath and nodded, not trusting her voice, and sat back down.

Another awkward moment followed.

"I don't know what you've been thinking, or how you feel about…what happened," Steve said, "but for the past ten days, I've felt like a leaf caught in a windstorm. My emotions are in turmoil…I can't stop remembering how good it was between us, and how right it felt to have you in my arms again. My instincts tell me that night was a fluke, and best forgotten. I just wish to hell I could."

Carol bowed her head, avoiding eye contact. "I've been thinking the same thing. As you said when you left, we should chalk it up to the love and goodwill that's synonymous with the season. But the holidays are over and I can't stop thinking about it, either."

"The loving always was terrific, wasn't it?"

He didn't sound as though he wanted to admit even that much, as if he preferred to discount anything positive about their lives together. Carol understood the impulse. She'd done the same thing since their divorce; it helped ease the pain of the separation.

Grudgingly she nodded. "Unfortunately the lovemaking is only a small part of any marriage. I think Christmas Eve gave me hope that you and I might be able to work everything out. I'd like to resolve the past and find a way to heal the wounds." They'd been apart for over a year, but Carol's heart felt as bloodied and bruised as if their divorce had been decreed yesterday.

"God knows, I want to forget the past..."

Hope clamored in her breast and she raised her eyes to meet Steve's, but his gaze was as weary and doubtful as her own.

His eyes fell. "But I don't think I can. I don't know if I'll ever be able to get over finding Todd in our bedroom."

"He was in the shower," Carol corrected through clenched teeth. "And the only reason he was there was because the shower head in the other bathroom wasn't working properly."

"What the hell difference does it make?" Steve shouted. "He spent the night here. You've never bothered to deny that."

"But nothing happened...if you'd stayed long enough to ask Todd, he would have explained."

"If I'd stayed any longer, I would have killed him."

He said it with such conviction that Carol didn't doubt him. Long before, she'd promised herself she wouldn't defend her actions again. Todd had been her employer and her friend. She'd known Todd and his wife, Joyce, were having marital troubles. But she cared about them both and didn't want to get caught in the middle of their problems. Todd, however, had cast her there when he showed up on her doorstep, drunk out of his mind, wanting to talk. Alarmed, Carol had brought him inside and phoned Joyce, who suggested Todd sleep it off at Carol's house. It had seemed like a reasonable solution, although she wasn't keen on the idea. Steve was away and due back to Seattle in a couple of days.

But Steve had arrived home early–and assumed the worst.

The sadness that settled over her was profound, and when she spoke, her voice was little more than a whisper. "You tried and found me guilty on circumstantial evidence, Steve. For the first couple of weeks, I tried to put myself in your place...I could understand how you read the scene that morning, but you were wrong."

It looked for a moment as though he was going to argue with her. She could almost see the wheels spinning in his mind, stirring up the doubts, building skyscrapers on sand foundations.

"Other things started to add up," he admitted reluctantly, still not looking at her.

Carol could all but see him close his mind to common sense. It seemed that just when they were beginning to make headway, Steve would pull something else into their argument or make some completely ridiculous comment that made absolutely no sense to her. The last time they'd tried to discuss this in a reasonable, nonconfrontational manner, Steve had hinted that she'd been Todd's lover for months. He'd suggested that she hadn't been as eager to welcome him home from his last cruise, which was ridiculous. They may have had problems, but none had extended to the bedroom.

"What 'other things' do you mean now?" she asked, defeat coating her words.

He ignored her question. His mouth formed a cocky smile, devoid of amusement. "I will say one thing for ol' Todd–he taught you well."

She gasped at the unexpected pain his words inflicted.

Steve paled and looked away. "I shouldn't have said that–I didn't mean it."

"Todd did teach me," she countered, doing her best to keep her bottom lip from quivering. "He taught me that a marriage not based on mutual trust isn't worth the ink that prints the certificate. He taught me that it takes more than a few words murmured by a man of God to make a relationship work."

"That's not what I meant."

"I know what you meant. Your jealousy has you tied up in such tight knots that you're incapable of reasoning any of this out."

Steve ignored that comment. "I'm not jealous of Todd–he can have you if he wants."

Carol thought she was going to be sick to her stomach. Indignation filled her throat, choking off any possible reply.

Steve stood and walked across the kitchen, his hands knotted into fists at his sides. He closed his eyes briefly, and when he opened them, he looked like a stranger, his inner torment was so keen.

"I didn't mean that," he said unevenly. "I don't know why I say such ugly things to you."

Carol heard the throb of pain in her voice. "I don't know why you do, either. If you're trying to hurt me, then congratulations. You've succeeded beyond your expectations."

Steve stood silently a few moments, then delivered his untouched coffee to the sink. His hesitation surprised Carol. She'd assumed he would walk out–that was the way their arguments usually ended.

Instead he turned to face her and asked, "Are Todd and Joyce still married?"

She'd gotten a Christmas card from them a couple of weeks earlier. Until she'd seen both their names at the bottom of the greeting, she hadn't been sure if their marriage had weathered better than hers and Steve's. "They're still together."

Steve frowned and nodded. "I know that makes everything more difficult for you."

"Stop it, Steve!" This new list of questions irritated her almost as much as his tireless insinuations. "All the years we were married, not once did I accuse you of being unfaithful, even though you were gone half the time."

"It's difficult to find a woman willing to fool around 400 feet under water."

"That's not my point. I trusted you. I always did, and I assumed that you trusted me, too. That's all I've ever asked of you, all I ever wanted."

He was quiet for so long that Carol wondered if he'd chosen to ignore her rather than come up with an appropriate answer.

"You didn't discover another woman lounging around in a see-through nightie while I showered, either. You may be able to explain away some of what happened, but as far as I'm concerned there are gaping holes in your story."

Carol clenched her teeth so tightly that her jaw ached. She'd already broken a promise to herself by discussing Todd with Steve. When the divorce was final, Carol had determined then that no amount of justifying would ever satisfy her ex-husband. Discussing Todd had yet to settle a single problem, and in the end she only hurt herself.

"I don't think we're going to solve anything by rehashing this now," she told him calmly. "Unless our love is firmly grounded in a foundation of trust, there's no use even trying to work things out."

"It doesn't seem to be helping, does it? I wanted us—"

"I know," she interrupted softly, sadly. "I wanted it, too. The other night only served to remind us how much we'd loved each other."

They shared a discouraged smile, and Carol felt as though her heart was breaking in half.

He took a few steps toward the front door. "I'll be leaving in less than three weeks."

"How long will you be away?" For a long time she hadn't felt comfortable asking him this kind of question, but he seemed more open to discussion now.

"Three months." He buried his hands in his pockets and Carol got the impression that the action was to keep him from reaching for her and kissing her goodbye. He paused, turned toward her and said, "If you need anything…"

"I won't."

Her answer didn't appear to please him. "No, I don't suppose you will. You always could take care of yourself. I used to be proud of you for being so capable, but it intimidated me, too."

"What do you mean?"

He hedged, as if searching his reserve of memories to find the perfect example, then shook his head. "Never mind, it isn't important now."

Carol walked him to the front door, her heart heavy. "I wish it could be different for us."

"I do, too."

Steve stood, unmoving, in the entryway. Inches from him, Carol felt an inner yearning more potent than anything she'd ever experienced engulf her, filling her heart with regret. Once more she would have to watch the man she loved walk away from her. Once more she must freely allow him to go.

Steve must have sensed the intense longing, because he gently rested his hands on the curve of her shoulders. She smiled and tilted her chin toward him, silently offering him her mouth.

Slowly, without hurry, Steve lowered his face to hers, drawing out each second as though he were relaxing a hold on his considerable pride, admitting his need to kiss her. It was as if he had to prove, if only to himself, that he had control of the situation.

Then his mouth grazed hers. Lightly. Briefly. Coming back for more when it became apparent the teasing kisses weren't going to satisfy either of them.

What shocked Carol most was the gentleness of his kiss. He touched and held her as he would a delicate piece of porcelain, slipping his arms around her waist, drawing her close against him.

He broke off the kiss and Carol tucked her forehead against his chest. "Have a safe trip." Silently she prayed for his protection and that he would come back to her.

"If you want, I'll phone when I return. That is…if you think I should?"

Maybe she could tell him about the baby then, depending on how things went between them. "Yes, by all means, phone and let me know that you made it back in one piece."

His gaze centered on her mouth and again he bent his head toward her. This time his kiss was hungry, lingering, insistent. Carol whimpered when his tongue, like a soft flame, entered her mouth, sending hot sparks of desire shooting up her spine. Her knees weakened and she nearly collapsed when Steve abruptly released her.

"For once, maybe you could miss me," he said, with a sad note of bitterness.

The following morning, Carol woke feeling queasy. It'd been that way almost since Christmas morning. She reached for the two soda crackers on the nightstand and nibbled on them before climbing out of bed. Her hand rested lovingly on her flat stomach.

She'd wanted to schedule an appointment with the doctor, but the receptionist had told her to wait until her monthly cycle was a week late. She was only overdue by a day, but naturally she wouldn't be having her period. As far as Carol was concerned, another week was too long to wait, even if she was certain she bore the desired fruit from her night with Steve.

In an effort to confirm what she already knew, Carol had purchased a home-pregnancy test. Now she climbed out of bed, read the instructions through twice, did what the package told her and waited.

The waiting was the worst part. Thirty minutes had never seemed to take so long.

Humming a catchy tune, she dressed for work, poured herself a glass of milk, then went back to the bathroom to read the test results.

She felt so cocky, so sure of what the test would tell her that her heart was already pounding with excitement.

The negative reading claimed her breath. She blinked, certain she'd misread it.

Stunned, she sat on the edge of the bathtub and took several deep breaths. She started to tremble, and tears of disappointment filled her eyes. She must be pregnant–she had to be. All the symptoms were there–everything she'd read had supported her belief.

Once more she examined the test results.

Negative.

After everything she'd gone through, after all the sweet potatoes she'd forced down her throat, after the weeks of planning, the plotting, the scheduling…

There wasn't going to be any baby. There never had been. Her plan had failed.

There was only one thing left to do.

Try again.

Chapter Five

It took courage for Carol to drive to Steve's apartment. Someone should award medals for this brand of lionheartedness, she murmured to herself–although she was more interested in playing the role of a tigress than a lion. If this second venture was anything like the first, Steve wouldn't know what hit him. At least, she hoped he wouldn't guess.

She straightened her shoulders, pinched some color into her cheeks and pasted on a smile. Then she rang the doorbell.

To say Steve looked surprised to see her when he opened the door would be an understatement, Carol acknowledged. His eyes rounded, his mouth relaxed and fell open, and for a moment he was utterly speechless. "Carol?"

"I suppose I should have phoned first…"

"No, come in." He stepped aside so that she could enter the apartment.

Beyond his obvious astonishment, Carol found it difficult to read Steve's reaction. She stepped inside gingerly, praying that her plastic smile wouldn't crack. The first thing she noticed was the large picture window in the living room, offering an unobstructed view of the Seattle waterfront. It made Elliott Bay seem close, so vivid that she could almost smell the seaweed and feel the salty spray in the air. A large green-and-white ferry boat plowed its way through the dark waters, enhancing the picture.

"Oh...this is nice." Carol turned around to face him. "Have you lived here long?"

He nodded. "Rush had the apartment first. I moved in after you and I split and sort of inherited it when Rush and Lindy moved into their own place recently."

The last thing Carol wanted to remind him of was their divorce, and she quickly steered the conversation to the reason for her visit. "I found something I thought might be yours," she said hurriedly, fumbling with the snap of her eel-skin purse to bring out the button. It was a weak excuse, but she was desperate. Retrieving the small gray button from inside her coin purse, she handed it over to him.

Steve's brow pleated into a frown and he stiffened. "No... this isn't mine. It must belong to another man," he said coldly.

A bad move, Carol realized, taking back the button. "There's only been one man at my house, and that's you," she said, trying to stay calm. "If it isn't yours, then it must have fallen off something of my own."

Hands in his pockets, Steve nodded.

An uneasy pause followed.

Steve didn't suggest she take off her coat, didn't offer her any refreshment or any excuse to linger. Feeling crestfallen and defeated, Carol knew there was nothing more to do but leave.

"Well, I suppose I should think about getting myself some dinner. There's a new Mexican restaurant close to here I thought I might try," she said with feigned enthusiasm, and glanced up at him through thick lashes. Steve loved enchiladas, and she prayed he would take the bait. God knew, she couldn't have been any more obvious had she issued the invitation straight out.

"I ate earlier," he announced starkly.

Steve rarely had dinner before six. He was either wise to her ways or lying.

"I see." She took a step toward the exit, wondering what else she could do to delay the inevitable. "When does the *Atlantis* leave?"

"Monday."

Three days. She had only three days to carry out her plan. Three days to get him into bed and convince him it was all his idea. Three miserable days. Her fingers curled into impotent fists of frustration inside her coat pocket.

"Have a safe trip, Steve," she said softly. "I'll… I'll be thinking of you."

It had been a mistake to come to his place, a mistake not to have plotted the evening more carefully. It was apparent from the stiff way Steve treated her, he couldn't wait to get her out of his apartment. Since it was Friday night, he might have a date. The thought of Steve with another woman produced a gut-wrenching pain that she did her best to ignore. Dropping by unexpectedly like this wasn't helping her cause.

She'd hoped they could make love tonight. Her temperature was elevated and she was as fertile as she was going to get this month.

Swallowing her considerable pride, she paused, her hand on the door handle. "There's a new spy thriller showing at the Fifth Avenue Theater…. You always used to like espionage films."

Steve's eyes narrowed as he studied her. It was difficult for Carol to meet his heated gaze and not wilt from sheer nerves. She was sure her cheeks were hot pink. Coming to his apartment was the most difficult thing she'd done in years. Her heart felt as if it was going to hammer its way right out of her chest, and her fingers were shaking so badly that she didn't dare remove them from her pockets.

"Why are you here?" His question was soft, suspicious, uncertain.

"I found the button." One glance told her he didn't believe her, as well he shouldn't. That excuse was so weak it wouldn't carry feathers.

"What is it you *really* want, Carol?"

"I…I…" Her voice trembled from her lips, and her heart, which had been pounding so furiously a second before, seemed to stop completely. She swallowed and forced her gaze to meet his before dropping it. When she finally managed to speak, her voice was low and meaningful. "I thought with you going away…." Good grief, woman, her mind shouted, quit playing games. Give him the truth.

She raised her chin, and her gaze locked with his. "I'm not wearing any underwear."

Steve went stock-still, holding his jaw tight and hard. The inner conflict that played over his face was as vivid as the picturesque scene she'd viewed from his living-room window. The few feet of distance between them seemed to stretch wider than a mile.

It felt as if an eternity passed as Carol waited for his reaction, and she felt paralyzed with misgivings. She'd exposed her hand and left her pride completely vulnerable to him.

She saw it then–a flicker of his eyes, a movement in the line of his jaw, a softening in his tightly controlled facial features. He wanted her, too–wanted her with a desperation that made him as weak as she was. Her heart leaped wildly with joy.

Steve lifted his hand and held it out to her, and Carol thought she would collapse with relief as she hurried toward him. He crushed her in his arms and his mouth hungrily came down on hers. His eager lips smothered her cry of happiness. Equally greedy, Carol returned his kiss, reveling in his embrace. She twined her arms around his neck, her softness melding against the hardened contours of his body.

His hands tightened around her possessively, stroking her

spine, then lowered over the rounded firmness of her buttocks. He gathered her pelvis as close to him as was humanly possible.

"Dear God, I've gone crazy."

Carol raised her hands to frame his face and gazed lovingly into his eyes. "Me, too," she whispered before spreading a circle of light kisses over his forehead, chin and mouth.

"I shouldn't be doing this."

"Yes, you should."

Steve groaned and clasped her tighter. He kissed her, plunging his tongue into the sweet softness of her mouth, exploring it with a desperate urgency. Carol met his tongue with her own in a silent duel that left them both exhausted.

While they were still kissing, Steve unfastened the buttons of her coat, slipped it from her shoulders and dropped it to the floor. His hands clawed at the back of her skirt, lifting it away from her legs, then settled once again, cupping her bare bottom.

He moaned, his breath seemed to jam in his throat, and his eyes darkened with passion. "You weren't kidding."

Carol bit her lower lip as a wealth of sensation fired through her from the touch of his cool hands against her heated flesh. She rotated her lower body shamelessly against the rigid evidence of his desire.

His hands closed over her breasts and her nipples rose as though to greet him, to welcome him. His eager but uncooperative fingers fiddled with the fastenings of her blouse. Smiling, content but just as eager, Carol gently brushed his hands aside and completed the task for him. He pulled the silk material free of her waistline and disposed of it as effectively as he had her coat. Her breasts sprang to life in his hands and when he moaned, the sound of it excited her so much that it throbbed in her ears.

The moist heat of his mouth closed over her nipple and she gasped. The exquisite pleasure nearly caused her knees to buckle. Blood roared through her veins, and liquid fire scorched her until she was certain she would soon explode. She lifted one leg and wrapped it around his thigh, anchoring her weight against him.

Steve's fingers reached for her and instinctively she opened herself to him. He teased her womanhood, toyed with her, tormented her with delicate strokes that drove her over the brink. Within seconds, she tossed back her head and groaned as the pulsating climax rocked through her, sending out rippling waves of release.

By the time Steve carried her into his bedroom, Carol was panting. He didn't waste any time, discarding his clothes with an urgency that thrilled her. When he moved to the bed, his features were keen with desire.

Carol lifted her arms to welcome him, loving him with a tenderness that came from the very marrow of her bones.

Steve shifted his weight over her and captured her mouth in a consuming kiss that sent Carol down into a whirlpool of the sweetest oblivion. Anxious and eager, she parted her thighs for him and couldn't hold back a small cry as he sheathed himself inside her, slipping the proud heat of his manhood into her moist softness.

He waited, as though to prolong the pleasure and soak in her love before he started to move. The feelings that wrapped themselves around her were so incredible that Carol had to struggle to hold back the tears. With each delicious stroke the tension mounted and slowly, methodically began to uncurl within her until she was thrashing her head against his pillow and arching her hips to meet each plunging thrust.

Steve groaned and threw back his head, struggling to regain control, but soon he, too, was over the edge. When he cried out his voice harmonized with hers in a song that was as ageless as mankind.

Breathless, he collapsed on top of her. Her arms slipped around his neck and she buried her face in the hollow of his throat, kissing him, hugging him, needing him desperately. Tears slipped silently from the corners of her eyes. They spoke the words that she couldn't, eloquently telling him of all the love buried in her heart–words Carol feared she would never be able to voice again.

When Steve moved to lift himself off of her, she wouldn't let him. She held him tightly, her fingers gripping his shoulders.

"I'm too heavy," he protested.

"No…hold me."

With his arms wrapped around her, he rolled over, carrying her with him in one continuous motion until their positions were reversed.

Content for the moment, Carol pressed her ear over his chest, listening to the strong, steady beat of his heart.

Neither spoke.

His hand moved up and down her spine in a tender caress as though he had to keep touching her to know she was real. Her tears slid onto his shoulder, but neither mentioned it.

In her soul, Carol had to believe that something this beautiful would create a child. At this moment everything seemed perfect and healed between them, the way it had been two years before.

Gently Steve kissed her forehead, and she snuggled closer, flattening her hands over his chest.

He wrapped his arms around her and his thumb tenderly wiped the moisture from her cheek. Tucking his finger under her chin, he lifted it enough to find her mouth and kiss her. Sweetly.

"I tried, but I never could stop loving you," he whispered in a voice raw with emotion. "I hated myself for being so weak, but I don't anymore."

"I'll always love you," she answered. "I can't help myself. This year has been the worst of my entire life. I've felt as if I was trapped in a freezer, never able to get warm."

"No more," he said, his eyes trapping hers.

"No more," she agreed, and her heart leaped with unleashed joy.

They rested for a full hour, their legs entwined, their arms wrapped around each other. Every now and again, Steve would kiss her, his lips playing over hers. Then Carol would kiss him back, darting her tongue in and out of his mouth and doing all the things she knew he enjoyed. She raised herself up on her elbows and brushed a thick swatch of dark hair from his brow. It felt so good to be able to touch him this freely.

"What's the name of that Mexican restaurant you mentioned earlier?" Steve asked.

Carol smiled smugly. "You are so predictable."

"How's that?"

"Making love never fails to make you hungry!"

"True," he growled into her ear, "but often my appetite isn't for food." His index finger circled her nipple, teasing it to a rose-colored pebble. "I've got a year's worth of loving stored up for you, and the way you make me feel tonight, we may never leave this bedroom."

And they didn't.

Carol woke when Steve pressed a soft kiss on her lips.

"Hmm," she said, not opening her eyes. She smiled up at him, sated and unbelievably happy. She wore the look of a woman who loves wisely and who knows that her love is returned. "Is it morning yet?"

"It was morning the last time we made love." Steve laughed and leaned over to kiss her again, as if one sample wasn't nearly enough to satisfy him.

"It was?" she asked lazily. They'd slept intermittently, waking every few hours, holding and kissing each other. While asleep, Carol would roll over and forget Steve was at her side. Their discovery each time was worth far more than a few semiprecious hours of sleep. And Steve seemed equally excited about her being there with him.

"Currently," he said, dragging her back to reality, "it's going on noon."

"Noon!" She bolted upright. She'd been in her teens the last time she'd slept this late.

"I'm sorry to wake you, honey, but I've got to get to the sub."

Carol was surprised to see that he was dressed and prepared to leave. He handed her a fresh cup of coffee, which she readily took from him. "You'll be back, won't you?"

"Not until tomorrow morning."

"Will you…could you stop off and see me one more time, before you leave?"

His dark gaze caressed her. "Honest to God, Carol, I don't think I could stay away."

As Steve walked away from his parked car at the Navy base in Bangor, less than ten miles north of Bremerton, he was convinced his strut would put a rooster to shame. Lord, he felt good.

Carol had come to him, wanted him, loved him as much as he'd always loved and wanted her. All the world felt good to him.

For the first time since they'd divorced, he felt whole. He'd been a crazed fool to harp on the subject of Todd Larson to Carol. From this moment on, he vowed never to mention the other man's name again. Obviously whatever had been between the two was over, and she hadn't wanted Todd back. Okay, so she'd made a mistake. Lord knew, he'd committed his share, and a lot of them had to do with Carol. He'd been wrong to think he could flippantly cast her out of his life.

In his pain, he'd lashed out at her, acted like a heel, refused to have anything to do with her because of his foolish pride. But Carol had been woman enough to forgive him. He couldn't do anything less than be man enough to forget the past. The love they shared was too precious to muddy with doubts. They'd both made mistakes, and the time had come to rectify those and learn from them.

Dear God, he felt ready to soar. He shouldn't be on a nuclear submarine–a feeling this good was meant for rockets.

Carol found herself humming as she whipped the cream into a frothy topping for Steve's favorite dessert: French pudding. She licked her index finger, grinned lazily to herself and leaned her hip against the kitchen counter, feeling happier than she could remember being in a long time.

Friday night had been incredible. Steve had been incredible. The only cost had been her bruised pride when she'd arrived at his apartment with such a flimsy excuse. The price had been minor, the rewards major.

Not once during the entire evening had Steve mentioned Todd's name. Maybe, just maybe, he was ready to put that all behind them now.

If she was pregnant from their Friday night lovemaking, which she sincerely prayed she was, it would be best for the baby to know "her" father. Originally Carol had intended to raise the child without Steve. She wasn't sure she would ever have told him. Now the thought of suppressing the information seemed both childish and petty. But she wasn't going to use the baby as a convenient excuse for a reconciliation. They would settle matters first–then she would tell him.

Steve would make a good father; she'd watched him around children and had often been amazed by his patience. He'd wanted a family almost from the first. Carol had been the one who'd insisted on waiting, afraid she wouldn't be able to manage her job, a home and a baby with her husband away so much of the time, although she'd never admitted it to Steve. She knew how important it was for him to believe in her strength and independence. But this past year had matured her. Now she was ready for the responsibility.

Naturally hindsight was twenty-twenty, and she regretted having put off Steve's desire to start a family. The roots of their marriage might have been strong enough to withstand what had happened if there'd been children binding them together. But it did no good to second-guess fate.

Children. Carol hadn't dared think beyond one baby. But if she and Steve were to get back together–something that was beginning to look like a distinct possibility–then they could plan on having a houseful of kids!

It was early afternoon by the time Steve made it to Carol's house. A cold wind from the north whistled through the tops of the trees and the sky was darkening with a brewing storm.

Carol tossed aside her knitting and flew across the room the minute she heard a car door close, knowing it had to be Steve. By the time he was to the porch, she had the front door open for him.

He wore his uniform, which told her he hadn't stopped off at his apartment to change. Obviously he was eager to see her again, Carol thought, immeasurably pleased.

"I'm glad to see you're waiting for me," he said, and his words formed a soft fog around his mouth. He took the steps two at a time and rubbed his bare hands together.

"I can't believe how cold it is." Carol pulled him inside the house and closed the door.

His gaze sought hers. "Warm me, then."

She didn't require a second invitation, and stood on the tips of her toes to kiss him, leaning her weight into his. Steve wrapped her in his embrace, kissing her back greedily, as if they had been apart six weeks instead of a single day. When he finished, they were both breathless.

"It feels like you missed me."

"I did," she assured him. "Give me your coat and I'll hang it up for you."

He gave her the thick wool jacket and strolled into the living room. "What's this?" he asked, looking at her knitting.

Carol's heart leaped to her throat. "A baby blanket."

"For who?"

"A...friend." She considered herself a friend, so that was at least a half-truth. She'd been working on the blanket in her spare time since before Christmas. It had helped her feel as if she was doing something constructive toward her goal.

Suddenly she felt as if she had a million things to tell him. "I got energetic and cleaned house. I don't know what's wrong with me lately, but I don't have the energy I used to have."

"Have you been sick?"

She loved him for the concern in his voice. "No, I'm in perfect health...I've just been tired lately...not getting enough vitamins, I suppose. But it doesn't matter now because I feel fantastic, full of ambition–I even made you French pudding."

"Carol, I think you should see a doctor."

"And if he advises bed rest, do you promise to, er...rest with me?"

"Good heavens, woman, you've become insatiable."

"I know." She laughed and slipped her arm around his waist. "I was always that way around you."

"Always?" he teased. "I don't seem to recall that."

"Then I'll just have to remind you." She steered him toward the bedroom, crawled onto the mattress and knelt there. "If you want French pudding, fellow, you're going to have to work for it."

The alarm went off at six. Carol blindly reached out and, after a couple of wide swipes, managed to hit the switch that would turn off the electronic beeping.

Steve stirred at her side. "It's time," she said in a small, sad voice. This would be their last morning together for three months.

"It's six already?" Steve moaned.

"I'm afraid so."

He reached for her and brought her close to his side. His hand found hers and he laced her fingers with his. "Carol, listen, we only have a little time left and there's so much I should have said, so much I wanted to tell you."

"I wanted to talk to you, too." In all the years they were married, no parting had been less welcome. Carol yearned to wrap her arms around him and beg him not to leave her. It was times like this that she wished Steve had chosen a career outside the Navy. In a few hours he would sail out of Hood Canal, and she wouldn't hear from him for the entire length of his deployment. Other than hearsay, Carol wasn't even to know where he would be sailing. For reasons of national security, all submarine deployments were regarded as top secret.

"When I return from this tour, Carol, I'd like us to have a serious talk about getting back together. I know I've been a jerk, and you deserve someone better, but I'd like you to think about it while I'm away. Will you do that for me?"

She couldn't believe how close she was to breaking into tears. "Yes," she whispered. "I'll think about it very seriously. I want everything to be right…the second time."

"I do, too." He raised her hand to his mouth and kissed her knuckles. "Another thing…make an appointment for a physical. I don't remember you being this thin."

"I lost fifteen pounds when we were divorced; I can't seem to gain it back." The tears broke through the surface and she sobbed out the words, ending in a hiccup. Embarrassed, she pressed her fingertips over her lips. "I've been a wreck without you, Steve Kyle…I suppose it makes you happy to know how miserable and lonely this past year has been."

"I was just as miserable and lonely," he admitted. "We can't allow anything to do this to us again. I love you too damn much to spend another year like the last one." His touch was so tender, so loving that she melted into his embrace.

"You have to trust me, Steve. I can't have you coming back and even suspecting I'd see another man."

"I know…I do trust you."

She closed her eyes at the relief his words gave her. "Thank you for that."

He kissed her then and, with a reluctance that tore at her heart, pulled away from her and started to dress.

She reached for her robe, not looking at him as she slipped her arms into the long sleeves. "If we do decide to make another go at marriage, I'd like to seriously think about starting a family right away. What would you say to that?"

Steve hesitated. Carol turned around to search out his gaze in the stirring light of early morning, and the tender look he wore melted any lingering doubts she harbored.

"Just picturing you with my child in your arms," he whispered hoarsely, "is enough to keep me going for the next three months."

Chapter Six

A week after Steve sailed, Carol began experiencing symptoms that again suggested she was pregnant. The early morning bouts of nausea returned. She found herself weeping over a rerun of *Magnum, P.I.* And she was continually tired, feeling worn-out at the end of the day. Everything she was going through seemed to point in one direction.

Self-diagnosis, however, had misled her a month earlier, and Carol feared her burning desire to bear a child was dictating her body's response a second time.

Each morning she pressed a hand over her stomach and whispered a fervent prayer that her weekend of lovemaking with Steve had found fertile ground. If she wasn't pregnant, then it would be April before they could try again, and that seemed like a thousand years away.

Carol was tempted to hurry out and buy another home pregnancy test. Then she would know almost immediately if her mind was playing tricks on her or if she really was pregnant. But she didn't. She couldn't explain—even to herself—

why she was content to wait it out this time. If her monthly cycle was a week late, she decided, then and only then would she make an appointment with her doctor. But until that time she was determined to be strong–no matter what the test results said.

The one thing that astonished Carol the most was that in the time since Steve's deployment she missed him dreadfully. For months she'd done her utmost to drive every memory of that man from her mind, and sometimes she'd succeeded. Since Christmas, however, thoughts of Steve had dominated every waking minute. Until their weekend, Carol had assumed that was only natural. Steve Kyle did play a major role in her scheme to get pregnant. But she considered having a baby more of a bonus now. The possibility of rebuilding her marriage–which she had once considered impossible to do–claimed precedence.

Missing Steve wasn't a new experience. Carol had always felt at loose ends when he was aboard the *Atlantis.* But never had she felt quite like this. Nothing compared to the emotion that wrapped itself around her heart when she thought about Steve on this tour. She missed him so much that it frightened her. For more than a year she'd lived in the house alone; now it felt like an empty shell because he wasn't there. In bed at night her longing for him grew even more intense. She lay with her eyes closed, savoring the memory of their last two nights together. A chill washed over her at how close they'd come to destroying the love between them. The only thing that seemed to lessen this terrible longing she felt for her ex-husband was constructing dreams that involved him to help ease the loneliness as she drifted off to sleep.

Friday morning Carol woke feeling rotten and couldn't seem to force herself out of bed. She pulled into the huge Boeing parking lot at the Renton plant ten minutes later than usual and hurriedly locked her car. She was walking toward her building, trying to find the energy to rush when she heard someone call out her name.

She turned, but didn't see anyone she recognized.

"Carol, is that you?"

"Lindy?" Carol could hardly believe her eyes. It was Steve's sister. "What are you doing here?"

"I was just about to ask you the same thing."

Lindy looked fantastic. It had been nearly two years since Carol had last seen her former sister-in-law. Lindy had been a senior in college at the time, girlish and fun loving that summer she and Steve had visited his family. Had that been only two summers ago? It felt as though a decade had passed. Lindy had always held a special place in Carol's heart, and she smiled and hugged her close. When she drew back, Carol was surprised at the new maturity Lindy's eyes revealed.

"I work here," Lindy said, squeezing Carol's fingers. "I have since this past summer."

"Me, too–for over a year now."

Lindy tossed the sky a chagrined look. "You mean to tell me we've been employed by the same company, working at the same plant, and we didn't even know it?"

Carol laughed. "It looks that way."

They started walking toward the main entrance, still bemused, laughing and joking like long-lost sisters…which they were of sorts.

"I'm going to kick Steve," Lindy muttered. "He didn't tell me you worked for Boeing."

"He doesn't know. I suppose he assumes I'm still at Larson's Sporting Goods. I quit…long before the divorce was final. We haven't talked about my job, and I didn't think to mention it."

"How are you?" Lindy asked, but didn't give her more than a second to respond. "Steve growls at me every time I mention your name, which by the way, tells me he's still crazy about you."

Carol needed to hear that. She grinned, savoring the warm feeling Lindy's words gave her. "I'm still crazy about him, too."

"Oh, Carol," Lindy said with a giant sigh. "I can't tell you how glad I am to hear that. Steve never told any of us why the two of you divorced, but it nearly destroyed him. I can't tell you how happy I was when you phoned last Christmas. He hasn't been the same since."

"The divorce was wrong…. We should never have gone through with it," Carol said softly. Steve had been the one who had insisted on ending their marriage, and Carol had been too hurt, too confused to fight him the way she should have. Not wanting to linger on the mistakes of the past, Carol added, "Steve told me about you and Rush. Congratulations."

"Thanks." Lindy's eyes softened at the mention of Rush's name, and translucent joy radiated from her smile. "You met Paul didn't you?"

Carol nodded, recalling the time she had been introduced to Lindy's ex-fiance in Minneapolis. She hadn't been overly impressed by him and, as she recalled, neither had Steve.

"He married…someone else," Lindy explained. "I was devastated, convinced my life was over. That's how I ended up in Seattle. I'm so happy I moved here. Paul did me the biggest favor of my life when he dumped me; I found Rush and we were meant to be together–we both know it."

Hold on to that feeling, Carol mused, saddened that she'd been foolish enough to allow Steve to walk away from her. It had been a mistake, and one they'd both paid for dearly. "I'm really pleased for you, Lindy," she said sincerely.

"Thank you…oh, Carol, I can't tell you how good it is to see you again."

They paused once they passed the security gate, delaying their parting. "What area are you working in?" Carol asked, stopping. The others flooding through the entrance gate walked a wide circle around them.

"Section B."

"F for me." Which meant they were headed in opposite directions.

"Perhaps we could meet for lunch one day," Lindy suggested, anxiously glancing at her watch.

"I'd like that. How about next Tuesday? I can't until then, I'm involved with a special project."

"Great. Call me. I'm on extension 314."

"Will do."

Steve walked past the captain's quarters and through the narrow hallway to his stateroom. Tired, he sat on the edge of his berth and rubbed his hand across his eyes. This was his favorite time of day. His shift was complete, and he had about an hour to kill before he thought about catching some sleep. For the past several days, he'd been writing Carol. His letter had become a journal of his thoughts. Chances were that he would be home long before the letter arrived. Because submarines spent their deployment submerged, there were few opportunities for the pickup or delivery of mail. Any emergencies were handled by radio transmission. There were occasions when they could receive mail, but it wasn't likely to happen this trip.

Steve felt good. From the moment his and Carol's divorce had been declared final, he'd felt as if he'd steered his life off course. He'd experienced the first turbulent storm and, instead of riding it out as he should have, he'd jumped overboard. Ever since, he'd felt out of sync with his inner self.

In his letter, he'd tried to explain that to Carol, but putting it in words had been as difficult as admitting it had been.

He didn't know what had happened between Todd and Carol. Frankly he didn't want to know. Whatever had been between them was over and Steve could have her back. Lord knew he wanted her. He was destined to go to his grave loving that woman.

When he'd sailed out of Hood Canal and into the Pacific Ocean, Steve had felt such an indescribable pull to the land. He loved his job, loved being a part of the Navy, but at that moment he would have surrendered his commission to have been able to stay in Seattle another month.

Although he'd told Carol that they should use this time apart to consider a reconciliation, he didn't need two seconds to know his own mind: he wanted them to remarry.

But first they had to talk, really talk, and not about Todd. There were some deep-rooted insecurities he'd faced the past couple of weeks that needed to be discussed.

One thing that had always bothered Steve was the fact that Carol had never seemed to need him. His peers continually related stories about how things fell apart at home while they were deployed. Upon their return, after the usual hugs and kisses, their wives handed them long lists of repairs needed around the house or relayed tales of horror they'd been left to deal with in their husband's absence.

Not Carol. She'd sent him off to sea, wearing a bright smile and greeted him with an identical one on his return. The impression she gave him was that it was great when he was home, but was equally pleasant if he wasn't.

Her easy acceptance of his life-style both pleased and irritated Steve. He appreciated the strength of her personality, and yet a small part of him wished she weren't quite so strong. He wasn't looking for a wife who was a clinging vine, but occasionally he wished for something less than Carol's sturdy oak-tree character. Just once he would have liked to hear her tell him how dreadful the weeks had been without him, or how she'd wished he'd been there to take care of the broken dryer or to change the oil in the car.

Instead she'd given him the impression that she'd been having a grand ol' time while he was at sea. She chatted about the classes she took, or how her herb garden was coming along. If he quizzed her about any problems, she brushed off his concern and assured him she'd already dealt with whatever turned up.

Steve knew Carol wasn't that involved in the Navy-wife activities. He figured it was up to her whether or not she joined. He hadn't pressed her, but he had wished she would make the effort to form friendships with the wives of his close friends.

Carol's apparent strength wasn't the only thing that troubled Steve, but it was one thing he felt they needed to discuss. The idea of telling his ex-wife that the least she could do was shed a few tears when he sailed away from her made him feel ungrateful. But swallowing his pride would be a small price to pay to straighten matters between them.

What she'd said about wanting a baby right away made him feel soft inside every time he thought about it. He'd yearned for them to start a family long before now, but Carol had always wanted to wait. Now she appeared eager. He didn't question her motivation. He was too damned grateful.

A knock on his door jerked his attention across the room. "Yes?"

Seaman Layle stepped forward. "The Captain would like to see you, sir."

Steve nodded and said, "I'll be right there."

Carol sat at the end of the examination table, holding a thin piece of tissue over her lap. The doctor would be in any minute to give her the news she'd been waiting to hear for the past month. Okay, so her period was two weeks late. There could be any number of reasons. For one thing, she'd been under a good deal of stress lately. For another…

Her thoughts came to a grinding halt as Dr. Stewart stepped into the room. His glasses were perched on the end of his nose and his brow compressed as he read over her chart.

"Well?" she asked, unable to disguise the trembling eagerness in her voice.

"Congratulations, Carol," he said, looking up with a grandfatherly smile. "You're going to be a mother."

Chapter Seven

Carol was almost afraid to believe what Dr. Stewart was telling her; her hand flew to her heart. "You mean, I'm pregnant?"

The doctor looked up at her over the edge of his bifocals. "This is a surprise?"

"Oh, no…I knew–or at least I thought I knew." The joy that bubbled through her was unlike anything she had ever known. Ready tears blurred her vision and she bit her lower lip to hold back the tide that threatened to overwhelm her.

The doctor took her hand and gently patted it. "You're not sure how you feel–is that it?"

"Of course I do," she said, in a voice half an octave higher than usual. "I'm so happy I could just…"

"Cry?" he inserted.

"Dance," she amended. "This is the most wonderful thing that's ever happened to me since…"

"Your high-school prom?"

"Since I got married. I'm divorced now, but… Steve, he's my ex-husband, will marry me again…at least, I think he will.

I'm not going to tell him about this right away. I don't want him to marry me again just because of the baby. I won't say a word about this. Or maybe I should? I don't know what to do, but thank you, Doctor, thank you so much."

A fresh smile began to form at the edges of his mouth. "You do whatever you think is best. Now, before we discuss anything else I want to go over some key points with you."

"Oh, of course, I'll do anything you say. I'll quit smoking and give up junk food, and take vitamins. If you really think it's necessary, I'll try to eat liver once a week."

His gaze reviewed her chart. "It says here you don't smoke."

"No, I don't, but I'd start just so I could quit if it would help the baby."

He chuckled. "I don't think that will be necessary, young lady."

Carol reached for his hand and pumped it several times. "I can't tell you how happy you've made me."

Still chuckling, the white-haired doctor said, "Tell me the same thing when you're in labor and I'll believe you."

Carol watched as Lindy entered the restaurant and paused to look around. Feeling a little self-conscious, she raised her hand. Lindy waved back and headed across the floor, weaving her way through the crowded tables.

"Hi. Sorry, I'm late."

"No problem." The extra time had given Carol a chance to study the menu. Her stomach had been so finicky lately that she had to be careful what she ate. This being pregnant was serious business and already the baby had made it clear "she" wasn't keen on particular foods–especially anything with tomatoes.

"Everything has been so hectic lately," Lindy said, picking up the menu, glancing at it and setting it aside almost immediately.

"That was quick," Carol commented, nodding her head toward the menu.

"I'm a woman who knows my own mind."

"Good for you," Carol said, swallowing a laugh. "What are you having?"

"I don't know. What are you ordering?"

"Soup and a sandwich," Carol answered, not fooled. Lindy wasn't interested in eating, she wanted answers. Steve's sister had been bursting with questions from the moment they'd met in the Boeing parking lot.

"Soup and a sandwich sounds good to me," Lindy said, obviously not wanting to waste time with idle chitchat.

Shaking her head, Carol studied Lindy. "Okay, go ahead and ask. I know you're dying to fire away."

Lindy unfolded the napkin and took pains spreading it over her lap. "Steve didn't come home Christmas Eve.... Well, he did, but it was early in the morning, and ever since that night he's been whistling 'Dixie.'" She paused and grinned. "Yet every time I said your name, he barked at me to mind my own business."

"We've seen each other since Christmas, too."

"You have?" Lindy pinched her lips together and sadly shook her head. "That brother of mine is so tight-lipped, I can't believe the two of us are related!"

Carol laughed. Unwittingly Lindy had pinpointed the crux of Carol and Steve's marital problems. They were each private people who preferred to keep problems inside rather than talking things out the way they should.

"So you've seen Steve since Christmas," Lindy prompted. "He must have contacted you after Rush and I moved."

"Actually I was the one who went to him."

"You did? Great."

"Yes," Carol nodded, blushing a little at the memory of how they'd spent that weekend. "It *was* great."

"Well, don't keep me in suspense here. Are you two going to get back together or what?"

"I think it's the 'or what.'"

"Oh." Lindy's gaze dropped abruptly and she frowned. "I don't mind telling you, I'm disappointed to hear that. I'd hoped you two would be able to work things out."

"We're heading in that direction, so don't despair. Steve and I are going to talk about a reconciliation when he returns."

"Oh, Carol, that's wonderful!"

"I think so, too."

"You two always seemed so right together. The first time I saw Steve after you were divorced, I could hardly recognize him. He was so cynical and unhappy. He'd sit around the apartment and watch television for hours, or stare out the window."

"Steve did?" Carol couldn't imagine that. Steve always had so many things going–he'd never taken the time to relax when they were living together. Another problem had been that they didn't share enough of the same interests. Carol blamed herself for that, but she was willing to compromise now that her marriage was about to have new life breathed into it.

"I wasn't joking when I told you he's been miserable. I don't know what prompted you to contact him at Christmastime, but I thank God you did."

Carol smoothed her hand across her abdomen and smiled almost shyly. "I'm glad I did, too."

Steve's letter to Carol was nearly fifty pages in length now. The days, as they often did aboard a submarine, blended together. It felt as if they were six months into this cruise instead of two, but his eagerness to return to Carol explained a good deal of this interminable feeling.

Carol. His heart felt as though it would melt inside his chest every time he thought about her mentioning a baby.

The first thing he was going to do after they'd talked was throw out her birth control pills. And then he was going to take her to bed and make slow, easy love to her.

Once he had her back, he wasn't going to risk losing her again.

In the past two months, Steve had made another decision. They needed to clear the air about Todd Larson. He'd promised her that he wouldn't mention the other man's name again, but he had to, just once, and then it would be finished. Laid to rest forever.

Finding Todd in their shower hadn't been the only thing that had led Steve to believe Carol and her employer were having an affair. There had been plenty of other clues. Steve just hadn't recognized them in the beginning.

For one, she'd been working a lot of overtime, and didn't seem to be getting paid for it. At first Steve hadn't given it much credence, although he'd been angry that often she couldn't see him off to sea properly. At the time, however, she'd seemed as sorry about it as he was.

His return home after a ten-week absence had been the real turning point. Until that tour, Carol had always been eager to make love after so many weeks apart. Normally they weren't in the house ten minutes before they found themselves in the bedroom. But not that time. Carol had greeted him with open arms, but she'd seemed reluctant to hurry to bed. He had gotten what he wanted, but fifteen minutes later she'd made some silly excuse about needing groceries and had left the house.

None of these events had made much sense at the time. Steve had suspected something might be wrong, but he hadn't known how to ask her, how to approach her without sounding like an insecure schoolboy. Soon afterward he'd flown east for a two-week communication class. It was when he'd arrived home unexpectedly early that he'd found Carol and Todd together.

The acid building up in his stomach seemed to explode with pain and Steve took in several deep breaths until the familiar ache passed. All these months he'd allowed Carol to believe he'd condemned her solely because he'd discovered another man in their home. It was more than that, much more, and it was time he freed his soul.

"Carol? Are you here?"

Carol remained sitting on the edge of the bathtub and pressed her hand over her forehead. "I'm in here." Her voice sounded weak and sick–which was exactly how she felt. The doctor had given her a prescription to help ease these dreadful bouts of morning sickness, but it didn't seem to be doing much good.

"Carol?" Once more Lindy's voice vibrated down the hallway and Carol heard the sound of approaching footsteps. "Carol, what's wrong? Should I call a doctor?"

"No…no, I'll be fine in a minute. My stomach has been a little queasy lately, is all."

"You look awful."

"I can't look any worse than I feel." Her feeble attempt at humor apparently didn't impress Lindy.

"I take it the sale at the Tacoma Mall doesn't interest you?"

"I tried to call," Carol explained, "but you'd already left. You go ahead without me."

"I'll do no such thing," Lindy answered vehemently. "You need someone to take care of you. When was the last time you had a decent meal?"

Carol pressed her hand over her stomach. "Please, don't even mention food."

"Sorry."

Lindy helped her back into a standing position and led her down the hallway to her bedroom. Carol was ashamed to have Steve's sister see the house when it looked as if a cyclone had gone through it, but she'd had so little energy lately. Getting to work and home again drained her. She went to bed almost immediately after dinner and woke up exhausted the next morning.

No one had told her being pregnant could be so demanding on her health. She'd never felt more sickly in her life. Her appointment with Dr. Stewart wasn't for another two weeks, but something had to be done. She couldn't go on like this much longer.

The April sun seemed to smile down on Steve as he stepped off the *Atlantis.* He paused and breathed in the glorious warmth of afternoon in the Pacific Northwest. Carol wouldn't be waiting for him, he knew. She had no way of knowing when he docked.

But she needn't come to him. He was going to her. The minute he got home, showered and shaved, he was driving over to her house. He was so ready for this.

They were going to talk, make love and get married. Maybe not quite that simply, but close.

He picked up his mail and let himself into the apartment. Standing beside the phone, he listened to the messages on his answering machine. Three were from Lindy, who insisted he call first thing when he returned home.

He reached for the phone while he flipped through his assorted mail.

"You rang?" he asked cheerfully, when his sister answered.

"Steve? I'm so glad you called."

"What's wrong? Has Rush decided he's made a terrible mistake and decided to give you back to your dear, older brother to straighten out?" His sister didn't have an immediate comeback or a scathing reply, which surprised him.

"Steve, it's Carol."

His blood ran cold with fear. "What happened?"

"I don't know, but I wanted to talk to you before you went to see her," she said and hesitated. "You were planning on going there right away, weren't you?"

"Yes. Now tell me what's the matter with Carol."

"She's been sick."

"How sick?" His heart was thundering against his chest with worry.

"I… don't think it's anything…serious, but I thought I should warn you before you surprise her with a visit. She's lost weight and looks terrible, and she'll never forgive you if you show up without warning her you're in town."

"Has she seen a doctor?"

"I…don't know," Lindy confessed. "She won't talk about it."

"What the hell could be wrong?"

The line seemed to vibrate with electricity. "If you want the truth, I suspect she's pregnant."

Chapter Eight

"Pregnant?" Steve repeated and the word boomeranged against the walls of his mind with such force that the mail he'd been sorting slipped from his fingers and fell to the floor. He said it again. "Pregnant. But…but…"

"I probably shouldn't have said anything." Lindy's soft voice relayed her confusion. "But honestly, Steve, I've been so worried about her. She looks green around the gills and she's much too thin to be losing so much weight. I told her she should see a doctor, but she just smiles and says there's nothing to worry about."

The wheels in Steve's mind were spinning fast. "The best thing I can do is talk to her, and find out what's happening."

"Do that, but for heaven's sake be gentle with her. She's too fragile for you to come at her like Hulk Hogan."

"I wouldn't do that."

"Steve, I'm your sister. I know you!"

"Okay, okay. I'll talk to you later." He hung up the phone but kept his hand on the receiver while he mulled over his sister's news. Carol had said she wanted to have a baby, and she knew how he felt about the subject. He'd longed for a family since the first year they were together.

However, they weren't married now. No problem. Getting remarried was a minor detail. All he had to do was talk to the chaplain and make the arrangements. And if what Lindy said was true, the sooner he saw the chaplain, the better.

Without forethought he jerked the receiver off the hook and jabbed out Carol's number with his index finger. After two rings, he decided this kind of discussion was better done in person.

He showered, changed clothes and was halfway out the door when he remembered what Lindy had said about letting Carol know he was coming. Good idea.

He marched back over to the phone and dialed her number one more time.

No answer.

"Damn." He started pacing the floor, feeling restless, excited and nervous. He couldn't stay in the apartment; the walls felt as if they were closing in on him. He'd spent the last three months buried in the belly of a nuclear submarine and hadn't experienced a twinge of claustrophobia. Twenty minutes inside his apartment, knowing what he now did, and he was going ape.

He had to get out there even if it meant parking outside Carol's house and waiting for her to return.

He rushed out to his car and was grateful when it started right away after sitting for three months.

He was going to be a father! His heart swelled with joy and he experienced such a sense of elation that he wanted to throw back his head and shout loud enough to bring down brick walls.

A baby. His and Carol's baby. His throat thickened with emotion, and he had to swallow several times to keep from breaking down and weeping right there on the freeway. A new life. They were going to bring a tiny little being into this world and be accountable for every aspect of the infant's life. The responsibility seemed awesome. His hands gripped the steering wheel and he sucked in a huge breath as he battled down his excitement and fears.

He was going to be a good father. Always loving and patient. Everything would be right for his son…or daughter. Male chauvinist that he was, he yearned for a son. They could have a daughter the second time, but the thought of Carol giving him a boy felt right in his mind.

But he had so much to learn, so much to take care of. First things first. Steve tried to marshal his disjointed thoughts. He had to see to Carol's health. If this pregnancy was as hard on her as Lindy implied, then he wanted Carol to quit her job. He made good money; she should stay home and build up her strength.

The drive to Carol's house took less than fifteen minutes, and when Steve pulled up and parked he noticed her car in the driveway with the passenger door opened. His heart felt like it was doing jumping jacks, he was so eager to see her.

The front door opened and Carol stepped outside and to her car, grabbing a bag of groceries.

"Carol." She hadn't seen him.

She turned abruptly at the sound of her name. "Steve," she cried out brokenly and dropped the brown shopping bag. Without the least bit of hesitation, she came flying across the lawn.

He met her halfway, and wrapping his arms around her waist, he closed his eyes to the welcome feel of her body against his. His happiness couldn't be contained and he swung her around. Her lips were all over his face, kissing him, loving him, welcoming him.

Steve drank in her love and it humbled him. He held her gently, fearing he would hurt her, and kissed her with an aching tenderness, his mouth playing over the dewy softness of hers.

His hands captured her face and her deep blue eyes filled with tears as she smiled tremulously at him. "I've missed you so much. These have been the longest three months of my life."

"Mine, too." His voice nearly choked, and he kissed her again in an effort to hide the tide of emotion he was experiencing.

Steve picked up the scattered groceries for her and they walked into the house together.

"Go ahead and put those in the kitchen. Are you hungry?"

She seemed nervous and flittered from one side of the room to the other.

"I could fix you something if you'd like," she suggested, her back braced against the kitchen counter.

Steve's eyes held hers, and the emotion that had rocked him earlier built with intensity every minute he was in her presence. "You know what I want," he whispered, hardly able to speak.

Carol relaxed, and blushed a little. "I want to make love with you so much."

He held his hands out to her and she walked toward him, locking her arms around his neck. She pressed her weight against him and Steve realized how slender she was, how fragile. Regret slammed into his chest with all the force of a wrecking ball against a concrete wall. She was nurturing his child within her womb, for God's sake, and all he could think about was getting her into bed. He hadn't even asked her how she was feeling. All he cared about was satisfying his own selfish lusts.

"Carol…" His breath was slow and labored. Gently he tried to break free, because he couldn't think straight when she was touching him.

"Hmm?" Her hands were already working at his belt buckle, and her mouth was equally busy.

He felt himself weakening. "Are you sure? I mean, if you'd rather not…"

She released his zipper and when her hands closed around his naked hardness, he thought he would faint. His eyes rolled toward the ceiling. "Don't…don't you think we should talk?" he managed to say.

"No."

"But–"

She broke away and looked up at him, her eyes hungry with demand. "Steven Kyle, what is your problem? Do you or do you not want to make love?"

"I think…we should probably talk first. Don't you?" He didn't know if she would take him seriously with his voice shaking the way it was.

She grinned, and when her gaze dropped to below his waistline, they rounded. "No. Because neither one of us is going to be able to say anything worth listening to until we take care of other things…."

It wasn't possible to love a woman any more than he did Carol at that moment, Steve thought. She reached for his hand and led him out of the kitchen and into the bedroom.

Like a lost sheep, he followed.

The newborn moon cast silvery shadows on the wall opposite the bed, and Steve sighed, feeling sated and utterly content. Carol slept at his side, her arm draped around his middle and her face nestled against his shoulder. Her tousled hair fell over his chest and he ran his fingers through it, letting the short, silky length slip through his hands.

Gently he brushed a blond curl off her cheek and twisted his head so that he could kiss her temple. She stirred and sighed in her sleep. He grinned. If he searched for a hundred years he would never find a woman who could satisfy him the way Carol did.

They hadn't talked, hadn't done anything but make love until they were both so exhausted that sleep dominated their minds. They may not have voiced the words, but the love between them was so secure it would take more than a bulldozer to rock it this time. Steve may not have had a chance to say the words, but his heart had been speaking them from the minute Carol had led him to bed.

Bringing the blanket more securely over her shoulders, he wrapped his arm around her and studied her profile in the fading moonlight. What Lindy told him was true. Carol had lost weight; she was as slender as a bamboo shoot, and much too pale. She needed someone to take care of her and, he vowed in his heart, he would be the one.

He almost wished she would roll over so that he could place his hand on her abdomen and feel for himself the life that was blossoming there. He felt weak with happiness every time he thought about their baby. He closed his eyes at the sudden longing that seared through his blood.

Carol hadn't yet told him that she was pregnant but he was sure she would in the morning. Until then, he would be content.

He closed his eyes and decided to sleep.

Steve woke first. Carol didn't so much as stir when he climbed out of bed and reached for his clothes. Silently he tiptoed out of the room and gently closed the door. She needed her sleep.

He made himself a pot of coffee and piddled around the kitchen, putting away the groceries that had been sitting on the counter all night. He pulled open the vegetable bin and carelessly tossed a head of lettuce in there. The drawer refused to close and he discovered the problem to be a huge shriveled up sweet potato. He took it out and, with an over the head loop shot Michael Jordan would have envied, tossed it into the garbage.

Carol and sweet potatoes. Honestly. The last time he'd looked inside her refrigerator, it had been filled with the stuff in every imaginable form.

He supposed he should get used to that kind of thing. It

was a well-known fact that women often experienced weird food cravings when they were pregnant. Sweet potatoes were only one step above pickles and ice cream.

Just a minute! That had been last Christmas…before Christmas.

Steve's heart seemed to stop and slowly he straightened. Chewing on the inside of his lip, he closed the refrigerator door. Carol had been stuffing down the sweet potatoes long before he'd accepted her dinner invitation. Weeks before, from the look of it.

His thoughts in chaos, he stumbled into the living room and slumped into the chair. An icy chill settled over him. No. He refused to believe it, refused to condemn her on anything so flimsy. Then his gaze fell on a pair of knitting needles. He reached for her pattern book and noted the many designs for infant wear.

His heart froze. The last time he'd been by the house, Carol had been knitting a baby blanket. When he'd asked her about it, she'd told him it was for a friend. His snort of laughter was mirthless. Sure, Carol! More lies, more deceit.

And come to think of it, on Christmas Eve she'd pushed her knitting aside so that he couldn't see it. She'd been knitting the *same* blanket for the *same* friend then, too.

He was still stewing when Carol appeared. She smiled at him so sweetly as she slipped her arms into her robe.

"Morning," she said with a yawn.

"Morning."

His gruffness must have stopped her. "Is something wrong?"

Such innocent eyes… She'd always been able to fool him with that look. No more.

"Steve?"

"You're pregnant, aren't you?"

She released her breath in a long, slow sigh. "I wondered if you'd guess. I suppose I should have told you right away, but…we got sidetracked, didn't we?"

He could hardly stand to look at her.

"You're not angry, are you?" she asked, her eyes suddenly reflecting uncertainty.

Again such innocence, such skill. "No, I suppose not."

"Oh, good," she said with a feeble smile, "you had me worried there for a minute."

"One question?"

"Sure."

"Just whose baby is it?"

Chapter Nine

"Whose baby is it?" Carol repeated, stunned. She couldn't believe Steve would dare to ask such a question when the answer was so obvious.

"That's what I want to know."

His face was drawn extremely tight—almost menacing. She moved into the room and sat across from him, her heart ready to explode with dread. She met his look squarely, asking no quarter, giving none. The prolonged moment magnified the silence.

"I'm three months pregnant. This child is yours," she said, struggling to keep her voice even.

"Don't lie to me, Carol. I'm not completely dense." The anger that seeped into his expression was fierce enough to frighten her. Steve vaulted to his feet and started pacing in military fashion, each step precise and clipped, as if the drill would put order to his thoughts and ultimately to his life.

Carol's fingernails dug into the fabric on the sides of the overstuffed chair and her pulse went crazy. Her expression, however, revealed none of the inner turmoil she was experiencing. When her throat felt as if it would cooperate with her tongue, she spoke. "How can you even think such a thing?"

Steve splayed his fingers and jerked them through his hair in an action that seemed savage enough to yank it out by the roots. "I should have known something was wrong when you first contacted me at Christmastime."

Carol felt some color flush into her cheeks; to her regret it probably convinced Steve she was as guilty as he believed.

"That excuse about not wanting to spend Christmas alone was damn convenient. And if that wasn't obvious enough, your little seduction scene should have been. God knows, I fell for it." He whirled around to face her. "You did plan that, didn't you?"

"I…I…"

"Didn't you?" he repeated, in harsh tones that demanded the truth.

Miserable and confused, Carol nodded. She had no choice but to admit to her scheme of seducing him.

One corner of his mouth curved up in a half smile, but there was no humor or amusement in the action. The love that had so recently shone from his eyes had been replaced by condemnation.

"If only you would let me explain." She tried again, shocked by this abrupt turn of events. Only a few hours before, they'd lain in each other's arms and spoken of a reconciliation. The promise that had sprung to life between them was wilting and she was powerless to stop it.

"What could you possibly say that would change the facts?" he demanded. "I was always a fool when it came to you. Even after a year apart I hadn't completely come to terms with the divorce and you, no doubt, knew that and used it to your advantage."

"Steve, I–"

"It's little wonder," he continued, not allowing her to finish speaking, "that you considered me that perfect patsy for this intrigue. You used my love for you against me."

"Okay, so I planned our lovemaking Christmas Eve. You're right about that. I suppose I was pretty obvious about the whole thing when you think about it. But I had a reason. A damn good one."

"Yes, I know."

Carol hadn't realized a man's eyes could be so cold.

"What do you know?" she asked.

"That cake you're baking in your oven isn't mine."

"Oh, honestly, Steve. Your paranoia is beginning to wear a little thin. I'm doing my damnedest to keep my cool here, but you're crazy if you think anyone else could be the father."

He raised his index finger. "You're good. You know that? You're really very good. That fervent look about you, as though I'm going off the deep end to even suspect you of such a hideous deed. Just the right amount of indignation while keeping your anger in check. Good, very good."

"Stop that," she shouted. "You're being ridiculous. When you get in this mood, nothing appeases you. Everything I say becomes suspect."

His hand wiped his face free of expression. "If I didn't know better, I could almost believe you."

She hated it when Steve was like this. He was so convinced he was right that no amount of arguing would ever persuade him otherwise. "I'm going to tell you one last time, and then I won't say it again. Not ever. We–as in you and I, Steve–are going to have a baby."

Steve stared at her for so long that she wasn't sure what he was thinking. He longed to believe her–she could recognize that yearning in his eyes–and yet something held him back. His Adam's apple moved up and down, and he clenched his jaw so tightly that the sides of his face went white. Still the inner struggle continued while he glared at her, as if commanding the truth–as if to say he could deal with anything as long as it was true.

Carol met that look, holding her gaze as steady and sure as was humanly possible. He wanted the truth, and she'd already given it to him. Nothing she could say would alter the facts: he was her baby's father.

Steve then turned his back on her. "The problem is, I desperately want to believe you. I'd give everything I've managed to accumulate in this life to know that baby was mine."

Everything about Steve, the way he stood with his shoulders hunched, his feet braced as if he expected a blow, told Carol he didn't believe her. Her integrity was suspect.

"I…my birthday–I was thirty," she said, faltering as she scrambled to make him recognize the truth. "It hit me then that my childbearing years were numbered. Since the divorce I've been so lonely, so unhappy, and I thought a baby would help fill the void in my life."

He turned to look at her as she spoke, then closed his eyes and nodded.

Just looking at the anguish in his face was almost more than Carol could bear. "I know you never believed me about Todd, but there's only been one lover in my life, and that's you. I figured that you owed me a baby. I thought if I invited you to spend Christmas with me and you accepted, that I could probably steer us into the bedroom. None of the problems we had in our marriage had extended there."

"Carol, don't–this isn't necessary. I already know you were–"

"Yes, it is. Please, Steve, you've got to listen to me. You've got to understand."

He turned away from her again, but Carol continued talking because it was the only thing lcft for her to do. If she didn't tell him now, there might never be another chance.

"I didn't count on anything more happening between us.

I'd convinced myself I was emotionally separated from you by that time and all I needed was the baby…"

"You must have been worried when I didn't fall into your scheme immediately."

"What do you mean?" Carol felt frantic and helpless.

"I didn't immediately suggest we get back together–that must have had you worried. After Christmas Eve we decided to leave things as they were." He walked away from her, but not before she saw the tilt of righteous indignation in his profile. "That visit to my apartment…what was your excuse? Ah yes, a button you'd found and thought might be mine. Come on, Carol, you should have been more original than that. As excuses go, that's about as flimsy as they get."

"All right, if you want me to admit I planned that seduction scene, too, then I will. I didn't get pregnant the way I planned in December…I had to try again. You had to know swallowing my pride and coming to you wasn't easy."

He nodded. "No, I don't suppose it was."

"Then you believe me?"

"No."

Carol hung her head in frustration.

"Naturally only one night of lovemaking wasn't enough," he said with a soft denunciation. "It made sense to plan more than one evening together in case I started questioning matters later. I'm pleased that you did credit me with some intelligence. Turning up pregnant after one time together would have seemed much too convenient. But twice… Well, that sounds far more likely."

Carol was speechless. Once more Steve had tried and found her guilty, choosing to believe the worst possible scenario.

"Fool that I am, I should have known something was up by how docile and loving you were. So willing to forget the past, forgive and go on with the future. Then there was all that talk about us starting a family. That sucked me right in, didn't it? You know, you've always known how much I want children."

"There's nothing I can say, is there?"

"No," he admitted bleakly. "I wonder what you would have told me next summer when you gave birth–although months premature, astonishingly the baby would weigh six or seven pounds and obviously be full term. Don't you think I would have questioned you then?"

She kept her mouth shut, refusing to be drawn into this kind of degrading verbal battle. From experience she knew nothing she could say would vindicate her.

"If you don't want to claim this child, Steve, that's fine, the loss is yours. My original intent was to raise her alone anyway. I'd thought…I'd hoped we could build a new life together, but it's obvious I was wrong."

"Dead wrong. I won't let you make a fool of me a second time."

A strained moment passed before Carol spoke, and when she did her voice was incredibly weak. "I think it would be best if you left now."

He answered her with an abrupt nod, turned away and went to her bedroom to retrieve his shirt and shoes.

Carol didn't follow him. She sat, feeling numb and growing more ill with each minute. The nausea swelled up inside her until she knew she was going to empty her stomach. Standing, she rushed into the bathroom and leaned over the toilet in a ritual that had become all too familiar.

When she'd finished, she discovered Steve waiting in the doorway, watching her. She didn't know how long he'd been there.

"Are you all right?"

She nodded, not looking at him, wanting him to leave so that she could curl into a tight ball and lick her wounds. No one could hurt her the way Steve did. No other man possessed the power.

He didn't seem to believe she was going to be fine, and slowly he came into the bathroom. He wet a washcloth and handed it to her, waiting while she wiped her face. Then, gently, he led her back into the bedroom and to the bed. Carol discovered that lying down did seem to ease the dizzy, sick feeling.

Steve took his own sweet time buttoning his shirt, apparently stalling so that he could stick by her in case she was sick a second time, although she knew he would never have admitted he cared. If she'd had the energy, Carol would have suggested he go, because for every minute he lingered it was more difficult for her to bear seeing him. She didn't want him to care about her–how could he when he believed the things he did? And yet, every now and again she would find him watching her guardedly, his eyes filled with worry.

"When do you see the doctor next?" He walked around the foot of the bed and resumed an alleged search for his socks.

"Two weeks." Her voice was faint and barely audible.

"Don't you think you should give him a call sooner?"

"No." She refused to look at him.

Steve apparently found what he wanted. He sat on the edge of the mattress and slowly, methodically put on his shoes. "How often does this sort of thing happen?" he asked next.

"It doesn't matter." Some of her energy returned, and she tested her strength by sitting up. "Listen, Steve, I appreciate your concern, but it just isn't necessary. My baby and I are going to be just fine."

He didn't look convinced. His brooding gaze revealed his thoughts, and when he looked at her, his expression softened perceptibly. It took a moment for his eyes to drop to her hand, which rested on her abdomen.

The change that came over him was a shock. His face tightened and his mouth thinned. A surge of anger shot through her. "You don't want to claim our daughter, then it's your loss."

"The baby isn't mine."

The anguish in his voice was nearly Carol's undoing. She bit her lower lip and shook her head with mounting despair.

"I can't believe you're actually saying that. But you'll never know, will you, Steve? All your life you're going to be left wondering. If she has dark eyes like yours and dark hair, that will only complicate your doubts. No doubt the Kyle nose will make you all the more suspicious. Someday you're going to have to face the fact that you've rejected your own child. If you can live with that, then so be it."

He twisted around and his fists were knotted into tight fists. "You were pregnant at Christmas and you're trying to pawn this pregnancy off on me."

"That is the most insulting thing you've ever said to me."

He didn't answer her for a long time. "You've insulted my intelligence. I may have loved you, but I'm not a blind fool."

"They don't come any blinder."

"Explain the milk?"

"What?" Carol hadn't a clue to what he was talking about.

"At Christmas, after we'd made love, we had a snack. Remember?"

Carol did.

"You poured yourself a glass of milk and I commented because you used to dislike it. We were married five years and the only time I can remember you having milk was with cold cereal. You could live your whole life without the stuff. All of a sudden you're drinking it by the glassful."

With deliberate calm Carol rolled her gaze toward the ceiling. "Talk about flimsy excuses. You honestly mean to say you're rejecting your own child because I drank a glass of milk an entire month before I was pregnant?"

"That isn't everything. I saw your knitting Christmas Eve, although you tried to hide it from me. Later, I asked you about it and you claimed it was a baby blanket. It was the same piece you were working on at Christmas, wasn't it?"

"Yes, but…"

"That blanket's for your baby isn't it, Carol? There never was any friend."

Frustration mounting in volcanic proportions, she yelled, "All right, it wasn't for any friend–that's what you want to hear."

"And then there were the sweet potatoes. Good God, you had six containers full of yams that night…pregnant women are said to experience silly cravings. And that's what it was, wasn't it–a craving?"

Standing, Carol felt the weight of defeat settle on her shoulders. No amount of arguing would change anything now. Steve had reasoned everything out in his own mind and found her answers lacking. There was no argument she could give him that would change what he'd already decided.

"Well?" he demanded. "Explain those things away, if you can."

She felt as if she were going to burst into helpless tears at any second. For six years she'd loved this man and given him the power to shatter her heart. "You're the only man I know who can put two and two together and come up with five, Steve," she said wearily.

"For God's sake, quit lying. Quit trying to make me doubt what's right before my eyes. You wanted to trick me into believing that baby is mine, and by God, it almost worked."

If he didn't leave soon, Carol was going to throw him out. "I think you should leave."

"Admit it!" he shouted.

Nothing less would satisfy him. She slapped her hands against her thighs and feigned a sorrowful sigh. "I guess you're just too smart for me. I should have known better than to try to fool you."

Steve turned and marched to the front door, but stopped, his hand gripping the knob. "What's he going to do about it?"

"Who?"

"Todd."

It took every dictate of Carol's control not to scream that her former employer had nothing to do with her being pregnant. "I don't have anything more to say to you."

"Is he going to divorce Joyce and marry you?"

With one hand cradled around her middle, Carol pointed to the door with the other.

"I have a right to know," Steve argued. "If he isn't going to help you, something should be done."

"I don't need anything–especially from you."

"As much as I'd like to walk away from you, I can't. If you find yourself in trouble, call me. I'll always be there for you."

"If you want to help me, then get out of my life. This baby is mine and mine alone." There was no anger in her words; her voice was low and controlled…and sad, unbelievably sad.

Steve hesitated and his lingering seemed to imply that something would change. Carol knew otherwise.

"Goodbye, Steve."

He paused, then whispered, "Goodbye."

The pain in his voice would haunt her all her days, she thought, as Steve turned and walked out of her life.

The loud pounding noise disrupted Steve's restless slumber and he sat up and glared at the front door of his apartment.

"Who is it?" he shouted, and the sound of his own voice sent shooting pains through his temple. He moaned, tried to sit up and in the process nearly fell off the sofa.

"Steve, I know you're in there. Open up."

Lindy. Damn, he should have known it would be his meddling sister. He wished to hell she would just leave him alone. He'd managed to put her off for the past week, avoiding talking to her, inventing excuses not to see her. Obviously that hadn't been good enough because here she was!

"Go away," he said, his voice less loud this time. "I'm sick." That at least was the truth. His head felt like someone had used it for batting practice.

"I have my own key and I'll use it unless you open this door right now."

Muttering under his breath, Steve weaved across the floor

until he reached the door. The carpet seemed to pitch and roll like a ship tossed about in a storm. He unbolted the lock and stepped aside so Lindy could let herself in. He knew she was about to parade into his apartment like an angel of mercy prepared to save him from hell and damnation.

He was right.

Lindy came into the room with the flourish of a suffragette marching for equality of the sexes. She stopped in the middle of the room, hands placed righteously on her hips, and studied him as though viewing the lowest form of human life. Then slowly she began to shake her head with obvious disdain.

"You look like hell," she announced.

Steve almost expected bugles to follow her decree. "Thank you, Mother Theresa."

"Sit down before you fall down."

Steve did as she ordered simply because he didn't have the energy to argue. "Would you mind not talking so loud?"

With one hand remaining on her hip, Lindy marched over to the window and pulled open the drapes.

Steve squinted under the force of the sunlight and shaded his eyes. "Was that really necessary?"

"Yes." She walked over to the coffee table and picked up an empty whiskey bottle, as though by touching it she was exposing herself to an incurable virus. With her nose pointed toward the ceiling, she walked into the kitchen and tossed it in the garbage. The bottle made a clanking sound as it hit against other bottles.

"How long do you intend to keep yourself holed up like this?" she demanded.

He shrugged. "As long as it takes."

"Steve, for heaven's sake be reasonable."

"Why?"

She couldn't seem to find an answer and that pleased him because he wasn't up to arguing with her. He knew there was a reason to get up, get dressed and eat, but he hadn't figured out what it was yet. He'd taken a week of leave in order to spend time with Carol. Now he would give anything to have to report to duty–anything to take his mind off his ex-wife.

His mouth felt like a sand dune had shifted there while he slept. He needed something cold and wet. With Lindy following him, he walked into the kitchen and got himself a beer.

To his utter amazement, his sister jerked it out of his hand and returned it to the refrigerator. "From the look of things, I'd say you've had enough to drink."

He was so stunned, he didn't know what to say.

She pointed her index finger toward a kitchen chair, silently ordering him to sit. From the determined look she wore, Steve decided not to test her.

Before he could object, she had a pot of coffee brewing and was rummaging through the refrigerator looking for God knew what. Eggs, he realized when she brought out a carton.

She insisted he eat, which he did, but he didn't like it. While he sat at the table like an obedient child, Lindy methodically started emptying his sink, which was piled faucet-high with dirty dishes.

"You don't need to do that," he objected.

"Yes, I know."

"Then don't…I can get by without any favors from you." Now that he had something in his stomach, he wasn't about to be led around like a bull with a ring through his nose.

"You need something," she countered. "I'm just not sure what. I suspect it's a swift kick in the seat of the pants."

"You and what army, little sister."

Lindy declined to answer. She poured herself a cup of coffee, replenished his and claimed the chair across the table from him. "Okay," she said, her shoulders rising with an elongated sigh. "What happened with Carol?"

At the mention of his former wife's name, Steve's stomach clenched in a painful knot. Just thinking about her carrying another man's child produced such an inner agony that the oxygen constricted his lungs and he couldn't breathe.

"Steve?"

"Nothing happened between us. Absolutely nothing."

"Don't give me that. The last time we talked, you were as excited as a puppy about her being pregnant. You could hardly wait to see her. What's happened since then?"

"I already told you–nothing!"

Lindy slumped forward and braced her hand against her forehead. "You've buried yourself in this apartment for an entire week and you honestly expect me to believe that?"

"I don't care what you believe."

"I'm to blame, aren't I?"

"What?"

"I shouldn't have said a word about Carol and the baby, but she'd been so sick and I've been so concerned about her." Lindy paused and lightly shook her head. "I still am."

Steve hated the way his heart reacted to the news that Carol was still sickly. He didn't want to care about her, didn't want to feel this instant surge of protectiveness when it came to his ex-wife. For the past week, he'd tried to erase every memory of her from his tortured mind. Obviously it hadn't worked, and the only thing he'd managed to develop was one hell of a hangover.

"I shouldn't have told you," Lindy repeated.

"It wouldn't have made one bit of difference; I would have found out sooner or later."

Lindy's hands cupped the coffee mug. "What are you going to do about it?"

Steve shrugged. "Nothing."

"Nothing? But Steve, that's your baby."

He let that pass, preferring not to correct his sister. "What's between Carol and me isn't any of your business. Leave it at that."

She seemed to weigh his words carefully. "I wish I could."

"What do you mean by that?"

"Carol looks awful. I really think she needs to see her doctor. Something's wrong, Steve. She shouldn't be this sick."

He shrugged with feigned indifference. "That's her problem."

Lindy's jaw sagged open. "I can't believe you. Carol is carrying your child and you're acting like she got pregnant all by herself."

Steve diverted his gaze to the blue sky outside his living-room window and shrugged. "Maybe she did," he whispered.

Chapter Ten

Carol sat at her desk and tried to concentrate on her work. This past seven days had been impossible. Steve honestly believed she was carrying another man's child, and nothing she could ever say would convince him otherwise. It was like history repeating itself and all the agony of her divorce had come back to haunt her.

Only this time Carol was smarter.

If Steve chose to believe such nonsense, that was his problem. She wanted this baby and from the first had been prepared to raise her daughter alone. Now if only she could get over these bouts of nausea and the sickly feeling that was with her almost every day and night. Most of it she attributed to the emotional upheaval in her life. Within a couple of weeks it would pass and she would feel a thousand times better—at least, that was what she kept telling herself.

"Hi."

A familiar, friendly voice invaded Carol's thoughts. "Lindy!"

she said, directing her attention to Steve's sister. "What are you doing here?"

"Risking my job and my neck. Can we meet later? I've got to talk to you. It's important."

As fond as Carol was of her former sister-in-law, she knew there was only one subject Lindy would want to discuss, and that was Steve. Her former husband was a topic Carol preferred to avoid. Nor was she willing to justify herself to his sister, if Lindy started questioning her about the baby's father. It would be better for everyone involved if she refused to meet her, but the desperate worry in Lindy's steady gaze frightened her.

"I suppose you want to ask me about Steve," Carol said slowly, thoughtfully. "I don't know that any amount of talking is going to change things. It'd be best just to leave things as they are."

"Not you, too."

"Too?"

"Steve's so closed mouthed you'd think your name was listed as classified information."

Carol picked up the clipboard and flipped over a page, in an effort to pretend she was exceptionally busy. "Maybe it's better this way," she murmured, but was unable to disguise the pain her words revealed.

"Listen, I've got to get back before someone important—like my supervisor—notices I'm missing," Lindy said, scribbling something on a pad and ripping off the sheet. "Here's the address to my apartment. Rush is on sea trials, so we'll be alone."

"Lindy..."

"If you care anything about my brother you'll come." Once more those piercing eyes spelled out his sister's concern.

Carol took the address, and frowned. "Let me tell you right now that if you're trying to orchestrate a reconciliation, neither one of us will appreciate it."

"I..."

"Is Steve going to mysteriously arrive around the same time as I do?"

"No. I promise he won't. Good grief, Carol, he won't even talk to me anymore. He isn't talking to anyone. I'm not kidding when I say I'm worried about him."

Carol soaked in that information and frowned, growing concerned herself.

"You'll come?"

Against her better judgment, she nodded. Like her ex-husband, she didn't want to talk to anyone, and especially not to someone related to Steve. The pain of his accusations was still too raw to share with someone else.

Yet she knew she would be there to talk about whatever it was Lindy found so important, although she also knew that nothing Lindy could say would alter her relationship with Steve.

At five-thirty, Carol parked her car outside Lindy's apartment building. She regretted agreeing to the meeting, but couldn't see any way of escaping without going back on her word.

Lindy opened the door and greeted her with a weak smile. "Come in and sit down. Would you like something cold to drink? I just finished making a pitcher of iced tea."

"That sounds fine." Carol still wasn't feeling well and would be glad when she saw her doctor for her regular appointment. She took a seat in the living room while Lindy disappeared into the kitchen.

Lindy returned a couple of minutes later with tall glasses filled with iced tea.

"I wish I could say you're looking better," Lindy said, handing Carol a glass and a colorful napkin.

"I wish I could say I was, too."

Lindy sat across from her and automatically crossed her long legs. "I take it the medication the doctor gave you for the nausea didn't help?"

"It helped some."

"But generally you're feeling all right?"

Carol shrugged. She'd never been pregnant before and had nothing to compare this experience to. "I suppose."

Lindy's fingers wiped away the condensation on the outside of her glass. She hedged, and her gaze drifted around the room. "I think the best way to start is to apologize."

"But what could you have possibly done to offend me?"

Lindy's gaze moved to Carol's, and she released a slow breath. "I told Steve I suspected you were pregnant."

"It's true," Carol answered with a gentle smile. She would be a single mother, and although she would have preferred to be married, she was pleased and proud to be carrying this child.

"I know...but it would have been far better coming from you. I left a message for Steve to call me once he returned from his deployment. I was afraid he was going to come at you with his usual caveman tactics and you've been so ill lately... It's a weak excuse, I know."

"Lindy, for goodness' sake, don't worry about it. This baby isn't a deep, dark secret." Remembering the life she was nurturing in her womb was what had gotten her through the bleakest hours of this past week. Steve might choose to reject his daughter, but he could never take away this precious gift he had unknowingly given her.

"I don't know what's going on with my brother," Lindy muttered, dropping her gaze to her tea. "I wish Rush were here. If anyone could talk some sense into him, it's my husband."

"Get used to him being away when you need him most. It's the lot of a Navy wife. The Navy blues doesn't always refer only to their dress uniform, you know."

Lindy nodded. "I'm learning that. I'm also learning I'm much stronger than I thought I was. Rush was involved in an accident last year in the Persian Gulf–you probably read about it in the papers–well, really that doesn't have anything to do with Steve, but he was with me the whole time when we didn't know if Rush was dead or alive. I can't even begin to tell you how good he was, how supportive. In a crisis, my brother can be a real trooper."

"Yes, I know." Carol paused and took a sip of her tea. On more than one occasion in their married life, she had come to admire Steve's levelheadedness in dealing with both major and minor emergencies. It was in other matters, like trust and confidence in her love, that he fell sadly short.

"I don't understand him anymore," Lindy admitted. "He was ecstatic when I mentioned my suspicions about you being pregnant…I thought he was going to go right through the ceiling he was so excited. He was bubbling over like a little kid. I know he drove over to your place right after that and then we didn't hear from him again. I phoned, but he just barked at me to leave him alone, and when I went to see him…well, that's another story entirely."

Carol stiffened. It was better to deal with Lindy honestly since it was apparent Steve hadn't told her. "He doesn't believe the baby is his."

Lindy's brow folded into a dark, brooding frown. "But that's ridiculous."

Carol found it somewhat amazing that her former sister-in-law would believe her without question and her ex-husband wouldn't.

"I…can't believe this." Lindy pressed her palm over her forehead, lifting her bangs, and her mouth sagged open. "But, sadly, it explains a good deal." As if she couldn't remain sitting any longer, Lindy got up and started walking around the room, moving from one side to the other without direction. "What is that man's problem? Good grief, someone should get him to face a few fundamental facts here."

Carol smiled. It felt good to have someone trust and believe her.

"What are you going to do? I mean, I assumed Steve was going to remarry you, but…"

"Obviously that's out of the question."

"But..."

"Single women give birth every day. It's rather commonplace now for a woman to choose to raise a child on her own. That was my original intention."

"But, Steve..."

"Steve is out of my life." Her hand moved to her stomach and a soft smile courted the edges of her mouth. "He gave me what I wanted. Someday he'll be smart enough to calculate dates, but when he does it'll be too late."

"Oh, Carol, don't say that. Steve loves you so much."

"He's hurt me for the last time. He can't love me and accuse me of the things he has. It's over for us, and there's no going back."

"But he does love you." Lindy walked around a bit more and then plopped down across from Carol. "When he wouldn't talk to me on the phone, I went over to the apartment. I've never seen him like this. He frightened me."

"What's wrong?" Carol was angry with herself for caring, but she did.

"He'd been drinking heavily."

"That's not like Steve."

"I know," Lindy said heatedly. "I didn't know when he'd eaten last, so I fixed him something, which was a mistake because once he had something in his stomach he got feisty again and wanted me to leave."

"Did you?"

"No." Lindy started nibbling on the corner of her mouth. "I kept asking him questions about you, which only made him more angry. I soon learned you were a subject best avoided."

"I can imagine."

"After a while, he fell asleep on the sofa and I stayed around and cleaned up the apartment. It was a mess. Then...I heard Steve. I thought at first he was in the middle of a bad dream and I went to wake him, but when I came into the living room, I found him sitting on the end of the davenport with his hands over his face. He was weeping, Carol. As I've never seen a man weep before–heart-wrenching sobs that came from the deepest part of his soul. I can't even describe it to you."

Carol lowered her gaze to her hands, which had begun to tremble.

"This is the first time I've seen my brother cry, and his sobs tore straight through my heart. I couldn't stand by and do nothing. I wanted to comfort him and find out what had hurt him so badly. I'm his sister, for heaven's sake–he should be able to talk to me. But he didn't want me anywhere near him and ordered me out of the apartment. I left, but I haven't been able to stop thinking about it since."

A tear spilled out of the corner of Carol's eye and left a moist trail down the side of her face.

"By the time I got home I was crying, too. I don't know what to do anymore."

Carol's throat thickened. "There's nothing you can do. This is something Steve has to work out himself."

"Can't you talk to him?" Lindy pleaded. "He loves you so much and it's eating him alive."

"It won't do any good." Carol spoke from bitter experience.

"How can two people who obviously love each other let this happen?"

"I wish I knew." Carol's voice dropped to a whispered sob.

"What about Steve and the baby?"

"He doesn't want to have anything to do with this pregnancy. That's his decision, Lindy."

"But it's the wrong one! Surely you can get him to realize that."

She shook her head sadly. "Once Steve decides on something, his mind is set. He's too stubborn to listen to reason."

"But you love him."

"I wish I could deny that, but I do care about him, with all my heart. Unfortunately that doesn't change a thing."

"How can you walk away from him like this?"

Carol's heart constricted with pain. "I've never left Steve. Not once. He's always been the one to walk away."

Chapter Eleven

"I'd do anything I could to make things right between me and Steve," Carol told Lindy, "but it isn't possible anymore."

"Why not?" Lindy pleaded. Carol knew it was hard for Lindy to understand when her own recent marriage was thriving. "You're both crazy in love with each other."

The truth in that statement was undeniable. Although Steve believed her capable of breaking her wedding vows and the worst kind of deceit, he continued to love her. For her part, Carol had little pride when it came to her ex-husband. She should have cut her losses the minute he'd accused her of having an affair, walked away from her and filed for the divorce. Instead she'd spent the next year of her life in limbo, licking her wounds, pretending the emotional scars had healed. It had taken Christmas Eve to show her how far she still had to go to get over loving Steve Kyle.

"You can't just walk away from him," Lindy pleaded. "What about the baby?"

"Steve doesn't want anything to do with my daughter."

"Give him time, Carol. You know Steve probably better than anyone. He can be such a stubborn fool sometimes. It just takes awhile for him to come to his senses. He'll wake up one morning and recognize the truth about the baby."

"I have to forget him for my own sanity." Carol stood, delivered her empty iced-tea glass to the kitchen and prepared to leave. There wasn't anything Lindy could say that would change the facts. Yes, she did love Steve and probably always would, but that didn't alter what he believed.

Lindy followed her to the front door. "If you need something, anything at all, please call me."

Carol nodded. "I will."

"Promise?"

"Promise." Carol knew that Lindy realized how difficult it was for her to ask for help. Impulsively she hugged Steve's sister. From now on, Lindy would be her only link to Steve and Carol was grateful for the friendship they shared.

Steve had to get out of the apartment before he went crazy. He'd spent the past few days drowning his misery in a bottle and the only thing it had brought him was more pain.

He showered, shaved and dressed. Walking would help clear his mind.

With no real destination in mind, he headed toward the waterfront. He got as far as Pike Place Market and aimlessly wandered among the thick crowds there. The colorful sights of the vegetable and meat displays and the sounds of cheerful vendors helped lift his spirits.

He bought a crisp, red Delicious apple and ate it as he ambled toward the booths that sold various craft items designed to attract the tourist trade. He paused and examined a sculpture made of volcanic ash from Mount Saint Helens. Another booth sold scenic photos of the Pacific Northwest, and another, thick, hand-knit Indian sweaters.

"Could I interest you in something?" a friendly older

woman asked. Her long silver hair framed her face, and she offered him a wide smile.

"No thanks, I'm just looking." Steve paused and glanced over the items on her table. Sterling silver jewelry dotted a black velvet cloth–necklaces, earrings and rings of all sizes and shapes.

"You can't buy silver anywhere for my prices," the woman said.

"It's very nice."

"If jewelry doesn't interest you, perhaps these will." She stood and pulled a box of silver objects from beneath the table, lifting it up for him to inspect.

The first thing Steve noticed was a sterling-silver piggy bank. He smiled recalling how he and Carol had dumped their spare change in a piggy bank for months in an effort to save enough for a vacation to Hawaii. They'd spent it instead for the closing costs on the house.

"This is a popular item," the woman told him, bringing out a baby rattle. "Lots of jewelry stores sell these, but no one can beat my prices."

"How much?" Steve couldn't believe he'd asked. What the hell would he do with a baby rattle–especially one made of sterling silver.

The woman stated a reasonable price. "I'll take it," he said, astonished to hear the words come out of his mouth.

"Would you like one with blue ribbon or pink?"

Already Steve regretted the impulse. What was he planning to do? Give it to Carol? He'd decided the best thing for him to do as far as his ex-wife was concerned was to never see her again.

"Sir? Blue or pink?"

"Blue," he answered in a hoarse whisper. For the son he would probably never father. Blue for the color of Carol's eyes when she smiled at him.

By the time Steve walked back to the apartment, the sack

containing the silver baby rattle felt like it weighed thirty pounds. By rights, he thought, he should toss the silly thing in the garbage. But he didn't.

He set it on the kitchen counter and opened the refrigerator, looking for something to eat, but nothing interested him. When he turned, the rattle seemed to draw his gaze. He stared at it for a long moment, yearning strongly to press it into the hand of his own child.

Blood thundered in his ears and his heart pounded so hard and fast that his chest ached. He would save the toy for Lindy and Rush whenever they had children, he decided.

Feeling only slightly better, he moved into the living room and turned on the television. He reached for the *TV Guide*, flipped through the pages, sighed and turned off the set. A second later, he rushed to his feet.

He didn't know who the hell he was trying to kid. That silver rattle with the pretty blue ribbon was for Carol and her baby, and it was going to torment him until he got rid of it.

He could mail her the toy and be done with the plaything. Or have Lindy give it to her without letting Carol know it had come from him. Or…or he could just set it on the porch and let her find it.

The last idea appealed to him. He would casually drive by her neighborhood, park his car around the block and wait until it was dark enough to sneak up and leave the rattle on the front step. He was the last person she would ever suspect would do something like that.

With his plan formulated, Steve drove to Carol's house. He was half a block away from her place when he noticed her car. She was leaving. This would work out even better. He could follow her and when she got where she was going, he could place the rattle inside her car. That way she would assume someone had mistaken her car for their own and inadvertently set the rattle inside. There wasn't anything she could do but take it home with her.

Carol headed north on Interstate 5, and her destination was a matter of simple deduction. She was going to the Northgate Mall. Lord, that woman loved to shop. The minute she steered onto the freeway on-ramp, Steve knew exactly where she was headed. They'd been married for five years, and their year apart hadn't changed her. The smug knowledge produced a smile.

But Carol exited before the mall.

Steve's heart started to pound. He was three cars behind her, but if she wasn't going shopping, he didn't know what she was planning. Maybe she was rendezvousing with Todd. Maybe all those times she'd told him she was shopping Carol had actually been meeting with her employer. The muscles in his stomach clenched into a knot so tight and painful that it stole his breath.

If there'd been any way to turn the car around, Steve would have done it, but he was trapped in the center lane of traffic and forced to follow the heavy flow.

It wasn't until they'd gone several blocks that Steve noticed the back side of the mall. Perhaps she'd found a shortcut and had never bothered to tell him about it.

Carol turned onto a busy side street, and against his better judgment, he followed her. A few minutes later, when Carol turned into the large parking lot at Northgate Mall, Steve felt almost giddy with relief.

She parked close to the J.C. Penney store, and Steve eased his vehicle into a slot four spaces over. On a whim, he decided to follow her inside. He'd always wondered what women found so intriguing about shopping.

He was far enough behind her on the escalator to almost lose her. Standing at the top, he searched until he found her standing in women's fashions, sorting through a rack of dresses. It took him a minute to realize they were maternity dresses. Although she'd lost several pounds, she must be having difficulty finding things that fit her, he realized. According to his calculations, she was five months pregnant—probably closer to six.

He lounged around while she took a handful of bright spring dresses and moved into the changing room. Fifteen minutes passed before she returned, and to Steve it felt like a lifetime.

When she returned, she went back to the rack and replaced all but one of the dresses. She held up a pretty blue one with a wide sailor's collar and red tie and studied it carefully. Apparently she changed her mind because she hung it back up with the others. Still she lingered an extra minute, continuing to examine the outfit. She ran her fingers down the sleeve to catch the price tag, read it, shook her head and reluctantly walked away.

The minute she was out of sight, Steve was at the clothing rack. Obviously she wanted the dress, yet she hadn't bought it. He checked the price tag and frowned. It was moderately priced, certainly not exorbitant. If she wanted it, which she apparently did, then she should have it.

For the second time in the same day, Steve found himself making a purchase that was difficult to rationalize. It wasn't as if he had any use for a maternity dress. But why not? he asked himself. If he left the rattle in her car it shouldn't make any difference if he added a dress. It wasn't likely that she would tie him to either purchase. Let her think her fairy godmother was gifting her.

From his position at the cash register, Steve saw Carol walk through the infant's department. She ran her hand over the top rail of a white Jenny Lind crib and examined it with a look of such sweet anticipation that Steve felt guilty for invading her privacy.

"Would you like this dress on the hanger or in a sack?" the salesclerk asked him.

It took Steve a moment to realize she was talking to him. "A sack, please." He couldn't very well walk through the mall carrying a maternity dress.

Carol bought something, too, but Steve couldn't see what it was. Infant T-shirts or something like that, he guessed. His vantage point in the furniture department wasn't the best. Carol started to walk toward him, and he turned abruptly and pretended to be testing out a recliner.

Apparently she didn't see him, and he settled into the seat and expelled a sigh of relief.

"Can I help you?" a salesclerk asked.

"Ah, no, thanks," he said, getting to his feet.

Carol headed down the escalator, and Steve scooted around a couple of women pushing baby strollers in an effort not to lose sight of her.

Carol's steps were filled with purpose as she moved down the wide aisle to women's shoes. She picked up a red low-heeled dress shoe that was on display, but when the clerk approached, she smiled and shook her head. Within a couple of minutes she was on her way.

Feeling more like a fool with every minute, Steve followed her out of the store and into the heart of the mall. The place was packed, as it generally was on Saturday afternoon. Usually Steve avoided the mall on weekends, preferring to do his shopping during the day or at night.

He saw Carol stop at a flower stand and buy herself a red rosebud. She'd always been fond of flowers, and he was pleased that she treated herself to something special.

She'd gone only a few steps when he noticed that her steps had slowed.

Something was wrong. He could tell from the way she walked. He cut across to the other side, where the flow of shoppers was heading in the opposite direction. Feeling like a secret government agent, he pressed himself against the storefront in an effort to watch her more closely. She had pressed her hand to her abdomen and her face had gone deathly pale. She was in serious pain, he determined as a sense of alarm filled him. Steve could feel it as strongly as if he were the one suffering.

Although he was certain she had full view of him, Carol didn't notice. She cut across the streams of shoppers to the benches that lined the middle of the concourse and sat. Her shoulders moved up and down as though she were taking in deep breaths in an effort to control her reaction to whatever was happening. She closed her eyes and bit her lower lip.

The alarm turned to panic. He didn't know what to do. He couldn't rush up to her and demand to know what was wrong. Nor could he casually stroll by and pretend he just happened to be shopping and had stumbled upon her. But something needed to be done–someone had to help her.

Steve had never felt more helpless in his life. Not knowing what else he could do, he walked up and plopped himself down next to her.

"Hi," he said in a falsely cheerful voice.

"Steve." She looked at him, her eyes brimming with tears. She reached for his hand, gripping it so hard her nails cut into his flesh.

All pretense was gone, wiped away by the stampeding fear he sensed in her.

"What's wrong?"

She shook her head. "I…I don't know."

Her eyes widened and he was struck by how yellow her skin was. He took her hand in both of his. "You're in pain?"

She nodded. Her fear palatable. "I'm so afraid."

"What do you want me to do?" He debated on whether he should could call for an ambulance or contact her doctor and have him meet them at the hospital.

"I…don't know what's wrong. I've had this pain twice, but it's always gone away after a couple of minutes." She closed her eyes. "Oh, Steve, I'm so afraid I'm going to lose my baby."

Chapter Twelve

Restless, Steve paced the corridor of the maternity ward in Overlake Hospital, his hands stuffed inside his pants pockets. He felt as though he were carrying the world on his shoulders. Each passing minute tightened the knot in his stomach until he was consumed with worry and dread.

He wanted to see Carol–he longed to talk to her–but there wasn't anything more for him to say. He'd done what he could for her, and by rights he should leave. But he couldn't walk away from her. Not now. Not when she needed him.

Not knowing what else to do, he found a pay phone and contacted his sister.

"Lindy, it's Steve."

"Steve, how are you? I'm so glad you phoned. I haven't stopped thinking about you."

She sounded so pleased to hear from him, and he swallowed down his guilt for the way he'd treated her. He'd been rude and unreasonable when she'd only been showing concern for him.

"I'm fine," he said hurriedly, "Listen, I'm at Overlake Hospital…"

"You're at the hospital? You're fine, but you're at Overlake? Good God, what happened? I knew it, I just knew something like this was going to happen. I felt it…"

"Lindy, shut up for a minute, would you?"

"No, I won't shut up–I'm family, Steve Kyle. Family. If you can't come to me when you're hurting, just who can you go to? You seem to think I'm too young to know anything about emotional pain, but you're wrong. When Paul dumped me it wasn't any Sunday-school picnic."

"I'm not the one in need of medical attention–it's Carol."

"Carol!" His blurted announcement seemed to sweep away all his sister's pent-up frustration. "What's wrong?" she asked quietly.

"I don't exactly know; the doctor's still with her. I think she might be losing the baby. She needs a woman–I'm the last person who should be here. I didn't know who else to call. Can you come?"

"Of course. I'll be there as fast as I can."

It seemed as though no more than a couple of minutes had passed before Lindy came rushing down the hall. He stood at the sight of her, immensely grateful. Relief washed over him and he wrapped his arms around her.

"The doctor hasn't come out yet," he explained before she could ask. He released her and checked his watch. "It's been over an hour now."

"What happened?"

"I'm not sure. Carol started having some kind of abdominal pains. I phoned her gynecologist, and after I explained what was happening, he suggested we meet him here."

"You said you thought Carol might be having a miscarriage?"

"Good Lord, I don't know anything about this woman stuff. All I can tell you is that she was in agony. I did the only thing I could–I got her here." The ten minutes it took to get Carol to the emergency room had been emotionally draining. She was terrified of losing the baby and had wept almost uncontrollably. Through her sobs she'd told him how much she wanted her baby and how this pregnancy would be her only opportunity. Little of what she'd said had made sense to Steve. He'd tried to find the words to assure her, but he hadn't really known what to say.

Just then Steve noticed Carol's physician, Dr. Stewart, push open the swinging door and walk toward the waiting area. He met him halfway.

"How is she?" he asked, his heart in his throat.

The gynecologist rubbed his hand down the side of his jaw and shook his head. His frown crowded his brows together. "She's as good as can be expected."

"The baby?"

"The pregnancy is progressing nicely…thus far."

Although the child wasn't his and Carol had tried to trick him into believing otherwise, Steve still felt greatly relieved knowing that her baby wasn't in any immediate danger.

"I'm sorry to keep you waiting so long, but quite frankly Carol's symptoms had me stumped. It's unusual for someone her age to suffer from this sort of problem."

"What problem?" Lindy blurted out.

"Gall bladder."

"Gall bladder," Steve repeated frowning. He didn't know what he'd expected, but it certainly hadn't been that.

"She tells me she's been suffering from flulike symptoms, which she accepted as morning sickness. There wasn't any reason for either of us to assume otherwise. Some of her other discomforts can be easily misinterpreted as well.

"The most serious threat at the moment is that she's dangerously close to being dehydrated. Predictably that has prompted other health risks."

"What do you mean?" Lindy asked.

"Her sodium and potassium levels have dropped and her heart rate is erratic. I've started an IV and that problem should take care of itself within a matter of hours."

"What's going to happen?"

Once more, Dr. Stewart ran a hand down the side of his face and shook his head. His kind eyes revealed his concern. "I've called in a surgeon friend of mine, and we're going to do a few more preliminary tests. But from what I'm seeing at this point, I don't think we can put off operating. Her gall bladder appears to be acutely swollen and is causing an obstruction."

"If you do the surgery, what will happen to the baby?" For Carol's sake, Steve prayed for the tiny life she was carrying.

Dr. Stewart's sober expression turned grim. "There's always a risk to the pregnancy when anesthesia is involved. I'd like to delay this, but I doubt that we can. Under normal conditions gall-bladder surgery can be scheduled at a patient's convenience, but not in Carol's case, I fear. But I want you to know, we'll do everything I can to save the child."

"Please try." Carol had looked at him with such terror and helplessness that he couldn't help being affected. He would do everything humanly possible to see that she carried this child to full term.

"Please do what you can," Lindy added her own plea. "This child means a great deal to her."

Dr. Stewart nodded. "Carol's sleeping now, but you can see her for a couple of minutes, if you'd like. One at a time."

Steve looked to Lindy, who gestured for him to go in first. He smiled his appreciation and followed the grandfatherly doctor into Carol's room.

As Dr. Stewart had explained, she was sleeping soundly. She looked incredibly fragile with tubes stretching down from an IV pole to connect with the veins in her arm.

Steve stood beside her for several minutes, loving her completely. Emotion clogged his throat and he turned away. He loved her; he always would. No matter what had happened in the past, he couldn't imagine a future without Carol.

"How is she?" Lindy asked when he came out of the room.

He found he couldn't answer her with anything more than a short nod.

Lindy disappeared and returned five minutes later. By then Steve had had a chance to form a plan of action, and he felt better for it.

As Lindy stepped toward him, he held her gaze with newfound determination. He and Carol were both fools if they thought they could stay apart. It wasn't going to work. Without Carol he was only half-alive. And she'd admitted how miserable she'd been during their year's separation.

"I'm going to marry her," Steve informed his sister brusquely.

"What?" Lindy looked at him as though she'd misheard him.

"I'm going to get the chaplain to come to the hospital, and I'm going to marry Carol."

Lindy studied him for several moments. "Don't you think she should have some say in this?"

"Yes…no."

"But I thought…Carol told me you didn't believe the baby is yours."

"It isn't."

Lindy rolled her eyes, then shook her head, her features tight with impatience. "That is the most ridiculous thing you've ever said. Honestly, Steve, where do you come up with these crazy ideas?"

"What idea? That the baby isn't mine, or remarrying Carol?"

"Both!"

"Whether or not I'm the father doesn't make one bit of difference. I've decided it doesn't matter. From here on out, I'm claiming her child as mine."

"But…"

"I don't care. I love Carol and I'll learn to love her baby. That's the end of it." Once the decision had been made, it felt right. The two of them had played a fool's game for over a year, but no more–he wouldn't stand for it. "I'm not going to put up with any arguments from you or from Carol. I want her as my wife–we were wrong ever to have gone through with the divorce. All I'm doing now is correcting a mistake that should never have happened," he told his sister in a voice that men jumped to obey.

Lindy took a moment to digest his words. "Don't you think you should discuss this in a rational matter with Carol? Don't you think she should have some input into her own life?"

"I suppose. But she needs me–although she isn't likely to admit it."

"You've had just as difficult a time recognizing that fact yourself."

"Not anymore."

"When do you plan to tell her?"

Steve didn't know. He'd only reached this conclusion in the last five minutes, but already he felt in control of his life again.

"Well?" his sister pressed.

"I haven't figured out when.... Before the surgery, I think, if it can be arranged."

"Steve, you're not thinking clearly. Carol isn't going to want to be married sitting in a hospital bed, looking all sickly and pale."

"The sooner we get this settled the better."

"For whom?" Lindy prompted.

"For both of us."

Lindy threw up her hands. "Sometimes the things you say utterly shock me."

"They do?" Steve didn't care–he felt as if he could float out of the hospital, he was so relieved. Carol would probably come through the surgery with flying colors and everything would fall into place the way it should have long ago.

This had certainly been a crazy day. He'd bought a sterling silver rattle, followed Carol around a shopping mall like an FBI agent, driven her to the hospital, then made a decision that would go a long way toward assuring their happy future. Steve sighed deeply, feeling suddenly weary.

"Is there any other bombshell you'd care to hit me with?" Lindy asked teasingly.

Steve paused and then surprised her by nodding. Some of the happiness he'd experienced earlier vanished. There was one other decision he'd made–one not as pleasant but equally necessary.

"Should I sit down for this one?" Lindy asked, still grinning. She slipped her arm around his waist and looked up at him.

"I don't think so."

"Well, don't keep me in suspense, big brother."

Steve regarded her soberly. "I'm leaving the Navy."

Chapter Thirteen

Carol opened her eyes slowly. The room was dim, the blinds over the window closed. She frowned when her gaze fell on the IV stand, and she tried to raise herself.

"You're in the hospital." Steve's voice was warm and caressing.

She lowered her head back to the pillow and turned toward the sound. Steve stood at her bedside. From the ragged, tired look about him, she guessed he'd been standing there all night.

"How long have you been here?" she asked hoarsely, testing her tongue.

"Not very long."

She closed her eyes and grinned. "You never could tell a decent lie."

He brushed the hair from her cheek and his fingers lingered on her face as though he needed to touch her. She knew she should ask him to leave, but his presence comforted her. She needed him. She didn't know how he'd happened to be at Northgate Mall, but she would always be grateful he'd found her when he did.

Her hand moved to her stomach, and she flattened it there. "The baby's all right?"

Steve didn't answer her for a moment, and a sickening sense of dread filled her. Her eyes flew open. The doctor had repeatedly assured her that the baby was safe, but something might have happened while she had slept. She'd been out for hours and much of what had taken place after they arrived at the hospital remained foggy in her mind.

"Everything's fine with the pregnancy."

"Thank God," she whispered fervently.

"Dr. Stewart said you were near exhaustion." He reached for her hand and laced his fingers with hers. His thumb worked back and forth on the inside of her wrist.

"I think I could sleep for a week," Carol said, her voice starting to sound more sure. It seemed as though it had been years since she'd had a decent rest. Even before her pregnancy had been confirmed she'd felt physically and emotionally drained, as if she were running on a treadmill, working as fast as her legs would carry her and getting nowhere.

"How do you feel now?"

Carol had to think about it. "Different. I don't know how to describe it. I'm not exactly sick and I'm not in any pain, but something's not right, either."

"You should have recognized that weeks ago. According to Dr. Stewart, you've probably been feeling ill for months."

"They know what's causing the problem?" Her heart started to work doubly hard. Not until the severe attack of pain in the shopping mall had she been willing to admit something could be wrong with her.

"Dr. Stewart thinks it could be your gall bladder."

"My what?"

"Gall bladder," he repeated softly. "I'm sure he can explain it far better than I can, but from what I understand it's a pear-shaped pouch close to the liver."

Carol arched her brows at his attempt at humor and offered him a weak smile. "That explains it."

Steve grinned back at her, and for a moment everything went still. His eyes held such tenderness that she dared to hope again—dared to believe he'd discovered the truth about her and their baby. Dared to let the love that was stored in her heart shine through her eyes.

"I never thought I'd see you again," she said, and her voice quivered with emotion.

Steve lowered his gaze briefly. "I couldn't stay away. I love you too much."

"Oh, Steve, how could we do this to each other? You think such terrible things of me and I can't bear it anymore. I keep telling myself the baby and I would be better off without you, and then I feel only half alive. When we're separated, nothing feels right in my life—nothing is good."

"When I'm not with you, I'm only a shell." He raised her hand to his lips and kissed her knuckles.

Carol felt the tears gather in her eyes and she turned her head away, unwilling to have Steve witness her emotion. No man would ever be more right for her, and no man could ever be so wrong.

She heard the sound of a chair being pushed to the side of the bed. "I want us to remarry," he said firmly. "I've thought it over. In fact, I haven't thought of anything else in the past fifteen hours—and I'm convinced this is the right thing for us to do."

Carol knew it was right, too. "But what about the baby?" she whispered. "You think—"

"From this moment on, the child is mine in my heart and in my soul. He's a part of you and that's the only important thing."

"She," Carol corrected absently. "I'm having a girl."

"Okay…whatever you want as long as we're together."

Carol's mind flooded with arguments, but she hadn't the strength to fight him. The intervening months would convince Steve that this child was his far better than any eloquent speeches she could give him now. By the time the baby was born, his doubts would have vanished completely. In the meantime they would find a way to settle matters–that was essential because they were both so miserable apart.

"Will you marry me, Carol, a second time?"

"I want to say yes. Everything within me is telling me it's the right thing to do…for me and for the baby. But I'm frightened, too."

"I'm going to be a good husband and father, I promise you that."

"I know you will."

"I made another decision yesterday–one that will greatly affect both our lives." His hand pressed against the side of her face and gently brushed the hair from her temple. "I'm leaving the Navy."

Carol couldn't believe her ears. The military was Steve's life; it had been his goal from the time he was a teenager. His dream. He'd never wanted to be or do anything else.

"But you love your work."

"I love you more," he countered.

"It's not an either-or situation, Steve. I've lived all these years as a Navy wife, I've adjusted."

A hint of a smile touched his face. "I won't be separated from you again."

For Steve's sake, Carol had always put on a happy face and seen him off with a cheerful wave, but she'd hated the life, dreading their months apart. Always had and always would. The promise of a more conventional marriage seemed too good to be true. Her head was swimming at the thought of him working a nine-to-five job. She wanted this–she wanted it badly.

"You're the most important person in my life. I'm getting out of the Navy so I can be the kind of husband and father I should be."

"Oh, Steve." The joy that cascaded through her at that moment brought tears to her eyes.

"I can't think of any other way to show you how serious I am."

Neither could Carol. Nevertheless his announcement worried her. Navy life was in Steve's blood, and she didn't know if he could find happiness outside the only career he'd ever known.

"Let's not make such a major decision now," she suggested reluctantly. "There'll be plenty of time to talk about this later."

Steve's eyes filled with tenderness. "Whatever you say."

Humming softly, a nurse wandered into the room and greeted them. "Good morning."

"Morning," Carol answered.

The room was bathed in the soft light of day as the middle-aged woman opened the blinds.

"I'm sorry, but there won't be any breakfast for you this morning. Dr. Stewart will be in later, and I'm sure he'll schedule something for you to eat this afternoon."

Carol didn't feel the least bit hungry. Her appetite had been almost nonexistent for months.

"I'll check on you in an hour," the woman said on her way out the door.

Carol nodded. "Thank you." She was filled with nagging questions about what was going to happen. Naturally she hoped Dr. Stewart could give her a prescription and send her home, but she had the feeling she was being overly optimistic.

Steve must have read the doubt in her eyes because he said, "From what Dr. Stewart told me, he's going to have you complete a series of tests this morning. Following those, we'll be able to make a decision."

"What kind of tests? What kind of decision?"

"Honey, I don't know, but don't worry. I'm not leaving you–not for a minute."

Carol hated to be such a weakling, but she was frightened. "Whatever happens, whatever they have to do, I can take it," she said a little shakily.

"I know you can, love. I know you can."

As promised, for the next few hours Carol underwent several tests. She was pinched, poked and prodded and wheeled to several corners of the hospital. As Steve promised, he was with her each time they took her into another and waiting when she returned.

"Quit looking so worried," she told him, when she'd been wheeled back to her room once more. "I'm going to be fine."

"I know."

She slept after that and woke late in the afternoon. Once more Steve was at her bedside, leaning forward, his face in his hands.

"Bad news?" she asked.

He smiled and Carol could tell by the stiff way his mouth moved that the action was forced.

"What's wrong?" she demanded.

He stood and came to stand beside her. She gave him her hand, her eyes wide with fear.

"Dr. Stewart assured me that under normal conditions, gall bladder surgery is optional. But not in your case. Your gall bladder is acutely swollen and is causing several complications to vital organs. It has to be removed, and the sooner the better."

Carol expelled her breath and nodded. She'd feared something like this, but she was young and healthy and strong; everything would be fine.

"He's called in a surgeon and they've scheduled the operating room for you first thing tomorrow morning."

Carol swallowed her worry. "I can handle that."

"This isn't minor surgery, Carol. I don't think you'd appreciate me minimizing the risks."

"No…no, I wouldn't."

"Dr. Stewart and his associate will be back later today to explain the details of what they'll be doing. It's major surgery, but you have several things in your favor."

She nodded, appreciating the fact that she would know precisely what the medical team would be doing to her body.

"What about the baby?"

Steve's expression tightened and he lifted his eyes from hers. "The pregnancy poses a problem."

"What kind of problem?"

"If the surgery could be delayed, Dr. Stewart would prefer to do that, but it can't be. Your life is at risk."

"What about the pregnancy?" Carol demanded. "I'm not agreeing to anything until I hear what will happen to my baby."

Steve's eyes revealed myriad emotions. Worry and fear dominated, but there was something else–something that took her an extended moment to analyze. Something that clouded his features and ravaged his face. Regret, she decided, then quickly changed her mind. It was more than that–a deep inner sorrow, even remorse.

When Steve spoke, it was as if each word had to be tugged from his mouth. "I'm not going to coat the truth. There's a chance the anesthesia will terminate the pregnancy."

"I won't do it," she cried automatically. "The whole thing's off. I'm not doing anything that will hurt my baby."

"Carol, listen to reason…"

"No." She twisted her head so that she wouldn't have to look at him. As long as she drew a single breath there was no way she would agree to do anything that would harm her daughter.

"Honey," he whispered. "We don't have any choice. If we delay the surgery, you could die."

"Then so be it."

"No." He almost shouted the word. "There's a risk to the baby, but one we're both going to have to take. There's no other choice."

She closed her eyes, unwilling to argue with him further. Her mind was made up.

"Carol, I don't like this any better than you do."

She refused to look at him and pinched her lips together, determined not to murmur a single word. Nothing he could say would change her mind.

The silence in the room was magnified to deafening proportions.

"I love you, Carol, and I can't allow you to chance your life for a baby. If the worst happens and the pregnancy is terminated, then we'll have to accept it. There'll be other children–lots more–and the next time there won't be any question about who the father is."

If Steve had driven a stake into her heart, he couldn't have hurt her more. No words had ever been more cruel. No wonder he was so willing to tell her he'd decided to accept this child as his own. She would likely lose the baby, and believing what he did, Steve no doubt felt that was for the best.

Carol jerked her head around so fast she nearly dislocated her neck. "The next time there won't be any questions?" she repeated in a small, still voice.

"I know this is painful for you, but–"

"I want *this* baby."

"Carol, please…"

"How long have you known about this danger?"

Steve looked stunned by her anger. "Dr. Stewart told me about the possibility after I brought you to the hospital yesterday."

Exactly what she'd expected. Everything Steve had done, everything he'd said from that point on was suddenly suspect. He wanted them to remarry and he was going to leave the Navy. His reasoning became as clear as water to her: he didn't really long for a change in their life-style, nor had his offer to leave the Navy been a decision based on his desire to build a strong marital relationship. He didn't dread their separations as she always had–he'd thrived on them. But if he wasn't in the military, then he could spend his days watching her. There would be no opportunity for her to have an affair. And when she became pregnant a second time, he would have the assurance that the baby was indeed his. His offer hadn't been made from love but from fear rooted in a lack of trust.

It amazed her, now that she thought about it, that he would be willing to give up such a promising career for her. He really did love her, in his own way, but not enough. Ultimately he would regret his decision, and so would she. But by then it would be too late.

"I'm probably doing a bad job of this," he said, and rammed his fingers through his hair. "I should have let Dr. Stewart explain everything to you."

"No," she said dispassionately. "What you've told me explains a good deal. You've been completely up-front with me and I appreciate what it cost you to tell me this. I…I think it's my turn to be honest with you now."

A dark frown contorted his features. "Carol…"

"No, it's time you finally learned the truth. I hesitated when you asked me to marry you and there's a reason. You don't need to worry about me, Steve. You never had to. My baby's father has promised to take care of me. When my plan to trick you didn't work, I contacted him and told him I was pregnant. He thought about it for a couple of days and has decided to marry me himself. I appreciate your offer, but it isn't necessary."

Steve looked as if she'd slipped a knife into his stomach. "You're lying."

"No, for once I'm telling you the truth. Go back to your life and I'll go on with mine. We'll both be far happier this way."

He didn't move for several minutes. His hands curved around the raised railing at the side of the bed and she swore his grip was strong enough to permanently mark the bars. His eyes hardened to chips of glacial ice.

"Who is the father?" he demanded.

Carol closed her eyes, determined not to answer.

"Who is he?"

She looked away, but his fingers closed around her chin and forced her face back toward him.

"Todd?"

She was sick of hearing that name. "No."

"Who?"

"No one you know," she shouted.

"Is he married?"

"No."

A pounding, vibrating silence followed.

"Is this what you really want?"

"Yes," she told him. "Yes...."

A year seemed to pass before she heard him leave the room. When he did, each step he took away from her sounded like nails being pounded into a coffin.

It was finished. There was no going back now. Steve Kyle was out of her life and she'd made certain he would never come back.

Carol felt as if she were walking through a thick bog, every step was hindered, her progress painstakingly slow. A mist rose from the marsh, blocking her view, and she struggled to look into the distance, seeking the light, but she was met instead by more fog.

A soft cry–like that of a small animal–reverberated around her, and it took her a minute to realize she was the one who had made the sound.

She wasn't in any pain. Not physically anyway.

The agony she suffered came from deep inside–a weight

of grief so heavy no human should ever be expected to carry it. Carol couldn't understand what had happened or why she felt this crippling sense of loss.

Then it came to her.

Her baby…they couldn't delay the surgery. The fog parted and a piece of her memory slipped into place. Steve had walked away from her, and soon after he'd gone she'd suffered another attack that had doubled her over with excruciating pain. The hospital staff had called for Dr. Stewart and surgery had been arranged immediately. The option of waiting for even one day had been taken out of her hands.

Now Steve was out of her life and she'd lost her baby, too.

Moisture ran down the side of her face, but when she tried to lift her hand, she found she hadn't the strength.

A sob came, wrenched from her soul. There would be no more children for her. She was destined to live alone for the rest of her life.

"Nurse, do something. She's in pain."

The words drifted from a great distance, and she tossed her head to and fro in an effort to discover the source. She saw no one in the fog. No one.

Once more the debilitating sense of loneliness overtook her and she was alone. Whoever had been there had left her to find her own way through the darkness.

More sobs came–her own, she realized–erupting in deafening sound all around her.

Then she felt something–a hand she thought–warm and gentle, press over her abdomen. The weight of it was a comfort she couldn't describe.

"Your baby's alive," the voice told her. "Can you feel him? He's going to live and so are you!"

It was a voice of authority, a voice of a man who spoke with confidence; a voice few would question.

A familiar voice.

The dark fog started to close in again and Carol wanted

to shout for it to stop. She stumbled toward the light, but it was shut off from her, and she found herself trapped in a black void, defenseless and lost. She didn't know if she would ever have the strength to escape it.

A persistent squeak interrupted Carol's sleep. A wheel far off in the distance was badly in need of oil. The irritating ruckus grew louder until Carol decided it would be useless to try to ignore it any longer.

She opened her eyes to discover Steve's sister standing over her.

"Lindy?"

"Carol, oh, Carol, you're awake."

"Shouldn't I be?" she asked. Her former sister-in-law looked as if she were about to burst into tears.

"I can't believe it. We've been so worried.... No one thought you were going to make it." Lindy cupped her hands over her mouth and nose. "We nearly lost you, Carol Kyle!"

"You did?" This was news to her. She had little memory. The dreadful pain had returned–she remembered that. And then she'd been trapped in that marsh, lost and confused, but it hadn't felt so bad. She had been hot–so terribly hot–she recalled, but there were pleasant memories there, too. Someone had called out to her from there, assured her. She couldn't place what the voice had said, but she remembered how she'd struggled to walk toward the sound of it. The voice hadn't always been comforting. Carol recalled how one time it had shouted at her, harsh and demanding. She hadn't wanted to obey it then and had tried to escape, but the voice had followed her relentlessly, refusing to leave her alone.

"How do you feel?"

"Like I've been asleep for a week."

"Make that two."

"Two?" Carol echoed, shocked. "That long?"

"All right, *almost* two weeks. It's actually been ten days. You had emergency surgery and then everything that could go wrong did. Oh, Carol, you nearly died."

"My baby's okay, isn't she?" From somewhere deep inside her heart came the reassurance that whatever else had happened, the child had survived. Carol vividly remembered the voice telling her so.

"Your baby is one hell of a little fighter."

Carol smiled. "Good."

Lindy moved a chair closer to the bed and sat down. "The doctor said he felt you'd come out of it today. You made a turn for the better around midnight."

"What time is it now?"

Lindy checked her watch. "About 9:00 a.m."

Already her eyes felt incredibly heavy. "I think I could sleep some more."

"As well you should."

Carol tried to smile. "So my daughter is a fighter…. Maybe I'll name her Sugar Ray Kyle."

"Go ahead and get some rest. I'll be here when you wake up."

Already Carol felt herself drifting off, but it was a pleasant sensation. The warm black folds closed their arms around her in a welcoming embrace.

When she stirred a second time, she discovered Lindy was at her bedside reading.

"Is this a vigil or something?" she asked, grinning. "Every time I wake up, you're here."

"I wanted to be sure you were really coming out of it," Lindy told her.

"I feel much better."

"You *look* much better."

The inside of her mouth felt like a sewer. "Do you have any idea how long it'll be before I can go home?"

"You won't. You're coming to live with Rush and me for

a couple of weeks until you regain your strength. And we won't take no for an answer."

"But–"

"No arguing!" Lindy's smile softened her brook-no-nonsense tone.

"I don't deserve a friend as good as you," Carol murmured, awed by Lindy's generosity.

"We should be sisters, and you know it."

Carol chose not to answer that. She preferred to push any thoughts of her ex-husband from her mind.

"This probably isn't the time to talk about Steve."

It wasn't, but Carol didn't stop her.

"I don't know what you said to him, but he doesn't seem to think you want to see him again. Carol, he's been worried sick over you. Won't you at least talk to him?"

A lump the size of a goose egg formed in her throat. "No," she whispered. "I don't want to have anything to do with Steve. We're better off divorced."

Chapter Fourteen

"I'm not an invalid," Carol insisted, frowning at her ex-sister-in-law as she carried her own breakfast dishes to the sink.

"But you've only been out of the hospital a week," Lindy argued, flittering around her like a mother hen protecting her smallest chick.

"For heaven's sake, sit down," Carol cried, "before you drive me crazy!"

"All right, all right."

Carol shared a knowing smile with Rush Callaghan, Lindy's husband. He was a different man than the Rush Carol had known before his marriage to Lindy. He smiled openly now. Laughed. Carol had been fond of Rush, but he'd always been so very serious–all Navy. The military wouldn't find a man more loyal than Rush, but loving Lindy had changed him–and for the better. Lindy had brought sunshine and laughter into his life and brightened his world in a wide spectrum of rainbow colors.

"Come on, Lindy," Rush said, "you can walk me to the door and kiss me goodbye."

With an eagerness that made Carol smile, her good friend escorted Rush to the front door and lingered there several minutes.

When she returned, Lindy walked blindly into the kitchen, wearing a dazed, contented grin. She plopped herself down in a chair, reached for her empty coffee cup and sighed. "He'll be gone for a couple of days."

"Are you going to suffer those Navy blues?"

"I suppose," Lindy said. She lifted her mug and rested her elbows on the table. "I'm a little giddy this morning because Rush and I reached a major decision last night." She smiled and the sun seemed to shine through her eyes. "We're going to start a family. Our first wedding anniversary is coming up soon, and we thought this would be a good way to celebrate."

"Sweet potatoes," Carol said, grinning from ear to ear. "They worked for me."

Lindy gave her a look that insinuated that perhaps Carol should return to the hospital for much-needed psychiatric treatment. "What was that?"

"Sweet potatoes. You know–yams. I heard a medical report over the news last year that reported the results of a study done on a tribe in Africa whose diet staple was sweet potatoes. The results revealed a higher estrogen level in the women and they attributed that fact to the yams."

"I see."

Lindy continued to study her closely. Carol giggled. "I'm not joking! They really work. I wanted to get pregnant and I couldn't count on anything more from Steve than Christmas Eve, so I ate enough sweet potatoes for my body to float in the hormone."

"One night did it?" Lindy's interest was piqued, although she struggled not to show it.

"Two actually–but who knows how long it would have taken otherwise. I ate that vegetable in every imaginable form–including some I wouldn't recommend. If you want, I'll loan you my collection of recipes."

A slow smile spread over Lindy's face, catching in her lovely brown eyes. "I want!"

Carol rinsed her plate and stuck it inside the dishwasher.

"Let me do that!" Lindy insisted, jumping to her feet. "Honest to goodness, Carol. You're so stubborn."

"No, please, I want to help. It makes me feel like I'm being useful." She never had been one to sit and do nothing. This period of convalescence had been troubling enough without Lindy babying her.

"You're recovering from major surgery for heaven's sake!" Steve's sister insisted.

"I'm fine."

"Now, maybe, but a week ago...."

Even now Carol had a difficult time realizing how close she'd come to losing her life. It was the voice that had pulled her back, refusing to let her slip into the darkness, the voice that had urged her to live. Something deep within her subconscious had demanded she cling to life when it would have been so easy to surrender.

"Lindy, I need to ask you something." Unexpectedly Carol's mind was buzzing with doubts about the future.

"Sure, what is it?"

"If anything were to happen to me after the baby's born–"

"Nothing's going to happen to you," Lindy argued.

"Probably not." Carol pulled out the kitchen chair and sat down. She didn't want to sound as though she had a death wish, but with the baby came a responsibility she hadn't thought of before her illness. "I don't have much in the way of family. My mother died several years ago–soon after Steve...soon after I was married. She and my father were divorced years before, and I hardly know him. He has another family and I rarely hear from him."

Lindy nodded. "Dr. Elgin, the surgeon, asked us to contact any close family members and Steve phoned your father. He…he couldn't come."

"He's a busy man," Carol said, willingly offering an excuse for her father, the way she had for most of her life. "But if I were to die," she persisted, "there'd be no one to raise my baby."

"Steve…"

Carol shook her head. "No. He'll probably marry again and have his own family someday. And if he doesn't, he'll be so involved in the Navy he won't be much good for raising a child." It was so much to ask of anyone, even a friend as near and dear as Lindy. "Would you and Rush consider being her guardians?"

"Of course, Carol," Lindy assured her warmly. "But nothing's going to happen to you."

Carol smiled. "I certainly plan on living a long, productive life, but something like this surgery hits close to home."

"I'll talk it over with Rush, but I'm sure he'll be more than willing for us to be your baby's guardians."

"Thank you," Carol said, and impulsively hugged Lindy. Steve's family had always been good to her.

"Okay, now that that's settled, how about a hot game of gin rummy? I feel lucky."

"Sure…" Carol paused and her eyes rounded. Her hand moved to the slight curve of her stomach as her heart filled with happiness.

"Are you all right?"

"I'm fine. The baby just moved–she does that quite a bit now–but never this strong."

"Does it hurt?"

Carol shook her head. "Not in the least. I don't know how to describe it, but every time she decides to explore her little world, I get excited. In four short months I'll be holding my daughter. Oh, Lindy, I can hardly believe it…I can hardly wait."

"Have you ever considered the possibility that *she* might be a *he*?"

"Nope. Not once. The moment I decided to get pregnant, I put my order in for a girl. The least Steve could do was get that right." His name slipped out unnoticed, but as soon as it left her lips, Carol stiffened. She was doing her utmost to disentangle him from her life, peeling away the threads that were so securely wrapped around her soul. There was no going back now, she realized. She'd confirmed every insulting thing he'd ever accused her of.

The mention of Steve seemed to subdue them both.

"Have you chosen a name for the baby?" Lindy asked a little too brightly in an all too apparent effort to change the subject.

Carol dropped her gaze. She'd originally intended to name the baby Stephanie, after Steve, but she'd since decided against that. There would be enough reminders that Steve was her baby's father without using his name. "Not yet," she answered.

"And you're feeling better?"

"Much." Although she was enjoying staying with Lindy and Rush, Carol longed to go back to her own home. Now that Steve was completely out of her life, living with his sister was flirting with misery. Twice Lindy had tried to casually bring Steve into their conversation. Carol had swiftly stopped her both times, but she didn't know who it was harder on–Lindy or herself. She didn't want to hear about Steve, didn't want to think about him.

Not anymore. Not again.

"So how are you feeling, young lady?" Dr. Stewart asked as he walked into the examination room. "I'll have you know you gave us all quite a scare."

"That's what I hear." This was her first appointment to see Dr. Stewart since she'd left the hospital. She'd been through a series of visits with the surgeon, Dr. Elgin, and everything was progressing as it should with the post-surgery healing.

"And how's that little fighter been treating you lately?" he asked with an affectionate chuckle, eyeing Carol's tummy. "Is the baby moving regularly now?"

She nodded eagerly. "All the time."

"Excellent."

"She seems determined to make herself felt."

"This is only the beginning," Dr. Stewart said chuckling. "Wait a few months and then tell me what you think."

The nurse came into the room and Carol lay back on the examination table while the doctor listened for the baby's heartbeat. He grinned and Carol smiled back. Her world might be crumbling around the edges, but the baby filled her with purpose and hope for a brighter future.

"You've returned to work?"

She nodded. "Part-time for the next couple of weeks, then full-time depending on how tired I get. Despite everything, I actually feel terrific."

He helped her into an upright position. "It's little wonder after what you went through–anything is bound to be an improvement." As he spoke he made several notations in her file. "You were one sick young lady. I don't mind telling you," Dr. Stewart added, looking up from her chart, "I was greatly impressed with that young man of yours."

Carol's smile was forced and her heart lurched at the reference to Steve. "Thank you."

"He wouldn't leave your side–not for a moment. Dr. Elgin commented on the fact just the other day. We both believe it was his love that got you through those darkest hours. He was determined that you live." He paused and chuckled softly. "I don't think God Himself would have dared to claim you."

Carol dropped her gaze, not knowing how to comment.

"He's a fine young man. Navy?"

"Yes."

"Give him my regards, will you?"

Carol nodded, her eyes avoiding his.

"Continue with the vitamins and make an appointment to see me in a couple of weeks." He gently patted Carol's hand and moved out of the room.

From the doctor's office, Carol returned to work. But when she pulled into the Boeing parking lot, she sat in her car for several moments, mulling over what Dr. Stewart had told her.

It was Steve's voice that called to her in the dark fog. Steve had been the one who'd comforted her. And when she'd felt the pull of the night, it was he who had demanded she return to the light. According to Dr. Stewart, he'd refused to leave her side.

Carol hadn't known.

She was stunned. She'd purposely lied to him, wanting to hurt him for being so insensitive about the possibility of the surgery claiming their baby's life. She'd been confused and angry because so much of what he wanted for her revealed his lack of faith in her integrity.

She'd sent him away and yet he'd refused to leave her to suffer through the ordeal alone.

Before she returned to her own job section, Carol stopped off to see Lindy.

"Hi," Lindy greeted, looking up from her desk. "What did the doctor have to say?"

"Take your vitamins and see me in two weeks."

"That sounds profound."

Carol scooted a chair toward Lindy's desk and clasped her purse tightly between her hands. The action produced a wide-eyed stare from her former sister-in-law.

"Something Dr. Stewart did say was profound," Carol stated in even tones, although the information Dr. Stewart had given her had shaken her soul.

"Oh? What?"

"He told me Steve was with me every minute after the surgery. He claimed it was Steve who got me through it alive."

"He was there, all right," Lindy confirmed readily. "No one could get him to leave you. You know how stubborn he is. I think he was afraid that if he walked away, you'd die."

"You didn't tell me that."

"Of course I didn't! If you'll recall, I've been forbidden to even mention his name. You practically have a seizure if I so much as hint that there could be someone named Steve distantly related to either of us."

"But I'd told him the baby wasn't his…. I sent him away."

"You told him what?" Lindy demanded, her eyes as round as dinner plates. "Why? Carol, how could you? Oh, good grief–it isn't any wonder you two have problems. It's like watching a boxing match. You seem to take turns throwing punches at each other."

"He…didn't say anything?"

"No. Steve never tells me what's going on in his life. No matter what's happened between you two, he won't say a word. I still don't know the reason you divorced in the first place. Even Rush isn't sure what happened. Steve's like that–he keeps everything to himself."

"And he stayed with me, even after I said I wouldn't remarry him," Carol murmured, feeling worse by the moment.

"There will never be anyone else for him but you, Carol," Lindy murmured. Some of the indignation had left her, but she still carried an affronted look, as if she wanted to stand up and defend her brother.

Carol didn't need Lindy's outrage in order to feel guilty. Lying had never set well with her, but Steve had hurt her so badly. She would like to think that she'd been delirious with pain at the time and not herself, but that wasn't the case. When she'd told Steve that she was going to accept another man's marriage proposal, she'd known exactly what she was doing.

"I owe him so much," Carol murmured absentmindedly.

"According to the surgeon and Dr. Stewart, you owe Steve your life."

Carol's gaze held Lindy's. "Why didn't you say something earlier?"

Lindy tossed her hands into the air. "You wouldn't let me. Remember?"

"I know…I'm sorry." Carol felt like weeping. Lindy was right, so very right. Her relationship with Steve was like a championship boxing match. Although they loved each other, they continued to strike out in a battle of words and deeds.

It wasn't until after she got home and had time to think matters through that Carol decided what she needed to do—what she had to do.

It wouldn't be easy.

Steve read the directions on the back of the frozen dinner entrée and turned the dial on the oven to the appropriate setting. He never had been much of a cook, choosing to eat most of his meals out. Lately, however, even that was more of an effort than he wanted to make. He'd been reduced to frozen TV dinners.

While they were married, Carol had—

Steve ground his thoughts to a screeching halt as he forced the name of his ex-wife from his mind. It astonished him how easily she slipped in where he desperately didn't want her. Yet he was doing everything he could to try to forget the portion of his life that they'd shared.

But that was more easily said than done.

He hadn't asked Lindy about Carol since she'd been released from the hospital. He wanted to know if Todd Larson was giving her the time she needed from work to heal properly. The amount of control it demanded to avoid the subject of Carol with his sister depleted his energy. He was like a man lost in the middle of a desert, dying of thirst. And water was well within sight, but he dared not drink.

Carol had her own life, and now that she and the baby were safe, she was free to seek her own happiness. As he could–only there would be little contentment in his life without her.

The sound of the doorbell caught him by surprise. He tossed the frozen dinner into the oven and headed to the front door, determined to get rid of whoever was there. He wasn't in any mood for company.

"Hello, Steve."

Carol stood on the other side of the threshold, and he was so shocked to see her that someone could have blown him over with the toot of a toy whistle.

"Carol…how are you?" he asked, his voice stiff, his body tense as though mentally preparing for pain.

"I'm doing much better."

She answered him with a gentle smile that spoke of reluctance and regret. Just looking at her tore through his middle.

"Would you like to come in?" he asked. Refusing her entry would be rude, and they'd done more than their share of hurting each other.

"Please."

He stepped aside, pressing himself against the door. She looked well, her coloring once more pink and healthy. Her eyes were soft and appealing when he dared to meet her gaze, which took effort to avoid.

Carol stood in the center of his living room, staring out the window at the panorama of the city. Steve had the impression, though, that she wasn't really looking at the view.

"Would you like something to drink?" he asked when she didn't speak immediately.

"No thanks…this will only take a moment."

Now that he'd found his bearings, Steve forced himself to relax.

"I was in to see Dr. Stewart this afternoon," she said, and her voice pitched a little as if she were struggling to get everything out. "He…he told me how you were with me after the surgery."

"Listen, Carol, if you've come to thank me, it isn't necessary. If you'd told me who the baby's father is, I would have gone for him. He could have stayed with you, but–"

"I lied," Carol interrupted, squaring her shoulders.

He let her words soak into his mind before he responded. "About what?"

"Marrying the baby's father. I told you that because I was so hurt by what you'd said."

"What I'd said?" He couldn't recall doing or saying anything to anger her. The fact was, he'd done everything possible to show her how much he loved and cared about her.

"You suggested it would be better if I did lose this child," she murmured, and her voice trembled even more, "because next time you could be certain you were the father."

She seemed to want him to respond to that.

"I remember saying something along those lines."

Carol closed her eyes as if her patience was depleted and she was seeking another share. "I couldn't take any more of your insults, Steve."

Everything he said and did was wrong when it came to Carol. He wanted to explain, but doubted that it would do any good. "My concern was for you. Any husband would have felt the same way, pregnancy or no pregnancy."

"You aren't my husband."

"I wanted to be."

"That was another insult!" she cried, and a sheen of tears brightened her eyes.

"My marriage proposal was an insult?" he shouted, hurt and stunned.

"Yes…no. The offer to leave the Navy was what bothered me most."

"Then far be it from me to offend you again." There was no understanding this woman. He was willing to give up everything that had ever been important to him for her sake, and she threw the offer back in his face with some ridiculous claim. To hear her tell it, he'd scorned her by asking her to share his life.

The silence stretched interminably. They stood only a few feet apart, but the expanse of the Grand Canyon could have stretched between them for all the communicating they were doing.

The problem, Steve recognized, was that they were both so battle scarred that it was almost impossible for them to talk to each other. Every word they muttered became suspect. No subject was safe. They weren't capable of discussing the weather without finding something to fight about.

"I didn't come here to argue with you," Carol said in weary, reluctant tones. "I wanted to thank you for everything you did. I apologize for lying to you–it was a rotten thing to do."

It was on the tip of his tongue to suggest that he'd gotten accustomed to her lies, but he swallowed the cruel barb. He'd said and done enough to cause her pain in the last couple of years–there was no reason to hurt her more. He would only regret it later. She would look at him with those big blue eyes of hers and he would see all the way to her soul and know the agony he viewed there was of his making. Her look would haunt him for days afterward.

She turned and started to walk away, and Steve knew that if he let her go there would be no turning back. His heart and mind were racing. His heart with dread, his mind with an excuse to keep her. Any excuse.

"Carol–"

Already she was at the front door. "Yes?"

"I...have you eaten?"

Her brow creased, as if food was the last thing on her mind. Her gaze was weary as though she couldn't trust him. "Not yet."

"Would you like to go out with me? For dinner?"

She hesitated.

"The last time you were at the apartment, you said something about a restaurant you wanted to try close to here," he said, reminding her. She'd come to his place with a silly button in her hand and lovemaking on her mind. Things had been bad between them then, and had gone steadily downhill ever since.

She nodded. "The Mexican Lindo."

"Shall we?"

Still she didn't look convinced. "Are you sure this is what you want?"

Now it was his turn to nod. He wanted it so much he could have wept. "Yes, I want this," he admitted.

Some of the tiredness left her eyes and a gentle smile touched her lovely face. "I want it, too."

Steve felt like leaping in the air and clicking his heels. "I'll be just a minute," he said hurriedly. He walked into his kitchen and with a quick twist of his wrist, he turned off the oven. He would toss the aluminum meal later.

For now, he had a dinner date with the most beautiful woman in the world.

Chapter Fifteen

Elaborately decorated Mexican hats adorned the white stucco walls of the restaurant. A spicy, tangy scent wafted through the dining area as Carol and Steve read the plastic-coated menu.

Steve made his decision first.

"Cheese enchiladas," Carol guessed, her eyes linking with his.

"Right. What are you going to have?"

She set aside the menu. "The same thing–enchiladas sound good."

The air between them remained strained and awkward, but Carol could sense how desperately they were each trying to ignore it.

"How are you feeling?" Steve asked after a cumbersome moment of silence. His eyes were warm and tender and seemed to caress her every time he looked in her direction.

"A thousand times better."

He nodded. "I'm glad." He lifted the fork and absently ran his fingers down the tines.

"Dr. Stewart asked me to give you his regards," Carol said in an effort to make conversation. There were so few safe topics for them.

"I like him. He's got a lot of common sense."

"The feeling's mutual–Dr. Stewart couldn't say enough good things about you."

Steve chuckled. "You sound surprised."

"No. I know the kind of man you are." Loving, loyal, determined, proud. Stubborn. She hadn't spent five years of her life married to a stranger.

The waitress came to take their order, and returned a couple of minutes later with a glass of milk for Carol and iced tea for Steve.

"I'm pleased we have this opportunity to talk before I'm deployed," he said, and his hand closed around the tall glass.

"When will you be leaving?"

"In a couple of weeks."

Carol nodded. She was nearly six months pregnant now and if Steve was at sea for the usual three, he might not be home when the baby was born. It all depended on when he sailed.

"I used to hate it when you went to sea." The words slipped from her lips without thought. She hadn't meant to make a comment one way or the other about his tour. It was a part of his life and one she had accepted when she agreed to marry him.

"You hated my leaving?" He repeated her words as though he was certain he'd heard her incorrectly. His gaze narrowed. "You used to see me off with the biggest smile this side of the Mississippi. I always thought you were happy to get me out of your hair."

"That was what I wanted you to think," she confessed with some reluctance. "I might have been smiling on the outside, but on the inside I was dreading every minute of the separation."

"You were?"

"Three months may not seem like a long time to you, but my life felt so empty when you were on the *Atlantis*." The first few years of their marriage, Carol had likened Steve's duty to his sub to a deep affection for another woman who whimsically demanded his attention whenever she wanted him. It wasn't until later that she realized how silly it was to be jealous of a nuclear submarine. She'd done everything possible to keep occupied when he was at sea.

"But you took all those community classes," he argued, breaking into her thoughts. "I swear you had something scheduled every night of the week."

"I had to do something to fill the time so I wouldn't go stir crazy."

"You honestly missed me?"

"Oh, Steve, how could you have doubted it?"

He flattened his hands on the table and slowly shook his head. "But I thought…I honestly believed you enjoyed it when I was away. You used to tell me it was the only time you could get anything accomplished." His voice remained low and incredulous. "My being underfoot seemed to be a detriment to all your plans."

"You had to know how I felt, or you wouldn't have suggested leaving the Navy."

Steve lowered his gaze and shrugged. "That offer was for me as much as you."

"So you could keep an eye on me–I figured that out on my own. If you held a regular nine-to-five job, then you could keep track of my every move and make sure there wasn't any opportunity for me to meet someone else."

"I imagine you found that insulting."

She nodded. "I don't know any woman who wouldn't."

A heavy silence followed, broken only by the waitress delivering their meals and reminding them that the plates were hot.

Steve studied the steaming food. "I suppose that was what you meant when you said my marriage proposal was an insult?"

Carol nodded, regretting those fiery words now. It wasn't the proposal, but what had followed that she'd taken offense to. "I could have put it a little more tactfully, but generally, yes."

Steve expelled his breath forcefully and reached for his fork. "I can't say I blame you. I guess I wasn't thinking straight. All I knew was that I loved…love you," he corrected. "And I wanted us to get married. Leaving the Navy seemed an obvious solution."

Carol let that knowledge soak into her thoughts as she ate. They were both quiet, contemplative, but the silence, for once, wasn't oppressive.

"I dreaded your coming home, too," Carol confessed partway through her meal.

Steve's narrowed gaze locked with hers, and his jaw clenched until she was sure he would damage his teeth, but he made no comment. It took her a moment to identify his anger. He'd misconstrued her comments and assumed the worst–the way he always did with her. He thought she was referring to the guilt she must have experienced upon his return. Hot frustration pooled in the pit of her stomach, but she forced herself to remain calm and explain.

"I could never tell what you were thinking when you returned from a deployment," she whispered, her voice choked and weak. "You never seemed overly pleased to be back."

"You're crazy. I couldn't wait to see you."

"It's true you couldn't get me in bed fast enough, but I meant in other ways."

"What ways?"

She shrugged. "For the first few days and sometimes even longer, it was like you were a different man. You would always be so quiet…so detached. There was so little emotion in your voice–or your actions."

"Honey, I'd just spent a good portion of that tour four hundred feet below sea level. We're trained to speak in subdued, monotone voices. If my voice inflections bothered you, why didn't you say something?"

She dropped her gaze and shrugged. "I was so pleased to have you back that I didn't want to say or do anything to cause an argument. It was such a small thing, and I would have felt like a fool for mentioning it."

Steve took a deep breath. "I know what you mean–I couldn't very well comment on how glad you were to see me leave without sounding like an insecure jerk–which I was. But that's neither here nor there."

"I wish I'd said something now, but I was trying so hard to be the kind of wife you wanted. Please know that I was always desperately lonely without you."

Steve took a couple more bites, but his interest in the food had obviously waned. "I can understand why you felt the need for…companionship."

Carol froze and a thread of righteous anger weaved its way down her spine. "I'm going to forget you said that," she murmured, having difficulty controlling her trembling voice.

Steve looked genuinely surprised. "Said what?"

Carol simply shook her head. They would only argue if she pressed the subject, and she didn't have the strength for it. "Never mind."

Her appetite gone, she pushed her plate aside. "You used to sit and stare at the wall."

"I beg your pardon?" Steve was finished with his meal, too, and scooted his plate aside.

"When you came home from a tour," she explained. "For days afterward, you hardly did a thing. You were so detached."

"I was?" Steve mulled over that bit of insight. "Yes, I guess you're right. It always takes me a few days to separate myself from my duties aboard the *Atlantis.* It's different aboard the sub, Carol. I'm different. When I'm home, especially after being at sea several weeks, it takes time to make the adjustment."

"You're so unfeeling…I don't know how to explain it. Nothing I'd say or do would get much reaction from you. If I proudly showed off some project I'd completed in your absence, you'd smile and nod your head or say something like 'That's nice, dear.'"

Steve grinned, but the action revealed little amusement. "Reaction is something stringently avoided aboard the sub, too. I'm an officer. If I panic, everyone panics. We're trained from the time we're cadets to perform our duties no matter what else is happening. There's no room for emotion."

Carol chewed on the corner of her lower lip.

"Can you understand that?"

She nodded. "I wish I'd asked you about all this years ago."

"I didn't realize I behaved any differently. It was always so good to get home to you that I didn't stop to analyze my behavior."

The waitress came and took away their plates.

"We should have been honest with each other instead of trying to be what we thought the other person wanted," Carol commented, feeling chagrined that they'd been married five years and had never really understood each other.

"Yes, we should have," he agreed. "I'm hoping it isn't too late for us to learn. We could start over right now, determined to be open and honest with each other."

"I think we should," Carol agreed, and smiled.

Steve's hand reached across the table for hers. "I'd like us to start over in other ways, too—get to know each other. We could start dating again the way we did in the beginning."

"I think that's a good idea."

"How about walking down to the waterfront for an ice-cream cone?" he suggested after he'd paid the tab.

Carol was stuffed from their dinner, but did not want their evening to end. Their love had been given a second chance, and she was grabbing hold of it with both hands. They were wiser this time, more mature and prepared to proceed cautiously.

"Are you insinuating that I need fattening up?" she teased, lacing her fingers with his.

"Yes," he admitted honestly.

"How can you say that?" she asked with a soft laugh. She may have lost weight with the surgery, but the baby was filling out her tummy nicely, and it was obvious that she was pregnant. "I eat all the time now. I didn't realize how sick I'd been and now everything tastes so good."

"Cherry vanilla?"

"Ooo, that sounds wonderful. Double-decker?"

"Triple," Steve answered and squeezed her hand.

Lacing their fingers like high-school sweethearts, they strolled down to the steep hill toward the waterfront like young lovers eager to explore the world.

As he promised, Steve bought them each huge ice-cream cones. They sat on one of the benches that lined the pier and watched the gulls circle overhead.

Carol took a long, slow lick of the cool dessert and smiled when she noted Steve watching her. "I told you I've really come to appreciate my food lately."

His gaze fell to the rounded swell of her stomach. "What did Dr. Stewart have to say about the baby?"

Carol flattened her hand over her abdomen and glowed with an inner happiness that came to her whenever she thought about her child. "This kid is going to be just fine."

He darted his gaze away as though he was uncomfortable even discussing the pregnancy. "I'm pleased for you both. You'll be a good mother, Carol."

Once more frustration settled on her shoulders like a dark shroud. Steve still didn't believe the baby was his. She wasn't going to argue with him. He was smart enough to figure it out.

"Do you need anything?" he surprised her by asking next. "I'd be happy to do what I can to help. I'm sure the medical expenses wreaked havoc with your budget, and you're probably counting on that income to buy things for the baby. I'd like to pitch in, if you'd let me."

His offer touched her heart and she took a minute to swallow the tears that burned the back of her eyes at his generosity.

"Thank you, Steve, that means a lot to me, but I'm all right financially. It'll be tight for a couple of months, but nothing I can't handle. I've managed to save quite a bit over the past year."

He stood, buried his hands in his pockets and walked along the edge of the pier. Carol joined him, licking the last of the ice cream off her fingertips.

Steve looked down and smiled into her eyes. "Here," he said and used his index finger to wipe away a smudge near the corner of her mouth.

He paused and his gaze seemed to consume her face. His eyes, so dark and compelling, studied her as if she were some angelic being and he was forbidden to do anything more than gaze upon her. His brow compressed and his eyes shifted to her mouth. As if against his will, he ran his thumb along the seam of her lower lip and gasped softly when her tongue traced his handiwork. He tested the slickness with the tip of his finger, slowly sliding it back and forth, creating a delicate kind of friction.

Carol was filled with breathless anticipation. Everything around them, the sights, the sounds, the smells of the waterfront, seemed to dissolve with the feeling. He wanted to kiss her, she could feel it with every beat of her heart. But he held back.

Then, in a voice that was so low, so quiet, it could hardly be counted as sound, he said, "Can I?"

In response, Carol turned and slipped her arm around his neck. His eyes watched her, and a fire seemed to leap from them, a feral glow that excited her all the more.

She could feel the tension in him, his whole body seemed to vibrate with it.

His mouth came down on hers, open and eager. Carol

groaned and instinctively swayed closer to him. His tongue plunged quickly and deeply into her mouth and she met it greedily. He tasted and teased and withdrew, then repeated the game until the savage hunger in them both had been pitched to a fevered level. Still his lips played over hers, and once the urgent need had been appeased, the kiss took on a new quality. His mouth played a slow, seductive rhythm over hers–a tune with which they were both achingly familiar.

He couldn't seem to get enough of her and even after the kiss had ended, he continued to take short, sweet samples of her lips, reluctant to part for even a minute. Finally he buried his head in the curve of her neck and took in short raspy breaths.

Carol surfaced in slow, reluctant degrees, her head buzzing. She clung to him as tightly as he held on to her.

"We have an audience," Steve whispered with no element of alarm apparent in his tone or action.

Carol opened her eyes to find a little girl about five years old staring up at them.

"My mom and dad do that sometimes," she said, her face wrinkled with displeasure, "but not where lots of people can see them."

"I think you have a smart mom and dad," Steve answered, his voice filled with chagrin. Gently he pulled away from Carol and wrapped his arm around her waist, keeping her close to his side. "'Bye," he told the preschooler.

"'Bye," she said with a friendly wave, and then ran back to a boy who appeared to be an older brother who was shouting to gain her attention.

The sun was setting, casting a rose-red hue over the green water.

They walked back to where Steve had parked his car and he opened her door for her. "Can I see you again?" he asked, with an endearing shyness.

"Yes."

He looked almost surprised. "How about tomorrow night? We could go to a movie."

"I'd like that. Are you going to buy me popcorn?"

He smiled, and from the look in his eyes he would be willing to buy her the whole theater if he could.

Chapter Sixteen

Steve found himself whistling as he strolled up the walkway to Carol's house. He felt as carefree as a college senior about to graduate. Grand adventures awaited him. He had every detail of their evening planned. He would escort Carol to the movies, as they'd agreed, then afterward he would take her out for something to eat. She needed to gain a few pounds and it made him feel good to spend money on her.

When they arrived back at the house, she would invite him in for coffee and naturally he would agree. Once inside it would take him ten…fifteen minutes at the most to steer her into the bedroom. He was starved for her love, famished by his need for her.

The kiss they'd shared the night before had convinced him this was necessary. He was so crazy in love with this woman that he couldn't wait another night to take her to bed. She was right about them starting over–he was willing to do that. It was the going-nice-and-slow part he objected to. He understood exactly what she intended when she decided they could start over. It was waiting for the lovemaking that confused him. Good Lord, they'd been married five years. It wasn't as if they were virgins anticipating their wedding night.

"Hi," Carol said and smiled, opening the door for him.

"Hi." Steve couldn't take his eyes off her. She was wearing the blue maternity dress he'd bought for her the day he'd followed her around like the KGB. "You look beautiful," he said in what had to be the understatement of the year. He'd heard about women having a special glow about them when they were pregnant–Carol had never been more lovely than she was at that moment.

"Do you like it?" she asked and slowly whirled around showing off the dress to full advantage. "Lindy bought it for me. She said she found it on sale and couldn't resist. It was the craziest thing because I'd tried on this very dress and loved it, but decided I really couldn't afford to be spending money on myself. She gave me a silver baby rattle, too. I have a feeling Aunt Lindy is going to spoil this baby."

"You look…marvelous."

"I'm getting so fat," she said, and chuckled. To prove her point, she scooped her hands under the soft swell of her abdomen and turned sideways to show him. She smiled, and her eyes sparkled as she jerked her head toward him and announced, "The baby just kicked."

"Can I feel?" Steve had done everything he could to convince himiself this child was his. Unfortunately he knew otherwise. But he loved Carol, and he'd love her baby. He would learn to–already he truly cared about her child. Without this pregnancy there was no way of knowing if they would ever have gotten back together.

"Here." She reached for his hand and placed it over the top of her stomach. "Feel anything?"

He shook his head. "Nothing."

"Naturally she's going to play a game of cat and mouse now."

Steve removed his hand and flexed his fingers. Some of the

happiness he'd experienced earlier seeped out of him, replaced with a low-grade despondency. He wanted her baby to be his with a desperation that threatened to destroy him. But he couldn't change the facts.

"I checked the paper and the movie starts at seven," Carol said, interrupting his thoughts.

He glanced at his watch. "We'd better not waste any time then." While Carol opened the entryway closet and removed a light sweater and her purse, Steve noted the two gallons of paint sitting on the floor.

"What are you painting?" he asked.

"The baby's room. I thought I'd tackle that project this weekend. I suddenly realized how much I have to do yet to get ready."

"Do you want any help?" He made a halfhearted offer, and wished almost immediately that he hadn't. It wasn't the painting that dissuaded him. Every time Carol so much as mentioned anything that had to do with the baby, her eyes lit up like the Fourth of July. His reaction was just as automatic, too. He was jealous, and that was the last thing he wanted Carol to know.

She closed the closet door and studied him, searching his eyes. He boldly met her look, although it was difficult, and wasn't disappointed when she shook her head. "No thanks, I've got everything under control."

"You're sure?"

"Very."

There was no fooling Carol. She might as well have read his thoughts, because she knew and her look told him as much.

"I'm trying," he said, striving for honesty. "I really am trying."

"I know," she murmured softly.

They barely spoke on the way to the theater and Carol hardly noticed what was happening with the movie. She'd witnessed that look on Steve's face before when she started talking about the baby. So many subjects were open to them except that one. She didn't know any man more blind than Steve Kyle. If she were to stand up in the middle of the show and shout out that she was having his child, he wouldn't hear her. He'd buried his head so deep in the sand when it came to her pregnancy that his brain was plugged.

Time would teach him, if only she could hold on to her patience until then.

Steve didn't seem to be enjoying the movie any more than she was. He shifted in his seat a couple of times, crossed and uncrossed his legs and munched on his popcorn as if he were chewing bullets.

Carol shifted, too. She was almost six months pregnant and felt eight. The theater seat was uncomfortable and the baby had decided to play baseball, using Carol's ribs for batting practice.

She braced her hands against her rib cage and leaned to one side and then scooted to the other.

"Are you all right?" Steve whispered halfway through the feature film.

Carol nodded. She wanted to explain that the baby was having a field day, exploring and kicking and struggling in the tight confines of her compact world, but she avoided any mention of the pregnancy.

"Do you want some more popcorn?"

Carol shook her head. "No thanks."

Ten minutes passed in which Carol did her utmost to pay attention to the show. She'd missed so much of the plot already that it was difficult to understand what was happening.

Feeling Steve's stare, Carol diverted her attention to him. He was glaring at her abdomen, his eyes wide and curious. "I saw him move," he whispered, his voice filled with awe. "I couldn't believe it. He's so strong."

"She," Carol corrected automatically, smiling. She took his hand and pressed it where she'd last felt the baby kick. He didn't pull away but there was some reluctance in his look.

The baby moved again, and Carol nearly laughed aloud at the astonishment that played over Steve's handsome features.

"My goodness," he whispered. "I had no idea."

"Trust me," she answered, and grinned. "I didn't, either."

Irritated by the way they were disrupting the movie, the woman in the row in front of them turned around to press her finger over her lips. But when she saw Steve's hand on Carol's stomach, she grinned indulgently and whispered, "Never mind."

Steve didn't take his hand away. When the baby punched her fist on the other side of Carol's belly, she slid his hand over there. She loved the slow, lazy grin that curved up the edges of his mouth. The action caused her to smile too. She tucked her hand over his and soon they both went back to watching the action on the screen. But Steve kept his fingers where they were for the rest of the movie, gently caressing the rounded circle of her tummy.

By the time the film was over, Carol's head was resting on Steve's shoulder. Although the surgery had been weeks before, it continued to surprise her how quickly she tired. She'd worked that day and was exhausted. It irritated her that she could be so weak. Steve had mentioned getting something to eat after the movie, but she was having difficulty hiding her yawns from him.

"I think I'd better take you home," he commented once they were outside the theater.

"I'm sorry," she murmured, holding her hand to her mouth in a futile effort to hold in her tiredness. "I'm not used to being out so late two nights running."

Steve slipped his arm around her shoulders. "Me, either."

He steered her toward his car and opened the passenger door for her. Once she was inside, he gently placed a kiss on her cheek.

She nearly fell asleep on the short ride home.

"Do you want to come in for some coffee?" she offered when he pulled up to the curb in front of her house.

"You're sure you're up to this?" he asked, looking doubtful.

"I'm sure."

Carol thought she detected a bounce to his step as he came around to help her out of the car, but she couldn't be sure. Steve Kyle said and did the most unpredictable things at times.

Once inside he took her sweater, and while he was hanging it up for her, she went into the kitchen and got down the coffee from the cupboard. Steve moved behind her and slipped his arms around her waist.

"I don't really want coffee," he whispered and gently caught her earlobe between his teeth.

"You don't?"

"No," he murmured.

His hands explored her stomach in a loving caress and Carol felt herself go weak. "I…I wish you'd said something earlier."

"It was a pretense." His mouth blazed a moist trail down the side of her neck.

"Pretense," she repeated in a daze.

As if he were a puppet master directing her actions, Carol turned in his arms and raised her face to his, anticipating his kiss. Her whole body felt as if it were rocking with the force of her heartbeat, anticipating the touch of his mouth over hers.

Steve didn't keep her waiting long. His hands cradled her neck and his lips found hers, exploring them as though he wished to memorize their shape. She parted her mouth in welcome, and his tongue touched hers, then delicately probed deeper in a sweet, unhurried exploration that did incredible things to her. Desire created a churning, boiling pool deep in the center of her body.

His fingers slipped from her nape to tangle with her hair. Again and again, he ran his mouth back and forth over hers, pausing now and again to tease her with a fleck of his tongue against the seam of her lips. "I thought about doing this all day," he confessed.

"Oh, Steve."

His hands searched her back, grasping at the material of her dress as he claimed her mouth in a kiss that threatened to burst them both into searing flames. With a frustrated groan, he drew his arms around her front, searching. His breath came in ragged, thwarted gasps.

Carol could feel the heavy pounding of his heart and she pressed her open mouth to the hollow at the base of his throat, loving the way she could feel his pulse hammer there.

"Damn," he muttered, exasperated. "Where's the opening to this dress?"

It took Carol a moment to understand his question. "There is none."

"What?"

"I slip it on over my head…there aren't any buttons."

"No zipper?"

"None."

He muffled a groan against her neck and Carol felt the soft puffs of warm air as he chuckled. "This serves me right," he protested.

"What does?"

He didn't answer her. Instead, he cradled her breasts in his palms, bunching the material of her dress in the process. Slowly he rotated his thumb over her swollen, sensitive nipples until she gasped, first with shock and surprise, then with the sweet sigh of pleasure.

"Is it good, honey?" he asked, then kissed her, teasing her with his tongue until she was ready to collapse in his arms.

"It's very good," she told him when she could manage to speak, although her voice was incredibly low.

"I want you." He took her hand and pressed it down over his zipper so that she could feel for herself his bulging hardness.

"Oh, Steve." She ran her long fingernails over him.

Exquisitely aroused, he made small hungry sounds and

whispered in a voice that shook with desire. "Come on, honey, I want to make love in a bed."

She made a weak sound of protest. "No." It demanded every ounce of fortitude she possessed to murmur the small word.

"No?" he repeated stunned.

"No." There was more conviction in her voice this time. "So many of our discussions end up in the bedroom."

"Carol, dear God, talking was the last thing I had in mind."

"I know what you want," she whispered. "I think we should wait…it's too soon."

"Wait," he murmured, dragging in a deep breath. "Wait," he said again. "All right, if that's what you honestly want—then fine, anything you say." Reluctantly he released her. "I'm going to have to get out of here while I still can, though. Walk me to the door, will you?"

Carol escorted him to her front door and his hungry kiss revealed all his pent-up frustration.

"You're sure?" he asked one last time, giving her a round-eyed look that would put a puppy to shame.

"No…I'm not the least bit sure," she admitted, and when his eyes widened even more, she laughed aloud at the excitement that flared to life so readily. "I don't like this any better than you do," she told him, "but I honestly think it's necessary. When the time's right we'll know it."

He shut his eyes and nodded. "I was afraid of that."

Chapter Seventeen

Carol woke before seven Saturday morning, determined to get an early start on painting the baby's bedroom. She dressed in a old pair of summer shorts with a wide elastic band and a Seahawk T-shirt that had once been Steve's. A western bandana knotted at the base of her skull covered her blond hair. She looked like something out of the movie *Aliens*, she decided, smiling.

Oh, well, she wouldn't be seeing Steve. She regretted turning down his offer of help now, but it was too late for second thoughts. She hadn't seen him since the night they'd gone to the movies, nor had he phoned. That concerned her a little, but she tried not to let it bother her.

He was probably angry about her not letting him spend the night. Well, for his information, she'd been just as frustrated as he was. She'd honestly wanted him to stay–in fact, she'd tossed and turned in bed for a good hour after he'd left her, mulling over her decision. It may have been the right one, but it didn't take away this ache of loneliness, or ease her own sexual frustration.

For six years the only real communication between them had been on a mattress. It was long past time they started building a solid foundation of love and trust. Those qualities were basic to a lifetime relationship, and they'd both suffered for not cultivating them.

By nine, Carol had the bedroom floor carpeted with a layer of newspapers. The windows were taped and she was prepared to do the cutting in around the corners and ceiling.

She carried the stepladder to the far side of the room and, humming softly, started brushing on the pale pink paint.

"What are you doing on that ladder?"

The voice startled her so much that she nearly toppled from her precarious perch. "Steve Kyle," she cried, violently expelling her breath. "You scared me half out of my mind."

"Sorry," he mumbled, frowning.

"What are you doing here?"

"I…I thought you could use some help." He held up a white sack. "Knowing you, you probably forgot to eat breakfast. I brought you something."

Now that she thought about it, Carol realized she hadn't had anything to eat.

"Thanks," she said grinning, grateful to see him. "I'm starved."

Climbing down the stepladder, she set aside the paint and brush and reached for the sack. "Milk," she said taking out a small carton, "and a muffin with egg and cheese." She smiled up at him and brushed her mouth over his cheek. "Thanks."

"Sit," he ordered, turning over a cardboard box as a mock table for her.

"What about you?"

"I had orange juice and coffee on the way over here." Hands on his hips, he surveyed her efforts. "Good grief, woman, you must have been at this for hours."

"Since seven," she said between bites. "It's going to be a scorcher today, and I wanted to get an early start."

He nodded absently, then turned the cap he was wearing around so that the brim pointed toward his back. Next, he picked up the paintbrush and coffee can she'd been using to hold paint. "I don't want you on that ladder, understand?"

"Aye, aye, Captain."

He responded to her light sarcasm with a soft chuckle. "Have you missed me?" he asked, turning momentarily to face her.

Carol dropped her gaze and nodded. "I thought you might be angry about the other night when you wanted to stay and–"

"Carol, no," he objected immediately. "I understood and you were right. I couldn't call–I've had twenty-four-hour duty."

Almost immediately Carol's spirits lifted and she placed the wrapper from her breakfast inside the paper sack. "Did you miss *me*?" she asked, loving the way his eyes brightened at her question.

"Come here and I'll show you how much."

Laughing, she shook her head. "No way, fellow. I'd like my baby's bedroom painted before she makes her debut." Carol noted the way Steve's face still tightened at the mention of her pregnancy and some of the happiness she'd experienced by his unexpected visit evaporated. He'd told her he was trying to accept her child and she believed him, but her patience was wearing perilously thin. After all, this child was his, too, and it was time he acknowledged the fact.

Pride drove her chin so high that the back of her neck ached. She reached for another paintbrush, her shoulders stiff with frustration. "I can do this myself, you know."

"I know," he returned.

"It isn't like I'm helpless."

"I know that, too."

Her voice trembled a little. "It isn't like you really want this baby."

An electric silence vibrated between them, arcing and spitting tension. Steve reacted to it first by lowering his brush.

"Carol, I'm sorry. I didn't mean to say or do anything to upset you. My offer to help is sincere–I'd like to do what I can, if you'll let me."

She bit into her lower lip and nodded. "I…I was being oversensitive, I guess."

"No," he hurried to correct her, "the problem is mine, but I'm dealing with it the best way I know how. I need time, that's all."

His gaze dropped to her protruding stomach and Carol saw a look of anguish flitter through his eyes, one so fleeting, so transient that for a second she was sure she was mistaken.

"Well," she said, drawing in a deep breath. "Are we going to paint or are we going to sit here and grumble at each other all day?"

"Paint," Steve answered, swiping the air with his brush, as if he were warding off pirates.

Carol smiled, then placed the back of her hand over her forehead and sighed. "My hero," she said teasingly.

By noon the last of the walls were covered and the white trim complete around the window and door.

Carol stepped back to survey their work. "Oh, Steve," she said with an elongated sigh. She slipped her arm around his waist. "It's lovely."

"I sincerely hope you get the girl you want so much, because a boy could take offense at all this pink."

"I am having a girl."

"You're sure?" He cocked his eyebrows with the question, his expression dubious.

"No-o-o, but my odds are fifty-fifty, and I'm choosing to think positive."

His arm tightened around her waist. "You've got paint in your hair," he said, looking down at her.

Wrinkling her nose, she riffled her fingers through her bangs. Steve's hand stopped her. His eyes lovingly stroked her face as if he meant to study each feature and commit it to memory. His gaze filled with such longing, such adoration that Carol felt as if she were some heavenly creature he'd been forbidden to touch. He raised his hand to her mouth and she stopped breathing for a moment.

His touch was unbelievably delicate as he rubbed the back of his knuckles over her moist lips. He released her and backed away, his breath audible.

Carol lifted her hand to the side of his face and he closed his eyes when the tips of her fingers grazed his cheek.

"Thank you for being here," she whispered. "Thank you for helping."

"I always want to be with you." He placed his hand over hers, intertwining their fingers. Tenderly, almost against his will, he lowered his knuckles to her breast, dragging them across the rigid, sensitive tip. Slowly. Gently. Back and forth. Again and again.

Carol sucked in her breath at the wild sensation that galloped through her blood. Her control was slipping. Fast. She felt weak, as though she would drop to the floor, and yet she didn't let go of his hand, pinning it against her throbbing nipple.

"How does that feel?" he asked, and he rotated his thumb around and around, intensifying the pleasure.

"…so good," she told him, her voice husky and barely audible.

"It's good for me, too."

His eyes were closed. As Carol watched his face harden with desire she knew her features were equally sharp.

He kissed her then, and the taste of him was so sweet, so incredibly good. His lips teased hers, his tongue probing her mouth, tracing first her upper and then her lower lip in a leisurely exercise. The kiss grew sweeter yet, and deeper.

Steve broke away and pressed his forehead against hers while taking in huge, ragged puffs of air. "There's something you should know."

"What?" She wrapped her hands around his middle, craving the feel of his body against her own.

"The orders for the *Atlantis* came in. I have to leave tomorrow."

Carol went stock-still. "Tomorrow?"

"I'm sorry, honey. I'd do anything I could to get out of this, but I can't."

"I…know."

"I got some Family-grams so you can let me know when the baby's born."

Carol remembered completing the short telegramlike messages while they were married. She was allowed to send a handful during the course of a tour, but under strict conditions. She wasn't allowed to use any codes, and she was prohibited from relaying any unpleasant news. She had forty-six words to tell him everything that was happening in her life. Forty-six words to tell him when his daughter was born, forty-six words to convince him this baby was his.

His hand slipped inside the waistband of her summer shorts and flattened over the baby. "I'll be waiting to hear."

Carol didn't know what to tell him. The baby could very well be born while he was away. It all depended on his schedule.

"I'd like to be here for you."

"I'll be fine…. Both of us will." Carol felt as if she was going to dissolve into tears, her anguish was so keen. Her hand reached for his face and she traced his eyebrows, the arch of his cheek, his nose and his mouth with fingers that trembled with the strength of her love.

His hands slid behind her and cupped her buttocks, lifting her so that the junction between her thighs was nestled against the strong evidence of his desire.

"I want to make love," she whispered into his mouth, and then kissed him.

He shut his eyes. "Carol, no–you were right, we should wait. We've done this too often before… we…"

She hooked her left leg around his thigh and felt a surge of triumph at the shudder that went through him.

"Carol..."

Before he could think or move, she jerked the T-shirt off her head and quickly disposed of her bra. Her mouth worked frantically over his, darting her tongue in and out of his mouth, kissing him with a hunger that had been building within her for months. Her fingers worked feverishly at the buttons of his shirt. Once it was unfastened, she pulled his shirttails free of his waistband and bared his chest. Having achieved her objective, she leaned toward him just enough so that her bare breasts grazed his chest.

The low rumbling sound in Steve's throat made her smile. Slowly then, with unhurried ease, she swayed her torso, taking her pleasure by rubbing her distended nipples over the tense muscles of his upper body.

Steve's breathing came in short, rasping gasps as he spoke. "Maybe I was a bit hasty..."

Carol locked her hands behind his head. "How long will you be gone?" she asked, knowing full well the answer.

"Three months."

"You were too hasty."

"Does this mean...you're willing?"

"I was willing the other night."

"Oh, dear God, Carol, I want you so much."

She rubbed her thigh over his engorged manhood and he groaned. "I know what you want." She kissed him with all the pent-up longings of her heart. "I want you, too. Do you have any idea how much?"

He darted his tongue over one rigid nipple, feasting and sucking at her until she gave a small cry.

He lifted his head and chuckled. "Good, then the feeling's mutual."

With that, he swung her into his arms and carried her into the bedroom. Very gently he laid her atop the mattress and leaned over her, his upper body pinning her to the bed.

He stared down at her and his eyes darkened, but not with passion. It was something more, an emotion she couldn't readily identify.

"Will I…is there any chance I'll hurt the baby?" He whispered the question, his gaze narrowed and filled with concern.

"None."

He sighed his relief. "Oh, Carol, I love you so much."

She closed her eyes and directed his mouth to hers. She loved him, too, and she was about to prove how much.

Carol woke an hour before the alarm was set to ring. Steve slept soundly at her side, cuddling her spoon-fashion, his hand cupping the warm underside of her breast.

They'd spent the lazy afternoon making slow, leisurely love. Then they'd showered, eaten and made love again, with the desperation that comes of knowing it would be three months before they saw each other again.

It was morning. Soon he would be leaving her again. A lump of pain began to unflower inside her. It was always this way when Steve left. For years she'd hid her sorrow behind a cheerful smile, but she couldn't do that anymore. She couldn't disguise how weak and vulnerable she was without him.

Not again.

When it became impossible to hold back the tears, she silently slipped from the bed, donned her robe and moved into the kitchen. Once there, she put on a pot of coffee just so she'd be doing something.

Steve found her sitting at the table with a large pile of tissues stacked next to her coffee cup. She looked up at him, and sobbed once, and reached for another Kleenex.

"G-g-good m-morning," she blubbered. "D-did you sleep well?"

Obviously bewildered, Steve nodded. "You didn't?"

"I s-slept okay."

Watching her closely, he walked over to the table. "You're crying."

"I know that," she managed between sobs.

"But why?"

If he wasn't smart enough to figure that out then he didn't deserve to know.

"Carol, are you upset because I'm leaving?"

She nodded vigorously. "Bingo–give the man a Kewpie doll."

He knelt down beside her, took her free hand and kissed the back of it. He rubbed his thumb over her knuckles and waited until she swallowed and found her voice.

"I hate it when you have to leave me," she confessed when she could talk. "Every time I think we're getting somewhere you sail off into the sunset."

"I'm coming back."

"Not for three months." She jerked the tissue down both sides of her face. "I always c-cry when you go. You just never see me. This t-time I can't… h-hold it in a minute longer."

Steve knelt in front of her and wrapped his arms around her middle. With his head pressed over her breast, one hand rested on top of her rounded stomach.

"I'll be back, Carol."

"I…know."

"But this time when I return, it'll be special."

She nodded because speaking had become impossible.

"We'll have a family."

She sucked in her breath and nodded.

"Dammit, Carol, don't you know that I hate leaving you, too?"

She shrugged.

"And worse, every time I go, I regret that we aren't married. Don't you think we should take care of that next time?"

She hiccuped. "Maybe we should."

Chapter Eighteen

"This works out great," Lindy said, standing in line for coffee aboard the ferry *Yakima* as it eased away from the Seattle wharf, heading toward Bremerton. "You can drop me off at Susan's and I can ride home with Rush. I couldn't have planned this any better myself."

"Glad to help," Steve answered, but his thoughts weren't on his sister. Carol continued to dominate his mind. He'd left her only a couple of hours earlier and it felt as if years had passed–years or simply minutes, he couldn't decide which.

She'd stood on the front porch as he walked across the lawn to his car. The morning sunlight had silhouetted her figure against the house. Tears had brightened her eyes and a shaky smile wobbled over her mouth. When he'd opened the car door and looked back, she'd raised a hand in silent farewell and done her best to send him off with a proud smile.

Steve had stood there paralyzed, not wanting to leave her, loving her more than he thought it was possible to care about anyone. His gaze centered on her abdomen and the child she carried and his heart lurched with such pain that he nearly dropped to his knees. There stood Carol, the woman he loved and would always love, and she carried another man's child. The anguish built up inside him like steam ready to explode out of a teakettle. But as quickly as the emotion came, it left him. The baby was Carol's, a part of her, an innocent. This child deserved his love. It shouldn't matter who the father was. If Steve was going to marry Carol–which he fully intended to do–she came as part of a package deal. Carol and the baby. He sucked in his breath, determined to do his best for them both.

Now, hours later, the picture of her standing there on the porch continued to scorch his mind.

"Lindy," he said, as they reached a table, "I need you to do something for me."

"Sure. Anything."

Steve pulled out his checkbook and set it on the table. "I want you to go to the J.C. Penney store and buy a crib, and a few other things."

"Steve, listen…"

"The crib's called the Jenny Lind–at least I think it was." The picture of Carol running her hand over the railing that day he'd followed her came to his mind. "It's white, I remember that much. I don't think you'll have any trouble knowing which one I mean once you see their selection."

"I take it you want the crib for Carol?"

"Of course. And while you're there, pick out a high chair and stroller and whatever else you can find that you think she could use."

"Steve, no."

"No!" He couldn't believe his sister. "Why the hell not?"

"When I agreed to do you a favor, I thought you wanted me to pick up your cleaning or check on the apartment–that sort of thing. If you want to buy things for Carol, I'm refusing you point-blank. I won't have anything to do with it."

"Why?" Lindy and Carol were the best of friends. His sister couldn't have shocked him more if she'd suggested he leap off the ferry.

"Remember the dress?" Lindy asked, and her chest heaved with undisguised resentment. "I felt like a real heel giving her that, and worse, lying about it." Her face bunched into a tight frown. "Carol was as excited as a kid at Christmas over that maternity dress, and I had to tell her I'd seen it on sale and thought of her and how I hoped against hope that it would fit." She paused and glared at him accusingly. "You know I'm not the least bit good at lying. It's a wonder Carol didn't figure it out. And if I didn't feel bad enough about the dress, the rattle really did it."

Steve frowned, too. He'd asked Lindy to make up some story about the dress and the toy so that Carol wouldn't know he'd been following her that afternoon. Those had been dark days for him–and for Carol.

"Did you know," Lindy demanded, cutting into his thoughts and waving her finger under his nose, "Carol got all misty over that silver rattle?" The look she gave Steve accused him of being a coward. "*I* nearly started crying by the time she finished."

Steve's hand cupped the Styrofoam container of coffee. "I'm glad she liked it."

"It was the first thing anyone had given her for the baby, and she was so pleased that she could barely talk." Lindy paused and slowly shook her head. "I felt like the biggest idiot alive to take credit for that."

"If you'll recall, sister dearest, Carol didn't want to have anything to do with me at the time."

Lindy's eyes rounded with outrage. "And little wonder. You are so dense sometimes, Steve Kyle."

Steve ignored his sister's sarcasm and wrote out a check, doubling the amount he'd originally intended. "Buy her a bunch of baby clothes while you're at it…and send her a huge bouquet of roses when she's in the hospital, too."

"Steve…I don't know."

He refused to argue with her. Instead, he tore off the check, and slipped it across the table.

Lindy took it and studied the amount. She arched her eyebrows and released a soft, low whistle. "I'm not hiding this. I'm going to tell Carol all these gifts are from you. I refuse to lie this time."

"Fine…do what you think is best."

Steve watched as she folded the check in half and stuck it inside a huge bag she called her purse.

"Actually you may be sorry you trusted me with this task later," Lindy announced, looking inordinately pleased about something.

She said this with a soft smile, and her eyes sparkled with mischief.

"Why's that?"

Lindy rested her elbows on the tabletop and sighed. "Rush and I are planning to start our family."

The thought of his little sister pregnant did funny things to Steve. She was ten years younger than he was and he'd always thought of her as a baby herself. An equally strange image flittered into this mind–one of his friend Rush holding an infant in his arms. The thought brought a warm smile with it. When it came to the Navy, Rush knew everything there was to know. Every rule, every regulation–he loved military life. Rush was destined to command ships and men. But when it came to babies–why, Rush Callaghan wouldn't know one end from the other. One thing Steve did know about his friend, though–he knew Rush would love his children with the same intensity that he loved Lindy. Any brother and uncle-to-be couldn't ask for anything more.

"Rush will be a good father," Steve murmured, still smiling.

"So will you," Lindy countered.

Blood drained from his heart and brain at his sister's comment. "Yes," Steve admitted, and the word felt as if it had been ripped from his soul. He was going to love Carol's child; he accepted the baby then as surely as he knew the moon circled the earth. When the little one was born, he was going to be as proud and as pleased as if she were his own seed.

"Yes," he repeated, stronger this time, his heart throbbing with a newly discovered joy. "I plan on taking this parenting business seriously."

"Good," Lindy said, and opened her purse once more. She drew out a plastic dish and spoon. "I take it you and Carol are talking to each other now."

Smiling, Steve took a sip of his coffee and nodded, thinking about how well they'd "communicated" the day before. "You could say that," he answered, leaning back in his chair, content in the knowledge that once he returned they would remarry.

"There were times when I was ready to give up on you both," Lindy said, shaking her head. "I don't know anyone more stubborn than you. And Carol's so damn proud; there's no reasoning with her, either."

They'd both learned lessons in those areas. Painful ones.

"Take care of her for me, Lindy," he said, his eyes appealing to his sister. "I'm worried about her. She's so fragile now, delicate in body and spirit."

"I don't think she'll be working much longer, but I'll make a point of stopping in and seeing her as often as I can without being obvious about it."

Her job had been an area they'd both avoided discussing, because ultimately it involved Todd. As much as possible, Steve avoided all thoughts of the sporting goods store where Carol was employed.

"I'd appreciate that," he murmured.

"If you think it's necessary, I could suggest picking her up and driving her to work with me."

"That's miles out of your way."

"No, it isn't," she returned, giving him an odd look. "Rush's and my apartment is less than a mile from Carol's place. In fact, I drive right past her street on my way to work anyway. It wouldn't be any trouble to swing by and pick her up."

"True, but Larson's is the opposite direction from the Boeing plant."

"Larson's? What's Larson's?"

"Larson's Sporting Goods where Carol works." Even saying it brought an unreasonable surge of anger. It had always bothered him to think of Carol having anything to do with the store.

"Carol doesn't work at a sporting goods store. She works for Boeing," Lindy informed him crisply, looking at him as though he'd recently landed from Mars. "She's been there over a year now."

"Boeing?" Steve repeated. "She works for Boeing? I…I didn't know that."

"Is Larson's the place she used to work?"

Steve nodded, wondering how much his sister knew about Carol's relationship with the owner.

"I think she mentioned it once. As I recall, they were having lots of financial troubles. She was putting in all kinds of extra hours and not getting paid. Not that it mattered, she told me. The couple who owned the place were friends and she was doing what she could to help out. I understand they're still in business. Carol never told me why she decided to change jobs."

Steve chewed on that information. Apparently for all their talk about honest communication they'd done a poor job of it. Again.

Lindy removed the lid from the Tupperware dish and started stirring some orange concoction that faintly resembled mashed carrots.

"Good Lord, that looks awful."

"This?" She pointed the spoon at the container. "Trust me, it's dreadful stuff."

"What is it?"

Lindy's gaze linked with his. "You mean you don't know?"

"If I did, do you think I'd be asking?"

"It's sweet potatoes."

"Sweet potatoes?" he echoed, wrinkling his nose. "What are you doing eating them at this time of year? I thought they were a holiday food."

"I just told you."

"No, you didn't." He didn't know what kind of guessing game Lindy was playing now, but apparently he'd missed some important clues.

"Rush and I are trying to get me pregnant."

"Congratulations, you already told me that."

"That's why I'm eating the sweet potatoes," Lindy went on to explain in a voice that was slow and clear, as though she were explaining this to a preschooler.

Steve scratched the area behind his left ear. "Obviously I'm missing something here."

"Obviously!"

"Well, don't keep me in suspense. You want to have a baby so you're eating sweet potatoes."

Lindy nodded. "Three times a day. At least, that was what Carol recommended."

"Why would she do that?"

Lindy offered him another one of those looks usually reserved for errant children or unusually dense adults. "Because she told me how well eating this little vegetable worked for her."

Steve's brow folded into a wary frown.

"Apparently she heard this report on the radio about yams raising a woman's estrogen level and she ate them by the bowlful getting ready for Christmas Eve with you." Lindy reached inside her purse and pulled out several index cards.

"She was generous enough to copy down some recipes for me. How does sweet potato and ham casserole sound?" she asked, and rolled her eyes. "I don't think I'll be sampling that."

"Sweet potatoes," he repeated.

Lindy's gaze narrowed to thin slits. "That's what I just got done saying."

If she'd slammed a hammer over his head, the effect would have been less dramatic. Steve's heart felt as if it was about to explode. His mind whirled at the speed of a thousand exploding stars. A supernova–his own. Everything made sense then. All the pieces to the bizarre and intricate puzzle slipped neatly into place.

Slowly he rose to his feet, while bracing his hands against the edge of the table. His gaze stretched toward Seattle and the outline of the city as it faded from view.

"Steve?" Lindy asked, concern coating her voice. "Is something wrong?"

He shook his head. "Lindy," he said reaching for her hand and pumping it several times. "Lindy. Oh, Lindy," he cried, his voice trembling with emotion. "I'm about to become a father."

Chapter Nineteen

An overwhelming sense of frustration swamped Steve as the *Atlantis* sailed out of Hood Canal. As he sat at his station, prepared to serve his country for another tour, two key facts were prominent in his mind. The first was that he was soon to become a father and the second, that it would be three interminable months before he could talk to Carol.

He'd been a blind fool. He'd taken a series of circumstantial evidence about Carol's pregnancy and based his assumption solely on a series of events he'd misinterpreted. He remembered so clearly the morning he'd made his less-than-brilliant discovery. He'd gone into Carol's living room and sat there, his heart and mind rebelling at what he'd discovered…what he thought he'd learned.

Carol had come to him warm from bed, her eyes filled with love and laughter. He'd barely been able to tolerate the sight of her. He recalled the stunned look she'd given him when he first spoke to her. The shock of his anger had made her head reel back as though he'd slapped her. Then she'd stood before him, her body braced, her shoulders rigid, the proud tilt of her chin unyielding while he'd blasted his accusations at her like fiery balls from a hot cannon.

He'd been so confident. The sweet potatoes were only the beginning. There was the knitting and the milk and a hundred little things she'd said and done that pointed to one thing.

His heart ached at the memory of how she'd swallowed her self-respect and tried to reason with him. Her hand had reached out to him, implored him to listen. The memory of the look in her eyes was like the merciless sting of a whip as he relived that horrible scene.

Dear God, the horrible things he'd said to her.

He hadn't been able to stop taunting her until she'd told him what he wanted to hear. Repeatedly he'd shouted at her to confirm what he believed until she'd finally admitted he was too smart for her.

Steve closed his eyes to the agony that scene produced in his mind. She'd silently stood there until her voice had come in desperate, throat-burning rasps that sounded like sobs. That scene had been shockingly similar to another in which he'd set his mind based on a set of circumstances and refused to believe her.

Steve rubbed a hand wearily across his face. Carol had never had an affair with Todd. She'd tried to tell him, begged him to believe her, and he'd refused.

"Oh, God," he whispered aloud, tormented by the memory. He buried his face in his hands. Carol had endured all that from him and more.

So much more.

Carol was miserable. She had six weeks of this pregnancy left to endure and each day that passed seemed like a year. Next time she decided to have a baby, she was going to plan the event so that she wouldn't spend the hottest days of the summer with her belly under her nose.

She no longer walked–she waddled. Getting in and out of a chair was a major production. Rolling over in bed was like trying to flip hotcakes with a toothpick. By the time she made it from one position to another, she was panting and exhausted.

It was a good thing Steve wasn't around. She was tired and irritable and ugly. So ugly. If he saw her like this he would take one look and be glad they were divorced.

The doorbell chimed and Carol expelled her breath, determined to find a way to come to a standing position from the sofa in a ladylike manner.

"Don't bother to get up," Lindy said, letting herself in the front door. "It's only me."

"Hi," Carol said, doing her best to smile, and failing.

"How do you feel?"

She planted her hands on her beach-ball-size stomach. "Let me put it this way–I have a much greater appreciation of what my mother went through. I can also understand why I'm an only child!"

Lindy giggled and plopped down on the chair. "I can't believe this heat," she said, waving her hand in front of her face.

"*You* can't! I can't see my feet anymore, but I swear my ankles look like tree trunks." She held one out for Lindy's inspection.

"Yup–oak trees!"

"Thanks," Carol groaned. "I needed that."

"I have something that may brighten your day. A preordered surprise."

With an energy Carol envied, Steve's sister leaped out of the chair and held open the front door.

"Okay, boys," she cried. "Follow me."

Two men marched through the house carrying a huge box.

"What's that?" Carol asked, struggling to get out of her chair, forgetting her earlier determination to be a lady about it.

"This is the first part of your surprise," Lindy called from the hallway.

Carol found the trio in the baby's bedroom. The oblong shaped box was propped against the wall. "A Jenny Lind crib," she murmured, reading the writing on the outside of the package. For months, every time she was in the J.C. Penney store she'd looked at the Jenny Lind crib. It was priced far beyond anything she could afford, but she hadn't seen any harm in dreaming.

"Excuse me," the delivery man said, scooting past Carol.

She hadn't been able to afford a new crib and had borrowed one from a friend, who'd promised to deliver it the following weekend.

"Lindy, I can't allow you to do this," Carol protested, although her voice vibrated with excitement.

"I didn't." She looked past Carol and pointed to the other side of the bedroom. "Go ahead and put the dresser there."

"Dresser!" Carol whirled around to find the same two men carrying in another huge box. "This is way too much."

"This, my dear, is only the beginning," Lindy told her, and her smile was that of a Cheshire cat.

"The beginning?"

One delivery man was back, this time with a mattress and several sacks.

Rush followed on the man's heels, carrying a toolbox in his hand. "Have screwdriver, will travel," he explained, grinning.

"The stroller, high chair and car seat can go over in that corner," Lindy instructed with all the authority of a company foreman.

Carol stood in the middle of the bedroom with her hand pressed over her heart. She was so overcome she couldn't speak.

"Are you surprised?" Lindy asked, once the delivery men had completed their task.

Carol nodded. "This isn't from you?"

"Nope. My darling brother gave me specific instructions on what he wanted me to buy for you–right down to the model and color. Before the *Atlantis* sailed he wrote out a check and listed the items he wanted me to purchase. Rush and I had a heyday in that store."

"Steve had you do this?" Carol pressed her lips tightly together and exhaled slowly through her nose in an effort to hold in the emotion. She missed him so much; each day was worse than the one before. The morning he'd left, she'd cried until her eyes burned. He probably wouldn't be back in time for the baby's birth. But even if he was, it really wouldn't matter because Steve Kyle was such an idiot, he still hadn't figured out this child was his own.

"And while we're on the subject of my dim-witted brother," Lindy said, turning serious, "I think you should know he was the one who bought you the maternity dress and the rattle, too."

"Steve did?"

Lindy nodded. "You two were going through a rough period and he didn't think you'd accept them if you knew he was the one who bought them."

"We're always going through a rough period," Carol reported sadly.

"I wouldn't say that Steve is so dim-witted," Rush broke in, holding up the instructions for assembling the crib. "Otherwise, he'd be the one trying to make sense out of this instead of me."

"Consider this practice, Rush Callaghan, since you'll be assembling another one in a few months."

The screwdriver hit the floor with a loud clink. "Lindy," Rush breathed in a burst of excitement. "Does this mean what I think it does?"

Steve wrote a journal addressed to Carol every day. It was the only thing that kept him sane. He poured out his heart and begged her forgiveness for being so stupid and so blind. It was his insecurities and doubts that had kept him from realizing the truth. Now that he'd accepted what had always been right before his eyes, he was astonished. No man had ever been so obtuse.

Every time Steve thought about Carol and the baby, which was continually, he would go all soft inside and get weak in the knees. Steve didn't know what his men thought. He wasn't himself. His mood swung from high highs to lower lows and back again. All the training he'd received paid off because he did his job without pause, but his mind was several thousand miles away in Seattle, with Carol and his baby.

His baby.

He repeated that phrase several times each night, letting the sound of it roll around in his mind, comforting him so he could sleep.

Somehow, someway, Steve was going to make this up to Carol. One thing he did know–the minute he was back home, he was grabbing a wedding license and a chaplain. They were getting married.

The last day that Carol was scheduled to work, the girls in the office held a baby shower in her honor. She was astonished by their generosity and humbled by what good friends she had.

Because she couldn't afford anything more than a three-month leave of absence, she was scheduled to return. A temporary had been hired to fill her position and Carol had spent the week training her.

"The shower surprised you, didn't it?" Lindy commented on the way out to the parking lot.

"I don't think I realized I had so many friends."

"This baby is special."

Carol flattened her hands over her abdomen. "Two weeks, Lindy. Can you believe in just two short weeks, I'll be holding my own baby?"

"Steve's due home around that time."

Carol didn't dare to hope that Steve could be with her when her time came. Her feelings on the subject were equally divided. She wanted him, needed him, but she would rather endure labor alone than have Steve with her, believing she was delivering another man's child.

"He'll be here," Lindy said with an unshakable confidence.

Carol bit into her lower lip and shook her head. "No, he won't. Steve Kyle's got the worst timing of any man I've ever known."

Carol let herself into the house and set her purse down. She ambled across the living room and caught a glimpse of herself in the hallway mirror as she walked toward the baby's bedroom. She stopped, astonished at the image that flashed back at her.

She looked as wide as a battleship. Everyone had been so concerned about the weight she lost when she'd been so sick. Well, she'd gained all that back and more. She'd become a walking, breathing Goodyear blimp.

Her hair needed washing and hung in limp blond strands, and her maternity top was spotted with dressing from the salad she'd eaten at lunch. She looked and felt like a slob. And she felt weird. She didn't know how to explain it. Her back ached and her feet throbbed.

Tired, hungry and depressed, she tried to lift her spirits by strolling around the baby's room, gliding her hand over the crib railing and restacking the neatly folded diapers.

According to Lindy and Rush, the *Atlantis* was due into port any day. Carol was so anxious to see Steve. She needed him so much. For the past two years, she'd been trying to convince herself she could live a good life without him. It took days like this one–when the sky had been dark with thunderclouds all afternoon, she'd gained two pounds that she didn't deserve and she felt so…so pregnant–to remind her how much she did need her ex-husband.

The doorbell chimed once, but before Carol could make it halfway across the living room, the front door flew open.

"Carol." Steve burst into the room and slowly dropped

his sea bag to the floor when he saw her. His eyes rounded with shock.

Carol knew she looked dreadful.

"Honey," he said, taking one step toward her. "I'm home."

"Steve Kyle, how could you do this to me?" she cried and unceremoniously burst into tears.

Chapter Twenty

Steve was so bewildered by Carol's tears that he stood where he was, not moving, barely thinking, unsure how to proceed. Handling a pregnant woman was not something listed in the Navy operational manual.

"Go away," she bellowed.

"You want me to leave?" he asked, his voice tight and strained with disbelief. This couldn't be happening–he was prepared to fall at her knees, and she was tossing him out on his ear!

With hands held protectively over her face, Carol nodded vigorously.

For three months he'd fantasized about this moment, dreamed of holding her in his arms and kissing her. He'd envisioned placing his hands over her extended belly and begging her and the baby's forgiveness. The last thing he'd ever imagined was that she wouldn't even listen to him. He couldn't let her do it.

Cautiously, as though approaching a lost and frightened kitten, Steve advanced a couple of steps.

Carol must have noticed because she whirled around, refusing to face him.

"I…I know the baby's mine," he said softly, hoping to entice her with what he'd learned before sailing.

In response, she gave a strangled cry of rage. "Just go. Get out of my house."

"Carol, please, I love you…I love the baby."

That didn't appease her, either. She turned sideways and jerked her index finger toward the door.

"All right, all right." Angry now, he stormed out of the house and slammed the door, but he didn't feel any better for having vented his irritation. Fine. If she wanted to treat him this way, she could do without the man who loved her. Their baby could do without a father!

He made it all the way to his car, which was parked in the driveway. He opened the door on the driver's side and paused, his gaze centered on the house. The frustration nearly drowned him.

Hell, he didn't know what he'd done that was so terrible. Well, he did…but he was willing to make it up to her. In fact, he was dying to do just that.

He slammed the car door and headed back to the house, getting as far as the front steps. He stood there a couple of minutes, jerked his hand through his hair hard enough to bruise his scalp, then returned to his car. It was obvious his presence wasn't sought or appreciated.

Not knowing where else to go, Steve drove to Lindy's.

Rush opened the door and Steve burst past him without a word of greeting. If anyone understood Carol it was his sister, and Steve needed to know what he'd done that was so wrong, before he went crazy.

"What the hell's the matter with Carol?" he demanded of Lindy, who was in the kitchen. "I was just there and she kicked me out."

Lindy's gaze sought her husband's, then her eyes widened

with a righteousness that was barely contained. "All right, Steve, what did you say to her this time?"

"Terrible things like I loved her and the baby. She wouldn't even look at me. All she could do was cover her face and weep." He started pacing in a kitchen that was much too small to hold three people, one of whom refused to stand still.

"You're sure you didn't say anything to insult her?"

"I'm sure, dammit." He splayed his fingers through his hair, nearly uprooting a handful.

Once more Lindy looked to Rush. "I think I better go over and talk to her."

Rush nodded. "Whatever you think."

Lindy reached for her purse and left the apartment.

"Women," Steve muttered. "I can't understand them."

"Carol's pregnant," Rush responded, as though that explained everything.

"She's been pregnant for nine months, for God's sake. What's so different now?"

Rush shrugged. "Don't ask me." He walked across the kitchen, opened the fridge and took out a beer, silently offering it to Steve.

Steve shook his head. He wasn't interested in drinking anything. All he wanted was for this situation to be squared away with Carol.

Rush helped himself to a beer and moved into the living room, claiming the recliner. A slow smile spread across his face. "In case you haven't heard, Lindy's pregnant."

Steve stopped pacing long enough to share a grin with his friend. "Congratulations."

"Thanks. I'm surprised you didn't notice."

"Good grief, man, she could only be a few months along."

"Not her," Rush teased. "Me. The guys on the *Mitchell* claim I've got that certain glow about me."

Despite his own troubles, Steve chuckled. He paused, standing in the middle of the room, and checked his watch.

"What could be taking Lindy so long? She should have phoned long before now."

Rush studied his own timepiece. "She's only been gone a few minutes. Relax, will you?"

Steve honestly tried. He sat on the edge of the sofa and draped his hands over his bent knees. "I suppose I'm only getting what I deserve." His fingers went through his hair once more. If this continued he would be bald before morning.

The national news came on and Rush commented on a recent senate vote. Hell, Steve didn't even know what his friend was talking about. Didn't care, either.

The phone rang and Steve bounced off the sofa as if the telephone had an electronic device that sent a shot of electricity straight through him.

"Answer that," Rush said, chuckling. "It might be a phone call."

Steve didn't take time to say something sarcastic. "Lindy?" he demanded.

"Oh, hi, Steve. Yes, it's Lindy."

"What's wrong with Carol?"

"Well, for one thing she's having a baby."

"Everyone keeps telling me that. It isn't any deep, dark secret, you know. Of course she's having a baby. My baby!"

"I mean she's having the baby *now*."

"Now?" Steve suddenly felt so weak, he sat back down. "Well, for God's sake she should be at the hospital. Have you phoned the doctor? How far apart are the contractions? What does she plan to do about this?"

"Which question do you want me to answer first?"

"Hell, I don't know." His voice sounded like a rusty door hinge. His knees were shaking, his hands were trembling and he'd never felt so unsure about anything in his life.

"I did phone Dr. Stewart," Lindy went on to say, "if that makes you feel any better."

It did. "What did he say?"

"Not much, but he said Carol could leave for the hospital anytime."

"Okay…okay," Steve said, pushing down the panic that threatened to consume him. "But I want to be the one to drive her there. This is my baby–I should have the right."

"Oh, that won't be any problem, but take your time getting here. Carol wants to wash her hair first."

"What?" Steve shouted, bolting to his feet.

"There's no need to scream in my ear, Steven Kyle," Lindy informed him primly.

Steve's breath came in short, uneven rasps. "I'm on my way…don't leave without me."

"Don't worry. Now, before you hang up on me, put Rush on the line."

Whatever Lindy said flew out his other ear. Carol was in labor–their baby was going to be born anytime, and she was styling her hair! Steve dropped the phone to the carpet and headed toward the front door.

"What's happening?" Rush asked, standing.

Steve paused. "Lindy's with Carol. Carol's hair is in labor and the baby's getting washed."

"That explains everything," Rush said, and picked up the phone.

By the time Steve arrived at the house, his heart was pounding so violently, his rib cage was in danger of being damaged. He leaped out of the car, left the door open and sprinted toward the house.

"Where is she?" he demanded of Lindy. He'd nearly taken the front door off its hinges, he'd come into the house so fast.

His sister pointed in the direction of the bedroom.

"Carol," he called. He'd repeated her name four more times before he walked into the bedroom. She was sitting on the edge of the mattress, her hands resting on her abdomen, taking in slow, even breaths.

Steve fell to his knees in front of her. "Are you all right?"

She gave him a weak smile. "I'm fine. How about you?"

He placed his hands over hers, closed his eyes and expelled his breath. "I think I'm going to be all right now."

Carol brushed a hand over his face, gently caressing his jawline. "I'm sorry about earlier…I felt so ugly and I didn't want you to see me until I'd had a chance to clean up."

The frenzy and panic left him and he reached up a hand and hooked it around her neck. Gently he lowered her mouth to his and kissed her in a leisurely exploration. "I love you, Carol Kyle." He released her and lifted her maternity top enough to kiss her swollen stomach. "And I love you, Baby Kyle."

Carol's eyes filled with tears.

"Come on," he said, helping her into an upright position. "We've got a new life to bring into the world and we're going to do it together."

Sometime around noon the following day, Carol woke in the hospital to discover Steve sleeping across the room from her, sprawled in the most uncomfortable position imaginable. His head was tossed back, his mouth open. His leg was hooked over the side of the chair and his arms dangled like cooked noodles at his side, the knuckles of his left hand brushing the floor.

"Steve," she whispered, hating to wake him. But if he stayed in that position much longer, he wouldn't be able to move his neck for a week.

Steve jerked himself awake. His leg dropped to the floor with a loud thud. He looked around him as though he couldn't remember where he was or even who he was.

"Hi," Carol said, feeling marvelous.

"Hi." He wiped a hand over his face, then apparently remembered what he was doing in her hospital room. A slow, satisfied smile crept over his features. "Are you feeling all right?"

"I feel fantastic."

He moved to her side and claimed her hand with both of his. "We have a daughter," he said, and his voice was raw with remembered emotion. "I've never seen a more beautiful little girl in my life."

"Stephanie Anne Kyle," she told him. "Stephanie for her father and Anne for my mother."

"Stephanie," Steve repeated slowly, then nodded. "She's incredible. You're incredible."

"You cried," Carol whispered, remembering the tears that had run down the side of Steve's face when Dr. Stewart handed him their daughter.

"I never felt any emotion more powerful in my life," he answered. "I can't even begin to explain it." He raised her hand to his lips and briefly closed his eyes. "You'd worked so hard and so long and then Stephanie was born and squalling like crazy. I'd been so concerned about you that I'd hardly noticed her and then Dr. Stewart wrapped her in a blanket and gave her to me. Carol, the minute I touched her something happened in my heart. I felt so humble, so awed, that I'd been entrusted with this tiny life." He placed his hand over his heart as if it were marked by their daughter's birth and she would notice the change in him. "Stephanie is such a beautiful baby. We'd been up most of the night and you were exhausted. But I felt like I could fly, I was so excited. Poor Rush and Lindy, I think I talked their heads off."

"I was surprised you slept here."

He ran the tips of his fingers over her cheek. "I had to be with you. I kept thinking about everything I'd put you through. I was so wrong, so very wrong about everything, and yet you loved me through it all. I should have known from the first that you were innocent of everything bad I've ever believed. I was such a fool…such an idiot. I nearly ruined both our lives."

"It's in the past and forgotten."

"We're getting married." He said it as if he expected an argument.

"I think we should," Carol agreed, "seeing that we have a daughter."

"I never felt unmarried," Steve admitted. "There's only one woman in my life, and that's the way it'll always be."

"We may have divorce papers, but I never stopped being your wife."

The nurse walked into the room, tenderly cradling a soft pink bundle. "Are you ready for your daughter, Mrs. Kyle?"

"Oh, yes." Carol reached for the button that would raise the hospital bed to an upright position. As soon as she was settled, the nurse placed Stephanie Anne Kyle in her mother's arms.

Following the nurse's instructions, Carol bared her breast and gasped softly as Stephanie accepted her mother's nipple and sucked greedily.

"She's more beautiful every time I see her," Steve said, his voice filled with wonder. The rugged lines of his face softened as he gazed down on his daughter. Gently he drew one finger over her velvet-smooth cheek. "But she'll never be as beautiful as her mother is to me right this minute."

Love and joy flooded Carol's soul and she gently kissed the top of her daughter's head.

"We're going to be all right," Steve whispered.

"Yes, we are," Carol agreed. "We're going to be just fine—all three of us."

NAVY BRAT

For Marcia, Catherine, Kathy and Pam
and others like them,
who've picked up the pieces of their lives
and
taught me the meaning of the word *courage.*

Special thanks to
Gene Romano, Senior Chief Journalist,
Naval Base Seattle

Barbara Davis,
Kitsap County Community Action Program
and
The Olympic College
Women in Transition Group

Plus
navy wives
Rose Marie Harris
Jan Evans

Chapter One

He was the handsomest man in the bar, and he couldn't keep his eyes off her.

It was all Erin MacNamera could do to keep her own coffee-brown eyes trained away from him. He sat on the bar stool, his back to the multitiered display of ornamental liquor bottles. His elbows were braced against the polished mahogany counter, and he nonchalantly held a bottle of imported German beer in his hand.

Against her will, Erin's gaze meandered back to him. He seemed to be waiting for her attention, and he smiled, his mouth lifting sensuously at the edges. Erin quickly looked away and tried to concentrate on what her friend was saying.

"...Steve and me."

Erin hadn't a clue as to what she'd missed. Aimee was in the habit of talking nonstop, especially when she was upset. The reason Erin and her co-worker were meeting was that Aimee wanted to discuss the problems she was having in her ten-year marriage.

Marriage was something Erin fully intended to avoid, at least for a good long while. She was focusing her energies on her career and on teaching a class titled Women in Transition two evenings a week at South Seattle Community College. With a master's degree clutched in her hot little hand, and her ideals and enthusiasm high, Erin had applied to and been accepted by the King County Community Action Program as an employment counselor, working mainly with displaced women. Ninety percent of those she worked with were on public assistance.

Her dream was to give hope and support to those who had lost both. A friend to the friendless. An encourager to the disheartened. Erin's real love, however, was the Women In Transition course. In the past few years she'd watched several women undergo the metamorphosis from lost and confused individuals to purpose-filled adults holding on tight to a second chance at life.

Erin knew better than to take the credit or the blame for the transformation she saw in these women's lives. She was just part of the Ways and Means Committee.

Her father enjoyed teasing her, claiming his eldest daughter was destined to become the next Florence Nightingale and Mother Teresa all rolled into one tenacious, determined, confident female.

Casey MacNamera was only partially right. Erin certainly didn't see herself as any crusader, fighting against the injustices of life.

Nor was Erin fooling herself about finances. She didn't intend to become wealthy, at least not monetarily. Nobody went into social work for the money. The hours were long and the rewards sporadic, but when she saw people's lives turned around for good she couldn't help being uplifted.

Helping others through a time of painful transition was

what Erin had been born to do. It had been her dream from early in her college career and had followed her through graduate school and her first job.

"Erin," Aimee said, her voice dipping to a whisper, "there's a man at the bar staring at us."

Erin pretended not to have noticed. "Oh?"

Aimee stirred the swizzle stick in her strawberry daiquiri, then licked the end as she stared across the room, her eyes studying the good-looking man with the imported ale. Her smile was slow and deliberate, but it didn't last long. She sighed and said, "It's you who interests him."

"How can you be so sure?"

"Because I'm married."

"He doesn't know that," Erin argued.

"Sure he does." Aimee uncrossed her long legs and leaned across the minuscule table. "Married women give off vibes, and single men pick them up like sonar. I tried to send him a signal, but it didn't work. He knew immediately. You, on the other hand, are giving off single vibes, and he's zeroing in on that like a bee does pollen."

"I'm sure you're wrong."

"Maybe," Aimee agreed in a thin whisper, "but I doubt it." She took one last sip of her drink and stood hurriedly. "I'm leaving now, and we'll test my theory and see what happens. My guess is that the minute I'm out of here he's going to make a *beeline* for you." She paused, smiled at her own wit, then added, "The pun was an accident, clever but unintentional."

"Aimee, I thought you wanted to talk…." Erin, however, wasn't quick enough to convince her friend to stay. Before she'd finished, Aimee had reached for her purse. "We'll talk some other time." With a natural flair, she draped the strap of her imitation-snakeskin handbag over her shoulder and winked suggestively. "Good luck."

"Ah…" Erin was at a loss as to what to do. She was twenty-seven, but for the majority of her adult life she'd avoided romantic relationships. Not by design. It had just worked out that way.

She met men frequently, but she dated only occasionally. Not once had she met a man in a bar. Cocktail lounges weren't her scene. In her entire life she'd probably been inside one only a couple of times.

Her social life had been sadly neglected from the time she was in junior high and fell in love for the first time. Howie Riverside had asked her to the Valentine's Day dance, and her tender young heart had been all aflutter.

Then it had happened. The way it always had. Her father, a career navy man, had been transferred, and they'd moved three days before the dance.

Somehow Erin had never quite regained her stride with the opposite sex. Of course, three moves in the next four years–unusual even for the navy–hadn't been exactly conducive to a thriving relationship. They'd been shuffled from Alaska to Guam to Pensacola and back again.

College could have, and probably should have, been the opportunity to make up for lost time, but by then Erin had felt like a social pygmy when it came to dealing with men. She hadn't known how to meet them, how to flirt with them or how to make small talk. Nor had she acquired a number of the other necessary graces.

"Hello."

She hadn't even had time to collect her thoughts, let alone her purse. Mr. Imported Beer was standing next to her table, smiling down on her like some mythological Greek god. He certainly resembled one. He was tall, naturally. Weren't they all? Easily six-four, she guessed, and muscular. His dark hair was neatly trimmed, his brown eyes warm and friendly. He was so handsome, he might well have posed for one of those hunk calendars that were currently the rage with all the women in the office.

"Hi," she managed, hoping she sounded a whole lot less flustered than she was feeling. Erin knew herself well, and she couldn't imagine what it was about her that had attracted this gorgeous man.

Few would have described Erin as a beautiful sophisticate. Her features were distinctively Irish, comely and appealing, but she wasn't anywhere close to being strikingly beautiful. Naturally long curly chestnut-red hair, straight white teeth and a smidgen of freckles across the bridge of her Gaelic nose were her most distinctive features. She was reasonably attractive, but no more so than any of the other women who populated the cocktail lounge.

"Do you mind if I join you?"

"Ah…sure." She reached for her glass of Chablis and held on to it with one hand. "And you are…"

"Brandon Davis." He claimed the chair recently vacated by Aimee. "Most folks call me Brand."

"Erin MacNamera," she supplied, and noticed several envious stares coming her way from the women in the crowd. Even if nothing came from this exchange, Erin couldn't help being flattered by his attention. "Most folks call me Erin."

He smiled.

"Is it true? Was I really giving off vibes?" she asked, surprising herself. Obviously it was the wine talking. Generally she wasn't even close to being this direct with a man she didn't know.

Brand didn't answer her right away, which wasn't any wonder. She'd probably caught him off guard, which was only fair, since he was throwing her completely off balance.

"My friend was saying men in bars pick up vibes like a

radar detector," she explained, "and I was wondering what messages I was signaling."

"None."

"Oh." She couldn't help being disappointed. For a moment there, she'd thought she'd stumbled upon some latent talent she hadn't known she possessed. Apparently that wasn't the case.

"Then why were you staring at me?" He'd probably ruin everything by informing her she had a run in her nylons, or her skirt was unzipped, or something else thoroughly embarrassing.

"Because you're Irish and it's St. Patrick's Day."

So much for padding her ego. Naturally. It was the in thing to be seen with an Irish girl on a day that traditionally celebrated her ancestors.

"You're not wearing green," he added.

"I'm not?" Erin's gaze dropped to her blue striped business suit. She hadn't given a thought to it being St. Patrick's Day when she'd dressed that morning. "I'm not," she agreed, surprised she'd forgotten something so basic to her heritage.

Brand laughed lightly, and the sound of it was so refreshing, Erin couldn't keep from smiling herself. She didn't know a whole lot about this sort of thing, but her best guess suggested Brand Davis wasn't the type of man who lounged around bars picking up women. First of all, he didn't need to. With his good looks and innate charm, women would naturally flock to him.

She decided to test her suspicion. "I don't believe I've seen you here before." That wasn't too surprising. Since this was her first time at the Blue Lagoon, the chances of their having crossed each other's paths at the bar were pretty slender.

"It's my first time."

"I see."

"What about you?"

It took Erin a second to realize he was asking her how often she frequented the cocktail lounge. "Every now and again," she answered, striving to sound urbane, or at least a tad more sophisticated than she'd been at age fourteen.

The waitress stepped up to the table, and before Erin could answer one way or the other Brand ordered two more of the same. Generally, one glass of wine was Erin's limit, but she was willing to break a few rules. It wasn't often she ran into a Greek god.

"I'm new to the area," Brand explained before Erin could think fast enough to formulate a question.

She looked at him and smiled blandly. The wine had dulled her senses, but then, making small talk had always been difficult for her. She wished she could think of some intelligent comment to make. Instead, her gaze fell on a poster on the other side of the room, and she blurted out the first thing that came to her mind.

"I love ferries." Then, realizing he might think she was referring to leprechauns, she felt compelled to explain. "When I first moved to Seattle, I was enthralled by the ferryboats. Whenever I needed to think something over, I'd ride one over to Winslow or Bremerton and hash everything out in my mind."

"It helps?"

Whatever you do, don't let her know you're navy. Casey MacNamera's voice echoed in Brand's mind like a Chinese gong. The MCPO–masterchief petty officer–was a good friend of Brand's. They'd worked together for three years early in his career, and they'd kept in touch ever since.

As soon as Casey had learned Brand had been given his special assignment at Naval Station Puget Sound at Sand Point in Seattle, the old Irishman had contacted him, concerned about his eldest daughter.

She's working too hard, not taking care of herself. Give an old man some peace of mind and check up on her. Only, for the love of heaven, don't let her know I sent you.

Personally, Brand wasn't much into this detective business. But, as a favor to his friend, he'd reluctantly agreed to look up Erin MacNamera.

He'd been ready to enter her office building when she'd stepped outside. Brand had never met Casey's daughter, but one look at that thick thatch of auburn hair and he'd immediately known that this woman was a close relative of his friend. So he'd followed her into the Blue Lagoon.

He studied her for several minutes, noticing little things about her. She was delicate. Not dainty or fragile, as the word implied. Erin MacNamera was exquisite. That wasn't a word he used often. Her gaze had met his once, and he'd managed to hold her look for just a second. She'd stared back at him, surprise darkening her eyes, before she'd jerked her gaze away. When he'd stepped up to her table, she'd been flustered, and she'd striven hard not to show it.

The more time he spent with her, the more he learned about her that amazed him. Brand wasn't entirely sure what he'd expected from Casey's daughter, but certainly not the enchanting red-haired beauty who sat across from him. Erin was as different from her old man as silk was from leather. Casey was a potbellied, boisterous MCPO, while his daughter was a graceful creature with eyes as shiny and dark as the sea at midnight.

Another thing, Casey had warned. *Remember, this is my daughter, not one of your cupcakes.*

Brand couldn't help grinning at that. He didn't have cupcakes. At thirty-two, he couldn't say he'd never been in love. He'd fallen in love a handful of times over the years, but there had never been one woman who'd captured his heart for more than a few months. None that he'd ever seriously considered spending the rest of his life with.

Be careful what you say, Casey had advised. *My Erin's got her mother's temper.*

Brand didn't feel good about this minor deception. The sensation intensified as they sat and talked over their drinks. An hour after he'd sat down with her, Erin glanced at her watch and flatly announced she had to be leaving.

As far as Brand was concerned, his duty was done. He'd looked up his friend's daughter, talked to her long enough to assure her father, when he wrote next, that Erin was in good health. But when she stood to leave, Brand discovered he didn't want her to go. He'd thoroughly enjoyed her company.

"How about dinner?" he found himself asking.

Twin spots of color appeared in her cheeks, and her eyes darkened slightly as though she'd been caught off guard. "Ah…not tonight. Thanks anyway."

"Tomorrow?"

Her silence didn't fool him. She appeared outwardly calm, as if she were considering his invitation, but Brand could feel the resistance radiating from her. That in itself was unusual. Women generally were eager to date him.

"No thanks." Her soft smile took any sting out of her rejection–or at least it was meant to. Unfortunately, it didn't work.

She stood, smiled sweetly and tucked her purse under her arm. "Thanks for the drink."

Before Brand had time to respond, she was out the door. He couldn't remember a woman turning him down in fifteen years of dating. Not once. Most members of the opposite sex treated him as if he were Prince Charming. He'd certainly gone out of his way to be captivating to MacNamera's daughter.

Who the hell did she think she was?

Standing, Brand started out the cocktail lounge after her. She was halfway down the block on the sidewalk, her pace clipped. Brand ran a few steps, then slowed to a walk. Soon his stride matched hers.

"Why?"

She paused and looked up at him, revealing no surprise that he'd joined her.

"You're navy."

Brand was shocked, and he did a poor job of disguising it. "How'd you know?"

"I was raised in the military. I know the lingo, the jargon."

"I didn't use any."

"Not consciously. It was more than that...the way you held your beer bottle should have told me, but it was when we started talking about the ferries crossing Puget Sound that I knew for sure."

"So I'm navy. Is that so bad?"

"No. Actually, with most women it's a plus. From what I understand, a lot of females go for guys in uniform. You won't have any problems meeting someone. Bremerton? Sand Point? Or Whidbey Island?"

Brand ignored the question of where he was stationed and instead asked one of his own. "Most women are attracted to a man in uniform, but not you?"

Her eyes flickered, and she laughed curtly. "Sorry. It lost its appeal when I was around six."

She was walking so fast that he was losing his breath just keeping up with her. "Do you hate the navy so much?"

His question apparently caught her by surprise, because she stopped abruptly, turned to him and raised wide brown eyes to study him. "I don't hate it at all."

"But you won't even have dinner with someone in the service?"

"Listen, I don't mean to be rude. You seem like a perfectly nice–"

"You're not being rude. I'm just curious, is all." He glanced around them. They'd stopped in the middle of the sidewalk on a busy street in downtown Seattle. Several people were forced to walk around them. "I really would be interested in hearing your views. How about if we find a coffee shop and sit down and talk?"

She looked at her watch pointedly.

"This isn't dinner. Just coffee." Unwilling to be put off quite so easily a second time, Brand gifted her with one of his most dazzling smiles. For the majority of his adult life, women had claimed he had a smile potent enough to melt the polar ice cap. He issued it now, full strength, and waited for the usual results.

Nothing.

This woman was downright dangerous to his ego. He tried another tactic. "In case you didn't notice, we're causing something of a traffic jam here."

"I'll pay for my own coffee," she insisted in a tone that implied she was going against her better judgment to agree to talk to him at all.

"If you insist."

The lunch counter at Woolworth's was still open, and they shared a tiny booth designed for two. While the waitress delivered their coffee, Brand reached for a menu, reading over the list of sandwiches. The picture of the turkey, piled high with lettuce and tomato slices between thick slices of bread, looked appetizing, and he reluctantly set it aside.

"Officer?" Erin asked, studying him while he stirred cream into his coffee.

"Adding cream to my coffee told you that?" Casey's daughter ought to be in intelligence. He'd never met anyone quite like her.

"No. The way you talk. The way you act. Lieutenant j.g. would be my guess?"

He was impressed again. "How'd you know that?"

"Your age. What are you, thirty? Thirty-one?"

"Thirty-two." This was getting to be downright embarrassing. He'd climbed through the ranks at the normal rate of speed and received a number of special assignments over the years. Since the navy was considering closing down its station at Sand Point, Brand had been sent by the admiral to conduct a feasibility survey. His duties in the area would last only a few weeks. Most of that time had already been spent.

"I take it you weren't raised in the navy?" Erin questioned.

"No."

"I might have guessed."

She sure as hell was batting a thousand with those guesses of hers. Her eyes briefly met his, and Brand was struck once more by how hauntingly dark they were. A spark, a hint of pain–something he couldn't quite name–touched an emotional chord deep within him.

"Listen," she said softly, regretfully, "it's been interesting talking to you, but I should have been home an hour ago." She was ready to stand when Brand reached across the table and gripped her hand.

The action was as much a shock to Brand as it was to her. She raised her head a fraction of an inch so that their eyes could meet. Hers were wide and questioning, his…he didn't know. Unrelenting, stubborn, he guessed. Brand wasn't thinking clearly, and hadn't been from the moment he'd followed her into the Blue Lagoon.

"We haven't talked."

"There isn't any need to. You weren't raised in the military. I was. You couldn't possibly understand what it's like unless you were carted from one corner of the world to another."

"I'd love it."

Her smile was sardonic. "Most *men* do."

"I want to see you again."

She didn't hesitate, didn't think about it. Nor did she delay answering. "No."

"I apologize if I'm bruising your ego," she added, "but frankly, I promised myself a long time ago to stay away from men in the military. It's a hard-and-fast rule I live by. Trust me, it's nothing personal."

Brand sure as hell was taking it personally. "I don't even tempt you?"

She hesitated and smiled gently before tugging her hand free from his grasp. "A little," she admitted.

Brand had the feeling she was saying that to cater to his pride, which she'd managed to bruise every time she'd opened her mouth.

"As far as looks go, you've got an interesting face."

An interesting face. Didn't she know handsome when she saw it? Women had made pests of themselves in an effort to attract his attention for years. Some of his best friends had even admitted they hesitated before introducing him to their girlfriends.

"I'll walk you to your car," he said stiffly.

"It isn't necessary, I–"

"I said I'd walk you to your car." He stood and slapped two dollar bills on the table. Brand liked to think of himself as a tolerant man, but this woman was getting under his skin, and he didn't like it. Not one damn bit. There were plenty of fish in the sea, and he was far more interested in lobster than he was in Irish stew.

Erin MacNamera wasn't even that attractive. Hell, he wouldn't even be seeing her if he wasn't doing a favor for her father. If she didn't want to see him again, fine. Great.

Wonderful. He could live with that. What Erin had said earlier was true enough. Women went for guys in uniform.

He was attractive. He wore a uniform.

He didn't need Erin MacNamera.

Satisfied with that, he held open the glass door that led outside.

"This really isn't necessary," she whispered.

"Probably not, but as an officer and a gentleman I insist."

"My father's an enlisted man."

She announced the fact as if she were looking for some response.

"So?" he demanded.

"So…I just wanted you to know that."

"Do you think that's going to make me change my mind about walking you to your car?"

"No." Her hands were buried in her pockets. "I…just wanted you to know. It might make a difference to some men."

"Not me."

She nodded. "My car's in the lot near Yesler."

Brand didn't know Seattle well, but he knew enough to recognize that that area of town wasn't the best place for a woman to be walking alone at night. He was glad he'd insisted on escorting her to her car, although even now he wasn't completely sure of his motives.

They turned off the main street and onto a small, narrower one that sloped sharply down to the Seattle waterfront.

"You park here often?" As prickly as she was, Erin would probably resent his pointing out the all-too-obvious dangers of the area.

"Every day, but generally I'm gone shortly after five. It's still light then."

"Tonight?"

"Tonight," she said with a sigh, "I met you."

Brand nodded. He found the parking lot, which by now was nearly deserted. The spaces were tightly angled between two brick buildings. The entire lot was illuminated by a single dim light.

Erin pulled her keys from her purse and clenched them in her hands. "My car is the one in the back," she explained.

Brand's gaze located the small blue Toyota in the rear of the lot, facing a two-story brick structure. Once more he was forced to swallow a chastising warning.

"I didn't want to say anything earlier, but I'm grateful you walked with me."

A small–damn small–sense of satisfaction filled him. "You're welcome."

She inserted the key into the driver's door and unlocked her car. Pausing, she glanced up at him and smiled shyly.

Brand looked down on the slender young woman at his side and read her confusion and her regret. The desire to pull her close was so strong that it was nearly impossible to ignore.

"I'm sorry the navy hurt you."

"It didn't. Not as much as I led you to believe. I just want to be on the safe side. For the first time in my life I have a real home with real furniture that I purchased without thinking about how well it would travel." She hesitated and smiled. "I don't worry about being transferred every other year, and–" She hesitated again and shook her head as though to suggest he wouldn't understand. "I apologize if I wounded your ego. You're really very nice."

"A kiss would go a long way toward repairing the damage." Brand couldn't believe he'd suggested that, but what the hell. Why not?

"A kiss?"

Brand nearly laughed out loud at the shocked look that came over her features. It was downright comical, as if she'd never been kissed before, or at least it had been a good long while. Not taking the time to decide which it was, he cradled her face between his large hands.

Her mouth was moist and parted, welcoming. Her eyes weren't. They were filled with doubts, but he chose to ignore her unspoken questions, fearing that if he took the time to reassure her he'd talk himself out of kissing her.

Brand wanted this kiss.

If Erin had questions, he was experiencing a few of his own. She was his friend's daughter, and he was risking Casey's wrath with this little game. But none of that seemed to matter. What did concern him was the woman staring boldly up at him.

Tenderness filled him. A strange tenderness, one he didn't fully understand or recognize. Slowly he lowered his mouth to hers. He felt her go tense with anticipation as their lips clung.

She was soft, warm and incredibly sweet. He opened his mouth a little more, slanting his lips over hers as he plowed his fingers through her thick hair.

Her first response was tentative, as if she'd been caught unprepared, but then she sighed and sagged against him. She flattened her hands over his chest, then flexed her fingers, her long nails scraping his sweater.

Gradually she opened to him, like a hothouse flower blossoming in his arms. Yet it was she who broke the contact. Her eyes were wide and soft as she stared up at him. A feeling of surprise and tenderness and need washed through him.

"I…was just thinking," she said in a lacy whisper.

Just now, thinking could be dangerous. Brand knew that from experience. He silenced her with a kiss that was so thorough it left them both trembling in its aftermath.

Once again, Erin was clinging to him, her hands gripping the V of his sweater as if she needed to hold on to something in order to remain upright.

"The rules you have about dating military men?" he asked, rubbing his open mouth over her honeyed lips. "How about altering them?"

"Altering them?" she echoed slowly, her eyes closed.

He kissed her again for good measure. "Make it a guideline instead," he suggested.

Chapter Two

As an adult, Erin had made several decisions about how she intended to live her life. She followed the Golden Rule, and she never used her credit cards if she couldn't pay off the balance the following month.

And she didn't date men in the military.

Her life wasn't encumbered with a lot of restrictions. Everything that was important and necessary was wrapped up in these relatively simple rules.

Then why, she asked herself, had she agreed to have dinner with Brand Davis? Lieutenant Davis, J.G., she reminded herself disparagingly.

"Why?" she repeated aloud, stacking papers against the edge of her desk with enough force to bend them in half.

"Heavens, don't ask me," Aimee answered, grinning impishly. After a day spent interviewing job applicants, talking aloud to oneself was an accepted form of behavior.

"I'm supposed to meet him tonight, you know," Erin said

in a low, thought-filled voice. If there had been an easy way out of this, she'd have grabbed it.

If only Brand hadn't kissed her. No one had ever told her kissing could be so…so pleasant. First her knees had gone weak, and then her formidable will of iron had melted and pooled at her feet. Before she'd even realized what she was doing, she'd mindlessly walked into Brand's trap. It was just like a navy man to zero in on her weakest point and attack.

Rolling her antique oak chair away from her desk, Aimee relaxed against its rail back and angled her head to one side as she studied Erin. "Are you still lamenting the fact you agreed to have dinner with that gorgeous hunk? Honey, trust me in this, you should be counting your blessings."

"He's military."

"I know." Aimee rotated a pen between her hands as she gazed dreamily into the distance. A contented look stole over her features as she released a long-drawn-out sigh. "I can just picture him in a uniform, standing at attention. Why, it's enough to make my heart go pitter-patter."

Erin refused to look at her friend. If Aimee wanted Brand, she was welcome to him. Of course, her friend wasn't truly interested, since she was already married to Steve and had been for a decade. "If I could think of a plausible excuse to get out of this, I would."

"You've got to be kidding."

She wasn't. "You have dinner with him."

Aimee shook her head eagerly. "Trust me, if I were five years younger I'd take you up on that."

Since Aimee's marriage was going through some rocky times, Erin didn't think it was necessary to remind her friend that dating wasn't something that should interest her.

"Relax, would you?" Aimee admonished her.

"I can't." Erin tucked her stapler and several pens neatly

inside her desk drawer. "As far as I'm concerned, this evening is going to be a total waste of time." She could be doing something important, like…like laundry or answering mail. It was just her luck that Brand had suggested Wednesday night. Tuesday was the first class for the new session for the Women In Transition course. Thursday night was the second session. Naturally, Brand had chosen to ask her out the one night of the week when she was free.

"You're so tense," Aimee chastised. "You might as well be walking around in a suit of armor."

"I'll be okay," Erin said, not listening to her fellow worker. She stood and planted her hands against the side of her desk before sighing heavily. "This is what I'm going to do. I'll meet him just the way we arranged."

"That's a good start," Aimee teased.

"We'll find a restaurant, and I'll order right away, eat and then make my excuses as soon as I can. I don't want to insult him, but at the same time I want him to understand I regret ever having agreed to this date." She waited for a response. When Aimee didn't give her one, she arched her brows expectantly. "Well?"

"It sounds good to me." But the look Aimee gave her said otherwise.

It was amazing how much a person could say with a look. Erin didn't want to take the time to dwell on the fact, especially now, when she was thinking about the messages she'd given Brand the night he'd kissed her. Apparently she'd encouraged him enough to ask her out to dinner a second time.

Erin didn't want to dwell on that night. It embarrassed her to think about the way she'd responded so openly to his touch. Her face grew hot just remembering. She shouldn't think about it–she was running late as it was. Reaching for her purse, she checked her watch and hurried toward the elevator.

"Don't get started in the morning until we've had a chance to talk," Aimee called out after her.

They generally clocked in at eight, reviewed files and then spent a large portion of the day with job applicants or meeting with prospective employers. Sometimes she wasn't back in the office until after four.

"I won't," Erin promised without looking back. Walking briskly, she raised her hand in farewell.

"Have a good time," Aimee called out in a provocative, teasing tone that attracted the notice of their peers.

This time Erin did turn back to discover her co-worker sitting on the edge of her desk, her arms folded, one leg swinging. A mischievous grin brightened her round, cheerful face.

But Erin wasn't counting on this evening being much fun.

Once outside the revolving glass door of the tall office complex, Erin paused and glanced around. Brand had said he'd be waiting for her there. She didn't see him right away, and she was beginning to think he wasn't going to show.

It must have been wishful thinking on her part, because no sooner had the thought entered her mind than he stepped away from the building and sauntered toward her.

His gaze found hers, and Erin was struck afresh by what a devilishly handsome man Brandon Davis was. If she wasn't careful, she might find herself attracted to him. She wasn't immune to good looks and charm, and they seemed to ooze from every pore of his muscular body.

"Hi," she greeted stiffly. Her defenses were in place as she deliberately kept her eyes trained away from his smile. It was compelling enough to dazzle the most stouthearted. Erin hadn't had enough experience with the opposite sex to build up a resistance to a man like Brand.

"I wasn't sure you'd show," he said when he reached her side.

"I wasn't sure I would, either." That was stretching the

truth. She was a navy brat. Responsibility, promptness and duty had been programmed into her the way most children were taught to brush their teeth and make their beds. No one could live on a military base and not be affected by the value system promoted there.

"I'm glad you did decide to meet me." His eyes were warm and genuine, and she hurriedly looked away before she could be affected by them.

"Where would you like to eat?" To Erin's way of thinking, the sooner they arrived at the restaurant, the sooner she could leave. She wanted this evening to be cut-and-dried, without a lot of room for discussion.

"Ever been to Joe's Grill?"

Erin's gaze widened with delight. "Yes, as a matter of fact, I have, but it's been years." Since she was ten by her best guess. Her father had been stationed at Sand Point, and whenever there was something to celebrate he'd taken the family out to eat at Joe's. Generally restaurants weren't something a child would remember, but it seemed her family had a special place in each of the cities where they'd been stationed through the years. Joe's Grill had been their Seattle favorite.

"I asked around and heard the food there is great," Brand said, placing his hand at her elbow.

She felt his touch, and although it was light and impersonal it still affected her. "You mean the guys from Sand Point still eat there?"

"Apparently so."

A flood of happy memories filled Erin's mind. For her tenth birthday, Joe himself had baked her a double-decker chocolate cake. She could still remember him proudly carrying it out of the kitchen as if he'd been asked to give away the bride. Visiting the restaurant had crossed her mind half a dozen times since she'd moved to Seattle, but with her hectic schedule she hadn't gotten around to it.

"Joe's Grill," she repeated, fighting the strong desire to fill in the details about her birthday and the cake to Brand. Her eyes met his, and mutual smiles emerged, despite Erin's attempts to the contrary. She had to keep her head out of the clouds when it came to dealing with this handsome lieutenant j.g. Reminding herself of that was apparently something that was going to be necessary all evening.

Brand's car was parked on a side street. He held open the passenger door for her and gently closed it once she was inside.

He did most of the talking as he drove to the restaurant. Every once in a while Erin would feel herself start to relax in his company, a sure sign she was headed for trouble. She'd give herself a hard mental shake and instantly put herself back on track.

When Brand eased the vehicle into Joe's crowded parking lot, Erin looked around her and nearly drowned in nostalgia. She swore the restaurant hadn't changed in nearly twenty years. The same neon sign flashed from above the flat-topped roof, with a huge T-bone steak lit up in red and *Joe's Grill* flashing off and on every two seconds.

"As I recall, the steaks here are so thick they resemble roasts, and the baked potatoes were larger than a boxer's fist." She was confident that was an exaggeration, but in her ten-year-old mind that was the way it seemed.

"That's what my friend said," Brand said, climbing out of the car.

The inside was much as Erin remembered. A huge fish tank built into the wall was filled with a wide variety of colorful saltwater fish. The cash register rested on top of a large glass display case full of tempting candy and gum. Erin never had understood why a restaurant that served wonderful meals would want to sell candy to its customers afterward.

The hostess escorted them to a table by a picture window that revealed a breath-taking panorama of Lake Union.

Erin didn't open her menu right away. Instead, she looked around, soaking up the ambience, feeling as if she were a kid all over again.

"This reminds me of a little place on Guam," Brand said, his gaze following hers. "The tables have the same red tablecloths under a glass covering."

"Not…" She had to stop and think.

"The Trattoria," Brand supplied.

"Yes." Erin was impressed he'd even heard of it, but then he probably had since everyone stationed on Guam ate there at one time or another. "They serve a clam spaghetti my father swore he would die for. My mom tried for years to duplicate the recipe and finally gave up. Who would ever believe a tiny restaurant on the island of Guam would serve the best Italian food in the world?"

"Better even than Miceli's in Rome?" he probed.

"You've been to Miceli's?" she asked excitedly. Obviously he had, otherwise he wouldn't have mentioned it. The fresh-from-the-oven-bread was what she remembered about Miceli's. The aroma would drift through the narrow cobblestoned streets of the Italian town like nothing Erin had ever known. Her stomach growled just thinking about it.

"I've been in the navy nearly fifteen years," he reminded her.

Mentioning the fact that he was navy was like slapping a cold rag across her face and forcing her back to reality. Her reaction was immediate. She reached for the menu, jerked it open and decided what she intended to order in three seconds flat. She looked up, hoping to catch the waitress's eye.

"I can't decide if I'm hungry enough for the T-bone or not," Brand remarked conversationally. He glanced over the menu a second time before looking to her. "You've decided?"

"Yes. I'll have the peppercorn filet."

Brand nodded, apparently saluting her choice. "That sounds good. I'll have the same."

"No," Erin said, surprised by how adamant she sounded. "Have the T-bone. It's probably the best of any place in town. And since you're only going to be in Seattle a few weeks, you really should sample Joe's specialty."

"All right, I will." Brand smiled at her, and Erin's heart started to pound like a giant sledgehammer, a fact she chose to ignore.

The waitress arrived to take their order, and Brand suggested a bottle of wine.

"No, thanks, none for me," Erin said quickly. After what had happened the night they'd met, she'd considered living her entire life without drinking wine again. It was probably ridiculous to blame two glasses of Chablis for the eager way she'd responded to Brand's kisses. But it was an excuse, and she badly needed one. She certainly wasn't looking for a repeat performance. Her objective was to get through this dinner, thank Brand and then go her own way. Naturally she wanted them to part with the understanding she didn't ever intend to date him again. But she wanted to be sure he realized it was nothing personal.

The conversation that followed was polite, if a tad stilted. Erin's hand circled the water glass, and her gaze flittered across the restaurant, gathering in the memories.

"I made a mistake," Brand announced out of the blue, capturing her attention. "I shouldn't have reminded you I'm navy. You were enjoying yourself until then."

Erin lowered her gaze to the red linen napkin in her lap. "Actually, I'm grateful. It's far too easy to forget with you." As she spoke, Erin could hear a thread of resentment and fear in her own voice.

"I was hoping we might be able to forget about that."

"No," she answered, softly, regretfully. "I can't allow myself to forget. You're here for how long? Two, three weeks?" She asked this as a reminder to herself of how foolish it would be to become involved with Brand.

"Two weeks."

"That's what I thought." Her gaze drifted toward the kitchen in a silent appeal to the chef to hurry with their order. The more time she spent with Brand, the more susceptible she was to his charm. He was everything she feared. Appealing. Attractive. *Charming*. She was beginning to hate that word, but it seemed to fit him so well.

He asked her about the places she'd lived, and she answered him as straightforwardly as she could, trying not to let the resentment seep into her voice. Her answers were abridged, clipped.

Their meal arrived, and none too soon, as far as Erin was concerned.

Brand's steak was delicious. As delicious as Erin had promised, cooked to perfection. He didn't know what to make of Erin MacNamera, however. Hell, he didn't know what to make of himself. She'd made her views on seeing him plain enough. He didn't know what it was about her that affected him so strongly. The challenge, perhaps. There weren't many women who turned him down flat the way she had.

The challenge was there, he'd admit that, but it was something else, too. Something he couldn't quite put his finger on. Whatever it was, Erin was driving him crazy.

They'd agreed to meet outside her office building, and Brand had half expected her to stand him up. When she had shown, he'd noted regretfully that it wasn't out of any desire to spend time with him. At first she'd been tense. They'd started talking, and she'd lowered her guard and been beginning to relax. Then he'd blown it by reminding her he was in the navy.

From that point on he might as well have been sitting across the table from a robot. He'd asked her something, and she'd answered him with one-word replies or by simply shrugging her shoulders. After a while he'd given up the effort. If she wanted conversation with her dinner, then she could damn well carry it on her own.

It didn't come as any surprise to Brand that she was ready to leave the minute they finished. He collected the bill, left a generous tip and escorted Erin to the car.

"Are you parked at the same lot off Yesler?" he asked once they were in traffic.

"Yes. You can drop me off there, if you don't mind."

"I don't." Brand noted that she sounded downright eager to part company with him. This woman was definitely a detriment to his ego. Fine, he got the message. He wasn't exactly sure why he'd even suggested this dinner date. As Erin had taken pains to remind him, he would be in Seattle only a couple of weeks. The implication being that he'd be out of her life forever then. Apparently that was exactly what she wanted.

In retrospect, Brand was willing to admit why he'd asked her out to dinner.

It was the kiss.

Her response, so tentative in the beginning, so hesitant and unsure, had thrown him for a loop. If Casey was ever to find out Brand had kissed his red-haired daughter, there would be hell to pay. The sure wrath of his friend hadn't altered the fact Brand had wanted to kiss Erin. And kiss her he had, until his knees had been knocking and his heart had been roaring like a runaway train.

What had started out as a challenge had left him depleted and shaken. Numb with surprise and wonder. Erin had flowered in his arms like a rare tropical plant. She was incredibly sweet, and so soft that he'd been forced to use every ounce of restraint he possessed not to crush her in his arms.

This dinner date was a different story. She could hardly wait to get out of his car. Fine. He'd let her go, because frankly he wasn't much into cultivating a relationship with a woman who clearly didn't want to have anything to do with him.

He pulled off First Avenue onto the lot and left the engine running, hoping she'd get his message, as well.

Her hand was already closed around the door handle. "Thank you for dinner."

"You're welcome," was his stiff reply. His tone bordered on the sarcastic, but if she noticed she didn't comment.

"I'm sorry I was such poor company."

He didn't claim otherwise. She hesitated, and for a wild moment Brand thought she might lean over and gently kiss him goodbye. It would have been a nice gesture on her part.

She didn't.

Instead she scooted out of the car, fiddled with the snap of her purse and retrieved her key chain, all while he sat waiting for her. When she'd opened the door to her Toyota, she twisted around and smiled sadly, as if she wanted to say something more. She didn't, however. She just climbed inside resolutely.

Brand had to back up his car in order for her to pull out of the parking space. He did so with ease, reversing his way directly into the street. She came out after him and headed in the opposite direction.

His hand tightened around the steering wheel as she drove off into the night.

"Goodbye, Erin. We might have been friends," he murmured, and regret settled over his shoulders like a heavy wool jacket.

Once he was back at his room in the officers' quarters, Brand showered and climbed into bed. He read for a while, but the novel, which had been touted as excellent, didn't hold his interest. After fifteen minutes, he turned out the light.

He should have kissed her.

The thought flashed through his mind like a shot from a ray gun.

Hell, no. It was apparent Erin didn't want to have anything to do with him. Wonderful. Great. He was man enough to accept her decision.

Forcefully, he punched up the pillow under his head and closed his eyes.

Before he realized what he was doing, a slight smile curved his lips. She should count herself lucky he hadn't taken it upon himself to prove her wrong and kiss her again. If he had, she would have been putty in his hands, just the way she had been the first time. Erin MacNamera might well have believed she had the situation under control, but she hadn't. She'd been tense and uneasy, and for no other reason than the fear that Brand was going to take her in his arms again.

He should have. He'd wanted to. Until now he hadn't been willing to admit how damn much he had longed to taste her again.

Brand rolled over onto his stomach and nuzzled his face into the thick softness of the pillow. Erin had been feather-soft. When she'd moved against him, her breasts had lightly cushioned his chest. The memory of her softness clouded his mind.

Burying his face in the pillow added fuel to his imagination, and he abruptly rolled over. He firmly shut his eyes and sighed as he started to drift off.

It didn't work. Instead, he saw Erin's sweet Irish face looking back at him.

Her eyes were an unusual shade of brown. Man-enticing brown, he decided. With her curly red hair and her pale, peach-smooth complexion, her eye color was something of a surprise. He'd expected blue or green, not dark brown.

Beautiful brown eyes…so readable, so clear, looking back at him, as if she were suffering from a wealth of regrets just before she'd climbed into her car.

Brand was suffering from a few regrets of his own. He hadn't kissed her. Nor had he suggested they see each other again.

Damn his pride. He should have done something, anything, to persuade her. Now she was gone….

Sleep danced around him until he was on the verge of drifting off completely. Then his eyes snapped open, and a slow, satisfied smile turned up the edges of his mouth.

He knew exactly what he intended to do.

Erin remembered Marilyn Amundson from the first session of the Women in Transition course on Tuesday evening. The middle-aged woman with pain-dulled blue eyes and fashionably styled hair had sat at the back of the room, in the last row. Throughout most of the class, she'd kept her gaze lowered. Erin noted that the woman took copious notes as she outlined the sixteen-session course. Every now and again, the older woman would pause, dab a tissue at the corner of her eyes and visibly struggle to maintain her aplomb.

At nine, when class was dismissed, Marilyn had slowly gathered her things and hurried outside the classroom. Later Erin had seen a car stop in front of the college to pick her up.

It was Erin's guess that Marilyn didn't drive. It wasn't unusual for the women who signed up for the course to have to rely on someone else for transportation.

Most of the women were making a new life for themselves. Some came devastated by divorce, others from the death of a loved one. Whatever the reason, they all shared common ground and had come to learn and help each other. When the sessions were finished, the classes continued to meet as a monthly support group.

The greatest rewards Erin had had as a social worker were from the Women in Transition course. The transformation she'd seen in the participants' lives in the short two months she taught the class reminded her of the metamorphosis of a cocoon into a butterfly.

The first few classes were always the most difficult. The women came feeling empty inside, fearful, tormented by the thought of facing an unknown future. Many were angry, some came guilt-ridden, and there were always a few who were restless, despairing and pessimistic.

What a good portion of those who signed up for the course didn't understand when they first arrived was how balanced life was. Whenever there was a loss, the stage was set for something to be gained. A new day was born, the night was lost. A flower blossomed, the bud was lost. In nature and in all aspects of life an advantage could be found in a loss. A balance, oftentimes not one easily explained or understood, but a symmetry nevertheless, was waiting to be discovered and explored. It was Erin's privilege to teach these women to look for the gain.

"I was wondering if I could talk to you?"

Erin paused. "Of course. You're Marilyn Amundson?"

"Yes." The older woman reached for a tissue and ran it beneath her nose. Her fingers were trembling, and it was several moments before she spoke. "I can't seem to stop crying. I sit in class and all I do is cry.... I want to apologize for that."

"You don't need to. I understand."

Marilyn smiled weakly. "Some of the other women in class look so…like they've got it all together, while I'm a basket case. My husband…" She paused when her voice faltered. "He asked me for a divorce two weeks ago. We've been married over thirty years. Apparently he met someone else five or six years ago, and they've been seeing each other ever since…only I didn't know."

This was a story Erin had heard several times over, but it wouldn't lessen Marilyn's pain for Erin to imply that she was another statistic. What she did need to hear was that others had survived this ordeal, and so would she.

"I'd…gone out shopping. The bus stops right outside our house, and when I returned home, Richard was there. I knew right away something was wrong. Richard only rarely wears his suit. I asked him what he was doing home in the middle of the day, and all he could do was stand there and stare at me. Then…then he said he was sorry to do it this way, and he handed me the divorce papers. Just like that–without any warning. I didn't know about the other woman…. I suppose I should have, but I…I trusted him."

Erin's heart twisted at the torment that echoed in the other woman's voice. Marilyn struggled to hold back the tears, her lips quivering with the effort.

"Although this may feel like the worst moment of your life, you will survive," Erin said gently, hugging her briefly. "I promise you that. The healing process is like everything else, there's a beginning, a middle and an end. It feels like the whole world has caved in on you now."

"That's exactly the way I feel. Richard is my whole life…was my whole life. I just don't know what I'm going to do."

"Have you seen an attorney?"

Marilyn shook her head. "Not yet…My pastor suggested I take this course, and find my footing, so to speak."

"In session twelve a lawyer will visit the class. You can ask any questions you like then."

"I wanted to thank you, too," Marilyn went on, once she'd composed herself. "What you said about the balance of things, how nature and life even things out… well, it made a lot of sense to me. Few things do these days."

Erin reached for her coat, slipping her arms into the satin-lined sleeves. She smiled, hoping the gesture would offer Marilyn some reassurance. "I'm pleased you're finding the class helpful."

"I don't think I could have made it through this last week without it." She retreated a few steps and smiled again. This time it came across stronger. "Thank you again."

"You're welcome. I'll see you Tuesday."

"I'll be here." Buttoning up her own coat, Marilyn headed out the classroom door.

Erin watched the older woman. Her heart ached for Marilyn, but, although she was devastated and shaky now, Erin saw in her a deep inner strength. Marilyn hadn't realized it was there, not yet. Soon she would discover it and draw upon the deep pool of courage. For now her thoughts were full of self-condemnation, self-deprecation and worry. From experience, Erin knew Marilyn would wallow in those for a while, but the time would come when she'd pick herself up by the bootstraps. Then that inner strength, the grit she saw in the other woman's weary eyes, would come alive.

As if sensing Erin's thoughts, Marilyn paused at the classroom door and turned back. "Do you mind if I ask you a personal question?"

"Sure, go ahead."

"Have you ever been in love?"

"No," Erin answered, regretfully. "Not even close, I'm afraid."

Marilyn nodded, then squared her shoulders. "Don't ever let it happen," she advised gruffly, yet softly. "It hurts too damn much."

Chapter Three

The envelope arrived at Erin's office, hand-delivered by the downstairs receptionist. Erin stared at her name scrawled across the front and knew beyond a doubt the handwriting belonged to Brand Davis. She held the plain white envelope in her hand several moments, her heart pounding. It'd been two days since her dinner date with Brand, and she hadn't been able to stop thinking about him. She'd been so awful, so aloof and unfriendly, when he'd been trying so hard to be cordial and helpful.

When he'd dropped her off where she'd parked her car, she'd practically leaped out of his in her eagerness to get away from him. Exactly what had he done that was so terrible? Well, first off, he'd been pleasant and fun–horrible crimes, indeed–while she'd behaved like a cantankerous old biddy. She wasn't proud of herself; in fact, Erin felt wretched about the whole thing.

"Go ahead and open it," she said aloud.

"You talking to yourself again?" Aimee chastised. "You generally don't do that until the end of the day."

"Brand sent me a note." She held it up for her friend's inspection as though she were holding on to a hand grenade and expected it to explode in her face at any moment.

"I thought the receptionist looked envious. He's probably downstairs waiting for you right now."

"Ah..." That thought didn't bear contemplating.

"For heaven's sake," Aimee said eagerly, "don't just sit there, open it."

Erin did, with an enthusiasm she didn't dare question. Her gaze scanned the short message before she looked up to her friend. "He wants to give me a tour of Sand Point before the opportunity is gone. You know there's a distinct possibility the navy may close down the base. He says I should have a look at it for nostalgia's sake."

"When?"

"Tomorrow...You're right, he's downstairs waiting for my answer."

"Are you going to do it?" Aimee's question hung in midair like a dangling spider.

Erin didn't know. Then she did know. Longing welled deep within her, not a physical longing, but an emotional stirring that left her feeling empty inside. She didn't want to have anything to do with this lieutenant j.g., didn't want to be trapped in the whirlpool of his strong, sensual appeal. Nevertheless, she had been from the first moment they'd kissed, despite her best efforts.

He paralyzed her; he challenged her. He was everything she claimed she didn't want in a man, and everything she'd ever hope to find.

"Well?" Aimee probed. "What are you going to do?"

"I...I'm going to take that tour."

Aimee let loose with a loud cheer that attracted the attention of nearly everyone in the huge open room. Several people stuck their heads out from behind office doors to discover what was causing all the excitement.

Shaking on the inside, but outwardly composed, Erin took the elevator to the ground floor. Brand was waiting in the foyer. He had his back to her and was standing in front of the directory. He wore his dress uniform, and his hands were joined behind his back, holding his garrison cap.

He must have sensed her presence, because he turned around.

"Hello," she said, her heart as heavy as the humid air of the rainy Seattle morning.

"Hi," he responded, his own voice low and throaty.

She dropped her gaze, unexpectedly nervous. "I got your note."

"You look surprised to hear from me."

"After the way I behaved the other night, I didn't expect to… I can't understand why you want anything to do with me."

"You weren't so bad." His lazy grin took a long time coming, but when it did it contradicted every word he'd spoken.

She found his smile infectious and doubted any woman could resist this man when he put his mind to it–and his mind was definitely to it!

"Are you free tomorrow?"

"And if I said I wasn't?" She answered him with a question of her own, thinking that was safer than admitting how pleased she was to see him.

"I'd ask you out again later."

"Why?" Erin couldn't understand why he'd continue to risk rejection from her. Especially when she was quite ordinary. Erin wasn't selling herself short. She was a warm, generous person, but she hadn't been with him. Yet he'd returned twice now, enduring her disdain, and she had yet to understand why.

Gradually she raised her eyes to his. And what she viewed confused her even more. Brand was thinking and feeling the same things she was, the same bewilderment, the same confusion. The same everything.

The smile faded, and his face tightened slightly, as if this were a question he'd often asked himself. "Why do I keep coming back?" He leveled his gaze on her. "I wish the hell I knew. Will you come to Sand Point tomorrow?"

Erin nodded, then emphasized her response by saying, "Yes. At ten?"

"Perfect." Then he added with a slight smile, "There'll be a pass waiting for you at the gate."

"Good," she said, taking a step back, feeling nervous and not knowing how to explain it. "I'll see you tomorrow, then."

"Tomorrow."

It wasn't until Erin was inside the elevator, a smile trembling on her lips, that she remembered Marilyn's parting words from the night before.

Don't ever fall in love, Marilyn had warned her, *it hurts too damn much.* Erin felt somewhat comforted to realize she was a long way from falling in love with Brand Davis. But she would definitely have to be careful.

"Well, is it the way you remembered?" Brand asked after a two-hour tour of Naval Station Puget Sound at Sand Point. He'd given her a history lesson, too. Sand Point had originally been acquired by King County back in 1920 as an airport and later leased to the navy as a reserve. Brand had explained that only a few hundred men were based there now, support personnel for the base at Everett. Brand was assigned to the admiral's staff–SINCPAC, out of Hawaii–

and sent to do an independent study in preparation for the possible closure of the base.

Erin had been on the base itself only a handful of times as a child. It amazed her how familiar the base felt to her, even though it had been sixteen years since she'd moved away from the area.

"It hasn't changed all that much over the years."

"That surprises you?"

"Not really." What did catch her unawares was the feeling of homecoming. There had never been one single base her family had been assigned to through the years that gave Erin this sort of abstract feeling of home. From the time she could remember, her life had belonged to the navy. Her father would receive shipping orders, and without a pause her family would pack up everything they owned and head wherever her father's commanding officer decreed. Erin had hated it with a fierceness that went beyond description. Nothing was ever her own, there was no sense of permanency in her life, no sense of security. What she had one day–her friends, her school, her neighbors–could be taken from her the next.

Brand's fingers reached for hers and squeezed tightly. "You look sad."

"I do?" She forced a note of cheerfulness into her voice, needing to define her feelings. Brand had brought her here. For the first time since she'd left her family, she'd returned to a navy base. She'd agreed to Brand's suggestion of a tour with flippant disregard for any emotions she might experience.

The wounds of her youth, although she knew she was being somewhat melodramatic to refer to them that way, had been properly bandaged with time. She'd set the course of her life and hadn't looked back since. Then, out of the blue, Brand Davis had popped in, determined, it seemed, to untie the compress so carefully wrapped around her heart.

As she stood outside the Sand Point grounds, she could almost feel the bandages slackening. Her first instinct was to tug them back into place, but she couldn't do that with the memories. Happy memories, carefree memories, came at her from every angle. The longer she stood there, the longer she soaked in the feelings, the more likely the bandage was to drop to her feet. Erin couldn't allow that to happen.

"I'd forgotten how much I enjoyed living in Seattle," she whispered, barely aware she was speaking.

"Where were you stationed afterward?"

Erin had to think about it. "Guam, as I recall…. No, we went to Alaska first."

"You hated it there?"

"Not exactly. Don't get me wrong, it wasn't my favorite place in the world, but it was tolerable…. We weren't there long." The sun actually did shine at midnight, and the mosquito was teasingly referred to as the Alaska state bird. Actually, Erin had loved Alaska, but they'd been there such a short while.

"How long?"

"Four months, I'd guess. There was some screwup, and almost overnight we were given orders and shipped to Guam. Now that was one place I really did enjoy."

"Did you ever take picnics on Guam?"

Erin had to think that one over, and she couldn't actually remember one way or the other. "I suppose we did."

"And how did you enjoy those?"

Erin glanced in Brand's direction and studied him through narrowed eyes. "Why do I have the funny feeling this is a leading question?"

"Because it is." Brand grinned at her, and the sun broke through whatever clouds there were that day. "I packed us a lunch, and I was hoping to persuade you to go on a picnic with me."

"Where?" Not that it mattered. The question was a delaying tactic to give her time to sort through her scattered feelings. A tour of Sand Point was one thing, but lying down on the grass feeding each other grapes was another.

"Anywhere you want."

"Ah?" Her mind scurried as she tried to come up with the names of parks, but for the life of her Erin couldn't remove the picture of Brand pressing a grape to her lips and then bending over to kiss her and share the juicy flavor.

"Erin?"

"How about Woodland Park? If you haven't visited the zoo, you should. Seattle has one of the country's best." That way she could feed the animals and take her mind off Brand. The choice was a good one for another reason, as well. Woodland Park was sure to be crowded on a day as bright and sunny as this one.

Erin was right. They were fortunate to find parking. Brand frowned as he glanced around them, and she could almost hear his thoughts. He'd been hoping she'd lead him to a secluded hideaway, and she'd greatly disappointed him. He might as well become accustomed to it. Erin had agreed to see him again, but she absolutely refused to become romantically involved.

"Just who do you think you're kidding?" she muttered under her breath. Her stomach had been tied up in knots for the last hour while she'd replayed over and over again in her mind this ridiculous scene about them sharing grapes. For all she knew, he might have brought along apples, or oranges, or omitted fruit altogether.

"You said something?" Brand asked, giving her an odd look.

"No..."

"I thought you did."

She was going to have to examine this need to talk out loud

to herself. As far as she could see, the best tactic was to change the subject. "I'm starved."

"Me too." But when he glanced her way, his gaze rested squarely on her mouth, as if to say he was eager to eat all right, but his need wasn't for food.

Her beautiful Irish eyes were moody, Brand decided. Moody and guarded. Brand didn't know what he'd done–or hadn't done–that disturbed Erin so much. From the moment they'd driven away from the naval station, he'd toyed with the idea of asking her what was wrong. He hadn't, simply because he knew she'd deny that anything was troubling her.

Brand wasn't pleased with her choice of parks for their picnic. The zoo was a place for family and kids. He'd be lucky if they found five minutes alone together. But then, that was exactly the reason Erin had chosen it.

Brand, on the other hand, wanted seclusion and privacy. He wanted to kiss Erin again. Hell, he *needed* to kiss Erin again. The thought had dominated his mind for days. She was so incredibly soft and sweet. He swore he'd never kissed another woman who tasted of honey the way she did. The sample she'd given him hadn't been nearly enough to satisfy his need. For days he'd been telling himself he'd blown the kiss up in his mind, way out of proportion. Nothing could have been that good.

"Anyplace around here will do," she said.

He followed her into the park, his gaze scanning the rolling green landscape and falling on a large pond. The space under the trees near the shore looked the most promising. He suggested there.

"Sure," she responded, but she sounded uncertain.

Brand smoothed out the gray navy-issue blanket on the lawn and set the wicker basket in the center of it.

"If you'd said something earlier, I would have baked brownies," Erin said, striving, Brand thought, to sound conversational.

"You can next time." The implication was there, as blatant as he could make it. He would be seeing her again. Often. As frequently as their schedules allowed. He planned on it, and he wanted her to do the same.

"What did you pack for us?" Her voice sounded hollow, as if it were coming from an abandoned well.

"Nothing all that fabulous." Kneeling on the blanket, he opened the basket and set out sandwiches, a couple of cans of cold pop, potato chips and two oranges.

Erin's gaze rested on the oranges for the longest moment. They were the large Florida variety, juicy, she suspected, and sweet.

"Do you want the turkey on white or the corned beef on whole wheat?"

"The turkey," she answered.

Next Brand opened the chips and handed her the bag. She grabbed a handful and set them on top of a napkin. For all her claims about being famished, Brand noted, she barely touched her food.

He sat, leaning his back against the base of the tree, and stretched his long legs out in front of him, crossing his ankles. "You're looking thoughtful."

Her responding smile was weak. "I…I was just thinking about something one of the women in my class told me."

"What was that?"

Her head came up, and her gaze collided with his. "Ah… it's difficult to explain."

"This class means a lot to you, doesn't it?"

Erin nodded. "One of the women has been on my mind the last couple of days. She hasn't centered herself yet, and–"

"Centered herself?"

"It's a counseling term. Basically, what it means is that she hasn't come to grips with who and what she is and needs to brace herself for whatever comes her way. Right now she's suffering from shock and emotional pain, and the smallest problem overpowers her. Frankly, I'm worried."

"Tell me about her." Brand held out his arm, wanting Erin to scoot close and rest her head on his chest. He'd been looking for a subtle, natural way of doing so without putting Erin on red alert.

He was almost surprised when she did move toward him. She didn't exactly cuddle up in his arms, but she braced her back against his chest and stretched her legs out in front of her. His arm reached across her shoulder blades.

"She's taking my class because after thirty-odd years of marriage her husband is leaving her. From what I understand there's another woman involved."

"I didn't know people would divorce after staying married for so many years. Frankly, it doesn't make a lot of sense."

"It happens," Erin explained softly, "more than you'd guess."

"Go on, I didn't mean to interrupt you. Tell me about…"

"I'll call her Margo. That isn't her name, of course."

Brand nodded. It felt so good to have Erin in his arms. He'd been fantasizing about it for days. The hold wasn't as intimate as he would have liked, but with this sweet Irish miss he'd need to go slowly.

"She's in her early fifties and never worked outside the home. All she knows how to be is a homemaker and a wife. I'd venture to guess that she's never written a check. I know for a fact she doesn't drive. At a time in her life when she was looking forward to retirement, she needs to find a career and make a home for herself."

"What about children? Surely, they'd stick by their mother at a time like this."

"Two daughters. They're both married and live outside the state. From what I can remember, one lives in California and the other someplace in Texas. Margo's completely alone, probably for the first time in her life."

"How's she handling it?"

"It's hard to tell. We're only two classes into the course, but as I said before, she's shaky and fragile. Time will help."

"My parents were divorced." Brand seldom spoke of his family, and even more rarely of the trauma that had ripped his life apart at such a tender age. "I was just a kid at the time."

"Was it bad?"

He answered her with a short nod. Without a doubt, it was the worst ordeal Brand could ever remember happening to him. His whole world had been shattered. He'd become a weapon to be used against one parent or the other. And he'd only been eleven at the time. Far too young to understand, far too old to cry.

"I rarely saw my father afterward. Every time he and my mother were in the same room together, they'd start arguing. My guess is that it was easier for him to move as far away as possible than to deal with her."

"So when he divorced your mother, he divorced you, too?"

Once again, Brand responded with a short nod. His life had been filled with one trauma after another after his father had moved out of the state. A year or two later, when his mother had remarried, all communication and child support had stopped. Brand had been made to feel guilty for every bit of food he ate or each pair of shoes he outgrew. While attending college, he'd become involved in the officers' training program offered by the navy. His life had changed from that moment forward. For the better.

Brand found security and acceptance in the navy. What the military had given him, it had taken away from Erin. He understood her complaints well. She hated moving, never planting roots or building lasting relationships. Brand thrived on the security. The navy was his home. The navy was his life. No one would ever take that away from him. There would always be a navy. Budget cuts hurt, bases were being closed down all across the country and military spending was being decreased, but he was secure, more secure than he had been since childhood.

"But I have a feeling about Margo," Erin continued. "She's far stronger than she realizes. That knowledge will come in time, but she may travel some rough waters before this ordeal is finished."

"You're strong, too."

Erin leaned her head to examine his face, and Brand took advantage of the moment to press his hands gently to her rosy cheeks. Her eyes found his, and he read her confusion as clearly as he viewed her eagerness. She wanted this kiss as much as he wanted to kiss her.

Gently he pressed his mouth to hers. The kiss was deep and thorough, his lips sliding across hers with unhurried ease and a familiarity that belied their experience. Slowly he lifted his head and drew in a deep, stabilizing breath. A bolt of sizzling electricity arched between them.

"Oh, damn," Erin whispered, sounding very much as if she were about to weep. Her eyes remained closed, and Brand was tempted to kiss her moist lips a second time. In fact, he had to restrain himself from doing so.

"Damn?"

"I was afraid of this." Her words were hoarse, as if she were having trouble speaking. Her eyes fluttered open, and she gazed up longingly at him. Irish eyes. Sweet Irish eyes.

"Don't be afraid," he whispered, just before he kissed her a second time. And a third. A fourth. His hands were in her hair, loving the silky feel of it as he ran his fingers through the lengthy curls.

Gradually he felt her opening up to him, like the satin petals of a rosebud. Either she'd had poor teachers or she was inexperienced in the art of kissing. Brand didn't know which, didn't care.

Positioned as they were against the tree, he couldn't get close enough to her. The need to cradle her softness grew until every part of his body ached. He wanted her beneath him, warm and willing. Open and sweet.

With their mouths joined, he rolled away from the tree, taking her with him. Erin gave a small cry of alarm, and when she opened her mouth he groaned and thrust his tongue deep into the moist warmth.

She rebelled for a moment, not having expected this new intimacy. It took her a second to adjust before she responded, meekly at first, by giving him her tongue. They touched, stroked and played against each other in an erotic game until Brand deepened the kiss to a level neither of them would be able to tolerate for long.

Her hands clenched his shirt, and Brand wondered if she could feel how hard and fiercely his heart was beating. He could feel hers, excited and chaotic, pounding against his chest. Her pulse wasn't the only thing he could feel. Her nipples had pearled and stood out. The need to slip his hand under her sweater and fill his palm with her breast ate at him like lye. He couldn't…not here.

He longed to feel her and taste her. Sweet heaven, if he didn't stop now he'd end up *really* frightening her. He probably had already. He was as hard as concrete against her thigh. The way they were lying, there wasn't any way he could hide what she was doing to him. Only years of training and self-discipline kept him still. He longed to rotate his hips to help ease the terrible ache in his loins.

He kissed Erin again, struggling within himself to take it slow and easy. His mouth gentled over hers, in sharp contrast to the wild, uncontrolled kisses they'd shared seconds earlier. She groaned and moved against him, causing Brand to moan himself. His innocent Irish miss hadn't a clue of the torment she was putting him through. Dear heaven, she was sweet. So warm and moist.

Brand had fully intended to cool their lovemaking, but he made a single tactical error that was nearly his undoing. Just because a kiss was gentle, it didn't make it any less sensual, or any less devastating.

By the time Brand lifted his head, he was weak, depleted, yet at the same time exhilarated. Shocked eyes stared up at him. He smiled and noted how the edges of her delectable mouth quivered slightly.

She raised her hand, and her fingertips grazed his face. Her touch was as smooth and light as a velvet glove. Unable to resist, Brand kissed her again.

"Are you going to say damn again?" he teased.

Her grin widened. "No."

"But you should?"

She nodded, then closed her eyes and slowly expelled her breath. "I don't know how this happened."

"You don't?"

"I'd hoped…"

He pressed a finger across her lips. "I know what you hoped! You couldn't have picked a more public place and for obvious reasons, which I fear have backfired on us both. As it is, I may have to lie on my belly the rest of the afternoon."

"You will?" As the meaning of his words sank into her

brain, Erin's cheeks blossomed with color. "I…I shouldn't have said anything." As if she needed something to occupy her hands, she reached for one of the oranges, peeling it open. She held out a dripping slice to him. "Want one?"

Sitting Indian-fashion, with his legs folded in front of him, Brand nodded. He thought Erin meant to hand it to him, but instead she leaned forward to feed him personally. Her eyes were locked with his. A second slice followed the first, but when the juice flowed from the edge of his mouth she bent toward him and licked it away.

When her tongue scraped the side of his lips, Brand's heart went still. She offered him another slice, but he took it from her fingers and fed it to her. He watched as she chewed and swallowed, and then he leaned forward to kiss her. She tasted of orange and woman. He deepened the kiss and was gratified when she opened up to him in excited welcome. His tongue swept her mouth in slow, even strokes, conquering as it plundered.

Erin looped her arms around his neck and melted in his arms. "I promised myself this wouldn't happen."

"And now that it has?" He angled his head to one side and dropped a series of long, slow kisses on her neck, working his way under her chin and to her ear. "Do you want me to stop?"

"No."

The satisfaction that one word gave him was worth a thousand from anyone else. "Let's get out of here."

"Why?" How afraid she sounded.

His mouth hovered a scant inch from hers. "Because there are other places I want to kiss you, and I don't think you'd appreciate me doing so in public."

His lips inched back to hers in breath-stealing increments. The closer his mouth edged toward hers, the choppier her breath became.

"Brand…I don't think this is such a good–"

He silenced any protest with a hot, need-filled kiss. She welcomed his tongue, and was panting by the time he dragged his mouth from hers.

"Come on," he said, vaulting to his feet. He reached for her hand, pulling her upright. "Let's get out of here."

"Where…will we go?"

"Your place."

"Brand…I don't know."

He turned and planted his hands squarely on her shoulders, his eyes refusing to release hers. "I'm not going to make love to you, yet. That's a promise. We need to talk, and when we do, I want it to be in private."

She might have had objections to the high-handed manner in which he was issuing orders, but she didn't voice any. Nor did she speak while he drove to her house in West Seattle, although the ride took nearly thirty minutes. The only words she did manage were to relay her address and give directions once he was in the vicinity.

It wasn't until he helped her out of the car that she did chance a look in his direction. Brand had to smile. Her eyes seemed so round and wide, an aircraft carrier could have sailed through them.

"He said *yet,* you idiot." She repeated the sentence two or three times once they were inside the house. Brand found it amusing the way she talked to herself. Without telling him what she was doing, she walked, as if in a daze, into the kitchen and started assembling a pot of coffee.

Brand hadn't a clue what she was mumbling about. He wasn't interested in coffee, either, but since she hadn't asked him, he didn't say so.

"There's something you should know," he began. Then he changed his mind. This wasn't the time. He needed to taste her again.

"What?" She sounded as though she were coming out of a coma.

"Come here first."

She walked over to him as though she were sleepwalking, her steps sluggish and her look disoriented.

"Kiss me first," Brand whispered, "then I'll tell you."

As if she were in a stupor, she planted her hands on his chest, then stood on tiptoe and brushed her lips lightly over his. Unable to hold himself back any longer, Brand wrapped his arms around her, pulled her close and buried his face in her neck, savoring her softness.

For the last several days he'd been wondering what it was about Erin that preyed so heavily on his mind. After kissing her, he understood. He felt strong when he was with her. Strong emotionally. Strong physically. When they were together, he became another Samson. She gave him a feeling of being needed.

She needed him, too. She'd never admit it, of course, never deliberately tell him as much, but it was true.

"You said we needed to talk," she reminded him. With what seemed like a good deal of effort, she moved away from him.

"Yes," Brand answered softly, and rubbed a hand along the back of his neck. "What are you doing every day for the next four days?"

"Why?" A worried look dominated her face. Then her eyes, which had been so gentle and submissive only seconds before, flashed to life with a fire that all but scorched Brand. "You don't need to tell me. You're only going to be in Seattle four more days."

Chapter Four

"Why are you so angry?" Brand demanded, not understanding Erin. He was being as honest as he knew how to be with her, and she was looking at him as though he'd just announced he was an ax murderer.

"You know… You know…" She walked over to the cupboard and slammed two ceramic mugs down with enough force to crack the kitchen counter. "From the beginning you've known how I feel about navy men."

"I didn't mislead you," he reminded her in as reasonable a tone as he could muster. "You knew from the first I was on a short assignment."

Grudgingly she answered him with an abrupt nod.

If Brand was upset about anything, it was the fact that he'd waited so long to do as his friend Casey MacNamera had asked and checked up on the old man's daughter. If Brand had contacted her the first week he'd arrived in Seattle, a lot of things might have worked out differently.

"Here's your coffee." The hot liquid sloshed over the edges of the mug when Erin set it on the glass table top.

He pulled out a beige cushioned chair and sat. His hands cupped the mug while he waited, giving Erin the time she needed to sort through her feelings.

It took her far longer than he expected. She paced the kitchen ten or fifteen times, pausing twice, her eyes revealing her confusion and her doubt. Both times she glared at him as though he'd committed unspeakable crimes. After a while, her brisk steps slowed, and she started talking to herself, mumbling something unintelligible.

"Am I forgiven?" Brand asked when she sat in the chair across the table from him.

"Sure," she answered, giving him a weak smile. "What's there to forgive?"

"I'm pleased you feel that way." Because of the abrupt switch in her behavior, Brand didn't feel as confident.

"Meeting you has…been an interesting experience" was all she'd say.

Brand felt the same way himself. "Can I see you tomorrow?"

"I'm busy."

Brand frowned, and a sinking sensation attacked the pit of his stomach. "Doing what?"

"I don't believe that's any of your concern."

Oh, boy, here it comes, he mused. "But it is. If you're attending church services, then I'll go with you. If you've promised a friend you'd help them move, then I'll cart boxes myself." If Erin thought the Irish could be stubborn, she had yet to butt heads with the German in him.

"Brand, please don't make this any more difficult than it already is. I can't change who I am for you. I told you from the first I don't want to become involved with anyone in the military, and I meant it. I don't know why you can't accept that. And I don't even want to know. You're leaving, and when it comes right down to it, I'm glad. It's for the best."

"I'm stationed in Hawaii. It's not all that–"

"I have no intention of flying off to the islands for an occasional weekend, nor can I afford to, so don't even suggest it."

"The only thing I was going to suggest was the two of us getting to know each other better." He strove to sound casual, although there wasn't a single bone in his entire body that was indifferent to Erin. She affected him far more strongly than any other woman he'd ever known. Generally he was the one seeking an out in the relationship.

Erin sipped her coffee, more relaxed now. *Centered* was the term she'd used earlier, and he could see it in her. She'd made her decision, and neither hell nor high water would sway her from it.

"Will you see me again?" He didn't like asking a second time. It went against his pride, but he was learning that when it came to Erin MacNamera he was willing to give more than with anyone else.

Her nod took a long time coming, but when it did, Brand felt the tension ease.

"On one condition," she added.

"Name it."

Her beautiful dark eyes found his, and he noted how lost and bewildered she looked. "What is it?"

"No more…of what happened today in the park."

"You don't want me to kiss you again?" Brand was sure he'd misunderstood her. They were just beginning to know each other, learn about each other, and it seemed ridiculous for them to put their relationship into a holding pattern now.

"I'm offering you my friendship, Brand, nothing more." He wanted Erin for more than a friend, but saying so would likely cut off any chance he had with her. If those were the ground rules she was setting, then far be it for him to argue with her. He fully intended to do whatever he could to change her mind, but she'd learn that soon enough.

"All right," he said, grinning at her. "We'll be friends."

"No more of that, either," she countered sharply.

"What?" Brand hadn't a clue what she was talking about.

"That smile. The navy could launch missiles with that smile of yours."

Was that a fact? Brand mused. He'd have to remember that and use it often.

Agreeing to this dinner date wasn't one of her most brilliant moves, Erin decided later. Brand was scheduled to fly out of the Whidbey Island Naval Station early the following morning. They'd talked several times by phone, but she hadn't seen Brand since their date on Saturday afternoon.

Erin hated admitting what a good time she'd had with the lieutenant j.g. They'd toured Sand Point and had a picnic at Woodland Park Zoo, although the only animal she'd encountered was of the human variety. And something else had happened Saturday, something she kept trying to forget and couldn't.

Brand had kissed her senseless.

It caused her cheeks to burn every time she thought about the way she'd abandoned herself in his arms. No one had ever told her kissing could be so wonderful…especially the way Brand was doing it. She felt achy and restless every time she dwelled on it. Her heart would start to beat, slow and sluggish, and the heat would start creeping through her. A warm excitement would fill her, and she could find no way of explaining it. The heat started low in her abdomen and grew into an achy restlessness that disturbed her beyond anything she'd ever experienced.

Then her breasts would start throbbing the way they had when he'd pressed her against the blanket and whispered there were other places he longed to kiss her, too. It had been all she could do not to ask him to take her nipples in his mouth... She wished he had–which was a crazy idea, since they'd been in a public place.

It wouldn't have stopped there. Erin knew that as well as she knew her own name.

Brand awoke carnal instincts in her. She'd never guessed she was capable of feeling sensual sensations as strong as this. Erin had always assumed she knew herself well. Apparently that wasn't the case after all. Not if Brand could evoke such an overwhelming reaction in her with a series of wet kisses.

The doorbell chimed, and, inhaling softly, she braced herself, walked across the living room and opened the front door to Brand.

"Hi." His gaze gave her an appreciative sweep. "Are you ready?"

She nodded. Damn, it was good to see him again. She hated to admit that much, and she gave herself a quick mental shake. Somehow, someway, she was going to get through this evening, and once she did it would be over between them. He could go his way and she could go hers, and never the twain would meet.

Once they were in the car, Erin suggested a Mexican restaurant that was less than a mile from her house. The food was good and cheap. All Erin was looking to do was to survive this evening with her heart intact.

The walls of the El Lindo were made of white stucco and decorated with several huge sombreros in bright shades of turquoise and gold. Erin studied the pictures on the wall, which were displayed in wide, bulky frames, in an effort to avoid looking at Brand. She dared not allow her eyes to meet his for fear of reviving memories from their last encounter.

"So where are you headed to next?" she asked, making sure her voice contained just the right amount of friendliness. A tortilla chip commanded her full attention as she dipped it in salsa.

"Probably San Francisco."

"When?" It felt good to have the upper hand in the conversation, Erin mused.

"Soon. A month or two from now, maybe less. Have you been there?"

"I don't think there are more than a handful of naval bases where I *haven't* been." She made light of the fact, when in reality it was a source of fierce bitterness. The comment was made with just enough sarcasm for Brand to recognize she wouldn't return to that life-style again for anything or anyone in the world, including him. He must have gotten the message, because his face tightened into a frown.

Erin ordered the cheese-and-onion enchiladas, her favorite, and Brand asked for the chili verde. Both dinners were excellent, and they lingered over coffee, talking about a variety of bland but safe subjects. Brand told her about his two best friends, Alex Romano and Catherine Fredrickson. Like him, Alex was a surface warfare officer. Catherine was an attorney. All three had been stationed in Hawaii for four years.

When Brand pulled into the driveway in front of her house, her hand was already on the handle. She had a farewell, so-glad-we-had-this-chance-to-meet talk all prepared, but she wasn't allowed to say one word of it.

Brand reached across the seat and gripped her hand. "Invite me in for coffee."

"We just finished having a cup."

"Invite me in anyway."

"I...don't know if that's such a good idea."

"Yes, it is. Trust me."

"All right." But she wasn't pleased about it.

She led the way into her compact home. Buying a house was one of the first things she'd done after being hired for the Community Action Program. The payments were high, but Erin didn't mind the sacrifice, because for the first time in her life she didn't have to worry about being forced to move. No one was going to casually announce it was time to relocate. She didn't need to worry that everything she owned was going to be stripped away from her almost overnight.

For the first time in her life, she was planting roots. They weren't as deep as she wanted, not yet, but she intended for them to be. This home was hers and hers alone. It was her security, her defense, her shelter. Falling crazy in love with a navy man would threaten everything she'd strived to build for herself in the past several years, and she adamantly refused to allow it to happen.

Once they were inside, Erin turned on the lights and pointed to the bulky stuffed chair angled in front of the television. "Make yourself comfortable. Would you like some coffee?"

"Please."

Brand followed her into the kitchen. "We've avoided the subject all evening," he said, standing directly behind her. He wasn't actually pinning her against the counter, but he made it plain he could if he wanted to.

"We don't need to talk about it."

"We do," he countered swiftly. "I'm leaving. Trust me, I don't want to go, but I am. It's part of my job. I don't know when I'll be back, but I will be."

She tried to look as uninterested as she could. "Look me up when you do," she said flippantly.

Brand frowned anew. "Erin MacNamera, that wasn't nice."

"I apologize." She didn't completely understand what she'd

said that was so wrong. If Brand thought she was going to sit around moping for him, he was dead wrong.

Yes, she enjoyed his company, and when he left she'd miss him for a while, but after a week or so she wouldn't give him more than the occasional fleeting thought.

"Kiss me," Brand instructed.

Erin's heart went still. She'd prefer leaping off the Tacoma Narrows Bridge to granting Brand Davis the privileges she had the day of their picnic. He might as well ask her to light a stick of dynamite and wave it around for everyone to see what a fool she was.

She tried to break away from him. "I can't…I have no intention of kissing you."

"Just once, to say goodbye."

"Brand…"

His hands drifted up and down her lifeless arms, bringing her against him. Erin didn't know who moved, him or her.

"If you won't kiss me, then you leave me no choice but to kiss you." He angled his head to one side and placed his moist, hot mouth over hers.

The kiss was unbearably good; it was all Erin could do not to melt at his feet. Somehow she managed to stand stiff and straight, not granting him an inch.

Brand appeared unconcerned by her lack of response. He drew her wrists up and placed her hands around his neck, then locked his own arms tight around her waist, lifting her against him.

Erin didn't want to respond, had promised herself she wouldn't, but before she knew what was happening her lips had parted and her tongue was eagerly searching out his. If only he weren't so gentle. So tender and generous. Erin felt as if she were drowning in sheer ecstasy. She moaned, and the sound seemed to encourage Brand all the more.

He kissed her again and again, and it was even better than his lovemaking had been in the park. Even more wonderful, and she hadn't thought that was possible. Brand's kisses were long and deep, and before she knew it Erin was clinging to him mindlessly.

He released her slowly, letting her slide down his front. Once her feet were firmly planted on the floor, his hand closed over her breast. Erin whimpered–it was a soft sound of pleasure–as he battled with the buttons of her silk blouse, peeling it open. He unfastened her bra and filled his palms with her lush fullness. His sigh went through her like a spear, and as hard as she tried, she couldn't keep from reacting.

Her nipples were so hard, they burned and throbbed and ached in a way she'd never experienced until now. Her hands were in Brand's hair and her head was thrown back as she squirmed against him. She wanted his mouth on her breasts, just the way she'd imagined. Just the way she'd dreamed about for the past two nights.

As if reading her thoughts, Brand gave her what she yearned to experience, drawing her nipple into his moist, warm mouth and sucking lightly, then strongly, then lightly again. A sensation of pleasure so hot it bordered on pain flashed through her like lightning. It was all Erin could do to hold still. If he continued this much longer, she'd be climbing the walls. Literally.

The sensation was incredible, beyond description. She wanted him, needed him. Soon her own fingers were busy. She was so impatient, she nearly ripped the buttons off his shirt. It became imperative that she do to him what he was doing to her. She didn't know if this was something women did to men, but she longed to return the pleasure he was giving her.

With her arms wrapped securely around his neck, she nuzzled the hollow at his throat, sliding her tongue back and forth in lazy circles while she fiddled with the opening on his shirt. Once it was free, she spread it back from his shoulders.

Erin had never seen a man as close to perfect as Brand. He was stronger than anyone she'd ever known. And he smelled so good, of spice and bay rum. He'd probably sprayed himself with an aphrodisiac before meeting her for dinner, but Erin was beyond the point of caring.

Brand's muscular body felt hot to the touch. She was unable to keep her hands still. They roamed up and down the sides of his waist, then over the lightly haired planes of his broad chest until she inadvertently touched the tight buds of his nipples. When she did, she was gratified by the shudder that went through him, starting with a rippling motion in his massive shoulders and working its way down.

"Erin," he pleaded, "no more."

She ignored him. After all, he ignored her, and fair was fair. Her mouth fastened over the tight pearl of his nipple, and she gave him the same treatment he had given her. He tasted as wonderful as he smelled.

"Erin," he pleaded a second time. She paused long enough to sigh, loving the sound of his voice, so low and husky. It spurred her on more powerfully than any words he might have said.

"We've got to stop before it's too late," he warned, working his hands between them.

Her response was to curl her fingers more tightly in the hair on his chest and tug lightly.

"Erin."

This time something in his voice did capture her attention. His hands were on her shoulders, and he heaved a giant breath as he wrapped his arms around her waist. Erin buried her face in his neck, embarrassed by the things she'd done and allowed him to do.

She rarely cried, but she felt the salty wetness coat her cheeks.

"Casey would shoot me dead if he knew how close I've come to making love to you."

Erin abruptly broke away from him, her eyes clouded with confusion. She nearly stumbled, finding herself off balance. Nevertheless, she glared up at Brand. "How did you know my father's name is Casey?"

Brand closed his eyes slowly, as if he'd inadvertently allowed a top government secret to pass from his lips. "That's a long story."

Erin jerked away and turned her back to him while her fingers frantically worked to assemble her bra and blouse. Her hands were trembling so badly, it made the task nearly impossible. When she'd finished, she walked across the room and removed her mug from the table, simply because she needed something to cling to. She felt as if she were being beaten by an invisible force, shaken so hard her teeth were rattling.

"How do you know my father?" she demanded a second time, and her voice trembled as severely as her fingers.

"We're friends. We worked together a few years back, hit it off, and have kept in touch ever since," Brand announced, looking none too pleased. If anything, he looked downright irritated. "When Casey learned I was flying into Seattle for this assignment, he asked me to check up on you. Apparently he's worried that you're working too hard. Your father's a good man, Erin."

That wasn't exactly the way Erin would have described him at the moment. He was a meddling, interfering old fool who couldn't keep out of her life!

"So Dad sent you out to spy on me?" she demanded coolly.

Brand nodded reluctantly.

"When we met at the Blue Lagoon…it wasn't by chance?"

"Not exactly. I followed you there."

Erin closed her eyes and placed her hand over her mouth. "Dear heaven."

"I know it sounds bad."

"Bad?" she cried. "You…I was set up by my own father!" She started pacing, because standing still was impossible. Turning abruptly, she glared at him with eyes she was sure conveyed her feelings exactly. "What about everything else? The kissing, the…petting. Did Dad ask you to indoctrinate me into—"

"Erin, no." He expelled his breath sharply and jammed his fingers into his scalp with enough force to remove a fistful of hair. "Okay, I made a mistake. I should have told you the first night that your father and I are friends. If you want to condemn me for that, go ahead, I deserve it. But everything else was for real."

Erin didn't know whether she believed him or not, but at this point it didn't matter. She crossed her arms and glared at the ceiling, trying fruitlessly to gather her thoughts and make sense of what had happened between them.

"I liked you the minute I saw you," Brand admitted slowly, "and the feeling has intensified each and every day since. I don't know what's happening between us. It's crazy, but I feel… Hell, I don't know what I feel, other than the fact I don't want to lose you."

"That's what I can't make you understand," she cried. "You lost me the minute I realized you were navy."

"Erin…"

"I think you should go." The lump in her throat made it impossible for her to speak distinctly. When Brand didn't budge, she pointed the way to the door. "Please, just leave."

Brand hesitated, then nodded. "All right, I can see I've really messed this up. At the rate I'm going, I'll only make matters worse. I'll try to give you a call before I leave tomorrow."

She nodded, although she hadn't a clue what she was agreeing to.

"I've got your address."

Once more she moved her head, willing to concede anything as long as he would get out of her home, her safe haven, and leave her alone. She felt shocked as she rarely had been. Shaken and hurt. To the best of her knowledge, her father had never done anything like this before. Once she got through with him, she would damn well make sure he wouldn't again.

Brand paused at the front door. "I'm not saying goodbye to you, Erin." He stood there for the longest moment without moving. His eyes were filled with regret. It seemed that he wanted to say something more but changed his mind.

Erin looked away, not wanting to encourage him to do anything but leave her in peace. Or whatever was left of that precious commodity.

The door closed, and she glanced up to discover that Brand was gone. A breath rattled through her lungs as she continued to stare into space.

It was over. Brand Davis had left.

Brand closed his eyes as he listened to the message on Erin's answering machine for the tenth time. He was paying long-distance rates to speak to a stupid tape recorder. Not that it had done any good. Not once had she returned his call.

She hadn't even tried.

He'd contacted her every day since he'd returned to Hawaii, but he hadn't spoken to her yet. It didn't seem to matter what time of the day he phoned, she wasn't home. Or if she was, she wasn't answering.

He'd tried writing too. Brand wasn't much of a letter writer, but each night since he'd been back he had sat down faithfully and written to Erin. Not just short notes, either. Real letters, sometimes two and three pages each. He wrote about things he'd rarely shared with longtime friends. He wasn't revealing deep, dark secrets, just feelings. Feelings a man wouldn't easily convey to another human being unless that person was someone special. Erin was more than special. Until he'd left Seattle, Brand hadn't realized how important Casey's daughter had become to him.

Ten days into his letter-writing campaign, he had yet to receive so much as a postcard from her. It didn't take a master's degree for him to figure out that his sweet Irish rose had no intention of answering his letters, either.

Rarely had Brand felt more discouraged. He was frustrated enough to contact Casey MacNamera.

"Casey, you old goat, it's Brand," he said, speaking into the telephone receiver. The long-distance wire hummed between them. Casey had retired in Pensacola, Florida.

"Well if it isn't Face Davis, himself. How you doing, boy?"

"Good. Real good." Which was only a slight exaggeration.

"I take it you told Erin about me asking you to check up on her. Good grief, that girl nearly had a conniption right on the phone. I don't think I've ever heard her more shooting mad. Nearly shouted me ears off, she did." The pot-bellied MCPO paused to chuckle, as if the whole matter were one of great amusement.

"I didn't mean to give it away," Brand said by way of apology. "We sort of hit it off… Erin and me." He paused, hoping Casey would make some comment either way. He didn't.

"That oldest girl of mine has got a temper on her. If you ever cross her, the best advice I can give you is to stand back and protect yourself from the fireworks."

"Speaking of Erin," Brand said, delicately leading into the purpose of this call, "how is she?"

"I can't rightly say." Casey paused and chuckled again. "She didn't get around to telling me anything about her health. She was far more concerned about giving me a solid piece of her mind."

"Did she say anything about me?"

Casey paused. "Not really. Only that she didn't appreciate the fact I'd sent you her way."

"I appreciated it."

"You did?" Casey's voice lowered suspiciously. "What makes you say that?"

"Erin and I dated two or three times. You've done yourself proud, you old goat. Erin's a wonderful woman."

"She's not your type."

Brand was about to take offense at that. "Why isn't she?"

"I thought you liked your women sleek and sophisticated. Erin's not like that. Not in the least. The girl's meat-and-potatoes."

"I like Erin. In fact, I like her a whole lot. I hope that doesn't offend you, because I intend to see more of her."

Brand expected a long list of possible responses from Casey. It didn't include laughter, but laugh was exactly what Casey MacNamera did. In fact, he burst into loud chuckles, as if Brand had just told the funniest joke of the year.

"Good luck, Brand. You're going to need it with my Erin. That woman's stubborner than a Tennessee mule. I don't want to discourage you, but she won't have anything to do with someone in the navy."

"I plan to change her mind."

"As far as I can see, you've got a snowball's chance in hell of ever doing that. Now, before I forget it, tell me how it is you got chosen for this cushy assignment. I should have known that handsome face of yours was going to get you a boondoggle one of these days. Where you headed to next?"

"San Francisco." And none too soon, as far as Brand was concerned, because the city was only six hundred miles from Seattle. And that was a hell of a lot closer than Hawaii.

"Oh, please, don't let there be another letter from Brand," Erin prayed aloud as she pulled into her driveway. For twenty days straight, she'd received a letter from him every day.

Twenty days.

She walked up to the mailbox on her porch and lifted the lid. Two flyers and a bill. There wasn't a letter.

Unreasonably disappointed, she sorted through everything again, and then stuck her hand back inside the mailbox. It was there, tucked down in the back.

Erin didn't know whether she should be upset or relieved. What did it matter? She'd been of two minds from the moment she'd met Brand Davis.

Two minds and one heart.

Opening her front door with her key, Erin walked inside her home and slapped everything down on the kitchen counter. Making herself a cup of tea, she leafed through the flyers and set the bill aside.

Once the tea was made, she reached for Brand's letter, opening it with her index finger. She counted five pages. Five long, single-spaced, handwritten pages. Wouldn't he ever stop?

"Oh, please, make him stop writing," she pleaded once more as her gaze hungrily scanned each word, canceling out her prayer.

When the first letter had arrived, Erin had righteously marched to the outside garbage can and tossed it inside.

She'd refused to read a single line of what that deceiver had written. From there, she'd made herself dinner, muttering sanctimonious epithets directed at the lieutenant j.g. and then headed off to her Women in Transition class, feeling downright pious about having tossed out the letter.

The feeling hadn't lasted long.

At nine-thirty, when she'd returned from class, she'd reached for her flashlight and, without a pause, started rooting through the garbage until she found the envelope.

She'd called herself every word for fool that she could think of in the days since. As much as she hated to admit it, each night she rushed home, eager for word from Brand.

She was living in a fool's paradise. Nothing would come of this. First off, she had no intention of ever answering him.

Nor did she intend to see him again. Their differences were irreconcilable, as far as she could discern. There were no compromises for her and Brand. He was military, and she adamantly refused to fall in love with someone in the armed services–especially someone in the navy.

Each and every time they'd been together, they'd hashed over their differences. There was no way to arbitrate this issue, no meeting in the middle. Nothing he could say would change her mind. Nothing she could say would alter his. Rehashing their differences would only be a waste of time and energy, and Erin had enough on her mind as it was.

The phone rang just as she was turning the last page of his letter. He was giving a humorous account of something he and his friend Alex had done. Without thinking, she reached for the receiver, not giving a thought to letting the recorder answer for her as had been her habit of late.

"Hello," she said softly.

"Erin? Erin, is that really you?"

It was Brand, and he sounded absolutely amazed that she'd answered the phone.

Chapter Five

"Ah…" Erin stammered, resisting the urge to replace the receiver and escape talking to Brand. That would be a coward's way of handling the situation. She and Brand were bound to have a showdown one time or another, and the longer she delayed the confrontation the more difficult it would be.

"Okay, just listen," Brand said, speaking with authority, his voice slightly high-pitched, his words rushed. "I've got everything I want to say all planned."

"Brand, please…"

"You can tell me whatever it is you want when I'm finished, okay?"

She nodded, closed her eyes, then whispered, "All right."

"You asked me once why I continued to ask you out. Do you remember that?"

"Yes." She did, all too well.

"I thought I had it figured out before I left Seattle. I liked you from the first. You're a caring, warm, generous woman, and anyone spending time with you would soon realize that. I noticed it long before the day at the zoo when you were telling me about the older woman in your class who's going through such a difficult time. You barely knew her, yet you sincerely cared about her and her problems."

"What has all this got to do with anything?"

"Just be patient. I'm coming to that."

Erin was so stiff, the muscles in her lower spine were starting to ache. She stood and pressed her hand to the small of her back and paced, walking as far as the telephone cord would stretch and then back again. She longed to rush him along, longed for this to be over as soon as possible. How painful it was, how much more difficult than she'd thought it would be.

"I realized shortly after our picnic that being with you makes me feel strong and good. Strong emotionally, strong physically. I realize that doesn't make a whole lot of sense to you right now. I'm not even sure I can explain it any better than that. Maybe later I can, but for now it isn't the most important thing." Brand paused and inhaled a single, choppy breath. He was speaking so fast that it was difficult for Erin to understand him. And the long-distance hum wasn't helping matters any.

"Brand..."

"Let me finish."

Erin's mind filled with enough arguments to sink a battleship. "All right." Only she wished he'd hurry so she could say what needed to be said and be finished with it.

"The last three weeks away from you have taught me some valuable lessons. I've written you every day."

She didn't need to be reminded of that. Every single message he'd mailed her was neatly stacked on her desk. She'd reread them so often, most had been committed to memory.

"Sitting down and putting my thoughts on paper has cleared up a lot of the confusion I've been feeling since I returned to Hawaii. It hit me almost immediately that…" He hesitated, as though he were fearful of her response. "I'm in love with you, Erin."

"In love with me?" she repeated, as though in a trance.

"I know you don't want to hear that, but I can't and won't apologize for the way I feel. For the first time in my life, I'm in love. I *thought* I was a hundred times before, but this is different. Better. Did you hear me, Erin? I love you."

Erin squeezed her eyes closed. Of all the things he had to say, all the nonsensical, absurd, foolish things…why, oh, why, did he have to tell her that?

"Say something," he pleaded. "Anything."

All the arguments she had lined up in her mind fell like dominoes, crashing against one another, tumbling into nothingness. She was left speechless.

"Erin, sweetheart, are you still there?"

"Yes." Her voice rose an octave above its normal range. "I'm here."

"I know it's something of a shock, blurting it out like this over the phone, but I swear to you I couldn't hold it inside another second. Haven't you noticed how I've signed my letters recently?"

She had. She'd preferred to ignore the obvious, even when it was slapping her in the face.

"A relationship won't work with us… We're too different."

"We'll make it work."

Just the way he said it, without leaving room for doubt, caused Erin to wonder if it was possible. Was loving someone enough to alleviate all the problems? Was it enough to gain a compromise where there wasn't one? Maybe it was, after all. Brand sounded so confident, so convinced.

Erin's hold tightened around the telephone receiver. "I don't see how."

"Erin, sweetheart…damn, I wish I was there right now. It's hell being so far away from you."

"You'll always be away from me." The truth was as cold and lifeless as ice water. How easy it was to forget he was navy. For a moment, just the slightest moment, she could feel herself lulled into believing a relationship was possible for them. If she allowed this false thinking to continue, he'd talk her out of everything that was important to her, everything she'd struggled to build. In the nick of time she realized what she was doing and pulled herself up short.

"I'll be away, yes," Brand argued, "but not all the time, and when we're together I'll make up for lost time."

"No."

"What do you mean, no?"

"Claiming you love me doesn't change anything." The words were easy enough to say, but she wasn't completely sure they were true. What she had to do was pretend they were and pray he didn't challenge her with a lot of questions.

"It does as far as I'm concerned."

"Brand, I'm sorry, I really am, but I can't see where discussing this is going to make a difference. You love the navy. I don't. You want to stay in the service, and I'd rather leap off a cliff naked than involve my life with anything that has to do with the military. We can talk until we're blue in the face, but it isn't going to change who or what we are."

Her words were greeted by a strained silence.

"You'd prefer to leap off a cliff *naked?*" Amusement echoed behind his words.

Perhaps it wasn't the best way to explain her feelings, but it was one of the worst things she could think of doing, although she had to admit it was nonsensical.

"Sweetheart, listen to me."

"No, please, I can't. It won't do any good. The best thing you can do for the both of us is forget we ever met. It isn't going to work, and prolonging the inevitable will only cause us both more pain."

"I love you. I can't–"

"You're not listening to me," she cried, hating the way her voice trembled. "You never have listened to me, and that's the problem."

Once more Brand was silent, and this time the lack of sound seemed to throb between them like a living thing.

"All right, Erin, I'm listening."

She drew in a tattered breath and started again. "What I'm trying to explain is the plain truth, as painful as it is to accept. It will never work between us. Neither of us can adjust our needs because we happen to be physically attracted to each other."

"I'm more than physically attracted to you."

Erin decided the best thing to do was ignore that statement. "I'm honored that you would feel as strongly about me as you apparently do. Personally, I think you're wonderful, too, but that doesn't make everything right. It just doesn't… even though that's what we want."

A moment passed before he spoke. "In other words, you're saying you don't love me. Or, more appropriately phrased, you *won't* love me."

"Yes."

He used a one-word expletive that was meant to shock her, and did. "You're in love with me, Erin. You can deny it if you want, but it's the truth."

"I imagine your ego chooses to believe that. If that's the case, then all I can say is fine, believe what you want." She might have sounded as confident as a judge, but on the inside she'd rarely been more unnerved.

"Say it to me, then."

Erin closed her eyes and swallowed tightly. "Say what?"

"That you don't love me." A strained silence passed before he demanded it of her again. "Say it!"

God help her, Erin couldn't do it.

"Be sure and put enough emphasis on the words to make it believable," he advised, "because I know you're lying, if not to me, then to yourself."

"You have such colossal nerve." She tried to make her statement sound as if she were highly amused by his attitude.

"Say it," he demanded a third time.

A moment passed before she was able to do as he requested. She tried to speak once, but when she opened her mouth she felt her throat start to close up, and she aborted the effort.

"Erin?"

"All right, if you insist. I don't love you."

"Do you mean it?" he asked her softly, sounding almost amused.

If only he didn't make it so damn difficult. She was furious with him, furious enough to put an end to this torment. "Yes, I'm sure. Now kindly leave me alone."

"As you wish." His voice was incredibly low, filled with so many emotions that she couldn't identify them all. "Goodbye, my sweet Irish rose. Have a good life–I sure as hell plan to."

The line was disconnected while she stood holding on to the receiver. For the longest time Erin didn't move. She stood exactly as she was, the phone pressed to her ear, the drone of the line buzzing like angry, swarming bees around her.

The wetness that spilled onto her face came as a surprise. She raised her hand, and her fingertips smeared the moisture across the high arch of her cheek.

"I *will* have a good life," she choked out. "I promise I will."

* * *

"I hate to keep troubling you," Marilyn said, stepping up to Erin's scarred desk. The class had been dismissed for the evening, and Erin was sticking the leftover handouts inside her leather briefcase.

Over the past several weeks, Erin had been keeping close tabs on Marilyn, charting her progress. The older woman had looked something like a baked apple when she'd first come into class. Shriveled up and burdened by the weight of her problems. She'd worn the same dress and the same pair of shoes and little, if any, makeup. All that had gradually changed over the weeks. Marilyn had hired an attorney, gotten a part-time job with a department store and signed up for driving school. She walked a little taller and held her head higher. The going hadn't been easy. Subject to depression and fits of rage, she'd recently confessed to Erin that she'd destroyed one entire wall of the family home.

"It's no trouble, Marilyn. It's always good to talk to you."

"I just wanted you to know I got my driver's license this afternoon."

"Congratulations!"

Marilyn's grin went from ear to ear. "I didn't ever think I'd be able to do it, but the examiner who gave me the road test was very understanding." Excitement lit up her eyes. "I don't mind telling you, I was nervous in the beginning. I backed out of the parking space the wrong way and then went over the curb on the way out of the parking lot. I thought for sure the examiner was going to fail me, but then I got to thinking about the things you've been saying in class, and I decided to make the best of it."

"And you passed?"

"By two points. They didn't exactly throw a parade in my honor, and the examiner did talk to me two or three minutes afterward, suggesting that I take it nice and easy for a while, which I intend to do. When he told me I'd passed the test, I got so excited, I nearly kissed the man."

The picture that scene presented in Erin's mind was amusing enough to bring a smile to her lips. She hadn't been doing a lot of smiling lately. Not since her phone conversation with Brand.

Over and over she'd played back their discussion in her mind. There were better ways of handling the situation with Brand. Yet she'd accomplished what she'd set out to do. Her methods hadn't been the best, but then, she'd never handled anything like this before.

A few days after speaking to Brand for the last time, she'd sat down and written her father a letter hot enough to blister the mailman's fingers. She'd poured out her outrage, claimed he'd insulted her intelligence and her sense of pride and demanded that he stay out of her life.

In the morning she'd tossed the letter into the garbage where it belonged. Her father couldn't be blamed because she'd fallen in love with Brand Davis. As much as she'd like to fault her overprotective parent, all he'd done was ask Brand to check up on her. Everything else that had happened was strictly between her and the lieutenant j.g.

Feeling pleased for Marilyn, Erin drove back to her house, showered and readied for bed. She hadn't eaten anything before class, and an inspection of the freezer disclosed one frozen Salisbury steak entrée with sick-looking watery mashed potatoes and cubed carrots. The entrée looked as though it might have been left by the previous owner of the house.

Unable to shake the melancholy feeling, Erin hadn't taken the time to buy groceries that weekend. And she didn't want to traipse into the local grocery store in her flannel nightgown at this late hour.

It was either the entrée or a can of lima beans.

"Why would you buy lima beans?" she asked herself aloud. "You don't even like them."

The habit of talking to herself was becoming more pronounced, she noted, wondering what she should do about it, if anything.

Standing in front of the microwave in her bare feet, her hair wet and glistening from her shower, Erin watched the digital numbers count down. The smell of the Salisbury steak wasn't proving to be all that promising.

The timer on the microwave dinged at the same time as the doorbell chimed. It took Erin a second to realize the direction of the second bell. Her gaze swiveled from the microwave to the front door and then back again while her mind raced.

No one she knew would be visiting this time of night. But then, it wasn't likely that a burglar would announce himself, either.

Walking barefoot across the carpet, she squinted and peered out the peephole to find an eye from the other side looking back at her. She leaped back and placed her hand over her heart. She'd have recognized that eye anywhere.

Brand.

"Come on, Erin, open up. I'm in no mood to be left standing on your porch."

Pulling back the dead bolt, Erin yanked open the door. She held on to the knob and resisted the urge to launch herself straight into his arms. That fact alone answered every question she'd been taunting herself with the last two days.

Brand walked inside and set down his bag. He looked like hell. Worse. As if he'd been dragged under a car or forced to sleep in an upright position for three nights straight. A two-day beard darkened his face, and his eyes were bloodshot.

"What's that god-awful smell?" he demanded.

"My dinner." She couldn't keep from staring at him. Even though she'd never seen him look worse, he was still the most incredibly handsome man she'd even seen in her life. Incredibly wonderful, too.

"What are you doing eating dinner this late?"

"What time is it?"

"Hell, I don't know. I just spent the last twenty hours on every conceivable means of transportation you can name. For all I know, it could be noon sometime in July."

"It's April."

"Fool's Day, no doubt."

"No." As hard as she tried, she couldn't stop staring at him. Even now, while they were carrying on a two-way conversation, she couldn't be entirely sure it was really him and not some figment of her imagination. She resisted the urge to reach out and touch him, which was even more powerful than the need to be in his arms.

"What are you doing here?"

His eyes met hers. "I don't know anymore. I asked myself that same question about the time I was on my third means of military transport."

"How long is your pass for?"

"Four days, but to be honest, I don't know how much of that time is left. Maybe I should just say what I want to say and be done with it, then get the hell out of here."

"Do you want something to eat?" That she should offer him anything was something of a joke, considering that she was warming a prehistoric frozen entrée for herself.

"Not if you're planning on serving the same thing you're eating. It smells like…" He left the rest unsaid, because it was apparent what he meant.

"I'll order a pizza." Somehow that made perfect sense to

Erin. The fact that he was with her, standing inside her home, didn't, but she hadn't figured out a way to deal with that just yet.

"I think I should sit down," Brand announced unexpectedly. He walked across her carpet and lowered himself onto the sofa, which was against the outside wall. Then he paused and looked around, as if he couldn't quite believe he was with her.

"I'll just be a minute," she said, walking backward, thinking he might vanish if she took her eyes away from him. The flyer she'd received in the mail a few days earlier from a national pizza chain was pinned to her bulletin board along with the discount coupon. With that in hand, she punched out the phone number and ordered a deluxe pepperoni pizza.

By the time she returned to the living room, Brand was sound asleep on her sofa.

Brand woke not knowing where he was. He sat bolt upright, kicking aside several blankets, and glanced around him. He still didn't know. The feeling was an eerie one.

Exhausted, he rubbed a hand down his face and gave his eyes time to adjust to the thick darkness, then slowly, thoughtfully, reviewed what he did remember.

In a flash it came to him. He was at Erin's house.

Erin. If anyone had told him even two months ago that he'd go through so many trials to get to a woman, he would have sworn they were nuts. If he'd ever doubted his love for her, making it from Hawaii to Seattle by way of Japan and Alaska proved otherwise.

And for what? He wasn't going to be able to talk any sense into her. Nothing had worked yet, but that wasn't going to stop him. Casey had claimed she was as stubborn as a Tennessee mule, and the old man was right.

But, damn it all, Brand couldn't turn his back on love and

simply walk away. The way he figured it, he had only one chance with her, and that was face-to-face.

Standing, he turned on a couple of lights and noted the time. Five a.m. He found his suitcase and showered.

By the time Erin stirred, he had a pot of coffee brewed.

"Good morning," she said, standing in the doorway. She raised the back of her hand to her mouth and yawned loudly. "There's some leftover pizza in the refrigerator if you're hungry."

"You should have woke me."

"What makes you think I didn't try."

"I wouldn't wake up?"

"The entire Third Infantry couldn't have stirred you."

He felt a bit sheepish about that. "I'm sorry. I didn't mean to crash at your place."

"Don't worry about it. If nothing else, you've given my neighbors a reason to introduce themselves." Yawning once more, she made her way into the bathroom.

It was difficult for Brand to keep his eyes off her. She was disheveled and warm from her bed. Without the least bit of trouble, his imagination kicked into gear. It was much too easy to picture himself in bed with Erin. He could feel her cuddled up against him, her warm, pale skin caressing his. He would put his hands on her breasts and lift them so that they filled his palms. Her nipples would tighten even before he could graze them with his thumbs.

Brand's breath became quick and shallow, and he half closed his eyes, savoring the fantasy. Desire throbbed through him, tightening the muscles of his thighs and his abdomen.

He felt a deep, almost painful sense of yearning for her. Not a physical need. Hell, what was he thinking? Yes, he did need her physically. He'd never wanted a woman as bad as he did Erin. But what he was experiencing now was a higher plane of yearning, a profound longing. An emotional, spiritual craving he'd never understood fully until this moment. It troubled him, knowing how much was at stake in this brief time with Erin.

A few minutes later, she returned to the kitchen, dressed in a dark blue business suit. The skirt was straight and emphasized her long legs and the rounded curves of her hips and buttocks. The jacket was tailored, and the shoulders were padded. Brand poured her a cup of coffee in an effort to break the spell she had over him.

"Thanks," she whispered, pulled out a chair and sat down.

"I suppose you're wondering what I'm doing here?" he asked, realizing he sounded defensive. He was treading on thin ice with Erin, and he knew it. One wrong word and he could lose her, and that was what Brand feared most.

"I can't help wondering why you came." She braced her elbows against the glass tabletop and poised the mug of steaming coffee in front of her lips.

Brand fully intended to answer her, launch into his campaign of reason, but for the life of him he couldn't take his eyes off her mouth. Those sweet, delectable lips of hers were driving him insane.

"Would you mind if I kiss you first?"

She lowered her head so fast it was amazing her chin didn't collide with her coffee mug. "I don't think that would be a good idea."

"Why not?" he questioned softly. He pulled out the chair next to her, twisted it around and straddled it.

"You know why," she countered swiftly.

His sweet Irish rose looked so professional and imperturbable that it was enough to challenge any red-blooded male. He couldn't help himself. He pressed his index finger under her chin and raised her gaze to his. Then he leaned forward slightly and gently brushed his mouth over hers.

She released a soft sigh, and when Brand moved back he noted that her eyes remained closed and her mouth was moist and ready for further exploration.

Brand was willing, more than willing to comply.

He took her mouth again, applying a subtle pressure. He heard her coffee mug hit the table, but if it spilled or not he didn't know. Erin moaned and parted her lips for him, inviting the investigation of his tongue.

It was amazing, Brand thought, that they could be so intimate while sitting in chairs and leaning toward each other. Her hands were braced against his shoulders and his were in her hair as he slowly rotated his mouth over hers, molding her lips with his, deepening and demanding even more from her.

Erin didn't disappoint him. She'd learned her lessons well.

Somehow Brand managed to get them into an upright position. Her arms locked around his neck, and she was squirming against him in the most tantalizing way, with a hunger that matched his own. Brand groaned, tormented by a heavy load of frustration.

Brand didn't know what he'd expected when they started, certainly not this fire that threatened to consume him. He'd felt rock-hard and aching from the moment their lips had met, and the pressure wasn't getting any better, only worse.

When he couldn't tolerate it any longer, Brand jerked his head back and battled for control. After dragging several deep breaths through his lungs, he bent forward and pressed his forehead to hers.

"I…I told you that kissing wasn't a good idea," she reminded him in a husky whisper. "Now you know why."

"I knew it before, but that didn't stop me." He smiled to

himself as he opened his eyes enough to study her. Hungry desire was on her face. Her eyes, her nose and her delicate chin all seemed pronounced with it. Her carefully styled hair was tousled from his roving fingers, and her pink lips were the color of rose petals moist from the dew.

Her arms remained fastened around his neck, her fingers buried in his nape. Neither of them seemed capable of movement, which suited Brand just fine. He'd dreamed about holding Erin just like this a thousand times since he'd left.

"Call the office and tell them you need the day off," he told her. "Make any excuse you want, but spend the day with me."

She nodded, her eyes closed. "Aimee's furious with me."

"Why?" He couldn't resist the temptation to kiss the very tip of her nose.

"She thinks I'm a fool to let you go."

"Luckily, I didn't believe you. You do love me, don't you, Erin MacNamera?"

She took a long time answering, much longer than he deemed it should take to admit the truth.

"I shouldn't have anything to do with you."

"But you will." He made it sound as much like a command as he dared.

"I don't know," she sobbed, and her soft, slender body shook. "I just don't know. I can't believe how much I've missed you since you've been gone. I…I thought I could put you out of my mind, and then you started sending me those beautiful letters. Every night there was one waiting for me. I prayed and prayed that you'd get discouraged when I didn't answer. Yet I'd hurry home every night and be so grateful to hear from you again."

It might have been a little egotistical on his part, but Brand was damn proud of those letters.

"Tell me you love me, Erin," he urged, bringing her back into the shelter of his arms. "Let me hear you say it. I need that."

She bent her head against his throat and began to cry softly. "I do love you, so damn much. And you're navy."

"It could be worse," he whispered close to her ear. He'd never loved her more than he did at this moment.

He cradled her until she sniffed and gently broke away from him. "We'll spend the day together?" Her eyes avoided his.

"All day."

"Good." She smiled up at him shyly, then started to unfasten her suit jacket. Brand didn't fully comprehend what she was doing until she pulled the white silk blouse free of her waistband.

"Erin?" His voice shook noticeably. "You're undressing."

"I know." She still wouldn't look him in the eye.

His Adam's apple worked up and down his throat a couple of times. "Is there a particular reason why?"

"Yes."

It seemed every muscle in his body went tense at the same moment. She wanted to make love. He wasn't going to argue with her: good grief, he'd been thinking about the same thing from the moment she'd walked out in her flannel nightgown, all tousled and sweet this morning.

"You're sure?" He had to ask! A man shouldn't question a woman's willingness, even though he fully suspected Erin was a virgin.

"I'm s-sure."

The ache in his loins intensified.

"I…didn't know men questioned a woman about this sort of thing." Her voice quivered slightly.

"Normally…they don't, but there are certain factors we need to decide."

"Can't we do that later?" The zipper in the back of her skirt made a snakelike sound as she glided it open. She slipped the straight skirt over her hips and let it drop to her feet. Then she carefully lifted it from the floor and folded it over the back of the chair.

"You want to talk later?" he repeated. If she removed her teddy, there wouldn't be time to wait for anything. She resembled a goddess, her skin so pale it was translucent, so creamy and white. He couldn't resist her. Hell, he didn't even know why he was putting forth the effort. This was the woman he planned to love for the remainder of his life. The woman who would mother his children.

"You'll go slowly?" she asked, her voice liquid and warm.

Brand tenderly brought her into his arms. "Yes, we'll go slow, real slow. Are you sure you don't want to wait?"

"For what?"

"For us to marry." The way he figured it, they could have everything arranged within a month or so.

"Married?" Erin cried. "I–I never said anything about the two of us getting married."

Chapter Six

Erin couldn't have shocked Brand more had she announced she was an alien from Mars. "I…thought, I…assumed we'd… you know." The last time Brand had stammered like this had been in the third grade. He couldn't seem to get the words past his tongue without twisting and misshaping them.

"I'd assumed…you wanted to make love." Erin's cheeks were a shiny fire-engine red.

"I do." He couldn't argue with her over that point. He'd been half out of his mind with wanting her from the day they'd gone to the zoo. These lengthy weeks apart had intensified the longing.

"If you want to make love, then why are you standing here arguing with me over a silly thing like us being married?" She folded her arms around her middle and rooted her gaze on everything in the kitchen but him.

"We're not arguing." At least not yet. It took Brand a few more minutes to gather his wits. In an effort to do so, he had to look away from Erin. Having her this close, and this willing, was temptation enough. He couldn't glance her way and not ache inside. His hands longed to touch her, hold her, give her everything she was asking for and more.

Her head was bowed, and the way she was standing with her arms shielding her waist brought out every protective instinct Brand possessed.

"If we're not arguing, then why are we…you know–waiting?"

Brand was asking himself the same question. Oh, hell, who did he think he was kidding? He wanted her. One sample of her willingness wasn't nearly enough to satisfy him. She was so damned beautiful, standing in the middle of the kitchen in her teddy, her skin so pale and baby soft. There were so many places yet to taste her and caress her, so much to teach her and for her to teach him.

The physical frustration was growing more painful, and try as he might, Brand couldn't get the picture of what she was offering him out of his mind.

He yearned to fill his palms with the lush heaviness of her breasts and take her nipples into his mouth and have her nourish him in ways he had yet to fully appreciate or understand. He wanted her legs wrapped tight around his waist and to bury himself so deep in her moist heat that he'd reach all the way to her soul. He yearned for all of those things with a hunger that was threatening to consume him, and in that instant he knew he couldn't have them.

"Get dressed, Erin."

Shocked, she blinked, and he recognized the flash of pain as it lit her beautiful brown eyes.

"Why?" she demanded.

"I believe we have a stalemate here, my dear." He strove

to sound unaffected, casual, but it was a front, and a fragile one at that.

"Do you mean to tell me you refuse to make love to me simply because I'm not ready to marry you?"

"Not exactly. We're not ready to make love–not when there's so much left unresolved between us." If she didn't hurry and do as he asked and get dressed, she just might learn how precariously weak his principles actually were.

"Wh-what do you mean?" She reached for her blouse, and Brand swallowed a tight sigh of relief. He was already beginning to question his decision. He'd hurt her, shamed her for making herself vulnerable to him, and that was the last thing he'd meant to do. Hell, he thought he was being virtuous and noble.

He brought her into the circle of his arms and drew his fingers through her hair. "I didn't mean to embarrass you," he whispered. "I love you, Erin."

"You're a–a wart on a woman's pride."

He struggled to hide a grin, not daring to let her know he was amused. "You're right," he agreed.

"Any other man would have been glad to make love to me."

"I'd be glad, too."

"Then why aren't you?"

Brand didn't know how to explain to her what he found so confusing himself. He wanted her. Needed her. Craved her. There didn't seem to be any answers to the questions that plagued him.

Holding her certainly wasn't helping matters any. The peaks of her soft breasts were pressing into his chest, and their rich abundance felt soft and swollen. Every time she breathed, her chest would nuzzle his and he'd experience an added degree of torment. She must know what she was doing to him, because she seemed to be breathing so hard and so often.

Unable to stop himself, he kissed her throat, pushing back her hair and twisting the length around his fist. Erin moaned softly. She removed her arms from around his waist, rotated her shoulders back and forth a couple of times, and before Brand realized what she'd done, her blouse lay on the floor.

"Kiss me there," she pleaded softly in a siren's voice. He was a sailor and he knew he should know better, but when she beckoned, he felt powerless to resist.

"There," she repeated.

She didn't need to explain where she meant. Brand knew. He found her breasts through the silk teddy, his tongue lapping the excited peak, drawing it into his mouth and sucking gently. Erin arched and whimpered, and when she did, her hips rubbed against the hot swell of his manhood.

Brand groaned and lost himself in her body, thoughtlessly throwing his concern and fears into a forty-knot wind. The delicious heat of desire was the only direction he needed. Slowly he slid his hand past her waistband and into the silky crevice between her thighs.

His thumb caressed the dewy mound until she softly cried out and arched upward, silently begging for what her virgin mind had yet to grasp. His finger located the apex of her femininity and slipped inside the folded layers of her heat.

She was hot and moist, and Brand groaned, or at least he thought he did. Maybe it was Erin. Perhaps both of them. It didn't matter. What did matter was the way she closed her legs convulsively around his invading hand, her hips jerking awkwardly in abruptly, frantic movements. Brand calmed her with a few whispered words of instruction then moved his hand, slowly at first, not wanting to injure or frighten her.

"Brand?" His name was a husky question on her lips.

"It's all right, sweetheart," he assured her. "It only gets better after this."

His finger slid smoothly through the moist heat as she gently rolled and swayed her hips, seeking her own satisfaction. Lightly he pushed and explored, going deeper and deeper, again and again. In and out, in an age-old rhythm.

Her hands tightened into a painful grip at his shoulders. Her long nails dug into his flesh as she arched and, with a strangled moan, tossed back her head and panted, cried out as release exploded within her.

There was no such deliverance for Brand, however, and his body throbbed with frustration and denial. He held her for several moments more until her breathing had calmed. Then he broke away from her, walked over to the sink and braced his hands against the edge as he drew in deep, even breaths.

"Brand?" Erin's silky smooth voice reached out to him. "Thank you…I never knew…I've never done anything like that with a man. I've never…"

His smile was weak at best, and when he spoke, his voice was husky and low. "I know."

"You did?"

He nodded.

"Can I do anything like that…for you?"

Brand shook his head fast and hard, the temptation so strong it nearly consumed his will. Nearly all his worthy intentions had been destroyed as it was.

"Can I?" she repeated.

He squeezed his eyes closed and shook his head. For good measure, he added verbally, "No."

"You're sure?"

Hell, no, he wasn't sure of anything at this point, but his mind was beginning to interject cool reason, and he took hold of it with both hands. How easy it would be for him to set aside their problems and make love to her until she saw matters his way. Once they'd crossed the physical barriers, Brand was certain, he could convince her to marry him. If he'd been a different kind of man, he might have done it, but Brand was convinced he'd hate himself for manipulating her, and eventually so would Erin. He couldn't risk that.

Once he'd composed himself, he turned around and held out his hand to her. She slipped into his embrace, her arms cradling his middle.

"Why?"

Once again Brand didn't require an explanation. She was asking why he hadn't made love to her.

"We're not ready."

He felt her lips form a smile against the hollow of his throat. "You could have fooled me."

Brand eased her away from him, holding her at arm's length, his hands braced against her shoulders. "We'll make love when we've reached a compromise. I'm not going to fall into the habit of settling our differences in bed, and that's exactly what would happen. I'm not looking to have an affair with you, Erin. I want a permanent relationship."

Her shoulders sagged, and her head dropped. "There isn't any compromise for us."

"There is if we want it bad enough."

Erin felt herself weakening against the powerful force of Brand's personality. If only Brand weren't so incredibly stubborn. He claimed he didn't want them to complicate their feelings for each other by hopping into bed with one another. Good grief, a woman was supposed to be the one seeking commitment. If she wanted to make love, which she obviously had, then he should "damn the torpedoes" and comply with her wishes. But oh, no, he wouldn't do that! He had to complicate everything by being decent and honorable.

If she'd had her way, they'd be in bed this very moment. She was so eager to relinquish her virginity that she'd practically thrown herself at him. Erin's cheeks grew pink as she remembered the way she'd begged him to make love to her. She'd never been so brazen with anyone in her life. Not even in her wildest fantasies with Neal.

Neal was her make-believe lover. Okay, it was silly–stupid, even–but during college, she and her best friend, Terry, had read several books about setting goals and achieving dreams. Each and every one of those self-help books had claimed that one had to learn to visualize whatever it was one wanted in life.

One Saturday afternoon, when they were bored and lonely, convinced they were destined to live their lives alone, Erin and Terry had conjured up the perfect husband. Terry had named her lover Earl, and Erin had chosen Neal, because she liked the sound of the name on her tongue.

Last summer Terry had met and married a man she claimed was exactly like the one she'd created. Erin had flown to New Mexico for the wedding.

Brand, however, had little in common with her dream lover. Both men were tall, dark and handsome, naturally. If it were the physical attributes that concerned her most, then Brand would fill the bill perfectly. In fact, he was more attractive than anything she'd ever expected in a man.

Neal, however, had roots buried so deep they reached all the way to the center of the earth. He was from a well-established pioneer family. His great-great-grandfather had battled Indians and helped settle the area–not Seattle in particular, but *any* area.

He'd been born and raised in the same house. A home built on a corner, bordered by a tall, fenced backyard. Erin didn't know why she'd decided on the corner house with the fenced yard, but it had a nice secure feel to it.

Once they were married, she and Neal would buy a house

themselves, and it, too, would be on a corner. Once children arrived, they'd fence it, as well.

Her ideal man would have been popular in school, and his senior-class president. He was well liked and trusted by all who knew him. As for his profession, Erin saw him as a banker or an attorney or something equally stable. If he was offered a huge promotion, if it meant moving, he'd never accept it. His home and his extended family were everything to him. He wouldn't dream of uprooting his wife and children for something as fleeting as a career opportunity.

Neal wasn't wealthy. Money had never concerned Erin much, although it would be nice if he did happen to have a healthy savings account, since she tended to live paycheck-to-paycheck.

For the past several years, whenever Erin had dated someone new–which she hated to admit hadn't been that often–she'd compared him to Neal. Her ideal man. The visualization of her dream husband.

Although Brand and Neal might be relatively close in physical attributes, they were worlds apart in every other area.

"What did you just say?" Brand asked, nuzzling her ear with his nose. They were sitting on the sofa, watching an old television movie. Most of the day had been spent walking around the Seattle Center, the site of the 1962 World's Fair, and talking. Although they'd talked for hours on end, neither of them had spoken about their situation again or discussed their options.

"I said something?" Erin asked, surprised.

"Yes. It sounded like 'Tell Brand about Neal.'"

"I said that out loud?" She scooted away from him and sat on the edge of the cushion, pressing her elbows into her knees. This habit of voicing her thoughts was growing worse all the time. Nothing was sacred anymore.

"Who's Neal?"

"A…friend," she stammered, not daring to look at him. If she were to let Brand know that Neal was just part of her fantasy world, he'd book her into the nearest hospital and request a mental evaluation.

"A friend," Brand repeated thoughtfully. "Competition?"

"In a manner of speaking."

"Why didn't you mention him before now?" Brand's voice had tightened slightly.

It seemed the perfect opportunity to pretend Neal was real, but that would mean lying to Brand, and Erin didn't know that she could do it. She'd had such little practice at telling lies, and Brand would probably see through it in a second.

"I haven't seen Neal in a while," she answered, stalling for time. She had to think fast, milk this opportunity for all it was worth and prove to Brand that she wasn't as naive or as guileless as he seemed to believe.

"So he's a friend you haven't seen in a while?"

"That's correct. Are you jealous?"

"Insanely so. Do I need to worry about him?"

"That depends."

"On what?" he demanded.

"Several things." She stretched and, leaning back, relaxed against him, tucking her feet beneath her.

It was all the invitation Brand needed. His hands stroked the length of her arms as he buried his mouth against her hair and said, "I'm not too worried."

"Good. There's really no reason for you to be."

Brand slipped his mouth a little higher and nibbled at her earlobe. At the heated flow of tingling pleasure, she carefully edged away from him, unfolding her feet.

Brand caught her by the shoulders and brought her back against him. He pushed his fingers through her hair, lifting it away from the side of her neck, and kissed her there, his tongue moist and hot.

"As I said before," Brand murmured against her throat. "I'm not concerned."

"Maybe you should be. He's got a steady job. Roots."

"So do I."

A tiny smile edged up her lips. "Perhaps, but your roots are shallow and easily transplanted. Maybe you should consider Neal competition."

"Is that so?" He twisted her around and pressed her back against the sofa cushion, poising himself above her. His eyes held hers, reading her as best he could. Erin didn't dare blink.

Slowly he lowered his head to the valley between her breasts and flicked his tongue over the warm flesh. His fingers laid open her lacy bra with a dexterity that should have shocked her, and in fact, did.

Erin clasped his head and sighed with welcome and relief as his mouth latched hungrily on a nipple and feasted heavily. The things he did to her breasts felt so good, so wonderful. To have him come to her like this, as if he were familiar with every part of her womanly body, as if the passion and the intimacy they shared made everything right. She arched and buckled beneath him, having trouble thinking coherently. He didn't help matters any by transferring his attention to the other breast.

Brand made everything feel right. Such thinking was bound to lead her into trouble. Erin might as well believe she could walk on water or leap off a tall building without the least bit of worry as have him make love to her like this.

As nonsensical as it was, having Brand touch her caused all the problems in the world to fade from view. All the conflict between them shriveled up and died a quick and silent death. With her breasts filling his mouth and his hands creating a magic and a heat that threatened to bring her to that earth-shattering sensual explosion, there was no room for anything but feeling. No room for doubt. No room for fear. No room for questions.

His kiss raked her mouth while his hands shaped and molded her breasts, lifting them so that the hardened, excited peaks rubbed against the rough fabric of his shirt. She longed to feel her flesh against his, and she worked toward that end, nearly tearing the material as she tugged it free from his waist. After she popped one button, Brand pushed her eager hands aside and unfastened the few remaining buttons himself. With his help, she was able to peel off the only barrier between them, thin as it was.

Brand lowered himself to her, and the sensation of her warm, heated flesh against the masculine roughness of his hard chest caused her to close her eyes and cry out in pleasure.

Brand subdued her whimper with a kiss, plunging his tongue deep in her mouth. His hips moved against hers, telegraphing his urgent need for her. Erin wanted him, too, and instinctively countered each of his movements with one of her own.

Pressing her hand between them, she stroked the hard outline of his maleness. Brand groaned against her mouth, and when he drew in a deep breath, she could feel the rumbling in his chest against the softness of her breasts. She reached for the snap of his jeans, but he pushed her fumbling hand aside and released it himself.

He kissed the side of her jaw and teased the seam of her lips with his tongue. "You're proving to be too much of a temptation."

"Me? Really?" She couldn't help sounding surprised. As far as she knew, she'd never enticed a man. Certainly not to the point of arousal Brand had reached. It made her feel beautiful when she knew she wasn't, and powerful when she'd never experienced a weakness more profound.

Slowly, as if her hand weighed a great deal more than it did, he lifted it away from him and pinned it between them, flattening her palm against his chest.

"Now," he said, drawing in a slow, even breath, "reassure me."

She frowned. "About what?"

"Neal."

Her face relaxed into a slow smile. "Neal is...Let me put it this way..." No, she decided, it was too difficult to explain. "You don't need to worry about him."

"He wants you, doesn't he?"

She lowered her lashes and shook her head. "No. I shouldn't have said anything. It was a slip of the tongue, remember? Not meant for your ears."

"I don't care. I want to know who he is."

"Trust me, you don't need to worry about him. I promise."

"Is he married to someone else?"

She was beginning to regret the whole episode, especially since she'd known from the first that she wasn't going to be able to pull it off and she'd persisted anyway. Brand deserved the truth, no matter how unflattering it was.

"Neal isn't real. I made him up a long time ago when I wrote down a list of the personality traits I wanted in a husband. I shouldn't have carried it this far– It was a poor joke."

"What?" Brand exploded. After a shocked moment, he laughed, then kissed the curve of her shoulder and lightly bit her skin.

She yelped, though he hadn't hurt her.

"That's what you deserve."

"I couldn't help it. You fell into my hands."

"That isn't the only thing we fell into. Sweet heaven, Erin, either we resolve something soon, or I'm going back to Hawaii unfit for military service."

The reminder that he would be leaving within a few hours robbed them of laughter and fun and shared passions like a thief in the night.

Slowly, reluctantly, he eased himself off her and then helped Erin into a sitting position. He continued to hold her for several minutes, his chin resting against the crown of her head.

Neither spoke. But the silence wasn't an uneasy one. Both of them seemed not to want or need to fill the void with idle chatter. Perhaps because they were afraid of what there was to say.

He was leaving, and it was something Erin had to accept. If they were to continue their relationship, it would be something he'd do countless times. Soon she'd end up keeping tabs on the times they said goodbye.

Later, Brand insisted on taking her to a plush restaurant. The food was excellent. They talked some more, but once again they avoided the subject that was uppermost in their minds.

"So how's Margo?" he asked over coffee when a sudden silence fell between them.

"Margo…Oh, I'd forgotten I'd told you about her. She's doing better than I expected," Erin said, and then added, "but she's having her share of problems, too. Mostly she's having a difficult time dealing with her anger. A few weeks back I recommended she attend an anger-management course."

"Has she always had trouble with that?"

"Apparently not, but we're not dealing with someone with a hot temper. What Margo is experiencing is rage. There are times when she literally wants to kill her husband for what he's done to her and their marriage. As more and more of the details of his 'other life' come into play, she's having to face head-on the deception and the pain, and that isn't easy for anyone. She feels betrayed and abandoned, in addition to being confused and lost. There was one bright spot, however. She got her driver's license recently, and I believe once she experiences the freedom a car will give her she's going to adjust a whole lot better."

Brand sipped his coffee, his eyes warm and thoughtful. "Doesn't being around these women affect you?"

"How do you mean?"

"Your attitude?"

"Toward marriage?"

Brand nodded.

"I've seen plenty of good marriages, my own mother and father's included. I–"

"Just a minute," Brand interrupted. "You mean to say your parents, who've been married how many years?"

"Thirty."

"They've been married thirty years and they're happy."

It didn't take a genius to see where Brand was leading the conversation. "You can stop right now, Brandon Davis. My mother is a special kind of woman. She thrived on adventure, and don't let anyone kid you, transporting everything you own from one port to another is an adventure, mostly the unpleasant variety."

"She liked it?"

"Liked isn't the word I'd use. Mom accepted it. When Dad announced he had shipping orders, she'd simply smile and dutifully do what had to be done, without question, without regret."

"I see. And you–"

She raised her hand. "Don't even ask." A short silence fell over them. "We're doing it again," Erin said after several tension-filled moments.

"Arguing?"

"No," she answered, her coffee capturing her attention. "We've done it almost the entire length of your stay."

"Done what?"

"Talked about everything else." After he'd first arrived, they'd discussed their relationship only briefly. It was something of a wonder how they'd masterfully avoided the subject for as long as they had. They'd talked about her Women In Transition class, her job with the King County Community Action Program and Marilyn–alias Margo–at length. Even Aimee and her troubled marriage had entered into their conversation.

Sometimes they'd spend hours on a single subject. Brand was an easy person to talk to. He listened and seemed genuinely interested in every aspect of her life, sharing her love and concern for others.

In retrospect, she understood their reluctance to discuss their own relationship, or rather their lack of one.

"There's no solution for us," she said, swamped with melancholy. They couldn't continue to fool themselves. Sooner or later they'd be forced to face the impossibility of their situation. Brand was one hundred percent Navy. As it had been with her father, it was with him. The military was far more than his career; it was his life.

"Of course, there's a solution," Brand countered.

"You could leave the navy and find work here in Seattle," she offered, but even as she spoke, Erin realized that plan wasn't feasible. Brand would be miserable outside of the military, just as unhappy as she'd be as part of it.

He mulled over her suggestion for a time. "I wish settling in Seattle was that easy, but it isn't."

"I know," she answered bitterly. Glancing at her watch, she moved her gaze from her wrist to him. "Shouldn't we be leaving?"

Brand looked at his own watch. "We still have time."

Erin wasn't convinced of that. But she wasn't as worried about Brand making his transport plane as she was about having to tell him goodbye. This time was going to be far more difficult than the first, and the third even more heart-wrenching than the second. It would go on and on and on until they were both so much in love and so wretched they'd be willing to agree to anything just to end the heartache.

"There'll never be any easy answers for us," she whispered through the tightening knot of truth. "One of us will end up giving in to the other and spending the rest of our lives wishing we hadn't."

"You're right," Brand announced abruptly. "Now that you mention it, I believe it is time we left." He stood and slapped his linen napkin on the table.

Erin noted how tense the muscles of his jaw had become. Silently she did as he asked, excusing herself while he paid the tab.

Once she was inside the powder room, Erin leaned against the sink, needing its support. If she didn't compose herself, she was going to break down and weep right there.

She had to put an end to this torment for both their sakes. Brand didn't seem to want to listen to reason. From everything he'd said, he seemed to believe a magical, mystical fairy godmother would swoop down out of the heavens and declare the perfect solution and they'd all live happily ever after. It simply wasn't going to happen.

By the time she reappeared, Brand was standing outside waiting for her. The night was cool, the stars obliterated by a thick overcast and the threat of rain hung heavy in the air.

Brand greeted her with "I think it would be best if we said goodbye here."

Her heart objected loud and strong, but she didn't voice a single doubt. "You're probably right."

"Well," he said after expelling his breath. "This is it."

"Right," she returned. "Have a safe trip."

"I will."

How stiff and unemotional he sounded, as if they were little more than acquaintances.

"Are you sure you don't want me to go to the airport with–"

"No."

She nodded, feeling wretched. This was worse than she'd ever believed it would be. Her throat had closed off, and she couldn't have carried on a conversation had her life depended on it. One- or two-word replies were all she could manage.

"Yes," he countered, just as quickly. "Come with me. God help us both, Erin. I can't bear to say goodbye to you like this."

Chapter Seven

The phone was ringing when Erin walked in the door that evening. She rushed into the kitchen to answer it, her heart racing like a steam engine. She frantically prayed it was Brand and that he wouldn't give up before she could make it to the phone. All the while she was dashing across the house she cursed herself, because she was famished for the sound of his voice, eager to accept each little crumb he tossed her way, despite all her vows to the contrary.

She'd gone to the airport with him, kissed him goodbye, then stood and waited until his plane had taxied down the runway and shot into the sky, taking him away from her. Like a fool, she'd stood there for what seemed like an eternity, her heart aching, while she chided herself for caring so damn much. Now she was doing it all again. Running through her own home, risking life and limb in an effort to reach the phone, praying it was Brand who was trying to contact her.

"Hello," she answered breathlessly, nearly tearing the

phone off the wall in her eagerness to get to it in time. While her breathing returned to normal, she was forced to listen to a twenty-second campaign from a professional carpet-cleaning company.

By the time she replaced the receiver, Erin was shaking with irritation. Not because she was angry with the salesperson, but simply because the caller hadn't been Brand.

He'd left two weeks earlier, and she'd heard from him twice by phone. A handful of letters had arrived, and although she treasured each one, she found something important was lacking in this second batch. Something Erin couldn't quite put her finger on. Each letter was filled with details of his life, but she felt Brand was holding back a part of himself from her, protecting his heart in much the same way she was shielding hers.

She'd written him a number of times herself, but she'd always been careful about what she told him. Anyone reading her letters would assume she and Brand were nothing more than good friends.

After he'd left the second time, she'd battled with the right and wrong of continuing a long-distance relationship. Over the years she'd repeatedly promised herself she wouldn't allow this very thing to happen, yet here she was involved with a navy man! Her principles had vanished like topsoil in a flash flood. Past experience had taught her that Brand wouldn't give up on her, and frankly, she hadn't the strength to sever things on her own.

Her plan was to subtly phase herself out of his life. But the strategy had backfired on her. Each day she found herself hungering for word from him, convinced this separation was far more difficult than the one before.

Erin dreamed of Brand that night. He'd come to her when she was in bed, warm and cozy, missing him dreadfully. Slipping under the covers, he'd reached for her, his eyes wide with unspoken need. His kisses were hot and hungry as he buried his mouth in hers.

In the beginning, Erin had tried to hold back, not wanting the kisses to deepen for fear of where they would lead. Gradually, without Brand ever saying a word, she felt herself opening to him. She was lost in the wonder of his arms, and he seemed to be equally absorbed in hers. Both seemed on the brink of being found, of discovering heaven.

His body had moved over hers, his skin hot to the touch and as smooth as velvet. The clothes that had been a protective barrier between them seemed to melt away. Bare, heated skin had met bare, heated skin, and they'd both sighed at the mysterious joy found in such simple pleasure.

His hands caressed her, his touch light and unbelievably gentle. His kisses robbed her of her sanity, and when he moved above her, she parted her thighs and moaned in welcome.

"Do you like this?" he whispered close to her ear.

"Oh…yes," she assured him.

His hands cupped her buttocks while his kiss raked her mouth. By the time he finished, Erin was panting and weak with longing. "Make love to me," she pleaded. "Brand, please, don't make me wait…not again."

In response, he lowered his sleek, muscular body to hers. Thrilled and excited, Erin opened to him, wanting him so badly she clawed at his back, needing him to hurry and give her what she craved.

To her dismay, he didn't enter her. She squirmed and closed her legs around the hot staff of his manhood, arching and buckling as he began to move, sliding between her thighs, the friction moistened by her excitement and need.

"Brand," she pleaded again, her voice hoarse as she clutched at him, breathing hard and fast. "Give me what I want."

"No…" His voice was that of a man in torment.

"Yes." She thought to outwit him, and she rotated her hips so that his thrust met the apex of her womanhood. If he were to continue, penetration couldn't be avoided, and he would fill her the way she craved. Arching her neck, she lifted her hips, coaxing him to completion, wanting him so much she couldn't think clearly.

"Please," she begged, tilting her hips higher and higher, but he stopped short. "I want to feel all of you…. Oh, Brand…"

"No…no…" He sounded like a man pounding against the gates of heaven, lost for all eternity. "We can't… It isn't right, not now, not yet. Soon," he promised. "Soon."

"We can…we must."

Her cries and pleas seemed to have no effect on him, and try as she might with her body, pushing her hips forward, inviting him, even demanding that he give her what she sought, did no good.

He was full and hard, and he teased her until a violent release delivered her physically from the prison of unfulfilled desire. She lay panting, her eyes closed, physically relieved but emotionally starving.

It was then that Erin had woken.

For a long while, she stared up at the ceiling, her head spinning, her heart pounding. She'd never been one to put a lot of stock in dreams, but this one had been so vivid, so real, that she couldn't help being affected.

This was the way it would be with Brand. It wasn't that he'd cruelly refuse to make love to her, but he'd never be able to satisfy the deep inner longings of her soul.

She required more than he could ever supply.

And they both knew it.

Each day that followed, Erin reassured herself nothing good would be accomplished by loving Brand. She'd made a decent life for herself, and she wasn't going to leave the only security she'd ever found because a few hormones refused to let her forget she was a woman.

She repeated the same tired arguments to herself in the mirror every morning and then went about her day. But when the nights arrived, her dreams were filled with loving Brand. Not all her dreams were wild sexual romps. When they did come, she found herself left frustrated and miserable. More often, her nights would be full of memories of him and the scant time they had spent together. Brand and she would be walking, hand in hand, along the beach together, talking, laughing, appreciating the love they'd discovered in each other. Then Brand would take her in his arms and kiss her until her mouth was moist and swollen. His eyes would delve into hers while his hands tenderly brushed the red curls from the side of her face.

They'd kiss, and their lips would cling, then kiss again, slowly, lazily, savoring each other.

Each morning, when Erin woke, it was the ending.

Each night, when she climbed beneath the sheets, was the beginning.

Stunned, Brand sat at his desk, reading over the same words two and three times. He felt numb. He'd been assigned duty aboard the command ship USS *Blue Ridge*. The *Blue Ridge* was the flagship of the Seventh Fleet and was being deployed in the western Pacific. Tour of duty–six months.

This couldn't have come at a worse time for him. Without a doubt, he knew he was going to lose Erin.

There wasn't a damn thing he could do about it.

A feeling of helplessness and frustration engulfed him like a tidal wave.

He'd left Seattle with matters unsettled, but that couldn't be avoided. He'd continued to write her every day since, and all he'd gotten in return were chatty letters that didn't say a damn thing about what she was feeling or thinking. He might as well be corresponding with a troop of Girl Scouts. Reading Erin's letters was like reading the newspaper. Just the facts, listed as unemotionally as possible. She even signed off with "Best Wishes." Well, Brand had a few wishes of his own, but Erin didn't seem to be interested in fulfilling any of those.

"Six months," he said aloud. It might as well be an eternity. Erin would refuse to wait for him; she'd made that clear from the first. She'd start dating other men, and the thought produced an ache that cut through his heart and his pride.

Although Brand had made light of it when she'd brought up this Neal character, he'd been jealous as hell. When he'd learned Neal was a figment of her imagination, the relief he'd felt was overwhelming.

Erin was a rare jewel, undiscovered and unappreciated by those around her. At first glance, few would have declared her beautiful. Her hair was a little too red, her nose a bit too sharp, her mouth a tad too full, for her beauty to be considered classic. But upon closer examination, she was a precious pearl, worth selling everything he owned to possess.

Brand understood from the things she'd told him how seldom she dated. She was endearingly shy. Warm, gracious, caring.

And Brand loved her.

He loved her so much he hadn't been able to function properly since he'd returned from his evaluation assignment at Sand Point.

He had to tell her about being assigned sea duty, of course, and he tried doing so in a letter several times. After attempting to phrase it a number of ways, jokingly, seriously, thoughtfully and playfully, Brand resigned himself to contacting her by phone.

He delayed it, probably longer than he should have.

He announced it flat out, without preamble.

And waited.

"Well," he said, speaking into the receiver. "Say something."

"Bon voyage."

"Come on, Erin, I'm serious."

"So am I."

She had this flippant way about her when she was upset and trying not to show it. Brand had anticipated it and allowed for her sarcasm, but she was precariously close to angering him.

"You want me to act surprised?" Erin questioned. "I can't find it in me. We both knew sooner or later that you'd get your shipping orders. You are in the navy. You should expect sea duty."

"I want you to wait for me." There, he'd said it. He hadn't softened it with romantic words or sent the message attached to a dozen red roses. Just the plain truth. These were going to be the longest months of his life, simply because he'd never left a woman he loved behind until now. He didn't like the feeling. Not one damn bit.

Erin didn't respond.

"Did you hear me?" he asked her, raising his voice. "I want you to wait for me."

"No." She said it so matter-of-factly, as if the answer took little, if any, thought or consideration.

That pricked Brand's pride, but he should have been used to it by now with Erin. Offhand he could have named two or three women who would have broken into tears when they learned he'd been assigned sea duty. In a few cases, the women had promised undying faithfulness and loyalty. They'd stood on the pier weeping as he'd pulled out of port, and they'd been there happy and excited upon his return. Brand hadn't expected the same reaction from Erin–in fact, hysterical women were a turnoff as far as he was concerned–but he needed something more than what Erin was offering him.

"So in other words you plan to date someone else?" he demanded.

"Yes."

"Who?"

"That's none of your business."

"The hell it isn't." His voice was raised and angry. "I'm in love with you, Erin MacNamera, and–"

"I didn't ask you to love me. I'm not even sure I want you to love me. Go ahead, go off and play navy for the next six months, but I'm telling you right now, Brand Davis, I won't sit home twiddling my thumbs waiting for you."

When Erin replaced the telephone receiver, there were tears glistening in her eyes. She hated being weak, hated the emotion that clogged her throat and knotted her fists at her side.

So Brand would be spending the next six months sailing between Hong Kong, the Philippines and several other exotic ports. Great. She was pleased for him. Happy, even.

It was the end for them. It was over. Done. Finished.

At first, when she'd answered the phone, the excitement she felt hearing Brand's voice had taken the sting from his words. He must have known how she would react to his news and been worried about telling her, because he'd barely answered her greeting before launching into the dreary details of this six-month assignment. To be fair, he hadn't sounded any too pleased about going out to sea himself, but that didn't change anything.

He'd leave without a qualm and without question. Why? Because the navy owned him the way it did her father and everyone else she'd grown up with, and she hated it.

But the United States Navy would never own her again. Never!

Brand had paused after telling her–waiting, it seemed, for some response from her. Her reaction had been immediate, but she'd shared damn little of it with Brand. When reality had begun to sink in, a deep sense of anger, loss, resentment and fear had crowded in around her like teenagers against the stage at a rock concert.

It was the same indescribable sensation that had come over her every time her father had announced he'd received a new assignment and they'd be moving.

Those identical emotions stormed at her once again. She felt like a casualty of a major disaster. Homeless. Lost emotionally and physically. Wandering around in the blue haze of insecurities that came when everything familiar, everything comfortable, had been pulled out from under her feet.

Erin had thought to escape that feeling for the rest of her life. She couldn't, wouldn't, allow Brand to drag her back into that crazy lifestyle.

"I'm going to miss loving you," she spoke into the stillness of the room.

She *would* miss Brand. As silly as it seemed, she'd miss the loneliness of waiting for his calls. The joy of his coming and the pain of his leaving. All those were part of the man she had to learn to stop loving.

The following morning, Erin called in sick. Unfortunately, it was Aimee who answered the phone.

"You don't sound sick," her friend announced first thing. "In fact, you sound as if you've sat up all night crying. I can hear it in your voice."

"I...Just write me down as sick, would you? Tell Eve I've

got the flu, or make up some other excuse." She finished by hiccuping on a sob.

"Aha! So I was right, you have been crying. What's wrong, sweetie?"

"Nothing."

"You think you're fooling me? Think again, girl!"

"Come on, Aimee," Erin mumbled. "Be nice. I don't want to talk about it."

"It must be Brand. What did he do that was so terrible this time? Send you roses? Tell you you're beautiful?"

"He's going out to sea for six months," she blurted out, as though someone should arrest him for even considering leaving her feeling the way she did. "He hasn't had sea duty in two years. He met me, and wham–the navy puts the kiss of death on anything developing between us. I... couldn't be more pleased.... It couldn't have come at a better time."

"You don't mean a word of that. Listen, I've got a light schedule this morning. How about if I drop in and we have one of our heart-to-heart talks. It sounds like you could use one."

"All right," Erin agreed, "only...hurry, would you?"

Aimee arrived around ten. Erin was dressed in her housecoat and her fuzzy pink slippers with the open toes. Her mother had sent her the shoes the Christmas before last, and just then Erin needed something from home.

She carried the tissue box with her to the door, blew her nose and then carelessly tossed the used Kleenex on the carpet.

Aimee walked into the house and followed the trail of discarded tissues into the kitchen. "Good grief, it looks like you held a wake in here."

"The funny part is," Erin said, sobbing and laughing both at the same time, "I don't even know why I'm crying. So

Brand's going off to sea. Big deal. It isn't like I didn't anticipate he would. He's navy."

"You're in love with him is why." Standing on tiptoe, Aimee reached inside Erin's tallest cupboard and brought down a teapot. "Sit down," she said, pointing toward the table. "I'll brew us some tea."

"There's coffee made."

"You need tea."

Erin wasn't sure she understood, but she wasn't in any mood to question her friend's illogical wisdom. If Aimee wanted to brew her a strong cup of tea, then far be it from her to argue.

"I've learned something important," Erin announced once Aimee had joined her.

"Oh?" Her co-worker reached across the table for the sugar bowl and added a liberal amount to Erin's cup. "Tell me."

"I've decided falling in love is the most wonderful, most…creative, most incredible feeling in the world."

"Yes," Aimee agreed with some reluctance. "It can be."

"But at the same time it's the most destructive, painful, distressing emotion I've ever experienced."

"Welcome to the real world. If it were only the first part, we'd all make a point of falling in love regularly. Unfortunately, it involves a whole lot more."

"I always thought it was roses and sunshine and sharing a glass of expensive wine while sitting in front of a brick fireplace. I had no idea it was so…so painful."

"It can be." Aimee held the delicate china cup with both hands. "Trust me, I know exactly what you're going through."

"You do?"

Her friend nodded. "Steve moved out of the house last weekend. We've decided to contact our respective lawyers.

It's going to be a challenge to see which one of us can file for the divorce first."

Erin couldn't hold back her gasp of surprise. "You didn't say anything earlier in the week."

"What's there to say? It isn't something I want to announce to the office, not that you'd spread the word. The way I figure it, everyone's going to find out sooner or later anyway, and personally, I prefer later."

"How are you feeling?"

Aimee gave an inelegant shrug. "All right, I guess. It isn't like this mess happened overnight. Steve and I haven't been getting along for the last couple of years. Frankly, it's something of a relief that he's gone."

Erin could understand what her friend was saying. The break with Brand had been inevitable. She'd delayed it too long as it was, hoping they'd come up with a solution, a means of compromise, anything that would make what they shared work.

"What we need is a plan of action," Aimee announced with characteristic enthusiasm. "Something that's going to get us both through this with our minds intact."

"Shopping?" Erin suggested.

"You're joking? I can't afford panty hose until payday, and on the advice of my attorney I dare not use the credit cards."

"What, then?" Everything Erin could think of involved money.

Gnawing at the corner of her mouth, Aimee mulled over their dilemma. "I think we should start dating again."

"Dating?" Erin sounded doubtful. "But you're still married, and I'm not interested right now… Maybe later."

"You're right. Dating is a bit drastic. It sounds simple enough, but where the hell would we find men? The bowling alley?"

"But I don't think we should rule out casual relationships," Erin qualified. "Nothing serious, of course."

"Next month, then. We'll give ourselves a few weeks to mentally prepare for reentering the dating scene. We'll diet and change our hair and get beautiful all over again and wow 'em."

In a month Erin might consider the idea, but for now it left her cold. "What about now? How are we going to get through…today?"

"Well…" Aimee paused. "I think we're both going to have to learn to survive," she said, and her small voice quavered.

Erin handed her a fresh tissue. They hugged each other, promising to support one another.

"Love is hell," Erin blubbered.

"So is being alone," Aimee whispered.

Brand stood in front of the telephone and stared at the numbers for a long while. He'd had a couple of drinks, and although his mind was crystal-clear, he wasn't sure contacting Erin was the thing to do, especially now.

Damn it all, the woman had him tied up in knots a sailor couldn't undo. He was due to ship out in a few days, but if he didn't clear up this matter with Erin, it would hang over his head for the entire six months. He couldn't go to sea with matters unsettled between them the way they were.

More than likely she'd slam the phone down in his ear.

What the hell? It was either phone her or regret the fact he hadn't. Brand had learned early in his career that it wasn't the things he'd done that he regretted, it was the things he *hadn't* done.

"What's the worst that can happen?" he asked himself aloud, amused that he'd picked up Erin's habit of talking to herself.

He answered himself. "She can say no."

"She's as good as turned you down before," his other self argued.

"Quit talking and just do it."

Following his own advice, Brand punched out the numbers that would connect him with his beautiful Irish rose. The phone rang seven times before she answered.

"Hello." She sounded groggy, as if he'd gotten her out of bed. The picture of her standing there in her kitchen, her hair mussed and her body warm and supple, was enough to tighten his loins.

"Erin? It's Brand."

"Brand?" She elevated her voice with what Brand felt certain must be happiness. She loved him. She might try to convince herself otherwise, but she was crazy about him.

"Hello, darling."

"Do you have any idea what time it is?" she demanded.

"Nope. Is it late?"

"You've been drinking."

Now that sounded like an accusation, one he didn't take kindly to. "I've had a couple of drinks. I was celebrating."

"Why'd you call me? You sound three sheets to the wind, Lieutenant."

Brand closed his eyes and leaned his shoulder against the wall. If he tried hard enough, he might be able to pretend Erin was in the same room with him. He needed her. He loved her, and, damn it all, he wanted her with him, especially when he wasn't going to be able to hold or kiss her for six long months.

"Brand," she repeated. "I'm standing here in my stocking feet, shivering. I'd bet cold cash you didn't phone because you were looking for a way to waste your hard-earned money, now did you?"

"I love you, darling."

His words were met with silence.

"Come on, Erin, don't be so cruel. Tell me what you feel. I need to hear it."

"I think we should both go back to bed and forget we ever had this conversation."

Brand groaned. "Come on, sweetheart. I never realized how stingy you are with your affections."

"Brand..."

"All right, all right, if you insist, I'll tell you why I phoned. Only– Hold on a minute, will you?" He set the phone down on the table, then climbed down on one knee. It took some doing, because the floor insisted upon buckling under his feet. He didn't drink often, and a few shots of good Irish whiskey had affected him far more than he'd realized.

"Brand, what the hell are you doing?"

"I'm ready now," he whispered. Drawing in a deep breath, he started speaking once more. "Can you hear me?"

"Of course I can hear you."

"Good." Now that it had come time, Brand discovered he was shaking like a leaf caught in a whirlwind. His heart was pounding like an automatic hammer. "Erin MacNamera, I love you, and I'm asking you on bended knee to become my wife."

Chapter Eight

Standing on the bridge, a pair of binoculars clenched tightly in his hands, Brand stared at mile upon mile of open sea. The horizon was marked by an endless expanse of blue, cloudless sky. The wind was brisk, carrying with it the scent of salt and sea. Taking in deep breaths, Brand dragged several lungfuls of the fresh air through his chest.

This was his second week sailing the waters of the Pacific. Generally Brand relished sea duty. There was a special part of his soul that found solace while at sea. He felt removed from the frantic activity of life on the land, set apart in a time and place for reconciliation with himself and his world.

Brand was grateful for sea duty, especially now, with the way matters had worked out with Erin. These next few months would give him the necessary time to heal.

Erin was out of his life. But he still loved her. He probably always would feel something very special for her. He'd analyzed his feelings a thousand times, hoping to gain perspective. He'd discovered that the depth, the strength, of his love wasn't logical or even reasonable. She'd made her views plain from the day they met, yet he'd egotistically disregarded everything she'd claimed and fallen for her anyway. Now he had to work like hell to get her out of his mind.

She'd flatly turned down his proposal of marriage. At first, after he'd asked her on bended knee, she'd tried to make light of it, claiming it was the liquor talking. Brand had assured her otherwise. He loved her enough to want to spend the rest of his life with her. He wanted her to be the mother of his children and to grow old with him. She'd gotten serious then and started to weep softly. At least Brand chose to believe those were tears, although Erin had tried hard to make him believe she was actually laughing at the implausibility of them ever finding happiness together.

She claimed his proposal was a last-ditch effort on his part, and on that account Erin might have been right. The fear of losing her had consumed him from the moment he'd received his orders. Rightly so, as it had worked out.

So Erin was out of his life. He'd given it his best shot, been willing to do almost anything to keep her, but it hadn't worked. In retrospect, he could be pragmatic about their relationship. It was time to move on. Heal. Grow. Internalize what he'd learned from loving her.

One thing was sure. Brand wasn't going to fall in love again any time soon. It hurt too damn much.

The breeze picked up, and the wind whipped around his face. He squinted into the sun, more determined than ever to set Erin from his mind.

Erin's philosophy in life was relatively simple. Take one day at a time and treat others as she expected to be treated herself. The part about not dating anyone in the military and not overcharging her credit cards was an uncomplicated down-to-earth approach to knowing herself.

Then why had she bought a grand piano?

Erin had asked herself that question ten times over the past several days. She'd been innocently walking through the mall one Saturday afternoon, browsing. She certainly hadn't intended to make a major purchase. Innocently she'd happened into a music store, looking for a cassette tape by one of her favorite artists, and paused in front of the polished mahogany piano.

There must have been something about her that caught the salesman's attention, because he'd sauntered over and casually asked her if she played.

Erin didn't, but she'd always wanted to learn. From that point until the moment the piano was scheduled to be delivered to the house, Erin had repeatedly asked herself what she was doing purchasing an ultraexpensive grand piano.

"How many credit cards did it take?" Aimee had asked her, aghast, when she heard what Erin had done.

"Three. I'd purposely kept the amount I could borrow low on all my cards. I never dreamed I'd spend that much money at one time."

Running her hand over the keyboard, Aimee slowly shook her head. "It's a beautiful piece of furniture."

"The salesman gave me the name of a lady who teaches piano lessons, and before you know it I'll be another Van Cliburn." Erin forced a note of enthusiasm into her voice, but it fell short of any real excitement.

"That sounds great." Aimee's own level of zeal was decidedly low.

In retrospect, Erin understood why she'd done something so crazy as to buy an expensive musical instrument on her credit cards. The two men who'd delivered the piano had explained it to her without even knowing her psychological makeup.

"I hope you don't intend to move for a long time, lady," the short, round-faced man had said once they'd maneuvered the piano up her front steps.

Getting the piano into the house had been even more of a problem. Her living room was compact as it was, and the deliverymen had been forced to remove the desk and rearrange the furniture before they found space enough for the overly large piano.

"If you do decide to move, I'd include the piano in the sale of the house," the second man had said to her as he used his kerchief to wipe the sweat from his brow. His face had been red and glistening with perspiration.

"I don't plan on moving," she'd been quick to assure them both.

"It's a damn good thing," the first had muttered on his way out the door.

"If you do plan on moving out of the area, don't call us," the second had joked.

Brand had been gone one month, and Erin had maxed out three credit cards with the purchase of one grand piano. It didn't matter that she couldn't have located middle C on the keyboard to save her soul. Nor did it concern her that she'd be making payments for three years at interest rates that made the local banks giddy with glee. What did matter, Erin discovered, was that she was making a statement to herself and to Brand.

She had no intention of ever leaving Seattle. And she certainly wasn't going to allow a little thing like the United States Navy stand in the way of finding happiness. Not if it meant leaving the only roots she'd ever planted!

If Erin was actually in love with Brand—and that *if* was as tall as the Empire State Building–then she was going to force herself to fall out of love with him.

The piano was symbolic of that. Her first move had been to reject his marriage proposal. Her second had been to purchase the piano.

Friday night Erin and Aimee met at a Mexican restaurant and ordered nachos. They'd decided earlier in the day to make an effort to have fun, drown their sorrows in good Mexican beer, and if they happened to stumble across a couple of decent-looking men, then it wouldn't hurt anyone if they were to flirt a little. For fun, Aimee had promised to give Erin lessons in attracting the opposite sex.

"We can have a good time without Steve and Brand," she insisted.

"You're absolutely right," Erin agreed. But the two of them had looked and acted so forlorn that they'd had trouble attracting a waiter's attention, let alone any good-looking, eligible men.

"You know what our problem is?" Aimee asked before stuffing a nacho in her mouth.

Erin couldn't help being flippant. "Too many jalapeños and not enough cheese?"

Aimee was quick to reply. "No. We're not trying hard enough. Then again, maybe we're trying too hard. I'm out of touch...I don't know what we're doing wrong."

For her part, if Erin tried any harder, the bank was going to confiscate her credit cards. As it was, she was in debt up to her eyebrows for a piano she couldn't play.

"We're trying," Erin insisted. She scanned the restaurant and frowned. It seemed every man there was sitting with a woman. Aimee was the one who claimed this place was great for meeting men, but then, her friend had been out of the singles' world for over a decade. Apparently everyone who'd met there had married and returned as couples.

"Oh, my–" Aimee gave a small cry and scooted down so far in the crescent-shaped booth that she nearly slid under the table.

"What is it?"

"Steve's here."

"Where?" Erin demanded, frantically looking around. She didn't see him in any of the booths.

"He just walked in, and…he's with a woman."

Erin had never met Aimee's husband, but she'd seen several pictures of him. She picked him out immediately. He was standing against the white stucco wall with a tall, thin blonde at his side. Tall and thin. Every woman's nightmare.

"You can't stay under the table the rest of the night," Erin insisted in a low whisper. "Why should you? You don't have anything to hide."

A tense moment passed before Aimee righted herself. "You're absolutely right. I'm not the one out with a floozy." Riffling her fingers through her hair, Aimee squared her shoulders and nonchalantly reached for a nacho. She did a good job of masquerading her pain, but it was apparent, at least to Erin, that her friend was far more ruffled than she let on.

As luck would have it, Steve and his blonde strolled directly past their booth. Aimee stared straight ahead, refusing to acknowledge her husband. Erin, however, glared at him with eyes hot enough to form glass figurines.

Steve, tall and muscular, glanced over his shoulder and nearly faltered when he saw Aimee. His gaze quickly moved to Erin, and although she could have been imagining it, Erin thought he looked relieved to discover that his wife wasn't with a man.

His mouth opened, and he hesitated, apparently at a loss for words. After whispering something to his companion, he returned to Aimee and Erin's table.

"Hello, Aimee."

"Hello," she answered calmly, smiling serenely in his direction. Erin nearly did a double take. Her co-worker had been hiding under the table only a few seconds earlier.

"I…You look well."

"So do you. You remember me mentioning Erin MacNamera, don't you?"

"Of course." Steve briefly nodded in Erin's direction, but it was clear he was far more interested in talking to his wife than in exchanging pleasantries with Erin. "I…thought I should explain about Danielle," he said, rushing the words. "This isn't actually a date, and–"

"Steve, please, you don't owe me an explanation. Remember, you're divorcing me. It doesn't matter if you're seeing someone else. Truly it doesn't."

"I thought you were the one divorcing me."

"Are we going to squabble over every single detail? It seems a bit ridiculous, don't you think? But technically I suppose you're right. I am the one filing, so that does mean I am the one divorcing you."

"I don't want you to have the wrong impression about me and Danielle. We–"

"Don't worry about it. I'm dating again myself."

"You are?" Steve asked the question before Erin could. He straightened and frowned before continuing. "I didn't know…I'm sorry to have troubled you."

"It was no trouble." Once more she leveled a serene smile at him, and then she intentionally looked away, casually dismissing him. Steve returned to the blond bombshell, and Erin stared curiously at Aimee.

"You're dating yourself?" Erin muttered under her breath. "I never expected you'd lie."

"I fully intend to date again," Aimee countered sharply. "Someday. I'm just not ready for it yet, but I will be soon enough and–" Her voice faltered, and she bit mercilessly into her lower lip. "Actually, I've lost my appetite. Would you mind terribly if we called it an evening?"

"Of course I don't mind," Erin said, glaring heatedly at Steve, who was sitting several booths down from them. But when it came right down to it, Erin didn't know who she was angriest with–Aimee, for pretending Steve didn't have the power to hurt her any longer, or Steve, who appeared equally afraid to let his wife know how much he cared. As a casual observer, Erin had to resist the urge to slap the pair of them.

The dreams returned that night. The ones where Brand climbed into bed with Erin, slipping his arms around her and nestling close to her side. There was little that was sexual about these romantic encounters, although he kissed her several times and promised to make love to her soon.

Erin woke with tears in her eyes. She didn't understand how a man who was several thousand miles away could make her feel so cherished and appreciated. Especially when she'd let it be known she didn't want anything more to do with him.

It got so that Erin welcomed the nights, praying as she drifted off to sleep that Brand would come to her as he often did.

Reality returned each morning, but it didn't seem to matter, because there were always the nights, and they were filled with such wonderful fantasies.

The letter from her father arrived a couple of weeks later.

"I received word from Brand," her father wrote in his sharply slanted scrawl. "He claims there's nothing between the two of you any longer and that's the way you want it. He was frank enough to admit he loves you, but must abide by your wishes. I couldn't believe my own eyes. Brand Davis is more man than you're likely to find in five lifetimes, and you refused his proposal? I feel I'm the one to blame for all this. I should have kept my nose out of your business. Your mother would have my hide if she knew I'd asked Brand to check up on you when he was in Seattle. To be honest, I was hoping the two of you would hit it off. If I were to handpick a husband for you, Erin, I couldn't find a better man than Brand Davis. All right, I'm a meddling old man. Your mother's right, who you date isn't any of my damn business.

"You're my daughter, Erin," he continued, "and I'll love you no matter what you decide to do in this life, but I'm telling you right now, lass, I'm downright disappointed in you."

"I've disappointed you before, Dad, and I'm likely to do so again," Erin said aloud when she'd finished the letter.

Tears smarted her eyes, but she managed to blink them back. Her father rarely spoke harshly to her, but it was apparent he'd thought long and hard about writing her this letter. It wasn't what he'd said, Erin realized, but what he'd left unsaid, that cut so deep.

Feeling restless and melancholy, Erin went for a drive that afternoon. Before she knew it, she was halfway to Oregon. Taking a side route, she drove on a twisting, narrow road that led down the Washington coast.

For a long time she sat on the beach, facing the roaring sea. The breeze whipped her hair around her face and chilled her to the bone, yet she stayed, conscious every second that somewhere out in the vast stretch of water sailed Brand, the man she was dangerously close to loving. She could pretend otherwise, buy out every store in Seattle and act as foolish as Aimee and her husband, and it wouldn't alter the fact that she loved Brand Davis.

Wrapping her arms around her bent legs, Erin rested her chin on her knees and mulled over her thoughts. The waves clamored and roared, putting up a fuss, before relinquishing and gently caressing the smooth, sandy shore. Again and again, in abject protest, the waves raged with fury and temper before ebbing. Then, tranquilly, like velvet-gloved fingers, the waves stroked the beach, leaving only a thin line of foam as a memory.

For hours, Erin sat watching the sea. In the end, before she headed back to Seattle, she hadn't reached any conclusions. She was beginning to doubt her doubts and suffer second thoughts about her second thoughts. Why, oh, why did life have to be so complicated? And why did she find the grand piano an eyesore when she walked in her front door?

Brand found order in life at sea. Internally his world felt chaotic as he struggled with his feelings for Erin. Each day that passed he grew stronger, more confident in himself.

Gradually the routine of military life gave him a strong sense of order, something to hold on to while time progressed.

Admittedly, the first weeks were rough. He found himself short-tempered, impatient and generally bad company. He worked hard and fell into his bunk at night, too tired to dream. When he did, his nights were full of Erin.

Erin at the zoo. Erin standing in the doorway of her kitchen dressed in a sexless flannel nightgown. Erin with eyes dark enough to trap a man's soul.

He had to forget her, get her out of his system, get on with his life.

"You still hung up on MacNamera's daughter?" Brand's friend Alex Romano demanded a couple of days before they were due to dock in Hong Kong.

"Not in the least," Brand snapped, instantly regretting his

short-fused temper. He smiled an apology. "Maybe I am," he admitted with some reluctance.

Alex answered with a short laugh. "I never thought I'd see the great Brand Davis go soft over a woman. It warms my heart, if you want to know the truth."

"Why's that?" Brand wasn't in the mood to play word games with his friend, but talking about Erin, even with someone who'd never met her, seemed to help. She'd dominated his thoughts for so long, he was beginning to question his own sanity.

"For one thing, it points out the fact you're human like the rest of us. We've all had women problems one time or another. But never you. At least until now. Generally women fight between themselves to fall at your feet. Personally, I never could understand it, but then I'm not much of a ladies' man."

"Ginger will be glad to hear that." Alex and Ginger had been married for ten years and had three toddlers. Brand was godfather to the oldest boy. Although Brand was sure Alex didn't know it, in a lot of ways he was envious of his friend, of the happiness he'd found with Ginger, of the fact that there was someone waiting for him at the end of his sea duty. There was a lot to covet.

"So?" Alex pressed. "What you gonna do about MacNamera's daughter?"

Brand expelled his breath in a slow, drawn-out exercise. He'd asked Erin to marry him, offered her his heart on a silver platter, and she'd turned him down. She hadn't even needed time to think about it.

"Not a damn thing," he answered flippantly.

"Oh, dear," Alex said, and chuckled, apparently amused. "It's worse than I thought."

Maybe it was, only Brand was too stupid to admit it.

Hong Kong didn't help. During three days of shore leave,

all he could do was think of Erin. He sat in a bar, nursing a glass of good Irish whiskey and thinking he should take up drinking something else, because Erin was Irish. Damn little good that would do. Everything reminded Brand of Erin. He walked through the crowded streets, and when a merchant proudly brought out a piece of silk, the only thing he could picture was Erin wearing a suit made in that precise color.

The sooner they returned to sea, the better it would be.

He was wrong.

They'd sailed out of Hong Kong when her letter arrived. Brand held it in his hand for a long moment before tucking it in his shirt pocket to read later. He felt almost light-headed by the time he made it to his cabin, where a little privacy was afforded him.

Sitting at the end of his berth, he reached for the envelope and carefully tore open the end before slipping the single sheet from inside.

Dear Brand:

I pray I'm doing the right thing by writing you. You've been gone several weeks now, and I thought, I hoped, I'd stop thinking about you.

What's troubling me most is the way our last conversation went. I'm feeling terribly guilty about the way I behaved. I was heartless and unnecessarily cruel when I didn't mean to be. Your proposal came as a shock. My only excuse is that it caught me unaware, and I didn't know what to say or how to act and so I pretended it was all a big joke. I've regretted that countless times and can only ask your forgiveness.

I bought a grand piano. I've never had lessons and can barely play a single note. Everyone who knows me tells me I'm crazy. It wasn't until after it was delivered that I realized why I'd done anything so foolish. It was an expensive but valuable lesson. I'm taking classes now on Saturday mornings. Me and about five preteens. I strongly suspect I'm older than my teacher, but frankly I haven't gotten up enough gumption to ask. I don't know if my ego could handle that.

The others seem to find me something of a weirdo. None of them would be there if their parents weren't forcing them to take lessons. I, on the other hand, want to learn badly enough to actually pay to do so. The kids don't understand that. In four months, when you return, I should be well into book 2, and I hope to impress the hell out of you with my rendition of "Country Garden" or something swanky from Mozart. At the rate I'm progressing, I might end up playing in a cocktail lounge by age forty. Can't you just see me pounding out "Feelings" to a group of men attending an American Legion convention?

Oh, before I forget, you'll be pleased to know Margo is coming along nicely. She has her own apartment now and found a full-time job selling drapes at the J.C. Penney store. The difference in her from the first time she walked into the class until now is dramatic. She's still struggling with the pain and an occasional bout of anger, but for the most part she's doing so well. We're all proud of her. I thought you might like to hear how she's doing.

Although I've written far more than I thought I would, the real purpose of this letter is to apologize for the way our last conversation went. I can't be your wife, Brand, but I'd like to be your friend. If you can accept my friendship, then I'll be waiting to hear from you. If not, I'll understand.

Warm wishes,
Erin

Brand read through the letter twice before neatly folding it and replacing it inside the envelope. So she wanted to be friends.

He didn't. Not in the least.

He wasn't looking for a pal, a buddy, a sidekick. He wanted a wife, a woman who would stand at his side for the rest of his life. Someone to double the joy of the good times and divide the burden of the bad. When his ship pulled into port, he wanted her standing on the dock with the other wives and families, so eager to see him she'd be jumping up and down, hoping for a glimpse of him. When he walked down the gangplank, he wanted her to come rushing to his arms, unable to wait a second longer.

Erin wasn't offering him any of that. She had some milquetoast idea about them being pals. Well, he wanted no part of it. If she wanted a buddy, then she could look elsewhere.

Disgusted with the whole idea, Brand tossed her letter on his bunk. Erin MacNamera was going to have to offer him a whole lot more than friendship if she wanted any kind of relationship with him.

For a solid week, Erin rushed home from work to check her mail. She didn't try to fool herself by pretending she didn't care if Brand answered her letter or not. She did care, more than she wanted to admit. The way she figured it, he'd received her letter a week earlier. He'd take a few days to think matters over, and if everything went according to schedule, she'd have a letter back by the end of the following week.

No letter had arrived. At least not from Brand. Junk mail.

Bills. Bank statements. They'd all made their way to Erin's address, but nothing from the one who mattered most.

"You might as well face it," she admonished herself. "He has no intention of answering your letter."

"What did you expect?" she asked herself a few minutes later. She knew what she'd expected. Letters. Hordes of them, filled, as they had been before, with humorous bits of wisdom that warmed her heart.

No such letters arrived. Not even a postcard.

Erin had never felt more melancholy in her life.

Erin's one-page letter had arrived exactly one month before. And for precisely thirty days Brand had been taking the letter out and reading it over again. Then he would methodically fold it and slip it back inside the envelope. After reading it so many times, he'd memorized every line.

At first keeping the letter was a show of strength on his part. He could hold it and touch a part of Erin. It felt good to be strong enough to stand his ground. He was unwilling to settle for second best with her. He wanted her heart… All right, he was willing to admit he needed more… He wanted her love for him to be so strong she was willing to relinquish everything. Frankly, he wasn't about to settle for anything less.

It was all or nothing, and that was the way it was meant to be. He was tired of going to her on bended knee. Tired of always being the one to compromise and give in. If anyone was going to make an effort to settle their differences, it would have to be Erin.

Besides, the way Brand figured it, Erin needed this time apart to realize they were meant for each other. She'd had two months to forget they'd ever met, and apparently that hadn't worked. Hadn't she said she'd been trying to forget him? She'd also claimed it wasn't working. Brand figured he'd let time enhance his chances with his brown-eyed beauty. She was his, all right; she just had to figure that much out for herself.

Nevertheless, Brand watched the mail, hoping Erin would write him a second time. She wouldn't, but he couldn't keep from hoping.

It wasn't Erin he heard from, but her father.

Dear Brand:

I'm sorry I haven't written in a while, but you know me. I never was much good at writing, unless it's something important. This time it is. I owe you an apology. Forgive an old man, will you? I had no business setting you up with my daughter. That was my intent from the beginning, and I suspect you knew it. My Erin's a stubborn lass, and I thought if anyone could catch her eye, it would be your handsome face.

When I heard what happened, I wanted to shake that daughter of mine, but she's her own woman and she's got to make her own decisions, and her own mistakes. I just never thought my Erin could be such a fool. I wrote and told her as much myself.

She isn't happy. That much I know for a fact. She has this friend, Aimee–you might have met her yourself. Apparently, Aimee and her husband have split, and so the two girls are in cahoots. To my way of thinking, no good's going to come of those two prowling around Seattle, looking for new relationships. Erin's a sweet thing, and I can't help worrying about her, although she wouldn't appreciate it if she knew. She'll do just fine. She's not as beautiful as some, but when she puts her mind to it, she'll find herself a catch that will make this old man proud.

Frankly, the wife and I are looking forward to some grandchildren.

The last time we spoke, Erin mentioned she'd written you. Seems a shame things didn't work out between the two of you. A damn shame.

Keep in touch, will you? Give Romano and the others my regards.

Casey

Erin and Aimee were in cahoots? Brand definitely didn't like the sound of this. Not in the least. He read the letter a second time, and the not-so-subtle messages seemed to slap him in the face. Erin was unhappy and looking for a new relationship. If Aimee weren't involved, that fact wouldn't concern him nearly as much. Alone, Erin was a novice in the ways of attracting men, but with Aimee spurring her on, anything could happen.

Brand liked Aimee, he just wasn't sure he could trust her. The other woman had made a blatant effort to catch his eye that first afternoon when he'd followed Erin into the Blue Lagoon. He had the feeling that if he'd paid her the least bit of attention she would have run out of the place with her tail between her legs, but that wasn't what concerned him now. The fact that the two of them were out prowling around looking for action did trouble him.

Damn it all. This could ruin everything. Casey mentioning grandchildren hadn't helped matters, any, either. Damn it all, if Erin was going to be making love, it would be with him. If she was so keen on having children, then he'd be the one to father them, not some… stranger.

"I brought along something for us to drink," Aimee said as she walked in Erin's front door. "Friday night," she grumbled, "and we're reduced to renting movies."

"Don't complain. We're going to have a good time."

"Right." Erin carried a large bowl of popcorn into the living room, having to weave her way around the piano.

"I hope you rented something uplifting–something that's going to make us laugh and forget our troubles. You know, these might be difficult times for us, but we've got a whole lot to be grateful for."

"I do." Erin couldn't help but agree.

"By the way, what movies did you rent?"

Erin picked up the two videos and read the titles. "*Terms of Endearment* and *Beaches*."

Chapter Nine

July was half spent, and summer had yet to make an appearance in the Pacific Northwest. The skies had been overcast all afternoon, threatening rain. Erin had been running behind schedule most of the day and had gone directly from work to her Women In Transition class at South Seattle Community College.

By the time she arrived home, she was hungry and exhausted. By rote, she carried the mail into the house with her and set it on the counter as she searched the cupboards for something interesting for dinner. Chicken noodle soup was her best option, and she dumped the contents of the can into a saucepan and set it on the burner while she idly sorted through her mail.

The letter from Brand caught her unaware. For a moment all she could do was stare at it while her heart casually slipped into double time. Ripping open the envelope, her hands trembling, she slowly lowered herself into the cushioned chair and read.

Dearest Erin,

I kept telling myself I wouldn't write. Frankly, I was hoping the two of us could start on fresh ground once I returned. I've discovered I can't wait. It was either write or go mad. Romano insists I give it one last shot. He's a friend of mine, and he knows your dad, too.

The last three months have been the longest of my life. I've always enjoyed sea duty, but not this time, not when matters between us have been left so unsettled.

All right, I'll admit it. I'm selfish and thoughtless, but damn it all, I love you. Believe me, I wish I didn't. I wish I could turn my back on you and walk away without a regret. I tried that, but it didn't work. Later, after you wrote, I reasoned I would give us both breathing room to settle matters in our own minds. That hasn't worked, either. And so what are we left with? Damned if I know.

I haven't a clue what's right anymore. I want another chance with you. If you're willing to give it a second shot, let me know. Only do it soon, would you? I'm about to go out of my mind.

Brand

Dearest Brand,

I don't know what's right anymore, either. All I do know is how wretched I feel ninety-nine percent of the time. I thought I could forget you, too, only it didn't work out that way. Believe me, I've tried. Nothing seems to work. I'll be so glad when we can sit down and talk face-to-face. I've never felt like this.

You might remind your friend Romano that we have met. Obviously he doesn't remember. I attended his wedding with my mom and dad. It must have been ten years or so ago.

Write me again soon. I need to hear from you.

Erin

"What do you mean you've tried to forget me?" The sharp question was followed by an eerie long-distance hum that echoed in Erin's ear.

"Brand? Is that you?" The phone had woken her, and Erin hadn't yet had time to clear her thoughts. She brushed the hair out of her face and focused her gaze on the illuminated dial of her clock radio. It was the wee hours of the morning.

"Yes, it's me."

"Where are you?"

"Standing in some pay phone in the Philippines." His voice softened somewhat. "How are you?"

"Fine." Especially now that she'd heard his voice. It had taken her several seconds to ascertain that he was real and not part of the wildly romantic dreams she shared with him. She'd fantasized a hundred times talking to Brand and woken hours later disillusioned by the knowledge that several thousand miles separated them. "How are you?"

"Fine. So you've tried to forget me."

"Yes… Oh, Brand, it's so good to talk to you." She scrambled to her knees, pressing the phone to her ear as if that would magically bring him closer. She felt like weeping, as nonsensical as it sounded. "I've been so miserable, and then you didn't write and didn't write and I swear I thought I was going crazy."

"Sweet heaven, Erin, I don't know what we're going to do. I wish to hell–" He was interrupted by someone in the background. Whoever it was seemed to be arguing with Brand.

"Brand?"

"Hold on, sweetheart. Romano's here, and he's giving me hell."

"Giving you hell! Why?"

Brand chuckled softly. "He seems to think it's important

you know I've been behaving like a jealous idiot ever since I got your letter."

"You're jealous? Whatever for?" Erin found this piece of information nothing short of incredible. For all intents and purposes, she'd been living the life of a nun for three solid months.

Brand hesitated before explaining, "It all started when I heard from your dad. He told me Aimee and her husband had split up and that you two women had gone out on the prowl. Then your letter arrived, and you claimed you'd tried to forget me, and I put two and two together—"

"And came up with ten," Erin teased, having trouble hiding her delight. "Let me assure you, you don't have a thing to worry about."

"I can't help the way I feel," Brand admitted grudgingly. "No one's ever mattered to me as much as you. My mind got to wandering, and I couldn't help thinking… To make a long story short, I guess I've been a bit cross lately."

Once more the conversation was interrupted by Brand's friend. "All right, all right," Brand said. "According to half the men on the *Blue Ridge* I've been acting like a real bastard. Romano insisted I call you and find out exactly what's been going on before I jump to conclusions."

"Were you really jealous?" Erin still had a difficult time believing it.

"I already said I was," he snapped.

"If anyone should be worried, it's me. You're the one sailing to all those tropical islands. From what I remember, those native women are beautiful enough to turn any sailor's head."

"I swear to you, Erin, I haven't so much as spoken to a single woman since we left port. How can I when all I think about is you?"

"Two and a half more months," she reminded him.

"I know. I can't remember any tour taking so long."

"Me either. I've got a couple of letters off to you this week, and I baked some chocolate chip cookies. Dad always loved it when Mom mailed him cookies.... I thought maybe you would too. Old habits die hard, I guess."

"I picked up something for you while we were in port, but I'd rather give it to you in person. Do you mind waiting?"

"No." But Erin noted that neither of them was willing to discuss how long it would be before they'd see each other again. Erin couldn't afford to fly off to Hawaii, especially after purchasing the piano. And Brand might not be able to get leave.

"Listen, Irish eyes, I've got to go."

"I know," she said, expelling a sigh of regret. "I'm so glad you phoned."

"I am, too. Write me."

"I will, I promise."

Yet both were reluctant to hang up the line until Erin heard Romano arguing with Brand in the background.

"Hey, Face, aren't you going to tell her you love her?"

Romano's question was followed by a short pause before Brand said, "She already knows."

Smiling to herself, Erin relaxed and grinned sheepishly. Yes, she did know, but it wouldn't have done any harm to have heard him tell her one more time.

Dearest Erin,

The cookies arrived today. You never told me you could bake like this. They're fabulous. I can't tell you how much it means to me that you'd send me cookies.

I don't know what the men think of me. For the first part of the cruise I was an ill-tempered bear, snapping at everyone. These days I walk around wearing a silly grin, passing out cookies like a first-grade teacher to her favorite pupils.

By the way, you haven't mentioned the piano lately. Did you know I play? My mother forced me to take lessons for five years. I hated it then but have had reason to be grateful since.

I'm sorry this is so short, but the mail's due to be picked up anytime and I wanted to get this off so you'd know how much I appreciate the cookies.

Miss you,
Brand

P.S. The next time you write, send me your picture.

"Well?" Erin asked for the third time as Aimee reviewed the stack of snapshots. Brand had been hounding her for weeks for a photo. She'd tried to put him off, explaining that she really didn't take a good picture, but he wouldn't listen, claiming that if she didn't send one he'd write and ask her family for a photo. It didn't take much thinking on her part to realize that her dad would take delight in sending off a whole series of pictures, no doubt starting with naked baby shots. "Which one is the best?"

Aimee shrugged laconically. "They're all about the same."

"I know, but which one makes me look sexy and glamorous and every lieutenant's dream?"

Aimee's questioning gaze rose steadily to meet Erin's. "He asked for *your* picture, you know, not one of Madonna in her brass-tipped bra."

"I realize that, but I wanted something special, something that made me look attractive."

"You are attractive."

"More than attractive," Erin added sheepishly. "Sexy."

"Erin, sweetheart, at the risk of offending you, I'd like to remind you we took these photos with my camera, which cost all of forty dollars. If you're looking for someone to airbrush the finish, you should have contacted a professional."

"It's just that–"

"Hey, sweetie, you don't need to explain anything to mc."

Erin knew she didn't, but she couldn't help feeling a twinge of guilt. Aimee's divorce was progressing smoothly enough. Matters, however, were starting to heat up now that the attorneys were involved.

"So have you heard from the sailor boy lately?" Aimee asked with a hint of sarcasm. She sorted through the pictures again and selected three, setting them aside. Falling in love wasn't a subject that interested Aimee these days. The divorce was proving to be far more painful than she'd ever expected.

"He writes often."

"And you?"

"I...I write often, too."

"How much longer before he's back in Hawaii?"

Erin had it figured out right down to the number of hours, although it would do her little good. "About six weeks."

Aimee nodded, but Erin wasn't completely sure her friend had even heard her.

"This one," Aimee said unexpectedly, handing her the snapshot. Erin was standing in front of a rosebush in her yard, where all of the photos had been taken.

She was wearing a dress in a soft shade of olive green, which nicely complemented her coloring. Her sleeves were rolled up past her elbow, and a narrow row of buttons ran down the length of the front. The outfit was complemented by a woven belt and a matching large-brimmed hat that shaded her face.

"This one. Really?" Erin questioned. It wasn't the one she would have chosen. Her eyes were lowered, unlike in the other photos, and her mouth was curved slightly upward in a subtle smile.

"He'll love it," Aimee insisted.

Dearest Erin,

The picture arrived in today's letter. I'd forgotten how beautiful you are. I couldn't take my eyes off you. It made me miss you so much more than I do already. An empty feeling came over me. One so big an earthmover couldn't fill it. I don't know how to explain it. I'm not sure I can.

All I know is I love you so much it frightens me. Somehow, someway, we're going to come up with a solution to all this. We have to. I can't bear to think of not having you in my life.

I'm sorry to hear about Aimee and her husband and hope they can patch things up.

And no, I haven't seen any women in grass skirts lately. Haven't you figured it out yet, my sweet Irish rose? I only have eyes for you.

Love,
Brand

Brand taped Erin's picture to the wall next to his berth. He'd seen other guys do the same thing and had never understood what led mature men to do something so juvenile. Now he understood. Love did. The last person he saw when he went to sleep at night was Erin, and she was the first one to greet him each morning. Sometimes he'd linger a few moments extra just staring at her.

He loved the picture. Just the way she was standing with her back to the sun, bright shreds of light folding golden arms around her. Her eyes were downcast, and she had the look of a woman longing to be kissed.

Brand ran his tongue around the outside of his lips. It had been so long since he'd kissed Erin he'd almost forgotten what it was like.

Almost forgotten.

What he did remember was enough to prompt a pronounced tightness in his pants. Although she was wearing a very proper olive-green dress in the snapshot, the image of her standing in the sunlight reminded him of the morning she'd wandered into the kitchen in her flannel gown. She'd smelled of lavender and musk, and the yoke of her prim gown had been embroidered in satin threads that emphasized her perky breasts. Erin had beautiful breasts, and the sudden need Brand experienced to taste and feel them was enough to produce a harsh groan. His breath fled. It was time to take a cold shower, something he seemed to be doing a lot of lately. He pressed his fingers to his lips and then bounced them against Erin's pictures, doubting that she had a clue how crazy he was about her.

Dear Erin,

You don't know me. At least I don't think we've ever met. I'm Ginger Romano. My husband, Alex, and Brand Davis are both aboard the *Blue Ridge*. By now you've probably heard about Brand's promotion. He's been promoted to full-grade lieutenant.

Brand's real popular with the guys, and they wanted to do something special for him. That's why Alex wrote me about you. A few of Brand's friends decided to get together and throw a surprise party for him to celebrate his promotion.

Someone thought it might be fun if they hired a

woman to jump out of a cake. That's when Alex came up with a much better idea. They're going to throw that party, and there's going to be a woman there all right, but we want to surprise him with *you*. Everyone went together and pitched in and we have enough for your airplane ticket. You're welcome to stay at the house here with Alex and me, if you don't mind kids. We have three, and they're a handful, but the welcome mat's out and we'd really be pleased if you could.

Let me know at your earliest opportunity if it's the least bit feasible for you to arrive the second week of October. We'll need to know soon, though, so we can book your flight. Please remember this is a surprise.

I'm looking forward to meeting you.

Sincerely,
Ginger Romano

"You're going?" Aimee asked again, as if she still couldn't believe Erin had agreed to this crazy, spur-of-the-moment plan. "You're honestly going?"

Maybe it was a crazy thing to do, but Erin couldn't resist. She could never have afforded the airplane ticket herself, and this seemed her golden opportunity to spend time with Brand. They'd been apart so many months, and they'd trudged over a mountain range of emotions and doubts.

She had his picture, but she wasn't exactly sure she remembered what he looked like. He'd contacted her by phone only one time in the last six months. Was she flying to him? In a heartbeat!

"I'm going," she assured Aimee, tucking her curling iron in her suitcase.

"I don't suppose you need a friend to tag along for moral support?"

"I do, but I can't afford you," Erin joked.

"Don't worry, I can't afford me, either. Apparently no one can, not even Steve." She was trying to make light of the facts with a joke, but it fell flat.

"Don't worry," Erin promised, "I'll be back in time for the settlement hearing. I won't let you go through this alone."

Aimee's eyes filled with appreciation. "Thanks. I'm counting on you." She glanced around the bedroom one last time. "Well, it looks like you've got everything under control." Aimee made it sound like a sharp contrast to her own life, and Erin struggled with a sudden twinge of guilt.

"Hey," Aimee said with a short, pathetic laugh, "don't look so woebegone. It isn't every day you get an opportunity like this. Enjoy it while you can. Play in the sun, relax, stroll along the beach. I'll be fine… You don't need to worry about little ol' me."

"Aimee!"

"All right, all right, I'm being ridiculous. I do want you to have fun. It's just that I'm going to miss you something terrible."

"I'm going to miss you, too, but it's only a week."

Erin glanced around one last time to be sure she'd packed everything she needed. Aimee was driving her to the airport and dropping her off. In less than two hours she'd be boarding the flight. Several hours later, she'd step off the Boeing 747 in Honolulu, where Ginger would be waiting to pick her up. She'd be leaving the cold rain of Seattle behind and disembarking in balmy eighty-degree sunshine.

Not a bad trade.

The flight seemed to take an eternity. Several times Erin had to pinch herself to make sure all this was real. She felt like a game-show winner who hadn't expected anything more than the consolation prize. Yet here she was flying to Brand with seven uninterrupted days of heaven stretching out in front of her.

The *Blue Ridge* was due to sail into Pearl Harbor sometime late Wednesday afternoon. The party was scheduled for Thursday evening. Ginger had taken care of most of the details, along with a couple of other navy wives and Lieutenant Commander Catherine Fredrickson, another of Brand's friends. For the past month, Erin had been corresponding with Ginger, and she liked her immensely.

The hardest part was keeping the fact that Erin was in Hawaii a secret until Thursday evening.

"I don't know where the hell she could be," Brand told Romano Thursday morning. "I tried phoning every hour all night. She didn't mention she was going away."

"Maybe something came up."

"Obviously," he barked. Brand was in a sour mood. For days he'd been looking forward to phoning Erin. It was the first thing he'd done when he'd walked into his apartment. The anticipation of hearing her voice was the only thing that had gotten him through those last few weeks. Rarely had he ever been more restless or more ready for a tour to end.

Each night for three weeks he'd dreamed of listening to the soft catch in her voice when she realized it was him on the line. For the first time in six hellish months he could speak to her freely without someone standing over his shoulder the way Alex had in the Philippines. He hoped that when they spoke this time they might accomplish something.

At the very least they could discuss what they had to do to see each other again.

For several long months he'd thought of little else but being with Erin again. Yet, when the time arrived, she was gone. Vanished. No one seemed to know where she was.

Brand had gone so far as to contact her family. Casey didn't sound the least bit concerned, claiming Erin often had to travel out of town on business trips. But, now that Brand mentioned it, Casey did seem to remember Erin saying something about flying off to Spokane sometime soon.

If that was the case, she hadn't bothered to tell Brand.

"How about going out for a couple of beers?" Romano suggested late that same afternoon.

"Ginger's going to let you?" he asked disbelievingly.

"She won't care. Bobby's at soccer practice, and frankly, what she doesn't know won't hurt her."

Brand didn't know what had gotten into his friend. Usually Alex couldn't wait to get home to his family, and once he was back, he spent plenty of time with the youngsters. Brand had always admired the fact Romano was a good family man. He hoped when the time came he'd be as conscientious a husband and father.

Brand considered his options. It was either hang around his apartment all night, hoping Erin would contact him, or visit the Officers' Club and talk shop with a few old friends. The second option was by far the most appealing, yet something elemental tugged at his heart. He hated the thought he might miss Erin, if she should happen to call.

"Well?" Romano pressed impatiently. "What's your choice?"

"I don't suppose one beer would hurt."

A twinkling light flashed in Alex's sea green eyes. "Nope, I don't think it will, either."

As soon as Brand had fastened his seat belt, Romano started the engine and drove past the Officers' Club and outside the navy compound. "Hey, where are we going?"

"For a beer," Alex reminded him, doing his best to hide a grin.

Something was up. Brand might not have a whole lot to

do with Navy intelligence, but he didn't need a master's degree in human nature to determine that something was awry.

"All right, Romano," Brand insisted, "tell me what's going on here."

"What makes you think anything is?"

"Let's start with the fact you're free the second night we're in port?"

"All right, all right, if you must know, the guys went together and planned a small party in your honor, *Lieutenant* Davis."

Amused, Brand chuckled. He should have known a long time before now that his friends wouldn't let that pass without making some kind of fuss. "Who's in on this?"

"Just about everyone. Only…"

"Only what?"

"There's one small problem, if you want to call it that." Romano hesitated. "It's a little bit embarrassing, but the guys wanted to make this special, so they hired a woman."

"They did what?" Brand demanded.

"Someone got the bright idea that it would be fun to see your face if they rolled in a cake and had a woman leap out of the top."

Brand slowly shook his head. "I certainly hope you're kidding."

"Sorry, I'm not. I couldn't talk them out of it."

Brand set his hand over his eyes and slowly shook his head. He should be amused by all this. "A woman?"

"You got it, buddy."

Brand mulled over the information and chuckled. There wasn't much he could do about it now, but he appreciated the warning. "Whatever happens, don't ever let Erin find out about it, understand?"

"You've got my word of honor."

The Cliff House was a restaurant with a reputation for excellent food and an extensive list of imported wine. Brand was mildly surprised that the establishment would sanction the type of entertainment his friends had planned.

The receptionist smiled warmly when Romano announced Brand's name, and she gingerly led them to a banquet room off the main dining room.

"Hey, you guys went all out," Brand muttered under his breath as they followed the petite Chinese woman.

"Nothing but the best," Romano assured him, still grinning.

Several shouts and cheers of welcome went out when the two men walked into the room. Brand was handed a bottle of imported German beer and a basket of thick pretzels and led to a table in the front of the room.

"Are you ready to be entertained?" Romano asked, claiming the empty chair beside him. He reached for a bowl of mixed nuts and leaned back, eager for the show.

Brand nodded. He might as well get this over with first thing and be done with it. He forced a smile and a relaxed pose while two of the crewmen from the *Blue Ridge* rolled out a six-foot-tall box tied up with a large red bow. It wasn't a cake, but close enough.

"You're supposed to untie the ribbon," Romano explained, urging him forward.

Reluctantly Brand stood and walked up to the front of the room. There must have been fifty men—and several women—all standing around, intently watching him. He tried to act nonchalant, as if he did this sort of thing every day.

He lifted one end of the broad red ribbon and tugged, expecting it to fall open. It didn't, and he was offered loud bits of advice by the men on the floor.

Brand tried a second time, tugging harder. The ribbon fell away, and the four sides of the box lazily folded open. Brand wasn't exactly sure what he expected. His mind filled with several possibilities for which he was mentally prepared. But what did appear left him speechless with shock.

"Hello, Brand," Erin greeted with a warm smile as she stepped forward. She was wearing the same olive-green dress as in the picture she'd sent. For a wild moment, Brand was convinced she was a figment of his imagination. She had to be.

"Say something," Romano shouted. "Don't just stand there looking like a bump on a log."

"Erin?"

Her brown eyes had never been wider. "You're disappointed?"

"Sweet heaven, no," he groaned, reaching for her, dragging her into the shelter of his arms.

Chapter Ten

Brand blinked, unable to believe Erin was so soft against his body. Perhaps he was hallucinating. All the lonely months they'd spent apart might have dulled his senses. Was he so desperate for her that his mind had mystically forced her to materialize?

Brand didn't know, but he was about to find out. In a heartbeat, his mouth came crashing down on hers. She was real. More real than he dared remember. Soft. Sweet. And in his arms.

Low, guttural sounds made their way up his throat as he slanted his mouth over hers. The men behind him were hooting and cheering, but Brand barely heard them above Erin's small cry of welcome.

He felt the tears slide down her face, and he loved her so much that it was all he could do not to break down and weep himself. He kissed her again, sliding his tongue along hers, deep, deeper, into the honey-sweet depths of her mouth.

The boisterous shouts from behind him reminded Brand that, no matter how much he wanted to, he couldn't continue to make love to Erin. At least not in front of several dozen of his peers. Pulling away from her was the hardest thing he'd ever done.

"Are you surprised?" Romano teased, joining him in the front of the room and slapping him hard across the back.

Unable to speak, Brand nodded. His eyes, insatiable and greedy, locked with Erin's. He couldn't resist hugging her once more. Wrapping his arms around her, he closed his eyes and breathed in the scent of lavender and musk that was hers alone. He'd dreamed of this moment so often and now it was all coming to pass, and he couldn't believe it was happening.

He gazed into the sea of faces watching him, unable to express the gratitude in his heart.

"Come on, Lieutenant," Catherine Fredrickson instructed, "sit down before you make a fool of yourself. Dinner's about to be served." He and Catherine had worked together for nearly four years, and he was an admirer of hers. Their relationship was probably a little unusual, when he thought about it. Catherine was a friend, and he'd never thought of her as anything more. It worried him that Erin might feel threatened by the lieutenant commander.

"We brought out the dessert early," another friend teasingly called out to him.

Keeping Erin close to his side, Brand led the way to their table. Several friends came forward, eager to introduce themselves to Erin. Many had worked with her father at one time or another and were interested in news of the fun-loving Casey MacNamera.

No matter how many people spoke to him, or commanded his attention, Brand couldn't take his eyes off his beautiful

Irish miss for more than a few seconds. His gaze was magnetically drawn back to her again and again.

Erin's gaze seemed equally hungry. A myriad of emotions scored Brand, many of which he couldn't have identified. All he knew, all he wanted to know, was that Erin was sitting at his side. His heart swelled with a love so strong that it made him weak.

Men gathered around him. Friends asked him questions. Dinner was served. Brand laughed, talked, ate and did everything else that was required of him. But every now and again his eyes would slide to Erin's, and they'd nearly drown in each other's presence.

She was even more beautiful than he remembered. Not so strikingly attractive that her loveliness called attention to herself, but her rare inner quality of strength and gentleness shone through.

"How long have you known about this?" he whispered, twining their fingers.

"A month." She smiled shyly. "The longest month of my life."

"Mine, too." He braced his forehead against hers and breathed in the warm scent of her. It was in his mind, then and there, to tell her how much he loved and needed her. But emotion constricted the muscles of his throat, making speech difficult.

"Here," Romano said, slapping a set of keys on the tabletop.

Brand didn't understand.

"Take the car," he instructed.

"Your car? But how will you get home?" Brand realized his speech was too sporadic to make sense.

"Ginger," Romano answered with a chuckle. "Now get out of here before someone gives you a reason to stay."

Brand didn't need a second invitation. He stood, his fingers linked with Erin's. He took a long detour around the room, shaking hands with his comrades, wanting to thank his friends for the biggest–and by far the best–surprise of his life.

When he'd finished, he walked purposefully out of the restaurant.

"Oh, Brand…" Erin whispered once they were alone together. She seemed at a loss to continue.

Brand understood. For weeks he'd been planning what he wanted to say to her. His intention was to logically, intellectually lead her to the conclusion that they should do as he'd suggested months earlier and marry. He planned to tackle each one of her objections with sound reasoning and irrefutable logic. But every word he'd prepared sailed straight into the sunset without ever reaching his lips. All that mattered to Brand in that moment was holding her, loving her.

He gently brought her into his arms and buried his face in the delicate curve of her neck. Brand felt the series of quivers that racked her shoulders and moved down her spine. He pulled her flush against him in an effort to comfort her. Her tears dampened his neck, and her warm breath fanned his throat.

Holding her this close was torment of another kind. Her soft breasts caressed his hard chest, and her stomach was flattened against his. All torture should be this incredibly sweet, he reasoned.

He laid his hand on her hair, filled his fingers with it, savoring the silky smoothness of the thick auburn tresses.

"Let's get out of here," Brand whispered when he could endure the pleasure of holding her no longer.

"Where?"

If they went back to his place, there was no question in his mind that she'd spend the night in his bed. No doubt Romano and the others assumed that was exactly what would happen. Maybe Erin was thinking the same thing herself. He didn't know.

His heart and body were greedy for her. But his need wasn't so voracious that it blocked out sound judgment. He wanted Erin as his lover, but sharing a bed with her wasn't nearly enough to satisfy him. If he was looking for sexual gratification, he could find that with any number of women.

He yearned for much more from Erin. He wanted her for his wife, and he wasn't willing to settle for anything less.

Brand helped her into the car. He noted when he started the engine that Erin's hands were clenched together in her lap. She was nervous. A slow smile worked its way across his mouth. What the hell, he was as tense as she was. Only in his case he was too sophisticated to show it.

"Where are we going?" she asked in a voice so small he could scarcely make out the words.

"The beach."

She relaxed at that, tucking her hand under his arm and leaning her head on his shoulder as he steered the car out of the parking lot. The warm, soothing wind whipped past them as Brand drove the narrow, twisting road down the steep hillside. Palm trees swayed in the breeze, and the silver light of a full moon reflected against the crashing waves of the surf.

Walking hand in hand down the sandy embankment, Brand led the way toward the water. The night was warm and the beach empty.

Brand paused once they reached the ocean, faced her and wrapped his arms around her trim waist, holding on to her. Her eyes met his, and he read the confusion and the doubts. Now wasn't the time for either.

"There's so much I planned to tell you," Erin murmured, seeming to search for the right words to say to him.

"Later," he whispered before his mouth met hers. "We have all the time in the world to straighten out our problems. For now, love me."

She moaned and slipped her arms up his chest, leaning into him as she gave him her mouth. Their kiss was like spontaneous combustion, their need for each other fierce and compelling. His tongue breached the barrier of her lips and plundered deep and long. All ten of his fingers sank into her hair as their kisses, tempered with tenderness, delved deeper and deeper. Sweeter than anything Brand had ever known. Slowly he ran his hands over her shoulders and the sides of her waist to her hips, finally cupping her buttocks. He drew her up slightly until her abdomen settled naturally over the hard imprint of his growing need. For an elongated second neither of them moved. Then Erin, his sweet, innocent Erin, started to rub against him, creating a hot friction, a burning need, that all but devoured him. Each sway of her hips, each rotation, eradicated every shred of reason Brand possessed.

"Ah, Erin," he rasped. Feverishly he tore his mouth from hers, hoping the cool air would clear his head. But it did little to help.

Her mouth. Her sweet, delectable mouth tasted even better than he'd fantasized. He couldn't seem to taste enough of her, and each kiss only quickened his appetite for more.

Even through the thick fabric of her dress he could feel her nipples harden. Her breasts felt lush and full, pressed as they were against his chest. Ripe. He remembered how they felt in his hands, how they'd filled his palms, spilled over. Unable to resist, his thumbs skirted over her nipples.

She moaned softly as his fingers fumbled with the row of buttons until the first several were free. He slipped the top partway down her shoulders and was challenged by her teddy and bra.

"Are so many clothes necessary?" he moaned, then alternated his attention from one breast to the other, his mouth closing over the material, making wet circles in the satin.

"Yes, all these clothes are necessary," she whispered, and he could hear the laughter in her voice.

He wanted her. Then. There. His need was so great that a thin film of sweat broke out over his body. Brand closed his eyes and gnashed his teeth in an effort to rein in the desire that coursed through him like liquid fire, gathering inevitably in his loins.

Erin stepped away from him and slowly, purposefully, unfastened the buttons of her dress, letting it slip to the sand.

"W-what are you doing?" Dear sweet heaven, she was going to make this impossible.

She smiled boldly up at him. "Let's swim."

Brand was about to remind her that neither of them had a suit when she started running toward the water.

"Erin," he called after her, and at the same moment he sank to the sand and started unlacing his shoes. Five years in Hawaii and he'd never once done anything so crazy. She was out in the surf, splashing away like a dolphin, and he was struggling to remove his pants, which he sent flying into the night. Without bothering to unbutton his shirt, he slipped it over his head, balled it in his fist and impatiently hurled it down on the beach.

By the time he joined her, Erin was waist-deep in the surf, holding her arms out to him. "Come in, Lieutenant, the water's fine."

"If you'd wanted to swim, I'd have preferred to wait until I had on a suit, and not a double-breasted one."

"I'm double-breasted," she teased, leaping up and down in the water like a porpoise to give him a tantalizing view of her breasts. Brand was certain she had no idea how much she was revealing. When wet, the white satin material of her bra was as transparent as glass. She might as well be nude for all the cover her underthings afforded her.

With unhurried strides, Brand walked toward her. The tide slapped against his long legs, but he refused to pause, his pace uniform and steady.

"Besides," she added with a taunting grin. "We both needed to cool off, don't you agree?"

"I had everything under control."

"No, you didn't, and neither did I." She rubbed her hands up and down her arms as a tiny shiver went through her.

"This craziness is supposed to cool us off?" he muttered under his breath. If anything, Brand was hotter than ever. Her nipples had beaded, the dark aureoles pointing directly at him, commanding his attention. The ends of her hair were wet and dripping lazily onto her smooth shoulders. The salt water rolled down her creamy white neck and into the valley between her breasts. Everything seemed to point in that direction, including his gaze.

When she was a few yards away from him, Erin floated into his arms. Her body was warm and slippery as she locked her arms around his neck, and her long legs folded over his hips. The instant her weight settled against him, she felt the strength of him. Slowly she raised her soft gaze to his, and her eyes widened slightly.

"Brand?"

"As you can see, your plans have backfired, my dear."

"Now what?"

She shifted her weight slightly, scooting her derriere over the protrusion, and in the process nearly unmanned him. She was too innocent to understand what she was doing to him. If this continued much longer, they'd end up making love while standing waist-deep in the surf.

"Let me taste you," he pleaded, his voice low and guttural.

As though in a trance, Erin nodded. She reached back and unfastened her bra. Her breasts fell free of the restraining material and settled against the water-slicked planes of his chest. Her nipples, pouting prettily, felt so hot, so gloriously wonderful against his cool skin, that for a second he forgot to breathe.

She must have felt it, too, because her breath caught softly then. Clenching handfuls of his hair, she began to move, circling her breasts against him, creating a delicious, indescribable friction.

"Oh, baby," he groaned as he lifted her higher, sliding his open mouth across her breasts, creating a slick trail, sucking lightly from one breast and then the other, loving the taste of her. His mouth closed around her, and he gloried in the untamed eagerness of her response.

Her hands were in his hair, and she was making low whimpering sounds. He languidly paid attention to each breast, rolling his tongue around the passion-beaded nipple, sucking strongly, then gentling the action.

Between sighs and moans Erin encouraged him to take more and more of her into his mouth, her voice soft and trembling as she pleaded, rotating her hips against him, her feet digging into the small of his back.

Brand had reached the limit of his endurance. "Erin," he begged, "Oh, baby, hold still…please."

"No…oh, Brand, I…don't think I can… It feels so good."

"I know, baby, I know. Too good."

She gently thrashed against him. "Kiss me," she whispered.

Brand willingly complied. Her mouth opened under the force of his, and her tongue met his in joyous union. The slow, smooth gyration of her hips against him caused the blood to rush to his head until he feared he would lose his footing. He felt as powerless against Erin as he was against the flow of the tide.

His hand slipped inside the wide leg of her tap pants and

over her bare derriere. Then, slowly, gradually, he slipped his fingers toward the warm, moist opening of her womanhood. She opened to him like a rosebud responding to the warming rays of the sun. Her pulsating warmth closed around him, and she started to whimper as he gently claimed possession of the innermost part of her body.

Making panting sounds, Erin squeezed her eyes closed and began to move against him, her actions countering his. Her nails dug deep into the thick muscles of his shoulders, but he felt no discomfort as her mouth hungrily latched on to his, her tongue boldly searching out his. He felt her climax and sensed the pulsating waves of undiluted pleasure as she relaxed heavily against him.

Gradually, her eyes opened, and their gazes held for a long moment. Brand loved her so much that he thought his pounding heart would explode in his chest. She smiled at him. Shyly. Almost apologetically. Her look was so tender that he could have drowned in it.

The sound of laughter coming from behind them on the shore brought Brand rudely back to reality.

"There are people coming," Erin whispered in a panic.

"I told you before this isn't such a good idea."

"But…Brand, I'm nearly naked."

"For all intents and purposes, you are indeed naked."

"Do something."

"You're joking."

"We can't just stand here."

"Why not? With any luck they'll stroll past and not notice two crazy people lolling around in the surf. Forget it, they'll notice."

Erin expelled a sharp breath and pressed her forehead against Brand's. "This is all my fault."

"I know," he whispered, kissing her soundly. "But I forgive

you." He hugged her close, amused. Her face was beet red; even her breasts were rosy with embarrassment. He waited until the sound of voices had faded, and then he carried Erin effortlessly back onto the beach.

Erin was in the kitchen with Ginger Romano, slicing pineapple into a large stainless-steel bowl for a fresh fruit salad they were making for the evening meal. Ginger was shaping hamburger patties, pressing the meat firmly together between the palms of her hands.

"You're quiet this afternoon," Ginger said, smiling warmly in Erin's direction. The two had been standing side by side for the past ten minutes without a word passing between them. The silence, however, was a comfortable one. Erin and Ginger had become fast friends in the past few days.

For the first time that afternoon the house was relatively quiet. The two youngest Romano children were napping. Alex and Brand had taken six-year-old Bobby to the grocery store with them to buy charcoal briquettes for the barbecue.

Erin smiled lazily over at her friend. "I don't mean to be so uncommunicative. I was just thinking, I guess." She was due to leave Oahu in two short days. She didn't want to go. Seattle was her home, and she loved living in the Pacific Northwest, but she'd forgotten how beautiful Hawaii could be.

"Who are you trying to kid?" Erin muttered under her breath. It wasn't Hawaii she found so relaxing and stimulating. It was being with Brand.

"Did you say something?" Ginger asked.

"Not really… I sometimes talk to myself."

"I do that myself when I'm thinking. Usually I do it when something's worrying me."

"I was just wondering what's going to become of me and Brand." No one had said anything, but Erin couldn't shake the feeling that everyone was waiting for them to announce their wedding plans. The pressure was there; it was low-key and subtle, but nevertheless Erin could feel it as strongly as she'd felt the tide against her legs when in the ocean.

"I take it you've enjoyed yourself this week?" Ginger asked, setting the plate of hamburger patties aside.

"Everyone's been wonderful."

"You've been quite a hit yourself. We were all eager to meet you."

"In other words," Erin said with a teasing smile, "Brand's friends were more curious than generous when it came to sending me that airplane ticket."

"Exactly! I do hope you enjoyed this week in Hawaii."

"What's there not to enjoy?" Erin teased.

"Then you might consider moving here," she suggested boldly.

"No way." Erin was quick to discount the suggestion. "Seattle's home."

"Have you lived there long?"

"Two years. I graduated from the University of Texas, but spent the first two years in Florida before transferring."

"You did your graduate work in Texas, too?"

"No, I finished up in New York, so you can see why I'm happy to settle in Seattle at last. It's my first home, and I intend to stay put for a good long while."

"I can understand that," Ginger said thoughtfully. "You were certainly a hit. We're going to be sorry to see you go."

"I passed muster, then?"

"With flying colors. It does my heart good to see the mighty Brandon Davis fall in love. I was beginning to doubt it would ever happen. He's such a stubborn cuss. He'd date a woman for a few weeks, then lose interest and drop her. I knew from the moment he mentioned your name, you were different, and so did everyone else."

"Brand is special." She licked the juice from her fingers and set the paring knife in the sink. "Frankly, I can't help worrying that I'm simply more of a challenge to him than the other women he's dated. I'm not like the others. I refused to fall at his feet." Although she attempted to make light of the fact, she considered it the bona fide truth.

"I don't think that's it, exactly," Ginger countered quickly. She paused and leaned her hip against the counter. "In some ways, perhaps, but not completely. Now that I've gotten to know you, I can understand why Brand's so enthralled with you. You two complement each other. You seem to balance each other. Brand's outgoing, you're a little withdrawn. Not unsociable–don't misunderstand me. Brand's one hundred percent Navy–"

"I'm one hundred percent not."

Ginger paused, and her smooth brow pleated in a frown. "It really troubles you, doesn't it?"

Erin nodded. "If I hadn't grown up around the military, I probably would naively accept this lifestyle as part of what it means to love Brand. But I've been there. The navy expects certain concessions from a wife and family, and frankly, I refuse to make those. I'm a navy brat, and I know what it means to marry a man in the military. It's one of life's cruel practical jokes that I'd meet Brand this way and fall for him."

"I don't look at it that way," Ginger said, scooting out a stool and sitting down. "Before I married Alex, I thought long and hard about accepting his proposal. I wasn't keen on marrying a navy man, knowing from the first that I would always place second in his life."

"Exactly," Erin agreed, but it was so much more than that. If she did marry Brand, her life would no longer be her own.

"I prefer to think of Alex and myself as a team. We're contributors to the defense and security of our country. I'm proud of Alex and the role he plays, but I'm equally satisfied with my own contribution. If it weren't for my talents, my enthusiasm, my dedication, and that of the other wives and families, the navy would lose its effectiveness. I realize I sound like a propaganda machine, but frankly, it's the truth."

"I grew up hearing and believing all that." Erin straightened and ceremoniously squared her shoulders, keeping her eyes trained straight ahead. In a monotone, she recited what she could remember of the Navy Wifeline creed. "I believe that through better understanding of the navy, wives will enjoy and accept more enthusiastically the navy way of life, and we pledge our efforts…Blah, blah, blah."

"You do know it," Ginger said with a smile.

"For eighteen years I was part and parcel of the demanding tempo of navy life. I was uprooted more times than I can remember. I've lived on more bases than some admirals. It was one move after another, and frankly, I don't know if I'm willing to make that kind of sacrifice a second time."

Erin was being as honest as she knew how to be. Yes, she loved Brand, loved him with all her heart, but being in love didn't solve the problem.

"What are you going to do?"

"I don't know," she whispered, suddenly miserable.

Things had changed between Brand and Erin after their night on the beach. Never again had either of them allowed their lovemaking to progress to that level.

They spent every available moment together, but they did little more than kiss and hold hands. Although she'd seen the tourist attractions a number of times before, Brand escorted

Erin all over the island. It was as though they both needed to see and appreciate the beauty and the splendor of Oahu through one another's eyes.

"I wish I knew what I could say that would help you," Ginger said, crossing her legs. She folded her arms around her middle and stared into space. "The thing that impresses me most about you and Brand is that it's like the two of you have been married for years and years. You seem to read one another's thoughts. It's uncanny. Forgive me for saying this, but it's almost as if you were meant to be together."

"It isn't as dramatic as you think," Erin argued. "I know the way a man in the navy thinks."

And behaves. Brand wasn't fooling her any. They hadn't talked once about the very subject that had driven them apart. Brand was biding his time, waiting until her defenses were lowered and she was weakest. His game plan was one Erin recognized well from her own father's school of strategy. Brand assumed that if he let matters follow a natural progression, things would work out his way. He seemed to believe that once she was head over heels in love with him, the fact he was navy wouldn't matter.

Wrong. It mattered a whole lot. Only she didn't want to spend their first time together in six months arguing. Apparently Brand didn't, either, and so the subject was one they'd both avoided. Brand by design. Erin…she didn't know. For selfish reasons, she guessed.

The front door opened, followed by the sound of running feet. "Mommy, we're home." Six-year-old Bobby burst into the kitchen like a pistol shot.

Brand and Alex followed closely behind. Alex carried a large bag of briquettes.

Slipping up behind Erin, Brand wrapped his arms around her waist and kissed her cheek. "Did you miss me?"

"Dreadfully."

"That's what I hoped." He smiled wickedly and turned her around to reward her with a kiss. The intensity caught Erin off guard.

When Brand released her, his eyes held hers. "We need some time alone."

She nodded. The following afternoon she was scheduled to return to Seattle. The day of reckoning had arrived.

Erin was barely able to down her dinner. The four adults sat around the picnic table, lingering over their coffee, while the three youngsters ran wild in the backyard.

"Hawaii is beautiful this time of year," Erin remarked lazily, catching Brand's eye.

He slipped her hand into his and squeezed tightly. "It's beautiful any time of year." His look suggested they make their excuses, but Erin wasn't falling into his game plan quite so easily.

She stood and carried Brand's and her plate into the kitchen, rinsing them off and stacking them in the dishwasher.

"You've been quiet this afternoon," Brand commented, sticking their iced-tea glasses in the top rack. "Is something troubling you?"

She nodded sadly. "I don't want to leave you." It plagued her more than she dared admit. She couldn't stay. Seattle was her home, not Hawaii. Her house and her piano awaited her return. As did Aimee and her job.

Brand reached for her shoulders, turning her toward him. His eyes were hot and fervent as they stared into hers. "Then don't go back."

"It's not that simple," Erin protested.

"Why isn't it?"

Frantic for an excuse, Erin said the first thing that came to mind. "Because of Catherine Fredrickson."

"What the hell has she got to do with anything?" Brand demanded harshly.

Chapter Eleven

"Catherine's in love with you."

Brand stared at Erin stupidly, as if he weren't certain he'd heard her correctly. His expression was first astonished and then incredulous. "What the hell are you talking about? As I recall, the conversation went something along the lines that you didn't want to leave Hawaii, to which I had the simple solution. Don't go. As I recall, Catherine's name didn't once enter the conversation."

"She's in love with you."

"She's not, and even if she was, what has that got to do with anything?" Brand demanded, holding tight reins on his patience. He glanced over his shoulder as if he feared Alex or Ginger might make an appearance. Plainly the subject was one he didn't want them listening in on.

"It's...something a woman likes to know when she's interested in a man herself."

Brand made a harsh sound that was a groan of abject frustration.

"I...I think you should marry her." Erin thought nothing of the sort, but said so for shock value. It seemed to have the desired effect. Brand looked as if he wanted to take her by the shoulders and shake her until her teeth rattled.

Instead he marched to the other side of the kitchen and rammed his hand through his hair with enough force that if he did it a few more times he'd require a hair transplant. He turned, opened his mouth as though he wanted to say something, but quickly snapped it shut.

"She's perfect for you." Even as she spoke, Erin realized how true that was. It hurt to admit it, more than she dared concede. Almost from the beginning Brand had mentioned his two friends, Romano and Catherine, blending their names together as if the two were actually one. It was understandable. The three worked together. They were the very best of friends. Alex was married to Ginger, but that left Brand free for Catherine.

"Erin–"

"No," she interrupted. "I mean it. Catherine is the perfect woman for you. First of all, she's navy, and–"

"I don't happen to be in love with her," he barked. His long legs ate up the distance between them in three giant strides. "Hasn't the last week told you anything? The last week, nothing," he corrected sharply. "The last seven months!"

His anger did little to faze her. The more she dwelled on the subject of Brand and Catherine, the more sense it made to her. In fact, she didn't know why it hadn't occurred to her much sooner. It wasn't until she'd met the other woman that Erin had recognized the truth.

"I'm serious, Brand."

"I'm not," he snapped. "I've never so much as kissed Catherine. It would be like dating my own sister. I'm sure she feels the same way."

"Wrong." Breaking out of his hold, she reached for the coffeepot. As if she hadn't a care in the world, Erin ran water and measured the grounds, hoping the activity would hide the pain that was crowding her heart. The thought of Brand loving another woman nearly crippled her emotionally, yet she pressed the subject, driven by some unknown force.

"All right," Brand conceded, slowly, thoughtfully. "Let's say you're right, and Catherine does hold some romantic feelings for me–although I want you to know right now I think that's crazy. But for the sake of argument I'll accept that premise. We've been working together for nearly three years–"

"Make that four," Erin interrupted, continuing to busy herself by clearing away what remained of the dinner dishes.

"Okay, four years." His gaze narrowed, but apparently he wasn't willing to argue over minute details. "If I haven't fallen for Catherine in all that time, then what makes you assume I'd ever consider marrying her, especially now that I'm in love with you?"

"It's so obvious."

"What is?" he cried impatiently.

"That you and Catherine should be together. It all fits. I doubt you'd ever find anyone who suits you better." Gaining momentum, she continued, "It's true, you and I share a certain amount of physical attraction, but beyond that we seem to constantly be at odds."

Brand made the growling sound a second time, and then shocked her by stepping forward and gripping her hard by the shoulders. He squeezed so tightly that he half lifted her from the floor. "You know what you're doing, don't you?" he demanded.

She stared up at him mutely, stunned by this sudden show of force. It was so unlike Brand, which revealed how accomplished she was at getting a reaction from him.

"You're avoiding another confrontation," he told her, his voice firm and angry. "You don't want to leave Hawaii, or more appropriately, you don't want to leave me. Wonderful, because frankly, I don't want you to go, either. I love you. I have for so long I can't remember what it was like to not love you. I refuse to think of marrying anyone but you. To have you suggest I take Catherine as my wife makes damn little sense." His hold on her relaxed, and her feet were once again safely planted on the linoleum.

Erin lowered her gaze, realizing he was right but hating like hell to admit it. She was looking to avoid a showdown, and that was exactly what would have happened had their discussion followed the lead he'd taken. Admitting how badly she wanted to remain in the islands with him had left the door wide open for trouble. Brand wanted her to stay, too.

She remained stiff in his arms for a moment. Then a sigh raked her shoulders and she relaxed against him, wrapping her arms around his middle.

"You're right," she whispered. "I'm sorry…so sorry."

Brand froze briefly and muttered something under his breath that Erin couldn't detect. As though he couldn't bear the tension another moment, he buried his hands in her hair and drew her firmly into contact with his muscular, trim body. She tilted her head to smile up at him, and Brand took advantage of the movement by placing his mouth over hers.

His kiss revealed a storehouse of need. His tongue probed her mouth, and she opened to him as naturally as a castle gate opens to an arriving king. A wide host of familiar sensations warmed her, a heat so intense it frightened her. It had always been this way between them. He touched her, and it was like fire licking at dry kindling. Her response to Brand continued to amaze Erin. He'd kiss her, and the excitement seemed to explode throughout her body. In the beginning, his kisses had produced a warm sort of pleasure, but since their six-month separation, every time he held her in his arms her response was one of hungry need.

She nestled into his embrace the way a robin settles into her nest, spreading its wings, securing itself against the storm. It felt so incredibly good to have him hold her. Nothing she had ever known compared to the feelings of security he supplied.

She dragged in a deep breath, savoring the scent of warm musk that was uniquely his. Brand groaned and deepened the kiss, and Erin welcomed the intimacy of his tongue stroking hers. Unable to remain still, she started to move against him. Her nipples had hardened and were tingling, and the only way to relieve that shocking pleasure was to rotate the upper half of her body against him.

A low, rough sound rumbled through his throat as he gripped her by the hips and pressed her flush against him, adjusting her stance to graphically demonstrate his powerful need for her.

It felt familiar and so very good. Erin locked her arms around his neck and moved with him, her grinding hips contrasting the action of his own, enhancing the pleasure a hundredfold. Erin felt as though she were on fire, hot and aching, wanting everything at once.

"Oh, baby," he whispered in a voice that was guttural.

The noise from behind was as unexpected as it was unwelcome. Brand jerked his head back and ground his teeth in wretched frustration.

"Hello," Bobby greeted enthusiastically, closing the sliding glass door as he casually strolled into the kitchen. "Dad sent me in here to ask what was taking you two so long."

Brand's gaze narrowed menacingly. "Tell your dad…"

"We'll be right out," Erin completed for him.

"When are we going to have the ice cream?" the youngster wanted to know, walking over to the freezer, opening the door and staring inside. "It's time we had dessert, don't you think?"

Erin nodded. "If you want, I'll dish it up now and you can help me carry it out to everyone."

The boy eagerly nodded his head. Then, glancing at Brand, he seemed to change his mind. "Only don't let Uncle Brand help you. He might kiss you again and then you'd both forget."

"I won't let him kiss me," Erin promised.

"Wanna bet?" Brand teased under his breath.

Bobby studied the two of them quizzically. "Uncle Brand?"

"Yes, Bob."

"Are you going to marry Erin?"

"Ah…"

"I think you should, and so does my dad."

A moment of tense silence filled the room. Erin swallowed the lump that threatened to choke her. Her eyes were locked with Brand's, and she struggled to look away, but his gaze refused to release her.

"I…Let's get that ice cream," Erin suggested, hoping she sounded carefree and enthusiastic when she felt neither.

Erin's suitcases were packed and ready for her flight as she walked through Alex and Ginger's home one last time before Brand arrived to drive her to the airport. She'd woken that morning with a heavy feeling in her chest that had only grown worse as the day progressed. She dared not question its origin or what she needed to do to relieve it.

She knew the answer as clearly as if a doctor had given her a written diagnosis. Leaving Brand was far more difficult than she'd ever dreamed it would be.

He hadn't pressured her to marry him. Not once. In fact,

she was the one who'd brought up the subject, when she'd suggested he consider Catherine for his wife. That idea had all too quickly backfired in her face. And rightly so. She'd been an utter fool to suggest Brand romantically involve himself with another woman. Even now, just musing over the thought brought with it an instant flash of regret and pain.

Erin liked Catherine, enjoyed her company and wished her well, but when it came to Brand, Erin had discovered she was far more territorial than she ever realized. The awareness came as something of a shock.

Brand arrived and loaded Erin's suitcases into the trunk of his car. If he was unusually quiet on the drive to Honolulu International, she didn't notice, since she didn't seem to have much she wanted to say, either.

They sat next to each other in the crowded gate area, tightly holding hands while waiting for her flight number to be called. Erin's throat was so tight, she couldn't have carried on a conversation had the fate of world peace depended on it.

Each second that ticked away seemed to suck the energy right out of the room. Apparently no one else noticed except Brand.

When her flight was called, those gathered around her stood and reached for their personal items and brought out their tickets.

The first few rows had boarded when Brand stood. "You'll need to go on board now." He stated it matter-of-factly, as if her going was of little importance to him.

She nodded and reluctantly came to her feet.

"You'll call once you arrive back in Seattle?"

Once again she nodded.

Brand smoothed his hands over her shoulders, and his gaze just managed to avoid hers. "I'm pulling as many strings as I can to transfer to one of the bases in Washington state."

He hadn't mentioned that earlier, and Erin's hopes soared. If Brand lived on any of the navy bases near Seattle, even if it was one across Puget Sound, it would help ease the impossible situation between them. Then they would have the luxury of allowing their relationship to develop naturally without thousands of miles stretching between them like a giant, unyielding void.

"You didn't say anything about that earlier," she said, hating the way the eagerness crept into her voice. That he was prepared to leave the admiral's staff to be closer to her spoke volumes about his commitment to her.

"I didn't mention it before because it isn't the least bit probable."

"Oh." Her hope and excitement quickly diminished.

The final boarding call for her flight was announced. Erin glanced over her shoulder, wanting more than she'd ever wanted anything to remain with Brand. Yet she knew she had to leave.

"I don't suppose…" Brand began enthusiastically, then stopped abruptly.

"You don't suppose what?"

"Never mind."

"Never mind? Obviously you had something you wanted to say."

"That won't work, either."

"What won't work?" she demanded impatiently.

"Have you ever considered moving to Hawaii?" he asked, without revealing the least bit of emotion either way.

She was so stunned by the suggestion that it left her breathless. "Moving to Hawaii?" she gasped.

As crazy as it seemed, the first thought that filtered into her brain was that she'd be forced to sell her grand piano with the house, and frankly, not that many folks would be interested in something that large, especially when it dominated a good portion of the living room.

"Never mind," Brand said irritably. "I already said that wouldn't work."

She stared up at him, wondering why he was so quick to downplay his own suggestion until she realized how unfeasible the idea actually was. She had her job and her home and her sturdy, hard-to-move furniture. What about the roots she was so carefully planting in the Seattle area? Her friends? The Women In Transition classes she taught evenings?

"I can't move."

Brand frowned and nodded. "I know. It was a stupid idea. Forget I suggested it."

The way their courtship was progressing, she'd leave behind everything that was important to her for Brand and move to Hawaii just in time for him to be transferred to Alaska. Knowing the way the navy worked, she could count on something like that happening.

The attendant's voice announcing the last call for her flight was an intrusion Erin didn't want or need.

"Why didn't you say something sooner?" she demanded. At least they could have discussed it without the pressure of her being forced to board the plane. As it was, they'd sat, holding hands, for an hour without uttering more than a few words.

"I shouldn't have said anything now." His gaze gentled, and he brushed the tips of his fingers across her cheek, his touch light and unbelievably tender. His eyes momentarily left hers. "You have to go," he told her in a voice that was low and gravelly.

"Yes…I know." But now that the time had arrived, Erin wasn't sure she could turn and walk away from Brand and manage to keep her dignity intact. Oh, hell, she didn't know what she was going to do. He was everything she ever dreamed she'd find in a man, and, at the same moment, her greatest fear.

He hugged her all too briefly, then dropped his arms and stepped away from her. Wanting more than anything to wear a smile when she left him, she beamed him one broad enough to challenge Miss America. Then, with a dignified turn, she headed for the jetway.

"Erin." Her name was issued in a low growl. He was at her side so fast it made her dizzy. He hauled her into his arms and kissed her with a hunger that left her weak and clinging.

"I'm sorry," the flight attendant said, standing at the gate. "You'll have to board now. The flight's ready to depart."

"Go ahead," Brand whispered, stepping away from her.

"Oh, Brand." Erin hated the way her eyes filled with ready tears. Mascara running down her cheeks ruined the image she was working so hard to leave in his mind.

"Go back to Seattle," Brand said harshly, "go ahead and go, before I end up pleading with you to stay."

"Where have you been all weekend?" Aimee demanded, walking directly past Erin and into her living room, carting a large paper sack in one hand and a cigarette in the other. "I must have called twenty times."

"I took a ride up to Vancouver."

"All by yourself?" She sounded incredulous. "Good grief, you just got back from a week's vacation in Hawaii. Don't tell me you needed to get away." She whirled around her, searching for some unknown object. "Where do you keep your ashtrays?"

Erin followed her friend into the kitchen while Aimee searched through a row of four drawers. She dragged the first one open, briefly scanning the contents, only to slam it closed.

Removing a small glass ashtray from the cupboard, Erin

held it out in the palm of her hand to her co-worker. "When did you start smoking?" She couldn't remember seeing Aimee with a cigarette before.

"I smoked years ago, when I was young and stupid. It's really a filthy habit. Trust me, whatever you do, don't start." Even as she was speaking, she opened her purse and brought out a pack. It was a brand designed especially for women, and the smokes were thin and long.

"Aimee!" Erin cried. "What's happened to you?"

As if she suddenly needed to talk, Aimee pulled out a chair and collapsed into it, automatically crossing her legs. Her foot started to swing like a precision timepiece, moving so fast she was creating a brisk breeze.

"I stopped off to show you my new outfit," Aimee announced. "I bought it to wear for the settlement hearing. If Steve's going to divorce me, I want to look my absolute best."

"In other words, you want him to regret it."

"Exactly." For the first time, a smile cracked the tight line of her mouth.

"Why don't you just come right out and tell him that?"

"You're joking!"

"I'm not," Erin assured her. She'd been away seven days, and upon her return she'd barely recognized her best friend. Aimee had lost a noticeable amount of weight and was so uptight she should be on tranquilizers. The fact she'd taken up smoking was a symptom of a much deeper problem.

"Steve and I are no longer on speaking terms."

"But I thought the two of you had never gotten along better."

"That was before," Aimee explained, grinding the cigarette butt in the ashtray.

"Before what?"

"Before...everything."

"Are you sure you're not misinterpreting the situation?" Erin didn't know Steve well, but she would have thought he was more fair-minded than that.

"That's not the half of it." The more Aimee talked, the faster her leg swung. Erin didn't dare focus her attention on the moving foot, lest it hypnotize her.

"You mean there's more?"

"Someone's moved into the duplex with him."

The pain was alive in Aimee's eyes. "A woman?" Erin asked softly.

"I…I don't know, but I imagine it must be. I know my husband–he enjoys regular bouts of sex."

"How'd you know someone moved in with him?" Erin couldn't help being curious. She strongly suspected that her friend was doing a bit of amateur detective work and coming up with all the wrong conclusions.

"I happened to be in the neighborhood and decided it wouldn't do any harm to drive by his place and see what Steve was up to. I'm glad I did, too, because there was a white convertible parked in his driveway." She blew a cloud of smoke at the ceiling, and when she set the cigarette down Erin noted that her hands were trembling.

"A white convertible?"

"Come on, Erin," Aimee said with a heavy note of sarcasm. "I'm not stupid. It was after midnight."

"That explains everything?"

"You and I both know a woman's more likely to drive a white car. Men like theirs black or red. The way I figure it, either Steve's got some cupcake shacked up with him or else he's having himself a little fun on the side. My guess is he's been into side dishes for a good long time."

"Aimee, that's ridiculous."

"Not according to my attorney."

"What makes him suggest anything like that? Honestly, I think this whole thing's gotten out of hand. Not so long ago you claimed Steve wasn't the type to mess around." The picture of the man who'd come to their table to correct a wrong impression the night they were in the Mexican restaurant played in Erin's mind.

"I called my lawyer first thing the following morning and gave him the license plate number. If Steve's fooling around, and I'm confident he is, then he's going to hear about it in court. If he wants another relationship, then the least he could do was wait for the ink to dry on the divorce decree."

Erin couldn't believe what she was hearing. Then again, it shouldn't shock her. Through the class she taught at the community college, she'd seen the emotional trauma, the bitterness and the pain of divorce cripple even the strongest women.

What surprised Erin was that this was Aimee. Calm, unruffled Aimee. In the time they'd worked together, Erin had seen her friend handle one explosive situation after another, competently, without accusation or blame.

"Anyway," Aimee said, reaching for the Nordstrom bag at her side, "I wanted you to see the new dress I got for the court date. God knows I can't afford it, but I bought it anyway." She carefully unwrapped the tissue from around the silk blouse and skirt that was a bright shade of turquoise.

"Oh, Aimee, it's gorgeous."

"I thought so, too. I'll look stunning, won't I?"

Erin nodded. She wouldn't be able to go inside the judge's chambers with her friend. According to court rules, Erin would have to wait in the hallway, but then, all Aimee really needed was emotional support before and after.

"By the way, what were you doing in Canada this weekend?" Aimee asked, waving the cigarette smoke away from

Erin's face. She glanced at the tip and extinguished it with a force that nearly pushed the ashtray from the table.

Erin hesitated, then decided that the truth was the best policy. "I needed to get away."

"I might remind you, you just spent the last week *away*."

"I know." In the five days since her return, Erin had spoken to Brand twice. Once, briefly, shortly after she'd arrived home. Then, later in the week, he'd contacted her again. He'd sounded tired and out of sorts. Although they'd spoken for several minutes, Erin had come away from the conversation feeling lonely and depressed.

As much as she tried to avoid doing so, Erin dwelt a good deal on what she'd suggested to Brand about him and Catherine. It hurt to think of Brand with another woman. *Hurt,* she decided, was too mild a word to describe the fiery pain that cut a wide path through her heart when she considered the situation. It would solve everything if the two of them were to fall in love. They had so much in common, including an appreciation of the many exciting aspects of navy life. Exciting to everyone, that is, who could accept the policies and the programs of a military lifestyle.

Someone who wasn't a navy brat. Someone who didn't know any better.

"Erin?" Aimee said softly. "Are you all right?"

"Oh, sure. I'm sorry," she said, forcefully bringing herself back to the present. "Were you saying something I missed?"

"No." But the other woman regarded her closely. "You never did tell me much about Hawaii. How was your time with Brand?"

"Wonderful." If anything, it had been too wonderful. She'd cherished each minute, greedy for time alone with him. They'd both been selfish, not wanting to share their precious days with others.

No one had seemed to mind. In fact, it had been as if Brand's friends were going out of their way to arrange it so.

"I hear Hawaii is really beautiful," Aimee continued. "At one time, Steve and I were planning a trip there for our tenth wedding anniversary."

"It is beautiful."

"But you wouldn't want to live there?"

The question took her by surprise. Erin blinked, not knowing how to answer. Could she live in Hawaii? Of course. The question didn't even need consideration. Anyone would enjoy paradise. If Brand were to own a business there, she'd marry him in a minute and plan on settling down and building an empire with him. But Brand was part of the military, and if she were to link her life with his, then she'd have to be willing to wholeheartedly embrace that lifestyle, and she didn't know if she could.

"Well?" Aimee pressed.

"No," Erin said automatically. "I don't think I could live in Hawaii."

"Me either," her friend muttered, and reached for a cigarette. "At least not now. Someplace cold and isolated interests me more at the minute."

"Greenland?"

"Greenland," Aimee echoed. "That would be perfect." She averted her eyes and pretended to remove a piece of lint from the leg of her slacks. "So," she said, expelling a breath sharply. "You'll meet me at the courthouse Monday morning?"

"I'll be there."

"Thanks. I knew I could count on you."

The phone rang just then, and Erin leaned toward the wall to reach for it.

"Hello," she said automatically.

There was no response for a couple of seconds, long enough for Erin to believe it was a crank call.

"Erin MacNamera?" Her name sounded as though it came from a long way off, but not long-distance. The telltale hum was decidedly missing.

"Yes, this is Erin MacNamera." The female voice was vaguely familiar, but Erin couldn't place it.

"This is Marilyn…from class. I'm really sorry to trouble you," she said, clearly trying to disguise the fact that she was weeping.

"It's no trouble, Marilyn. It's good to hear from you. How are you? I haven't talked to you in weeks."

"I'm fine." She paused and then gave a short, abrupt laugh. "No, I'm not…all right. In fact, I thought I should call someone. Do you have time to talk right now?"

Chapter Twelve

That night, after Aimee's settlement hearing, Erin woke from a sound sleep with tears in her eyes. She lay for several moments, trying to remember what she'd been dreaming that had been so bitterly sad. Whatever it was had escaped her. She rolled over and glanced at her clock, then sighed. It would be several hours yet before the alarm sounded.

Snuggling up with her pillow, she intended to go back to sleep, and was somewhat surprised to discover she couldn't. The tears returned, rolling down her cheek at an alarming pace.

Sitting up, she reached for a tissue, blowing her nose hard. She couldn't understand what was happening to her or why she would find it so necessary to weep. A parade of possible reasons marched through her mind. Hormones. She was missing Brand. Her experience with Aimee that morning. Marilyn. There were any number of excuses why she would wake up weeping. But none that she could readily understand.

She drew the covers over her shoulders and lay staring into

space. How she wished Brand were with her then. He'd take her in his arms and comfort her in a soft and reassuring way. He'd kiss away her doubts and her fears. Then he'd touch her in all the ways he knew would please her and gently coax the tears away with his warmth and his wit.

Erin missed him more in that moment than she had in the six months he'd been away at sea.

She closed her eyes, and faces and tension crowded her mind. They were the faces of the men and women she'd seen in court that morning. The eerie silence that had nearly stifled her as she'd waited for Aimee and Steve to come out of the judge's chambers.

The silence had been like nothing she'd ever experienced. Long rows of mahogany benches had lined the hallway. It was ironic that they should resemble church pews. Lawyers conferred with their clients while waiting their turn with the judge. Aimee must have crossed and uncrossed her legs a hundred times, she'd been so nervous. Then she'd started swinging her foot fast enough to cause a draft.

Later, when she and Steve had gone before the judge, Erin had been surrounded by the silence. The wounded, eerie silence of pain.

Erin was worried about Marilyn, too. The older woman had phoned needing to talk. The pain and the anger of her circumstances had gotten so oppressive she couldn't tolerate it another minute. Reaching out for help was something they'd discussed in class. Erin had spent almost an hour on the phone with Marilyn, listening while she talked out her pain.

Marilyn was just beginning to draw upon that well of inner strength. Erin had every confidence that the older woman would come away strong and secure. She wasn't so sure about the young woman she'd seen in the courthouse earlier that day, however.

The desperate look on the woman's face returned to haunt her now. She'd been weeping softly and trying to disguise her tears. Trembling. Shaken. She looked as if she'd been knocked off balance.

Erin's heart throbbed anew at the anguish she'd viewed in the young mother's eyes. She knew nothing of her circumstances, only what she'd overheard while waiting for Aimee. Yet the woman's red eyes and haunting look returned to torment Erin hours later.

After the hearing before the judge, Aimee had been shaken to the core, and Erin had suggested they go out for lunch instead of rushing back to the office. Aimee hadn't said much, and the two had eaten in silence. It was the same throbbing silence Erin had experienced earlier in the courtroom.

Now, hours later, in the wee hours of the morning, it was back again, nearly suffocating her with its intensity, and she hadn't a clue why.

Sitting at his desk, Brand had a vague uneasy feeling he couldn't quite place. He'd heard regularly from Erin since her return to the mainland.

When it came to dealing with his sweet Irish rose, he was playing his hand close to his chest. Being patient and not pressing her for a commitment was damned difficult.

He loved her, there was no question in his mind about that. He also knew it was asking a good deal of her to love him back. It would be a whole lot easier if he wasn't navy. Erin wanted stability, permanence, roots. All Brand had to do was prove to her she could have all that and still be his wife. The military had provided more security than he'd ever known as a civilian.

The navy was his life, and Brand believed that, in time, Erin would come around to his way of thinking. She loved him. A smile courted the edges of his mouth as he recalled their time together in the surf and Erin's eager response to his touch. They'd never come closer to making love than they had that night. It was something of a miracle that they hadn't.

When they'd first met and dated, the physical attraction between them had been nearly overpowering. He'd never experienced anything like it. If they were together for any length of time, he could be assured that the magnetism between them would reach explosive levels. That hadn't changed, but another dimension had been added in the months they'd known each other. They'd bonded emotionally. Erin had become a large part of Brand's life. She'd helped define who he was, how he thought and the way he governed his actions. She was the first person he thought of when he rolled out of bed in the morning. Generally, he woke regretting that she wasn't at his side, and mused how long it would take for her to come to her senses and marry him.

Thoughts of her followed him through most of the day. He lived for the mail. If there was a letter from her, he read it two and three times straight through, savoring each word. Often right then and there, with his concerns fresh in his mind, he sat down and wrote her back. Brand had never been much of a writer. Letters were time-consuming, and he sometimes had trouble expressing himself with the written word. Not wanting to be misinterpreted, he'd opt for a quick phone call instead. Sea duty this last time around had been a challenge for him in more ways than one, but he'd learned some valuable lessons. He needed to hear from Erin.

Not wanted. Needed.

While on duty aboard the *Blue Ridge,* he'd been forced to admit for the first time how much he did need her. He'd tried not to love her, he'd attempted to put her out of his mind and his life, but he'd discovered to his chagrin that he was unable to do so.

Erin MacNamera was the most important person in his world. Since he couldn't give her up, he had no other option but to be patient and bide his time.

The vague uneasy feeling persisted most of the afternoon. Catherine's news was equally unsettling.

"What do you mean you're being transferred to Bangor?" Brand demanded. He didn't use profanity often, but he couldn't hold back a couple of choice words when he learned Catherine was being stationed in Washington state.

"Hey," she argued, "I didn't ask for this. Personally, I'm not all that thrilled about it."

"You didn't ask for it, I *did*." Brand would have been willing to surrender his commission for the opportunity to move closer to Erin. It seemed he was thwarted at every turn when it came to loving her.

A letter from Erin was waiting for him when he arrived home that evening. He stared at the envelope, grateful that something good had come of this day. He'd been beginning to have his doubts.

Standing in the middle of his compact living room, he tore open the letter with his index finger and read:

Dearest Brand,

This is the most difficult letter I've ever written in my life. I've started it so many times, tried to make sense of my feelings, praying all the while that you'll understand and forgive me.

I woke up early the other morning, weeping. Aimee had needed me to go to the courthouse with her for her settlement hearing. I had waited outside in the hallway for her, and while I was there I saw a woman in her early twenties crying. Never have I had any experience affect me more profoundly. There was so much pain in that hallway. It seemed to reach out and grab hold of me. Perhaps it was because Aimee's settlement hearing followed on the heels of an episode with Margo. She's had her ups and downs over the last nine months, small triumphs followed by minor setbacks. I've worked with so many divorcing women since I started my job. I'm beginning to wonder if anyone stays married anymore. How can Margo's husband walk away after thirty years of marriage? How could he possibly abandon her now? It doesn't make sense to me.

Even Aimee surprises me. I knew she and Steve were having problems, but I never dreamed matters would go this far.

I suppose you're wondering what Aimee's settlement hearing and Margo's problems have to do with the fact I woke up crying. Trust me, it took a long time for me to make the connection myself.

Deep down, in the innermost part of my being, the trauma involving Aimee and Margo forced me to face up to my true feelings regarding our relationship. I do love you, Brand. So much so that it sometimes frightens me, but we can't continue, we can't go on pretending our differences are all going to magically disappear someday. Falling in love caught us both unaware. You certainly didn't intend to leave Seattle caring about me, and I never intended to love you. It happened, and we both let it. Now we're left to deal with the way we've tangled our two lives.

I realize my thoughts are all so scrambled yet, and you don't have a clue of what I'm trying to say. I'm not even sure I can explain it myself. I suppose I recognized it first when I talked to Margo late one evening when she was suffering from a bout of deep emotional pain. Following on the heels of that was Aimee's settlement hearing.

I know you're hoping we'll soon be married. You've been so patient and understanding. I knew how much you truly loved me when you stopped pressuring me to become your wife.

In the last few weeks, I've given a good deal of thought to your proposal, and to be honest was leaning in that direction.

I've made my decision, and it was the most heart-wrenching one of my life. I can't marry you, Brand. It came to me recently why. It isn't because I don't love you enough. Please believe that. Learning not to love you will likely take me a lifetime.

If we do marry, someday down the road we're going to divorce. Our differences are fundamental ones. You're a part of the navy. I honestly believe that what attracted me to you so strongly was your likeness to my father. You certainly don't resemble him physically, but on the inside you two could be mistaken for blood relatives. You think so much alike. Your lives don't belong to yourselves, or your family. They belong to good ol' Uncle Sam.

I had eighteen years of that, and I can't and won't accept that crazy lifestyle a second time. I hated it then, and I'll hate it now.

This isn't a new issue. It's the same one we've been pounding out almost from the moment we met. The problem is, I grew to love you so much I was willing to give in on this, thinking that if we married everything would work out all right. I was burying my head in the sand and pretending. But someday in the future, we'd both have paid dearly for my refusal to accept the truth. By then there'd probably be children, too. I couldn't bear for our children to suffer through a divorce.

It's ironic that I work almost exclusively with divorced women. Month after month, class after class, and it still didn't hit me how ugly and painful it is to dissolve a marriage until I saw what's happened to Aimee. She and Steve are in so much pain. It hurts me to see her suffer. I barely know Steve, and I hurt for him, too. My attitude toward marriage has gotten so sarcastic lately. I'm beginning to question if anyone should willingly commit their lives to another.

Aimee's so bitter now. I think she's convinced herself she hates Steve. The woman in the hallway at the courthouse, too. I felt something so strongly when I saw her. That sounds crazy, doesn't it? Everyone there was in such deep emotional pain. When I thought about it, I realized that so many of those men and women started out just the way we are. At one time they'd been as deeply in love as we are now. Only we'd be starting off with a mark against us, feeling the way I do about the navy.

Please accept my decision, Brand. Don't write me back. Don't call me. Please let this be the end.

It's been the most painful and difficult decision of my life. Yet deep in my heart I know it's the right one. You may disagree with me now, but someday, when you look back over this time, I believe you'll realize I'm doing the right thing for us both, although God help me, it's the most painful decision I've ever made.

Thank you for loving me. Thank you for teaching me about myself. And please, oh, please, be happy.

Erin

Brand closed his eyes. He felt as though a two-by-four had been slammed into his stomach. For one frenzied moment he thought he might be sick. It was the oddest sensation, as though he'd been physically attacked, badly injured, and was experiencing the first stages of shock.

It took him a couple of minutes to compose himself. His heart was pounding inside his chest like a huge Chinese gong. He paced back and forth in fruitless frustration, sorting through his limited options.

Before he leaped to conclusions, he needed to reread Erin's letter and determine how serious she actually was. He did so, sitting himself down at his desk and digested each word, seeking…hell, he didn't know what he was looking for. Loopholes? An indication, any evidence he might find, that she didn't mean what she wrote. A glimmer of hope.

The second reading, and later a third, told him otherwise. Erin meant every single word. She wanted out of the relationship, and for both their sakes, she didn't want to hear from him again.

A week had passed since Erin had mailed Brand the final letter.

"Coward," she muttered under her breath. This was what she got for not confronting him over the phone. She'd known from the first that she was taking the easy way out. Originally she'd told herself she was looking to avoid any arguments or lengthy discussions. Only later was she willing to admit that she was a wimp.

"Are you back to talking to yourself again?" Aimee muttered from her desk across the aisle from Erin's.

"What did I say this time?"

"Something about being a coward."

"Oh…I guess maybe I did." It was funny, really. Ironic, too, that she'd made the most courageous, and by far the most difficult, decision of her life, and a week later she was calling herself a coward.

"I would do the same thing all over again," she whispered, and her voice caught slightly. Caught on the pain. Caught on the regret.

"Are you still carrying on about Brand?" Aimee demanded unsympathetically.

Erin nodded.

"Trust me, all of womankind is better off without men. They use and abuse, in that order," Aimee said, and snickered softly. "I'm beginning to sound a bit jaded, aren't I? Sorry about that. You've been in the dumps all week, and I haven't been much help."

"Don't worry about it. You're having problems of your own."

"Not so much anymore. Steve and I have come to terms. The final papers are being drawn up, and the whole messy affair is going to be over. At last. I didn't think this was ever going to end."

"Are you doing anything after work?" Going home to an empty, dark house, even with a grand piano to greet her, had long since lost its appeal. Before she'd written the final letter to Brand, she'd hurried home, praying there'd be a letter waiting there for her. But there wouldn't be any more letters. At least not from Brand. Once she realized that, she'd suddenly started looking for excuses not to go home after work.

"What do you have in mind?" Aimee asked.

"James Bradshaw, the famous divorce attorney, is giving a workshop on prenuptial agreements. I recommended it to the women in my class. I thought you might like to join us."

"Hey, sorry, I can't do anything tonight," Aimee answered in a preoccupied voice. She shuffled a couple of files before she continued. "Prenuptial agreement? Good grief, Erin, you're not even married and you're planning for a divorce."

"Not me," Erin replied. "It's for the women in my class. After seeing what's happened to Marilyn and women like her, and now you, I think it's smart to have everything down in black and white."

Aimee busied herself at her desk. "Personally, I don't think it's a good idea to start out a marriage by planning for a divorce."

Erin stared at her friend, not knowing what to think. Aimee was at the tail end of a divorce that had cut her to the quick. If anyone understood the advisability of prenuptial agreements, Erin thought, it should be her friend.

"Listen–" Aimee rolled back her chair and sighed. "Forget I said that. I'm the last person in the world who should be giving romantic advice. My marriage is in shambles and…I feel like one of the walking wounded myself. Maybe the lecture isn't such a bad idea after all."

"Go on," Erin urged. "I'd be interested in hearing your opinion."

Aimee didn't look as if she trusted her own thoughts. "As I said, I don't think it's a good idea to start off a marriage by planning for divorce. I know that's an unpopular point of view, especially in this day and age, but it just doesn't feel right to me."

"How can you say that?" Erin cried. "You're going through a divorce yourself. Good grief, you've been through hell the last few months, and now all of a sudden you're making marriage sound like this glorious, wonderful state of being. As I recall, you and Steve can't carry on a civil conversation. What's changed?"

"A lot," Aimee announced solemnly. "And you, my friend, have the opportunity to gain from my experience."

Feeling uncomfortable, Erin looked away.

"We're both here day in and day out, working with women who are making new lives for themselves," Aimee continued. "But finding them a decent job is only the beginning. They've been traumatized, abandoned and left to deal with life on their own. If you want the truth, I'm beginning to believe our thinking's becoming jaded. Not everyone ends up divorced. Not everyone will have to go through what these women have. It's just that we deal with it each and every day until our own perception of married life has been warped."

"But you and Steve–"

"I know," Aimee argued. "Trust me, I know. I pray every day I'm doing the right thing by divorcing Steve."

Erin was praying the same thing herself for the both of them. "But if you're having second thoughts, shouldn't you be doing something?"

"Like what?" Aimee suggested, her voice flippant. "Steve's already involved with another woman."

"You don't know that."

"Deep down I do. You saw him the day we went to court. He wore that stupid green tie just to irritate me, and the looks he gave me…I can't begin to describe to you the way he glanced at me, as if…as if he couldn't believe he'd ever been married to me in the first place. He couldn't wait for the divorce to be final."

"But I thought this was a friendly divorce."

Aimee's gaze fell to her hands. "There's no such thing as a friendly divorce. It's too damn painful for everyone involved."

"Oh, Aimee, I feel so bad for you and Steve."

"Why should you?" she asked, the sarcastic edge back in her voice. "We're both getting exactly what we want."

Erin knew nothing more that she could say. She didn't have any excuse to linger around the office. The lecture wasn't until seven, and it was optional as far as her class was concerned. She didn't have to be there herself, but she thought it would help kill time, which was something that was weighing heavily on her these days.

Erin's thoughts were heavy as she walked outside the double glass doors of the fifteen-story office complex. The wind had picked up and was biting-cold. She hunched her shoulders and tucked her hands inside her coat pockets as she headed for the parking lot on Yesler.

With her head down, it was little wonder she didn't notice the tall, dark figure standing next to her car. It wasn't until she was directly in front of him that she realized someone was blocking her path.

When she looked up, her heart, in a frenzy, flew into her throat.

Brand stood there, his eyes as cold and biting as the north wind.

"Brand," she whispered, hardly able to speak, "what are you doing here?"

"You didn't want me to write you or contact you by phone. But you didn't say anything about not seeing you in person. If you want to break everything off, fine, I can accept that. Only you're going to have to do it to my face."

Chapter Thirteen

"You couldn't let it go, could you?" Erin cried, battling with an anger that threatened to consume her. Tears blurred Brand's image before her, and for a second she couldn't make out his features. When she did, her heart ached at the sight of him.

"No, I couldn't leave it," Brand returned harshly. "You want to end it, then fine, have it your way. But I'm not going to make it easy for you."

"Oh, Brand," she whispered, her anger vanishing as quickly as it had come, "do you honestly believe it was easy?"

"Say it, Erin. Tell me you want me out of your life."

He towered over her like a thundercloud, dark and menacing. Erin's feet felt as if they were planted ankle-deep in concrete. She needed to put a few inches of distance between them, grant them both necessary breathing room. As it was, she was having a difficult time getting oxygen into her lungs.

"Could we go someplace else and discuss this?" She barely

managed the tightly worded request. The urge to break down was nearly overwhelming. It hurt as much to talk as to breathe.

Of his own accord, Brand stepped away from her. "Where?"

"There's an…Italian restaurant not far from here." The suggestion came off the top of her head, and the minute she said it, Erin realized attempting to talk would be impossible there.

"I'm not discussing this with a roomful of people listening in on the conversation."

"All right, you choose." A restaurant hadn't been a brilliant idea, but Erin couldn't think of anyplace else they could go.

She wished with everything in her heart that Brand had accepted her letter and left it at that. Having him confront her unexpectedly like this made everything so much more difficult.

"If we're going to talk, it has to be someplace private," he insisted.

"Ah…" Erin hesitated.

"My hotel room," Brand suggested next, but he said it as though he expected her to argue with him.

"Okay," she agreed, not questioning the wisdom of his idea. Her primary thought was to get this over with as quickly as possible. It didn't matter where they spoke, because in her heart she knew it wouldn't take more than a few minutes. "I don't have a lot of time."

"You've got a date?" He bit out the question.

"No…I'm suppose to be at a lecture."

"When?"

"By seven."

"You'll be there." Brand took off walking, expecting her to follow behind. She did so reluctantly, wishing she could avoid this confrontation and knowing she couldn't.

His pace was brisk, and Erin practically had to trot in order to keep up with his long-legged strides. They'd gone four or five blocks when he entered the revolving glass door that led to the tastefully decorated hotel lobby.

He paused outside the elevator for Erin to catch up to him. She was breathless by the time she traipsed across the plush red-and-white carpet.

In all the time she'd known Brand, she'd never seen him quite like this. He was so unemotional, so unfeeling. Aloof, as if nothing she could say or do would disconcert him.

His room was on the tenth floor. He unlocked and held open the door for her, and she walked inside. It was a standard room with a double bed, a nightstand and a dresser. In the corner, next to the window were a table and two olive-green upholstered chairs.

"Go ahead and sit down," he instructed brusquely. "I'll have room service send up some coffee."

Erin nodded, walked across the room and settled in the crescent-shaped chair.

Brand picked up the phone, pushed a button and requested the coffee. When he'd finished, he surprised her by sauntering to the other side of the compact room and sitting on the edge of the mattress.

Erin's gaze fell to her hands. "I wish it didn't have to be this way. I'm so sorry, Brand," she said in a small voice.

"I didn't come all this way for an apology."

He seemed to be waiting for something more, but Erin didn't know what it was, and even if she had, she wasn't sure she could have supplied it. The strained silence was so loud, it was all Erin could do not to press her hands over her ears.

"Say something," she pleaded. "Don't just sit there looking so angry you could bite my head off."

"I'm not angry," he corrected, clenching his fists, "I'm downright furious." He bounded to his feet and stalked across the compact room. "A letter," he said bitingly, and turned to glare down at her. "You didn't have the decency to talk this out with me. Instead, you did it in a letter."

"I…was afraid…"

She wasn't allowed to finish. Brand advanced two steps toward her, then stopped. "Have I ever given you a reason to fear me? Ever? Am I so damn difficult to talk to? Is that it?"

"I wasn't afraid of you."

"A letter doesn't make a whole lot of sense."

"I know," she whispered woefully. "It seemed the best way at the time. I didn't mean to hurt you. Trust me, it hasn't exactly been a piece of cake for me, either."

"Explain it to me, Erin, because I'm telling you right now, I can't make heads or tails out of that letter. You love me, but you can't marry me because you're afraid we'll end up divorcing someday and you don't want to put our children through the trauma. Do you realize how crazy that sounds?"

"It isn't crazy," she cried, vaulting to her feet. "Okay, so maybe I didn't explain myself very well, but you weren't there. You don't know."

"I wasn't where?"

"In the courthouse that day with Aimee." She covered her face with her hands and shook her head, trying to dispel the ready images that popped into her head. The same ones that had returned to haunt her so often. The young mother, who was consulting with her attorney and trying so hard to disguise the fact that she was crying. Aimee, her legs swinging like a pendulum gone berserk while she smoked like a chimney the whole time, pretending she was as cool as a milkshake. The heartache. The pain that was all so tangible. And the silence. That horrible, wounded silence.

"What makes you so certain we'll divorce?" Brand demanded.

Lowering her hands, she sadly shook her head. "Because you're Navy."

"I'm getting damn tired of that argument."

"That's because you've ignored my feelings about the military from the first. I told you the night we met how I felt about dating anyone in the military. I warned you…but you insisted. You refused to leave well enough alone–"

"Come on, Erin," he argued bitterly, "I didn't exactly kidnap you and force you to date me. You were as eager to get to know me as I was you."

"But I–"

"You don't have a single quarrel. You wanted this. You can argue until you're blue in the face, but it won't make a damn bit of difference."

"I can't marry you."

"Fine, then we'll be lovers." He jerked off his blue uniform jacket and started on the buttons of his military-issue shirt.

Stunned, Erin didn't move. She couldn't believe what she was seeing. "I…I…what about the coffee?"

"Right. I'll cancel it." He walked over to the phone and dialed room service. When he turned back to her, he seemed surprised that she was still wearing her coat. "Go on," he urged. "Get undressed."

Erin's mind raced for an excuse. "You're not serious," she said, crowding the words together.

"The hell I'm not. I don't suppose you're protected," he said, pausing momentarily. "Well, don't worry about it. I'll take care of it." He sat on the end of the bed and removed his shoes, then stood and methodically undid his belt. While she stood stunned, barely able to believe what she was viewing, he unzipped his pants and calmly stepped out of them.

Erin sucked in a sharp breath and backed up two or three paces. Brand must have sensed her movement, because he glanced up, seemingly surprised to find her standing so far away from him.

"Take off your clothes," he ordered. He stood before her in his boxer shorts and T-shirt, seemingly impatient for her to remove her own things.

"Brand, I…can't do this."

"Why not?" he demanded. "You were plenty eager before. As I recall, you once told me you'd rather we were lovers. I was the one fool enough to insist we marry."

"Not like this," she pleaded. "Not when you're so…cold."

"Trust me, Erin, a few kisses will warm us both right up." He walked over to her and systematically unbuttoned her coat. She stood, numb with disbelief. This couldn't actually be happening, could it? In answer to her silent question, her coat fell to the floor.

Brand's eyes were on hers, and she noted that the anger was gone, replaced with some emotion she couldn't name. With his gaze continuing to hold hers, Brand reached behind her for the zipper at the back of her dress. The hissing sound of it gliding open filled the room as though a swarm of bees were directly behind them. She raised her hands in a weak protest, but Brand ignored her.

Easing the material over her smooth shoulders, he paused midway in his journey to press his moist, hot mouth to the hollow of her throat. Tense and frightened, Erin jerked slightly, then reached out and gripped the edge of the table to steady herself.

"Brand," she pleaded once more. "Please don't…not like this."

"You'll be saying a lot more than please before we're finished," he assured her.

His mouth traveled at a leisurely pace up the side of her neck, across the sensitized skin at the underside of her jaw. Despite everything, his nearness warmed her blood.

Everything was different now. He was loving and gentle and so incredibly male. He smelled of musk. Erin had forgotten how much she enjoyed the manly fragrance that was Brand. He turned his head and nuzzled her ear with his nose, and unable to resist him any longer, Erin slipped her arms around his middle and tentatively held on to his waist.

He rewarded her with a soft kiss and braced his feet slightly apart. Then, dragging her by the hips, he urged her forward until she was tucked snugly between his parted thighs. Once she was secure, he slipped her arms free of the restricting material of her dress and slowly eased it over her hips.

Erin wasn't ready for this new intimacy and resisted. Brand reacted by kissing her several times until she willingly parted her mouth to eagerly receive his kisses. The gathered silk material of her dress pooled at her feet.

His hands were at the waistband of her tap pants when he paused as though he expected her to resist him anew. "I think we should stop now," she whispered, knowing that if the loving continued much longer they'd both be lost.

"That's the problem," he whispered, his mouth scant inches from her own. "We both think too much. This time we're going to feel."

"Oh, Brand…" She was confused and uncertain but too needy to care.

"I want you, Erin, and by heaven, I fully intend to have you."

If she pushed him away or made the slightest protest, Erin was convinced, Brand would immediately cease their lovemaking. But she seemed incapable of doing either. All she could seem to manage was a weak mewling sound deep in her throat that encouraged Brand to take further liberties with her. She felt torn between the dictates of her body and the decree of her pride. She couldn't allow this to happen, and yet she was powerless to stop him.

He kissed her again and again. A trembling started in her knees, spreading to her thighs until she could barely support herself. She sagged against Brand. He accepted her weight, and without her quite figuring out how he managed it, Erin found herself sprawled across the mattress with Brand lying alongside her.

"My sweet Erin, oh, my love," he whispered, his eyes tender. "Tell me you want me. I need you to say it…just this once. Give me that to remember you by." The words were issued in sweet challenge between wild, carnal kisses.

"Oh, Brand." She breathed his name when she could, but talking, indeed breathing, had become less and less important.

"Say it," he demanded again, easing his hands over her flat, smooth stomach to caress the womanly part of her.

"Do you want me?" he whispered.

"Yes…oh, yes."

Erin had never felt as she did at that moment. Never so needy or so feminine. He kissed her and moved over her, his hands in her hair, lifting her mouth upward to meet his. Brand made her feel as if she were exploding from the inside out. This feeling, so beautiful, so brilliant and warm, filled her eyes with tears that splashed onto her cheeks.

He straddled her, eager now, his hands gripping the waistband of her tap pants. He paused when he noticed her tears.

Slowly he eased himself off her and sat on the edge of the mattress, his eyes closed. "I can't do it. Dear God in heaven, I can't do it."

Erin couldn't move. Her breasts were heaving, and tears rained down the side of her face and leaked onto the bedspread. "It would never work between us, Brand. I couldn't bear to go through a divorce." She paused and twisted her head away so that she wouldn't have to look at him.

"You honestly believe that, don't you?" He slowly shook his head.

"I do mean it. Would I put us through this torture if I didn't?"

"Honest to God, I don't know." Before she fully realized his intention, Brand moved off the bed and reached for his clothes.

Erin sat up, distributing her weight on the palms of her hands. He was actually dressing. A few moments earlier he'd been preparing to make love to her, and now he was dressing. "I want you, Erin," he said when he'd finished. "I'll probably regret not making love to you to the day they lower me into my grave."

"But why…aren't you?"

"Damned if I know. Maybe it's because I count your father as a friend." He paused and rubbed his hand across his face. "More likely I'm afraid if we make love, once would never be enough, and we'd spend the rest of our lives the way we have the last eight months. Personally, I can't deal with that. I don't think you could, either."

He was right; she'd never been so miserable.

"Go ahead and get dressed."

"First you demand that I undress, now you want me to dress. I wish you'd kindly make up your mind," she muttered peevishly. She scooted off the mattress and reached for her clothes, jerking them on impatiently.

"You claimed you wanted to talk," she reminded him once she'd finished.

He nodded. "Coming here wasn't a brilliant idea." His smile was decidedly off center. He hesitated, his eyes sad. "My anger frightened you?"

"Only at first, when you seemed so indifferent."

He nodded and leaned against the wall, as if standing upright were becoming too much of a burden for him. "You meant what you said in that letter?"

Erin closed her eyes and nodded.

"I was afraid of that."

"Brand, I'd give anything if I could be different. Anything, but–"

"Don't," he said, cutting her off. "It isn't necessary."

"Please try to understand," she pleaded softly. "I went through hell. For nights on end I'd wake up weeping and not know why, and then I realized it all boiled down to what was happening to you and me. Deep down I knew it would be that way."

Brand said nothing. She'd pleaded with him not to argue with her, begged him to accept the inevitable, but his silence now was like having a knife plunged directly into her soul.

"There isn't anything more to say then, is there?" he said, his back as stiff as a flagpole as he walked over to the closet and removed his suitcase.

"You're leaving?" It wasn't her most brilliant deduction in the past year.

"There isn't any reason to stay."

No, she admitted miserably to herself. There wasn't. Reluctantly, she stood, her heart aching as it never had. Before she left him, before she walked out of his life, she had to say one last thing. When she spoke, her voice wavered slightly, then leveled out. "You probably hate me now…. I wouldn't blame you if you did. But please, in the future, when you can, try to think kindly of me. Please know that more than anything I want you to be happy."

"I will be happy," he said forcefully. "Damn happy."

She nodded, although she didn't believe it would be true for a good long while for either of them.

"Go ahead and marry your stockbroker, or attorney, or whoever it is who interests you," he continued. "Settle down in your four-bedroom colonial with your two point five children and live the good life." Brand's words were biting and sharp. Forcefully he shoved his clothes inside the suitcase, not taking the time to fold them properly. "Plant those roots so deep they'll reach all the way to China."

Erin blinked back tears. He was so bitter, and there was nothing she could say to make it better. She stiffened, knowing he needed to vent his frustration and his pain.

"By all means, marry your stockbroker," he repeated forcefully. "Security is everything. Tell yourself that often, because I have the feeling you're going to need to remember it."

Erin knotted her fists at her side. The lump in her throat had grown to gargantuan proportions.

"Goodbye, Erin," he whispered as he eased the lid of the suitcase closed. He looked toward the door, silently asking that she walk out of his room as willingly as she was walking out of his life.

"I know it hurts, but it's better this way," she whispered, her voice low and choppy.

He paused and grudgingly smiled at her. "Far better," he agreed.

Chapter Fourteen

"Come on, Erin," Aimee urged. "It's December. Liven up a little, would you?"

"I'm alive." Which was stretching the truth. Oh, she functioned day to day and had for the past several weeks, since she'd last seen Brand. The emotional pain had been intolerable in the beginning, but, as expected, the intensity had lessened. She'd counted on being much better by now, however.

Severing the relationship with Brand was what she wanted, she reminded herself. Marrying Brand would have been the biggest mistake of her life. It was amazing how many times a day she was forced to remind herself of that.

"How about doing some Christmas shopping after work?" Aimee suggested.

"Thanks anyway, but I finished mine last week." Erin appreciated the offer, but try as she would, she couldn't muster much enthusiasm for the holidays. The crowds irritated her, and she hated being impatient and grumpy when everyone around her was filled with good cheer.

Bah, humbug! Erin had always loved the holidays.

As hard as she tried not to, she couldn't help wondering about Brand. Was he still in Hawaii? Had he started dating? Was he happy?

By force of will, Erin managed to avoid thoughts of him during the day. Every time her mind turned to the Hawaii-based lieutenant, she immediately focussed on another subject. World peace. Jalapeño jelly. Scissors. Anything and everything but Brand.

It was later, when she was about to slip into the welcome void of sleep, that she found herself most vulnerable. She'd be wandering between the two worlds when Brand would casually stroll into her mind.

He didn't speak; not once had he uttered a word. He just stood there, straight and tall, dressed in his uniform. Proud. Strong. Earnest.

Erin tried to make his image disappear. More than once she'd sat bolt upright in bed and demanded that he clear out of her mind. He always did, without question, but when she lay back down, she always regretted that he was gone.

There had been one improvement, if she could call it that. The episodes when she woke in the middle of the night weeping for no apparent reason had passed. But it was damn little comfort for all the lonely days and nights those unexplained bouts had spawned.

Erin and Aimee walked out of the office together. The air was filled with a joyous holiday flavor. Bells chimed at every street corner. Storefronts were decorated with large swags of evergreen draped above doorways, stretching from one business to the other. Huge red plastic bells adorned streetlights. Erin walked past it all, barely noticing.

"Call me if you change your mind," Aimee said before heading in the opposite direction.

"I will, thanks." But Erin already had her plans for the evening. She was going home, cuddling up in front of the television and mindlessly viewing situation comedies until it was bedtime. It wasn't exciting, nor was it inspiring, but a quiet dinner and television were the only things she could effectively deal with that night. After months of teaching sessions on self-acceptance and being kind to oneself, Erin was determined to follow her own advice.

Erin's mail contained three Christmas cards. The first was from Terry, an old college friend. Terry had married the previous year, and her printed Christmas letter shared the happy news of her pregnancy.

"Terry with a baby," Erin mused aloud, remembering distinctly how they'd both been certain they were destined to remain single the rest of their natural lives.

The second card was from Marilyn. Erin read her brief note with interest. The older woman was forming friendships and had attended a dance with a woman friend who had been widowed several years earlier. Marilyn's note ended with the happy news that she'd danced three times. She claimed she felt more like a wallflower than like Cinderella, but she was ready to attend another dance the following week.

The third Christmas card was from her parents. Erin read over the greeting and was pleased to note that her father had included a short typed sheet along with her mother's much thicker letter. She read her father's letter first.

Dear Erin,

Happy holidays. Your mother and I mailed off a package to you this afternoon, which should arrive in plenty of time for Christmas. I wish we could be together, but that's what happens when kids grow up and leave home. Your mother and I are going to miss being with you this year.

I don't have much news. Your mother will tell you everything that's up with your brother and sister. They're well and happy, and that's all that counts.

Now what's this I hear about you putting your house up for sale? I remember when you bought it you claimed you were going to live there for the next thirty years. You've only been there two years. I'm afraid you've got more navy blood in you than you realize.

The last bit of information may come as something of a shock. I thought about letting you hear it from someone else but decided that would be cruel. I heard through the grapevine Brand Davis is engaged to Catherine Fredrickson. Apparently they've been friends for a long time. I'm sorry if this news hurts you, baby, but I thought you'd want to know.

Have a good time opening up that box of goodies your mother and I mailed.

Love,
Dad

Erin didn't feel anything. Nothing whatsoever. So Brand was marrying Catherine. It was what Erin herself had suggested months earlier. He certainly hadn't allowed any grass to grow under his feet, she mused somewhat bitterly.

A numbing pain took hold and, deciding to ignore it, Erin set aside the mail and fixed herself a dinner consisting of soup and a turkey sandwich. When she finished, she stared at the bowl and plate and decided she couldn't force herself to eat it. Watching television had lost its appeal, too.

Being alone felt intolerable, and she decided to go for a

drive. Mingling with other people seemed important all of a sudden. She wandered through a small shopping complex close to her house, bought a couple of cards at the Hallmark store and strolled back to the parking lot.

"Brand is marrying Catherine," she said aloud in the confines of her car as she drove home. "More than anything, I want him to be happy." She had to say it aloud to remind herself that it was true.

Erin drove past the street where she should have turned off, but for some unknown reason she continued driving, her destination unclear.

An hour passed, and when she found herself close to Aimee's she decided her subconscious was telling her she needed to talk over Brand's engagement with her best friend.

Although Aimee's car was parked in front of her house, she didn't answer the doorbell for several minutes. When she did appear, she was dressed in her housecoat and slippers.

"Erin?" she cried after opening the door. "What are you doing here? Good grief, you look like you've seen a ghost. Come on in." She skillfully steered her through the living room and into the kitchen.

It seemed to Erin that Aimee didn't want her in the living room, which was preposterous, but in case she was arriving at a bad time she asked, "Should I come back later?"

"Of course not," Aimee returned quickly.

A little too quickly, Erin thought. "You look like you were taking a bath."

"No…no."

Erin's gaze narrowed suspiciously. "Then why are you wearing a robe?" It wasn't anywhere near time for bed.

Aimee glanced down at the purple velvet as if she'd never seen it before. "Ah…"

"Aimee," Erin whispered heatedly. A sinking feeling attacked the pit of her stomach, and she looked around. "Have you got a man in your bedroom?"

The dedicated social worker squeezed her eyes closed and nodded several times.

"Why didn't you say something?" Erin felt like a complete idiot. She wanted to crawl under the carpet and hide.

"I couldn't say anything," Aimee protested at length. "You wouldn't drop by unexpectedly like this unless it was something important. One look at you, and I knew you were upset."

"I'm more upset now than I was before I arrived. It would have been better if you hadn't answered the door."

"May I remind you that you're my best friend," Aimee countered heatedly, although they both continued to whisper in an effort not to be overheard by the mystery man in Aimee's bedroom.

Erin couldn't be more surprised by her friend's actions had she announced she was considering entering a convent. To the best of Erin's knowledge, Aimee had never fooled around. She'd been asked out on a date once or twice but had always declined, claiming she wasn't ready for the singles scene just yet.

It wouldn't be the first time Aimee had surprised her, but until now the surprises had all been pleasant ones. Her friend's divorce was only days from being finalized. Perhaps the pain of what was happening between her and Steve had led her friend into an act completely out of character.

For some time now, Erin had sensed that something was developing in Aimee's life, but she wouldn't have suspected for the world that it was another man. Aimee had given up smoking and was calmer than she had been a few months earlier. Erin had attributed the changes to part of the healing process.

"It's not what you're thinking," Aimee muttered, chastising Erin with a single look. She glanced over her shoulder. "Steve, kindly come out here and save my reputation."

"Steve?" Erin repeated, stunned. "You and Steve? You're divorcing him, remember?"

"Yes, me and Steve," Aimee confirmed. "Steve," she called a second time.

"Honey, if I come out now, I may save your reputation, but it sure as hell will ruin mine."

Aimee actually blushed. Erin couldn't believe it. Her best friend's cheeks went a bright shade of pink.

"Steve?" Erin repeated Aimee's husband's name, still unable to believe what she was hearing.

Aimee nodded, then walked over to the kitchen counter and assembled a pot of coffee.

"You and Steve are…" Erin motioned with her hand, as if that would complete the sentence for her. A tardy smile quivered at the corners of her mouth. "When did all this get started?"

"Will you kindly quit looking at me like you're going to burst out laughing?"

"I can't help it. The last time you mentioned Steve's name it was to claim he was involved with another woman. What about the white car parked outside his apartment? You were convinced he wore that ugly green tie to the settlement hearing to irritate you, and–"

"That was before," Aimee reminded her. "That car belonged to his brother, and hell, I should have known better. I was eager to leap to all the wrong conclusions."

"As I recall, you two were finished, and you couldn't wait to sign the final papers."

"We still might."

"What?" Aimee was certainly full of shocking surprises this evening.

"We were talking about it earlier. It might be wise to start on fresh ground–bury the past, so to speak. We haven't decided yet, but we're leaning toward staying married for…for a couple of reasons."

"But what happened to change everything?"

A slow, almost silly smile lit up Aimee's eyes. "About a month ago–"

"A month?" Erin echoed in strained disbelief. It was hard to imagine that she hadn't suspected something earlier. The two were best friends, and Erin felt she really knew Aimee. "You two have been chummy for a month?"

"Longer, actually," Aimee admitted, keeping her voice low. "Steve called about six weeks ago, needing to come over to the house and pick up some things. The atmosphere was cool between us then, to say the least. We arranged a time suitable to us both. I wasn't keen on being here alone with him, but someone had to be here. I didn't trust him not to take more than what he'd come for, and so I gritted my teeth and met him myself."

"You should have asked me." As matters had turned out, Erin was grateful her friend hadn't.

"I know," Aimee agreed, "but it was shortly after Brand left, and you were still so raw. I didn't want to burden you with my problems."

"We've been burdening each other for a good long time. But go on. I'm dying to find out what happened."

Aimee smiled. It was the same silly smile as before. "It got worse before it got better. Actually, it got a whole lot worse. Steve arrived, and we got in this huge fight about a light fixture, of all things. I told him he could have the stupid thing. He claimed he didn't want it, but I refused to let that pass. He was still arguing with me when I dragged out the chair and started to remove it from the wall."

"Aimee!"

"I know, I know. My expertise doesn't involve anything electrical, which Steve took delight in reminding me. At the moment, I think, he was hoping I'd electrocute myself. Fortunately, I fell before that happened."

"You fell?"

"Conveniently into Steve's arms, and we both went crashing to the floor. I was furious and outraged and blamed him. I started listing his legion of faults, and he kissed me just to shut me up so he could see if I'd been hurt."

The picture that formed in Erin's mind was a wildly romantic one. Aimee hopping mad, and Steve more interested in making sure she hadn't been hurt in the fall than in listening to her tirade.

"One thing led to another, and before we knew it we were in bed together."

"Oh, Aimee that's so romantic."

"Romantic, nothing. I was furious, claiming he'd seduced me. Steve adamantly denied it and said I was the one who'd seduced him. Before the night was over, we'd seduced each other a second time. Both of us were more than a little chagrined over what happened. Steve left the following morning without taking any of the things he claimed he needed so badly. I called him the next day, and he returned for the items…only he ended up spending the night again."

"But what about everything that led up to the divorce? You were miserable together. Remember?"

"Nothing's really changed," Aimee explained. "Only our attitude has. We're committed to working out our problems. Steve's willing to see a counselor. In fact, he's the one who suggested it."

"So you've talked everything out?"

"We talked, among other things," Steve inserted as he walked into the kitchen. Standing behind Aimee, he slipped his arms around her waist and cuddled her close. "Should we tell her?" he asked his wife.

"Nothing's for sure yet," Aimee said, twisting her head around to look up at him.

"I'm sure of it."

Erin hadn't a clue what the two were discussing. "Tell me what?"

"Aimee's pregnant. At least we think she is."

"Steve, I haven't been to the doctor yet. You can't go around announcing it until I've been in to see Dr. Larson."

"All those pregnancy test kits you bought claim you are. That's good enough for me." He broke away from his wife and strutted around the kitchen in a walk that would have done a rooster proud.

Delight brightened Aimee's eyes as she held out her hands to Erin. "After ten years. I can't believe it: We tried so hard and for so long." Her face broke into an eager smile. "Oh, Erin, I'm going to have a baby."

The two gripped hands, and Erin felt tears of shared happiness fill her eyes.

"Hey, you two, kindly give credit where credit is due." A light shone in Steven's eyes, one that had been decidedly missing the other times Erin had seen him.

"I couldn't be happier for the two of you," Erin said, sincerely meaning every word, but at the same time the pain she felt knowing Brand was marrying Catherine felt like a heavy chain tightening around her heart. First Terry, and now Aimee.

"You didn't come over here because you suspected anything was developing between Steve and me," Aimee reminded her, scooting out a chair at the table. By now the coffee had brewed, and Aimee automatically brought down mugs.

Steve kissed his wife's cheek. "I'll leave you two to talk," he said, and smiled warmly at Erin before returning to the living room.

"Brand's engaged," Erin announced, her voice trembling

slightly. "My dad wrote and told me. He claimed it was better I hear the news from him than someone else."

"Oh, Erin, I'm so sorry."

"What's to be sorry about?" she asked with a shaky laugh. "If marrying Catherine is what it takes to make Brand happy, then why should I feel bad?"

"You love him."

"I know."

Aimee was quiet for a moment. "Have you given any more thought to what I said all those weeks ago about having our jobs taint our views on marriage?"

Erin hadn't. She'd been sifting through so much emotion and pain that she'd filed her friend's thoughts away in the farthest corner of her mind. "Not really."

"Then do. Not all marriages end in misery and heartache."

"It sometimes seems that way."

"I know," Aimee was quick to agree. "Think about it, Erin. You haven't been at this job long enough to gain perspective yet. That comes with time. I fell into that same trap myself.

"There are plenty of good marriages out there that work because the two people involved are prepared to do whatever they have to to see that it does."

Erin drew in a deep breath. "It's too late now for Brand and me."

"That's what I thought," Aimee reminded her.

"I want Brand to marry Catherine," Erin murmured, telling the biggest lie of her life. "They're perfect together... I said so from the first."

A Christmas card to Brand wouldn't hurt, Erin decided later. One with a brief note of congratulations. It took her nearly three days to compose the few lines.

Dear Brand,

Merry Christmas. I always claimed you and Catherine were perfect together. Now Dad tells me he heard through the grapevine that the two of you have set the big date. Congratulations.

I honestly mean that. I wish you only the best. You deserve it.

Erin

P.S. Neal and I are getting along famously.

Neal, Brand mused, reading over the short message a second time. He didn't know what tricks Erin was up to now, but he wasn't in the mood for it. He'd put her out of his life, and he was managing nicely.

"Who the hell are you kidding?" he asked out loud.

"You say something?" Romano asked.

"Nothing that concerns you," Brand barked. "Who the hell leaked out information about me and Catherine?"

"What kind of information?"

"That we're marrying."

"Hell, I don't know who'd say anything. Is it true?"

Brand answered that with a single intense look.

"Hey, don't get mad at me. I was just asking." Alex scooted away from his desk. "What's with you today, anyway?"

Brand debated on whether he'd let his friend know or not, then decided he owed everyone around him an explanation. He hadn't been the best company the past few weeks. "I got a Christmas card from Erin."

Romano responded with a low whistle. "No wonder you've been acting like a wounded bear all day. What'd she have to say?"

"Congratulations to me and Cath," he answered with a low snicker.

"You going to write and let her know the truth?"

"No," Brand answered without hesitating. If Erin wanted to believe he was marrying Catherine, he'd let her.

"I take it you don't plan on looking her up next week, either?"

"Hell, no." Brand had cursed the assignment that was taking him into Seattle. The timing couldn't have been worse. Two months, and he was only now getting to the point that he could go a small portion of the day without dwelling on the situation between him and Erin. He wasn't about to set himself up for more pain. He'd had all he could take.

Brand altered that decision, however, shortly after he checked into the Seattle hotel. He had a rental car, and with time to kill he decided it wouldn't hurt to swing past Erin's house. If luck was with him, he might catch a glimpse of her.

Luck, however, hadn't exactly been tossing charms his way lately, he was quick to note.

"You're acting like a lovesick fool," he told himself as he exited from the freeway and climbed the twisting roadway that led to West Seattle. "Why the hell shouldn't you?" He asked himself next. "You've been a lovesick fool from the moment you met Erin MacNamera."

By the time he was on the side street that led to her house, Brand was having third and fourth thoughts. They vanished the minute he saw the For Sale sign.

He waited until the blazing anger that raged through him had dissipated enough for him to think clearly. When it had, he stepped out of the car and marched to her front door and rapped hard against the wooden structure.

She took her sweet time answering. Her complexion went pale when she saw him, and his name was only a voiceless movement of her lips.

"What's that For Sale sign doing on the front lawn?" he demanded.

Erin looked up at him as if she were sorely tempted to reach out and touch him to be sure he wasn't a figment of her imagination.

"The For Sale sign," he repeated harshly, pointing to it in case she wasn't aware it was there.

"I'm selling the house," she whispered, then blinked twice. "What are you doing here?"

"I'm on assignment. I want to know why the hell you're moving."

"It's…well, it's not easy to explain."

She stepped aside for him to come into the house. Brand had no intention of doing so. He was walking a fine line as it was. His anger had carried him all the way to her front door, but being this close to Erin, loving her as much as he did and loathing her for the hell she'd put him through, wasn't exactly conducive to them being alone together. He'd forgotten how beautiful she was, with her rich auburn hair and her expressive dark eyes. They registered a multitude of emotions.

"I can't…explain it out here," she said when he doggedly remained where he was. "Come inside. There's coffee."

"If you don't mind, I'd prefer not to. Just kindly tell me why you're moving?"

"You don't want to come inside?" Erin sounded hurt and incredulous.

"No." Once again he pointed to the sign.

"I have to sell," she explained haltingly. "Well, I don't exactly have to… Actually, if you want the truth, I'm sick of the grand piano. It takes up the entire living room, I don't have the time for lessons, and I lack talent."

"That isn't any reason to sell. A few months ago a bulldozer was the only thing that would get you out of this house."

"It isn't the house that was so important to me."

"Then what the hell was it?"

"Roots," she shouted back, just as angry and impatient with him as he was with her.

Brand wasn't buying that for one minute. "Now we both know, don't we, Erin? All this business about needing security was bull. You don't have any more roots in Seattle than you did anyplace else. You can pretend all you want after today, sweetheart, but for right now, you're going to admit the truth."

She frowned as if she hadn't a clue what he was saying.

"You're bored and restless," he elaborated.

She denied that with a hard shake of her head. "That's not true."

"Sorry, sweetheart, I should have recognized the symptoms, but I was so damn much in love with you, a battleship would have escaped me."

A lone tear ran down the side of her face, but Brand was in no mood to react to her anguish. Perhaps deep down he was pleased to see her crying, although he didn't like to think that was true. She'd put him through hell, and if she was suffering a little, then so much the better.

"You thrive on change, you always have, only you refused to admit it. You're looking for a challenge, because it's the only thing you've ever known. You grew up learning how to adjust to situations, and now all of a sudden there's nothing new. Everything is the same, one day after the next, and you're looking for a way out, only you're sugarcoating it with the idea that you don't have enough room in your living room. Did it ever occur to you that you might sell the piano?"

"No," she whispered in a tight, strained voice.

"I didn't think it would." She thought more like a navy wife than Brand had ever realized.

Neither of them spoke for several tense moments. Brand

knew he should turn and walk away from her. He'd said everything he wanted to and more. Erin stood before him as pale as a canvas sail bleached by the sun, holding herself proud, her head high and regal.

He started to move, but every step felt as if he were dragging an anchor with him. Part of him yearned to shout back at her, tell her she'd never find a man who loved her as much as he did, but she'd rejected his love once, and he was too damn proud to hand her the power to injure him again.

He was halfway to his car when she called out to him. "Brand…"

He twisted around and discovered that she'd walked down the steps toward him. "What?" he demanded brusquely.

She shook her head. Then, using the back of her hands, she wiped the moisture from her face. "I'm so–"

"Don't apologize," he said, in as cutting a voice as he could manage. He could take anything but that. She didn't want him, didn't love him enough. By God, he wasn't about to let her water down her regrets by telling him how sorry she was.

"I wasn't," she whispered brokenly. "Just be happy."

Something broke within Brand, something deep and fundamental that had been wounded that afternoon in the Seattle hotel. "Be happy," he shouted, marching up to her. He gripped her hard by the shoulders. The power of the emotion had a stranglehold on all his good intentions to turn and aloofly walk away from her. He had damn little pride left when it came to Erin, but for once he was determined to close himself off from her. After all the times she'd hurt him, it felt good to be the one in control. He struggled to remain indifferent and detached.

He ruined everything by announcing the truth. "Do you honestly believe I can be happy without you in my life?" he demanded. "Fat chance, sweetheart."

She blinked up at him, her eyes stricken and wide. "But you're marrying Catherine."

He snickered loudly. "Your father should know by now not to trust everything he hears."

"You mean you're not?"

"Not anytime soon," he bit out caustically.

Indescribable joy crowded Erin's face before she gave a hoarse shriek. She tossed her arms around his neck and shocked him by spreading madcap kisses all over his face. Her hands were splayed over his ears as her sweet mouth bestowed a fleeting succession of kisses wherever her lips happened to land. Tears mingled with those first kisses and mumbled, unintelligible words.

"Erin, stop," he demanded. At the first touch of her mouth, the hard protective shell he'd erected around his heart cracked. He'd worked like a madman to fortify it from the moment he'd knocked on her front door. He didn't know how much longer he could hold out with her touching him like this.

Her lips found his, and he opened to her, hungry and eager and too battle-weary to fight her any longer. He took control of the kiss, plowing his hands into her hair and slanting his mouth over hers. She sighed and locked her arms around his neck and kissed him back with a need that made Brand bitterly regret the fact they were outside her house.

"You're going to marry me," he told her forcefully.

"Yes…yes," she answered, as if there had never been any question about it. "Only let's make the wedding soon."

Brand frowned. He couldn't believe what he was hearing. "I'm probably going to get transferred."

"I know."

"In the next twenty years I may be stationed from here to kingdom come. We'll move any number of times."

"No doubt we will, but I'm used to that."

The rigid control he'd maintained early on had melted and puddled at his feet, but Brand wasn't completely convinced this was for real. He wasn't leaving anything to speculation. "There are going to be children."

"I certainly hope so."

"You wanted roots, remember?"

"I've got them, only they're wound around you."

Brand felt dizzy with relief and a profound sense of completeness. "Why?"

She laughed softly, and he heard the pain mingled with the joy. "You're right…you were right all along, only I was too blind to realize it. For months I've been restless and bored, just like you said. I wanted to blame that feeling on you, but it started long before we met. Nearly every weekend I was taking long drives. Last month I put the house on the market, thinking once it sold I'd put in my notice at the office and move to Oregon.

"I was wrong about so many things. Aimee was right–I hadn't been with the Community Action Program long enough to realize some marriages do work. People can stay in love forever. I'd forgotten that and so many other things. Did you know I attended four different universities? Can you believe that? All along I kept claiming I wanted roots, but I was too blind to see how bored I get in one place. When I did realize that, it was too late–I'd heard about you and Catherine. Oh, Brand, I'm so ready to be your wife. So ready to settle down."

"The only place you're going to settle is with me."

"Aye, aye, Lieutenant," she whispered. Her mouth claimed his for a lengthy series of delicate, nibbling kisses.

Epilogue

"Here we are again," a smiling Ginger Romano commented to Erin as they stood on the crowded pier. The two were part of a large gathering of family members waiting for the crew of the *Blue Ridge* to disembark after a lengthy cruise. The ship was returning from monitoring sea trials and had been gone nearly five months.

Erin was eager for Brand's return for more than the usual reasons. She'd missed her husband the way she always missed him when he was away for any length of time. They'd been blissfully happy in the two years since their marriage. Becoming Brand's wife had taught Erin several valuable lessons about herself. She loved navy life. Thrived on it, just the way he'd claimed she would. She was home, where she'd always meant to be. The navy was in her blood, the same way it was in her father's and in Brand's. She might not have a whole lot to do with national defense, but she, and the other wives like her, were as important to the navy as the entire Pacific fleet.

"There's Daddy," Ginger shrieked, pointing to Alex as he walked down the gangplank. Bobby and the two little ones went racing toward their father.

Brand was directly behind Alex. He paused and searched the crowd for Erin. Her heart sped as she started toward him at a dignified gait. Soon, however, she broke into a run as Brand started rushing toward her. He caught her by the waist and lifted her high above his head; their mouths found and clung to each other in a love feast of longing and need.

"Welcome home, Lieutenant," she said when she could, wiping the moisture from her face. Generally she wasn't emotional at these reunions, and she didn't want to give away her secret too quickly.

Slowly Brand lowered her to the ground, but he didn't release her. "You missed me?"

"Like crazy."

"You're pale." His hand tenderly caressed her cheek. "You haven't been overdoing this volunteer work, have you?"

"I love working with the Chaplain's Office."

"That didn't answer my question."

"Quit arguing and kindly kiss me."

Brand was all too eager to comply, pulling her flush against him, his mouth greedy over hers. When he raised his head, his eyes were narrowed and questioning.

"Erin?"

"Yes." She smiled saucily up at him.

"You've gained weight?"

"Is that a question or a statement?"

He stepped back from her, and Erin watched as his gaze shifted from her swollen breasts to the slight swell of her smoothly rounded stomach. He splayed his fingers over the mound and stared at her as if he'd never seen a pregnant woman in his entire life.

"Yes, my darling, we're pregnant."

"A baby," he whispered haltingly. "But…you never said a word."

"I didn't find out until after you'd left, and then I thought a pregnant wife would make a delightful surprise for your homecoming."

"A baby," he whispered a second time, and seemed to be struggling for words. He gently cupped her face in his hands and brushed the pads of his thumbs across the slick tears that streamed down her cheeks. "I love you, Erin MacNamera Davis, more and more each day. Thank God you came to your senses and married me."

Erin thanked God, too. Her husband's large hand flattened across her abdomen as he brought her protectively into the circle of his arms. "A baby," he whispered, as if he still couldn't believe it was true.

"Our own navy brat," Erin added, just before their mouths merged.